PETERSBURG

"A fast-moving story . . . The action caroms from Russia to Paris to Geneva to Berlin as the characters are bound together in a web of destiny and intrigue."

San Francisco Chronicle

"A brilliant historic study of a Russian culture in the throes of violent transition."

Los Angeles Times Book Review

"Not merely a good read, as every reader hopes for, but a great one."

The Pittsburgh Press

"Compelling . . . Lush and boldly imagined . . . Scenes of passion, plotting, violence in the streets and confrontations with the dreaded secret police succeed each other at a mounting pace."

Publishers Weekly

"Engaging characters . . . Engrossing historical events."

The Kirkus Reviews

PETERSBURG

Emily Hanlon

IVY BOOKS • NEW YORK

*To Ned, whose love and support—and not least of all his
listening ear on all those trips to and from Burlington—
are so much a part of this book.*

*And in sweet memory of his grandfather, Pyotr Petrovich
Tarasov, whose spirit was often with me.*

An Ivy Book
Published by Ballantine Books
Copyright © 1988 by Emily Hanlon

Library of Congress Catalog Card number: 88-2476

ISBN 0-8041-0484-0

This edition published by arrangement with G.P. Putnam's Sons

Manufactured in the United States of America

First Ballantine Books Edition: November 1989

Designed by Mary Jane DiMassi

Endpaper map illustrations © 1988 by Lisa Amoroso.

CONTENTS

CONTENTS

AUTHOR'S NOTE

Historical fiction, I discovered, is a rather amazing mix of reality and fiction, so much so that I soon found myself slipping around corners into turn-of-the-century Russia, hardly feeling the time warp. Imagination was reality for so long; yet, oddly, now that I read what I have written, like a traveler recalling a trip, scenes have become remembrances of the people I met along the way.

Several of the characters grew from composites of historical people. These include Alexei Kalinin, Dmitri Mayakovsky, Arkady Akimov, Leonti Yermolov, and some of the members of the Terrorist Brigade. Other characters appeared as they lived: Czar Nicholas II, the statesman Sergei Witte, the writer Maxim Gorky, the priest Georgi Gapon, the revolutionary Leon Trotsky, and Minister of the Interior V. K. Plehve.

The revolution against which the story unfolds took place in 1905, twelve years before the Bolshevik revolution that overthrew the Czar. This first Russian revolution, rising from the capital city of St. Petersburg, now called Leningrad, was bloody and far-reaching, and has been called the "dress rehearsal" for 1917; however, the 1905 uprising was ultimately brutally repressed by Czarist forces, and for many years afterward revolutionaries in Russia were forced underground.

Although the sweep of this history as depicted is accurate, and many events did occur as shown, other events are totally fabricated. I make no claim to have written a true history, although I am indebted to those who did. In writing this book I drew most heavily on three books: *Black Night, White Snow*, by Harrison Salisbury; *Land of the Firebird*, by Suzanne Massie; and *The Fortress*, by Robert Payne. Special thanks goes to Helen Tarasov Reed, for her help with the Russian names, and her recollections.

History notwithstanding, what spurred me most was the passion and paradox of a time when lives were swept up in the storm of events surrounding them. The result, I hope, is a good read.

CAST OF CHARACTERS

Alexei Yakovlevich Kalinin (*Alyosha*)

ALEXEI'S FAMILY

Zhenya Kirilovna, mother
Yakov Nikolaievich, father
Tolya (*Anatole Yakovlevich*), brother
Mousia, sister

Mikhail Anatolyevich Kalinin (*Misha*)

MISHA'S FAMILY

Tolya, father
Helena, mother
Nikita, Sasha, Mousia, Nadezhda, brothers and sisters

Irina Ilyanovna Rantzau (*Irinushka*)

IRINA'S FAMILY

Grand Duke Ilya Mikhailevich, father
Grand Duchess Tatyana Ivanovna, mother

Anna Petrovna Orlova (*Annochka*)

ANNA'S FAMILY

Count Pyotr Orlov, father
Countess Marya Dmitreyevna, mother
Petya and Boris, brothers

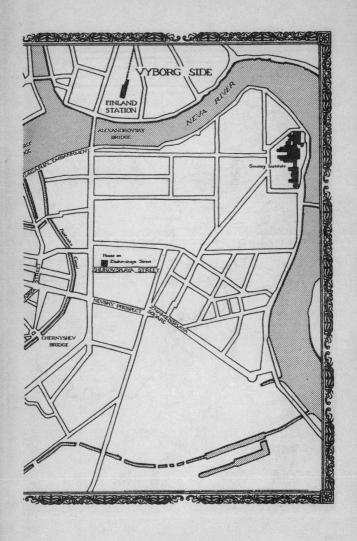

VYBORG SIDE

FINLAND STATION

NEVA RIVER

ALEXANDROVSKY BRIDGE

GAGARIN EMBANKMENT

Smolny Institute

House on Zhukovskaya Street

ZHUKOVSKAYA STREET

NEVSKY PROSPECT

ZNAMENSKAYA SQUARE

CHERNYSHEV BRIDGE

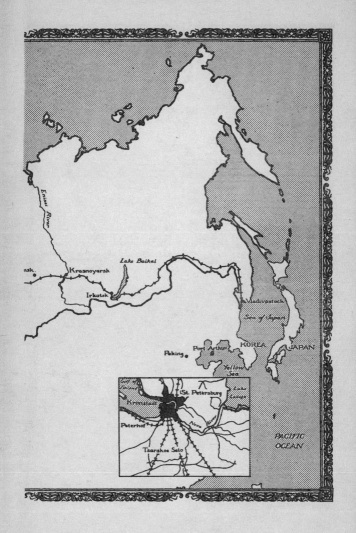

PROLOGUE

A MEETING

"What's the problem here?" Alexei approached a tight group of workers engaged in animated conversation.

The foreman snapped to attention in front of the great Alexei Yakovlevich Kalinin. An embarrassed, uncertain hush settled about the workers. They fingered their idle picks and sledgehammers and waited for the foreman, usually a talkative fellow, to respond. A bright March sun radiated off the rails lying in angled piles on the snowy stretch cutting through the deep Caucasian woods.

Alexei was dressed too heavily for the unseasonably warm day and he unwrapped the thick, cashmere scarf from his neck and flipped up the ear flaps of his sable hat. He set his foot on some track and, taking off one glove, flicked at the snow covering his boot. Casually eyeing the foreman, he chided, "Come now, Ippolit, I haven't all day. And neither have you." In truth, he was more irritated by the men's reticence than by their slackening off. They were a good crew.

"Yanson!" the foreman barked. "Tell Alexei Yakovlevich what you saw or your children will be on the streets next payday!"

"Praise God, sir, it was only my mind playing tricks!"

"Tell Alexei Yakovlevich, Yanson. Let him decide what is your dreams or not."

By now the entire crew working on the rails had stopped work to listen. It wasn't often the great Alexei Yakovlevich came to inspect his tracks. And this was such a conversation!

Yanson took a deep breath, and muttered, "Flesh eaters."

"How's that?" Alexei questioned.

"Flesh eaters, Alexei Yakovlevich," the foreman spoke up, more bold now that the secret was let out. "Yanson said he saw some flesh eaters in the woods. 'Course none of us believe him. Ain't no one seen them but Yanson. And we all know Yanson isn't all there in his brain—"

Alexei motioned the foreman to be still. Instinct told him that

1

Yanson was telling the truth. There was fear and submission in
the stance of the tall, brawny man; his eyes were downcast and
his ruddy, wind-chafed face was tinged with a nervous pallor.
He had seen something unsettling in the woods, something that
perhaps seemed like a poor soul selling human flesh, but this
was 1903. There was hunger, yes—there would be hunger in
Russia as long as there was a Czar—but there was no famine,
none of the desperation that had driven men to cannibalism during the 1890's.

Walking over to Yanson, Alexei said, "Perhaps you were mistaken. Perhaps the flesh looked human, but frozen—"

"I swear, I speak the truth, sir!"

"Then you could show me the place?"

Yanson eyed the foreman, who nodded. "If you like, sir. It's
but a mile or so into the woods."

"Ippolit," Alexei ordered, "pick out five men to come with
us. Bring picks and shovels. The rest of you, back to work."

The air was darker and colder inside the forest. The heavy
snow came halfway up the men's boots and bent the boughs of
the tall fir trees. Alexei walked first and the men followed in
silence. Their breaths froze. Ice crusted on their eyebrows, beards
and mustaches. Alexei wrapped his scarf about his chin and
mouth and turned up the fur collar of his coat. The same grim
anticipation that had quieted the men was causing his heart to
skip a beat. *Flesh eaters* . . . The grisly thought would not leave
his mind.

"It's just up ahead," Yanson whispered, and crossed himself.
The sun was shimmering through the trees, revealing a nearby
clearing.

Alexei walked slowly, bending under the branches, and suddenly stopped. He felt the frigid air expanding inside his chest
and throat as he gaped at bare, gray-white female legs and the
bony half-chest and shaved head of a man propped against the
side of a dilapidated cart. Inside the cart more stiffened arms
and legs stuck out like some bizarre sculpture, and Alexei's gaze
returned to the two hapless half-beings lying in the snow. The
man's eyes were flat; he was ageless, frozen in hacked death.
The rest of the woman had already been sold off, but one of the
man's legs and half his buttock lay in the snow like the bloodied
hind quarter of a steer. Beside him stood a hag bargaining with
two ill-clad, listless peasants, themselves little more than skele-
tons. The hag's mouth gaped toothlessly as she dickered, dangling a frozen, human arm in her hand.

The men gathered about Alexei as they might gather near a

bonfire for warmth. They crossed themselves. One muttered a prayer. Another retched.

The hag and the customer turned.

The peasant woman shrieked, grabbed her husband and ran, disappearing in the black woods.

The hag tossed down the arm, reached behind her for a rusted gun and held it on the men, who backed away, huddling over their shovels and picks. "Who the devil sent you?" she demanded hoarsely, her eyes set defiantly on Alexei.

Alexei tried to find the breath to speak, but his own stomach was rebelling. He pressed his scarf to his lips, closing his eyes against the soft, sweet-smelling fabric, but the horror pursued him in the shape of frozen limbs silhouetted against the blackness of his mind.

"Take another step and I'll shoot you!" the hag was yelling, waving the ancient rifle wildly in the air.

Forcing out his hand in a gesture of peace, Alexei promised, "I swear, old woman, I'm not the police, and I've no intention of hurting you."

She screeched then, a thin, high-pitched cry of a desperate animal.

The men drew back farther into the protection of the woods.

Alexei moved slowly toward her, his eyes returning again and again to the curve of the frozen buttock. He could see the chipped hipbone protruding, and swallowing hard, he said in an even tone, "I'd like to buy your entire load, old woman."

"Hee-hee!" she cackled. "And what would you be wantin' with the wares I peddle, eh, you in yer fine clothes and boots. Yer scarf alone would bring enough to feed me for a week."

"Here, it's yours then."

She cocked her head and peered like a chicken at his offering. "Throw it to me," she said warily.

Rolling it into a ball, he hurled it toward her, but the folds opened and the scarf floated in a delicate blue curve.

The hag hobbled quickly, snagged it with the tip of the rifle and dragged it to her feet. Then she picked it up and held it to her nose. "Clean as spring, it is." She laughed giddily.

"How much do you think it's worth?" Alexei went on. "Wagon and contents."

The old hag's face grew somber. She took a few steps closer and said warily, "You give me a price."

"Fifty rubles."

Her eyes widened, then narrowed. "Hundred or I'm off quicker than a rabbit who smells the fox."

Purposefully, Alexei took out his wallet, counted the rubles and handed them to the woman.

She grabbed them, pressing them between her hands, and furtively hobbled off.

Alexei watched until the hag was swallowed by the great, still woods. Slowly his gaze returned to the misery she'd left behind. It was the shaved head with its vacant eyes that attracted him like a magnet now. What tale could the wretch tell if he could speak? Perhaps he was better off dead. Better off than one who must stoop to sell his miserable flesh. Better off than those driven by starvation to buy and eat it.

"We could follow her, Alexei Yakovlevich!" Ippolit spoke up, reminding Alexei he was not alone. "We could bring her to the authorities."

"Leave her be," Alexei said, feeling suddenly weary.

"Then what do we do, Alexei Yakovlevich?"

"Bury the remains in the snow and burn the sled."

The foreman looked uneasily to his men and back to Alexei. "It's a dirty task you ask of us, sir."

"Think of it as a service to God, Ippolit. And here on earth, I'll see that you're all properly rewarded." He meant to look into the face of each of the men as he spoke, he wanted to thank them personally, but saw only a streak of features as he turned and left. He walked purposefully until he was well beyond the clearing and then he slowed, stopping suddenly to lean against a tree. The air about him grew dim. His legs were giving way, and pressing his head to the tree trunk, he slid to the ground. Above him the sky was clouding and scarred with bare, black branches, spindly like starvation. *Dear God, dear God in heaven, has Russia truly come to this again?* he lamented. His shoulders heaved with a desperate sob. His head fell down upon his knees, and he wrapped his arms about his knees, but no tears came. It was a dry, painful mourning.

PART ONE

PARTICULAR PASSIONS

CHAPTER ONE

Alexei was early, as per the instructions. The vast, gilded, columnated hall of the palace of the Grand Duke Ilya Mikhailevich was ablaze with lights and warmed by burning birch wood. The air was heavy with the dizzying scent of jasmine and roses; plants overflowed from ornate pots hanging from the ceiling and spreading against lavender crystal. Although it was not yet midnight, the room was beginning to swell with guests. Alexei lingered about the edges of the hall, chuckling inwardly at his easy capitulation to the Grand Duchess's specially annotated invitation.

> *Alexei darling,*
> *I have a delightful surprise for you, one which you would forever regret if you were to miss it. I promise you an evening to be remembered.*
>
> *Ever your adoring friend,*
> *Tatyana*

It was years since he had attended one of Tatyana's fetes, always finding a last-minute emergency to prevent his going. The assemblage of sparkling Petersburg guests, the firmament which he'd once zealously clamored to reach, had lost its appeal. The young women were growing foolishly younger with each passing year, increasingly transparent and doomed to the fate of their mothers and aunts. Alexei saw the decay threatening beneath the flawless surfaces; he saw the vain matrons they would become, their aging in piteous contrast to the heavy glitter of jewels and lavish gowns straining with the weight of puffy arms, chests and waists.

Russian men, he thought, fared better, or perhaps it was the simple, crisp fit of uniforms. Uniforms abounded, many encrusted with gold embroidery; chests gleamed with jeweled medals. Young Hussar officers, the muscles of their youthful bodies seductively taut beneath skintight elkskin britches, wore scarlet-and-blue tunics and boots polished to the sheen of black ice. There were representatives of the elegant Circassian and Mongol officer corps in their exotic Oriental uniforms mingling with the wasp-waisted, red-sleeved Chevaliers Gardes. The Grand Duke Ilya's birthday ball was a highlight of the fall season in St. Petersburg, closely rivaling festivities at the Winter Palace. Epaulets were everywhere amid fur-trimmed capes and hems, crimson sashes, laces, silks, velvets and satins.

Once, years before, Alexei had dreamed of a uniform, but he'd never worn one, neither civil nor private nor military. Uniforms were, he'd come to think, an obsessive affectation of his countrymen, and like the autocracy that spawned it, doomed to extinction with the arrival of the twentieth century. He smoothed his palm along the front of his black dress suit distinguished by its expensive European tailoring. An enormous diamond stud held fast his tie.

Alexei was a tall, broad, yet fit man, appearing far younger than his forty-two years. His incurable addiction to rich foods, fine wines and vodka was kept in balance by his boundless energy. He thought nothing of walking miles on a subzero day to personally inspect new track or the building of a station house. Unlike most residents of Petersburg, Alexei Kalinin walked everywhere, his boots permanently scarred with the water marks of winter ice and spring mud.

Alexei's peasant roots, scarcely a generation old, were evident in the rough, thick fingers, the dark complexion and heavyset eyes. Though he never hesitated to look a man directly in the face, Alexei's eyelids drooped involuntarily, his intense introspection and guardedness often mistaken for subservience. It was a trait he'd learned to use to his advantage. Even those who knew of his keen, often ruthless business sense were disarmed by his apparent peasant brooding that might at any moment fade like a morning fog, revealing a dazzling refinement. His striking good looks made many men uneasy, but women twittered about him like love-struck schoolgirls or fawned seductively.

Age had only added to Alexei's allure, sculpturing his youthful beauty into a rugged, dark handsomeness complementing, even defying middle age. Yet women, the easy seduction, now bored him along with money and power. He despaired of the boredom, as if a part of him had chilled or atrophied before truly flowering. At the age of forty-two, Alexei Kalinin still had fantasies of the romantic love that life seemed to guard jealously from him. Love, a family, sons of his own, were the price God or the devil had exacted.

Leaning against a wall, Alexei sipped champagne and continued his solitary observations, his eyes carefully scanning the swelling crowd. He knew Tatyana's surprise would be a person. One of her fortes was mixing the finest cross section of the Petersburg elite, everyone from the Czar and his nobility to the most-talked-of artists and philosophers, even a mild-mannered revolutionary or two. Alexei wouldn't be surprised if a worker and his wife, or an awestruck contingent from a Vyborg cotton factory appeared clustered together in their best Sunday dress. But Tatyana was not a liberal. Alexei doubted a class-conscious thought ever crossed her mind. She was an exhibitionist.

Alexei and Tatyana Ivanovna had long been friends, almost since he'd moved to Petersburg twenty years before. Ten years his senior, she'd sought him out, eager to embrace the young, upstart inventor/industrialist from the provinces of Moscow as her own; but the affair had not gone well. He was both tormented and terrified by Tatyana Ivanovna's allure. Beautiful, cultured and married to the Grand Duke Ilya Mikhailevich, cousin of the Czar, she was too boldly hedonistic and larger-than-life, making everything she touched seem deliriously lush, exotic and forbidden. He felt like an awkward, frightened boy with her, as if all his startling financial success and power were rooted in quicksand.

Often during those early years, Alexei left Tatyana's bed feeling breathless, feeling he'd been running to escape for hours. In desperation, he'd sought out the comforts of whores and later his little provincial mistresses, awed young dancers in the corps de ballet, daughters of the petty bourgeoisie come to Petersburg to paint, or write poetry, perhaps to sing. He prided himself on his caring of them. Money, it seemed then, bought everything: power, women, and comfort, everything except acceptance in courtly society. For that he needed the Grand Duchess Tatyana Ivanovna, and the affair had gone on painfully for years.

"Oh, Alexei Yakovlevich . . ." Tatyana had sighed as she'd peered intently into his eyes one hot August afternoon. He had come to visit her in her villa in Tsarkeyo Selo. Running her finger across his lips, then smoothing her hands along his shoulders and down his chest, she went on despairingly, "It's no good anymore, is it? Horribly no good. With everyone but me, you have the eye of a man who knows he's wanted and admired. That's the irony of this sorry liaison, isn't it? All the ladies' tongues wag deliciously about us. I see their eyes light on us with envy. Ah, if they only knew when you touch me, I feel an emptiness that makes me want to kill. No

man has ever treated me so badly as you, Alyosha. Am I so
unattractive?''

"No, no, you know that's not true."

"It's how you make me feel."

"I'm sorry," he insisted, avoiding her eyes.

"It's odd, even in your denial of me, you lack passion, yet
I know there's a brooding wolf within you. I see it sometimes
when you think no one is looking. I feel it in the stony silence
that answers my questions about your past. Yet none of that
frightens me. It's why I could be so good for you. Nothing
you have done or could do would ever shock or frighten me.
In fact, it would only make me want you more. You're safe
with me, Alyosha. I could unleash the passion if you'd only
let me.''

"You see too much. You make more of me than I am,"
he answered blandly.

Her expression hardened into a look of hatred such as
Alexei had never seen in her before, and she snarled, "The
truth is, I *have* made more of you than you are! I have given
you a respectability none of your gold can buy. I have taught
you everything, how to dress, how to eat. What art to appreciate. What wines to order. You would be nothing without
me!''

Tatyana's words pricked him more than he wanted to admit. "You have a vile tongue when you want, Duchess."

"Is the truth so vile, Alexei Yakovlevich? Yes . . ." She
snickered. "I think it is. Your truth, at least. You'll always
have one foot in the gutter you came from."

"And you?" He grabbed her arm tightly. "It's that gutter
that attracts you most, isn't it?"

She glared imperiously at his fingers pressing the skin of
her arm white, and he let her go. "Perhaps you're right. But
I tell you this, I've wallowed there too long with you."

"Yes, I think you're right." He threw off the covers and
started to leave the bed.

"I can destroy you, Alexei! I made you in Petersburg and
I can destroy you.''

Alexei hesitated. He knew Tatyana's words were all too
true. He also knew if he didn't break the hold she had on
him, he would be forever her slave. Breathing deeply to compose himself, he turned to her and smiled ingratiatingly. "I
suppose that's a chance I shall have to take."

"What bold words for a peasant in a nobleman's bedcham-
ber.''

"Nobleman, is it? When was the last time your husband

shared your bed? And, if I may be so bold as to remind you—it's you who invite me, time and time again."

Anger flared again in Tatyana's eyes, and she leapt from the bed, screaming, "You're finished in Petersburg, do you hear me? Finished!" Her nails streaked across his bare chest.

He grabbed her arm and she pulled back as if he were going to strike her. He only shook his head in dismay. "You do love the gutter, don't you, Duchess? You fight just like the cheapest streetwalker."

"I suppose you would know, with all the time you spend with them."

"Ah, so you've had me followed!" Alexei chuckled, hiding the indignation he felt at her invasion of his privacy. Letting go of her arms, he went on, "I'm flattered actually, that you care that much."

"Tell me, Alexei, do they satisfy you? Do your whores know how to please you so much better than I?"

"In many ways . . ."

She lunged for him again, but he easily blocked her attack, and taking her in his arms, he held her this time so she could not move. "You bring most of this pain down upon yourself, Tatyana," he said gently and apologetically. "You make me say things I never dreamed of saying. But if I've spent time in the gutter as you say, I've been faithful to you in the bedrooms of palaces. Do you know how many of your so-called friends have blatantly invited me to their chambers? But I've never, not once in all these years have I so much as accepted their invitations to tea." His words seemed to take the fight from her and she felt suddenly limp in his arms. He held her to him and, running his fingers through her hair, he kissed her gently. "I'll stay with you, Tatyana, for as long as you want. But I fear my feelings will never change. You're far too strong a woman. Your power chills my passion."

"Alyosha," she despaired, "you are the most beautiful liar God ever made." Tears filled her eyes.

"I promise you I'm not lying. I may keep things from you, but I've never lied to you."

"Make love to me once more, then you're free to go." She nestled against his shoulders. "I can't demean myself by demanding your attentions any longer. I ask only one thing. Help me keep up our little charade. You'll give me that much, won't you? We'll keep them wondering, all right. I like you too much to lose you completely. Why, I don't know, but I do."

Alexei nodded to one of the lushly clad, mauve-velveted servants carrying sparkling silver trays laden with crystal goblets of champagne and exchanged his empty glass for a full one. He felt tired, sluggish, yet occasionally he had to favor Tatyana, if only to soothe his own conscience. How paltry few people there were with whom he had the slightest inclination to talk. There were far more whom he fervently wanted to avoid, those who wanted something of him or from him, those who had something to sell him; they all bored him. Tatyana's surprise had better be a good one, else he'd find an excuse to slip away early. He should have brought Misha with him. He should have insisted the boy come. Alexei didn't see enough of his nephew lately; Misha was having his time in the world. In due course, the boy would have to settle down, but now Misha was scarcely twenty; Alexei wanted to afford him the freedom of youth he himself had never had.

"Ah, if it isn't the conscience of the capitalists," a familiar voice teased as a hand clapped Alexei on the back in greeting.

"Sergei Yurievich!" Alexei turned, enthusiastically shaking the hand of Sergei Witte, one of the few men other than the Czar's six-foot-six-inch cousin, the Grand Duke Nikolai Nikolaievich, who made Alexei feel on the slight side. Sergei Witte was not only tall but also burly; his massive white-suited chest sparkling with medals made his head, unwieldy on any other man, seem undersized.

Alexei's welcome of Witte was sincere. He liked the Czar's Minister of Finance, though he didn't trust him. Witte, like Alexei, was a self-made man, and unquestionably the most brilliant and realistic adviser in the Czar's employ. Each saw the other as a counterpart in the struggle to modernize Russia. Witte was a staunch monarchist, committed to shoring up the Imperial system through modifying the Czar's powers. Alexei, although careful never to preach revolution publicly, believed only a republic shorn of any remnants of Czarist Russia would carry Russia to her destiny as the industrial Goliath of the twentieth century.

"What brings you to one of Tatyana's extravaganzas? I thought you forswore Petersburg society!" Witte laughed heartily. "Don't tell me you've been teased back to Tatyana's web. Only a fool would return for more."

Alexei's smile hardened. The one aspect of society he despised more than its affectations was its gossip. Everyone's bedroom, it seemed, had walls of glass.

"Come, come, I don't mean to pry, my friend. You always were too private. Petersburg likes a good scandal, but you've never allowed its tawdry little paws to rake you over the coals long. You don't know how to play, my friend. It's made you many enemies. But come . . ." Witte tightened his hold on Alexei's arm. "The night's barely taken flight. Do you think our hostess would mind if I stole you for a few minutes?"

"Oh, no, Sergei Yurievich, not tonight!" Alexei protested. "I've cleared my head of business and politics. I'm here to enjoy one of Tatyana's surprises, which will be no small pleasure, I'm certain."

"A minute of your time only, my friend. I've been wanting to talk to you for weeks, but you've been incognito."

"Patching up the government's bungled work on the rails from Irkutsk, which is of no small importance if the Czar wants to keep his rein on Manchuria."

"Precisely. The route to Manchuria more than touches on what I need to discuss." Witte's voice lowered as he replaced Alexei's champagne glass on a silver tray and expertly guided him across the room, past servants who looked like dolls in a toy-shop window, and whisked him into a small anteroom off the Grand Duke's study.

In the brighter light of the anteroom Alexei noticed the dark circles under Witte's eyes and a worried paleness to his skin.

"You know the Czar's fascination with Asian adventures, particularly since he forced the Japanese out of Port Arthur," Witte began, referring to the only ice-free port in the Russian Empire. Port Arthur was more than ten thousand miles away, on the Manchurian coast. Other than slow caravan routes, its only connection to western Russia was the as-yet-unfinished Trans-Siberian railroad.

"An Asian war is a fool's daydream!" Alexei snorted. "Russia is too backward to profit from any more expansion. We need tend to our own backyard to spur economic growth. When will your Czar see that?"

"The Czar's cousin, Willy . . ." Witte said, his tone filled with deprecation at the mention of Kaiser Wilhelm II of Germany, "is turning the Czar's head with letters filled with talk of Russia's 'mission in Asia being shaped by heaven.' This is a quote, Alexei Yakovlevich, and a frightening one, for I fear the Czar holds it as gospel. He showed me the letter from Wilhelm which said Russia's great task is to 'cultivate the Asian continent and defend Europe from the inroads of the Great Yellow Hordes.' Wilhelm promised Germany would always stand by Russia's side in a war with Japan—well, you can imagine we would have nothing but women, children, and old men left before Germany would lend a helping hand."

"You're his adviser, make him see sense. I thought that was what you did so well."

"He comes to me when the sewer is overflowing and expects me to perform magic."

"Then why do you stay?"

"Because the monarchy will stay, Alexei Yakovlevich. You're a fool to think otherwise. In the end, the Czar will modify his rule and share his power. It's the only way he can survive."

"You're too insistent, Sergei Yurievich. You must be standing on rather rocky ground to come to me this way."

Witte threw up his hands in dismay. "The court is overrun with dangerous adventurers who have the ear of the Czar and his Empress. Yet, as much as I fear their manipulations, I fear the power of some of those in the government more."

"Plehve." Alexei grimaced at the mention of the boldly reactionary Minister of Interior, whose recent unleashing of a pogrom against the Jews in the town of Kishinev had gone far to damage Russia's image internationally.

"Plehve and his cohort, Yermolov." Witte began pacing at the mention of Leonti Yermolov, head of the Okhrana, the Czar's powerful secret police force. When he spoke again, his voice was edged with uncertainty. "The Czar cannot survive long with men like Plehve and Yermolov holding the reins. Yet they are entrenched. And to tell you the truth, Yermolov scares me the most. At least Plehve as a minister is in the public eye, and he must watch himself more carefully after his debacle in Kishinev. But Yermolov has no one watching over him. By the very nature of his job, everything he does is covert. He's a cunning bastard with a healthy following amongst the nobility. There are powerful men who would like to see Yermolov in my job, I'll warrant."

"Is that a real danger?" Alexei asked with concern.

Witte was thoughtful. "Suffice to say, and I tell you this in the strictest confidentiality, there are those within the government, within the halls of the Okhrana itself, who are working to get Yermolov out." Witte drew closer, and his voice lowered. "I've some influence in the Okhrana myself of late."

"That surprises me. Agents and double agents seem hardly your milieu."

"These are precarious times, my friend. One must do what one must do. Besides . . ." Witte straightened. "Yermolov does more harm to the Czar than good. The secret police have their role, God knows, but pogroms, beatings, and butchery should never be part of it. If a terrorist bomb doesn't succeed in blowing Yermolov sky-high, I'm confident other factions in the Okhrana will push the man out."

"Or blow him out?"

"Oh, no, *I'll* not stoop to such extremes! An assassin will never be on my payroll, Alexei Yakovlevich, rest assured. But if there's a legal or even quasi-legal way to oust Yermolov, I'll take it!" The energy of the outburst seemed to tire Witte; he closed his eyes a moment and pressed his hand against his forehead. "But tell me, how is Misha? I hope he's not involved in all this brouhaha at the university."

"Praise God, he seems to fancy the ladies far more than revolution."

"Praise God, indeed. The universities have become hotbeds of socialism, and I tell you what I tell the Czar—we've no one but ourselves to blame. If I were a student today, being told what I can study and not, having half the most interesting courses deleted from the curriculum because some idiotic Minister of Education thinks stimulating the mind is a revolutionary act, I would most certainly be marching and throwing bricks. Why, it's the same thing we've done with the Jews. They were probably the meekest of the Czar's flock until Plehve and Yermolov tried to erase them from the face of Russia. And to what end? They've turned an entire generation of young Jews, who would have liked nothing better than to stay in their ghettos, into the bulwark of the revolution!"

Alexei could not help but chuckle.

"Personally, I can't see the humor in all this."

"It's you, Sergei, listening to you. You sound like a revolutionary yourself."

"Ach, and you, are you not filled with contradictions too, my friend? For all your republican sentiments, I daresay you've oppressed more than a few of your precious workers in your factories and on your railroads."

"It's the system, Sergei Yurievich," Alexei insisted defensively. "The monarchy is an anachronism and rotten to its core. I could turn over my factories to the workers. I could give my entire fortune away to the poor, and it would be but a drop in the bucket, quickly swallowed up in the mire of poverty and backwardness that is Russia."

"But why not give it a try, Alexei Yakovlevich, eh? Why not hand over your factories to the workers?" Witte prodded, and he reached for a cigar from a humidor on the Grand Duke's writing table.

Witte's mind game was beginning to grate on Alexei's nerves. The man's arrogance was sometimes unbearable and Alexei felt the need to strike back. "I will tell you a story, my friend. Not a pleasant one, I'm afraid. Still, I think you will find it of interest," he began mildly. "I was out checking the laying of new track that went through a Caucasian forest last March. There was some commotion among the workers and I was told there was a seller of human flesh not far away."

Witte raised his eyebrows dubiously and poked a hole in the end of his cigar.

"I asked to see her, and was led to a clearing deep in the woods where some bone-thin peasants were standing with an old hag about a wagon. Inside the wagon were two female legs and the upper torso and head of a man."

Witte's nostrils twitched in revulsion, and he opened his mouth to speak.

"Wait until you hear it all before you protest," Alexei insisted. "I assume the rest of the unfortunate woman had already been sold off. But half of the man, one side of him from his waist to his toes, was lying in the snow at the hag's feet. She was about to sell an arm to the unfortunate peasants, who ran when they saw us. I proceeded to buy the entire load from the hag, and had my men bury what was left of the bodies."

Witte frowned. "This is not a subject to jest about, Alexei."

"As God is my witness, I saw it all, just as I told you."

"And I tell you that you saw falsely," Witte glowered. "There is *no* starvation in Russia. There are *no* flesh eaters. There haven't been since the Volga famine a decade ago."

"Deny it all you want. It will not change the truth."

Witte grumbled and tried to light his cigar. The match wouldn't catch and he crushed it in his hand, snapping, "Dammit, then, I'll have all the villages near where you saw this"—he groped for the right word—"this hideous exchange searched! And if there's any cannibalism . . ."

"What will you do? Proclaim starvation a crime?"

"Arrest the damn hag who did the selling!"

"Ah, Sergei Yurievich, you know as well as I that she was just a hapless victim, one step higher than those poor souls to whom she sold her wretched wares. Arresting her would do no good, if you could find her, which I doubt."

"Well, perhaps you're right. Besides . . ." Witte was chewing on the end of his still-unlit cigar. "I'm certain she's the exception." Eyeing Alexei uncertainly, he questioned, "You haven't told anyone of this?"

"It's bad enough that the memory haunts me. You see, I'm like you, Sergei. I pray what I saw was an exception, a bizarre occurrence. What terrifies me is that it is an exception that portends the future."

Witte shuddered and settled into a chair. His heavy body seemed almost to deflate. "Alexei Yakovlevich, this is just one more nightmare to fill my days. Let me give you an example of what I am up against. Each morning I go in to talk to the Czar. I advise him of the danger of some of his policies. I advise him of the corruption about him. I advise him that his people are starving, that the workers are clamoring for food and jobs, and do you know what he does? He smiles politely as if I were some ninny and begins talking to me about the weather, or a lovely canoe ride he took with one of his daughters, or of a fine new dessert his Empress has ordered for him, or . . ." He paused before going on. His face hardened in anger. "Of Russia's mission in Asia. That's what obsesses him—not poverty or revolution on his doorstep, but war. And most of his cabinet feed into his dreams, as if Russia were on some glorious mission of God in Manchuria." Witte leaned forward and peered intently at Alexei. "I need the Symposium's help in forestalling the war with Japan, Alexei Yakovlevich," Witte implored.

"Why the Symposium?"

"Some of the richest, most influential businessmen in Russia have banded with you, Alexander Ryabushinsky and Andre Bobrinsky in the Symposium. The Czar may not like the criticism he gets from you, but you're well within the law. And he knows he can't succeed in an Asian war without bankers and industry. He needs your support."

"Not to mention the railroad across Siberia—a rather weak link to the front if it remains incomplete." Alexei snorted.

"Which is why he's pushing like hell to complete it. It would be suicide to go to war in Manchuria without it. If you could just talk to those in the Symposium, Alexei, convince them it is in their best interests *not* to support a war with Japan, I daresay the Czar will think twice."

Alexei shrugged. "I think not."

"I don't understand you, Alexei Yakovlevich. You've just waxed poetic on the starving masses, and now, when I ask your help in saving the lives of their sons . . ." Witte rose in exasperation. "If we don't do something to stop this insane march toward war, there'll be more to fill the flesh eaters' wagons, and I'm not talking about the bodies on the front."

"Russia *is* already starving. How much worse can it get than the flesh eaters? I will not help you forestall this war, Sergei Yurievich. My most devout hope is that if it comes, it brings the monarchy to its knees. In the end, more will be saved than perish. Now, I have one of the most powerful women in Petersburg waiting for me. I don't want to make her crosser than I most assuredly already have. Good evening, Mr. Minister.'' Alexei nodded and was gone.

CHAPTER TWO

''The Czar and his foreign adventures be damned,'' Alexei muttered as he started back to the ballroom, feeling the memory of the flesh eaters clatter like chains about his spirit. In hopes of regaining his equilibrium, he headed toward the tables spread with mounds of caviar, black oysters, pickled and smoked fish, hams, mushrooms, candied fruit and colorful patterns of vegetables ripened to perfection in the Grand Duke's greenhouse.

''Alexei Yakovlevich, Alexei Yakovlevich . . .'' People smiled, touched his arm, spoke words which made as much sense to him as Chinese.

He merely nodded, smiled back politely, loaded his plate and searched for a place to eat unnoticed. He found some privacy near a wall shadowed by the enormous fronds of the Grand Duke Ilya's spectacular palm trees; but as he stared down at his plate, he was overcome with the nausea he'd felt for several days after he'd seen the old hag and her wagon of butchered arms and legs. Some champagne was what he needed, a lot of champagne, he told himself as he stepped from his hiding place to grab a glass from a passing tray. ''Take this for me, won't you?'' He handed the servant his plate. ''But wait a moment like a good fellow.'' He quickly downed two glasses of champagne and was starting to sip his third when, out of the corner of his eye, he caught sight of a reflection in a wall of milky glass.

A shiver of recognition held tight his body, and he moved to get a better view of the young woman. He'd seen her only once, months before at the Yusupovs' fete to mark the end of the White Nights. He had not forgotten, could not forget her. She'd been playing the piano, a suite from *Swan Lake*, with a power that had drawn Alexei from his conversation. To his amazement, the pianist herself had been as unforgettable as her music. Silken, flaxen hair surrounded a delicate face; pale skin was drawn smoothly across broad cheekbones; there was a regal sweep to her high forehead; her lips were full, sensuous, but her smile, like the depth of her unsettling blue eyes, was far too serious for her years. She was tall and girlishly slim. Fully filled, she would be stately.

Although the girl had disappeared that night before Alexei could be introduced, he'd been delighted to discover she was the daughter of Count Orlov, Tatyana's brother. "Oh, yes, Anna's quite talented," Tatyana had agreed. "And lovely too. I saw you gaping at her. If you like, I could arrange a meeting sometime, although it's not easy. Her mother keeps her on a tight rein, even though Anna is perfection itself. In fact, the poor child leaves for the Crimea tomorrow to summer with her mother. You know, of course, my brother and his wife no longer live together. Marya Dmitreyevna keeps the estate in the Crimea with some awful Siberian mystic, Zinaida Golovnina. Come the fall, Anna will be sent back to the Smolny Institute, which is no better than a convent. Still, I shall see what I can do for you, my dove."

Alexei knew in an instant that the girl was Tatyana's surprise, and her presence helped sweep away the ghosts of the flesh eaters. Anna was lovelier than he had remembered, appearing like a vision in a gown of sunray-pleated ivory satin; delicate lace swept off her girlish shoulders in short flower-petal sleeves. Compared to the jewels on the women around her, she appeared almost unadorned with a simple strand of pearls about her neck, cascading clusters of pearls on her ears, and more woven on velvet through the back of her golden upswept hair. She was obviously uncomfortable with the extreme décolletage that she kept on pulling in little yanks or covering with rapid waves of her fan. Her attention was never on the conversation with a dour, ashen-faced matron and her stout, bald-headed husband. Rather Anna turned constantly, as if looking for someone. On more than one occasion during her anxious visual sweeps through the room, her eyes met Alexei's.

He smiled and nodded at her.

Each time her deep blue eyes widened before looking hurriedly away. Her pale skin flushed a rosy pink from the full swells of her breasts to her neck to her cheeks.

"So you've peeked at my surprise, have you?" Tatyana's arm encircled his waist.

"I've just figured it out." He kissed her on the cheek.

"I promised you, didn't I? She's ripe, isn't she, even more so than last spring."

"She's a child . . ." he insisted, feeling strangely compelled to lie.

"Seventeen, Alyosha. No longer a child, and I daresay no man here tonight will look on her as one. She's the main entertainment. It's why I thought to invite you. You were so taken with her playing at the Yusupovs'. Happily, she's chosen something by Mozart. As I recall, you've a passion for Mozart."

"Could your recall have anything to do with her choice?" he teased, feeling that twinge of sadness he felt on seeing Tatyana lately. The years had not been kind—lines prematurely webbed her once porcelain skin, an aging which no amount of powder and rouge could hide.

"Of course, I take care of my friends!" she exclaimed, but her smile faded into a pout as she gazed about the ballroom. "Where's Misha?" Tatyana grimaced. "I thought he was coming tonight. Oh, Alexei . . ." she despaired. "Don't tell me he's turned me down again."

"Ach!" Alexei tapped his forehead in forgetfulness. "It totally slipped my mind. He announced at the last minute he had plans he simply couldn't break."

"You allow that boy too much freedom, Alexei. He runs wild, I hear, breaking girls' hearts all over Petersburg. And not unlike his uncle. A fine example you set for him, never settling down yourself. I tell you, it's time to put that boy on the right track. There's hardly a mother here tonight who wouldn't give her fortune for her daughter to marry your nephew. You could align your family with the best in all Petersburg, Alexei. You know that."

"Misha is far too young to settle down yet."

"You'll be sorry, I tell you, letting him waste his time on riffraff."

"Pretty little dancers . . ."

"Gypsies and whores is what I hear."

"Come now, Tatyana . . ." He slipped his arm through hers. "If I'd known Misha's presence was so important . . ."

"Oh, it's not," she scolded, and her voice lowered to a whisper. "It's you, of course. It's been you all these years and, I suppose, it always shall be. I have to hold out the promise of some tantalizing young fruit to have you come and see me anymore. Do you think I have no feelings?"

"I don't stay away intentionally, you know that." He smiled endearingly. "It's business. I'm a slave, as always, to my work."

"Ah, yes, I've heard about your business—practically stole the rebuilding of the route through Irkutsk from poor Pavel

Botkin. I have my spies, you know, and they tell me it's a race between your steam engines and the socialists to see who wins control of Russia. I daresay the Czar and everyone here is rooting for you!'' She urged him forward. ''Come, let me introduce you to Anna. But I warn you, Alyosha, you will fall in love instantly. She's your type, I warrant, beautiful, talented . . .''

''And seventeen.''

''When has that ever stopped you?''

''Often in the past few years,'' he assured her.

Tatyana rolled her eyes disbelievingly, and went on, ''Anna is rare perfection. If only I had been blessed with such a daughter, but God saw fit to give me Irina. Did I tell you that Princess Bordova's daughter, Alexandra, saw Irina in Paris this summer? At first Alexandra quite thought she had the wrong girl. Irina has become a perfectly slovenly bohemian. But I'm not surprised. She was hanging on the arm of some young man, naturally—quite common, by his dress. Irina seemed not to want to waste a moment speaking to Alexandra and never so much as introduced the young man. Well, that's Irina's style. I tell Ilya that he should demand she come home and marry. He says it would do no good. She'll not marry until she's ready. Of course, she would if Ilya cut off her allowance, but he has such a soft spot in his heart for the girl. I swear, he's why Irina's incorrigible. If only she were more like Anna . . .'' she mused, and her face wrinkled into a crooked smile. ''A bit of young flesh would be a comfort to ease you into your declining years, Alyosha. And don't think decline is so far away. One day the peak is still barely in sight, and then next morning you wake up teetering on the brink. Old age, my sweet, it attacks without warning. Marry the girl. It could be arranged.''

''Tatyana, I've never even met her! Besides, marriage is no more a priority for me than it is for Misha.''

Tatyana tossed him a disgruntled look, and slipped away. ''Anna, darling!'' she called. ''I want you to meet Alexei Kalinin, a great admirer of yours. . . .''

Anna was not certain whether she was relieved or still more unnerved by the fact that the man who'd been watching her every movement was the very man she'd been brought to meet. She'd noticed him the moment he arrived. He was the only man not wearing some kind of uniform, and although he was not unpleasant to look at, there was something foreboding about him. Perhaps it was his eyes, that watched without watching. He was very tall, too, with long arms and large hands seeming not to fit. It was hard to imagine him as one of Aunt Tatyana's "oldest, dearest of friends."

"Alexei Yakovlevich is quite a fine gentleman, and he's amassed one of the greatest fortunes in Russia," Aunt Tatyana had informed Anna on a recent visit to school. The visit in itself had been a shock. In the six years Anna had been in Smolny, Aunt Tatyana had visited three, perhaps four times. "Alexei Yakovlevich's weakness is the arts, music in particular," Aunt Tatyana had explained. "He once fancied himself some kind of composer, so you see your advantage. He was quite taken with you, Anna, with your playing at the Yusupovs' last spring. I'm sure he could be a great support."

Anna had been confused.

"For your music," Aunt Tatyana had explained, the insistent pitch of her voice breaking the hush shrouding the Smolny Institute for Young Ladies. "It would be important for you to have a patron."

"But a patron . . . Why?"

"You shan't be in this place forever. Then what are your choices? To throw yourself into the arms of some handsome young Hussar—no, no, I'm afraid that's my Irina, but not you. Are you then to be married to some fat old prince?"

"Mama said when it's time, she'll return to Petersburg."

"I know Marya Dmitreyevna. She'll never return. She'll drag you to Ravens Head, where you'll fade away with your mama and Zinaida Golovnina. Is that what you want, to lead a life no better than that of a nun? God has given you a great gift, Anna. The greatest sin would be not to spread His glory through your music for everyone to hear. Now, I have arranged, or rather your papa has arranged for you to come home the weekend of your Uncle Ilya's birthday ball. Lydia Karlovna knows all about it and has agreed that you be allowed more hours to practice."

"For what?"

"You are to perform. Early on, of course. The Czar never stays long. His Empress tires with her growing belly, as if a Russian winter were a hex." Aunt Tatyana had sneered. "The Hessian prude. It would serve her right if she never conceived a son."

"But, Aunt Tatyana . . . Uncle Ilya's ball . . . all those people . . . the Czar . . . I can't play for the Czar. . . ."

"Of course you can, darling. I have the utmost confidence. The evening shall surely shine, with you its reigning star. You've a fitting tomorrow with Madame Brissac. Her prices are highway robbery, even the Empress has complained, I'll give her that, but what can one do. . . ."

* * *

Anna trembled as Alexei Kalinin bowed, then slipped her gloved hand into his. "Lovely—strong fingers. The mark of a true pianist." He held her hand lightly to his lips.

She gasped and drew away. Her face drained of color. "Please excuse me, but I have to go now, Alexei Yakovlevich. I must!" Turning, she grabbed her skirts and began pushing her way through the crowded ballroom.

"Anna!" Tatyana called in annoyance. "Anna, come here!"

Anna didn't stop. She hurried past guests and out the ballroom, racing by statuelike servants and down the long velvet-carpeted corridor, through silk-and-satined drawing rooms and parlors. She knew where she was going and, taking her skirts in both hands, she ran like a boy, knees bent high, until she came to two heavy oak doors. Pushing them open, she stepped breathlessly into a darkness laden with the perfume of lilies laced with a humid, earthy scent. She stood against a moist wall, relaxing in her newly found safety. No one would think to look for her here, in Uncle Ilya's greenhouse. As children, she and her cousin Irina used to play here for hours. Now she could stay until it was too late to perform, and then she would face Aunt Tatyana's wrath.

Anna was about to turn on the lights, when she heard a gentle knocking on the door. Closing her eyes, she held her breath and sank in between some ferns. The knocking came again.

"Anna Petrovna, may I come in? I know you're in there. It's me, Alexei Yakovlevich. Please, I only want to talk to you." The knob turned and the door pushed slowly open. "It seems you might be in need of a friendly shoulder to cry on," his melodic voice cajoled.

For a moment she considered hiding; it would be hard for Alexei Kalinin to find her amidst the large, twisted stems and wide leaves of her uncle's plants. But that was too foolish. Taking a deep breath, she slipped from the ferns with a swish of her skirts and reached for the light. The vaulted room was aglow, and Alexei Kalinin came into view, his dark eyes riveted so intensely on her, she thought something was wrong. She reached behind her neck to push escaping hairs back in place.

"I suspect I've intruded in a private place, Anna, but I would like to stay, if I may?" His voice was oddly soothing, and he took a few steps toward her, the deepness of his gaze causing a strangely pleasurable shudder to flow through her.

"Why don't we sit?" he suggested, holding his hand toward several straight-backed chairs.

Reluctantly she did as he bade. Sitting very tall, she said with determination, "Alexei Yakovlevich, I wish you hadn't followed me."

"Your aunt is concerned."

"I've disappointed her. I'm sorry, truly. But there's nothing I can do."

"Well, of course, your aunt will forgive, but the Czar—Nicholas himself has come to hear you play."

"The Czar will forgive much more readily than Aunt Tatyana," Anna replied, feeling her eyes grow watery. "I tried to tell her this would happen." She sighed despairingly. "If only my mama were here . . ." Strands of hair escaped the pins and hung like corn silk down her shoulders. "Mama's the only one who understands . . ." She broke off, fumbling in her sleeve for her handkerchief.

"You might want to explain it to me, if it's about music. I understand a bit myself. Oh, I haven't your talent, but I've great understanding. I love music as much as I love anything in the world."

She bit her lip as if to stop the tears. "I'm not so talented really, Alexei Yakovlevich. It's a trick, a horrible hoax—I know it is, and one day I shan't be able to play at all." She began to nervously twist the handkerchief. "My music will all be gone, even from inside my head."

"Who told you such a thing?"

"No one told me. It's what I know. You're lucky. Aunt Tatyana says you have composed, but I can't do that. I can never write down what I hear. I try. But it's awful, all wrong." She was pleading, a frightening desperation disfiguring her lovely face. Pressing her hands to her lips, she implored, "I must go now, Alexei Yakovlevich. I shouldn't be talking to you."

"Why not?"

"I shouldn't even be here. Don't you see, I don't belong here anymore! I should be at school, asleep. How shall I stay up all night to dance, much less play for the Czar?"

Alexei waited until the confused tumult of words ceased, and he asked, "Anna, has anyone ever taught you to write music?"

"Mama." The question caught her off guard.

"And is she very good? Composing is a very, very special talent. I try, but I'm not very good. I'd never presume to teach anyone."

"Mama has taught me everything. I would never play if it weren't for her!"

"Of course, Anna. I only meant, even those who love us the best are not the best teachers. I have friends who are. Rimsky-Korsakov is one of the very best teachers at the Conservatory and he is a dear friend of mine. Have you ever thought of attending the Conservatory?"

"Mama would never allow it."

"And your papa?"

Anna didn't answer.

"It's odd, I think, your papa here in Petersburg and your mama hundreds and hundreds of miles away in the Crimea, yet it's your mama who decides everything."

Anna stood up. "I must go, Alexei Yakovlevich."

"What if I wrote to your mama?"

"No, no! You must never do that!"

"You belong at the Conservatory, Anna. I could help you get in. I'd like to help you as I've helped many talented young people before you."

"Thank you, Alexei Yakovlevich. I appreciate your offer, but I don't need such help. I play only for myself and my mama."

"And the Czar and your Uncle Ilya and the hundreds of your aunt's and uncle's guests who are waiting for you now."

"But I can't!"

"I say you can. I say—"

"All right, I'll tell you then!" The color flared suddenly in her cheeks and she seemed more a woman than a child. "Sometimes I think my playing is magnificent, I truly do. I know that's prideful, but I feel so glorious when I'm playing, as if God has truly blessed me. And then, without warning, the keys become like red-hot pokers. All the magnificence and the perfection are gone. Everything crumbles."

"Only in your mind."

"Yes, yes, because I can't go back—I can never make it perfect!" She hurled the words at him, almost accusingly.

"And even if you did, it wouldn't matter. For the next moment holds more imperfection. I also promise you something else: there won't be a person in that room tonight who would pick up even the greatest mistake you made. Once you begin, you'll sweep them away."

"How do you know all this when you've only heard me play once!" she demanded.

"Once is enough, I promise you that. But once is surely not enough to fill my desire." He paused, studying the youthful beauty burning in her face; it clamored with the tenderness of beginnings. "I remember when I was in Paris, and I saw a great young Parisian performing *Hamlet*. Talk of mistakes—he made a terrible one. He totally forgot his lines and interjected about twenty lines from *The Tempest* in their place. No one—mind you, not even the greatest critics—knew what he had done. They all praised his performance as brilliant!"

"That can't be true—please, Alexei Yakovlevich, don't talk to me like I'm a child easily calmed by a silly nursery rhyme."

"I swear on the soul of my mother—it's the absolute truth. The actor told me. We were in a club after the performance, a group of us, and he told us all. We laughed and laughed. You see, for him, it was enough that he never lost his passion."

A sadness returned to her face. Her lovely lips drooped.

"You want to play tonight, don't you, Anna? There's something inside you which wants to perform as much as it wants to run."

She looked away, saying nothing.

"I was a perfectionist myself once." He chuckled. "It's awful, a self-imposed prison."

"Don't think you know me, Alexei Yakovlevich. I'm not that transparent!" she flared.

Alexei tightened, startled, but the shock quickly wore off, replaced by an invigorating delight. "You're an artist, Anna," he said almost reverently. "All you have to do is go out there and perform." His voice was mellow, his closeness both a comfort and a threat.

A sudden knocking on the door caused Anna to jump to her feet. "Papa!" she cried.

"Count Orlov, a pleasure." Alexei strode to greet him. "Anna and I were just discussing the passion of performing. I was telling her that passion is always ripe with imperfections, but she seems quite taken with the idea of perfection."

"That is her mother's obsession, I'm afraid." The count tittered. Shadows of Anna's beauty lay faded in the count's soft features. His once-blond hair was graying and thinning; his fair skin was toneless like muscles lax from disuse. Yet he had the self-confident look of a man long flattered and pampered.

"Well, Anna, the Czar has arrived. Tatyana is quite distraught. He expects to hear you play. What shall she tell him?"

"Tell her she's playing," Alexei announced.

"Now, that's my old Anna!" the count exclaimed, hugging his daughter and kissing away the outrage bubbling from her throat. "But you must have someone fix you up again, your hair and your face," the count called as he hurried out the door.

"How dare you!" Anna's eyes opened wide. Her chest was heaving.

"It's what you wanted to say, isn't it?"

"No, not at all! And now I have no choice! I shall make a fool of myself in front of the Czar and all Petersburg."

"Don't be so angry, Anna, I'm not going to leave you in the lurch. All the time you play, I shall be close by. I promise."

"I don't need you!"

"Still, I shall be there." He pushed some flyaway hairs back against her dampened head. "Your papa is right. Your hair needs fixing. Shall I tell your aunt to send someone to you?"

"No, I'm fine. I can fix it myself." She glared at him, and hurried from the room.

"Well, well, well, Pyotr Ivanovich, your daughter has grown delightfully. I wouldn't have recognized her. Where have you been keeping her?" Czar Nicholas smiled easily from Anna's father to Anna, his gently handsome face and reassuring welcome calming for the moment her fear and the stormy feelings aroused by Alexei Kalinin. She loved the Czar absolutely, as she loved her mother and father, perhaps more. He was at once a god and a man.

"Anna is at Smolny, your highness," Count Orlov replied graciously.

"Of course, of course, and your wife, the lovely Marya Dmitreyevna, she is well?"

"The weather of the Crimea continues to be more to her liking than Petersburg."

"If only we could all be so lucky as to spend our lives in the Crimea. It's a paradise, for certain. And, we are told, your wife is an angel to the dying in the sanatoriums there. Surely it makes her absence more tolerable, knowing she is selflessly caring for those sad, miserable victims. Anna, Tatyana Ivanovna tells me you shall please us with some Mozart."

"I pray that I might, your highness." Anna bowed on knees fragile as glass.

The Czar extended his gloved hand toward Anna, then led the Empress to one of the chairs near the grand piano.

As if on cue, the ballroom fell into a hushed silence. Gowns brushed along the polished floor; the circle of the audience pressed closer to the piano.

"You'll do fine, my sweetest pea." The count beamed.

"If only Mama were here," she whispered, her voice barely audible. A terrible shaking was beginning to overcome her. She was very cold, and her head felt light. In desperation, she looked for Alexei Kalinin, who seemed her only salvation; but she could not see beyond the blinding glare of jewels and crystal surrounding her. She thought of the Czar and tried to sit. Her heart throbbed painfully. Her throat grew tight. The shining black and white keys of the piano loomed like prison bars.

"It's all right, Anna," a low voice calmly reassured. A black-clad arm touched hers. "Just begin. You'll be fine once you begin."

A strange aching filled Anna's chest as she sat at Alexei's urging. His breathing seemed in rhythmic unison with her own.

She looked up.

The gentle flicker of a smile creased his fine, thin lips. "Forget the world, and begin," his melodic voice whispered as his dark eyes rested on hers, seeming to drink in her fear, leaving her filled with warm waves of yearning to please. "Now . . ." His gaze moved to the piano.

Instinctively, Anna's followed. Her fingers reached for the keys, and once touching them, began to fly effortlessly, calling forth the sweep of the music, glittering as from the sheen of a sun-drenched sea. She was a leaf of newborn spring enmeshed in a funnel of breezes dizzying in their speed. The crescendo built, caressing the lining of her brain and echoing on quivering blades of grass, white on black and the crimson of cats' eyes in the darkest night.

The applause was thundering. The Czar's praise was lavish. He led her in the opening polonaise. She felt blessed. Handsome young man after handsome young man asked for a dance, offered her champagne or a piece of delicately smoked fish. They buzzed about her, asking her questions which demanded no answers. She only had to smile, laugh or nod. The evening spun out in a dazzling array of sights, sounds and sensations. Now and again Alexei Kalinin passed near. He smiled; she smiled back. She wanted to thank him.

"Do you like the mazurka?" a deep, melodic voice questioned from behind.

She spun around in mid-sentence. "Alexei Yakovlevich!" She felt her own radiance reflecting off his "I love the mazurka!" She turned to her companions. "You'll excuse me?" she said, quickly taking her leave.

"You were marvelous," he bent over and whispered.

"I felt marvelous."

"Perfect?"

She laughed softly. "It didn't matter."

"They're beginning . . ." Alexei nodded toward the orchestra, and clasping her hand tightly, he threw back his head and thrust one foot forward, waiting for the fiery beat to begin. With a wild grin, he stomped his foot and flew into the air, whirling Anna deliriously about the room. He bounded first on one foot and then the other, tapping his heels and then spreading his legs, stopping short only to spin around again. He guided Anna first with his left hand and then his right, falling to one knee and twirling her about him, jumping to meet her in smooth, vibrant movements. They laughed as their dance encompassed the room. The world fragmented into a gossamer glitter. Onlookers jumped out of their way. Anna's skirt billowed. Sweat made Alexei's face shine. He was tireless. They danced set after set, stopping only for Alexei to swig down some vodka. Enthusiastic clapping urged them on. Anna twirled out, to see only two other couples still dancing. She was flying again, soaring with the rush of a speeding troika on a winter's night.

The mazurka led into a lively quadrille, then a galop. Alexei kept on appearing and reappearing as her partner. She missed him during supper. Aunt Tatyana had seated him at the far end of the dining room, at the head table with important people. "All of Petersburg shall be talking of you and Alexei Kalinin in the morning. I'm jealous!" a girlish voice whispered in her ear.

Supper was sumptuous. Decanters filled with countless flavors of vodka and the finest French wines were liberally distributed and constantly being refreshed. The meal began with several soups of young sturgeon with eelpout livers, duck puree, and mushroom bouillon, followed by miniature blini spread with butter and caviar, then fish and truffles and delicately boiled swan. There were bear steak and preserved peas, white asparagus, tongues cut in slices, grouse roasted in sour cream with cranberry sauce, and salted cucumbers. Dessert of melons, grapes, apples, and oranges piled in perfect pyramids on golden platters and an endless array of pastries was finished off with the entrance of a double line of brilliantly dressed servants carrying bowls of flaming champagne punch above their heads.

Anna, who was used to the simple meals at Smolny, could

barely get past the first course. She slipped in and out of a sweetly drugged sleep as the supper carried on through dawn. The last thing she remembered was a waltz with Alexei, in which he talked to her about something called "Evenings of Contemporary Music" held in Becker's music shop.

"The most avant-garde of the new music is played there, all the composers banned by our genteel Chamber Music Society. It's quite marvelous—the works of men like Debussy, Ravel, and d'Indy, and the most wonderful of the new Russians. We shall go sometime, Anna. Yes, I think you must. Music today is on the cutting edge of the new order. Poets and musicians are the priests of the future. Only they are dedicated to eternal truth."

CHAPTER THREE

Irina Rantzau sat by the window, trying to escape the heat of the small, crowded apartment, but it was a brutal day in Paris, the air outside as suffocating as the air within. Still, she could not listen to the excited murmuring about her. The pounding of her heart felt metallic, making it hard to swallow, making it feel like fear, but she wasn't afraid of killing or dying. Dear God, why was she shaking then? Pressing her hands together, she held her tall, graceful body taut; beads of perspiration dotted her skin. She drew a calming breath and focused her eyes on Savva Safanov, the messenger newly arrived from St. Petersburg. He was an extraordinarily angelic-looking young man with soft, curled blond hair, smooth cheeks and clear, almost aqua eyes. No one would imagine him an assassin, and he wasn't, yet. Savva, like Irina and most of the others, was a novice to terrorism. Of the seven, only Vera Martova and Stepan Ostravsky had killed before: Vera once, Stepan many times—no one knew for sure how many.

Prince Andre Maximov, a distant cousin of Irina's, had been one of Stepan's victims. Irina had felt no particular sympathy for the Prince even before she'd met his assassin. The Prince was notorious for his ill treatment of his peasants. In fact, when she'd read the account of the assassination in the newspaper, she'd been quite taken by the daring drama of the act: a rather handsome, well-dressed young man had walked up to the Prince outside the theater in Moscow, called him by name and, seeming to extend his hand in friendship, shot him through the heart. No one had seen the derringer concealed in the young man's hand and, in the confusion, he'd slipped into the crowd and disappeared. Blame was quickly laid on the notorious Stepan Ostravsky, and the Czar raised the bounty on Stepan from ten to twenty thousand rubles. Stepan was insulted. He felt his head worth a lot more.

Irina glanced at Stepan now, hoping to catch his eye, but he was absorbed in his own thoughts. One arm was stretched across the back of the couch; his long legs were crossed. His white shirt and beige trousers were crisp despite the heat, and as he pulled unconsciously at his beard, his dark eyes almost dreamy, he appeared more a young lawyer or doctor than a wild-eyed terrorist, the once-illiterate son of Georgian peasants.

Even if Stepan were not so engrossed, Irina knew he wouldn't be looking at her. He never looked at her during a meeting, unless speaking directly to her. He couldn't, he explained. Even a glance might catch up his mind, forcing him to break concentration, an act of suicide for a terrorist. They were living on the edge. Their first dedication was to the revolution, to freedom and equality; yet, despite Stepan's protestations, Irina knew his insistence on concentration in the safety of a Paris apartment had to do far more with erotic passion than with revolution and survival.

He was, if possible, more obsessed by her than she was by him. Stepan had told her in a rare, unguarded moment of tenderness that he'd never dreamed he would hold a duchess in his arms. He sometimes touched her body as if she were a work of art, insisting he'd never felt skin so soft nor smelled a perfume so rare as her scent. In times of deepest passion, he was awed like any peasant bedding his mistress. That was her hook, but she paid dearly for it. As much as Stepan wanted her, he also despised her, baiting her for her ancestry, warning that she might someday be called upon to execute one of her own family, insisting she was spoiled and tainted with a rottenness no amount of revolutionary cleansing could purge. He took her money without asking, almost daring her to question him, and worse, far worse, he cruelly and without warning or explanation barred her from his life for weeks on end.

Irina knew she didn't love Stepan; she didn't think her masochism ran that deep. But she wanted him as desperately as she had ever wanted a man. More than a lover, he was her teacher. Under his tutelage, revolution went beyond a lover's ideology, adorning a duchess like a new necklace. Terrorism was not just an act of rebellion, it was the answer, she believed, to a world gone mad, a world whose madness had almost destroyed her. Joining the Brigade gave order to her life and filled the void of her loneliness. She had been warmly welcomed by Stepan's comrades in those early days and soon became one of them, reading voraciously, staying up all night drinking wine and arguing politics. For the first time in her life, she'd felt intelligent; she'd been stunned when people fell silent as she talked, listened to what she had to say and even sought out her opinions. But perhaps, she thought sometimes, sweetest of all was the knowledge that she would never again wake up with a raging hangover in some strange man's bed. For these gifts, she could accept even Stepan's erratic loving. Eventually, always, he wanted her again.

They had been in a dry spell now for almost a month, since late August, a difficult time for Irina under the best of circumstances, a time when, despite all efforts to forget, events of the past sifted in ghostly visions from locked corridors of her mind. It had been a little more than six years ago, on August 16, 1897, when Irina's exile had begun. That was the day she had been discovered naked on the couch with her handsome tutor, Apollon. She had been all of fourteen at the time, and her mother, the Grand Duchess Tatyana, had been shocked. Her mother had no right to be shocked over anything anyone did, yet she had arranged to have Irina immediately shipped to school in Switzerland. Gradually Irina had come to the realization that it was more fear than shock that had caused her mother to act so swiftly and violently, fear that Irina in her budding womanhood would steal the pretty young men whom the Grand Duchess kept dangling about her.

Irina remembered pleading with her mother to let her stay, at least through mid-September and her father's birthday, Irina's favorite fete of the year. Everyone had a name-day ball, but only her father had a European-style birthday celebration. The Grand Duke's name day fell during Lent, when no dancing and little merriment of any sort were allowed, so Tatyana, not one to be denied anything, held a birthday ball. The Czar himself attended and, just as important, Irina's father helped her pick out her gown, and he danced the first dance with her. She sat at the head table beside him, and that year, the year of Irina's summary exile, she'd had romantic requests from several officers, promising young men who thought her much older than fourteen, to dance the night away.

Her mother refused to allow Irina to stay, despite her father's protest. Part of the punishment was that Irina should miss the ball. For years afterward, September 14, her father's birthday, loomed as a torturous reminder of all she'd left behind. Then one day it ceased to matter. Russia, home, mother, father, old friends ceased to matter. Irina considered herself a citizen of the world. September became like any other month, except, looking back, she was always at her most wild then, changing lovers with a spiraling madness; visiting places—Venice, London, Lisbon—because she had to keep moving. Last year in September she had met Stepan Ostravsky and joined the Terrorist Brigade. This year in September she was about to do something she had sworn she'd never do—return to Russia, to St. Petersburg—and therein lay her fear, she realized. Her heart pounded mercilessly as she contemplated home. The simplicity of it was almost ironic. She wasn't afraid of revolution; she wasn't afraid of destroying the world that had spawned her; she wasn't afraid of dying. She was afraid of returning home.

"Comrades, please, we are about to begin!" Vera Martova knocked her knuckles on the edge of the table. There was no need for such an action. The room was already hushed.

Savva cleared his throat. Trickles of sweat ran down the side of his face. "Dmitri Mayakovsky sends his regards to the Terrorist Brigade-in-Exile, and gives us, at last, the name of the target." His low voice settled religiously. In the silence that followed, no one breathed.

"Go on," Vera Martova finally urged.

"Our target is Leonti Yermolov, chief of the Okhrana. His death has been decreed unanimously by Dmitri Mayakovsky and the leadership of the Terrorist Brigade."

Josef Kidarsky, a pale, gaunt young man standing by the door, spit. "Yermolov is scum."

Kiril Zatov, sitting beside Katya, nodded his agreement. "The man gives new meaning to the word 'diabolic.' "

"Yes, he is most deserving." Savva's bright eyes smoldered to a sea blue. "But he's a difficult man to kill. Several attempts have already been made on his life. Some call him the Cat because he seems to have so many lives. The man lives in a cocoon of secrecy. He expects death at any moment, and never goes anywhere without his bodyguards."

Stepan sat up sharply, the elegant pose of his lean body

taking command. "It will bring me the sweetest of pleasures to blow the cur to bloody bits."

"More so than you might imagine," Vera said, a smile lighting her usually dour face. She was a pudgy young woman, whom Irina and her roommate, Katya, had dubbed "the pigeon"; but for all Vera's blandness, she was a brilliant strategist and a heroine. Born the bastard child of a landowner and a peasant girl, she had, at the age of nineteen, walked into the police chief's office in Minsk, pulled out a gun, and shot the chief in the neck, killing him instantly. The man was so universally hated that throngs of supporters mobbed the steps of the courthouse on the first day of the trial. In the fracas, Vera was separated from her guards and whisked out of Russia, first to Poland and finally to Paris, where she joined Stepan and the Terrorist Brigade-in-Exile. Leadership of the exiles teetered uneasily between Vera and Stepan. Now she held up a large brown envelope in her thick fingers, and eyeing Stepan, announced, "I have here a most interesting dossier on our friend Yermolov."

Stepan sat forward, his fingers clasping his knees, his brows furrowed.

Vera went on. "It was sent to me as the editor of *The People's Will*. Here, I will read you the letter." Color rose in her cheeks as she carefully opened the envelope and took out a thick layer of papers. "It's dated July 13, 1903, St. Petersburg. 'My dear Comrade Martova,' he begins. 'Although I work for no revolutionary organization, rebellion burns in my heart. I have been an unimportant secretary in the Okhrana for an unmentionable number of years. Yes, unimportant so no one notices. I am a fly on the wall, the eyes of the revolution within the citadel of reaction. As this fly, I have taken it on as my own personal banner to work up this dossier on the chief, Leonti Yermolov, who is lower than a maggot in a dead child's eye. It is with greatest honor and excitement—yes, Comrade Martova, I feel such excitement knowing this paper shall soon touch your hand. For I know *The People's Will* is truly the voice of the revolution. I send this to you, knowing you will use it in the interest of all Russia. Praise God! Down with the Czar! Long live the revolution!' Signed, 'A Comrade.' "

Vera took a deep breath as she finished reading and laid the cover letter on the table. "I have here reports of Yermolov's ordering the flogging of prisoners as well as his signed orders to have workers shot and peasants hanged for mere suspicion of revolutionary sympathies. I have here"— she paused dramatically and her cheeks heightened with color—"the founding charter of the Black Hundreds, with guess-who's signature on the bottom!"

"Yermolov!" Kiril gasped.

"The very man."

"My God!" Stepan was impressed. "Let me see that." He reached out, grabbing the paper from Vera, and when he finished, passed it on to Katya, who was across from him.

Irina hurried over and leaned above Katya; a shot of electricity caused her body to jerk as she spied Yermolov's scrawled signature. "The Black Hundreds . . ." she muttered softly. Long before Irina had given a thought to revolution or terrorism, she had known the Black Hundreds were a despicable lot. Her father, generally not a man moved to emotion of any sort, called the Black Hundreds "dogshit on the heels of the monarchy." He decried the Czar's covert support of the "worthless hooligans," mostly uneducated workers and peasants whose patriotic fervor was easily aroused. They roved in gangs through cities, beating up Jews, students and striking workers, often staging counterdemonstrations that ended in violent confrontations with anti-Czar sympathizers. At best, the police stood idly by; at worst, they joined the fray on the side of the Black Hundreds.

"When did you receive this?" Stepan demanded.

"Four days ago."

"Four days ago, and you kept it to yourself?"

"I was pondering it all, Stepan Stepanovich, and then when Savva told me who our target is, I knew it was time for all of us to talk."

Stepan's mouth twitched irritably. He was not one to be excluded from consideration of something so important as the Yermolov dossier, but Vera quickly went on, "There's one more document which I think equally startling as the Black Hundreds. It's dated November 1901. I read: 'An organization of workers, ostensibly independent but actually created and directed by members of the Okhrana, will be first set up among machine-shop and textile workers in Moscow. If successful, we will spread such police-organized unions to Petersburg, Kiev, Odessa and every major city and port, where we will affiliate with legitimate unions with the express purpose of infiltrating not only their ranks but also their leadership, ultimately turning them into police tools and impotent forces against the government.' This is signed by a man named A. V. Akimov."

"How insane!" Stepan chortled and reached for a cigarette. "Police unions! They could never happen. Yermolov is way over his head on this one."

"You think so?" Vera said hotly, as if her pride had been pricked. "I'll read another memorandum from this Akimov then. This one is dated August 3, 1902, just a year ago. 'Contact has been made with a seminary student, Father Georgi Apollonovich Gapon, who has agreed to organize the Society of Russian Factory and Plant Workers in Petersburg. This Father Gapon has a definite charisma to him. My only hesitancy is that he may not be completely compliant with the needs of the police.' "

"A priest working with the police!" said Irina disbelievingly.

"Why not?" asked Kiril. "Priests can have as rotten politics as the next man. In fact, they usually do."

"Who's Akimov?" Katya asked. "Savva, you know most of the chiefs and agents in the Okhrana. Have you heard of someone called Akimov?"

Savva shook his head. "Nor have I heard any rumor of police unions."

"I would assert they never got off the ground," Stepan argued haughtily.

Kiril nodded his agreement. "There's no way a policeman could pass for a true revolutionary worker, not once he opens his mouth."

"Don't underestimate the police, Kiril, especially the Okhrana. It could be fatal," Vera warned.

"Nor can we *overestimate* them, comrade, or allow them to take us away from our appointed goal—which is Yermolov. He's the target." Stepan's reminder sounded like a reprimand.

"Yes, I'm in agreement," Katya spoke next. "Besides, if word of police infiltration of unions gets out, it could dilute the energy of the workers needlessly. Suspicion will run rampant. Workers will start worrying that every union member is a cop. I say we say nothing of this in the newspaper."

"I'm not so certain," Irina interjected, feeling herself determinedly aligned with Vera. The idea of the police forming a union struck a chord of reality. "If there's any chance it's true, it's our duty to warn the workers."

"What do you feel, Josef?" Stepan asked quickly. "You're the only voice not accounted for."

Josef pressed his large, farmer's hands together. "I, too, think we should stick to our target. It's going to be hard enough to track Yermolov."

"Good, then!" Stepan's face lit up triumphantly. He slapped his hands on his thighs. "We have a clear majority. I say we drink to the cur's death—except . . . ." His eyes light-ened playfully and his lips drooped clownishly. "We happen to be out of vodka!" As he spoke, his eyes lighted on Irina. He tossed some francs on the table to start the collection.

"I'll pay!" she burst out, as if on cue.

"Splendid idea!" Stepan was already on his feet. "Nothing like the aristocracy unwittingly paying to toast their own downfall, eh? Come with me, Irina. We'll get some wine and cheese and bread, perhaps some sweets. We need to fortify ourselves for all our work ahead." Stepan tilted his head. His voice was inviting, his smile alive with intimacy.

Irina felt Vera's hard glance, and taking a deep breath, said, "Why not? I could use some fresh air."

Dusk was darkening to night in the respectable working-class neighborhood when Irina and Stepan left the building. The air was cooling slightly; women ushered resistant children inside; men sat on the stoops to smoke and argue. Irina edged from Stepan and walked in long strides, her hands thrust in her pockets.

"So you think this police-union fantasy has some truth to it then?" Stepan slipped his arm proprietorially through Irina's.

"I don't know. It may." She pulled away, feeling nervously protective of herself.

Stepan chuckled. "Think about it, Irinushka. What would the police really get out of it? Too much work for too little effort. I'm surprised Vera fell for it. Still, I liked to see you talk up like that. You looked quite beautiful siding with Vera against me as you did. I applaud you."

"It was hardly against you! Not everything Vera and I do is motivated by you."

He chuckled softly and hooked her arm again. "All for the better, then. It bodes well for our expedition in Petersburg. You and Vera will have to work closely together. We all will. It's important to rise above personal differences, especially petty ones."

"Sometimes you are the most arrogant man I've ever met." She tried again to pull from him.

His arm slipped familiarly to her waist. "And sometimes you can still surprise me. You know you looked ravishing in there."

"I wasn't aware that counted in such matters."

"Of course, always!" He chuckled and glanced quickly up and down the street before pulling her into an alleyway. Leaning her against the wall, he pressed against her, his arms enveloping her, the close muskiness of his skin as pervasive as the rich scent of earth after a summer rain. "I want you to stay with me tonight."

"Ha!" She laughed deprecatingly. "You decide you want me now after weeks of silence, and you think I'm like a dog who will come wagging my tail at a kind word!"

"I think you've missed me as desperately as I have missed you." He kissed her neck. His breath was sweetly heavy in her ear. "I'm sorry I'm cruel to you, my pet. It pains me to sleep without you, but I must. You know that." He was kissing her softly, nibbling at her skin.

She tried to push him away. "I don't understand you, Stepan, I don't understand why you do this to us."

"I don't either—I swear . . ." He kissed her, kneading his hands and arms about her as if their passion were brand new. His heat coiled inside her. His tongue licked and probed; his hand was pushing at the fabric of her skirt.

"Stepan, no!" She pushed him breathlessly away. "Are you mad?"

"Oh, come, Irinushka, please. It will be fun, the kind of madness you adore. A little back-alley girl. Come, play the part with me," he implored.

"Why? Won't Vera?" The words came out without forethought, sounding cheap and vindictive.

Stepan dropped his arms and snapped, "You demean yourself with such thoughts!"

"Then end it with her."

"We've been through this a thousand times." He reached into his pocket for his cigarettes, and holding one in his lips, he angrily lit a match. Inhaling deeply, he warned, "Vera never mentions you, although she has far more to fear from you than you from her. For all your fine breeding, you're less a lady than the bastard." He turned to leave the alley.

"No, Stepan, wait!" She grabbed him, wrapping her arms about his shoulders. "I'm sorry. You're right, my behavior was appalling—I just love you so much. Hold me, please," she begged, taking his hand and pressing it to her breast. "I've missed you. It's been so long."

He chuckled softly and smoothed his hand along the line of her chin and neck. "You see, I try to end it with you and I can't do that either." Taking her hand, he led her toward the back of the alley, and leaning her against the wall, began to slowly unbutton the top of her dress. "What if I tell you that in Petersburg we'll be together?"

"How do you mean?"

He undid the buttons to her waist. "Savva and I have already discussed Dmitri's plans. It's what we're going to talk about when we get back, but there's no harm in your having a little advance notice. You and Kiril will be the first to follow Savva back to Petersburg.''

"When?"

"I'm not sure." His hand slipped under her chemise and he rolled her hardened nipple between his fingers. "Savva and Dmitri must arrange certain matters." He kissed her neck. "But with your social connections, you're to set up a flat which is extremely fashionable and above suspicion, in a very posh district. The police will never look for us there. Olga Gambarova . . . you've heard of her."

"The Matriarch," she said, trying hard to keep her mind on what he was saying.

"Yes, she's been around since Adam and Eve." He slipped down the shoulder of her thin cotton dress. "Olga was with the Narodnaya Volya when they assassinated Alexander II. Dmitri has brilliantly recruited her to work with us. We're to be together in the house. You, me, Katya, Savva, and Olga. We'll all have parts to play. Lovers, housekeeper, valet, cook, you see." His lips were practically touching hers as he spoke.

"No, I don't see," she said, her voice low and quivering.

"I don't see either . . ." he murmured, his words lost to the wet warmth of his kiss and their bodies began moving in a slow, rhythmic dance. His fingers edged under the shoulders of her dress and chemise and pulled them, binding her arms. "God, you're beautiful, Irina. You're madness." He pulled down the lace chemise with his teeth, and his mouth covered her breast.

"This is crazy," she breathed as she tugged at his shirt until her palms were sticky with the sweat of his skin. "You're crazy, you know."

"You make me this way, you alone. You're a goddamned witch . . ." he swore, pushing her skirts to her waist.

'' 'Morning . . .'' Katya yawned as she stood in her night-gown in the kitchen doorway, her unbrushed hair half-covering her face. "When did you get in?"

"Are you my mother? Are you keeping track of me?" Irina snapped.

"Whoa! Hold on. It was only idle curiosity. If you don't want to tell me, that's fine," Katya assured, pouring herself a cup of coffee. Sitting at the table, she gazed down at some crumpled pages of paper covered with childish handwriting. "Ah, the words of the great man," she said with mock reverence. "Is that how he pays you for the glory of your body? He gives you his manifestos to rewrite."

"You're being cruel now." Irina had to fight back the sadness Katya's words evoked. It did seem the only reason Stepan had asked her back for the night was to entice her to decipher and edit his newest manifesto.

Katya turned the pages to look at the title. "Hmm, sounds interesting: 'Terrorism in the Twentieth Century: A Russian Resurgence.'"

"It is interesting," Irina said defensively. "It's brilliant."

"Or it will be—when you're finished with it."

"He can't help it if he can't structure a piece. How good would you be without an education?"

"There you go—defending him, and to me of all people! Just because I think Stepan Ostravsky is totally depraved when it comes to relationships with women, with you in particular, doesn't mean I don't think him a brilliant revolutionary. When are you going to learn not to confuse the two?" Katya asked sincerely. "You know, this passion of yours is all that keeps you from truly becoming a leader."

"That's ridiculous. I've done nothing to be a leader."

"Not yet, but you will. You've a wonderfully incisive mind, and people like you. You have a way about you that makes others feel alive. You'd see that if you'd just step out of Stepan's shadow. Don't you think he wants to keep you just where you are, rewriting his manifestos and feeding his passion whenever he needs a change from the pigeon?"

"If he'd only give her up," Irina lamented.

"You know he won't. They were lovers long before he came upon you. I'm sure he'll be with her long after he's forgotten about you. What you need is to forget about Stepan and funnel all your energy into the revolution. . . ." Katya reached for her hand. "The next time Stepan gives you one of his come-hither looks, tell him to go to hell, why don't you?"

"Because . . ." Irina slipped from Katya's hold and held herself tall. She wanted to sound strong, but tears watered the steely grayness of her eyes. "I'm sorry to disappoint you, Katya, but I don't think I'm ready for that. I don't even think I want that. And if you think he's using me, then consider this: I use him too. I want him. I like what I get from him. I liked last night—very much."

"There's a difference between needing and wanting. Needing makes life awfully complicated."

"And you don't need Josef?"

"I've never needed him. Friendship and trust are the true underpinnings of affection, not passion."

Irina wanted to snap back with some remark to hurt Katya,

but she couldn't. In the year since Irina had left the Art Institute, she'd come to depend on Katya's cool objectivity, and in her heart wished she could be like Katya, unemotional, untouched by the heartaches that doggedly followed Irina from man to man. Katya was satisfied with Josef Kidarsky, a gaunt young man with pained eyes seeming always to peer into places no one else saw. His clothes hung absurdly on his lanky frame. Katya was tall and pale, her nose crooked and her eyes a haunting blue-green; at the age of twenty-four she had already given in to middle-age spread. Yet her love for Josef seemed fulfilling if quiet; Irina had to give Katya that.

Katya and Josef had long been friends, ever since their student days in Moscow. Katya's father, a well-to-do fur merchant, had been enraged by the friendship. Josef was Jewish. Katya's father said she had to give up either the Jew or her family. She chose the Jew, who chose to follow her into exile when Katya was sentenced to five years in Siberia for organizing working men's and women's reading groups. It was Josef who helped her escape.

"You know what I miss most about Russia?" Irina asked impulsively.

"What?"

"Ice! Wouldn't you just die for a glass of truly iced lemonade right now? What kind of civilized country is it where you can't keep ice?" The two women laughed, the tension between them gone as quickly as it had come. They were friends again, and the easy connection settled softly about Irina.

She reached for Stepan's manifesto, her hand grazing Katya's as she did. "I appreciate what you tell me, Katya, truly I do. I know in my heart you're right. And someday, if I live long enough, maybe I'll be as strong as you. But now, I'm just the way I am. To try to be different would be more insane than even this passion of mine for Stepan is. Can you understand that?"

Katya warmly grasped Irina's hand. "Of course I can. But I'm not going to give up trying to make you see how wonderful you are all by yourself."

Irina smiled hopefully. "Perhaps it will all be different when we're back in Russia."

"Yes, home."

"Home." Irina laughed bitterly. "You know, it's funny. This little apartment seems as much home to me as anyplace I've ever lived."

"Will it be very hard for you to go back?"

Irina shrugged as if it did not matter. "In all of Russia,

there's only one person I'm truly looking forward to seeing again—my cousin Anna. We grew up together. We were closer than most sisters. After I was sent away, she wrote to me almost every day for months. But I never answered her," Irina said carelessly.

"Why not?"

"I don't know. Goodness, I don't even know why I brought that up!" She forced a laugh. "I haven't given Anna a thought in years."

"Maybe it's because you're going to see her soon."

"Well, probably I won't. After the heartless way I treated her, I can't imagine her ever wanting to speak to me again. It's why Stepan and I make such a good pair, I think. We hurt anyone we love."

Katya looked pained. "That isn't true, Irina. You've never hurt me, not once in all these months. I consider you the dearest friend I've ever had."

"Do you really?" Irina felt quieted.

"Absolutely. And it's why I think you'd be such a good leader. You've a good heart, Irina, and a quick mind. Now, tell me, will you make contact with your cousin when you get home?"

"Oh, she's most likely married by now. If I know my Aunt Marya, she's ushered poor Anna into some sterile, well-appointed marriage. Besides, I doubt she'd want to see me. What would Anna and I have in common anymore? We couldn't be truly friends. I would have to keep the most important part of my life from her."

"Not your love."

"Honestly, Katya, underneath all your hard bravado, you're a terrible romantic at heart!"

"I believe love is one of the things we're fighting for. The right for everyone to love whom they please. The right for rich and poor alike to live in a world where the pursuit of happiness knows no class bounds. If that's romanticism, then I wear the label proudly."

"I love you, Katya, you know that—the revolution needs more people like you. Stepan thinks talk of love and happiness is weakness."

"I think they are the heart of what we fight for."

"Yes, I do too."

They were quiet a few moments; it was an unsettling silence, as if a new and secret truth had been bared between them. Then, suddenly, the intimacy seemed exhilarating, and Irina exclaimed, "I'll tell you what, let's forget about Stepan . . ." She folded his pages and pushed them to the side of the table. "Let's forget the revolution and Yermolov and be terribly silly, like schoolgirls! We'll go shopping, and out to some very posh place for lunch, my treat. We'll order some fabulous wine and eat foods with cream sauces and the most delicious desserts. Maybe they'll have those strawberries you love dipped in dark chocolate. We'll eat until we burst. Oh, say you'll come with me, Katya. I need to do something naughty like that. It'll get me back into the mood of going home."

"I shouldn't. I've work to do for that meeting with the French Socialists tomorrow. I'm to go with Stepan, you know."

"First rule is, we don't mention Stepan, not once."

Katya was smiling and shaking her head in disbelief. "All right, then, I'll let you stuff me with some decadent bourgeois treats."

"Oh, Katya, what would I ever do without you?"

"And I without you?"

CHAPTER FOUR

"It's snowing!" Anna whispered excitedly into the darkness, relieved for a reason to break the torturously slow ticking of another lonely night. She knew by the slant of the moonlight across the domes of the cathedral that it was not yet one in the morning. Clambering from her bed to Valia's, she pulled at her roommate and pushed off the covers. "Wake up, wake up—it's snowing!"

Valia grumbled and kicked aimlessly.

"It's the first snow of winter! Come on, Valia, wake up. The moonlight is glorious! It makes everything seem the lightest shade of silver blue. We have to make a wish."

"I wish only to sleep and be warm."

"Don't be an old stick-in-the-mud. If you don't get up now, your wish will be useless." She yanked Valia to a sitting position.

"All right, all right. . . ." Valia sighed and pulled herself from the bed, complaining. "If my feet freeze off . . ."

Anna grabbed her friend across the bed. "There!" she cooed, folding back warm blankets to cover Valia, and then spreading out beside her. "It's beautiful, isn't it? By morning the snow will be covering everything and we shan't see the earth again until after Easter. The trees will crystallize, and even Smolny will look like a fairy garden. Oh, I love winter, don't you?"

"What are you going to wish?"

Anna shrugged and quickly turned her face to hide her smile. "I don't know," she lied. "What about you?"

Valia was silent a moment, and in a hushed tone sounding like a prayer, she said, "I shall wish for a handsome cadet from the Preobrazhensky Guards to catch my glance at the carriage procession during *Maslenitsa*. I'll have a card with my name and address, and when our eyes meet, I'll smile most daringly and quickly push open the carriage window and toss it to him."

"What good will that do?" Anna demanded, strangely annoyed by the impossibility of Valia's wish.

"He'll write to me, of course, and I'll write to him."

"Oh, yes!" Anna laughed bitterly. "I can just imagine Lydia Karlovna calling you and saying, 'Valia Vaslavna, there's a handsome young cadet in my office who swears undying love for you. Come see him. In fact, go for a stroll with him, go out for tea'—that's if you should catch a cadet's eye to begin with!"

"Are your fantasies any better?" Valia hotly demanded. "The Conservatory, no less!" She snickered. "You play before the Czar and all of a sudden you're a famous concert pianist. And where's your wonderful Alexei Kalinin? I thought he was to be your patron. I though he was to take you to some Evening of Contemporary Music with all the bohemian artists and poets—"

"Stop it!" Anna cried, covering her ears.

"Shush!" Valia pressed her hand against Anna's mouth and held her tightly.

The two girls sat grasped together scarcely breathing, waiting for the footsteps which inevitably came.

"Don't move," Valia warned, letting her hand slip from Anna's mouth; but just as she was walking from the bed, there was the urgent knock.

"Valentina Vaslavna! Anna Petrovna!" the doorknob turned.

Valia motioned Anna to lie down. She began moaning as Miss Heidlemann marched in, candle in hand.

"Valentina Vaslavna—is that you? If this is one of your

and Anna's tricks!'' She grabbed Valia's arm and held the candle to her face.

Valia moaned incoherently and took a few more steps until she reached the edge of her bed, and toppled over.

"Barefoot, too!" Miss Heidlemann complained as she pulled the covers out from under Valia, straightened her legs on the bed, and covered her up again. "You two are worse than any first-formers! The next time you wake me from my sleep, Lydia Karlovna shall be awakened too. Sleepwalking will be no excuse for Lydia Karlovna!"

Neither Anna nor Valia spoke until they were certain Miss Heidlemann was back in her room and snoring. "Thank you," Anna whispered, kneeling by Valia's bed.

"I didn't do it for you, Anna. I did it for myself. My papa is no happier over bad reports from Lydia Karlovna than is your mama. Now, go to bed."

"I'm sorry for what I said before, truly I am." She held Valia's hands and pressed them to her face.

"You can be the meanest person I know sometimes, Anna—especially since you played for the Czar. I think it's gone to your head."

"It's not the Czar."

"I don't want to hear any more. I just want to go to sleep." Valia pulled her hands free and turned her back, pulling the covers over her head.

Anna sat down on the bed. "I'm very cold," she whispered. "Can I come in with you? Remember when we used to snuggle up together to keep warm? We haven't done that for years."

"The bed isn't big enough for two of us anymore."

"Please, Valia. I'll sleep way over on the edge and hardly take up any room. Maybe if I'm close to you, I'll be able to sleep. I won't talk or bother you. I just can't stand another night of not sleeping. Please. . . ." Her voice was barely audible as the sadness which had been building inside her for weeks broke into inconsolable sobs. It wasn't until she lay cradled in Valia's arms that the tears began to lessen and her body relaxed. "I'm sorry I've been so mean lately." She grasped on tightly to her friend. "Nothing seems right anymore. I feel like I'm losing my mind. At night sometimes I think I'll suddenly race down the hall and start screaming, that I'll run into the night barefoot and with just my nightgown and keep running until a policeman stops me and sends me to a madhouse."

"It's Monsieur Kalinin, isn't it? You're in love with him. . . ."

"I don't know, I don't know anything anymore. But he's all I think about when I'm studying or in chapel or even practicing the piano: *Alexei Kalinin, Alexei Kalinin* . . . his name repeats itself in my mind like a maddening song. What if I never see him again?"

"Perhaps he's tried. You know this place. He might have written to you. Or perhaps he's off on business. You said he's an important businessman."

"He was toying with me," she said in a dull monotone. "It's just like Mama says about men. They play to hurt."

"I don't believe that."

"Maybe I do." Anna sat up and pressed her chin to her knees and stared out the window at the falling snow. "I hate this place, Valia."

"We've only another year."

"An eternity. I don't know if I can survive it. Oh, Valia, don't you see—St. Petersburg is out there, just beyond those miserable school gates—St. Petersburg, the grandest city in all the world, and we might as well be in China. It's not fair."

"Maybe you should talk to your papa. After all, you don't need Monsieur Kalinin to get you an audition at the Conservatory. Anyone can have an audition. And after you've played for the Czar."

"It wouldn't do any good. It's Mama I have to convince, and there's not a chance of that. Can you just imagine my writing and telling her I want to audition at the Conservatory?" Anna laughed bitterly. "Besides, it's not just the Conservatory. There are people, young people like ourselves, out there going to the theater and the ballet every night, dancing at balls and going for tea on Nevsky Prospect. My cousin Irina is in Paris. She's *been* in love, many times—not just dreamed about it. I daresay she's been kissed and adored passionately. I want to be like that too, Valia. I want to skate at night on the Neva and slide down the ice whenever I feel like it. I want to ride to the islands at night and drink champagne with the Gypsies. I want to be in love, I want it more than anything in the world!"

"Then why don't you write to Alexei Kalinin?"

"I don't want to be in love with him!" she snapped.

"Well, still you could write to him. Tell him you enjoyed his company and his help the night of your uncle's birthday ball, that you hope his health and business are doing well, and that you would be most interested in discussing his patronage at whatever time is convenient for him."

"I couldn't do that! What would he think of me?"

"You're an artist, Anna, he told you that, didn't he? Artists are different, they're allowed to be bold. I believe even Lydia Karlovna knows that. She lets you get away with more than anyone because your music brings her such praise."

"I don't know. . . ." Anna began biting at a nail. "Perhaps Alexei Yakovlevich has forgotten me already. Anyway, this is foolishness. I'm not in love with him at all. And tomorrow I shall spend all day in the cathedral praying. Then I'll be close to God again. My music will return, and I'll be happy. Yes, that's what's wrong—it's not Alexei Yakovlevich at all. It's my music. I haven't been playing. When I don't play I lose my place with God and the devil toys with my soul." She got out of bed.

"Where are you going?" Valia followed.

"To make my wish on the first falling snow." She sat on her bed and peered into the moonlit night. "I wish for God's love to fill my heart so I can be an obedient daughter. I wish never to anger or pain my mama again. I wish that the glory of God's love be my only salvation."

"This isn't right! I can't make it work!" Vera Martova burst out angrily, her bloodshot eyes straining as she crushed the editorial she'd been writing into a tiny ball and threw it into the already overflowing garbage. "This business about the police unions keeps on coming out of me, no matter how hard I try to keep it in. It's as if it has a life of its own."

It was very late, or early, past six in the morning of October 4. Vera, Irina, Katya and Josef had been working on the newest issue of *The People's Will* for over a week now, centering it around the Yermolov dossier. Vera was a stern taskmaster. Everything had to be perfect. Yet they had to have the mock-up of the newspaper up at the typesetter's by ten, a seemingly impossible task. Masses of papers lay on the table, the bed, the bureau, every available surface of Vera's small Paris apartment.

"You want to have a try at writing the editorial, Irina?" Vera rubbed her eyes in exhaustion. "I'm no good for anything anymore—"

Irina never had a chance to reply. Without warning, the front door was kicked in, followed by two large men brandishing guns. They were distinctly Russian, with round faces, thick lips and Slavic features. Their clean-shaven faces were sweating, the skin shining like slime; their prickly hair was closely cropped; their suits were a toneless gray and ill-fitted.

"What the hell!" Josef was on his feet.

"Shut up, Jew!" the taller of the two men ordered in Russian. The muscles in his arms and chest bulged. His teeth were large and nicotine-stained, his hands massive like dull, heavy swords; his eyes were small, the pupils looking like pinholes. "Close it!" he snapped the order to his partner, who eagerly kicked the door closed.

Vera stood up. "You're from the Okhrana!" Fear reddened the pallor of exhaustion. "I recognize your weapon." She laughed, an awkward, choked laugh as she stared fixedly at the man with the nicotine-stained teeth. "This is Paris. We're out of your jurisdiction."

"Which one of you is Martova?" he demanded, peering through his pinhole eyes.

"I am."

"Give me the material on Yermolov. All of it. I know what's in it. I've got a list. Ivan!" He snapped his fingers. "The list."

Without taking his stare off his captives, the smaller man, Ivan, who was only small in comparison with his cohort, pulled a list from his pocket.

"It's not here," Vera said boldly.

"Oh, yeah?" The pin-eyed man started for her.

Josef lunged.

"I told you to stay put, Jew!" he thundered, and with a flick of his wrist, the butt of his gun knocked Josef in the side of the head, sending him crashing into a chair. He lay there like a crumpled doll; blood trickled down his cheek.

"Josef!" Katya cried.

Ivan grabbed her as she darted toward Josef, and bent her arm behind her back.

Katya's face contorted as she cried in pain.

"Pigs! Scum!" Irina screamed.

"You wanna be next, missy? Huh?" The pin-eyed man waved his gun in Irina's face.

Wordlessly Irina stepped back. A tremor of fear sucked at her breath.

"Please, you're hurting me," Katya moaned.

"Shut her up," the pin-eyed man ordered.

Still twisting Katya's arm, Ivan wrapped his gun hand around her head and over her mouth.

Perhaps it was Katya's pain or Josef's crumpled body or Vera's defiant glare or the vile arrogance of the pumped-up slugs of captors—Irina didn't know what drove her to lunge, flailing at Ivan, feeling she could rip out his throat with her fingers. A primordial scream gurgled as her knees bent to propel her, but the scream doubled back inside her as Ivan's foot shot arrow-straight, his heel landing in her gut. Grabbing herself, she fell to the floor gasping for breath; the pain radiating in a swirling black murkiness. She bit her lip until it bled and prayed for relief from the agony.

"Now, *Comrade* Martova." The pin-eyed man snickered. "Your little Jew lovers are all accounted for." He grabbed Vera's chin in between his thumb and index finger. They dug deeply, causing the skin around them to swell red. "Get me the material on Yermolov."

"It's not here," Vera said dully.

"Hee-hee! You take me for a fool?" He grabbed her by her hair and bent back her head. "I don't feel like carrying all these papers back with me. Nor do I feel like reading through all your trash."

"Surprised you can read at all," Vera managed to say.

Yanking back her head, the pin-eyed man threw her against the wall. Then he cocked his gun and held it at Josef's head. "The Jew will go first, if you don't tell me, *Comrade* Martova. Then your girlfriend here. The pretty one next." He pointed to Irina. "Except she won't look so pretty when Ivan's done with her, I promise. He likes to cut, you see, carves pretty pictures, a real artist." Releasing Vera, he stepped toward Irina. "Get up," he ordered.

"In a pig's eye!" Irina spat.

With one quick movement he wrenched her helplessly to her feet and clamped his massive fingers into either side of her jaw. "A pretty face, eh, Ivan? Toss me your knife, but don't let go of that one's mouth."

Ivan flourished a shining five-inch blade and flipped it to the pin-eyed man, who caught it in his left hand while his right still held Irina's jaw in a painful, viselike grip. He brandished the blade before her eyes, then held the point to her cheek.

Irina felt encased in silence.

The pin-eyed man sweated. He reeked. He grinned. His teeth were grossly yellow and gray.

Her body stiffened at the cold piercing of the metal.

He was pressing, first the point; then he laid the whole razor-sharp edge against her cheek. "The papers!" he demanded.

The cold steel pressed, weighted by the silence.

"Where are the papers, Martova?"

The tension of the blade against Irina's cheek sharpened. The blade turned.

Irina screamed.

"All right!" Vera shouted. "I'll give it to you. Let her

go!'' She pointed to a large brown envelope by her feet. ''It's all there. I swear.''

The pin-eyed man shoved Irina against the wall and she fell. Instinctively her hand reached for her face. She felt only the imprint of the knife. No blood. No cut. Then Katya was hurled beside her. Wordlessly they touched hands, holding tightly, shaking uncontrollably as the two men examined the contents of the envelope. When everything was accounted for, the pin-eyed man clutched the envelope under his arm and ordered Ivan to take the remaining papers into the kitchen and burn them in the sink. That done, the two thugs brandished their knives one last time and backed from the room, vanishing as quickly as they had come.

Katya was the first to her feet as the door closed, and she raced to Josef. ''Are you all right?'' she pleaded, sobs verging on hysteria cracking her voice as she wiped the blood from his cheek with her skirt.

''Yes, I'm fine. It's only superficial,'' he calmly assured her as he used her arm to help pull himself to his feet. ''And you? Are you all right?''

''Fine, yes.'' Katya embraced Josef and held him tightly.

Slowly but firmly, he broke free and asked Vera, ''Are you sure they were Okhrana?''

''Positive.'' Vera's skin was a ghastly white color.

''Then why didn't they arrest you?''

''Paris is out of their jurisdiction,'' Vera said, her tone more questioning than affirmative. She hesitated. ''But more to the point . . .'' Her chest heaved. ''How did they know we had the Yermolov dossier? Only the seven of us knew of its existence. Did any of you mention it to anyone? Let it slip?''

''No!'' came the unanimous cry.

''Perhaps the man who sent it to us, the fly on the wall, was setting us up,'' Katya suggested.

''No, that makes no sense,'' Irina, who had finally pulled herself to her feet, said. Her knees felt weak and she had to quickly sit on the couch. Several times her fingers unconsciously smoothed the place where the knife had been. ''If he had sent us the material to set us up, surely more would have happened than the papers being stolen. They would have arrested Vera—''

''And Stepan,'' Vera interjected. ''If anything, they want Stepan more than me.''

Irina nodded in agreement. ''What if Savva was arrested on his way back to Russia and tortured for information?''

Vera shook her head. "If Savva hadn't made it back to Petersburg on schedule, Dmitri would have sent word to us."

A silence followed, unnerving, like a needle caught in the scratch of a record. Uncertainly Irina looked up. The quietly horrified expression on her comrades' faces underlined her own fear. "You don't suppose . . ." Irina began uncertainly. "I mean, it isn't possible that someone informed on us—you don't suppose one of us . . ." Her voice was throaty. She could not get the word "betrayed" from her lips.

"*If* Savva is free, *if* he arrived safely back in Petersburg, then I can't think of any other answer." Vera's voice was accusing. Her eyes narrowed as they moved from Irina to Katya to Josef.

"Surely you don't believe any of us . . ." Irina began.

"It is not up to me to believe anything. It is up to me to report the facts to Dmitri Andreievich. We must call a meeting of the others as quickly as possible, and then one of us must go back to Petersburg. This information must be delivered to Dmitri Andreievich in person."

Alexei was in Kharkov when Anna's letter reached him. He opened it carelessly, as he opened all his mail, never looking at the sender's name or address, but his eyes searched eagerly for the signature once he saw the flowing feminine writing.

October 5, 1903

Mon ami, Monsieur Kalinin,
 I hope you don't think me too bold for calling you mon ami, *for surely you led me to believe we were friends the night of September 14. The friendship of that evening remains with me still, for my success with our beloved Czar would never have happened if not for you. I received the most delightful note from the Czar himself, written in his own hand, and he sent me an exquisitely enameled pin in the shape of a strawberry in thanks. Of course, I expected nothing, and will treasure the gift always. I shall never wear it for fear of losing it. I know you are a busy man, but I wanted to thank you for your help and understanding. Should you ever have the time, I should be happy to hear from you.*

Your devoted friend,
Anna Petrovna Orlova

Alexei read the note several times, unaware of the intense flush of excitement Anna's handwriting and the sight of her

name were causing him. He focused instead on her obsequi-
ousness over the Czar's praise and his little enameled strawberry. He began to scribble:

> My dear Anna Petrovna,
>   If you rate your artistic success in terms of a musical
> illiterate such as the Czar, you will end up a pedagogic
> sycophant. I spoke to Rimsky-Korsakov about you before
> leaving Petersburg. He is most anxious to hear you play,
> but alas I will not be back for another three weeks. Devote
> yourself to your music—not to perfection, but to passion.
>   Respectfully,
>   Alexei Yakovlevich Kalinin

Alexei carried the unmailed letter to Anna in his pocket
for three days, not thinking of it until he stopped to look in
the window of a jewelry shop. By chance, he spotted an
enameled strawberry brooch. Although he found the pin most
unattractive, he went inside to inquire about the price.

"Five hundred rubles," the jeweler told him. "Would you
like to see it?"

"No, no." Alexei waved his hand, his eyes scanning the
cases glittering with precious jewels. "That ruby brooch,
there, in the shape of a flower."

"Oh, yes, Monsieur has the finest of taste. This is fashioned after a Fabergé piece made for the Czarina. Of course,
Fabergé's was priceless. This is a mere two thousand rubles."

"Fine, I'll take it. I want it sent immediately to this address. . . ." He dug into his pocket for the letter to Anna.
"Send it to the same party as is on this letter. And enclose
the letter with it."

CHAPTER FIVE

"Another worker was killed today on the Nikolaevsky Bridge.
Shot down in cold blood. That's what Ivan told me. He was
driving Mousia back from her dance class and the Cossacks

weren't letting no one by. Poor little Mousia had to sit in the freezing carriage for an hour before the streets got cleared.'' Zhenya Kalinina's aged eyes settled sympathetically on her granddaughter.

"But Ivan was fun!" Mousia piped up. "He wrapped me in the blanket and told me a story about bears and robbers. It was very funny, Grandma, and then we sang songs."

"Bet you were scared with all them Cossacks," Nikita insisted, his smooth round cheeks stained with gravy.

"Ivan said no one would dare hurt *me*."

"Oh, Lord, Lord, praise God!" Helena Kalinina's pale skin grew paler and a hint of life flashed in her flat gray eyes. She crossed herself several times. "You see, Alexei, you see what we live with day in and day out. It's fine for you, traveling about Russia, but a seven-year-old child has to suffer, and for what? For wanting to go to her dance lesson. You must move us from Petersburg, Alexei. You must. I fear for our lives hourly. Each morning when the boys go off to school, I fear I will never see them again." Tears glistened, and she crossed herself again.

"I wish I'd been there." Sasha pouted. "You're lucky, Mousia. I never see nothing, except the worker with the bloody head. Hey, remember that, Nikita?"

"Sasha!" Helena cried out. "I won't have it. I won't have talk like this at the dinner table. This was supposed to be a party to welcome Uncle Alexei home, and what do we talk about but revolution and killing. I won't have it, and neither will your father." She glanced at her husband, Tolya, sitting at the head of the table opposite Alexei.

Tolya Kalinin seemed hardly to hear his wife, yet a silence settled about the table as everyone waited for him to answer. It was a rare occasion for him to be dining with the family. When he wasn't out drinking in cheap bars by the railroad yards, he was holed up in his rooms with a bottle. It was unusual for the whole Kalinin family to eat together; and as much as Misha welcomed Uncle Alexei's sudden return, he despaired the family gathering. Misha could barely look at his father. The man repelled him. His blotchy, round, layered face was stubbled with two days' growth. His bleak eyes were vacant and red from drinking. His tie was barely knotted and his middle shirt buttons were open. His rough swollen hands were wrapped tightly about his wineglass.

"You're such a fool, Helena!" It was Zhenya who finally spoke, shaking her head disdainfully as she eyed Tolya, her oldest son. Her impatience, however, was directed at her daughter-in-law. "You think it's safer in Moscow or even in

the countryside? Misha read to me just the other day of a
group of peasants burning down the master's house and all
his fields. The militia was called in and the men were all
hanged in front of their wives and children, and what with
them half-starving. Half of Russia starves, yet the Czar talks
about seizing Manchuria and Persia.''

"Stories, newspaper headlines, trash!'' Helena protested.
"You shouldn't have Misha read you such stories, Mother.
It's better not to know such things.''

"And does not knowing make the truth go away?'' Zhenya
clucked, and her eyes brightened, the crags of skin seeming
to smooth in her growing agitation with her daughter-in-law.
"We're all dogs in the Czar's kennel—rich and poor alike,
even men like my Alexei—yes, even the richest can be arrested for whispering of a constitution or elections. Right
now, if the Czar's police knew we were talking like this
around our own dinner table, they could arrest us.''

"So don't talk, Mama,'' Tolya grumbled like a bear coming out of hibernation. He poured himself more wine.

"Yes, please, Mother, you frighten the children. Tell her,
Tolya, tell her she frightens the children.''

"Me! You're sitting next to her, Helena. You got a mouth.
Lord knows I hear it enough. Georgi!'' he thundered, calling
for the servant. "More wine!''

"You see, Alexei . . .'' Helena turned plaintively to her
brother-in-law, her watery eyes blinking nervously. Her long
thin fingers twisted about themselves. "You see how it is
when you're gone, Alexei.'' She bit her lower lip and pushed
a flyaway hair back into her bun. At thirty-seven, Helena
Kalinina looked more like sixty. She had none of the matronly padding of most women her age; rather she was worn
thin like weather-beaten shingles, the last glint of her youthful
beauty long tarnished by years of childbearing and the diffi-
culty of life with Tolya. Out of the ten children she had borne,
only five lived: Misha, Sasha, Nikita, Mousia, and the infant,
Nadezhda. "Someone must protect the children. I try, God
knows.'' Helena's hand lashed out, smacking ten-year-old Sasha and taking away the glass of milk into which he was
blowing bubbles.

"Who can protect anyone?'' Zhenya demanded. "As
mothers we have no choice. We must try and try to protect
our children, and in the end, they belong to the world. But
you, you think your children belong to you.'' Zhenya guffawed. "Look at Misha,'' she went on authoritatively. "He's
a man already and you and Tolya treat him like a child. He's
a man playing with life because that is all you allow him.''

Misha reddened. Along with Uncle Alexei, his grandmother was his greatest support, his only support when Uncle Alexei was gone. He wondered what he'd done to make her angry.

"Misha plays because he's had it too soft, like his mother," Tolya grumbled. "Never had to work a day in his life. Never known what it was to have his back aching and his legs crumble from exhaustion. If I had my way, I'd send him to the railroad yards, not the university."

"The world is different, Papa, from when—" Misha began.

"Different!" Tolya's eyes twitched as if trying to focus. A frightening life seemed to grip his bloated body. "You think because you don't see them, there aren't men doing just what your uncle and I used to do? You think because you live in this fine house with servants there aren't people living in hovels? Ach, you disgust me, Misha!" His voice rose threateningly. "You and your fine friends talking about revolution and strikes when you haven't lifted a finger to work your whole life. Revolution! You want revolution? Think, then, my fine fool. Think of your workers and peasants marching into this very room and taking what's yours and mine, looting what Alexei sacrificed for more than a namby-pamby piece of shit like you will ever know. Is that what you want? Is it?" Tolya was on his feet, his arms waving wildly.

"Tolya, Tolya . . ." Helena was by his side, meekly consoling him. "Sit, my heart. Have some drink. Yes, here . . ." She handed him his glass.

"*You*, Helena, it's your fault!" Tolya gruffly threw her arms off him. "Alexei thought he was doing me a favor when he found some fine lady for my wife." Tolya snorted disparagingly. "Some china fish is all he got me! Give me an honest whore anytime."

"Tolya!" Zhenya gasped.

"That's not fair, Papa!" Misha glared hotly, his fingers grasping the edges of the table. "You shouldn't talk that way about Mama."

"You, my son, daring to tell me!" Tolya lunged for Misha.

Instantly Alexei was between them, barring Tolya's way. "Sit down or go to your room," Alexei ordered, his voice barely above a whisper. He grabbed Tolya's arm roughly. "You're drunk. Stinking drunk. Enough, now, or so help me God, you'll regret I came home tonight."

For a moment Tolya looked ready to attack Alexei, but then his lips trembled and his face collapsed into a pitiful blubbering. "I'm sorry, Alyosha, my brother. Forgive me."

He hugged Alexei tightly, burying his face in his brother's massive shoulders. "I was drinking to celebrate your return only. A few drinks, I thought, to be happy. I have so little happiness, Alyosha. A few drinks is all I wanted. . . ."

"Come, come, it's all right, Tolya." Alexei slipped free of the tight hold and, propping him with one arm, led Tolya from the table. "Come, Misha," he called. "Help me put your father to bed."

Even after Tolya was safely tucked away for the night, Uncle Alexei was strangely preoccupied, and shortly after dinner, he changed to go out for the night.

"Will you be late, Uncle Alexei?" Misha asked as he sat on the bed while Alexei changed. "There are some things I want to talk to you about."

"I'll be at Ryabushinsky's. You know how long those meetings sometimes run. Why don't you come with me and we can go out for a drink afterward. I'd rather like that. I'm afraid I'll be leaving for Moscow on the morning train."

"You just came back for the meeting, then?"

"It's only slightly out of my way," he told Misha. "You're welcome if you want to come."

Misha shook his head. He had no interest in the endless arguing of the boring men in the Symposium. Misha had gone to a few meetings, because his uncle had invited him, but he felt uncomfortable with the middle-aged men who spoke of ways to "influence" the Czar, "suggestions" to curb military spending and the "introduction" of reforms aiding the expansion of capital. There was a coldness to their talk; rubles and gold seemed more their motivation than human welfare.

"I had plans with Mathilde," Misha replied, thinking perhaps this was not a good time to talk to Uncle Alexei about his failing grades anyway.

"Ah, Mathilde, yes, by all means. Don't let me keep you from such a delight!" Alexei winked through the mirror as he straightened his tie. "Still, if you'd like to come for a while, I think you'll be pleased. Ryabushinsky has drafted a position paper calling for representative government, freedom of speech and assembly. It's quite radical, and I might add, much of it was at your prompting."

"*My* prompting?"

Alexei smoothed his collar and turned smiling to Misha, feeling connected to the boy as he hadn't for a long time. Perhaps it was that he was feeling more connected to life. It was the young pianist, Anna Petrovna, he thought. Her talent excited him—no, not just talent, there was immortality in her soul. It burned, untouched, promising wealth unparalleled by his gold and rubles. Immortality wore no price tag. It shimmered with God's love and forgiveness, bringing peace to tortured souls. God, she was a find. Her music. In six lifetimes a man might not be able to touch, much less help mold, such a destiny.

"What do you mean, *my* prompting?" Misha asked.

Alexei stared a moment, unseeing. Then he remembered the discussion. It was important. "Don't you think I know the disdain in which you hold the Symposium? I can read your eyes; you tell me by your silence. And that's good, I think. You remind me of what I felt when I was your age, thinking everything had to happen now, immediately. Always impatient. Well, there's something to that. Nicholas Romanov is deadweight. Russia can't afford to carry him much longer. I wouldn't be surprised if a bomb were hurled at his head one of these days!"

The passion in Uncle Alexei's voice was mirrored in the layered shadows of his eyes. Misha was excited and strangely unnerved. "Do you think someone would really kill the Czar?"

"I'm sure there are plots afoot. Grand dukes and provincial governors are falling like flies to terrorist bombs."

"Do you approve?"

"How can one be a forward-thinking Russian these days and not? Terrorism has practically become a national pastime," Alexei replied flippantly, but his smile quickly faded, and his expression became pensive. "In truth, Misha, I believe terrorists have a place in times such as this—but don't let me hear you quoting me."

"But murdering someone, taking another's life."

Alexei grew still. "People do what they must to survive. Remember that, Misha. God grant it never happens, but someday you too may be faced with survival. Then there is no time for morality."

Misha tittered nervously, and burst out, "I bet Grandma would be a terrorist if she could! What do you think, Uncle Alexei? Can't you just imagine Grandma carrying a bomb underneath her coat!"

Alexei chuckled. "I wouldn't put anything past my mother!"

"Do you think that's why she's angry at me because I do nothing, like Papa said?"

"Ah, your father. You must block his drunken ravings from your mind."

"But it's true, I do nothing. We talk revolution at the university. And I feel it too. Sometimes when I see a worker or a small child in rags, I abhor my fine clothes, and I think: Today, tonight, I will do something finally. I will join a group. I will march. I will speak out for the freedoms I believe all Russians must have. But I don't. I can't. And it's not that I'm afraid, Uncle Alexei. I swear to you I'm not afraid. I just despise violence. And revolution is violent."

"Well, to tell you the truth, I'm just as glad you're not marching and handing out manifestos. Men have been arrested for less."

"But you and Monsieur Ryabushinsky and your manifesto . . ."

"It's unfair perhaps, but true, Misha, that those of us in the Symposium are protected by our position and power. There's always some risk, but the government needs us, and so the Czar tolerates us. Right now we're an irritating thorn in his side. But someday . . ." He settled next to Misha on the bed and took out his cigarettes. "Someday we shall rule Russia. Yes, someday there will be a freely elected government and men like you and I will represent the people! For that day, you must stay out of trouble, eh!"

Misha smiled halfheartedly and nodded. This was an old conversation after all: Uncle Alexei's dream about Misha's being a politician one day, an elected representative of the people. Misha had no desire to hold public office, not under the monarchy or in a republic, but he'd learned it was fruitless to argue with his uncle once he became intoxicated with such visions. It was far easier to change the subject, and Misha latched on to the first thing that came to his mind. "Why is Papa the way he is? Why does he say such things to Mama?"

"He was drunk," Alexei said sympathetically.

"He's always drunk. I hate him."

Alexei offered him a cigarette. Reaching for a match, he said, "It's more painful for you to hate him than love him, I promise you that. For better or worse, he's your father. There's no peace in hating your father."

"There'll be peace when he's dead," Misha growled.

"Believe me, your father is more to be pitied than hated." Alexei lit Misha's cigarette.

"Don't talk to me of such things, Uncle Alexei. Don't you tell me of his hard life. Whatever was done to him, he's done it sixfold to Mama and me and the others. Only when you're here is he docile."

"I know. I know," Alexei said sadly, stricken by the rage

he saw glinting in Misha's stare. "Still, he's your father. A man must make peace with his father."

"I can't. I'll never be able to. When I was a little boy, I used to pretend you were my father. Or I'd dream Papa was dead, and you adopted me."

"You might as well be. I'll never have a son of my own. You're as close to me as any son could be. In fact . . ." Alexei wrapped an arm around Misha. "I've been thinking, when school is out for the summer, I'd like you to start working with me. The business, all my holdings, will be yours someday. It's time you began finding out about what you will own, get a little taste of the power."

"I'm not sure I want such power."

"Of course you do. You've given up on school is all. It's time you were out in the world, making a little of that money you spend. It will be challenging, I promise. And then sometime, not right away, of course, but sometime, you must think about producing sons of your own."

"Oh, please, Uncle Alexei—marriage is the last thing on my mind."

"It needn't slow you down, my boy. Not in the least. Just so long as you know your sons are yours. Now, what was it you wanted to talk to me about?"

"Nothing really. It can wait. You're in a hurry, and so am I. I promised Mathilde I'd be there when the performance was over."

CHAPTER SIX

"The problem," Misha expounded as he sat eating a late-night supper at a Gypsy restaurant with Mathilde and a group of their friends, "is that a Russian must complicate the most straightforward situation. It's a quirk, and, I believe, a tragic flaw of the Russian personality," he added dramatically.

"Hear! Hear!" Sergei Denisov rose to his feet and held up his champagne. "We are going to hear the one and only Mikhail Anatolyevich Kalinin expound on the state of Russia!" He threw back his head and downed his glass.

Misha teasingly eyed Mathilde, then leaned over to kiss her.

There were hoots and clapping, Kolya Voronykhin reached for the hand organ he had recently borrowed from a Gypsy musician and flourished an introduction.

Misha stood and made a wobbly bow. "I say . . ." He lifted his glass. "We drink to the heroic worker who gave his life yesterday on the Nikolaevsky Bridge." Misha's words were slurring.

"To the worker!" Sergei Denisov echoed.

"To all workers!" Marie Popova rose to her feet.

"To the ballet!" Mathilde held up her glass.

"No, no, Mathilde, my love. We are toasting heroism now."

"And don't you think it's heroic for me to dance every night?" She slipped her arm around him, and kissed him. "Think of what it does to my poor toes. And besides, while you all gorge yourselves, Maria and I have to watch every morsel we put into our mouths. Don't you think that's heroic, Misha?" She giggled.

"No!" He thumped his fist on the table and sat down. "Ask Denisov. He's the authority. Denisov, do you think dancing at the Maryinsky qualifies as heroic?"

"No, but I think hanging out with one such as you does. For that, you are dubbed heroic, Mathilde."

Misha didn't laugh with the others; he pressed his hands to his head, trying to get control of his thoughts, flapping like slaps of mud, one on the other. He was drunk, very drunk. It was hard to think straight, yet he needed to. There was something he needed to say. His voice boomed suddenly. "If the Czar wants to hang on to his divine right, fine, but take away his secular power. That belongs to the people and the people alone. Russia needs free men, free workers, if we're to succeed in the twentieth century."

"Capitalism needs free workers, you mean," Denisov chided.

"Listen, my friend, I'm no socialist. I never pretended to be. And not everyone who wants to get rid of the Czar is a socialist either, not by a long shot. It's a revolution like the Americans had that we're after. Russians like the good life too much to give it up for the asceticism of socialism. Take away our vodka and our fine food and we'll die!" He downed the champagne.

Denisov slapped him on the back. "Spoken like the true heir to Russia's greatest fortune!"

"To hell with fortune! It's birth that counts, and despite

my mother's, I'm far more peasant than aristocratic,'' Misha went on, the loudness of his voice causing him to teeter precariously. ''After all, what did my mother's fine family have left but some title? The impoverished nobility.'' He snorted in disgust. ''They're the worst, eh, Mathilde? Only such a man as my grandfather would marry his daughter to a brute like my father. I have never forgiven my grandfather for sentencing my mother to a life of hell!'' he thundered angrily.

An embarrassed silence settled about the group. Mathilde tried to coax Misha down beside her. ''Come now, my heart. Sit by me and let's be jolly. We've all come to have some fun, and when you turn so serious . . .''

''Have I ever told you of my heritage?'' He grasped her shoulder roughly.

Denisov yanked Misha's hand and shoved him into his seat. ''You wax poetic on the peasants whenever you get drunk, my friend, and you're drunk now, stinking.''

Misha broke into a grin. ''So I am!'' He filled everyone's glass with champagne and ordered two more bottles. ''The rise of the proletariat may be inevitable, but it is the peasants who are the soul of Russia! My grandmother was born a peasant, and is illiterate to this day, but she's the finest woman you'll ever meet. Tell me, Mathilde, what do you think of terrorists?'' He set his chin on his hand and stared at her as if eager for her response.

''I think they are boring.''

''Oh, boring, is it! And if it was you they meant to kill?''

''Why would they want to kill me, for heaven's sake?'' She seemed shocked.

His laughter was derisive, and he turned to Kolya. ''Voronykhin, you come from generations of princes. A true blue blood. What do you think of terrorists?''

''They scare the hell out of me!'' He downed his drink. ''I should carry a red flag just to be sure they don't mistake me for the enemy.''

''Yes, Kolya!'' Marie Popova laughed merrily. ''A red flag and a sable coat!''

''It's done all the time, Marie,'' Kolya insisted. ''Besides, I happen to believe in the righteousness of the workers' cause. As a matter of fact, I could live on half my allowance and still not lose a whit of pleasure. I'd give half away if it would do any good.''

Misha stared; his eyeballs felt white-hot; his lids pressed to close. A wave of nausea threatened to overcome him.

''What do you think, Kalinin?'' Kolya was insisting. ''Do you think you could live on half your allowance?''

"No! Absolutely not!" Mathilde piped up. She wrapped an arm about Misha and kissed his ear as she whispered, "Tell Kolya you need twice as much to be truly happy."

Misha stared uncomprehendingly at Mathilde. She was swaying back and forth. Her red lips were grinning grotesquely. "Passion!" he cried. "We Russians muck it all up— we get so damned caught up in our own words and our damned passion. We can justify anything, even violence, terror and death! Yes, we glorify violence as if we were devil worshipers. It lurks within our souls, waiting to burst free and consume us!" He stopped abruptly. His head was pounding and his gut was twisting, threatening to spill out. Pushing himself from the table, he rushed from the tiny smoke-filled café, and made it outside the door before retching.

"Are you all right?" Denisov was beside him, holding his shoulders as the dry heaves threatened to suck out his insides. "I've never known you to get sick."

"Take me home, would you?" he pleaded, sweating despite the frigid air.

"Sure, sure, just let me get Mathilde."

"No, no, she'll want me to go back to her place. I don't think I can." He wiped his mouth with his sleeve and started shaking. "God, my head. It feels like a bomb's gone off." He leaned against the side of the café and began to slide to the ground. "Denisov . . ." He grabbed him desperately. "I have to do something!"

"What do you mean?"

"Something with my life, don't you see! I'm failing out of school. My uncle is talking about my working with him, even marrying. But there's something inside me . . ." Tears began streaming down his face; his fingers clamped on Sergei. "It blinds me, and I can't take a step forward or back. Like when my father starts hitting me, I can't stop him. I want to kill him, but I can't even defend myself. Do you think I'm going mad?"

"Let me get Mathilde. She'll want to be with you."

"No, no, not Mathilde. Sometimes I can't stand the little whore."

"Jesus, Misha, you're drunk. You don't know what you're saying. I've never seen you like this."

"Shit," he moaned, gray waves of nausea folding in on him. "I'm gonna be sick again."

Misha's head still felt like an exploding bomb the next morning, yet he dragged himself out of bed in time for his nine-o'clock economics exam. Better to go and get a 2, than not go and get a 0. His father took any 0 which Misha got as a personal insult. Misha considered flagging a cab, but the cold air helped clear his head. A fresh snow had fallen the night before, padding the roadway on the frozen Neva River and coating the bare branches of birches and the heavy boughs of firs. He slowly made his way along the embankment, walking in paths left by the street cleaners. Sledded carriages sped quietly by, the bells on the horses' harnesses ringing like crystal. Even the normally loud coachmen seemed quieted by the white peace cushioning the morning. The green-and-white Winter Palace and the Admiralty glistened. Misha stopped and stared across the Nikolaevsky Bridge, trying to envision the spot where the striking worker from the Putilov Iron Works had died, his blood blotted red in the snow.

Murdered, he thought, the word tightening a nagging knot someplace deep inside him. His eyes shifted uneasily from the bridge to the foreboding Peter and Paul Fortress buttressed against the other side of the frozen river. People, students he knew, were incarcerated there, their young lives stolen one day, swept up without warning, punished for the crime of caring. Some said they were better off dead. His grandmother said they were heroes. And they were. His grandmother said he was a child playing at life. And he was, failing at school, partying with dancers like Mathilde.

"Hey, Misha . . . Kalinin, is that you?"

He turned at the sound of Denisov's voice and waved.

"You look like hell," Denisov greeted him.

"I feel like it."

"I'm sure. I've never seen you drunker than last night. What the hell are you doing here? Don't tell me you're coming to the demonstration at Kazan Cathedral."

"You know me and demonstrations. Actually, I was on my way to my economics exam."

"Don't bother. I just went to my locker to pick up some leaflets and everything is shut down tight as a drum. I guess they're afraid we'll march from the cathedral back to school and start breaking windows—which wouldn't be a bad idea, eh! Well, so long as you're up and about, why don't you come along?"

"I don't know."

Denisov chuckled. "Come on, my friend, you'll love the camaraderie of the fight. Gets your blood going."

"Mathilde is more than adequate for that."

Denisov's lips tightened angrily. "I don't understand you, Misha. You're going to fight one day. We're all going to be called upon to fight in the end."

"When I'm called upon, I'll go."

"By the Czar," he accused. "Or will your uncle buy a substitute?"

"Look, Denisov, this is getting unfriendly."

"You're damn right it is. I'm sick of my best friend acting like some kind of damn pacifist."

"I appreciate your concern," he said derisively. "But we've had this discussion before. It ends with you trying to convince me to become an anarchist."

"It's the only answer to total freedom."

"Ah, yes, anarchism!" Misha sneered. "The ultimate pie-in-the-sky platform. Complete freedom. Freedom for you to kill me. Freedom for me to kill you. It's a lot of words! Such freedom doesn't exist on earth or in heaven. It can't. It's order we need. A different one from what we have, but order just the same. Society can't go on without it."

"I, at least, have the action to back the words."

"Meaning?"

"Meaning I'm sick of you sitting on your tail while the rest of us risk our necks. Dammit, Misha, I've been your friend for too long to not know that you're one of us at heart. Whatever's stopping you, I guarantee one march will free you. Come with me now. It's a worthy cause—an end to these damn temporary education rules and the end of the student draft. Aren't you tired of being taught by little bureaucrats who have as much interest in teaching as a snail?"

"I'll flunk out of school this semester anyway, so it won't affect me."

"Good then! Fine! Go on to Mathilde, why don't you!" He sneered. "Luxuriate between her legs while the rest of us get our heads beaten in!"

Misha's fist flew out, knocking Denisov onto the snowy roadway, where he lay stunned, blood trickling from his nose. Several passersby stopped and gaped. "Go on, go on, this is a personal matter!" Misha waved to them and then held out a hand to help Denisov up. "Look, I'm sorry . . ."

"Go to hell!" Denisov pulled himself to his feet and, brushing the snow from his trousers and jacket, he hurried away.

Misha went to the demonstration to look for Denisov and to apologize. He'd never meant to hit him. They had been friends for more than ten years and had few disagreements until they'd entered the university and Denisov discovered anarchism. Misha had willingly gone to some early meetings of the Anarchist Alliance, but he had little patience with the debating until dawn about the definition of freedom and the most arcane theoretical points of socialism. Still, he valued Denisov's friendship above all others, and if it meant marching in a few demonstrations to prove it, he'd go.

He was several blocks from Kazan Cathedral when he began to see black-uniformed policemen on foot and red-jacketed Cossacks on horseback. The agents of the Okhrana were not so easily recognizable, but Misha knew they were out in numbers, disguised as peddlers, coachmen, business-men, and students. They moved like shadows, striking with-out warning, making arrests on the basis of unsubstantiated rumors or whim. The name of their chief, Yermolov, could silence a room of the most ardent student activists.

Curious passersby, young and old, dressed in everything from furs to rags, milled about cordoned-off streets where rumors of student barricades at the cathedral were spreading rapidly. Misha was slipping around a police barrier when he was roughly pushed back.

"Can't you read? See, it says 'No entrance,'" a brawny cop told him.

"I need to get to the cathedral."

"Ain't no one else getting there. Chief's orders. Ain't no permit for the march as it is, so you best be on your way, sonny."

"You've got no right!"

"This club says I do!" The cop held it only inches from Misha's face, and instantly two other police came to his sup-port.

"All right, all right, I'm going!" Misha held out his hands as he backed away and faded into a crowd. His pace quick-ened as he headed down the Moika Canal to Nevsky Prospect and the other approach to the cathedral. "Damn bastards," he muttered, feeling his resentment toward the cops growing with each step. "Who the hell do they think they are? Damn bastards with their guns and their badges. Take away their guns and their badges—"

The swell of a chant interrupted his griping and as he neared Nevsky Prospect, he paused to listen. "We Demand Our Teachers Back! End the Draft Now!" Turning down Nevsky, he saw a large contingent of marchers held at bay by a line of well-armed Cossacks and police. Several banners reading "Students' Alliance for Freedom! End Punitive Drafting Now!" dotted the gray sky above the marchers. Red flags waved. Fists rose and fell to the beat of a new chant. "Let Us Through! Let Us Through! Let Us Through Now!" The tempo intensified. The air was electric with rebellion and

Misha began pushing his way into the middle of the marchers.

"What's happening?" he asked a young woman. White-
blond hair escaped her babushka. Her cheeks were ruddy, her
skin smooth.

"They won't let any more of us near the cathedral. Seems
they're busy busting heads in there already. We've got to get
through. We've got to support the others!" she insisted, the
energy of her voice mirrored in the brilliance of her eyes.
Turning from Misha, she shook her fist at the line of police
"Let Us Through! Let Us Through! Let Us Through Now!"

Misha was carried by her passion, and began chanting with
her. She smiled at him and her voice grew louder. His rose
to meet hers.

Some anxious minutes passed, with the marchers pushing
ahead a few steps, only to fall back again. Finally the message swept down the line. "Stay tight. We're breaking
through. Stay tight. There's strength in unity."

Arms linked and the chant thundered. "Let Us Through!
Let Us Through Now!"

Cossacks readied their whips.

Demonstrators packed closely and surged forward. "Don't
panic! Stay tight!" came the cry, and the girl squeezed
Misha's arm with her own. They stayed shoulder to shoulder
for a few hundred feet. Suddenly Cossacks on horseback,
arms waving whips, stormed, forcing the marchers to break
ranks. Misha lost sight of the girl with the vibrant voice as
he ran with a small group, darting around horses, ducking to
avoid whips and clubs. He ran until the cathedral came into
view. For a moment he felt exuberant, as if he'd reached
some long-appointed goal. Only then did he turn to see the
disaster behind him. Many of the demonstrators were lying
bloodied on the ground. Others were cordoned off by police
with guns drawn.

Praise God, how had he made it through? But he didn't
have time to ponder the question long. A student was surging
toward him with a look of hatred in his eyes. The student, he
knew, was a plainclothes cop and he raced ahead until he
found himself trapped, police behind and the cathedral ahead.
Cossacks swarmed over demonstrators on the steps of the
cathedral. Bodies tumbled like rocks in a slide and collided,
falling bloodied down steps and over the parapet; people
screamed, gun butts, fists, and whips pounded against flesh;
curses flew; people moaned. Misha saw the girl with the vibrant voice. She'd broken free too. Her babushka was gone;

her long blond hair flew in wisps like trails of snow flurries in the moonlight.

"Murderers!" she shrieked.

Misha watched the word form on her red lips and expand in waves of deafening sound.

"Murderers!" The vengefulness of her voice spread like a cannon blast; she was running through the tangled mass of people, up steps, down steps, and Misha was running toward her, propelled by an energy that made him feel invulnerable. Not even a burst of gunfire stopped him. He was running toward the girl, pushing past people until he saw the whip cut through the air and land across her neck and face.

A scream of horror caught in his throat and he froze as a red welt rose across her white skin. Blood began to ooze. Tiny drops appeared on the surface and spilled over in a stream of red tears, skin against bone. Still the Cossack grabbed her, beat her, called her the foulest of names.

Misha was running again, the rage seeming to burst from his gut and strain at his skin. Someone pulled at his shoulder and he swerved, blocking a club with his arm. His fist shot out, landing in the policeman's gut. As the policeman doubled in pain, Misha's fists pummeled the man's head. Then Misha was diving at the Cossack who was raising his whip on the girl once more. Just as his arms were about to crush around the Cossack's neck, Misha felt his own skull split in two and there was nothing.

"You must have one hell of a hangover," perfect rows of white teeth told him.

He felt the ground beneath him. It was hard, cold stone. Legs blurred his view, hundreds, millions of legs constantly shifting. The air was thick with smoke. The talk was loud and angry, spiked with spit.

"How are you feeling, brother?" The white teeth doubled and merged with lips.

Misha stared very hard, trying to focus. For a moment, the lips spread into a face holding the bluest eyes he had ever seen. Happy eyes, burning bright. They belonged to a god, a Nordic god with blue eyes and soft blond curls. Misha thought he was in heaven.

"What's your name?"

The vision split, the face dismembered. Misha closed his eyes, the shaft of blond hair sliced in half, white skin streaked with blood. The girl, heavenly Father, the girl had lost her face. He tried to move, to shake free of the image, but the pain in his head made his stomach surge.

"Better stay put. They've sent for a doctor. You never should have been brought here."

He opened his eyes and the god was still there. "Where are we?"

"Spassky station. Jail. There are hundreds of us."

Misha let the words settle in. This god was a man. They weren't in heaven.

"I'm Savva Safanov." The god-man pressed his hand on Misha's. "You have a name?"

"Mikhail Kalinin," he said without sound. The god-man named Savva was merging and splitting again.

"I saw you go down. The Cossack pig must have had a lead pipe or club. That's a bad bump you got." Savva touched Misha's head.

Misha closed his eyes. He wanted to sleep, to forget the girl, the blood, the screams.

"Don't fall asleep, brother." Savva shook him ever so slightly. "Now that you're awake, I think it's better you stay that way till the doc comes. There are a couple like you who should have been sent to the hospital. The filthy pigs, they had a heyday with us. You at the university?"

Misha thought he nodded his head. His mouth felt dry. He could barely swallow. "Water . . ."

"Sure—hey, someone bring some water over for a fallen comrade. But not too much. Just a sip, to wet the lips. . . ."

A hand slipped gently under his head; a cold metal cup was held to his mouth.

"Hey, Misha," a voice called. "It's me, Denisov."

"You know him?" asked Savva.

"Sure, Misha Kalinin."

"Kalinin, Kalinin . . . anyone I should know?"

"His uncle owns half the railroads and oil wells in Russia. He'll be out of here in no time . . ."

Denisov's voice floated like fragments of a foreign language. Misha wanted to talk to him. He wanted to tell him he was sorry. Then he felt someone by his side, and Denisov's voice again. "Come on, come on. . . ." Denisov shook him gently. "Don't sleep."

Misha raised his hand, groped for Denisov's, and when Denisov took it, Misha tried to squeeze it, but he had no strength.

"It's okay, my friend," Denisov whispered. "I understand. I'm sorry too. Look, we'll talk later when you're better."

Then Denisov slipped his hand away and someone else took his place. It was the god-man, Savva. "Look . . ."

Misha could feel his breath on his ear. "You probably won't remember this, but I saw you out there. You fight like a bull. I'm telling you the revolution could use you, brother . . ." The voice grew distant and loud at the same time. "Well, well, you're about to be saved! Here comes the doc and a stretcher. See you around, Misha Kalinin. . . ."

CHAPTER SEVEN

The concussion was severe, but he would recover; his eyesight would return to normal. He had recurring nightmares about the girl with half a face and a blue-eyed Nordic god whose saber dripped blood. At first he thought his mother was a nurse, and he pleaded with her as he pleaded with them all, "The girl. She was bleeding—her face—is she here? Can I see her?" He closed his eyes, feeling very tired.

"Misha!" an all-too-recognizable voice wailed.

He looked again, holding his eyes wide to focus the constantly shifting image appearing like feathers. He blinked, and in that moment, his mother became clear. She was wearing a hat made of huge ostrich plumes. Tears were streaming down her face.

Then his father entered his plane of sight. "Stop, stop, enough, Helena!" his father's voice boomed. He pulled at his wife's shoulder, pulling her away from Misha. "So?" he demanded.

Misha closed his eyes.

"Don't yell, Tolya. This is a hospital," Helena implored.

"Some kind of hospital, with a guard outside the door! He's under arrest plain and simple. The head will mend, but the consequences are far-reaching. There will be a trial—ah, the sins of the fathers . . ." Tolya grasped Misha's shoulder, digging in his fingers painfully. "Wait until Alexei hears of this. The ghost of the past has come to haunt the Kalinin family again. All Alexei's work to make us respectable, and you, his favorite, you drag us through the mud once more. . . ."

"Tolya, don't! Tolya, he's ill!" Helena was pleading as she

tried to pry his fingers from Misha's shoulder. "Nurse, nurse!" she cried, and ran from the room.

Misha looked again when she returned. His father was sitting in a chair beside the bed, head pressed against folded hands, sobbing.

Zhenya Kalinina visited Misha early the next morning. She was wearing a new, brightly colored lavender-and-blue dress for the occasion, and she carried a huge bouquet of long-stemmed roses. "Well!" She dropped the bouquet on the bed. "You look fine, Misha, just fine. From what your mother said, I expected to find you half dead." She bent over and kissed both cheeks, then his lips, and finally the bandage that wrapped around his head.

"I might have been if they'd stayed any longer." He smiled and reached for her hand, slipping his own inside her large, strong fingers. "How are Nikita and Sasha and Mousia? Are they convinced I'm a criminal and will be hanged next week?"

"Mousia, of course, was terrified. But I spoke to her after your father finished his carrying on. And the boys think you quite the hero."

"What do you think?"

"I say bravo! You have your first battle wound. And," she added, fussing with his pillows, "it was a long time in coming. Yet I knew it would come. Finally, always, a Russian fights. I believe that. Even when we crawled on the dirt under the yokes of the Mongol and Tatar dogs, we had freedom burning in our souls. There's no shame, only honor in fighting for freedom."

"Do you think Uncle Alexei will be angry with me?"

"Alexei—angry! Whatever for? A Cossack." She spit. "You attacked a Cossack no less. That makes you a hero, praise God!"

"Grandma." He urged her down beside him on the bed. "Why must men fight?"

"Because there is evil in the world. Evil doesn't go away by prayer alone. Why? I don't know. You'd have to ask God that. He gave us evil to appreciate the good. And to protect the good for our children, men must fight. It is the way. Not that I like it, but what can one do when faced with evil? Only cowards run. Like your father. Praise God, he's my son, but sometimes I wonder." She crossed herself. "He would kiss the Czar's arse if he had the chance. Me . . ." Her voice lowered. "I'd give any Romanov a good hard boot! So I say about your papa—he's your papa and my son, but he's a damned fool. Now . . ." She sighed contentedly. "I thought we could recite poetry to pass the time. Some Pushkin would be best. You remember the one called 'Message to Siberia'?" She reached for a rose, and breathed in deeply, then held it to Misha's nose, and laid it beside his head. "Remember, with Pushkin, the passion is there."

Misha smiled, feeling safe. This was always his grand-mother's preamble to a recitation of Pushkin. Although she couldn't read, Zhenya Kalinina knew volumes of Pushkin, Nekrasov and other great poets by heart. When Misha was a boy, she would sit on his bed every night and tell him stories or recite poetry. Pressing her hand to his lips, he said, "I love you, Grandma."

"Of course you do. Now, come . . ." She smoothed back the hair from his face. "Do you remember the poem?"

"I'm not sure."

"All right, then. I'll begin:

> *Deep in the Siberian mine.*
> *Keep your patience proud;*
> *The bitter toil shall not be lost,*
> *The rebel thought unbowed.*
>
> *The sister of misfortune, Hope,*
> *In the under-darkness dumb*
> *Speaks joyful courage to your heart;*
> *The day desired will come.*
>
> *And love and friendship pour to you*
> *Across the darkened doors,*
> *Even as round your galley-beds*
> *My free music pours.*
>
> *The heavy-hanging chains will fall,*
> *The walls will crumble at a word;*
> *And Freedom greets you in the light,*
> *And brothers give you back the sword."*

It was Mathilde who noticed the disappearance of the guard from outside Misha's hospital door five days after the dem-onstration.

"Uncle Alexei," Misha explained. "My parents must have gotten in touch with him, then."

"Well, I think it's grand the guard is gone. He made me dreadfully nervous, looking me up and down every time I came to visit you, and taking my name. That's all I need, you know, is to be involved with someone who's thought to be antisocial. If I didn't love you so much, Misha, I never would risk coming to see you.'' She weaved her fingers inside his and held them to her lips. Bending over, she whispered into his ear, ''I wish I could crawl beside you in this bed right now. I imagined that last night, sneaking into the hospital and being with you. Oh, but you missed a wonderful dinner last night. Prince Senn, you know, he's mad about Marie Popova all of a sudden. He took us all to Cubats. The supper was superb, but it was dreadful without you and Denisov. I was terribly bored. Everybody took pity on me, of course. They're as desperate as I am for you to get well.''

''Nobody's heard from Denisov, then?''

''Nobody. It's perfectly dreadful. We're all worried to death that something terrible's happened. You know how people can just disappear and never, never be heard from again. I should be moved to tears if that happened to Sergei. But praise God you're safe. I can't wait to have you out of here . . .'' Her face was very close to his. She smoothed her cheek against his.

Her skin grated and he pulled away, shocked at his own revulsion. ''Don't, Mathilde. I don't feel well. My head . . . I don't know.''

''It's your uncle. You're afraid now that your uncle knows—do you think he'll take your allowance away?'' She was concerned.

''No. . . .'' He closed his eyes, suddenly wanting her to leave.

''Good, because I don't see why he should. I mean, after all, just about anyone can get arrested in the streets today. If your uncle puts up a fuss, all you have to tell him is that it was all a mistake.''

''But it wasn't—I'd do it again.''

Her eyes closed. She frowned impatiently.

''You can't understand that, can you?'' He grabbed her hand.

''It's boring is all, like when Denisov gets talking about his anarchism. Besides, I don't believe you. It's the blow to your head. Once the swelling's gone down, you'll be your old self again.''

''I don't think so, Mathilde.''

Her laughter was grating. ''Oh, please, Misha, don't tell me you've decided to become a revolutionary. How terribly gauche! I just can't imagine you giving up the good life for . . . well, for what?''

Misha closed his eyes, wishing when he opened them that

she'd be gone. "Get me my overcoat, will you? It's in the closet."

"Whatever for? You're not thinking of walking out of the hospital!"

"Just get it, would you!"

"Well, all right, all right. . . . Here." She held it out to him.

He reached into his pocket, coming up with the key to her apartment.

"What's this?" She tittered uneasily.

"The key to your flat. I won't be needing it anymore."

"What?" Her face drained of color. "What do you mean?"

"I mean, I don't think we work very well together after all. When you take away the lust and my uncle's money, we really don't have very much, do we?"

"You little . . ." She spluttered.

"Shit," he filled in.

"Yes!" The color rushed to her face. "You'll regret this, Misha."

"Actually, I don't think so." He closed his eyes, not opening them until he heard her heels clicking down the hall.

Misha woke to someone nudging his shoulder. He looked up to see a young, short, stocky, dark-haired orderly watching over him. Misha couldn't remember seeing him before. He pushed himself to a sitting position. "Who are you?"

"I've been sent by a comrade, one who saw you fight. He sends his best wishes for your health and speedy recovery. He says to tell you that you are a fighter, and that the revolution needs all who fight. He says if you want to fight, you should ask your uncle about Dmitri Mayakovsky."

"Who's that?"

"I know no more. You are to ask your uncle. To the revolution! To victory!" The orderly kissed Misha on both cheeks, turned and left.

Misha was sitting on the edge of his bed, waiting. He'd been ready to leave the hospital for hours, but Uncle Alexei was late, as usual. He'd gone over the visit from the unnamed orderly a hundred times, just as he'd done for the past four days, trying to find a clue to this man Dmitri Mayakovsky, trying to ascertain for certain if the orderly were real or a dream. He racked his brain looking for something to connect Uncle Alexei to the name Dmitri Mayakovsky, but could not.

"Misha!" The call of the deep voice yanked him from his thoughts, and he jumped to his feet.

Uncle Alexei was hurrying toward him, arms outstretched. He hugged him and kissed him again and again. "So, a political prisoner, eh! What the hell were you doing attacking a goddamned Cossack? And what were you doing in the demonstration?"

"I'm not sure why I was there. Denisov and I had had an argument. It was unpleasant and I went searching for him."

"In the demonstration?"

Misha nodded. "I'm worried about Denisov, Uncle Alexei. He was arrested, that much I know. But no one's heard from him since. Is there any way you can find out something?"

"I'd say we have enough problems with you, my friend. Assaulting a Cossack is no small affair." He grimaced. "Anyway, I've already spoken to Yuri Dobrinsky. You've an appointment with him tomorrow to discuss your defense." Alexei reached for Misha's bag. "I'd like to be there, but I've a business meeting—"

"Uncle Alexei . . ." Misha touched his arm. He breathed deeply and forced out the question. "Have you ever heard of a man named Dmitri Mayakovsky?"

Alexei stiffened. His face froze in solemnity. "Who told you about Dmitri Mayakovsky?"

"I'm not certain. Someone dressed as an orderly appeared in my room. I was asleep and when I woke he was standing there looking at me. He told me I was a fighter and if I wanted to fight for the revolution I should ask you about Dmitri Mayakovsky."

Alexei gripped and ungripped his fingers, then sat down heavily on the bed. His brow furrowed.

Misha sat beside him. "You know this man, then."

"Yes." He peered, his eyelids drooping, and underneath, a darkness threatened like clenched fists. "But there's no reason for you to. Mayakovsky's a dangerous man. He doesn't play schoolboy games. He's not interested in marching, that much I promise you."

"What is he interested in?"

"Take my word for it, there is nothing about the man that you need to know. There is nothing that such knowledge would give you but more danger than you could ever want. Now, come, the carriage is waiting."

"Uncle Alexei, please—I'm not a child anymore. I can make my own decisions."

Alexei rose purposefully, walked over to the door and shut it tightly. Returning to Misha, he said, his voice threatening,

"*Your* decision-making has led you to a hospital bed with a jail sentence hanging over your head. *Your* decision-making told you to attack a Cossack. I would say *your* decision-making is hardly well-honed."

Misha colored deeply. "Grandma was proud of what I did. I had the feeling you were too."

"She's an old woman with romantic ideas. I shall speak to her as soon as we get home. I think she'll be shocked to find out that you took her seriously. Now, I want this discussion to end here and now. I don't want to hear another word about Mayakovsky."

"I mean no disrespect, but if you won't tell me about Dmitri Mayakovsky, then I'll find out another way."

"I forbid it!" Alexei's face drained of color. He was angrier than Misha had ever seen him before.

Oddly, Misha felt more dared than threatened, and he burst out, "It's my life. I make my own decisions!"

"Fine, then, make your own decisions about your allowance, because you'll be getting none from me."

Misha felt sickened by the threat. More than that, he felt sickened by such anger swooping around them like demons. Still, he could not stop himself. "I'll find this Dmitri Mayakovsky with or without you!"

"Do that!" Alexei thundered, and started for the door. His hand reached for the doorknob, and he stopped.

Misha watched his uncle's back heaving. Finally Alexei's shoulders slumped. Slowly he returned to the bed, tossed his hat on a chair and unbuttoned his sable-collared greatcoat. He sat in silence for a long time. "All right," he finally spoke. "I'll tell you." His voice was low, but each word was spoken with deliberate clarity. "Dmitri Mayakovsky is Yuri Dobrinsky—my lawyer and partner Yuri Dobrinsky and your Dmitri Mayakovsky are one and the same."

"I . . . I don't understand."

"Dmitri Mayakovsky is a terrorist."

Misha stared disbelievingly, and the image of Yuri Dobrinsky filled his mind. He was a rather unprepossessing man, bald, plump and round-shouldered, with bushy, peppered eyebrows growing over bland gray eyes. His reddish complexion was accented by a bulbous nose, thick lips, and large square teeth. His suits, like the man himself, always seemed crumpled. The collars of his shirts never met. More than that, Misha couldn't remember. Although Yuri Dobrinsky always had been in the shadows of Misha's life, Misha didn't know much about the man. He was Uncle Alexei's lawyer and partner. He came to the house on business sometimes, rarely if ever saying more than hello to Misha.

"Yuri Dobrinsky is a scrupulously honest man. I'd trust him with my last penny, but with my life or with yours?" Alexei questioned, and shrugged as if carrying a heavy load. "There's a ruthlessness about him, a determination. Underneath his shabby, slow-moving exterior, he's a fanatic. Yuri's ties to terrorism go way back. His father was an officer in the Imperial Guards who was exiled for plotting to assassinate Nicholas I. Dmitri was little more than an infant at the time. His mother took him to live with her father, who despised everything Yuri's father stood for. The grandfather forbade the mention of Yuri's father in his house and legally adopted Yuri, stripping him of his father's name. Dobrinsky is the grandfather's name. Yuri's real name is Mayakovsky. It's no wonder it's the name he uses in the revolution."

"What happened to his mother?"

"She died when he was about eight, and with her death he lost all ties to his father, except those that burned in his heart. Through his grandfather, Yuri was nominated for the Imperial Guards, but he insisted on a career in the law, thinking that as a lawyer he could defend men like his father. He had the potential for being a brilliant lawyer apparently, but he became so involved in revolutionary causes, no one but those who couldn't pay would touch his services."

"What about his father?"

"He died in prison. A few of the conspirators survived, and during a brief period of liberalization in the 1850's, they were released, but barred from returning to western Russia. I met Yuri in 1883. Alexander II had been assassinated only two years before. Being a revolutionary then was like signing your own death warrant. Yuri was practically penniless when I approached him through the daughter of one of his father's co-conspirators. I needed legal help in patenting my railroad track switch. He was as eager to help me as I was for his help. Yuri made enough money from my invention to set him up for life. Most of what he makes goes to the revolution."

"And he never involved you?"

"Oh, to a certain degree. One can't be around Yuri long without being persuaded. But terrorism, violence, simply wasn't an avenue open to me. Yuri and I accept our differences."

"How involved is he?"

"I'm not certain of the details. I know there's a connection between Yuri and the Terrorist Brigade—although God knows you must never mention that. It could mean Yuri's life. The Brigade is responsible for probably half the political assassinations in Russia. So, you understand why I was hesitant . . .''

"But why did he come to me?"

"I don't know. I haven't the foggiest idea. But believe me, I shall find out. Now, what do you say we forget the entire matter. Wipe it from your mind as if it never happened. I shall speak to Yuri, but you and I . . .'' He slapped Misha's knee. "We must get out of this place! It will sorely affect our mood soon. What you need is a brisk ride and some hearty food and fine wine. Then, perhaps, we should talk about a vacation for you, some time to recuperate. A trip to Italy or Greece perhaps, to lie in the sun. Then, when you return, you can spend some time with me and the business. Yes!'' He reached for Misha's suitcase. "I believe a European trip is quite the medicine for you. Oh, by the way . . .'' He paused as they reached the door. "I'm having a dinner party in a few weeks. There's someone I want you to meet. She's quite beautiful, and very talented. Anna Petrovna, Count Pyotr Orlov's daughter. But she's not one of your young hussies, my friend. Come on too strong and you'll lose her forever, I warn you. I suspect you'd have to wed her to bed her.''

CHAPTER EIGHT

Yuri Dobrinsky lived in a small, unadorned house on Vasilievsky Island not far from the university. His office was at the end of a long, dark hall. Papers, books, and folders cluttered the desk and the floor; layers of dust fogged on all surfaces; ashtrays were overflowing and half-filled coffee cups abounded. At first Misha had wondered how the old man did business in such a mess; but then he remembered that he had no clients other than Uncle Alexei, and terrorists for certain were not fussy. Besides, as soon as the conversation began, Misha forgot about the surroundings.

There was an authority to Yuri Dobrinsky that Misha had never noticed before. Perhaps it was the knowledge that in another life he was the terrorist Dmitri Mayakovsky. Yet, Yuri's normally unfocused eyes seemed to sharpen behind the thick lenses; they riveted on Misha as if drilling below the surface of expression and words. The inward roll of Yuri's shoulders expanded slowly as his questions became more pointed. He seemed to know the answers before they were asked, and he listened intently, his silence demanding Misha's total concentration.

"There is no question then that you attacked the Cossack?"

"No, none. I . . . I'm sorry."

"No apologies, not now, not ever. You did what you did, nothing more, nothing less. The facts are all we have to work on. The facts could send you to Siberia, but we shall do our best not to let that happen." Yuri Dobrinsky smiled as if the meeting had drawn to an end. He slowly stood, but Misha remained seated. "Is there something else, then?" Yuri questioned.

"Actually . . ." Misha cleared his throat and felt his skin grow hot. "Actually . . ." He forced himself to go on. "There is. It's rather confidential, however, and I'd appreciate it if you never mentioned it to Uncle Alexei."

Yuri Dobrinsky inhaled deeply on his cigarette and settled back down in his seat. "Yes, go on." A cloud of smoke surrounded his balding head. His fingers were stained with nicotine.

"Well, someone came to me when I was in the hospital. An orderly, except he wasn't an orderly. He was a revolutionary, I believe."

"Quite possibly. Revolutionaries have many disguises. What did this orderly tell you?" Yuri was crushing out his cigarette, but his eyes never left Misha's.

"He said I was a fighter." Misha returned the even stare. "He said if I wanted to fight in the revolution I should ask my uncle about Dmitri Mayakovsky."

"And what did your uncle say?"

"He told me Dmitri Mayakovsky was you. You're a terrorist—with the Terrorist Brigade. Or so he thinks," Misha hastily added.

"Oh, he thinks so, does he? And what else did Alexei Yakovlevich say? That you are to stay away from Dmitri Mayakovsky?"

"Yes."

"So why are you asking about him?" The question was mildly asked.

"I suppose curiosity would be the most honest answer. Was it you who sent me the message?"

"Yes."

The straightforwardness of Yuri's reply momentarily quieted Misha and he racked his brain to think of what to say next. "Why?" was all that came out.

"Our organization has a need for brave men and women. It isn't many who would attack a policeman and then turn on a Cossack as you did."

"Who told you I did that?"

"A comrade, one to be trusted, Savva Safanov. I believe you met him in the jail before you were taken to the hospital. He was quite impressed with you."

"I'm flattered, Yuri Nikolaievich, but in truth I have no desire to fight, and certainly not to join a terrorist organization."

"Then why did you bring up the matter?"

"As I said, I was curious. Especially since you are Uncle Alexei's partner, and you know this is something he wouldn't want me to do."

"Which is why you were directed to ask him about Dmitri Mayakovsky. I could not in good conscience have recruited you without your resolving the differences between your uncle and yourself on this matter."

"If I should join you, which I have no intention of doing, I could never tell Uncle Alexei."

"Alexei Yakovlevich is not opposed to terrorism in principle. He refuses to commit violence himself, and he's terrified at the thought of your life being in jeopardy. He loves you immensely."

"And I him."

"Still, Misha—and this is most important—you are a grown man now. It's all right for you to believe in that which your uncle does not. It's all right to follow your heart. No man can decide for another, no matter how great the love between them."

"There is nothing to decide. I have no desire to join you."

"I see. Well, then, this should complete our interview. Let me assure you, your decision shall in no way affect my ability to represent you. And I needn't remind you of the absolute necessity for secrecy on your part about my identity." Yuri leaned forward as if to stand.

Misha remained still. Despite his resolve, he felt more unsettled than before he'd come. "Why are you a terrorist, Yuri Nikolaievich?"

Yuri seemed not at all surprised by the question, and he answered simply, "I was following in my father's footsteps,

I suppose. I was driven to understand the dedication that
would drive a man to risk everything, his family, his life."

"Well . . ." Misha sighed uncertainly. "I think I feel more
confused than dedicated. As far as I'm concerned, there's
more than enough violence in the world. Why would a good
man deliberately choose to add more?"

"Ah, there's a basic misconception. Our only dedication
is to liberty and equality. My father's aim, our aim, is not
violence or chaos, but to overthrow the Czar and replace him
with a government of the people. If the Czar would peacefully hand over his rule, there would be no need for revolution."

"He'll never do that."

"Exactly. Instead, he will employ every means of violence
necessary to save his miserable neck. In fact, he is one of
the most vicious terrorists the country has ever seen." Yuri
steadied his eyes on Misha. "He employs terrorism daily and
calls it justice. He gives men such as the butcher Yermolov
the legal right to shoot workers, hang peasants and beat up
students. He gives the Okhrana the power no police force
should ever have. On the whim of Leonti Yermolov, you or I
or any citizen of Russia can be shaken from his bed, taken
from his loved ones in chains, and left to die in some prison
cell without ever even being accused. Perhaps the luckier ones
are those who are summarily shot. So if you want to talk
about violence, my young friend, if you wonder why good
men turn to terrorism, speak to a woman whose husband has
been taken away by the Okhrana. Speak to a father whose
son has vanished for the crime of protesting injustice. Speak
to a child who grew up without a father because his father
committed the crime of caring for his fellowman!"

Quiet followed, as if Yuri were waiting for Misha to respond, but Misha could say nothing. He was silenced by the
passion of Yuri's words and the poignancy of his argument.

"You see, Mikhail," Yuri concluded, "in truth what drives
us is responsibility to our fellowman. And when put in those
terms, the question becomes quite different, doesn't it? The
question is not why one becomes a terrorist, but whether one
is willing to suffer for his fellowman. If one understands the
burden that such suffering carries, then revolutionary violence becomes just one part of the fight for justice."

Misha rose to his feet. "But, you see, I'm not confused
about the morality of what you say, not even the politics. I
think, politically, I would find far more to agree with you
about than not. But feelings are different—how *I* felt at the
demonstration. You spoke about revolutionary violence being

orderly. But not for me. I was out of control. All I wanted to do was strike back, kill if I had to."

"And?" Yuri urged him gently on.

"And . . ." Misha was holding himself very tightly. "I don't want to be like that. I hate that men are like that."

"Or made to be like that."

Misha shook his head and sat back down again. He closed his eyes, wishing he could explain it all; he didn't want Yuri Nikolaievich to think him weak or a coward. But what would he say? That he'd grown up in a war zone, with his father in his drunken ravings letting loose more terror than Misha ever wanted to see. That he'd learned the burden of suffering for his fellowman when he was a small child and tried to beat his father for hitting his mother, and in return his mother had taught him and all her children to cower before the beast; she'd taught her children that survival lay in subservience to a madman. Even his grandmother, for all her strength of spirit, could not stop Tolya. She could comfort later, bathe the battered limbs and hold the nightmares at bay with her hugs and songs in the night, but she could not stop the terror that had bounded Misha's life for as long as he remembered.

He'd long ago stopped inviting his friends home unless he was certain Uncle Alexei would be there. If his father was drunk, or in one of his moods, even childish laughter annoyed him and he stormed into Misha's room and slapped him about in front of his friends. How could Misha explain that to Yuri Nikolaievich? How could he explain that he feared his father's madness was buried inside himself, that all too often he felt it seething? It was this that had burst loose on the Cossack, not bravery or heroism, but madness.

"What I hate is that I feel anger at all," Misha burst out, suddenly needing to fill the silence that had settled between them.

Yuri rubbed his pudgy finger thoughtfully across his lips. "The secret of anger, my friend, is learning how to control it. Then we can direct it and use it in a positive way."

"I mean no disrespect, Yuri Nikolaievich, but that sounds contradictory."

"Because you see anger only as something negative. I see it as a powerful human emotion, able to move mountains, as powerful as love. When men hate enough, when their hatred of their oppressors is so great they can no longer contain it, then we will have the revolution. Then men will flood into the streets and into the countryside and in a righteous rage take what should be theirs."

"And what if the result is chaos?"

"If their leaders are strong and true, the result will be a new form of government."

"Well, for some people, and perhaps even theoretically, what you say is true, but it isn't for me. A man can become a beast. I know that, Yuri Nikolaievich. I have seen anger devour love and what good there is within a man."

"And you fear that would happen in you? That your violence or rage could devour the good?"

"It's not something I'd like to find out."

"Being volatile does not make one evil. Take your uncle, for example. When I first met him, he was as wild and bull-headed as any lout you'd want to meet. Even now, his temper is not something many men want to find themselves confronted with."

"My uncle is a good man."

"Precisely, that's my point. His volatility does not make him any less good. And my feeling is that you and he are cast from the same emotional forge."

"Unfortunately, I'm my father's son, not my uncle's."

"I know something of your father . . ."

"He's a beast. I would say that to God himself."

"I think . . ." said Yuri slowly. "I think I understand your dilemma, Misha." He leaned back in his seat and pressed his fingers together. "I daresay it was mine as a young man too."

Misha sat forward so as not to miss a word.

"As small children, we have no control of the violence about us. We are its victim in much the same way a peasant is the victim of his landlord or a worker his boss. We must do as we are told or suffer the consequences. The adult world seems rather unreliable and cruel, and we think when we are grown, we will be different. When we are grown, everything shall be set straight, but oddly, as we grow, we find a need to turn our irrational anger on someone else. We don't mean to. We don't want to, but it's all we know. And when we do it, as you see yourself having done to the Cossack, then we live with the terrible understanding that we have the capability of becoming every bit as bad as those who victimized us. Would you agree with that?"

Nervously Misha nodded. Yuri's words were making him most uncomfortable.

"What you need is some control in your life. Something that allows you to funnel your anger. Perhaps it's like a man who takes up boxing, wouldn't you say? Some would call him a fool or a masochist for taking all that punishment. But perhaps he knows he has the need to punch a fellow out now and again. He also knows his strength is such that he could harm most men, or that once he begins hitting, he can't stop. So he does the best thing he can do. He becomes a boxer and is given the right to beat another man bloody.''

''Are you saying that I really want to hit someone and that joining your organization would give me that freedom?'' Misha asked doubtfully.

''I'm saying that like the boxer, you have a need to live your life in an organized fashion. You need to see that the very violence you fear, if channeled, can be positive and useful.''

''In killing someone.''

''In freeing Russia from the Czar's violence. You see, Misha, not every man can become a terrorist. Not many men can adhere to the discipline. We're not some haphazard group drawn together to hurl a bomb. Everything we do is carefully thought out. All the options, all the possibilities, all the results, are thought about and gone over again and again. As little as can be is left to chance. The spark of our devotion to the revolution is passionate, but our acts are always calculated. Each squad works as a team. And that team becomes your family. Only they know the truth of your life and you theirs, and, at the final moment, when one of you, one out of six or seven, hurls the bomb, the moment is orchestrated as carefully as a symphony or a ballet.''

Misha was trembling with an almost unbearable sense of hope as he listened to Yuri Dobrinsky. No one, not even Uncle Alexei, had ever explained the complexities of life with such precision and simplicity. It was as if Yuri saw into the labyrinth of Misha's soul and found its darkest chambers not vile after all.

''But I don't think I could ever kill, Yuri Nikolaievich,'' he said almost apologetically.

''You needn't, I promise. You will never be forced to do anything that counters your own morality. I want you as part of our team. You have talents, my boy, which we very much need. Now, I was wondering, do you have any free time today?''

''Well, yes. The whole day.''

''Good, then. There are some people I'd like you to meet.''

CHAPTER NINE

October 26, 1903

Dear Alexei Yakovlevich,
   It is with great sadness that I must decline your gracious invitation for Thursday, November 5. As you know, it is the rule for students at Smolny not to leave the school except for prescribed reasons. I shall remember you in my prayers.

                        Respectfully,
                        Anna Petrovna Orlova

Two days later Anna was called to the headmistress's office after tea. Nervously Anna rolled her eyes toward Valia, wondering what she had done. Whatever the lecture from Lydia Karlovna, it would be boring. Perhaps, Anna thought, she should turn and walk out on the fat old witch and be done with it. Expulsion couldn't be worse than the prison walls of Smolny growing narrower day by day. Even Alexei Yakovlevich didn't matter anymore. He wasn't her savior, not if he could speak to her as horribly as he did in that note—as if the brooch could make a difference! Anna was not some poor stagestruck girl who could be bought with rubies. She'd rather throw herself at her father's feet and beg him to send her to the Conservatory, or at the very least, beg him to keep her in Petersburg with him. *I will be your most obedient daughter,* she'd practiced saying in her mind. *I shall be as quiet as a mouse. You won't even know I'm here.* Taking a deep breath, she knocked on the headmistress's door.

"It's Anna Petrovna, Lydia Karlovna."

"Come in, my dear." Lydia Karlovna's voice was unusually singsongy and welcoming.

Anna pushed open the door, and to her shock, Alexei Kalinin was sitting in the seat beside Lydia Karlovna's desk. He rose, his long body unfolding as she walked in. He smiled and extended his hand.

Anna stopped. She was gaping. She couldn't help herself.

Lydia Karlovna was smiling. "You know Alexei Yakovlevich, Anna."

"Why, yes, of course." She didn't know what surprised her most: his presence at Smolny or the warm rush of delight his presence brought. He was not so tall as she remembered, or so old. His hair was curlier, his eyes deeper set, but lighting on her with that penetrating intensity which would have caused her to look away if not for his joyous smile, so open in his delight in seeing her. She was swept back to Uncle Ilya's birthday ball, to the explosive freedom and delirious happiness of her music. She returned his smile spontaneously, feeling as she did the breathlessness of her dancing with this strange yet familiar man; she was swirling about Aunt Tatyana's fantasy ballroom of mirrors, lights and chandeliers, feeling like a fairy-tale princess in her prince's arms.

"Well, I have some business to attend to. Monsieur Kalinin wishes a few words in private with you, Anna. I'm certain you'll find my office quite suitable, Alexei Yakovlevich." Lydia Karlovna smiled as she left.

In six years, Anna could never remember Lydia Karlovna smiling.

"I'm delighted to see you again, Anna Petrovna." Alexei was crossing the wide office in three steps. He took her hand and held it, gazing in wonder as he had the night of the ball. Then he kissed her hand in greeting. He was so handsome, so elegant in his crisp white shirt, navy cravat and light gray wool suit. "You look tired," he went on. "You haven't been ill, have you?"

"No." She swept her hand in front of her face, wishing he couldn't see her at all. She felt awkward and plain in her school uniform. "I . . . I want to thank you for your lovely present. But you shouldn't have. It was far too extravagant, Alexei Yakovlevich, and . . ." She shifted from foot to foot. "Why?" She breathed deeply. "Why have you come to see me?"

"Come, sit down." He led her to a chair and pulled another close. "So . . ." He leaned back and crossed his legs, the long length of his body flowing in the graceful cut of his suit. "You want to know why I've come to see you. That is a fine question. But I've a finer one. Why have you declined my invitation?"

"It's not possible." She turned to avert her eyes. Perhaps then the strange pounding of her heart would quiet. Who was this man that he could affect her so? "Surely Lydia Karlovna has told you. Smolny students are not allowed to leave except at prescribed times. A special exception was made for Uncle Ilya's birthday ball.''

"Yes, yes, I know. And I'm not nearly so special as the Czar.''

"Alexei Yakovlevich, nobody in all the world is so special as the Czar!''

"I see." His eyes opened wide.

"You mock me!''

"Goodness, no. I would never do that. I'm just constantly amazed that such an air-headed ninny as Nicholas Romanov could appear special to anyone. I assure you, without his title and his fine uniforms, you wouldn't look twice at him.''

"But he's the *Czar*!''

"Yes, yes, so he is. A quirk of fate that a country as great as Russia should have a ruler so weak as our Czar. But be that as it may, what if I told you my invitation for Thursday has been approved by Lydia Karlovna.''

"Then I should not go!'' She jumped to her feet. "I should never go anywhere with anyone who talked as you do about the Czar!''

"Anna!'' He pulled her to a stop. "I feel you're very angry at me for something which has nothing to do with my feelings about the Czar.''

"Please, Alexei Yakovlevich. I must go.''

"Not yet. Now, sit and compose yourself.''

Slowly and reluctantly she obeyed, more out of fear of Alexei Kalinin following her into the hall and making a scene with Lydia Karlovna than any desire to stay with him. He was too peculiar a man. His power to both calm and enrage her was frightening. She could feel the blood in her brain literally boiling, as it hadn't for years, not since she was a small child and deprived of something she passionately wanted. Yet, in truth, she did not want to leave him. She sat a moment, breathing deeply to regain her composure.

"Please, Anna, accept the invitation to my dinner party. There's someone I'm quite anxious for you to meet—my nephew Mikhail. He's only a few years older than you, and quite a gallant young man. I think you two should get along famously. Besides, there is still the Conservatory for us to discuss. I'm to talk with Rimsky-Korsakov this afternoon. But first I must have your promise to attend my dinner party.''

"You're bribing me,'' Anna said after a long silence.

"Exactly!''

"All right.'' Her lips tightened, but she could not look at him. "I shall attend your dinner party, but I shan't play. I shall not be your entertainment.''

"Agreed."

She became suddenly quiet, and began folding and unfolding her hands nervously. "I have an admission, Alexei Yakovlevich. It's not a pleasant one. But I'm afraid I couldn't be ready for an audition at the Conservatory for quite a while."

"Why is that?"

"I haven't been practicing." She blushed deeply. "I haven't played for weeks."

"I'm sorry, Anna. There's nothing worse than for an artist not to be able to practice his art. Who is teaching you here?"

"Miss Heidlemann."

"Is she any good?"

"Not very."

"Well, then—there's your problem. I'll have a real teacher sent over daily. Rimsky can suggest one this afternoon. That is . . ." He raised his eyebrows expectantly. "If you're the least bit interested."

Anna sighed and threw her hands into the air. "Of course I'm interested. How could I not be interested? Oh, you are a terrible man, Alexei Yakovlevich. Truly wicked. You've got me trapped in a box."

"Surely a happier one than that which surrounds you here." He scanned the walls of Lydia Karlovna's office, and rose. "Until the fifth, then, my dear."

"Papa!" she cried out almost as an afterthought. "Will he be coming to the dinner?"

"Your papa, your Aunt Tatyana and Uncle Ilya—oh, and I believe Tatyana said your cousin Irina is home."

"Irina, here in Petersburg!" she exclaimed with delight. "I haven't seen her in ever so many years. Oh, thank you, Alexei Yakovlevich, thank you. Now I'm truly happy you've invited me!"

Irina had to laugh at her fears of being drawn back into her old life. After a six-year absence, she was home scarcely two weeks and already she was fighting with her mother. Her father was more distant than she'd remembered, a shadowy figure lost behind smoke rings, newspapers, and reams of papers and folders. His hair had turned white, his stomach grown fatter. There seemed little for them to say to each other. He was continually apologizing for being on his way out.

Her mother was more shrill than before, always prying and criticizing. She didn't like the clothes that Irina had brought with her, and she didn't like the cut of her hair. She thought

Irina too thin and her color too pale. She wanted to know why Irina had dropped out of the Art Institute and who was the man whom Alexandra Bordova had seen her with. Her mother arranged teas and dinner parties with boring, eligible young and middle-aged men. She was obsessed with Irina's marrying and producing grandchildren.

"You never wanted me, Mama!" Irina finally cried out. "Why would you want my children?"

Her mother's face contorted, making her look horribly old and ugly. "Why don't you go back to Paris, then!" Tatyana spat.

Irina used all her concentration to control herself. It would not do for her to leave her parents' house yet. "I'm sorry, Mama," she said, walking to her mother and bending to kiss her. "It's my fault. I'm sorry. I never was a very good daughter. I shall try to be one now."

Tatyana merely nodded. "I heard you ordered a gown modeled after the peasant style of Novgorod for Alexei Kalinin's dinner party."

"Yes, I think you'll like it, Mama. Madame Brissac helped me, of course, but I did most of the design myself. It will be different, but lovely, I assure you. I've been gone so long, I felt like appearing terribly Russian."

"Madame Brissac told me to tell you she's having trouble fitting the rubies into the neck."

"Whatever she works out will be fine." Irina knelt down beside her mother and took her hands in her own. "We do love each other, don't we, Mama?"

"Of course we do." Tatyana's eyes flicked nervously, as if they could not rest on her daughter.

"Oh, Mama . . ." Irina sighed, resting her head on her mother's lap. "I've been gone such a long time. I missed you, you know. Not a day went by without my thinking of you and Papa."

"Well, my dear." Tatyana tapped Irina's head. "I must be going. I've a fitting myself in an hour."

"Shall I meet you for tea at Donan's, then?"

"Oh, that would be nice, but I've plans."

"Yes, yes, of course." Irina stood up. She watched her mother leave the room, and shuddered, rubbing her arms for warmth. It was a cold house. Even as a child, she remembered, it was a cold house. Purposefully she turned her mind to Misha Kalinin and the fortuitousness of his uncle's dinner party. It would give Misha and her a chance to meet publicly and start off their relationship for all of Petersburg to see.

She liked Misha Kalinin. He was a far better choice for

her lover than Savva Safanov had been. All Petersburg would take notice of an affair between the heir of Alexei Yakovlevich and the daughter of the Grand Duke Ilya Mikhailevich. Misha was handsome in a rakish way, intelligent, energetic, somebody to whom she might naturally find herself attracted, and Dmitri Mayakovsky was right: Misha's dedication would make up for his inexperience. Irina would teach him as she had been taught. There was much to teach and arrange before Stepan arrived. There was much to resolve, too. Dmitri was right about that also. The personal strain among Irina, Stepan, and Vera had to be smoothed out, now more than ever.

"Do you love Stepan Stepanovich?" Dmitri had casually asked as she'd sat in his study several days before. Bach was playing softly on the gramophone. The windows steamed. The clutter of Dmitri's study blurred. He seemed like a great bear with his rounded shoulders covered in a heavy brown sweater.

Irina didn't know how to respond. What was she to say to Dmitri Andreievich, after all? No, I don't love Stepan, but I lust after him with a madness even I can't understand. She could hardly talk of lust with Dmitri Andreievich, and so she said nothing.

Dmitri poured more tea. "I know this is a difficult conversation for you, my dear, and one which, perhaps, you think I have no business having."

"Oh, no, Dmitri Andreievich, not at all. It isn't easy between Stepan and me. It's never been easy."

"Yes, I imagine. I love Stepan like a son, and even that has its problems. His hardness runs deep. It's why he's so valuable. As a revolutionary, no one is better than Stepan Ostravsky. As a lover, perhaps none is worse."

Dmitri's words, so reminiscent of Katya's, made her feel suddenly cared for, and she blurted out, "The problem is, Dmitri Andreievich, I've tried to break it off with Stepan, many times. Sometimes my resolve is so strong, and then, well, it just never seems to work."

"Perhaps I can help, then. I'll talk to him when he returns. The squad must be unified, now more than ever. The attack in Vera's apartment and the theft of the Yermolov documents hit a raw nerve in each of us. Trust is no longer absolute."

"Oh, but it is for me! I know none of the comrades betrayed us."

"We all fervently want to believe that. Still, until we find out how Yermolov discovered we had the documents, there is that gray area of uncertainty. It can't be ignored if we are to survive. But . . ." He sighed as if he were suddenly tired.

"All that notwithstanding, Misha Kalinin is too green, not only politically but also emotionally. It would be awkward with all of you living together if you and Stepan were involved. Nothing can jeopardize the mission. Yes, I shall talk to Stepan Stepanovich when he returns. I'm sure he'll understand."

Anna was delighted by the sledded drozhki Alexei Kalinin sent for her. If she'd thought about it at all, which she hadn't, she would have assumed he'd send a covered carriage for her, but the ruddy-faced coachman, his silver buttons shining in the moonlight like the frost on his beard, led her to a sleek black open sled. The coachman's caftan matched the blue decorations of the fragile vehicle. On the floor was a thick Oriental carpet.

"Miss . . ." He held her arm as she climbed in, and wrapped her in a lush sable blanket. "My name is Mitya. My master says you like to drive fast. This is Shalamar. None is faster." He nodded proudly toward the large dark bay stallion whose flowing mane reached his shoulders, hiding his neck. A delicate harness, seeming more like ribbons, connected the horse to the wooden arch framing the proud head. Shalamar snorted impatiently and laid back his ears. The coachman laughed and hoisted his enormous body into the driver's seat with the ease of an acrobat. Smoothing his beard across his massive chest, he sat himself straight and reached for the reins. "Are you ready, miss?"

"Oh, yes!" Anna cried excitedly. It had been years since she'd been driven through the streets of Petersburg in a drozhki, huddled close to her father as they flew in a whirlwind, seeming hardly connected to the earth.

"Make way! Make way!" came the familiar cry of the coachman as he adroitly wove the sled along the boulevard, slipping in and out of traffic, never needing to stop. "Take care, citizens! There's a good fellow, Shalamar! Heigh ho, my fine beast, careful of that one straight ahead. Fly right and I shall reward thee with a fine bran mash!" The coachman spoke constantly to the horse, his voice mellow, gently urging the beast through the maze. The horse's head never lost its proud curve as his legs kicked up snow and surged forward in the crystal flurry of the night.

Anna held her breath as her eyes hungrily absorbed Petersburg streaking by in a paint smear of light and movement. She wanted the ride to never end.

* * *

"Anna! Anna!" Alexei greeted her, personally helping her out of her coat, hat and muff. He unwound her scarf from her neck and rubbed her frozen nose. "I see Shalamar did his job. He brought the color to your cheeks. You liked my beast?" he asked eagerly.

"He was wonderful and the ride was grand!" Anna breathed deeply, the warmth of the house making her skin tingle. The air was thick with lilies; the light was soft.

Alexei bent to kiss her hand. "Your skin needs warming." He held out his arm. "Come, have some champagne and I shall introduce you. Not many are here yet. You look lovely, Anna. Simply lovely."

"Thank you." She smiled, feeling the peace of her connection with this strange man flood her. She pressed her hand against the brooch pinned to her shoulder.

"It looks more lovely on you than I'd even imagined." He led her down the wide, carpeted hall, its walls lined with paintings. He talked to her of his art collection. They paused now and again in front of a picture. Aunt Tatyana had said Alexei had the finest collection of French Impressionists in all Russia. Anna could not focus on the paintings, or Alexei's talk, only the sound of his voice and the warmth radiating through her body from the spot where his arm wrapped about her.

"My mother, I shall introduce you to her first," he whispered as they entered the expansive parlor lush with purples, blues, and crimsons. His mother was a tall, rather stout old woman in a forest-green, satin gown and smoking a foul-smelling, Turkish cigarette. Her graying hair was thinning. She smiled easily at Anna, commenting on her brooch.

Anna waited for Alexei to say something about the gift, and when he didn't she merely returned the old woman's smile and said, "Yes, it's lovely, one of my favorites."

"You will excuse us now, Mama." Alexei kissed her. "I want Anna to meet Misha."

"Ah, yes, good, good. But beware of my grandson, Anna, you look too fine for the likes of him."

"Ignore the hag! She raves!" Alexei teased. "Mikhail is a dove, the old woman's favorite. She would die for him, and talks of nothing but his beauty. Misha!"

A tall, thin, aristocratic young man dressed in a fashionable, dark red, cut-velvet dinner jacket and sharply pressed, black trousers turned from a conversation with a group in front of the fireplace. He was fair, with a trim mustache and thick sandy-colored hair swept back from a broad forehead; his lively blue-green eyes opened wide when they lighted on Anna. His long fingers and slender hands held a cigarette on which he inhaled deeply before crushing it out. He seemed so unlike his uncle, yet as he walked in long strides toward Anna, there was the distinct echo of Alexei in the sharp line of his nose, the smoothness of his lips, and the broad, energetic smile.

"Anna Petrovna, my nephew Mikhail Anatolyevich."

"Call me Misha." His smile was unnerving. His eyes boldly met hers. "So, my uncle tells me you play the piano." He took a gold cigarette case from his coat pocket and offered one to Anna.

"No, thank you."

"Ah, yes, you're from Smolny. I don't suspect they allow such foul behavior as smoking."

"No." Anna shook her head, feeling a growing discomfort with the cockiness of the young man.

"Forgive me, but I must leave you two young people alone," Alexei said.

Anna cast him a pleading glance.

"I shan't be far. But I must attend to my other guests."

Misha proceeded to spend the next ten minutes talking of himself, his short career in the School of Commerce, some unknown girl who'd been beaten by the Cossacks, and the righteous struggle of the students. Now and again he laughed at something he said, and she stared back blankly, trying to understand the humor. She could barely listen to his droning. His chatter about the students was as insolent as was his uncle's arrogance over the Czar. She wondered if her father, Aunt Tatyana, and Uncle Ilya knew of the Kalinins' revolutionary beliefs. She tried to view Misha objectively and couldn't help wondering if beneath his elegant exterior there didn't burn a terrorist's heart. Well, she would escape his company the moment she could. He was crude, absolutely crude.

"Anna, my sweetest Anna! Is that truly you?" An impassioned cry caused her to turn, and even before she did, she knew, as if a photograph had snapped in her mind, she knew the husky voice belonged to her cousin Irina. She had not seen Irina for six years, and she felt her body smiling as she swirled around. In that first flash of recognition, it seemed Irina had changed drastically and had not changed at all. There was the same boldness of her smile behind shimmering red-painted lips. Her almond, almost Asian eyes were dramatically outlined with charcoal. In place of an evening gown, she wore an elegantly embroidered brocade dress after the style of the peasants of the Novgorod region. The full ivory sleeves were stitched with gold threads. There were rubies at

the neck, and the dress fell in a tent of deep red satin, a gold
scalloped fringe running down the center. Irina's hair was
hidden by the traditional haloed headpiece, studded with rubies, emeralds and diamonds.

"Irina!" She gasped, her hand flying to her mouth. Then
they were hugging and laughing. "What are you doing here?
Oh, and your dress—you look so gorgeous." She was smiling, almost crying with happiness as she stared into Irina's
eyes, and kissed her again.

"I'm here because I'm invited, you silly goose. Besides, I
heard you'd be here too. Do you like the dress?"

"It's marvelous."

Irina held up her arms. "Well, after six years abroad, I
wanted to feel truly Russian. How can one feel truly Russian
in a Parisian evening gown? Oh, Anna!" She hugged her
again. "It's good to see you. You've grown so. Oh, my little
cousin, you're all grown up, and so beautiful."

"What did you expect? That I would wait for you to come
home and lead me through the woods to fairyland? Besides,
I should be quite cross. You never wrote to me."

"I never wrote to anyone, but I missed you most. Of all
Petersburg, I missed you most. You must believe that—"

"I hate to be the one to interrupt this lovely reunion."
Misha stepped forward and bowed slightly to Irina. "I'm
Mikhail Anatolyevich. I live here. You must be Irina Ilyanovna, you truly must. All of Petersburg is talking of your
return."

"Really." Irina seemed bored.

"So, you've been abroad. Geneva?"

"Paris."

"I was there last summer."

"Many people were—but, Anna, darling . . ." Irina
slipped her arm through hers. "Come say hello to Mama and
Papa and then we must talk. I've been hearing such wonderful
things about you. I think Mama wants to shame me with your
feats."

"I have no feats, truly. I've nothing, Irina," she whispered, letting herself be drawn across the room by her cousin.

"Let's make a quick hello. Then you must tell me about
this Mikhail Kalinin. He's terribly attractive, don't you
think?"

CHAPTER TEN

"So, the families unite after all." Tatyana's smile was forced as she poured Alexei coffee.

"You don't approve, then, of the children's affair?"

"Approve!" she snorted, offering him the sugar. "I take no moral stand. How could I? I'm twisted with envy, Alyosha, but if you tell anyone that, I shall slit your throat."

"Ah, Tatyana, envy is such a wasted emotion."

She clicked her tongue and angrily reached for the servants' bell. "This coffee will only frazzle my nerves more." She rang furiously. "Some cognac!" she demanded as the servant slipped into the room. To Alexei she said, "It will make the brew more palatable."

The servant no sooner returned than she swept him away and began to pour the cognac herself. "Everything frazzles my nerves since Irina's been home." She filled both cups to the brim, then added another lump of sugar to her own. "Perhaps I was not the best of mothers, but my daughter is not a blank page to me. She doesn't love your Misha."

"I'm not so certain—from what he says, there seems to have been some kind of explosion between them. And Misha is not a novice to the game of love."

"She has none of the symptoms of a woman in love." Tatyana's eyes narrowed. "She'll hurt him, Alexei. I know my daughter. She's a viper when she wants. You must warn him!" Tatyana bristled with her rage.

Alexei took her hand and kissed her fingers. "It hurts me to see you so distressed."

"It is funny to hear you say that—when you have distressed me more than any man alive. But you, you're not better than my daughter. The two of you mock me—Irina with your blood, you with mine. The irony is too delicious."

"What do you mean?"

"Irina plays with your nephew, you play with my niece."

"Anna!" He sat back.

"You're mad for her. It's written all over your face. Not

94

only have you arranged an audition at the Conservatory with Rimsky-Korsakov, but you sit in on her music lessons. And that brooch you sent her. Really, Alexei—a piece like that as a thank-you for her playing! What did it cost you? Two thousand rubles at least!"

Alexei's body stiffened. He blushed for the first time in more years than he could remember.

"What are your intentions?"

"I'm impressed with her talent. I want to get her into the Conservatory."

"Liar."

"Well, since it was you who introduced us, Tatyana, perhaps you can tell me my intentions. And if I recall, it was you who suggested that I marry her."

"Marriage is one thing. Love is another."

"I am not in love with Anna."

"Of course you are! Ah, I know the workings of your mind. You love what you can own and you want to own Anna and her talent. You want to make her famous. You have an obsession with owning works of art. Anna is no different."

"I've had many artists as my mistresses," he said pointedly.

Her nostrils flared. "None that you've created. And not a musician. Ballerinas, painters. But music is your soul. Anna will be an extension of you. You'll merge her with yourself until you actually believe her talent is a part of yourself. For true talent is something you can't buy."

He drained his cup and eyed Tatyana angrily. "Perhaps I should warn Misha."

"How's that?"

"If Irina is anything like her mother, he's truly taking a viper to his heart."

"Oh, Alexei, what do you think I'm made of? You've rejected me all these years. You tell me of your little ballerina mistresses, and now you lust after my own niece. How much do you think any woman can take?"

"Perhaps, then, I should leave." He started to get up.

"No." She grasped his arm and stared at him long and hard. She seemed to want to say something, but her eyes filled with tears.

Alexei thought he should take her in his arms and comfort her, but he was too upset himself. Tatyana in her bitterness had touched a raw nerve. He felt exposed. Tatyana had a witch's eye for truth.

"Of course," she went on. "You will pursue this madness with Anna."

"The audition at the Conservatory is in three weeks," he said, careful to display no emotion.

"Well, I'll tell you this, then. Even should she get in, her mother will never allow it."

"I don't understand the Orlovs. Doesn't the Count have any control over his family?"

"My brother is a weak man. He knows how to fawn about people, which is why he does so well with women and in the Czar's service. Unfortunately, he does not do well with gambling. Neither does his son. They're in debt to the point of disaster. All they have left is the villa in the Crimea, which belongs to Marya Dmitreyevna's family, and the palace here in town. Yet . . ." She shrugged, grimacing. "Who knows if my brother even owns the roof above him anymore? I'm prepared for the day when he comes knocking on my door, begging for a bed. He probably couldn't pay for Anna's tuition at the Conservatory even if she did get in."

"Who pays for her support at Smolny?"

"Her mother. Marya Dmitreyevna retrieved some control of the money before she left my brother. Plus she received her mother's jewels when the old woman died. I've always abhorred Marya Dmitreyevna, even when she considered herself the belle of St. Petersburg. But I don't envy the poverty into which she's fallen and I don't blame her for leaving Petya. He's not a good father and is a worse husband. It was a matter of survival. If nothing else, Marya Dmitreyevna knows how to survive."

"But your brother is still the head of the family. He can make decisions about his daughter."

"I'm afraid he's more in need of a patron at this moment than Anna."

"What do his debts amount to?"

She thought for a moment, and said casually, "I could find out, if you're interested."

"Yes, yes, I would be."

"I shouldn't though," she scolded. "I shouldn't do anything for you ever again, Alyosha." Her expression softened. "Tell me you love me."

"I adore you." He kissed both her cheeks softly. "More than that, I like you and I need your friendship."

"One day it shan't be there. I warn you, Alyosha, one day even you will push me too far."

"The hours, Anna Petrovna—I want to know the hours you've practiced!" Anton Babichev burst into the practice room, not so much as acknowledging Alexei's presence.

"As much as I can," she offered timidly.

"Not enough, never enough! We are talking about your being accepted at the Petersburg Conservatory. There is always time to do more, Anna Petrovna, always. We are talking about dedicating your life to your art."

"But it's difficult here at school, Anton Grigorievich. If you—" she tried, her voice low.

"No excuses, no excuses—just begin," he ordered.

Anna stole a glance at Alexei as she seated herself again at the piano, relieved to find him smiling.

"The Bach sonata—begin with that." Babichev took his stand at the far end of the piano, and let his monocle drop from his eye. He listened attentively as she played, but no sooner had she completed the first movement than he lamented, "You drive an arrow into my soul, Anna Petrovna. Again, play it again!" His voice rumbled. He pounded the piano, making the room shudder.

Babichev was a very large man, taller than Alexei, with fiery, flyaway hair, a red mustache, beard, and swirls of red hair on his large fingers, which were the bane of his existence. "Ah, if I only had hands like yours!" he cried, taking Anna's strong yet slender fingers in his own, caressing them as if they were a work of art. "If only I had your hands with my soul. . . ." He dropped Anna's and squeezed his own tightly, thrusting them pleadingly toward the ceiling. "These hands were made for tilling fields or pounding iron—not for giving life to the passion of the soul. God has blessed you, Anna Petrovna, yet you have no appreciation. You should fall down on your knees and pray!" He pointed to the icon of the Virgin in the corner above the piano. "Instead, you laugh at me when you should be practicing. Yes, I can tell in an instant when you have been practicing enough. God may have damned me with these hands, but he made my ears His instrument. I know when you lie to me! I know on the first note. You have not practiced an hour. Do you hear that, Alexei Yakovlevich? I tell you it's a waste of your money, despite her talent. This girl hasn't the passion."

Anna felt her body shrink and tingle fearfully at the accusation. It was true, of course. She could not practice. She was terrified to practice. She was terrified of the audition, almost more afraid of being accepted than not. Yet she cried out to Babichev, "That's not true!" She turned to Alexei. "It's not true, I swear."

"Perhaps if you weren't so caustic, Anton Grigorievich," Alexei said, his voice startling in its calm. "Passion is a timid thing at times. One must find a safe place to let it free."

"I've been hired to teach, not to coddle, Alexei Yakovlevich." Babichev's face deepened to the color of his hair. "If you don't agree with my methods, you may dismiss me."

"Of course, my dear Babichev. . . ." Alexei rose to his feet and wrapped an arm about the man, leading him to the far corner of the room. "Your dismissal is furthest from my thought," he said with a lowered voice. "Besides, if you left, Anna would be distraught. I beg of you, do what you do so well. Teach." He slipped a handful of rubles into Babichev's hand. "I understand the pressures of an artist. I just ask for a little more patience, is all."

"Well, of course, of course. . . ." Babichev nodded and began pacing back and forth across the small practice room. "I understand I'm too insistent at times. But it's only because my soul bursts with perfection. To a finely tuned ear, the slightest mistake—and from such a talented musician as Anna Petrovna—you understand, Alexei Yakovlevich."

"Of course, perfection," Alexei replied with more than a hint of sarcasm.

Babichev breathed deeply and smoothed back his hair. He turned to Anna, pressed his hands together tightly, and squinted his eyes dramatically. When he spoke, his voice was almost melodic. "All right, we'll start from the beginning. And this time, you'll play it flawlessly. Can you even imagine a flawless Bach? It's ecstasy. Take a moment, Anna Petrovna. Hear it in your brain, feel it propelling you like endless curves of ecstasy. . . ."

Anna nestled into the protection of Alexei's arm as the drozhki flew along the desolate snow-laden road leading to Kamenny Island. In summertime, traffic barely moved, with workers and nobles alike leaving the crowded city streets for the estates and parks of the north. In winter, however, the island was a wasteland strangled by the frozen river and buffeted by the assaulting winds from the Gulf of Finland. To Anna the endless expanse felt like freedom. She watched Shalamar's long mane blow in the wind. The horse's breath seemed frozen in a halo about his head. The chiming of the harness bells mixed with the music in her mind.

It was a long journey for tea, but Anna never noticed. It seemed a miracle that she should be let out of school for tea, and the speed of the sled was exhilarating. Alexei drove as fast as her father, and the movement held her close to him. Every so often, she glanced up at him, their faces almost touching.

He looked down, smiled, rubbed her nose with his gloved

hand. "Don't let it freeze!" he warned, and pulled the sable blanket higher around her face.

"You either!" She reached up, rubbing his nose as if it were her job for the ride.

"Can't feel a thing. Is the nose still there?"

"Oh, yes," she promised, giggling.

"Good, a man needs his nose."

The Pelican Rest Inn was empty except for Anna and Alexei. Popavich, the innkeeper, welcomed them with open arms. The dining room was steaming with an inviting heat, and he hurried them to a table near the stove. The windows were covered against the winter, and candles lit the room.

"Some brandy for me, Popavich, and tea immediately for the young lady. Give us a minute to thaw and decide what it is we want to eat."

"Ach, there are no decisions to be made, my friend Alexei Yakovlevich. My wife has made you a feast to delight your taste sensations. It is good, I promise." He smiled and nodded as he hurried from the room.

"Do you come here often?" Anna asked, slipping out of her muff, but not yet ready to take off her coat.

"At times, but not for a while. Misha enjoys the place. There's a wonderful ice slide outside."

Anna looked away at the mention of Misha. She'd had a letter from Irina detailing her love affair. The thought of Irina free to love and be happy, free to do whatever she wanted, was tormenting. She wanted to be happy for Irina, but it was hard. Seeing Irina again, laughing and talking together that night of Alexei's dinner, had brought back memories Anna had all but forgotten. Next to them her life seemed more drab than ever. Irina was the glittering reminder of a happiness within her that yearned to break free.

From the time Anna was a toddler following Irina down hallways and across padded green lawns, she'd been attracted by her cousin's loud, bold manner, gangling, tomboy ways, and the freedom that Aunt Tatyana and Uncle Ilya allowed her. Summertime was the best, the strawberry-scented months spent at Ravens Head, her family's villa in the Crimea. Once Anna loved Ravens Head more than anyplace in the world. Even the boring days of train travel seemed worthwhile when the train chugged finally through the flat, empty expanse of the Ukrainian steppe into the lush hills and valleys of the Crimea, shimmering with the sun-drenched perfume of wildflowers, massive fruit trees, lilacs, wisteria and white acacia. Huge roses climbed along fences, trees and houses and dropped their petals in carpets of silky snow. Wild strawberries covered slopes in ribbons and grapes hung thickly on mile-long vines choking twisted mountain roads.

Ravens Head was nestled in a breezy grove of cypress trees high on a cliff above the sleepy seaside town of Yalta, not far from the Imperial Palace at Livadia. From her bedroom window Anna could see an endless expanse of water and, in the distance, tall pines on rugged mountain peaks which seemed thrust up by God from the blue-and-emerald waters of the Black Sea. In the mornings, lilacs filled air soft as a baby's smiles, and at night the heady scent of roses was carried on a warm sea breeze, wafting into every nook and cranny of the rambling house. Anna ran barefoot, slid down banisters, bounced balls on the wide sky-blue porch, and raced with her brother and Irina across the lawn to the cliff's edge, where they called to God through cupped hands.

There were boat rides and picnics on the beach, long morning swims with her father, and cool afternoons collecting berries and mushrooms in the woods with her mother. Anna's skin burned, then tanned; her hair bleached almost white and fell as soft as silk. She played badminton with Irina and rode horseback through the mountains, always insisting to her father they stop for water at one of the Tatar villages, whose whitewashed enclaves could be easily sighted by the delicately laced minarets of the mosques rising into the cloudless Crimean sky. Anna and Irina shuddered with awe, fear, and great excitement at the swarthy, sinewy Tatar men in their black hats, embroidered jackets, and tight white trousers. The women were strong and exotic, with red-dyed hair and dark eyes seeming to swim above floating veils. Irina believed the cascades of Tatars racing along the mountain trails rode on the breath of ancient warriors of pagan gods.

Except for Anna's music lessons and the required hour of practice each day, there seemed no reason for living in the Crimea other than to laugh, have parties, and play. Best, however, were the secret meetings of ''The Club,'' an elite gathering made up of Anna and Irina, Anna's brother, Petya, the twins Osip and Konstantin Chukovsky, and Mitya Tairov, who challenged Osip to a duel to prove his love for Irina. Mitya Tairov's older brother, Lev, had recently been killed in a duel in Moscow; Mitya was convinced he could refurbish the family name. The duel was to take place in the woods behind the Czar's estate; Osip and Mitya were walking their twenty paces and would most certainly have fired if a Czar's guard had not found them. Mitya's father whipped him brutally for his headstrong behavior, and Irina organized a picnic for him the next day, holding Mitya's hand the entire afternoon.

Anna never forgot the picnic. It was during the summer of her twelfth year.

Irina was fourteen, and taller than all the boys. She wore a long, sheer white dress over a lace chemise to the picnic, and tied her hair in thick, peasant braids. "For this one day, my heart belongs entirely to Mitya Tairov, who suffered so mightily for my love. His body is bruised, but his heart is true." Holding Mitya's hand, Irina led them in a snake dance to the seashore, where she insisted they take off their stockings and walk barefoot along the rocks. There was something hysterically funny about the trip. Anna never knew exactly what, but they were all laughing and joking, kicking water at each other until their clothes stuck to their bodies, especially Irina's. She fell into the water more than once, leaving the lace and thin summer fabric of her dress and undergarments almost transparent on her skin.

"Hey, you! Mitya, is that you?" a tall man with a broad hat called. He waved a walking cane in the air. "Mitya Tairov, is that you?"

"Let's get out of here!" Irina shouted, and started to run from the shore. She led them up the beach and along a secret trail up the cliffs, through fields and vineyards to a dark, still pond hidden under the cover of thick leafy trees and bushes. There they ate a lunch she had hidden of delicate sandwiches and rich, chocolate cakes. When they had finished, she took Mitya's hand and climbed to the highest rock. Smiling down on the rest of the assembly, she slipped her hand free and unclasped the clips from her braids, shaking her head so her hair fell about her shoulders in tangled waves.

"The great poet Pushkin wrote of this moment," she began solemnly. "He called it 'A Nereid,' which is what I am today, the daughter of Nereus, the sea god." Slipping off her dress, she stood in her lace chemise and stared at the others, her large, dark gray eyes sparkling, glowing with the power of some heavenly being, or so it seemed to Anna. Irina was frighteningly beautiful standing on the rock in that hidden glade, her auburn hair and flawless, apricot-tanned skin highlighted by the speckled, summer sun. The curves of her body were as mesmerizing as the low, melodious tempo of her voice while she recited:

Below the dawn-flushed sky, where the green billow lies
Caressing Tauris' flank, I saw a Nereid rise.
Breathless for joy I lay, hid in the olive trees,

And watched the demigoddess riding the rosy seas.
The waters lapped about her swan-white breast and young,
As from her long soft hair the wreaths of foam she wrung.

Smiling the way Anna had often seen Aunt Tatyana smile when she was surrounded by gentlemen, Irina turned to Mitya, and taking both his hands in hers, she kissed his lips. "Today, in praise of your bravery, we shall all be water nymphs."

Mitya looked confused. "But we haven't brought any swimming clothes," he insisted, his voice cracking as he spoke.

"Water nymphs don't wear clothes—not even lady and gentleman nymphs together," she said knowledgeably. "Who should go first? You or me? Then the rest will follow."

Mitya, who was thirteen, turned and ran from the rocks into the woods.

For a moment, Irina looked shocked, then enraged. "Wait here!" she ordered the others, and ran after him.

Mitya and Irina were gone for a very long time.

Anna sat alone on a far rock, watching her brother and the boys whispering and laughing. She waited, not certain what the whole adventure was about. The longer she waited, the more nervous she became, wondering if the servants had noticed their disappearance and what her mother would think if she knew she'd been walking through the woods barefoot.

What seemed like hours later, Irina and Mitya appeared. Wordlessly, and without looking at anyone, they climbed back to their rock and, to Anna's astonishment, slipped from their clothes. Holding hands, they dove in. Anna wasn't sure what riveted her most, their nakedness or the horrible, red welts across Mitya's back and buttocks.

"What happened to him?" she gasped, thinking perhaps Irina had done something to him in the woods.

"His father," Petya said, pulling his shirt over his head. "The old man beat him for dueling. Can you imagine Papa doing something like that? Now, come on, are you going in or what? I mean, if you're just going to stand here gaping, you better go home." Petya was glaring at Anna, his hands on his hips. He was wearing only his undershorts. Beyond him, Konstantin was tearing off the remainder of his clothes. Osip, stark naked, darted by her and with a wild man's shriek dove in.

"Come on, Petya!" Konstantin yelped, tugging at his shoulders.

"Be a baby if you want, then!" Petya snapped, pulled off his shorts, and dove in.

Anna felt paralyzed. Then Irina was standing beside her, the sunshine shimmering off the water streaming down her pointed white breasts. "Come on in," Irina whispered, giggling. "You don't want everyone to think you're a baby." Irina started to unbutton her dress.

Tears filled Anna's eyes and she ran into the woods.

Irina followed. "Are you afraid we'll be caught? Because we won't. I've come here plenty of times. Nobody else ever does."

Although she had seen Irina naked before, she could not stop looking at her. "I must go home, please let me go home!" She began to sob.

"No, I won't, not unless you tell me what's making you so sad."

"You're so beautiful, Irina. And I . . . I . . ." She wrapped her arms tightly about herself, wishing she could simply vanish.

"Oh, you silly." Irina kissed away her tears. "You'll be beautiful too, and very soon, I can tell," she said knowingly. "Besides, there's nothing terribly grown-up about those boys, not even Mitya." Her eyes opened wide and she giggled a naughty giggle. "Shall I tell you what we did in the woods?"

Anna wasn't sure she wanted to know.

"He was such a baby. I told him I just wanted to pretend to be sea nymphs, but he wouldn't get undressed. Can you imagine? So I did first. The dummy, he just stared at me and stared at me, and his little thing started to get bigger. It was all I could do not to laugh, because he's not a man at all, not at all. I've seen a real man."

"You have!" Anna gasped.

"Oh, yes, and I'm quite determined I shan't be a virgin much longer. But you can't tell anyone that, Anna. It's our secret."

All Anna could do was nod her head.

"Shall I tell you who it is?" Irina's face flushed a lovely pink. Her nipples grew harder.

Again, all Anna could do was nod.

"My tutor, Apollon Apollonovich. He said he's in love with me, and promises not to hurt me at all. What do you think, Anna? Shall I let him be the one?"

"Do you love him?" Anna's voice sounded very small.

"I'm terribly fond of him. Besides, he's the only grown man I know, besides Uncle Petya and Papa, of course, and their friends. They don't count. I was thinking of trying first with Mitya, in the woods, but when I kissed him, he was too scared. So we just played a little. I let him touch me, but in truth he tickled more than anything, not like Apollon. *His* kisses sear. . . .'' She closed her eyes and her whole body shuddered. ''They're like a vein of gold exploding in the sunlight! Apollon said the kiss is God's gift to mankind. He said God must be a socialist because he gave the kiss to everyone, rich and poor alike. The kiss makes every man and every woman a noble. Yes, that's the best way to describe it. Only God could have created an invention so wonderful. Have you ever been kissed?''

''Oh, no!''

''I didn't think so. I wasn't either when I was your age. But I wish I had been. You do want to be kissed?''

''Oh, yes.''

''Then you must come swimming with us.''

''Irina! Irina!'' the boys chanted from the pond.

''Oh, do come!'' Irina insisted. Throwing up her arms, she swirled around and around in the stream of sunlight cutting through the leafy cover of the woods.

Anna thought she looked beautiful.

''Come now, I insist.'' Irina began unbuttoning Anna's dress again, and this time Anna didn't stop her. ''There!'' she exclaimed, standing back to admire Anna when she was fully undressed. ''You are quite beautiful just the way you are. And see, it is beginning.'' She ran her finger across the tiny swell of Anna's breast, and grabbing her hand, raced with her through the woods.

The most delicious rush of happiness washed over Anna as she and Irina burst onto the rock to the admiring calls of the boys and dove into the pond. The water felt as smooth as silk.

For weeks after that, the Club met as often as they could escape the watchful eyes of the servants, and soon they were so used to their nakedness, they undressed even before they reached the pond. Once, just before the summer ended, Mitya Tairov kissed Anna. They were the last ones out of the pond. Anna was just climbing from the water when Mitya leaned over and pressed his lips on hers. They stared at each other a few moments.

''Can I do it again?'' Mitya asked uncertainly.

''Yes!'' Anna smiled happily.

The second time he rested his hand on her arm, but as he started to press her to him, she pulled away. ''Catch me if you can!'' she shouted.

Within seconds, he was up to her. Breathlessly they faced

each other. "You're very beautiful, Anna," he whispered, his eyes seeming to take in all of her body. "You're the most beautiful girl I've ever seen." He reached out, almost touching her nipple; then he blushed deeply and ran screeching like a wild man after the others. After that, he held her hand as they walked through the woods, and swam back and forth across the pond next to her, but they never kissed again.

Days later, Irina was sent back to St. Petersburg. Anna's mother told her Irina was sick. Petya told her that Irina had been caught naked on the couch in the study with her tutor, Apollon Volkov, and was being sent to school in Switzerland.

Anna didn't see Irina after that summer, and Mitya Tairov died in the winter of typhoid. That was also the first winter Anna's mother spent at Ravens Head, presumably because of her pregnancy; Boris was born in late January and Marya Dmitreyevna didn't return to Petersburg that spring. In fact, she never returned to Petersburg again. Anna was sent to the Smolny Institute, and when she returned to Ravens Head the following summer, everything had changed. With Irina abroad and poor Mitya Tairov dead, the Club ceased to meet. Even if it had, Anna knew she wouldn't have been able to go. Something dreadful had happened to her mother over the winter, something Anna couldn't understand. Although the baby was healthy, all life seemed sucked out of her mother, who gave herself totally to the care of her horrid new confidante, a growling Siberian mystic named Zinaida Golovnina.

Not only did Marya Dmitreyevna shed her pastel lace and silken gowns for the homespun garb of Zinaida Golovnina, but she dimmed Ravens Head with shades on the windows and gray covers on the furniture; she turned her parlor into a holy room paneled with icons and smelling of sickly-sweet incense, and she knelt in shadowy candlelight for hours, her incantations spiraling like tentacles through black sockets. The mesmerizing blue of her eyes had faded; her skin sallowed; her hair turned lusterless; her voice lost its lilt. The moldy darkness of the deep woods where she collected mushrooms became her perfume, and her fingertips were stained with the blues, browns, and reds of the berries and herbs which Anna was certain unleashed not the magic of healing, as Zinaida Golovnina promised, but rather a jagged descent, sharp like the carved bone of Zinaida Golovnina's cheeks and jaws, dusty, dry like the cracking skin of her bloodless lips.

While Marya Dmitreyevna prayed, gathered mushrooms and berries, and tended to the sick and dying in the tuberculosis sanatoriums, Zinaida cared for the baby and ran the house with an iron hand. There was an hour of morning prayer, followed by several hours of piano practice, something which Anna never minded until it was ordained by Zinaida Golovnina. The piano, like Ravens Head itself, felt like a prison, with Zinaida its guard and warden, always ready to deal out punishment, either hours of kneeling before the icon, or a swift rap of a rod across Anna's knuckles, or both. The first time Zinaida struck Anna, she was dumbfounded. Anna had never been hit in her entire life, and she'd run screaming to her mother.

"Do as Zinaida Ivanovna tells you," was all Marya Dmitreyevna said. "She is your mother and father until my strength returns."

"But where is Papa? When is he coming?"

"Your papa is dead."

"No, he's not. You know he's not, Mama! Why do you say that?" Anna threw herself on her mother, sobbing, until Zinaida came and pulled her away.

Although Anna occasionally saw her father in Petersburg—he surprised her every few months with tea at Myedved's or Donan's—he never returned to Ravens Head. When he came to the Crimea, he stayed with his sister, Tatyana, or Mitya's father, his friend, the brutal Prince Tairov. Anna wasn't allowed to see her father when he came to the Crimea. In fact, Anna rarely left the confines of Ravens Head during the summer. From being the happiest times of her life, summers became the worst, shrouded in a cover of gloom emanating from Zinaida Golovnina and her incense, her omnipresent praying, holy mutterings, and the quick, painful switch of her stick.

"What's wrong?" Alexei's question broke through her remembrances. "You look so sad."

"I do? Well, no, I'm not, not at all. In fact, I was just thinking about ice sliding. You said there's an ice slide here."

"Why, yes, a wonderful one. We'll ask Popavich about it, but it's most fun to come here at night. He has a blazing bonfire going and torches lining the slide. Perhaps one day we shall return at night." He reached across the table for her hand.

She jumped at his touch. "Here comes the tea. I think that's what I need." She forced a smile.

Alexei and Popavich began talking about the ice slide, but Anna wasn't listening. She felt herself fading, pulling herself inside herself. What was she doing here with Alexei Kalinin anyway? What did he want of her? Did he think she was like Irina? Did he think she was free to live, much less love?

Worse, what would her mother think? What would her mother do if she knew Anna was here with a strange man, alone in an empty inn in the middle of Kamenny Island?

"Do you think I'm modern?" Anna asked suddenly.

"Modern!" The question surprised Alexei. "What does that mean?"

"I don't know. It's just, well, you know my cousin Irina? She's very modern."

"That she is."

"You know about her and your nephew?"

"But of course. I fear I shall have the two of them to support."

"You . . ." She hesitated. "You don't think it's wrong what they're doing?"

"Do you?"

"I don't know. I mean, yes, I suppose I do," Anna said, surprising herself. She hadn't meant to say that.

"They love each other."

"Then they should be married."

"Oh, my dear Anna, one should never marry someone one loves. It ruins the whole affair."

"That's what Irina says." She dropped four sugars into her tea. "Can I ask you a question, Alexei Yakovlevich?" She spoke with calm formality although inside she was shaking.

"Anything."

"Have you ever been in love?"

"Oh, yes, many times."

"With whom? Can you tell me?"

He thought a moment, and frowned. "I'm afraid I don't remember. It was so long ago, when I was very young. Once any pretty young thing who tossed me a smile could cause me to fall madly in love!"

Anna giggled.

"What's so funny?"

"I don't know. It seems hard to imagine you like that."

"Young."

"No!" Anna cried seriously. "You're young now." Her papa was old; although still handsome, he had practically no hair left, and was always fussing about the few strands, letting them grow longer than they should. Alexei with his smoothly shaven skin and shining thick hair was more like her brother Petya, even handsomer. Petya was thin as a string bean, but Alexei was broad, firm, not fat like Uncle Ilya, and certainly not old.

"Hardly young!" Alexei was laughing. "But what about you? Are you in love with any clever young man?"

"Me! Goodness no. I never see any young men, clever or dull."

"Yes, but that will change soon. There are many young men at the Conservatory."

She nodded, feeling the uneasiness return. "Even if I get into the Conservatory, which I may not, probably I won't be able to go."

"Babichev is right, you know. Even I can hear you've not been practicing enough. The audition is only ten days away."

Anna blushed deeply, shocked by Alexei's bluntness. "But it's not my fault, Alexei Yakovlevich. They have us doing so many other things."

"I shall speak to Lydia Karlovna again, then. Your father has instructed her to allow you all the time you need. Is there something else wrong?"

"No." She lowered her eyes.

"This is very important to me, Anna. Rimsky-Korsakov has already gone out of his way for you, convincing Babichev to teach you. The man may be a fool, but he knows his music. I don't want you to let me down."

"I won't! I couldn't! It's just that my mama will never let me go. I know she won't. Then what will you tell Monsieur Rimsky-Korsakov?" Tears wet her eyes.

"I've spoken to your father, Anna, and to your aunt."

"They're not my mama. You don't know her. You don't!"

"There's nothing to worry about, Anna. I promise. I shall take care of your mama, even if I have to talk to the Czar himself. You are a very, very talented young lady. You belong at the Conservatory. You will make all of Russia proud. Not even your mama can stand between you and Russia. Here . . ." He handed her his handkerchief. "Dry your eyes and take off your coat. It's warm enough in here, I promise. Besides, here comes Popavich with a tray of his wife's specialties. And believe me, we must eat every morsel or Popavich will become distraught!" He winked.

As Popavich's boots thudded across the floor, Alexei got up to help Anna off with her coat. Bending over, he whispered, "It will be all right. I promise. You see, I'm a man who's used to getting what he wants, and I want this for you."

CHAPTER ELEVEN

"That's him. . . ." Irina nodded toward a vendor standing by an almost empty cart of frozen reindeer meat on the other side of Hay Market Square. "The one with the sleazy little Mongol eyes. He's from the Okhrana for certain. Kiril has driven him four times in the past week. He always gets off at Sadovaya Street and walks. Yesterday he was selling geese at the Shchukin market. I tell you, Kiril's getting hired as a driver at the Okhrana may be the break we need. He says half the street peddlers are police agents."

"And the other half are revolutionaries!" Misha teased.

"Come on." Irina readjusted the pack on her back, tied the scarf tighter about her head, and started across the square.

Savva, who was a master of disguise, had taught both Misha and Irina how to transform themselves into itinerant peddlers. He coached them in their speech and their makeup, and left peddler clothes and wares for them in a middle-class wool draper's shop; nobody seemed to notice that the young, well-dressed couple who walked into Kolya Pritkin's shop never came out again. Instead, two rather moth-eaten peddlers, a woman of indeterminable age, her head wrapped in layers of woolen scarves, her face streaked with dirt, and a tall man with vacant eyes, a long black beard, a worn fur cap practically covering his eyes, and a grease-stained sheepskin coat, exited by the back, quickly melding into the bustling crowds of the Gostinny Bazaar.

The woman sold religious and bridal items. A large brass cross stuck out of her sack and amulets hung about her neck and arms. The man sold secondhand boots and other leather goods. They traveled as a pair. The woman did most of the talking, gossiping with the other peddlers and complaining about the prices of milk and bread while bemoaning the fate of a son who was drafted, another who had run away, and a daughter who at seventeen was married to a brute and had three children.

"Aye, aye . . ." The peddler woman moaned, finishing

109

her tale of woe. "But never mind. Everything will pass. Glory to God. Eh, Daddy!" She chucked the vendor of frozen reindeer under the chin.

The vendor, who had only one piece of meat left, seemed to welcome the diversion of the chatty woman.

"I always told my son, the one who got hisself drafted, to become a policeman. If it pleases God, he still will. God knows, it's the likes of men like our chief who keep us honest. Aye, a pleasant-looking fellow, with his pockmarks!" She laughed hoarsely and poked the vendor with her elbow.

"And what do you know of such things, old hag?" He eyed her warily.

"God knows it wasn't so long ago I was a pretty lass meself." She held her face close and smiled.

The vendor pulled back. Her breath reeked of garlic.

"Ask my Igor." She nodded over her shoulder to where Misha stood, staring dumbly ahead. "A lass has to make a living with a man so . . ." She tapped her finger against her head and rolled her eyes. "Igor's a gentle soul, but he don't know much. God be praised, he'd give away all his leather if I didn't keep an eye on him. Don't you think I knew how to make a pretty roll of rubles once. Got some stashed away for a rainy day, I do, Daddy. I knew our chief when he was in Moscow, I did. I was a favorite of the lout's. Aye, and a lout he was, I'll tell you. Liked the nastiest sort of fun. You know the gent I mean?"

"Should I?"

Irina laughed raucously. "God knows the lout wouldn't like the likes of you. He's not that sort, unless it was to make yer rump swell red!" She guffawed and elbowed him. "He's got a reputation, he has—amazes even them that knows. I don't mind telling his name none. Shows me stuff if I strut a bit. Yermolov, he's the man. Leonti Yermolov, our darling chief of policemen."

The vendor shrugged as if the announcement were no surprise. "Well, everyone knows what he's got a taste for." Then he chortled. "So, old hag, you played around like that, did ya? Ever in the market for such fun anymore?" He put his arm about Irina.

"Aye, and you couldn't afford me!" She nestled against him.

"Give me a chance. Sure, you can't be so picky now."

"I gave you a story about the lout, God knows, Daddy. You give me one now, for a little exchange of fun. Life's hard enough without it, but never mind. So go on, give me a tidbit!" She eyed him with an expectant grin.

"About Yermolov, you mean."

"Who else?" She peered closer and ran her tongue across her lips. "Like to keep track of the bastard now that he's grown so high and mighty. Glory to God, but he gave me more than me share of pains and never paid me right, either, I'll tell you. Promised me more than I could stand the last time I asked him for me money. Bet he does a good job chopping up them revolutionaries and terrorists, if it pleases God. Bet the lout makes them dance pretty."

"Muscovite boots! First-rate! Step in and walk away!" Misha called out suddenly. Then he crossed himself and stared blankly ahead.

"*He* really goes with you?" the vendor asked.

Irina nodded and spit. "And always will. But I've been known to lose him for a few hours."

"Hey there, now!" He grabbed her wrist to pull her closer. "You're not such a bad looker once ya get close. I bet some soap and water and you'd be all right." He squeezed her tighter.

"You like to hurt too, Daddy." She smiled and blinked her eyes.

"It could be arranged." He lowered her arm, bending it behind her as he pulled her close. "What do you want to know?"

"I'd like to get me chance to see my own foul-faced Leonti Yurievich now that he's so dandy. I heard he dresses up to kill the ladies. I'd like to see him dressed to kill." She smiled broadly, and pressed her head on the vendor's chin.

"He's a hard man to see."

"Aye, and that I know. 'Tis why I ask around. God be praised, I get a hankering for him that tears at me memories."

"Perhaps I could ask around. Perhaps something could be arranged."

"You're a fine man, God knows." She lowered her voice and whispered expectantly, "How close could I see?"

"How close do you want?"

"Close enough to spit in his face!" She laughed hoarsely. "I could show you scars."

"I'd like to see them!"

"I see Yermolov first."

"Meet me here again in two days. I'll have something to report."

"What's your name, Daddy?"

"Boris Alexandrovich."

"Nice, Boris Alexandrovich. I'm Sonya Mikhailovna." She

lightly kissed his lips. "I've got to be going now. Igor gets upset if we stand around too long."

"You're awfully quiet," Irina said as she and Misha sat around a bonfire just outside the Flea Market eating greasy meat pies.

Misha shrugged and nibbled at the edge of the pie.

"Not so much as a 'job well done'?" She jostled him and smiled hopefully.

"It was—you were very good. I just worry is all, the way most of the peddlers are afraid to even mention Yermolov's name, and there you were bandying it about."

"With good cause, I thought. Everyone knows the reputation the scum has with women. Do you think it's so totally improbable that Sonya Mikhailovna could have once been his mistress and fallen on hard times?"

"I don't know, I suppose you're right," Misha said impatiently. "But I also think we should get out of here. If that guy Boris Alexandrovich suspects anything, he'll have his thugs on us in no time."

"Which is why we can't hurry away. Relax. Enjoy!" She held up her pie.

Their eyes met and, feeling his annoyance growing, he looked quickly away.

"Something's bothering you. I can tell." She wiped her greasy fingers on her coat. "Was I too convincing?"

Misha felt too embarrassed to answer. Irina's insight frightened him.

"Oh, my lovely Igor," she cooed, and slipped her arm through his. "You worry too much about me."

"Perhaps somebody has to. What if that guy Boris Alexandrovich wants his payment?"

Before Irina could answer, a sausage peddler sat beside them.

"Have a bit?" He sliced off a piece of meat and offered it to Irina.

"Thanks, Daddy." She grinned and bit half, handing the other to Misha, who shook his head. "My Igor has a touch of a stomach worm," she advised the peddler. Then, tugging at Misha, ordered, "Come on, come on, me fine fool. It's time we're off and working. And ya can carry me pack awhile!"

Wordlessly Misha stood and slung the two packs on his back.

"Good day to ya, Daddy." Irina smiled politely at the sausage peddler. "God be praised, but it's cold away from the fire!'' Her face grew serious as they started down the crowded street. It was the height of the shopping hour. The streets and stalls lining the market front were jammed with people buying and selling. Irina slipped close to Misha. ''I'm certain I saw that sausage man when we were buying the meat pies.''

''I know. I did too.''

''Don't look back!'' Irina grabbed his arm. ''Just let one of the packs slip.''

Misha made a motion as if to redistribute the weight and the pack of religious items fell off.

''Aye! Ya dumb brute!'' Irina shouted, punching him as she turned to pick up the pack. An old man jostled her, and she tripped, catching sight of the sausage peddler slipping into one of the market-front stalls. ''Quick,'' she whispered, grabbing her sack as she pulled Misha, who fell into a money changer's table and stumbled behind Irina into the nearest gate.

Inside the market the air was dimly lit with lanterns and heavy with the pungent odors of sauerkraut, leather, grease, spilled wine and vodka. Bearded men dressed in blue caftans called out bargains on everything from meat and fish to dried fruits, vodka, clothes, wolfskins, and housewares. Some ragged boys were kicking a ball. Old women prayed in front of paper icons. Irina and Misha walked fast, pushing against the current of the slowly moving mass of peasants, workers, and wanderers dressed in multicolored costumes and clogging the narrow alleyways. A drunk stumbled from a tavern and cursed them.

''I think he's after us still,'' Misha whispered, fear pounding in his body, even to his fingertips, which were tightly wrapped about Irina's.

''Let's go in there. . . .'' She dropped her pack as she pointed to a crowd standing outside an incense shop to watch a backgammon game. ''Maybe it leads into the street.''

''No!'' He grabbed her. ''I know this place. I used to come here as a boy. . . .'' For years Misha and his friends had haunted the common markets, looking for bargains, smoking cheap cigarettes and paying too much for swigs of vodka and wine and the caresses of girls. ''There's a tavern I know up ahead.'' As he started forward, he turned once more, trying to catch sight of the sausage peddler; when he looked ahead, a huge coachman was blocking their way.

''Where you going so fast now, practically knocking down folks.'' He held fast onto Irina's arm. ''Don't make a fuss, and it'll all be easier.'' The coachman smiled through his teeth. His fingers pressed on Irina's arm until she winced with the pain.

Misha's head swung around. The sausage man was pushing through the crowd, his arms flailing as he hurried toward them. With a sudden shove, Misha broke past the coachman's body block and dove into the crowd, where he fell to his knees and crawled into a fish store, then slipped out again, bending as he ran to hide his height. He turned into alleys, frantically searching for the tavern, but each turn seemed wrong. Panic was taking hold. Perhaps he shouldn't have left Irina. She'd think he was running, leaving her to take the fall, but he wasn't. He couldn't. He'd save her. He'd kill them if he had to, but they wouldn't take her away.

Finally the tavern appeared. He flattened against the wall and looked behind him. There was no sign of the sausage peddler or the coachman, no sign of anyone running, searching, and Misha went inside. The barkeep noticed him but didn't recognize him. Wordlessly Misha slipped through a door into the adjoining bridal shop.

The shopkeeper, a dumpy middle-aged woman, gasped.

"Do you have a jacket or coat in here?"

"Well, sure, if you're wanting to get married."

"That'll be fine. Just give me anything. Here . . ." He dug into his pocket and threw some rubles on the table. "This should more than pay for anything in the shop."

She nodded, and without further questions hurried to a rack of men's jackets.

Misha tore off the greasy peddler's jacket and slipped into the black frock coat. "Now, can you show me the back way out?"

"Up the stairs and out the roof."

He quickly raced up stairs littered with bolts of fabric and boxes of artificial flowers and sequins. Light from a small window cast shadows across the tiny attic crisscrossed with spiderwebs. Misha had to bend to walk, kicking aside dust-covered boxes and barrels. He pushed open the small door and burst onto a walkway leading to a wooden bridge some fifteen feet over Sadovaya Street.

It was hard to differentiate people in masses below, but soon his eyes caught sight of a woman struggling in between two men. One was the huge coachman, there was no doubt, dwarfing the woman. Misha ran back across the bridge, down the stairs of the bridal shop, through the bazaar and out the nearest exit to the street. He pushed people aside recklessly as he raced ahead looking for Irina or the towering height of the coachman. His only thought was to save her. His legs stretched as he ran, faster and faster, darting across the street here, running back, grabbing tall men, thrusting them aside. People stepped by to let him pass. He knew he looked like a madman without a proper coat, no hat, running, gasping; the frigid air would surely freeze his lungs.

He stopped abruptly. Not twenty feet away he saw the coachman opening the door to a carriage. The sausage peddler had a firm grip on Irina, who was still resisting the arrest.

Misha saw her foot reluctantly settle on the first step of the coach, and the scream barreled from his gut. "Run!" He hurtled forward, throwing himself against the sausage peddler and knocking him to the ground. "Run!" he screamed as he grabbed Irina.

Irina clutched her skirts and they ran, never letting go of each other's hand.

The coachman and the sausage peddler were close behind. Crowds opened about them.

"Catch them! Hold them!" the coachman screamed. "They're criminals!"

People fell still further back.

Footsteps pounded. Misha could hear the men gasping, or was it his own breath tearing at his chest, threatening to choke him? Then a sledded drozhki slowed beside them.

"Get in!" the driver yelled.

Without thinking, Irina threw herself in and Misha followed, scarcely having a grip when the drozhki took off, sending him crashing to the floor beside Irina. There was nothing to do but lie there holding on to each other so as not to fall out.

"Make way! Make way!" the driver shouted as he urged on his horse, weaving at angles in and out of traffic, not stopping until they were far from the center of Petersburg.

Only as the sled began to slow could Irina and Misha pull themselves to the seat. Shivering in his thin jacket only, Misha wrapped the carriage blanket about him.

"Well, that was a close call." The driver turned around.

"Josef!" Irina exclaimed breathlessly. "Where did you come from? How did you know? Lord, it's good to see you!" She gathered her skirts, and standing, she hugged him. "How did you find us?"

"Savva asked me to watch over you two today. He knew you were making your move on that cop."

"When did you get to Petersburg?"

"Two days ago. Say, are you all right?"

"Yes, yes, fine. Thanks to you and Misha. But you two don't know each other. Josef Kidarsky—Misha Kalinin."

"I've heard much about you from Savva." Josef extended his hand as Misha stood in the carriage to greet him. "You are a much-welcomed and needed addition to our little band."

"I'm honored for you to say so, but I feel I've done so little compared to the rest of you."

"Your time will come, I assure you. Besides, you saved Irina today. You were fine, really. I thought the two of you were goners when you disappeared inside that bazaar with the cur hot on your heels. But come, I could use a drink, eh— what about you? Some dark little tavern, someplace where a mismatched pair such as the likes of you would frequent!" he teased, eyeing their dress.

CHAPTER TWELVE

The apartment was advertised in the *Novoye Vremya* as an ideal setting for a young couple. It was the eighth one Irina and Misha had looked at, and, to their delight, it met all their requirements: a first floor with a wide view of the fashionable Zhukovskaya Street, large and airy, with enough room to easily accommodate the young couple, their housekeeper, valet, and cook and, most important, there were two separate exits to a back alley which forked quickly into the next streets over.

"You are recently married, no?" the landlady asked, smiling eagerly from Irina to Misha. Agafia Markovna was a stout elderly woman with a thick, regional accent. She lived on the floor above.

Irina looked shyly away.

"We are recently very much in love," Misha sidled up to the old woman and whispered as he handed her a fat wad of money. "There's two months' advance rent and a little something extra for yourself, Agafia Markovna. I'm away too often. My beloved may need some companionship."

"But of course, of course," the old woman assured. She looked at Irina sympathetically. "I myself am alone, you see. My husband died, oh, it's ten years now. I still mourn for him. But never mind, you're a lovely couple, lovely, yes. You will have servants?"

Misha nodded. "My old nanny, Fedora, has agreed to move in with us."

"Good, good. She can cook?"

"Excellently. And there'll be a girl servant, of course, and Jacob, my valet, a pleasant young lad, highly recommended from my uncle, Alexei Yakovlevich Kalinin."

The old woman drew in her breath. Her eyes opened wide. Her face crinkled. "Not Alexei Yakovlevich Kalinin who makes the railroads!"

"Yes, that is my uncle." Misha pretended modesty. "And my beloved is the daughter of the Grand Duke Ilya Mikhailovich Rantzau."

"Oh, Mikhail Anatolyevich." The old woman almost bowed. "I'm honored that you've chosen my house to be your house. And anything I can do, anything at all . . ."

"We shall let you know, Agafia Markovna. Mainly, we wish not to be disturbed."

"Of course, of course. I'm at your service, Mikhail Anatolyevich."

Irina was surprised when her mother, who had been in bed all morning with a headache, asked her to stay home and take tea with her. "Of course, if you have plans, I'll understand." Tatyana smiled endearingly.

The sweetness of tone and the smile set off danger signals in Irina's brain, and she hesitated.

"If your plans are with Misha, though, I'm sure he'll understand. He gets you all the time and I've seen so little of you since you've been home." Tatyana held out a limp hand to Irina. "Oh, I know it's my fault too, Irinushka. I've never been the kind of mother a girl would call a friend. But then, I've never been one to have many women friends. You'll stay the afternoon with me, won't you? We can talk, just the two of us. Goodness, it seems we haven't really talked for six years."

"More like twenty, Mama."

"Oh, Irinushka, it hurts so much when you reproach me," Tatyana pleaded petulantly. "I may not have been a good mother, but I am a mother nonetheless."

"You want something of me, Mama." Irina warily circled the end of the huge carved oak bed. Her mother's hair was down and her skin was pale from the headache. Her eyes seemed flat and, without makeup, she was pitiably old, older than a pampered, fifty-two-year-old woman ought to look, Irina thought.

"Sit, darling. Let's just talk, why don't we? But first ring for some tea. I think the tea might help my head. The damn powders don't do a thing." Tatyana made an effort to push up her pillows.

"Here, let me." Irina plumped the pillows and helped her mother get more comfortable.

"Just your being here makes it feel so much better."

Irina's reluctance soon faded as her mother began filling her in on the details of Petersburg gossip. For the next hour she talked with an ease which Irina found both astounding and delightful. They laughed raucously and Irina was drawn into an intimacy all the more deadly when she felt the rope being yanked about her neck. "I just need to know the truth, Irinushka." Tatyana patted Irina's hand. "I just need to know if Alexei's taken Anna to his bed. Anna won't tell me, of course. But she'd tell you. You'll ask her for me, won't you, my pet?"

"I shan't do anything of the sort, Mama!" Irina jumped to her feet. "If Anna needs or wants to confide in me, she shall, but I'd never pass her secrets on to you. Why is it so important that you know?"

"Do I have to spell it out for you, my own daughter? All of Petersburg knows the torch I carry for that man. And I suppose I shall until the day I die. Tell me truthfully, Irina." The tears Tatyana shed were painfully real. "Have you never been obsessed to distraction by a man?"

The question was so unexpected, Irina hadn't time to look away.

"Ah, yes, I thought so. I know my daughter better than she thinks. And tell me, Irina, was he anything like you imagined the man of your dreams to be?"

Staring at the floor, Irina shook her head.

"It's not even love, is it? I can't say I love a man who treats me as shabbily as Alexei does. It was some kind of madness from the moment I first saw him. He was so handsome, Irina, I can't begin to tell you. So dark and smooth, as if he'd been temporarily loaned to us mortals by the pagan gods. It was the Princess Kusova who discovered him. She was simply star-struck by her young buck, rude as a peasant, dripping with money and desperate to become cultured. We all thought she had something of a pet monkey about her. But I tell you, as soon as I laid eyes on him . . . ."

Irina wanted to tell her mother to stop as much as she wanted her to go on.

"What is more ravishing than ravishing youth?" Tatyana cried. "Yet it was odd. I could tell right from the beginning that I frightened him. Princess Kusova, the whiny little wench, was one thing. He could handle her. But he couldn't handle me," she said, pride coming into her voice for the first time. "Clearly, I was more woman than he'd ever had. Still, I thought if I gave him what he wanted, you see . . . Oh, it was all too clear what he wanted, the cunning bastard. He wanted a birthright, and I gave him the next best thing. I taught him the graces of society. I made sure he had the finest tailors and was on the best guest lists. I showered him with love, and he in return—he treated me like some common little whore from the first."

Irina felt sick as she watched the tears stream down her mother's wrinkled cheeks. She couldn't help wondering if at the age of fifty-two she would be so pathetic as to be carrying a torch for Stepan.

"And now!" Tatyana's voice took on strength as she threw off the covers and reached for her robe. "And now he makes love to my niece! The only thing worse would be if he had seduced you!" She jumped to her feet and swept the papers and pens from her writing table in a fit of rage. Then she stood, holding her head with her hands.

Irina thought she should help her mother, but she was powerless to move. "You don't know for sure that they're having an affair, Mama," she said with extreme calm. "After all, Smolny is practically a convent. Perhaps—"

"He picks her up for afternoon rides! Petya has told Lydia Karlovna it's all right. But it's my fault, all my fault. I introduced Petya to Alexei and I'm sure Alexei has loaned him money. In exchange, he's given Alexei the right to seduce his daughter in a carriage most likely!"

"Somehow I can't see Anna doing that."

"Sweet and innocent is exactly Alexei's type! I tell you, the man is a devil. He could beguile the Virgin herself. He'll ruin Anna and throw her into the gutter! Oh, I suppose I'll be to blame for bringing the two of them together."

"Mama, since when has an affair with someone like Alexei Kalinin ever ruined anyone?"

"Ach, you with your sluttish mind!" Still holding her head with one hand, Tatyana pointed an accusing finger at Irina. "You have no understanding of someone like Anna. And worse, you have no feelings for me. Right in the middle of this awful affair, you have to carry on with Misha! Must you move in with him, Irina? Must you sling the mud of your excesses in my face?"

"The mud of my excesses," Irina repeated in disbelief.

"Yes, you heard me!" Tatyana was pacing now. The long satin robe trailed behind her. "Don't think I don't know your devious ways! You don't love Misha. I know passion when I see it. You've none for Misha. You sleep with him only to torment me!"

"This is preposterous. You're mad, Mama, totally mad. I won't talk to you about it anymore." Irina started from her mother's chambers.

"Irina!" Tatyana screeched. "I forbid you to move in with Misha Kalinin! Forbid it, do you hear me?"

Usually when Misha came to Irina's house she greeted him with a peck on the cheek, but the servant had barely time to announce him when Irina flew into his arms and kissed his mouth warmly, her hands smoothing his neck and back. "Don't let me down," she whispered as she turned and took his hand. "Mama," she told her mother, who was closely watching the scene from the parlor chair. "Misha and I have decided to go out tonight."

"My dinner party!" the Grand Duchess exclaimed. "You're expected. Misha, Irina told you about my party."

"Why, yes . . ." Misha said, thinking the Grand Duchess didn't look well. She was pale beneath her makeup and had dark circles under her eyes.

"Misha and I have a private celebration, Mama. You understand." Irina held Misha's hand to her lips and kissed his fingers. "Your guests will not miss us in the least."

"You push me too far, Irina." Her voice rose erratically.

"What will you do? Kick me from the house? You see, it will do no good, for I'm already leaving. Will you cut off my allowance, then? If you do, Misha will see after me, won't you, my love?" She kissed him more passionately this time, and taking him by the hand, led him to the door.

"Irina!" The shrillness of the Grand Duchess's voice frightened Misha.

"Good night, Mama," Irina said.

"What was all that about?" Misha asked as they settled into the carriage.

"I hate her. I despise her!" Irina cried, holding his arm tightly. "I can't wait until I move out. It can't be a moment too soon."

"What happened?"

"I don't want to talk about it. I don't want that woman to ruin our evening. We're going to celebrate my leaving that house and our escape the other day, or rather your bold rescue." She paused then, staring hard out the carriage window as they pulled away from the palace. Absently she began weaving her fingers in and out of Misha's. When she turned to him, her smile was inviting. "You were quite marvelous that day, Misha, quite terrible and beautiful, like a warrior! Like Taras Bulba or Alexander Nevsky. I think we must celebrate. Don't you?"

The pleasurable feelings that Irina's new behavior was arousing in Misha made it hard to concentrate on what she was saying. The taste of her earlier kiss still lingered deliciously, despite the fact that he knew he was more a pawn in some argument between Irina and her mother than the object of Irina's desire. Although there'd been an easy camaraderie between them from the first, Irina had never been flirtatious. She was more the patient teacher, and her attitude sometimes turned annoyingly patronizing. Still, he enjoyed her companionship, as much as any he'd known. He loved their talks, their strategizing, and the roles they played; he loved the intensity of life moving from the underworld of peddlers to the finest drawing rooms of Petersburg. In retrospect, he even loved the danger of the chase and narrow escape from the police the other day. He loved the teamwork among himself, Irina, Savva and Josef. He knew it was an easy step from loving Irina to being in love with her. He also knew she was Stepan Ostravsky's mistress.

"Oh, Misha, take me to one of your haunts, to one of those Gypsy cafés across the river."

He nodded, feeling suddenly delighted with the idea. "Yes, I'd like to introduce you to my friends. I haven't seen them in weeks. Perhaps Denisov will be there."

"He's your friend, the one who was arrested with you?"

"Yes, and I haven't heard from him since." Misha tapped the top of the coach and then leaned out the window to give the driver the new address.

A biting wind swept in and Irina cried, "Oh, close it quickly!" She snuggled against him as he settled back into the carriage. "It's freezing." She pulled the fur blanket about them. "It will take some doing to get used to Petersburg winters again."

Misha pushed the blanket about her chin. "There, now. You'll be warm enough in a moment." He straightened himself, trying to put some space between them.

"I hope your announcement of our moving in together had a better welcome in your house than it did in mine," Irina chattered on.

"I haven't told them yet. I was thinking I'd wait until Uncle Alexei comes home in a few days. My mother . . . well, even though she's lived in town for twenty years, her values are quite provincial. She's never gotten used to the mores of Petersburg society. She prays daily for my soul."

"I think that would be nice, to have a mother who prays for me daily," Irina said with a bitter sadness. "Tell me about your family, Misha. I know your mother is a Zubova."

"Ah, yes, I come from a proud line of princes."

"The Zubovs used to be one of the most powerful families in Petersburg."

"Such a long time ago, I'm surprised you even know that."

"You look more like a Zubov than a Kalinin. They were all fair."

"How do you know?"

"Mama told me. There isn't a thing about anyone of note in Petersburg that my mother doesn't know."

"I didn't think the Zubovs were of note any longer."

"They're not, but the Kalinins most definitely are."

"And what do you know of the Kalinins?"

"My mother and your uncle were lovers. She still carries a torch for him. Did you know that? She's mad to distraction about his affection for my cousin Anna," Irina went on, and she took Misha's hand in hers, weaving their fingers together again.

"Yes. . . ." He slipped his hand away, pretending he needed to check something in his pocket. "Uncle Alexei seems quite taken with Anna Petrovna. That's all he talks of—Anna Petrovna and her audition at the Conservatory." Misha frowned.

"You don't approve?"

"About the Conservatory, well, I suppose that's fine. But love—he's more than twice her age."

"Oh, pooh! My father is more than twenty years older than my mother. Besides, one never marries for love. But I think I shall, if I ever marry, which I doubt. What about you, Misha?" Her face was very close to his.

He lit a cigarette to have something to do with his hands and offered her one.

She shook her head. "Will you marry for love?"

"I don't think of marriage, although my uncle does. At one point I think he had ideas of *my* marrying Anna Petrovna."

"That would be a brilliant match, socially speaking. But I wouldn't have allowed it. I'd never allow Anna to marry a terrorist!" she teased. "Do you know what my dream is,

Misha?'' Her voice sounded surprisingly childish. ''My dream is that we all find love after the revolution. I think about that often, after the revolution. It seems like a fairy tale to me, with happy endings for everyone. People will be free to live and love, no more hunger and loneliness.''

''Or cruelty. Perhaps when men are no longer frustrated with poverty, they won't hurt those they love most.''

''The poor hardly have the corner on cruelty!''

''Yes, of course, I didn't mean that. I only meant . . .'' He turned to her. He had no idea what he meant, and her expression had become so forlorn. ''Was it very painful for you before, with your mother?'' he asked gently.

''It has always been painful for me with my mother. But yes, today was very hard. She used me. I thought she wanted to be with me, but she only wanted something from me.''

''I'm sorry.''

Sighing, she pulled back and slipped into the corner of the carriage. She was quiet a moment and then began to laugh. It was a cold, self-deprecating laugh. ''You know what she said? The witch. She said I didn't love you. She said there was no passion between us and I was only moving in with you to get back at her.''

''How's that?''

''In her twisted mind, somehow, because you're Alexei Yakovlevich's nephew, and he's interested in Anna, who's my cousin, well, somehow we're all in a plot against her. Don't even try to make sense of it, Misha. It makes none. But she picked up on our lack of passion quickly enough.''

''The faster we move in together, the better, then.''

''Yes, but the last I heard, it won't be for another two weeks. Stepan, Katya, and Vera are finishing up on some work in Paris.''

''You must be very happy about Stepan's return.''

'' 'Happy' is not the word I would use about Stepan, but I will be happy to see Katya. The best I can say about Stepan's return is that then our work will truly begin. He was born to the streets. His plans never fail. He's a brilliant strategist.''

''I've read his manifestos.''

''Yes . . .'' She raised an eyebrow. ''So have I. He's brilliant, but not one to love.'' She sat forward, closer to Misha again, and asked, ''You know, Stepan and I were lovers.''

''Yes, I heard.''

''Well, that's over. I'm quite cured of Stepan Ostravsky,'' she said, as if making an announcement. Touching Misha's arm, she went on, her voice softer yet more intense. ''I want you to know that, Misha. There's nothing between Stepan and me, and there won't be, ever again.''

It was a Friday night and the café was noisy with a mostly student crowd, many of them friends of Misha's, and most of whom he hadn't seen since before the demonstration at Kazan Cathedral. News of his affair with Irina, however, had clearly preceded him, and she was immediately welcomed into the festivities. More champagne and oysters were ordered, and the conversation turned to events at the university over the past weeks. "Say," Misha called. "Have any of you heard about Denisov? I thought maybe he'd be here tonight.''

An uneasy silence fell about the table, and Clara Bartova glanced at Grigory Verigin, who was a friend of Misha's and Denisov's. Grigory seemed to pale, and then he said softly, "He's been sent to Siberia.''

"Siberia!'' Misha gasped. "That's not possible. My trial's not come up and I did far worse than he.''

"He wasn't sent for demonstrating. While in jail, he attacked a guard. He had a knife hidden in his boot and he went after a guard. Cut him up pretty badly, I hear.''

"You know Denisov.'' Clara laughed giddily. "He always said no jail could hold him.''

"Got twenty years,'' someone else said.

The table fell quiet again.

Irina reached out for Misha's hand, but before she could touch him, his fist rose into the air and slammed down on the table so hard, champagne spilled over the tops of glasses. "Damn fool! What the hell did he have to go and do something like that for?'' Then he was on his feet, glaring at the startled, silenced faces about him. Denisov's imprisonment was already old news to them. They wanted Misha to leave, he knew that, to depart with his grief so they could return to their partying.

"Misha . . .'' Irina was standing beside him. "Come, we'll go.'' She had his hat and coat in her arms along with her own and was urging him away.

"They don't care,'' he said angrily as they stepped into the cold air.

"It happens so much now, that's all. It's impossible to mourn for everyone.'' She was helping him on with his coat. "Come on, you'll freeze.''

"It's not everyone. It's Denisov! They all knew him. Twenty years in Siberia is a death sentence for him. He'll die before he finishes the first year. He'll do something crazy like attacking the guard, and they'll kill him.''

Irina motioned to the coachman, who was sitting about a bonfire with other coachmen, talking and drinking vodka. Then she hustled Misha inside the coach. "Just drive for a while, Volodya," Irina told the coachman.

She wrapped the blanket about Misha and herself and they sat without talking. The bells on the horse's harness jingled. The wind from the river battered the windows of the carriage. Suddenly Misha shuddered. A sob racked his body and he covered his face with his hands. For a moment he seemed able to stem the flow of tears and then he was lost to them. Turning from Irina, he buried his face in the back of the seat.

Irina reached to comfort him and he pushed her away.

"You don't know. You just don't know."

"You can tell me."

"I can't. God, I can't." He rocked back and forth, his sadness so intense that she feared crying herself.

"Please, Misha, let me help you."

As if exhausted, he turned face-forward again and slumped against the seat. Staring into the darkness, he said, "The last time I saw Denisov, we had a fight. I punched him out. It was my fault. It was the last time I saw him."

"How awful for you."

"I never meant to hit him. I never thought I'd never see him again." His voice quivered. "I love him."

"He knows that. You can't be the kind of friends you and he are without his knowing that."

Misha didn't answer, but this time when she took his hand, he didn't stop her. "This is just the beginning, Misha, and already so many are lost."

The gentleness of her voice and her touch soothed him, and he turned to her. Her face was fragile and beautiful in the pale light of the coach lamp, her eyes filled with understanding. It was as if he'd known her all his life. "I'm scared," he whispered. "Are you ever scared?"

"Oh, God, yes. Sometimes I wake in the middle of the night in a cold sweat, wondering if I've lost my mind, wondering if I'll be brave enough when the time comes, wondering if I truly want to risk death."

"The other day, when that cop had you, were you frightened?"

"Terrified."

"I was too."

There was a silence, a moment of bonding, and as naturally as if they had been intimate for a very long time, Irina slipped her arms under his and pressed her head against his chest. "What's so terrifying is that what happened to Denisov

can happen to any of us,'' she murmured. ''We can kill them
off one by one. But they can sweep us up anytime.''

Her face was close. Her eyes seemed to caress him. She
smoothed her fingers across his lips and he leaned down and
kissed her.

CHAPTER THIRTEEN

Anna hurried down the carpeted hallway to Lydia Karlovna's
office, feeling the flush of excitement warm her. She pressed
her hand to her burning cheek and opened her eyes wide,
almost giggling with pleasure. She was not expecting Alexei;
he'd said he had business to attend to all day; yet she knew
he was there, waiting for her. They'd been to tea at Kamenny
Island twice in the past week. He'd come to sit in on her
lessons almost daily. As Anna neared the headmistress's door,
she had to hold herself stiff to keep from running. It was far
too early for tea. Perhaps Alexei had something special in
mind. She knocked on the door.

''Yes, Anna, come in.''

Anna's smile faded, her whole body seemed to deflate as
she entered the office: the chair in front of the desk where
Alexei always sat was empty.

''Well, come in, Anna. Come in.'' Lydia Karlovna bustled. Waving Anna toward one of the large overstuffed chairs,
she announced, before Anna was fully seated, ''I had a message from your mother. She's in Petersburg. A carriage shall
be here shortly.'' Lydia Karlovna pressed her plump arms
across her thick waist. ''You're excused from the rest of the
day's classes.''

''But my lesson with Mr. Babichev!'' Anna burst out,
grabbing at the first coherent thought. Her mother, here, in
Petersburg! It was impossible. Not now, not yet. ''The interview at the Conservatory . . . it's only three days away.'' She
stumbled over words. Her voice snagged. Her stomach tightened.

''Surely your mama is more important than a piano lesson.
Now, I advise you to hurry and change. You don't want to

meet her after all these months in your school uniform. I shall send Sophie when your carriage arrives."

Anna tried to get up, but her energy was gone, the world turned cold; she looked in confusion to Lydia Karlovna, who seemed her last friend, her final refuge. She wanted to ask her: You do like Alexei Yakovlevich, don't you? And you will tell my mama, won't you? You'll tell her that he's a good man, a fine man? But when she opened her mouth to speak, the words "Mama . . . home?" came out like a question, splintering in reflection of her mother.

A shudder of dread more chilling than the bitter Petersburg air gripped Anna as the carriage turned finally onto Millionnaya Street and through the gates of the yellow palace with its rococo colonnades. Instinctively she looked through the fog to her mother's second-floor window, and imagined her, a pencil-thin shadow, standing there.

"Home at last, safe and sound!" Grigory, the coachman, opened the door and offered Anna his hand.

She felt her strength returning as her feet touched the ground. She didn't want her mother to see her weak. With a brusque, "That will be all, Grigory," she hurried up the palace steps and through the already open doorway, tossing her coat, hat, and muff into the waiting arms of a maid. "My mother is here, Krasina?"

"Yes, miss, she's up in her rooms, miss. The Countess says for you to come right up."

Breathing deeply, Anna felt in her pocket for Alexei's brooch, which she'd hidden there for good luck. Clutching it, she slowly climbed the steps.

"Yes, Anna," the Countess's voice responded to her knocking.

"I'm sorry I'm late, Mama, but Grigory said . . ." She burst in, only to meet the cold black stare of Zinaida Golovnina.

The elongated wraith of a woman stood stiffly between Anna and her mother; her knotted, man-size hands were clasped tightly as if in prayer. An oversize, wooden cross hung almost to the waist of the loose-fitting, homespun dress buttoned high about the neck.

"Say hello to Zinaida Ivanovna, Anna." The slight, straight lines of Countess Marya's back remained motionless as she stared out the window into the gray Petersburg afternoon. "She has traveled to her most hated of all places for you."

"Welcome, Zinaida Ivanovna." Anna curtsied and waited, hearing her short rapid breaths bouncing about the icy silence, feeling the bony fingers of Zinaida Golovnina sink into her heart.

"So . . ." The Countess turned slowly, her delicate face appearing pale. Dark circles nagged at her eyes, dulling their famed blueness. "Anna . . ." The slender jeweled fingers grasped the back of a chair. "This is not a trip either Zinaida Ivanovna or I expected to take."

Anna tried to swallow, but could not. "I'm sorry for being late, Mama! It's not my fault. . . ."

"It's not your lateness that concerns your mother," Zinaida warned, her husky voice filling the room. "We have prepared this letter for you to write to Alexei Kalinin." Zinaida held out a piece of the Countess's heavy lavender notepaper.

"Alexei . . ." The word faded hopelessly from Anna's tongue.

"How could you, Anna?" the Countess cried out suddenly, shrilly, accusingly. "How dare you accept invitations from Alexei Kalinin—and even *think* of a place like the Conservatory?" Her face sucked in grotesquely.

"Papa said—"

"Your papa!" she spit, her eyes like glass, the veins in her neck protruding like hackles. "How could you listen to him? Your papa's as bad as his sister. Tatyana . . ." She spoke the name with disgust. "*She* was with this man, Alexei Kalinin, for years. *She* was his mistress. Perhaps she still is!"

"That isn't true!" Anna pressed her hands to her ears, not wanting to hear any more. Why was her mama telling her this, her mama of all people? Why was her mama hurting her so?

"Don't be a fool, Anna." Marya Dmitreyevna grabbed her arms. "All of Petersburg knew of their cavorting. They were no better than beasts. Oh, he was handsome then, I'll give him that, as if the devil himself had bartered his soul for his beauty. All the ladies made a display of themselves before Alexei Yakovlevich . . ." She snorted as she spoke his name. "But your father's sister kept his bed. That's the way the Orlovs have always been, without morals, without shame—without regard to whom they hurt. But your father is the lowest of them, and now you." Marya Dmitreyevna shuddered, seeming to pull herself inside herself. "My worst fears have come true, Anna. You are too much an Orlova. May God have mercy on your soul!"

Anna shuddered, feeling an ugliness swimming up from

some deep, untouched place in her body, swimming up blind and sharp-toothed, devouring the wonder and excitement of the past months. She wanted to tell her mother about it, to prove her mother's accusations false. If only Zinaida weren't there. Maybe if Anna and her mother were alone without that woman's skeletal peering, Anna could tell how Alexei took her to tea all the way on Kamenny Island, how he listened to her so intently, and made her laugh, how he had found Mr. Babichev to give her lessons, and how much she had improved. If only Zinaida weren't there, Anna would sit right down at the piano and her mother would hear in the flawless sheen of her playing that Alexei was a good man. She would tell her mother how Alexei sat and listened to her practicing for hours, the intensity of his interest warming like the flame of life, warming as the Countess herself once had done. Indeed, Alexei seemed at times like her mother once had been, years before, when Anna and she were alone at the piano, when there was nothing but the music flowing ecstatically between them, no Papa and Petya, no Petersburg, no Zinaida Golovnina, nothing but God's music.

"The letter, take it, Anna," Zinaida's voice sternly demanded, hollow and devoid of emotion. "Copy it and sign it." Zinaida stuffed the paper into Anna's hand. "Read it, *now*."

Anna's eyes were so blurred with tears she could hardly make sense of the large, childish handwriting.

December 15, 1903

Monsieur Kalinin,
   It is with regret that I inform you I can never accept another invitation from you. Any efforts on your part to see or communicate with me in the future will be rebuffed.
                                  Cordially yours,
                                  Anna Petrovna Orlova

"But I can't send this! I can't, Mama!" she begged, the tears spilling down her face. "He's my friend and he hasn't done anything to deserve such a letter. Oh, if only you knew, Mama. He's just like you, I swear. He sits and listens to me play. He only wants to help me—"

"Hush!" Zinaida raised her hand above Anna. "Do as your mother bids, now."

"Mama—" Anna's words were cut off by the bony hand of Zinaida Golovnina clasped about her neck. "Mama, please!"

The Countess was standing, her face turned, staring out the window.

"Write the letter, Anna. Now."

"No! I can't. I won't!"

"Then we shall pray." Zinaida pressed her fingers painfully into Anna's shoulders as she ushered her toward the corner of the room where an icon of the Virgin hung surrounded by candles. "You will prostrate yourself before the holy Mother and beg her intervention in the salvation of your soul." Zinaida pushed Anna to her knees.

For hour upon endless hour, Zinaida Golovnina knelt praying, or prostrated herself, her hands seeming to claw the cold, hard floor before the icon. Her voice waxed and waned, filtering with the smoky light of the candles and fading into the shimmering gold halos of the Virgin and Child. Anna lost track of time. Minutes oozed like blackening resin on a scarred wound. Pain numbed her knees, thighs, and back, and the gnawing emptiness in her stomach became almost pleasurable. Anna was floating outside herself, away from the flood of Zinaida's incantations and the awful accusations.

"Did he touch you? Has Alexei Kalinin ever touched you?" Zinaida spit the name Alexei Kalinin as if it were caked in gutter mud. "Tell me, Anna, has the man Alexei Kalinin ever touched you?"

"He holds my hand sometimes, as he helps me in and out of the carriage."

"You go to tea with the man, Alexei Kalinin?"

"Yes."

"Where?"

"Donan's," Anna lied, praying to the Virgin to forgive and protect her. Anna could never tell a woman like Zinaida of her afternoons on Kamenny Island with Alexei. She had to keep the memory pure within her; for then, no matter what was done to her, even if her mother and Zinaida banished her to Ravens Head for the rest of her life, the joy would remain forever hers.

"Does he have an apartment?"

"I don't know."

"God sees all truths, child."

"I have told the truth, I swear."

"Have his lips ever touched yours?"

"No. No!"

"He is a seducer, Anna. He cuts out virgins' souls as he devours their bodies and tosses them to hell. . . ." Zinaida grabbed Anna's hand and pulled her to the floor. The rumble of Zinaida's incantations through the wooden planks burrowed like shiny black grubs into Anna's brain.

Alexei, Alexei, Alexei. . . . She held the brooch in her hand as she repeated the name in an effort to conjure up his face, his eyes, and the game they played together. It was a game she played at school; but with Alexei the game seemed more like life than anything she had known.

"It's called the seeing game," Anna had told him, laughing softly, her eyes already seeking his. They were sitting in the Pelican Rest. "It's really quite simple. All we do is sit here and look at each other. But you must look directly into my eyes. That's the hardest part, to look and not feel silly and giggle. You mustn't stare either. Staring ruins the game. You just look until you see into the other's soul."

"Oh, dear, I don't know about that. What if you don't like what you see?"

"I shall, of course, I shall!" She laughed heartily. "I'm very good at this game. I've already played it when you haven't been watching. I've seen wonderful things in your soul."

"Then you haven't looked deeply enough."

"It's just a game, really," she insisted, silenced by the immediacy with which their eyes joined. Beckoning shades of gray, blue and black floated in shifting layers, drawing her below the surface of his eyes, drawing her deeper and deeper. Until there was only the unbearable connection between them, as if life itself, shadowy and warm, started in that moment, opening slowly like the pale petals of a rose.

"You think of him still! His hold on your soul is far worse than I expected!" Zinaida was kneeling face-to-face with Anna, her voice, her dark eyes demanding attention. She lifted the wooden cross from her chest and held it out for Anna to kiss.

Anna felt her body swaying. Her eyes were heavy. She wanted to sleep. "May I have some water, please?"

"Pray!" Zinaida pressed the cross against Anna's lips, and slowly made the sign of the cross. "When I feel your soul releasing, you shall have water and sleep. Not until then." She let the cross drop back to her chest, and shook Anna fiercely. "Pray!"

Several times Anna fell asleep as she knelt in the smoky alcove beside Zinaida. Her eyes simply closed and her head nodded.

"Pray!" The clamp of a hand forced her awake. Then the question, again and again, "Will you write the letter to Alexei Kalinin?"

Anna had answered no so many times, she seemed to have no voice left, only the will, feeling like survival, to shake her head again and again.

"Pray, then, child. Pray to God and the holy Virgin to bless your soul. . . ." Zinaida's voice was dim, its words, their meaning, muffled by the flickering candles and the beauty of the icon glorified in a harmony of soft yellows, rich browns, crimsons, and celestial blues. This icon had long been one of Anna's favorites; as a child she'd sat before the portrait of the Virgin and Child, sang to them, told them stories. There was such compassion and love in the delicate lines of the Virgin's face; her loveliness radiated a depth of faith which Anna herself often desperately prayed to attain. The innocence and tenderness of the Mother and Child reached out to Anna; she felt safe, graced by the gentle eyes, blessed by the smiling mouth as if she were in the presence of holy truth.

Dear Jesus, our Lord in Heaven, make me strong. Save me with your ever-present love. Save me from this woman who cannot be your servant. For God is love, and protects His children. I am pure, dear Jesus. I have done no wrong. I offer myself to you in pledge of my love. Save me and my mama and Alexei Yakovlevich from the hatred of this woman, Zinaida Golovnina. . . .

"Anna . . ." Her mother's cool hand swept across her sweating brow. "Come with me, Anna." Her mother helped her to her feet.

Anna shuddered at the sweet scent of her mother's skin.

"Here, have some water," her mother offered, holding a glass to Anna's lips.

"Make her sign first."

"Drink, Anna." Her mother held the glass to Anna's lips. "Look at me, Annochka." Her mother was smiling. "This is very important, my dove. You do love me?"

"Yes, Mama, I love you! I always love you!" Anna quivered with the fragility of the moment. How could her mother doubt her love?

"Listen to me, then. You are too willful. You have always been too willful, and that frightens me. You have brought me such pain, Annochka. Please, no more. Do this for me. Write this letter for me, and I shall never leave you again. I promise. We will be together always, my dove, my sweetest soul. Please, Annochka. Please do this for me. I can't bear any more pain."

Anna took the pen from her mother's hand. The letters she

copied made little sense. Still, she wrote. Her mother was beside her, gently urging her on. When Anna finished, her mother cradled her, smoothing her hair and kissing her softly.

"Can I sleep now, Mama?"

"Of course. Come. I'll help you myself, and put you into my own bed."

Anna had to hold her mother one more time. She needed to wrap her arms around the slim shoulders and feel the familiar warmth. "I love you, Mama. I love you so much."

Alexei barely finished reading before crushing the lavender notepaper into a ball and hurling it to the floor. "Damn!" he thundered, grinding the paper with the heel of his shoe. "God damn them all!" His rage echoed through the marbled halls. Picking up a chair, Alexei raised it above his head and dashed it to the floor; its legs splintered. Then he ran from the room, colliding with a startled servant.

"Get me my coat!" he ordered.

Moments later, the trembling servant reappeared. "I told Sasha to harness Shalamar to the drozhki, sir."

Without answering, Alexei grabbed his coat, hat, scarf and gloves and was out the door; he faltered at the gate to his palace, peering into the dark of the bitterly cold night. To the left lay Smolny, where Anna might be, waiting for him. He could run there, push past a sputtering Lydia Karlovna, who surely must have been instructed to keep him away, and race through the darkened corridors calling Anna's name. She would appear from a line of rooms along a long hall, appear as if by magic, or in a drunken vision, draped in soft pastel folds of silk, appearing ancient in mists of fragrances, gliding toward him, her almond blue eyes laughing, her broad cheeks bright with color, her smile radiant.

"Master, Alexei Yakovlevich, the carriage, sir." The heavyset coachman was before him.

"Very good," Alexei snapped, embarrassed, as if the coachman had been privy to the images flooding his mind—stupid, schoolboy images filled with absurd yearnings. What was wrong with him lately? Sometimes he thought he was going mad. He closed his eyes a moment and images of Anna mixed and matched in his mind, pictures of the sweet young smoothness of her skin, her fingers flying across the keyboard, the surge of her laughter, the curve of her chin, all of it combining as it always did into the deafening applause, with Anna, his Anna standing alone, breathless on the stage beside the grand piano, the brilliance of the music calling all of Petersburg to its feet. He saw the audience, ecstatic as they rose, clapping, cheering, throwing roses. "Bravo! Bravo!" The audience, the world, enthralled.

Enthralled, he almost said out loud as he stared dumbly at the heavyset coachman, suddenly needing to explain himself. *Enthralled*, yes—he was pleased with the word. "Enthralled" was far more apt a description of his feelings about Anna than "love" or "infatuation." There was much in Anna to enthrall anyone, young or old, man or woman. He was enthralled with her as he had been once with money and power, and with the stallion Shalamar, whom he'd bought at a ridiculously high price and then had ridden into submission. Still, ten years later, he was enthralled with the brute. Enthralled, yes, the word calmed him, and he let his eyes focus on the coachman. "There won't be anything else, Sasha." He hurried to the courtyard where Shalamar was waiting.

It was almost ten by the time Alexei rang the bell to Count Orlov's palace. He rang twice before the heavy oak door was slowly opened.

"May I help you?" A low voice, more like a man's, flowed resonantly from an unusually thin, large-boned woman. Even in the shadows of the hall, Alexei could see she wasn't a servant. A large wooden cross pressed heavily on a coarsely clad, shapeless chest, and long black hair hung loosely like a gypsy's around her broad, bony shoulders; but it was her eyes, glowing in black on black, a black cat in the night, which unnerved him. They seemed to sear through him.

"I'm here to see Count Orlov," he asserted, his voice louder than he'd expected.

"The Count is not at home, Alexei Kalinin." She enunciated each syllable of his name, making the music of it seem foreboding.

"When is he expected?"

"He's not."

"Yet he knew I was coming."

"*I* knew you were coming. You received Anna's letter."

Alexei stiffened, turning his head to better make out the face in the light. "What do you know of Anna's letter?" He stepped closer. "Is Anna here?"

"Anna is none of your concern."

"Who are you?"

"Anna's protector."

"Is that so?" He chortled. "And your name? Surely Anna has mentioned you to me."

"The Countess has returned to Petersburg, Alexei Kalinin." Her eyes widened. "The spirit of God has returned with her. The house of Orlov is no longer open prey to the likes of Alexei Kalinin.'' Her lips widened as she spoke his name, widening and pressing against large yellow teeth.

"Then I shall speak with the Countess.''

"The Countess has nothing to say to you.''

"Tell the Countess I'm here. Let her decide for herself.''

"She knows you are here, Alexei Kalinin. She has no wish to see you, not now, not ever.''

"It was the Countess who ordered Anna to write that letter.''

"Good evening, Alexei Kalinin.'' The woman stepped back and started to close the door.

Alexei blocked its closing with his body. "I will see the Countess or Anna.'' He pushed still harder, expecting the woman to fall back under his pressure, but she held him at bay. They stood for several moments locked in a contest of strength. Alexei felt himself straining. The veins in his neck were stretching. His temples were pulsating. Who was this woman that she could keep him from Anna? He would kill her if he reached her, wrap his fingers around her neck, hold his thumb against that soft place until her body went limp.

The woman pressed harder.

Alexei was losing ground. "Then tell the Countess this, woman of God!'' He pounded his fist against the door. The rage spit from his lips. "Tell the Countess that should she dare keep Anna from her audition, or from any future engagement with me, I shall call in all her husband's notes immediately. Tell the Countess they are enough for me to take this palace and everything her husband owns twice over. And I will. Don't doubt that. The great house of Orlov will all too soon find itself in the streets!''

"Good night, Alexei Kalinin!'' she hissed, and exerting more pressure than he had thought possible, she shoved him out, slamming the door after him.

He swerved to pound his fists against the door, catching himself just in time. That woman, that serpentine bitch, would let him pound all night and leave him the fool. That woman, whoever she was! His fists rose again to pound the door, and he beat them into himself instead. *Alexei Kalinin*—he heard his name rolling off her tongue and recoiling in a hideous laugh. *Alexei Kalinin!* She hissed as if she knew.

His mind reeled, propelling him forward, down the palace steps and onto the dark, windy street.

Alexei Kalinin! The name pursued him like an incantation.

It was beginning, the unraveling, that spinning out like never-ending night.

He ran, his footsteps echoing through the empty, windblown street. The desperation tightened like fists, a hangman's noose, a scream of death. His fingers ached. His throat seared. It was his nightmare bursting from beneath the threshold of his consciousness.

Shalamar, he remembered. The horse was tethered at the Orlov palace, and he hurried back, grabbing the reins as he leapt into the drozhki. "Let's go, boy!" Alexei called, urging him on. The stallion whinnied and his hooves began to fly; Alexei guided him in and out of the back roads of Petersburg, through blackened slums, and to the country where the river flowed through lightless villages, scarcely more than bleak, muddied pinholes of hell in the landscape. The wind cut against his skin, whipping down the neck of his fur collar, under his hat, and through his gloves. His eyes teared; his nose ran; ice formed on his face. Still, he drove Shalamar on.

"He came." The low, deep voice found its way into the pounding crevices of Anna's brain.

For a moment, caught as she was in a fitful half-sleep, she thought the hand caressing her head, soothing the unbearable aching, was her mother's, and she smiled, trying to open her eyes, wanting to hold her mother close. "Mama . . ." She gasped. Her throat was parched. She grasped the hand and pulled it to her lips, realizing too late the long, gnarled fingers belonged to Zinaida Golovnina.

"He came, my child, just as I told you he would. He is just as I said he would be—if anything, more powerful. I could feel his power. The very fiber of his being was in battle with me." She clasped the wooden cross tightly. "I felt his evil, Anna. We must be careful. Kalinin is like a bomb those terrorists throw. One day, he will go off." Zinaida's voice floated discordantly from a flickering candle. The words made no sense.

"Where's Mama?" she begged, tears pressing against her eyes. The pain in her head made her stomach sick.

"She's dressing, as you must now. She'll be in soon. Come now, you don't want to disappoint your mama again. She'll expect to see you dressed."

"My head," Anna moaned as Zinaida tried to lift her. "My head hurts so."

"All right, here. I have some powders for you. But first you must get up and dress."

Why? Anna wanted to ask. *Where are we going?* But words grated like wires on raw nerves. She pushed herself up on the pillows. Her arms and legs were heavy, as if they did not belong, and the effort of dressing exhausted her.

"Here now, drink this." Zinaida handed her a glass. "The powder will help your head."

Obediently Anna drank, and her mother appeared, feeling of furs and smelling of perfume. Her mother helped Anna to her feet again and led her from her room and down the stairs to a waiting carriage. It was night. Anna's mouth was cottony. Her brain heavy like sludge. Thoughts drowned quickly. Her mother held her as the carriage sped through the ice-covered streets.

Anna drifted in and out of sleep. The world stopped and started. Strange noises clanked and thudded. Steam hissed. Damp dust dried inside her nose. Legs buckled and vanished. Strong, strange arms carried her. She cried for her mother, reaching out like a child.

"I'm here, Annochka." Her mother smiled.

The world slipped. Sunlight streamed through dirt-streaked glass.

Her mother watched and slept and read.

Darkness sped into light, day into night. Images raged in numbing blackness.

Zinaida Golovnina prayed.

"Are you hungry?" her mother asked.

Anna shook her head.

"Here, drink this. It's for your head." Zinaida held a glass to Anna's lips.

"Drink, Annochka," her mother said.

Anna drank and the nightmare continued. She cried, screamed and died. She floated and woke and slept again.

"Are you hungry?"

"No."

"Here, drink this. It's for your head." Zinaida held a glass to Anna's lips.

"I can't, no more."

"Drink, Annochka," her mother said.

Anna drank. There was no time. The world sped by, black into gray, into blue; snow into sun, green leaves, blue sky. The speeding slowed to bumps through spring breezes. Anna's neck and head were free of fur wraps. Her eyes opened. An engine hummed.

"Are you hungry, Anna?"

"No."

"Here, drink this. It's for your head." Zinaida held a glass to Anna's lips.

"I can't, no more"

"Drink, Annochka," her mother said.

Anna drank. More days and nights. Sleep finally filled with softness and throbbed with waking. Still she slept. Her mind was opening to the light.

"Alexei!" she screamed, sitting up in a bed in a room she knew. She blinked, thinking she was dreaming still, that terrible dream, a nightmare of being in her room at Ravens Head. She pulled at the covers and leapt from the bed, stumbling as she spun around. Her head was light, but she was awake. Her limbs were once more her own. She ran to the window. It wasn't a dream. The all-too-familiar trees of the Crimean woods were green and soft, and beyond, the Black Sea shimmered with morning sunlight. Birds chirped. Heat pricked her skin. She pressed her hands to her head. No dream! No dream! She was at Ravens Head. The trip from Petersburg to Ravens Head took five days. The audition . . . Alexei!

Racing barefoot from her room, she bolted down the wooden stairs.

"Anna!" Boris happily called, and left his toy trains to greet her. She bent to hug him, a frightening sadness welling as she nestled against his little-boy skin.

"Why are you sad, Anna? I've been waiting for you so long. Mama and Zinaida Ivanovna said you were staying forever."

She kissed her brother and tried to smile.

"Mama said you'll take me swimming."

"I will, yes, I promise. But I have to speak to Mama now. Where is she?"

"On the veranda with Zinaida Ivanovna."

"You stay here, all right, Boris? You play with your trains, and I'll be back very soon."

"Ah, Marya Dmitreyevna, Anna is awake." Zinaida smiled as Anna stepped onto the wide porch.

The air smelled of moist earth and summertime. Insects buzzed. The morning sun streamed through the trees and slanted across the table where Zinaida and her mother were breakfasting.

"Annochka!" Marya Dmitreyevna smiled, rising to greet her. Her hair was down, and she wore a pale pink dressing gown. Dark circles sagged under her eyes. Her cheeks were sunken. "I was beginning to think you'd sleep forever. But it was a long, tiring journey. Goodness, I'm hardly feeling myself yet. But I was thinking it would be nice to go collecting mushrooms this afternoon, Annochka. When the sun is hot, you and Boris and I can go into the cool of the woods.''

Anna shuddered as her mother kissed her.

"Come, sit down. Some coffee and something to eat. You haven't eaten for days, you know. Look how pale you are, Annochka, my soul." She caressed Anna's cheek. "I shall have Cook make you some blini with sturgeon and sour cream. Yes, a few weeks in the Crimea and you'll be looking just fine."

"Mama . . ." She breathed deeply, and bit her lip. "Mama . . ." She forced out the words. "Why am I here?"

"Really, Annochka, we needn't go into all that now. What's important is that you are here. Boris is so excited, especially to have you with us for Christmas. We'll have such a grand Christmas this year, just like we used to. Poor little Boris, he's never had his brother or sister around him for Christmas. He's such a lonely little boy, Annochka. You're just what he needs."

Opening her eyes wide to hold back the tears, Anna said with a determination that surprised her, "I want to go back to Petersburg, Mama."

"I'm afraid that's impossible."

"Why?"

"Just the impudence of your questioning is proof of the righteousness of Zinaida Ivanovna's guidance. I thought your willfullness would be bridled at Smolny, Anna, but it has only grown worse. To think you have shamed me so as to throw yourself at a man like Alexei Kalinin."

"I haven't thrown myself at him, Mama. I've done nothing with Alexei Yakovlevich I'm ashamed of. He wants to help me with my music, is all. And now . . ." She had to fight to hold back her tears. "Now I've missed my audition!"

"The Conservatory!" Marya Dmitreyevna's voice was quickly growing shrill.

"There's nothing wrong with the Conservatory. Papa said—"

"Don't mention your father's name to me, Anna, ever! Is that clear?" Her eyes shone wildly. "And don't mention the Conservatory either. Is that clear?"

"But why, Mama? Why can't we even talk about it?"

"It's a little late for talking now. Oh, Annochka, what do you think it did to my heart to hear from a friend that my own daughter was flaunting herself to the world with a man like Alexei Kalinin—and then, as if that isn't bad enough, to be told by the same friend that you are auditioning for the Conservatory!''

"What's wrong with the Conservatory, Mama? Just tell me that.''

"Your naiveté horrifies me. Such a place has nothing to do with music. It is little more than a hotbed of socialism. The girls who attend end up loose Gypsies playing ditties.''

"That's not true, Mama!'' Anna could scarcely see her mother through her tears. "You don't know anything! How could you, stuck away in this place with that horrible woman—''

The stinging smack of her mother's hand against her face sucked the breath from Anna.

Marya Dmitreyevna's face washed of color. Her blue eyes flashed angrily as she flung the words through narrowed lips. "I wash my hands of you, Anna. Do you understand? My life is pained enough without your prideful will. Until I hear of your humility, you are to obey the word of Zinaida Ivanovna. You are completely in her charge.'' She gathered the skirt of her dressing gown and left.

"Mama, please, wait! Mama, listen to me!'' Anna sobbed piteously as she pressed her hand to her still-stinging face. Her chest heaved and she slipped helplessly to the floor, what little energy she had flooding from her body. The sun-speckled woods whirled in a dizzying swarm of colors and sounds, seeming to blind her. There was no place to run, no place to hide. The woods, hills, and sea were endless. Zinaida Golovnina would always find her. "Alexei . . .'' she moaned, closing her eyes. She saw him then, his face, his smile, his massive shoulders. He felt so close, she could almost touch him. She would write to him. He would help her escape.

"Anna.'' Fingers clamped her arm. "Come, it is time to pray.''

"No.'' Anna shrank back.

Zinaida knelt beside her. "You will learn, child.'' She held the soft flesh under Anna's arm. "You will learn obedience.''

"I won't go with you.''

"Yes, you will. You will come with me now, child.'' Zinaida's eyes opened wide, seeming to burn into Anna's own. "Only I can cleanse you of your obsession with this Alexei Kalinin. Only I can bring you peace. You want that, Anna. I know you want peace. We all want peace. Come with me now. We shall pray for peace and guidance.''

"No!'' Anna struggled to break free.

"Pray, child, pray for forgiveness, then you shall eat and sleep."

"You can't make me go with you!"

"Then we shall pray here, on the earth." Zinaida dragged Anna across the veranda and down the stairs to the small garden of wildflowers. Kneeling, she pulled Anna to the ground beside her.

CHAPTER FOURTEEN

Each time with Irina was different from any other time, and always different from any other woman he had known. Misha had no desire to hurry away into the night. Instead he lay close, holding her, stroking her, talking about silly and unimportant things until he thought he would drift off to sleep cradled by her warmth; but she would touch him, her lips or fingers smooth against him, and desire would swirl like a silken whirlwind, beyond a game, beyond the moment of feeling good. Sensations lingered until life itself felt exquisitely taut, suspended across an abyss, and passion as calming as it was feverish burst forth, leaving him in a peace that seemed the quintessence of all he had and could ever experience.

This was love, he knew, but could not find the words to express it to Irina. *I love you* seemed a mockery of all they shared. Besides, he had professed love so easily to so many women before, the words themselves were meaningless, and he tried to think of others. Poetry came to mind. He dreamed poems to Irina and created such sweet sonnets as he walked the streets as Igor, the idiot leather man, that he often found himself biting back tears. For all their beauty, he never wrote down his poems or sonnets, never so much as whispered one in Irina's ear. He feared she would laugh. He feared her biting laughter. He feared her leaving him, and he would be a boy again.

Irina cursed herself daily for ever having started up with Misha Kalinin. Nothing was going as planned. A simple affair was all she'd wanted, something to fuel reality for her mother's witch-eyes, and, in truth, to steady herself for Stepan's return. Who would have thought she'd end up caring for someone like Misha as much as she did? Dear God, it was more than caring, it was a kind of loving, she despaired. His boyish adoration tugged at her heartstrings; she found herself thinking of him too often, recalling the smallest moment, breathlessly anticipating meetings and staring at him because his face brought her pleasure. He was a gentle lover, giving up his mind to her as readily as he gave his body. Their time together was slow and sweet. He stroked her, coaxing her to flower, as if that inner core which always felt locked might one day pour exuberantly into sunlight. They talked of living and dying, of childhood, and funny, sad and beautiful times. The endless, easy talking as they clung wrapped about each other was what frightened her most. She felt stripped, more exposed than she had with any man; and then she felt herself running from him, needing to hurt him. He was so easy to hurt.

"Why must I always take you home?" he asked as she sat up in the bed and reached for her corset. "In a few days we shall be living together."

"Because my mother expects me home. Her guests will still be there. You can come in and have drink. She'll like that."

"I won't. Your mother makes me nervous. She's always looking at me."

"She's giving you the evil eye, now that she knows we're in love!" Irina laughed nervously, catching herself on her effusion of words. "Which only goes to prove we're putting on a good show now," she went on more sternly. "Mama is not an easy woman to deceive." She stood up, fumbling hopelessly as she tried to make the sides of the corset meet.

"Here." Misha jumped to help with the hooks.

His happy smile was upsetting her. "You look like the cat that swallowed the canary." She frowned and pushed his hands away. "Look, Misha, if you're reading anything into what I just said—about our being in love—it didn't mean anything. It was a slip of the tongue. You know there is no place for love in the revolution."

Still he was smiling.

"Lord, I knew that was what you were thinking! And you must stop, you must—or you'll be more of a liability than an asset to the squad. Besides, Stepan will see through you right away. He'll slay you if you give him the slightest hint of weakness."

"Since when is loving a weakness?"

"Don't be naive, Misha!" She laughed mockingly as she grabbed a stocking. "You think because I've slept with you a few times, you know me? I give my body to any man I like. I've lost count of the men I've slept with. Don't think you're special—because you're not. There's nothing special about you, nothing!" She reached for her cigarettes.

"Why do you do this, Irina? Why do you run cold, then hot, then cold again? And don't tell me it's the revolution."

"All right, I won't. I won't tell you anything, because I've already told you everything and you don't want to listen. You don't want to hear the truth."

"Did Dmitri Mayakovsky tell you to sleep with me?" he asked suddenly. His voice quivered.

She laughed again, that husky, mocking laughter reminding him of Irina sidling up to the reindeer-meat vendor, Irina as the coarse, foul-mouthed peddler. "Dmitri would be harder on you than Stepan if he knew what a fool you're being." She crushed out her cigarette and began putting on her stocking again. "Look . . ." She turned to him. "I think this night should be the end of our personal relationship. Stepan is coming in any day now. Besides, it won't work once we're in that apartment with Stepan and Olga."

"I didn't expect it would." His voice was very soft.

"Well, if you're thinking I'll be with Stepan, you're wrong. None of us will be personally involved. Dmitri insists it's the only way. We're comrades. That's enough." She pulled on her dress and stood at the mirror brushing her hair.

"I think I should take you home," Misha said, fumbling through the jumble of covers for his underwear. "It wouldn't look good if you arrived alone."

They finished dressing in silence. Misha kept on looking over at Irina, thinking she would look at him, but she didn't.

"Are you ready?" she snapped. She was already in her hat, coat and muff.

He grabbed his coat and started for the door. "You know," he said, staring at her as his hand touched the knob, "it's not true that we must love only the revolution. We love the revolution because we're capable of loving."

"*I* have no problem in keeping love and sex separate, Misha."

His face tightened and grew a frightening color of pale. "Don't be so sure of that." His eyes narrowed. "You're very good at deceiving yourself, Irina. Perhaps that makes you more of a liability to the revolution than me."

* * *

"Misha!" he heard his father roar as he slipped into the house. "Misha, is that you?" came the angry, slurred voice.

Misha's skin prickled and his heart pounded fearfully. He'd known an explosion was coming. He'd felt the tension building for weeks, months even, perhaps since he'd come out of the hospital.

"It's me, Papa," Misha called in a hushed whisper as he stood at the bottom of the stairs.

There was no answer, and Misha slowly began up the stairs, wishing he'd thought to turn on the light. He could hear his father's labored breathing. "Papa, is everything all right?" He paused, the pounding in his own chest growing almost painful. "Papa, could you tell me what I've done? I know I've done something. Perhaps if we could talk about it . . ." Slowly his foot took the next step.

His father's breathing grew raspy. The stench of vodka on his breath was nauseating. "I want you in my room," came the low gurgling of a threat.

Misha listened to the shuffling of his father's steps, and he thought perhaps this time it would be different, perhaps this time they would talk.

He saw the bulk of his father lumped in the shadow of the candlelight. His father always sat alone, drinking by candlelight.

"Can I turn on the light, Papa?"

There was a grunt of assent.

Misha flicked on the light and the chandelier glowed. He chose a seat as far from his father as possible, not wanting to look at the wretched man, his hair dirty and uncombed, his unshaven face swollen, his eyes red, his shirt spotted and hanging out of trousers which sat below a bulging belly. His fly was half-unbuttoned and he was barefoot.

"Your mother is mad with misery," Tolya announced as he drained his glass and poured himself some more. "You must go and tell her now it isn't true. That you're moving into some apartment with a tart."

Misha groaned inwardly. He should have known better than to wait so long. He should have known his mother would hear the gossip. "She isn't a tart, Papa."

Tolya rose to his feet.

Misha rose at the same instant and drew defensively away. "Papa, Irina is the daughter of a grand duke. I love—"

Before he could finish, his father lunged for him, smashing his fist across his face with such force, Misha fell to the floor.

"You can't do this to me!" Misha screamed. "Not anymore. Not ever again!"

"Oh, can't I!" Tolya bellowed. "You yellow-bellied little fart!" He grabbed Misha as he stumbled to his feet, only to slap him down. Again and again, his fist slammed into Misha's head and shoulders. "You've brought shame to this family for the last time! You have no values! You think because you defy the Czar, you can defy your parents! You think you can get away with anything in life, that your uncle will always bail you out! And now you go to live with a tart and don't even tell your mother! You think with your pecker, as if that's all you've got! God, you disgust me!" He kneed Misha fiercely in the groin. "See what you can give your little whore now!" He snorted as he left the room.

Misha lay moaning as he held himself tightly. Tears of pain and rage rolled down his cheeks. He lay there until he felt the soft touch of his grandmother's hands on his head.

"Misha," she whispered, and kissed him. "Are you all right? Praise God, I knew this would happen. Tolya's been mad all day. I begged Alexei not to go, but he's as mad as the rest of them. He thinks only of that Orlova girl. Oh, Misha, Misha, bad will come from all this. Surely, it is life we fear, not death. Alexei is not himself. God be praised, I see specters from the past rising like demons. Oh, Misha, Misha, my purest soul, I've been so terrified. The vodka makes Tolya wild, as if the soul of his father comes from the bottle."

Slowly, he pushed himself to a sitting position and let his head fall against his grandmother. "Someday," he moaned. "Someday I will beat him back."

"Dear Lord our Savior, salvation is eternal . . ." she prayed as she held him and rocked him. Then she said, "It's true, then. Why have you taken an apartment with the daughter of the Grand Duke Ilya Mikhailevich?"

"Because I love her." A swell of sadness tightened his body, causing it to throb even more. A vision of Irina, of her loving him, touched him and then was gone.

"You should have told your mother. The shock of the news sent her to bed."

"The news would have shocked her at any time. Then he would have beat me regardless."

"Come. . . ." She helped him stand on his feet. "You'll wash and I'll warm your sheets. In the morning you'll go to the baths, then you'll feel better. God knows, perhaps Alexei will be home soon."

It was almost noon when Misha was awakened by a servant holding a notepaper which Misha recognized as Irina's. "The messenger said it was most urgent," Vassily advised.

"Yes, thank you. I'll ring if there's to be a response."
Misha waited until the servant left, then slowly pulled himself
to a sitting position. His whole body ached.

> *Misha,*
> *Pick me up in twenty minutes. No later. It's of the utmost*
> *urgency.*
>
> *Irina*

"Dmitri has called a meeting. Stepan has arrived, and we'll
surely see Katya and Vera," Irina whispered as she settled
into the back of the cab. "They've been here a week, but it's
all very hush-hush. They have a flat on the Vyborg side with
Josef until we set up shop on Zhukovskaya Street. I spoke to
Josef just yesterday."

"I see," he said flatly.

"Oh, don't pout," she scolded. Her gaze narrowed and
settled on his face. "Your cheek is swollen. Did you walk
into a door?"

"Yes."

"Seriously, what happened?" Her hand reached to touch
him. "Did somebody hit you?"

He pushed it away. "It's no concern of yours."

"Your father! The beast . . ." She tried to caress him
again.

"Don't judge what you don't know! And don't touch me."
He grabbed her wrist a moment.

"You're very angry with me."

"What did you expect?" His eyes searched her face;
her beauty filled him with a deep aching, and he looked
away.

"Would it help you to know I hardly slept last night?
It's . . ." She hesitated. "It's just better this way, Misha, not
only for the revolution, but for you too. You feel too much
for me and I'm not a good person to feel much for."

He laughed bitterly. "You make your own truths. They're
very convenient. I just ask one thing of you. Don't play games
with me with Stepan Ostravsky."

"I wouldn't do that. We're comrades."

"Tell me what that means, Irina. I'm confused." He
sneered.

"It doesn't mean being lovers. It means trust, absolute
trust. We may depend on each other for our very lives one
day. You *can* trust me, Misha."

"God grant you're a better comrade than you are a lover."

She turned from him, unable to bear the hardness of his gaze. "Perhaps it's better that you hate me," she said flatly as she stared out the window into the gray day, heavy with fog and threatening snow. Her head was beginning to ache. It was a familiar aching, tagged with Stepan's name. The tugging was beginning, that struggle between desire and disdain.

They rode in silence to a respectable workingmen's inn across the river, which was crowded with lunch patrons already merry with the Christmas spirit. "The main dining hall is too noisy. We are looking for something more intimate," she told the owner.

"Of course." The man nodded and wordlessly led them to a smoky room around the back of the stairs. He knocked three times, waited a moment and opened the door.

Irina's stomach tightened when she saw Stepan; he was his composed, even serene self as he sat beside Dmitri at the table. There was no sign of the wear of his journey from Paris. He appeared rested. His crisp white shirt was neatly pressed and perfectly fitted across his shoulders. His brown woolen vest was unbuttoned. His beard had grown a bit. God, but he was good to look at, damn him. She waited for him to glance up, and when he didn't, she called a general, "Hello, comrades," to all those sitting around the table, and laid her coat on the pile by the door.

Misha followed Irina, and sat in the empty seat next to her. He felt an uneasy tension as comrades nodded silently to him, then turned anxiously back to Dmitri. Misha knew all but two of the comrades. There was Savva, who looked pale and unusually somber, and Josef, who sat motionlessly, his head bent, his hands pressed angrily into his eyes. Kiril smoked relentlessly, and the matriarch, Olga Gambarova, solemnly nursed a glass of vodka. Misha didn't know the man next to Olga; he was in his late twenties, short, stocky and dressed in workingman's clothes. To his right and next to Dmitri Mayakovsky sat a tall, slim, strikingly handsome man with deep-set eyes, fine features and a dark beard, which he stroked unconsciously. He seemed oblivious of Misha and Irina's arrival. He was, Misha knew, Stepan Ostravsky.

"We are complete now, Viktor Ilyitch," Dmitri advised the innkeeper. "Thank you. There will be nothing else."

"It is my honor to serve, Dmitri Andreievich. I will see you are not disturbed." The innkeeper bowed slightly and backed from the room, closing the door tightly after him.

"Now that Misha and Irina are here, we can start," Dmitri Mayakovsky began, absently pushing his glasses up, then smoothing the puffy palm of his hand over his bald head. His hand seemed to glide. Large circles of sweat spread from under his arms, darkening his crumpled shirt.

It was very hot in the cramped room, despite the subfreezing temperatures outside. Coats, scarves and sweaters were piled on a vacant chair, ties were loosened, shirt sleeves rolled up and collar buttons undone. Wind-chafed faces glistened with perspiration.

Olga offered Misha and Irina the vodka.

Stepan took out a handkerchief and wiped his face. His eyes cruised noncommittally over the newcomers. He lit a cigarette, leaned back in his chair, and looked back to Dmitri.

"I had hoped this wouldn't be necessary, for us to all get together in a group so soon. It is always dangerous. Let me begin by making introductions, for some of you are new to one another. To my right is Kiril Zatov, then Olga Gambarova, Vladimir Ropshin, Savva Safanov you all know, and Josef Kidarsky. Finally, we have Irina Rantzau, Misha Kalinin and Stepan Ostravsky. There would be two more of our comrades with us: Vera Martova and Katya Kazen, but . . ." Dmitri paused ominously and fumbled for his cigarettes.

Seconds ticked endlessly. The boisterous voices of men and women drinking in the tavern outside hummed against the oppressive silence.

Dmitri inhaled deeply and, seeming to look at everyone in the same moment, he said, "It is with greatest sorrow I tell you comrades Martova and Kazen won't be with us." A pained expression tightened his mouth; his eyes were steady. "They were murdered last night, shot to death in their beds. Josef found them. We have cause to believe it was the work of the Okhrana. We suspect it was connected to the robberies in Paris."

Irina heard little else; the aching in her chest was unbearable. She was suffocating. Katya dead, her Katya. It wasn't possible. Even Vera, the pigeon . . . The room was fading beyond the fog of her tears. She pressed her twisted handkerchief to her mouth and the oddest sound came out. Then Savva was beside her.

"They were good friends," he whispered, slipping his arm about her shoulder.

She held on to him desperately, wishing he were Misha.

"Spies!" Josef's voice exploded, causing her to jump. Josef had been sitting motionlessly up until then, his gaze fixed on some unknown site. "Kiril!" he accused, his face washed of color; he shook his fist. "How did you get your job driving for the Okhrana?"

"Excuse me . . ."

"How did you get your job driving for the Okhrana?" Josef demanded shrilly. "You were in Paris even after I left. And then you arrived here in Petersburg and barely two weeks later you land a job as a driver for the Okhrana? How lucky, how convenient! Perhaps you'd like to explain your good fortune."

"I applied," Kiril spit. "At the suggestion of Dmitri Andreievich. He saw an advertisement for drivers in the newspaper. What do you think? I placed the ad myself?"

"Spies!" Josef was on his feet, lunging for Kiril.

Misha pulled him back.

"Everyone's a spy! No one's to be trusted! The revolution is constantly betrayed!" The vituperation of Josef's accusation crumbled suddenly into a mournful wail as he collapsed into his chair and his head flopped on his arms on the table. "Katya . . ." he intoned, his grief silencing all those around him.

It was Dmitri who finally spoke. His voice was quiet, but his meaning was clear. "This is the worst that can happen, accusations amongst us. Mistrust will destroy us sooner than the Okhrana."

"We are comrades!" Savva exclaimed.

"Vera Martova and Katya Kazen were heroic fighters of the revolution!" Kiril rose respectfully to his feet.

"The country will mourn their deaths!" Vladimir followed. "Vera Martova was a hero to the people!"

Stepan, Dmitri, Misha, Irina and Olga Gambarova rose to their feet.

"Ten, a hundred revolutionaries more will rise from their blood!" Olga cried passionately, holding her glass to her lips and tossing back her head as she downed the vodka.

Irina wanted to be with Misha when the meeting was over. She wanted to end their silly argument and lie in his arms, maybe cry, maybe talk, maybe just feel the peace and comfort of his love. But he was too distant.

"I'm sorry, Irina. I know Katya was your friend." His voice was mechanical.

All she could do was nod and watch him leave with Kiril.

"Need some company?" Savva asked, slipping an arm about her. "We can walk along the river."

She nodded. Perhaps it was best to be with Savva. They could walk and then get drunk and then cry, and Savva would talk in poetry about the holiness of their struggle. He would transform Katya into a warrior, a knight of the revolution, and for a moment Irina could hold Katya once again.

They were only a block from the inn when Stepan caught up with them. "Mind if I walk with you?" He slipped his arm through Irina's.

Savva looked embarrassed. "No, not at all. I was only keeping Irina company until something better came along. I'm sure you two have things to talk about. I'll just be hurrying on."

"No, really . . ." Irina began.

Savva was already starting away.

"Thanks, friend!" Stepan called, and Savva turned down a side street. A brisk wind was blowing; Stepan raised his collar about his neck. He gazed intently at Irina, his face filled with concern. "I'm sorry about Katya. I know how much she meant to you."

"Yes . . ." Irina nodded, feeling the sadness threatening to swamp her again. She started walking, eyes fixed on the ground. Stepan walked beside her. He put an arm protectively about her, and she allowed herself the luxury of his comfort. She was so tired. "Praise God you weren't staying with them, Stepan."

"Precisely for such reasons." He stopped walking and smiled down at her, smiling his boyish grin. "But you're looking well, considering. Come, let's go someplace warm and have a drink and catch up on the past months. I've missed you."

She felt conspicuous standing so close to Stepan in the middle of the street and she slipped free of him, insisting, "Thanks, but I think not. I need some time alone."

"Nonsense. Solitary mourning is totally unacceptable. In fact, mourning is unacceptable. Come back to my place, Irinushka. You'll soon forget."

"I don't want to forget, Stepan." She began walking again.

"But you do, you know you do." He slipped his hand through hers and eyed her seductively. "It's been months, and besides, you look beautiful."

"Don't, Stepan." She looked anxiously about at passersby and pulled back her hand. "Someone might see us." She lowered her voice. "Misha and I have worked very hard to prove to all Petersburg we're passionately in love."

"So I've heard. Dmitri has filled me in." His lips narrowed with an almost imperceptible hint of disdain. "Dmitri's quite filled me in on everything," he said pointedly.

"Then you understand why we can't anymore."

"I doubt anyone in *this* neighborhood would recognize you," he mocked.

"Still . . ." She folded her arms protectively about her waist.

"You're really serious." His eyes hardened, his face paled, and he stepped back as if to see her from a different perspective. "You know I was shocked, no, rather embarrassed when Dmitri lectured me as to how my relationship with you had to be strictly professional, comrade to comrade. Really, Irina, we're quite grown up, don't you think? Whom we sleep with is our own concern. You disappoint me that you need a papa to intervene for you."

"How can you be talking about such things now?" she demanded, feeling assaulted by his words and by the coldness of his feelings. "Vera's dead not twenty-four hours!"

"Better to care for another in life than in death. Funny . . ." Stepan reached into his pocket for his cigarettes. "You've always claimed I have no conscience except for the revolution. Then examine my relationship with Vera." He paused to light a cigarette, shielding the match against the wind. Inhaling deeply, he said as they began walking, "Vera was so intense, you know, but inside she was tight as a drum. I daresay I loosened her up a bit. For all my alleged crimes against women, I was kind to Vera Martova. She might have died a virgin without me."

"Oh, God, Stepan, if you don't mind, I'd rather not continue this conversation."

"Fine with me." He slipped his arm through hers again. "My place is not far from here. It's small, but homey."

She pulled free her arm and stopped short, demanding, "Don't you mourn her death?"

"Mourn, no—just as I expect no one to mourn me should my end come tomorrow. I feel nothing except the moment. It's the only way a revolutionary must be," he said calmly, taking her hand again and turning down a side street.

"That's not the direction I go in, Stepan. I told you, I want to be alone."

He chuckled arrogantly. "The problem with you, my love, is that you're still bound to the established social order, which ordains a period of mourning, a certain propriety. How many times have I told you that we must, from the very depth of our beings, cut ourselves off from all such bonds? You saw Josef, how entangled he is with Katya's death. He'll be a liability to us all if he doesn't get himself straight quickly. We must be like machines, Irinushka, dedicated to one objective and one objective alone—destruction of their filthy order. Immoral is anything which stands in the way of our cause." He smiled then, a relaxed, easy smile. "There, you see that pretty pink house at the end of the street? My room is the second floor front."

She shook her head. "I really must go." Her heart was beating very fast. Inside, she was shaking from the newness of her feelings. She was saying no to Stepan. How pleased Katya would have been.

"Is it your little boy, Misha Kalinin?" He was trying hard to be flippant, but his anger curled the edges of his smile. "How long can such a boy fulfill you, eh?"

"There's nothing between Misha and me."

"Which is not what I hear." He was already backing away from her. "But live out your foolish little fantasies, if you must." He tossed his cigarette into the snow and crushed it with the heel of his boot. "You'll see, I can live with you and your little boy lover in that house and it will be as if we never had a past. It's you who won't be able to. Yes!" His laughter bit the frigid air. "You'll come clawing at my door one night—I'll bank on that."

PART TWO

AN EXILE

CHAPTER FIFTEEN

His face pressed against the cold wooden floor. Saliva was frozen on his cheek. His sheepskin jacket had long come undone, and he was shaking uncontrollably. The stove was dying out, but he could not move. His fingers numbly held a bottle of vodka.

"Alexei Yakovlevich," a familiar voice called. A rough hand pressed his forehead. "Alexei Yakovlevich, you drunken souse!" The voice grew raspier.

There was a tugging at his arm. He tried to hold on to his bottle, but his fingers had no strength.

"Idiot! Drunken fool! Why God has sent me to save you, I'll never know."

There was more tugging and pulling.

"Alexei Yakovlevich, you shall freeze to death if you don't help me help you!"

Blows fell about his face and head. The stamp of a boot thundered through the floorboards, exploding in his brain like waves upon a shore.

He groaned and slowly brought his hand to his head. A boot kicked his side; the pain reverberated. A strong arm swung him over onto his back. The face of Kira Yurovna loomed grotesquely above him. She seemed all face, sharp and red wrapped in a fur hunting cap. Her head was ominously close to the ceiling.

"Have you come here to die, Alexei Yakovlevich?" She yanked angrily at his arms as she spoke. "Is that how you repay me? You give me your corpse!"

Gradually his body began to move with her pulling.

"You are fatter and I am older!" she spit, grabbing him under his arms and dragging him to the bed. "God, but you stink! What mess are you in, Alexei Yakovlevich?" The words burst from her like steam as she heaved him on the bed. Pushing his legs after his body, she pulled off his boots and socks and briskly rubbed his feet until a tremor of feeling returned. Then she threw some blankets over him. After stok-

155

ing the stove until it was blazing, she returned to undress him, mumbling all the time about his losing fingers and toes to the Siberian cold. She rubbed him down with some sweet-smelling vapors doused on a rough towel, rubbed and scrubbed until his skin began to tingle; the throbbing in his brain began to numb. Cursing him some more, she undressed herself and slipped into the bed beside him, covering them both with layers of blankets and holding her body warmly against his until the burning in his feet and hands turned pleasant and his skin no longer felt cold. Then he slept.

He felt ashamed as he watched Kira bustle about the steaming hut, straightening up the mess of his drunken ravings, tossing the legs of a chair into the stove, mending the curtains, sweeping up the broken bottles and dishes. She scrubbed the floor and walls and brewed him a foul-smelling and worse-tasting tea to which she added a touch of vodka. He drank without question. He had not spoken a word since he had awakened, his head feeling swollen to twice its size, his whole body aching from the hangover. He listened dutifully to Kira's accusations as if they were his punishment. God knows how many days he'd been drinking. There was enough broken glass strewn about to rival a barroom after a brawl.

"I tell you, you would have frozen to death one more night here alone, Alexei Yakovlevich!" She waved a pointed finger in his face, and sighed with exhaustion as she sat on the bed beside him. "Your head. Is it any better?"

He watched her through heavy eyes, wanting to lay his head on her wide lap. Her angular face muted behind a fantasy blur of his tears; she appeared young once more, and a feeling of selfless love which it seemed he had never known before swept through his body, causing him to shudder and sob.

"Tears now! Ach, Alyosha, what is a woman to do with you? After more than twenty years one would think you would have learned not to cry. But God is good. He has saved you once again." Her voice softened as she held him then, pressing him to her and cooing softly. Again he slept.

The pain in his body grew worse, and a fever set in. Kira never left him. Alexei sometimes did not know who she was. She changed in his mind and in his eyes, appearing sometimes as his mother when Alexei was a small boy. She sang and Alexei smiled, thinking he was singing with her. Then she was Tatyana, her face harshly painted as she swooped on his body, ripping his chest with taloned fingertips. Other times she was phantom thin and hissed his name, "Kalinin . . ." until he thought his ears would burst. Dead men laughed with blackened tongues and the snake hissed, "Kalinin," shattering walls of glass. When the glittering explosion settled, Anna came softly to his side, bending to whisper words he could not hear. Her silky locks brushed like finest spun gold against his cheek. Pleasure sparkled in the darkness, and he reached for her, only to pull back, ashamed at the coarseness of his touch. Anna's blue eyes laughed in childish happiness, and her music rose sweetly from a crystal sea, enveloping him with such ecstasy he thought he was dying.

"A priest!" he wailed. "Please, a priest!"

Kira came to him. She rocked him, laid cool wet cloths on his forehead, rubbed down his body, pressed snow about his head and wrists and feet, and promised him she would not let him die.

"Forgive me, Kira," he pleaded in between sobs. "Forgive me, please."

"There's nothing to forgive, Alyosha."

Her caring encompassed him like mother and father, wrapping him in the sweet innocence of childhood. Kira knew all his secrets. Suddenly he wanted nothing more than to merge with her, to live in her shadow, if only God would grant him life again.

Alexei Yakovlevich Kalinin grew up on the outskirts of Yaroslavl, an industrial town northeast of Moscow, and lived the first seventeen years of his life in the same house where his father, Yakov Nikolaievich Kalinin, had grown up. Yakov was the illegitimate son of a well-to-do engineer and a peasant girl. Although Yakov's father refused to give his son his name, he set up the boy and his mother in a small house in a poor artisan neighborhood. The one-story structure was in between a tavern and a fish market, and although crumbling on the outside, Yakov's mother kept the three tiny dark rooms spotless, saving the kopecks she brought home from her job dyeing wool to buy gilt-framed icons of the Virgin and Christ, pastel flowered curtains and a threadbare but once fine linen tablecloth. Any money Yakov's father, the engineer, gave her on his occasional visits, she saved for Yakov, to send him to school.

Yakov feared his father, a tall, impeccably dressed man with graying sideburns and a rumbling voice. His mother always cleaned the house for days before his father came, tossing out whatever drunken lout she'd taken in to temporarily father her son. They were all the same, broken men who lusted after his mother and smacked Yakov about when she wasn't looking, and sometimes when she was. Yakov wondered why she let them in. They brought nothing except pain.

His father was different. He always found a few minutes to talk to Yakov and go over his papers from school. If Yakov had done well, which he usually did, his father would nod humorlessly and hand him a few kopecks. "Go now," he would say, rising from his seat. "I want to be alone with your mother."

Yakov would hurry from the house, his heart pounding, wishing just once his father would touch him. Sometimes he dreamed of running into his father's arms as he bowed his head to enter the darkened house with its low ceilings. He dreamed of his father staying with them, and sometimes of taking them from their miserable existence to the elegant yellow dacha with the pond, the swans and long tree-lined drive which his mother once showed him.

"There, Yakov, there is where you father lives," she said proudly.

"Why can't we live there too, Mama?"

"Hush, don't think such thoughts. It is enough your father has not turned his back on us altogether. Make him proud of you. That is your only salvation in this wretched life. You are his son. He knows that. A man does not turn on his own flesh and blood, Yakov. Make him proud."

Yakov was a bright child, and like his father, quick with his numbers. After four years of secondary school, his father found him a post as an accountant's apprentice in a bookkeeping firm. In 1855, when he was seventeen, his mother died in childbirth. The infant, a boy, lived, or so Yakov was told. He never knew what happened to him. His mother was thirty-three years old.

His father came to see him several days after the funeral and gave him the deed to the house. "We are complete now, Yakov," the old man said, staring Yakov hard in the eyes. "There is nothing more between us. Is that clear? Don't expect anything else from me."

The house was desperately lonely and quickly fell into disrepair without his mother's constant care; Yakov resolved to quickly marry. He was drinking too much, he knew. Sometimes he could not wake up in the morning without a swig of vodka, and he could barely wait until lunch for more. Yet, drinking made him depressed and churlish. On more than one occasion he was tossed from a tavern into the dusty road.

Marriage was his only salvation. A woman, he knew, would change his brutish ways. The problem was to find one. Although broad and strong and not unpleasant to look at, he was painfully shy about women, and could do little more than stare at the young girls in the marketplace. He was amazed when one of them, an attractive peasant selling eggs and milk with her mother, returned his gaze and even smiled when he worked up the courage to let his eyes rest on hers.

Two weeks later, it was she who walked up to him. "Why do you watch me and never smile?" she demanded, hands on her rounded hips. It was summertime and a mustache of beaded sweat sparkled above her pretty upper lip, which seemed to be laughing at him; wisps of reddish hair escaped the thick, tightly woven braids.

Yakov stammered meaningless sounds.

"Cat got your tongue?"

"No! I didn't mean to stare!" he burst out.

"No crime in staring." Her hazel eyes glittered with a hint of green. "But there is a crime in not being friendly. A smile deserves a smile, don't you think?"

"Oh, yes." As if being watched by a demanding schoolteacher, he dutifully smiled back.

"Oh, you are a strange one. Do you have a name?"

"Yakov—Yakov Nikolaievich."

"My name is Zhenya Kirilovna. It's terribly hot. Wouldn't you like to buy me something cool to drink?"

"Oh, yes, yes, of course!"

A year later Yakov and Zhenya were married. Yakov felt truly blessed. Zhenya had a face like an angel, a body any sane man would never tire of, and her love of singing and dancing was as fervent as was her love of God. Yakov swore never to beat her, an oath he kept, even when drunk, for many years.

The only sadness during those early years was the deaths of their first three children, none of whom lived past the first few weeks. While Yakov thanked God for taking the lives of the infants instead of his wife, Zhenya quietly accepted the deaths as the will of God. Her own mother had lost nine out of thirteen children. Then Anatole was born, the first to live. Five years later, in 1861, the second child, Alexei, survived.

Although they still lived in the same run-down house, Yakov's career was blossoming. The railroad was coming to Yaroslavl, and by the time Alexei was four, Yakov was managing a staff of five at the main railroad office in town, and earned enough to move from the old neighborhood. Zhenya was desperate to move. She hated the poverty of the three cramped dark rooms of Yakov's house. Worse, she feared bringing up her children in a neighborhood where drinking, thievery and street brawls were the major forms of recreation, and easy women frequented the ubiquitous taverns. She wasn't sure for whom she feared most: Alexei, her jewel; Tolya, her heartache; or the infant, a girl named Mousia.

Alexei and Tolya were as different as two brothers could be. Whereas Tolya was surly and lumbering, Alexei was lithe and sprightly, an angel to look at from the first. His dark curls, rosy complexion, and large deep-set eyes fringed with long thick lashes turned the head of every matron in the town. Alexei loved music and mimicked his mother's singing with his own sweet voice. Even though Zhenya could not read herself, she sat looking at the brightly colored picture books Yakov brought home for the boys; she and Alexei spent hours spinning their own tales around the pictures.

Tolya, on the other hand, had no patience for books or learning of any sort, and Zhenya feared he was dim-witted. At the age of nine, he barely knew his letters, and despite frequent beatings, spent more time in the streets than in school. Big for his age and far stronger than he was bright, Tolya began tagging along with a group of older boys who haunted the riverfront and the taverns, taunting drunks, stealing, sneaking peeks at lovers, running errands for a cigarette or a swig of vodka or beer.

By the time Tolya was fourteen, he was as big as his father and the beatings Yakov dealt the boy were turning into fist-fights, which grew still worse should Yakov stumble home drunk. Then, if Tolya proved the victor over his father, Yakov would turn his blind rage on Zhenya or Alexei, sometimes on even little Mousia, who was always a frail child. Each winter the doctor warned she might not make it to spring. Still, Yakov lashed out at the child if Zhenya, Alexei, or Tolya didn't manage to hide her.

For Alexei, the change in his father was as abrupt as it was horrifying. Although his father had never been affectionate, Alexei knew he pleased him with his good grades in school. He worked to please his father, who seemed to enjoy nothing better than spending a Sunday afternoon exploring mathematics and physics with Alexei. It seemed as if they learned together, studying all the science needed to build the model railroad stations and tracks, which had been Yakov's and Alexei's project for years; they perfected the engines and even the track switches. The model, which traversed the floor of the main room of the house, became renowned throughout the neighborhood. Often on a Sunday, people stopped in after church to watch the railroad's progress.

Yakov had been enamored of railroads for years and had huge maps of the spreading Russian tracks which, by 1878, were reaching to the Urals. He kept clippings about the American railroads, especially the completion of the Union Pacific and Central Line, the first railroad to span a continent. "If Americans can tame their wild frontier, Russians can tame Siberia," he liked to say to Alexei. "Someday I shall take you there. Siberia is not only a place to send criminals, but it is the world where enterprising Russians make their fortunes. It is said that when God flew over Siberia, his hands grew so cold he dropped most of the riches he was carrying. They are still there, waiting for us. Gold, silver, sable—I hear the sables run so thick the hunters cannot shoot them fast enough to warm the bodies of the rich."

Yakov and Alexei spent days crisscrossing maps of Russia with designs of their own railroad systems. They carefully watched the progress of the building of the line from Moscow to Yaroslavl, and Yakov bought tickets as well as new outfits for the whole family to ride along with the Imperial family on the virgin trip between the two cities. For Alexei's eleventh name day, Yakov surprised him with a visit to St. Petersburg, riding first class on the all-night train.

That trip to St. Petersburg seemed in retrospect the high watermark of his life. The gaiety and luxury were matched only by the misery and poverty of their return. Everything on the trip, from the compartment on the train to the hotel where they stayed, to the circus, plays and concerts they saw, to the restaurants where they ate, was first class. Nothing seemed too expensive. They bought fine new clothes, and traveled by cab, coming back to the hotel room each night loaded with presents: dresses and china for his mother, dolls and books for Mousia, and even a new fur hat for Tolya. Alexei felt himself drunk on the good times, the eating, and the excitement, feeling certain the joy would last forever.

"Mama! Mousia! Tolya! We're home, and wait—wait till you see all we've bought!" he cried as he stepped from the cab on their return.

The foreboding stare of his mother standing hands on hips in the doorway to the cramped house, her dark eyes flashing, her cheeks flushed of color, made him stop in his tracks. "What's wrong, Mama?" His heart was beating very fast. He looked from his mother to his father. The presents suddenly felt heavy in his arms.

"Go inside, Alexei," she ordered, glaring past him to his father.

Huddling the packages to his chest, Alexei hurried by his mother without so much as a quick kiss.

Yakov, who had been drinking heavily all the train ride home, shouted threateningly as he walked down the rocky path, "Is this the kind of greeting a man expects from his wife? God knows, I've spoiled you by sparing the whip, Zhenya."

Alexei shuddered. He knew that tone in his father's voice all too well, and he dropped his gifts, falling backward into the shadowy corners of the dark room.

"What is this?" His mother was tearing like a madwoman at the bundles Alexei had so lovingly carried home from Petersburg. "You spend your money on satins and jewels and sweets when you won't have the money to feed your family!"

Alexei's body tightened and his brain blackened as his mother ripped the beautiful yellow gown he and his father had spent so many hours choosing for her. "Mama!" he cried, running to grab the gown, to protect the precious purchase from her wrath.

His mother looked as wild as he had ever seen her. The veins in her neck and forehead bulged and her teeth gritted. She seemed bloated, like a monstrous toad ready to leap. "Your father's lost his job!" she shrieked accusingly, tears streaming down her cheeks. "They fired him last week because he's drunk all the time. He doesn't have the money to put food on the table next week, but he takes you first class and buys this!" She tore at the bundles with still more vengeance, throwing the clothes and toys about the room.

Yakov yelped and leapt into the air, arms swinging. The madness began, tossing them into a nightmare which seemed unending. His father never again held down a steady job, and what little money he made, he drank away. He stumbled about the house cursing and lashing out, except when Tolya was home. In the abyss of his drunkenness, Yakov grew to fear his older son, and the wrath which he had once poured on Tolya, he turned on Alexei. He made frequent visits to the school to check up on Alexei and bound him to a chair and whipped him whenever his grades didn't meet Yakov's expectations. The whippings came more frequently when Alexei took on a job as an errand boy at the railroads to earn extra money. He worked there each day after school, and followed Tolya and his friends to the tavern at night.

He went not to drink or to be with Tolya. He felt out of place with the older boys. Rather, he went to play the piano.

It was a rather run-down, out-of-tune piano, but Alexei felt drawn to the keys. Since he was a small boy he'd taken weekly lessons, but now there was no money for such a luxury. Yet it often seemed the only peace he knew was those hours spent playing in the tavern. The tunes and melodies fired his imagination with sounds of his own making. Then he touched on happiness again, envisioning his music rising to the heavens and carrying himself and all his family with it.

The spring Alexei was fourteen, Mousia died. She'd been sick all winter, coughing off the flesh from her thin body, or so it seemed. Her death was a blessing; still Alexei sobbed miserably for days. His father didn't come to the funeral; the women in the neighborhood cared for his mother, and Alexei cut school for weeks to spend his days at the tavern playing the piano.

"I hear your poor little sister's in heaven now," Katerina Kasimirovna crooned, pushing her way onto the piano stool beside Alexei.

Alexei nodded and kept playing. Katerina was a whore who made her living working the taverns. She was one of Tolya's favorites, and Tolya had been encouraging Alexei to spend his tips from piano playing on a night with her. She was beautiful, with the most incredible red hair Alexei had ever seen. Her breasts were so big, there appeared not a garment that could fully contain them.

"You play such sad songs, Alyosha," she whispered, her breath hot in his ear. Her fingers brushing through his hair were maddening. "I should think you should be merry now, for your little sister. Her misery is over. She has left this wretched life and is in God's heaven. Play a happy song for her, why don't you?"

Alyosha tried, but he stumbled over the keys as he felt Katerina's breast press against his arm. When her tongue ran along his ear, he slammed closed the piano cover and jumped to his feet, mortified to find his pants sticking out like a tent. He started to run.

"Alexei, what's the matter?" Katerina caught up with him as he smashed into Lizaveta Vasilyevna, the tavern owner's wife.

"Hey, hey there, my pretty. What have you done that Katerina Kasimirovna should be after you in the middle of the afternoon? Have you stolen one of her jewels? Have you?" Lizaveta Vasilyevna shook him to a stop.

"No, no! I swear, on my mother's soul, I've done nothing." He looked pleadingly from Katerina to Lizaveta.

"He is too long in mourning, Lizaveta Vasilyevna. He's too young to mourn so long, and more of a man than a child, I'll wager. I was trying to tell him that when he ran from me with all the symptoms of a man who needs relief!" She eyed his crotch and the two women laughed raucously.

"But the poor boy has no money for such relief as you give, Katerina."

"Aye, and sure I can show some mercy and compassion. Besides, his lovely brother Tolya is such a good customer . . ." Katerina had her arm around Alexei, talking in words which no longer made sense. He knew only the incredible excitement her fingers caressing his neck and ears sent coursing through his body.

"I'd say you'd better hurry, or the poor boy shall waste his lovely load. Go, take him upstairs, Katerina. I've seen you eyeing him for months now."

Obediently Alexei followed Katerina up the stairs, feeling his excitement burst as she slipped her dress off her shoulders, exposing the two most beautiful breasts he could ever imagine.

Katerina laughed softly and wrapped her arms about him. "Do whatever you want to me, whatever your mind comes up with, Alyosha, for I shall do the same to you," Katerina moaned hotly in his ear, and her hands began to fondle and caress as she undressed him.

She was surely a devil or a goddess. Never in his wildest fantasies had he imagined such pleasure existed.

During the next year life pulsated schizophrenically between the pleasure of the whores and the rest of his world. He went to school, did his studies as best he could to avoid beatings from his father, sang in the choir, went to church with his mother, prayed devoutly with her each morning before the icon, and read poetry to her before going to the tavern at night. He prayed for three things. First that his father would give up drinking and become the father he had once loved, second that his mother would not die from the misery of her life, and third that the pleasure he found in the whores' arms would not damn him to eternal hell.

By the time Alexei was sixteen, he was almost six feet tall, and the soft, childish beauty of his face had matured into angular, manly handsomeness. His complexion was ruddy from working outside, his muscles strong. He had long since ceased being an errand boy at the railroad and worked alongside Tolya at the hardest labor he could get. His body, it seemed, would never stop growing. No sooner did his mother make him a new set of clothes than his shoulders began to ripple against the seams and the pants grew short and tight against his long, muscular legs. He yearned for the day when his fuzzy shadow of mustache would turn into whiskers, and patiently withstood the losing battle his mother waged against his dark, unruly curls. "Such eyes, such eyes, lashes fit for an empress! It's a crime against the angels to cover such beautiful eyes," his mother insisted as she brushed and combed, finally attacking the wayward locks with her scissors.

Alexei couldn't understand the power of his eyes, but he knew it was there, for not only his mother but also the whores carried on about their dark, exotic beauty, which left them hot and quivering inside. Young girls giggled and blushed when he stared hard at them, and matrons either turned hurriedly away or boldly returned his gaze. He knew the meaning of their looks, but he was never tempted. He felt beholden to the whores, who treated him so well, and besides, his heart was already taken. Alexei was in love with Nina Alexandrovna.

It seemed he'd loved her his entire life, even though he'd never spoken with her. Nina was new to his school. She had long dark curls, large blue eyes, pouting lips which broke into an easy smile, and the clearest skin he had ever seen. She was attractively plump, and her breasts bounced, even bound by corsets. But the images of Nina which haunted him were strangely not of her naked body; rather he saw himself walking with her hand in hand. He heard them laughing together, and imagined them sitting in a park and talking about the railroads. He would tell her not of the work he did each day after school, mending tracks and greasing wheels, but of the dreams he'd once shared with his father. He imagined talking to her about his father; and he imagined her listening.

"Nina Alexandrovna!" he burst out her name as they were about to leave history class one day.

She turned, startled, and her eyes locked on his. She did not answer. No one was allowed to speak out of turn, especially not in Mr. Fedotov's class. Fedotov liked nothing better than to catch a student with an infraction of the school code and bend him over the desk and whip him or let the rod crash down on a girl's knuckles.

Nina Alexandrovna turned her head and followed quietly behind the student in front of her.

The next day Alexei left a note on her desk as he passed to his own seat.

Nina Alexandrovna,
   Forgive me for my outburst. Believe me, I would have taken any and all punishment. I could never let anything harm you. All I wanted was to say hello.
                                    Respectfully,
                                    Alexei Yakovlevich

The next day Nina handed him a note as he passed her desk.

Alexei Yakovlevich,
   Thank you for the explanation. It does make sense, now that I think about it. You are a very bright boy, even though Mr. Fedotov doesn't like you. I think you are too smart for Mr. Fedotov. Hello to you too.
                                    Respectfully,
                                    Nina Alexandronva

Alexei handed her another note at the end of class.

Dear Nina Alexandrovna,
   Could I ever dare dream of talking to you?
                                    Respectfully,
                                    Alexei Yakovlevich

The next day, Nina's note read:

Alexei Yakovlevich,
   I go shopping with my mother on Saturday afternoons. She always spends forever in the market on Kazansky Prospect. Perhaps I shall be strolling outside as I wait for her at about one P.M. *If you happen to be there, we could talk.*
                                    Respectfully,
                                    Nina Alexandrovna

Alexei never met Nina outside the market. He never saw her again. On Friday night, his father was arrested for murder.

CHAPTER SIXTEEN

The facts were undeniable, if incredible. Yakov Kalinin walked, or more accurately stumbled, for he was very drunk, into the dacha of Grigory Berdeyev, a retired engineer, and brutally beat the old man to death. Although the old man was alone except for a few servants at the far end of the rambling estate, Yakov stole nothing except the old man's gold pocket watch inscribed with his name. Yakov was discovered wandering about the grounds, the watch clutched fiercely in his hand. Upon seeing the police, he threw himself at their feet and confessed to the murder amid a flood of self-flagellating tears. He became violent when the police tried to take the watch, insisting he only wanted "a remembrance." The police could make little sense of Yakov's ravings, which grew worse as time went on, and being able to establish no real motive for the murder, a judge sentenced Yakov to life in a prison for the criminally insane.

Zhenya, Alexei and Tolya knew that Yakov had murdered his father. They knew the dacha, if not the man. How many times had Yakov taken them past the elegant estate when the boys were small, bringing them so far as the front gate and proudly explaining it was the home of his father. Yakov liked to visit especially in the spring when the leaves were down and the yellow stone house shone brightly in the warming light. The tree-lined driveway curved gently before crossing a wooden bridge over a pond where geese and swans swam.

"One day," Yakov liked to say to Alexei, "one day my father shall see us standing here, and he will be so taken by your intelligent face that he shall stop and say, yes, of course, you are my grandson. Come, Yakov, come, my grandson—my house is your house."

Despite the countless trips and the hours walking back and forth in front of the estate, Alexei never got to see his grandfather; and he was happy when the trips stopped altogether. His father always grew agitated after the fruitless visits. His drinking became worse. Once during such a binge, Yakov

destroyed much of their model railroad; he and Alexei had to
build it up again almost from scratch. Alexei didn't mind.
They made improvements in the new model, especially on
the switches, which hadn't worked right before.

Alexei thought the shock of his grandfather's murder came
as much from the reality of the old man's life as from anything else. A part of Alexei was certain the great man, the
engineer, never had existed except in his father's mind. None
of them, not his mother, Tolya or Alexei, ever uttered a word
about the true identity of his father's victim. It was a terrible
truth, and if left unspoken, it might stay hidden forever.

The first time Yakov was allowed visitors, Alexei and his
mother went together. Alexei and Zhenya brought clean
clothes, some of Yakov's favorite food, cigarettes and vodka.
Yakov balked at seeing them, and the guards had to drag him
to the visitor's room, his legs and arms in chains.

Zhenya cried in horror at the sight of her husband and her
fingers grabbed Alexei's arm, grasping so tightly, it was all
Alexei could do not to pry them loose. Instead, he turned to
his mother and pulled her to him as if to shield her. There
was so little recognizable in the shattered shell that was his
father. The filthy prison clothes hung loosely about his ema-
ciated frame. His hair and beard were horribly matted. His
skin was colorless except for a rash of red sores. His eyes
were dull, sunken in the skeletal face. He stared at Zhenya
and Alexei a long time before great sobs burst from him and
he crumpled to the floor amidst the clanging of chains.

"Go, Mama, please. This is no place for you," Alexei
urged, filled with a terrible hatred, not for his father, but for
the two hulking guards staring at him, watching, listening as
if they had a right.

Zhenya breathed deeply and slowly pushed away. Her eyes
rested sadly on Alexei. "Don't leave me," she whispered,
and trembling visibly, she walked to Yakov and knelt beside
him.

"Go away!" he shrieked, a high-pitched shriek of terror
which brought the guards running toward Zhenya as if to
protect her.

"Leave them alone!" Alexei bounded in between the
guards and his parents and glared defiantly.

"He's one of the violent ones," the taller of the two guards
said as if by way of explanation.

"He's filthy," Alexei asserted, his eyes never leaving the
guards'. "I can hardly breathe his air. Isn't there anyplace
for him to bathe?"

They shrugged, seeming to grow uneasy under Alexei's constant stare. "We know nothing about such matters."

"My mother has brought some clothes and food for him, and some vodka."

"Leave them."

Alexei dug into his pocket and took out a five-ruble note. He stuck the money into the pocket of one of the guards. "I'll bring you more, then. Can you give him the vodka at least? Perhaps it will calm him."

"Leave it. Leave it all, until next time."

Alexei quit school to work full time at the railroad. He used almost all his extra money to assure that his father got his vodka, cigarettes, and food; but Yakov seemed to be growing weaker rather than stronger. Occasionally Alexei brought enough money to bribe the guards to leave him alone for a few minutes with his father. Usually his father did nothing but cry then, and Alexei cradled him in his arms.

Then, one day, Yakov began to talk. For the first time in the seven months since his arrest, his words made sense. "He was my father," Yakov said, his eyes focusing on Alexei, and taking on an almost lifelike brightness. "I . . . I didn't mean to harm him." His voice was pleading for understanding. "I only wanted to touch him once, his hand. He wouldn't let me. He called me a no-good bum and said I wasn't his son. I tried to tell him about you and our train. I thought if he knew about you, he would see how clean his blood ran in me. But he called me a bastard, a filthy bastard. He wouldn't listen to me, Alyosha, about you. I only wanted him to know about you. . . ."

Two days later Yakov was found hanging in his cell. He'd made a noose out of his shirt. His feet were still in chains.

Alexei stopped going to church with his mother when his father killed himself. He stopped praying before the icons. He told his mother there was no God.

Zhenya pounded him with her fists. "Leave my house if you believe such a thing!" she wailed. "God is our only salvation! God is love. God is all we have in this wretched life!" Her fists landed violently about his head and shoulders.

Alexei never moved.

"Go!" she shrieked. "You, too, Alexei, leave me to my misery!"

He went to the whores. He'd barely seen them since his father was arrested. He drank with them until he could hardly stand, and waited for Katerina to finish with her customer.

"Ah, Alyosha, my lovely boy." She kissed him sadly. "There is such unhappiness in your eyes. Tolya, of course, has told me everything."

"Tolya doesn't know everything. He never came, never once did he see our father!" His voice rumbled threateningly, and suddenly he wanted her with renewed desperation. He kissed her roughly and sucked at her nipple until she cried in pain. He pressed his hands hard against her shoulders and pushed apart her legs, thrusting himself inside her with a force he'd never known, wishing he could tear her apart. Desperation clawed like evil inside his brain. He hated her. He wanted to hit her. He wanted to smash his fist into her face. Instead, he threw on his clothes and ran from the room, swearing he was done with whores.

He slept by the river and returned home in the morning. His mother was sitting by the window, sewing. She looked up as he entered.

He could barely see her face in the shadows.

She held out her hand to him. "You're all I have left, Alyosha." Her voice broke.

He ran to her arms and knelt beside her, his head pressed on her lap.

"I feel God has forsaken us, Mama. I can't help it."

"We must be strong, you understand that, Alyosha. The poor have to be stronger than the rich. It's not that we can't find happiness on earth. We just have to fight harder."

"Why, Mama? I don't understand. That man, that rich man Papa killed—I can't even call him my grandfather. I can't believe I am related to such a man who would turn away his own flesh and blood. I think he deserved to suffer. I think he deserved what he got."

"Hush, Alyosha, don't say that."

"It's what I believe."

A plan was forming in Alexei's mind. He had been thinking of it for a long time, for over a year, since before his father was arrested. It had to do with the railroad, the track switches in particular. Not only did they easily freeze, causing great delays in winter, but they stuck too; the repair crews were constantly checking the switches. One day an accident would happen. It was only a matter of time. Alexei imagined the accident more and more lately, two engines heading at breakneck speed toward each other, the engineers never thinking to slow down, never imagining the switches wouldn't work, never imagining the tracks wouldn't split, and they'd crash into one another, metal and bodies mangled together, thrown into the air, lying scattered along the tracks.

Alexei talked about the problem obsessively, and waited daily for the arrival of the mechanics' grease he'd ordered from England. He'd read about the grease in a French magazine. It was a "miracle" grease, used to make the huge weaving machines run smoother and more efficiently. He was certain he could apply it to his switch.

His mother always listened, nodding as if she understood his ideas and calculations.

Tolya was impatient with Alexei's formulations. "And what are you going to do with your new switch if you come up with one? Who's going to listen to you, Alexei? A sixteen-year-old laborer and some 'miracle' grease! Besides, it makes me sick seeing that model you and Papa made all over the floor. I don't think you'll ever come up with anything. You're just trying to bring Papa back is all." He drained his beer. "I'd just as soon get rid of everything that ever reminded me of him. The man was a beast. I hated him! I'm glad he's dead!"

"Tolya!" Zhenya rose to her feet and grabbed his arm.

He shoved her roughly away.

In a second, Alexei was on top of him, and the two brothers were rolling angrily about the floor, hitting and punching. Tolya dragged Alexei to his feet and was about to hit him when Alexei swung first, knocking Tolya backward into the table, knocking all the food and dishes to the floor. Alexei was on Tolya again, hitting him again and again. Alexei felt like a madman, like the madness was exploding from him. He smashed his fist into Tolya's face until there was nothing but blood.

"I've got a working model of the switches," Alexei said to Tolya several weeks later. Tolya's nose was still swollen and the bruises on his face were turning a sickly yellow-green.

"It won't mean nothing to me," Tolya grunted from the bed where he'd been sleeping off a night of carousing.

"Still, I'd like to show you." Alexei sat beside him and set down the shining metal switch. "It's all in the spring mechanism here. Feel it." He took Tolya's hand and held it to the metal.

"It's freezing! My skin sticks!" He yanked his hand away.

"Yes, I've had it in the ice cellar for over three days. I even poured water over it to make it freeze, and it still works. See . . ." He moved Tolya's finger to the greased spring.

"See, that's fine. It's protected by that grease. The trick is the angle of the spring and setting it along with the grease. It works, Tolya, just as I said it would."

Tolya sat up in the bed to examine the model himself. "Perhaps it's just the grease."

"I thought that myself. So I greased a model of a regular switch and it didn't work much of the time when it was frozen. No, I'm certain it's the setting. I got the idea from the switches Papa and I made once—at least we tried to make it work. What we never had was the right grease. This stuff doesn't dry out for months, maybe years."

Tolya shrugged at the mention of his father. "So, what do you do now?"

"I'm not sure. You've been at the railroad longer than I have. You know more people. Who should I see?"

"Old man Matyushin. He owns it all. He's the one."

"Would you help me get to see him?"

Tolya swung his legs over Alexei's head. "Maybe. But if you really want my advice, store your switch away with your worm-eaten models and forget the whole thing."

"You've an appointment at ten in the morning on Tuesday," Tolya told Alexei as they broke from work for lunch a week later. "But the foreman says you'll be docked for any time off. And it could be a while. Matyushin isn't prompt with his appointments. You could be sitting outside the bastard's office all day, so think about it. Think if you want to be docked a day's pay for nothing."

There was no question of Alexei not keeping the appointment. He would have sat outside Matyushin's office for a week if it meant showing him his switch. His mother was so excited, she sewed him a new shirt and washed and pressed his dress suit. Alexei polished his dress shoes five times the night before the appointment and polished the metal of the model of the switch until it shone. He carried his clothes in a sack to work that day, and changed in a railroad car in the yard. He greased his hair and brushed it until his arm ached.

Tolya smiled approvingly when Alexei emerged, and exclaimed, "God be praised, but you look fine, Alexei Yakovlevich! I daresay Katerina would bow down and kiss your hand if she saw you looking like such a dandy. Yes, sir, you got a prince's blood in ya, little brother." Then Tolya embraced him, kissed him on both cheeks, and solemnly whispered, "God be with thee," as he embraced him. The seven other men on the crew did the same.

Hugging the switch to his side, Alexei set off for the railroad offices, picking his way through the muddy yard to keep the dirt and stones from smudging his shoes. As a small child, he'd often come to the railroad office with his father, but the last time he'd been there was to apply for a job as errand boy. Then, the woman at the desk had hardly noticed him. This time the woman, young and pretty, actually smiled and asked if she could help him.

"Yes, I'm here to see Konstantin Apollonovich Matyushin. My name is Alexei Yakovlevich Kalinin." He hoped his voice wasn't quivering as much as it sounded in his head.

She looked down at her desk. "Yes, yes, your name is right here. Konstantin Apollonovich's office is up the stairs and to the left, but I'm afraid you may have to wait awhile. Konstantin Apollonovich hasn't arrived yet, and he has a nine-o'clock and nine-thirty appointment already waiting. But you may go up."

"Thank you." Alexei bowed in his nervousness. Holding tight his sack, he turned and hurried so fast up the marble stairs, he almost slipped. The huge waiting room outside Matyushin's office was paneled in mahogany. Plush chairs and couches encircled the walls, as if Matyushin often expected many visitors to be waiting. The room was well-lit by crystal fixtures and a huge chandelier. Palms and assorted plants as well as freshly cut flowers were everywhere.

Alexei chose a seat away from Matyushin's nine and nine-thirty appointments, well-dressed middle-aged men with finely fitted suits and large diamond studs in their ties. They both glanced at Alexei when he walked in and then went back to their newspapers.

The minutes ticked by painfully slowly. It was eleven-thirty before Matyushin's nine-o'clock appointment was called in. He was inside for almost an hour, and then the young man at the desk announced that Konstantin Apollonovich would be going out for lunch and would resume his appointments at two o'clock sharp.

Alexei spent the next hour and a half walking around the block and smoking cigarette after cigarette. He bought himself some blini and hot tea from a street vendor. It was precisely two o'clock when he returned to Matyushin's office. He didn't get in to see the great man until a quarter to four.

Matyushin was younger than Alexei had imagined. He was enormously overweight, with flabby, clean-shaven reddish skin, and he wore a monocle. His ears stuck out beyond brown, woolly sideburns. One of his two front teeth was gold.

"So, you have some invention to show me, Kalinin." Matyushin spoke as Alexei stepped in the door of the huge, brightly lit office. The walls were covered with photographs of the railroad, and there were shelves of model engines and cars, as well as a gilt-framed picture of the Czar.

"Yes, sir."

"Well, show me, show me. . . ." Matyushin was intent on lighting a cigar, and did not look up. "I haven't got all day. Be quick with it."

Alexei's hands were shaking as he handed over his switch and blurted out, "Sir, I've been working in the yards for almost three years now, and we spend much of our time inspecting and greasing the switches. I've long thought there's something wrong with the design of the switch, and—"

"How old are you, boy?"

"Seventeen next week, sir."

"Seventeen and you've long thought there's something wrong with our switches, eh?" Matyushin's laughter was derisive.

"I've been interested in trains since I was a small boy. My father and I—"

"Yes, yes, I know all about your father, Kalinin."

Alexei felt himself blanch. He was beginning to sweat.

"So you've come up with a better switch than all our engineers, eh?"

"I think so, sir." He edged closer.

Matyushin laid his puffy hand on the model switch, then began playing with the spring mechanism. He rubbed the grease like balls in between his fingers and made the switch open and close countless times. Finally he casually asked, "What kind of grease is this? It seems to keep lubricating the more I rub it."

"It's from England, sir."

"England!" Matyushin seemed more angry than interested. "How did you get it?"

"Well, I read about it, sir. It isn't actually being used on the railroads, at least not to my knowledge. Maybe in America, but I've not come across it in my reading. The English are using it on such things as their mechanical looms and sewing machines. So I wrote to the manufacturer and he sent me some."

"Just like that?" Matyushin was puffing at his cigar.

"Yes, sir." Alexei thought he should apologize, but he wasn't sure for what, so he went on. "I've had the switch frozen and it still works, sir. It's the type of spring mechanism and the angle—"

"Yes, yes, I can see all that." Matyushin rose to his feet

and began washing his hands with water in a porcelain bowl. "I'd like to keep this model for a while. Test it a bit."

"Why, yes, of course, sir!"

"I'm not promising anything, Kalinin. I'm sure whatever you've come up with, my engineers have come up with. But I'll give it consideration, seeing that you've put in so much work. Pretty fair work, too. Come see me in about a week. I'll have an answer for you."

When Alexei returned to see Matyushin in a week's time, he was told to come back the next day, and then the next.

"Konstantin Apollonovich is a very busy man," was the receptionist's ready reply.

"Perhaps then if I make an appointment," Alexei finally got up the courage to suggest.

The receptionist glanced up haughtily and said, "I'm sorry, Konstantin Apollonovich is filled for the next month. And then he's going abroad. If you wait around, perhaps I can slip you in, but for an appointment you'll have to wait three months."

"But I must see him."

"You and all of Russia. I'm sorry. I can give you an appointment in three months. That is the best I can do." The young man rose to announce the ten-thirty appointment.

Alexei pushed past him into Matyushin's office and placed himself directly in front of the polished mahogany desk. "My switch, Konstantin Apollonovich. I've come for my track switch."

Matyushin lifted his monocle to his eye and peered with irritation.

"I . . . I'm sorry, Konstantin Apollonovich . . ." the receptionist stammered to Matyushin. "This boy claims you have something of his, and—"

"Ah, yes, Kalinin." Matyushin puffed on his cigar. "You were here several weeks ago, to see me about some invention."

"My track switch."

"Ah, yes!" The glimmer of recognition flashed across Matyushin's face. "That track switch. Now I remember. With that grease. Yes, it was just as I thought. Our own engineers had come up with the same idea. In fact, we're planning on putting it into work within months. I'm sorry, Kalinin. But you're young. You'll come up with other ideas." Matyushin flicked some ashes from his cigar and went back to his papers.

"There, you have your answer, Kalinin," the receptionist

said, regaining some of his authority. "Now, Konstantin Apollonovich is a busy man. You must be going."

"But my switch. I'd like it back," Alexei said, feeling suddenly confused.

Matyushin shrugged. "I'm afraid that's difficult, Kalinin. You see, it was inadvertently thrown out. I brought it to the shop, and somebody discarded it. But it's no great loss, is it? I'm sure you can make yourself a new one. Besides, you'll be working to install them in a few months, eh?" Matyushin chortled.

"Yes, yes, of course. . . ." Alexei was backing out, feeling his confusion blossom into embarrassment. How could he have been such a fool as to think he had invented something new, something important? It was garbage, was all, and it ended up where it always should have been. Bowing his head, he hurried past the receptionist and bounded across the room and down the steps.

"For a smart boy, you are one hell of a horse's ass!" Tolya roared as they sat about the table drinking late into the night. Their mother had long since gone to bed.

Alexei felt too tired to respond.

"Thrown in the garbage—what kind of a feeble excuse is that?"

Alexei shrugged.

"Don't you see, he's conning you. First he tells you to come back in a week, then he won't see you, so you have to burst into his office. Then he comes up with some ridiculous story about the switch being thrown away. And as for their coming up with new switches in a few months—we're the ones who'll be putting them in, and have we heard a word about new switches? Have we?" Tolya nudged him so hard he almost fell off his chair.

"What are you saying?" Alexei pressed his hands to his head, the confusion which had been plaguing him all day spinning around with the vodka in his brain.

"I'm saying Matyushin's pulling a fast one on you. I'm saying he's stealing your invention."

"Why would he do that?"

"It's as clear as the nose on your face! Don't you see, little brother? You've got something in that switch, something a man like Matyushin is willing to steal for. It's probably worth millions."

"But he's rich enough. Surely he wouldn't steal—"

Tolya jumped to his feet and began pacing back and forth in the small, dark room. He turned suddenly and grabbed

Alexei to his feet. "Matyushin's a cur! He's like any rich man who ever lived—you get that. Don't matter how much he has, he wants more. And he pegged you as a sucker. 'I'm sorry, Kalinin—your invention is no good, Kalinin. . . .' " Tolya was shouting in a high-pitched woman's voice. " 'I lost it, Kalinin. Got thrown away, don't you see!' "

The meaning of Tolya's words was slowly beginning to take form in Alexei's mind, and with it the reality which he'd feared was true all along. Alexei felt his body crumple, and he sat back on the chair, burying his face in his hands. "I can't believe I just handed my switch over to him—getting no receipt, nothing that says it's mine."

"Well, no sense your crying over spilled milk. The trick of it now is to get it back."

"But it's gone. Thrown away."

"Would you stop believing that cur's lies!" Tolya roared. "I'll wager you anything it's still in his office. And there's only one way to get it back. We're gonna go in there and take what's ours."

"You mean steal it."

"Well, now . . ." Tolya pulled out his chair and sat down beside Alexei. His face was very close. "I wouldn't use the word 'steal.' I mean, it's hardly stealing, considering you're only taking what's yours to begin with. The trick is not to get caught." A hint of a smile creased Tolya's lips, and in the shadow of the candle, Alexei thought Tolya looked so much like Papa.

CHAPTER SEVENTEEN

They dressed in black and slipped unseen through the spring night. The back streets of Yaroslavl were empty except for occasional drunks or groups of merrymakers. Alexei led Tolya around the side of the railroad offices and watched in wonder as Tolya effortlessly jimmied the window.

"While you were building your models with Papa, I had my own education." Tolya chuckled softly and ducked inside. Alexei quickly followed. They stood for a moment, letting their eyes grow accustomed to the moonless black.

"The stairs should be right around the corner," Alexei advised, feeling a shock of exhilaration replace the fear that had been hounding him for the past twenty-four hours. Suddenly it seemed so easy to reach out and take what was his.

They climbed the lightless staircase without so much as a creak from the marble beneath them, but Tolya stopped short as they turned into Matyushin's waiting room: a shaft of light was coming from the inner office. He pressed Alexei back into the stairway.

"Maybe it's the cleaning woman," Alexei breathed.

"At eleven-thirty at night?"

"Then it's Matyushin himself." The fear came rushing back, making it hard to swallow.

"Yes, I'll bet on that, and all to the better, I think. If the model is hidden away someplace, we'll make him tell."

"Perhaps we should just go. He'll see us. He could have us arrested."

"But he won't. He *stole* your invention."

"I've no proof."

"Of course you have. The whole crew in the yard saw you with that switch. They knew you were taking it to Matyushin. They'll stand by you, by God. Besides, little brother, I won't let anything go wrong tonight. You'll see, I'm good for something other than whoring." He hugged Alexei then, and kissed both his cheeks. "That switch belongs to you, and together we're gonna get it back. You're gonna make us all famous, Alyosha—just like the old man always said you were. Come on. . . ."

The thick carpet cushioned their steps; still, the walk seemed endless. Alexei kept grabbing at Tolya, and his stomach twisted violently.

Tolya paused to listen. Then they were at Matyushin's door, which was slightly ajar. Soft music was playing in the background. "Now!" Tolya whispered, and kicked open the door.

Matyushin looked up, fright gripping his flaccid face. His pen dropped from his hand. He jumped to his feet, knocking over a crystal goblet of wine. "What do you want?" His sight was set on Tolya, who, though shorter than Alexei, was far more massive.

"We've come for something which belongs to my brother here, Matyushin."

Only then did Matyushin notice Alexei. The fat man's lips creased into a quivering smile spread across his gold tooth. "I haven't the foggiest notion what you're talking about."

"Kalinin's the name," Tolya went on. "Seems my little brother here entrusted you with something that belongs to him. Seems he made the mistake of thinking you an honest man." Tolya took some threatening steps toward Matyushin. "Where's my brother's switch, Matyushin?"

"The switch—I told him, it was lost, thrown out by mistake."

"Yes, yes, I know that's what you told him, but what you didn't know was that he has a brother that can sniff out a lying cur a mile away. We know you still have the switch, so why don't you make it easy on us all and just give it back to us." Tolya grabbed him tightly by the collar.

"How dare you?" Matyushin tried to pull away. His skin was turning a ghastly gray. "You're fired, the two of you. I know about you, a murderer for a father. You think I won't have the police on you—"

Tolya shoved the palm of his broad hand in Matyushin's face, making him stumble as he fell backward, gasping for breath. He pulled Matyushin to his feet and hurled him into the leather chair. "Here, have some wine. It will calm your nerves. Then we can talk, all right?" Tolya sat on the edge of the desk and dangled his legs. "You see, we don't only want my brother's switch back. We want to know what you've done about it thus far. We want to know who you've told about it."

"No one, I swear!" His voice was trembling. He gasped as he gulped his wine. Sweat was beading his forehead and lips. "It's useless!"

"Where's the switch, Matyushin?" Tolya demanded.

"It's not here! I swear by God! I told you—"

"Watch him, Alexei. I'm gonna pull this place apart until I find it." Tolya jumped to his feet and with a sweep of his arm cleared off stacks of papers from the desk.

Matyushin lunged after him, only to be blocked by Alexei. "You guttersnipe . . . you son of a murdering swine!" Matyushin growled, growing more incensed with each crash. "Stop your brother! He's a madman. He's tearing my office apart."

"Then tell us where my switch is. We'll find it eventually. If not here, then it's at your home. We'll find it there, if you like that better. And then all of Yaroslavl will know what a thief you are. Many people saw me with that switch. The whole railroad yard knew I was bringing it to show you."

"I don't know what you're talking about," Matyushin snarled, but his face bloated red as Tolya ripped down books, threw papers and art objects, and turned out drawers.

"The only place it could be, Alexei, is in the safe," Tolya finally announced, his hands on his hips. "Would you be so kind?" Tolya grinned. "Would you be so kind as to open your safe?"

"I'll do no such thing—not for the likes of you!" He raised his fat arm threateningly.

Again Alexei blocked him, but this time Matyushin was more aggressive, swinging and striking Alexei in the neck. The force of the blow stunned Alexei a moment, and when he looked again, Matyushin was barreling with his head toward him. Throwing himself forward, Alexei wrapped his arms about the man's chest. They grappled fiercely, Tolya cheering Alexei on. Matyushin, for all his apparent middle-aged flabbiness, was a fiercer opponent than Alexei had imagined, and he landed a couple of painfully well-placed blows before Alexei felled him.

"Open the safe, you thief!" Alexei exploded breathlessly. His gut was aching, and he wanted to kill Matyushin for the pain he was suffering. He wanted his switch more. "Open it and give me what's mine!"

"I have nothing of yours!" Matyushin spit.

"It's mine, mine!" Alexei's fingers were wrapped about the man's throat. The neck felt fragile to his touch, the veins and skin pathetically fragile. Alexei pressed his fingers harder; Matyushin's guttural gasps and wide, popping eyes drove madly into Alexei's brain.

"Leave off!" Tolya was grabbing him. "You'll kill him. Alexei, leave off!"

Matyushin collapsed onto the floor, holding his neck as he gasped for breath.

"Get up, you cur. Next time I won't be able to save you!"

Trembling, Matyushin hung desperately on to Tolya. He tried to speak, but his voice wouldn't sound.

"Open the safe!" Tolya ordered.

Alexei fell back on the desk and pressed his hands into his eyes, needing to wipe away the touch of Matyushin's neck, the taut lines of the muscles and the veins, the straining well of his throat imprinted like an invisible scar. He had almost killed the man. He would have killed him if not for Tolya. He pressed harder on his eye sockets and down on his cheekbones until the pain blotted out the memory, the sensation, the need to kill. It was so easy, dear God, it was so easy after all, to kill a man, to cross that line and become sucked up into that darkness where there was nothing else, no sound, no feel, no scent, nothing human, only darkness.

"Alyosha, Alyosha, come look!" Tolya's voice sounded

far away. "Look at the riches, more than enough to fill ten lives, and this cur steals from you. It's here, Alyosha, my brother—your switch, and the cur's jewels, rubles—he's as rich as the Czar himself, and he steals from one so poor as you."

Alexei walked numbly across the room. Tolya was laughing as he held a diamond necklace about his neck. The safe door was swung open. On top of countless neat piles of rubles sat Alexei's switch.

"You have what you want! Go, leave now, and it will be the end of it!"

"Who have you told about it?" Alexei asked. His voice sounded tired. His eyes wanted to close.

Matyushin stepped back fearfully, pressed himself into the safe. "Nobody, nobody else knows. I swear. I didn't want to tell anyone else yet. It's brilliant, Kalinin, really brilliant. And so simple. Yes, take it and be done. Take it and you'll make your own millions. If you like . . ." Matyushin was talking to Alexei but eyeing Tolya dancing about the room with his necklace. "I'll even introduce you to the right people. Yes, it's what I had in mind all along. You and me as partners. I'd only take thirty percent. That's not much, considering you can't get far without—" He stopped short and his eyes and mouth opened wide. His gold tooth sparkled like a glittering void. "You can't do that!" he shrieked as Tolya stuck the necklace in his pocket.

"Sure, I can. I've done it. You want thirty percent of Alexei's invention—we want thirty percent of what you got here. Don't you think, little brother? Or maybe we should take some of them piles of rubles." Tolya started for the safe.

"Give him the necklace back," Alexei said coldly. "We're not thieves. We've got what we've come for." He dug into Tolya's pocket and pulled out the necklace, tossing it at Matyushin's feet. Then, taking Tolya's arm, he started across the room.

"Still, don't ya think we should take . . . ?" Tolya began mournfully and he turned around. "Watch out!" he screamed, pushing Alexei aside as a bullet rang out.

Alexei dove, and the switch went flying, landing midway between himself and Matyushin.

His gun pointed at Tolya, Matyushin ordered Alexei to kick the switch to him. "Easy now, and one funny move and I'll shoot your brother in his fat head. Then I'll shoot you. It'll be easy. You two filthy sons-of-a-bitch swine sons of a murderer came to rob me and kill me, just like your drunken father. Yes, you came into my office drunk and violent . . ."

Alexei kept blinking his eyes as if to keep Matyushin in focus, but he couldn't see the man anymore. There were only his voice and his laughter, his accusations, his lies, his power, far greater than that gun. A maddened cry exploded from his throat and he was leaping through the air, landing on Matyushin before the startled man could get off a shot. Alexei slammed Matyushin's wrist on the top of the metal safe, and the gun hurtled into the air.

"I'll kill you—so help me God!" Matyushin was screaming. He kicked Alexei and sank his teeth into Alexei's hand.

"Damn you!" Alexei fist flew out in revenge, landing in the blubber of the man's belly.

Matyushin fell back, but balanced himself and was on Alexei like a dog, lunging for his throat.

Alexei pried at Matyushin's fingers and pushed at his arms, heaving up his own legs suddenly and throwing off his attacker.

Matyushin grabbed him as he fell, and the two of them crashed to the floor, clamped ferociously together: hands on throats, rolling and gurgling, gasping. Alexei pressed harder and harder, his fingers in the soft spot, pressing so hard he could almost feel his own thumbs. But Matyushin in his madness was stronger. Alexei's head was filling with an airy darkness. He could not breathe.

"Alexei, Alexei!" Tolya was holding him fiercely, cradling Alexei in his arms as he kissed his face again and again. "Alexei, my brother, not you too. Don't go, God grant thee life. Oh, Mama, God grant thee peace. Alexei, Alexei . . ." Tolya was moaning.

Alexei opened his eyes and tried to speak, but his throat felt cut off from air still. He gasped uncontrollably as he squeezed Tolya's arm with the little strength that was returning.

"How is he?" Alexei pointed to Matyushin, lying motionlessly on the floor.

"I don't know. I forgot to look with my fear about you." Tolya knelt beside the body.

Only then did Alexei see Tolya's pockets bulging with rolls of rubles and the jewels.

"Come, you miserly fool—rather give up your life than your rubles, eh?" Tolya nudged Matyushin.

Matyushin didn't move.

"Come on, now, don't play no more games with us." He pulled Matyushin by one arm.

The fat man didn't move.

"He's dead," Tolya gasped as his eyes met Alexei's, and he dropped hold of the body as if it were poison. "Glory to God!" He jumped to his feet. "The cur's dead."

It wasn't until early the next morning that Alexei realized he didn't have his switch. He ran to Tolya's bed, and waking him with trembling hands, he whispered, "The switch—you have it, don't you? You must have it!"

Tolya sat up in bed. "I thought you had it. I took the money and jewels. I thought you had your switch. Mother of God." He crossed himself.

"It's early. We can go back and get it."

"No, we can't. You don't go near that railroad office, you understand. In fact, you don't go out my sight, not even to take a leak. I'm gonna be your shadow until this all blows over."

"What if it doesn't?"

Tolya closed his eyes a moment, then embraced Alexei and held him tightly.

Alexei went through the motions of life, but his reality was the churning of his mind, sweeping from images of memories to the fantasies and yearnings that were never to leave him for very long. Matyushin haunted him like a walking ghost. Alexei was afraid to close his eyes at night, but his dreams were not of the dead man, rather of his mother sitting by her window with her sewing, her knitting needles white like bones. He reached out to touch her, so close, but she never saw him. He heard her singing and watched her looking through her books; the pages were all black. His mother sat like death, no one to talk to.

Often in his waking dreams Alexei imagined the police arresting him. He saw them walking down the tracks to where he worked, wrapping his hands and legs in chains. He saw the judge, stern with eyes like coal, sentencing him to death, and he saw himself being hanged. Once he dreamed of Nina Alexandrovna. She was running barefoot through a field of yellow daisies. Her hair was auburn in the brilliant sun. She floated more than ran, stopping suddenly, her face contorting horribly in a scream of terror. At the other side of the flowery knoll, Alexei was hanging from a dead tree.

Other times, Alexei tried to think about his father, to imagine meeting him with God, but he could not. There were times when he could not remember what his father looked like except when he was in prison, almost dead.

* * *

Four days after Matyushin's death, Alexei was called to the police station.

"It's routine," Tolya advised. "The police are questioning everyone who had an appointment with Matyushin in the past month. Just answer all the questions and keep as much to the truth as you can. Act normal."

Alexei felt strangely unthreatened by the police interview. There were people whom he recognized in the station house: the receptionist, Pavel Petrovich, who had lost his haughty glow and seemed skittish, like a trapped rabbit, and the two well-dressed businessmen with their diamond-studded ties. The police kept them waiting almost as long as had Matyushin. Every so often, Alexei gazed up to find the receptionist, Pavel, looking at him. Then Pavel was sitting on the bench next to him. He looked much younger than Alexei remembered, not much older than Alexei himself.

"Terrible business, terrible," Pavel lamented. "I'm out of a job, with no one to recommend me. I worked hard for the bastard," he grumbled. "And now no one's to know." Then, leaning closer to Alexei, he whispered, "He had your switch, Kalinin. Had it all along. Just as I suspected." Pavel shrugged and took out his cigarettes, offering one to Alexei. " 'Course, I wasn't about to cross the bastard for one like you, but he had your switch, he did. All along." Pavel leaned back on the chipping wall and inhaled deeply.

Alexei felt relieved when he was called in before Pavel. The questioning was over quickly, scarcely before Alexei had time to feel the terror creeping up from the soles of his feet.

"You may go. We'll call you if we need you," the officer in charge snapped, as if Alexei's presence were nothing more than an annoyance.

Two weeks later, he was summoned to the police station again.

"Alexei Yakovlevich!" a beefy-faced sergeant called.

Alexei rose fearfully to his feet and was led into the interrogation room.

Two men, one in a captain's uniform and one in a dark suit, looked up from a desk cluttered with papers.

Alexei dared not meet their eyes.

"That switch, Sergeant, or whatever it was Matyushin's receptionist was talking about," the Captain ordered.

The Sergeant left Alexei's side, went to a closet, and came back with the switch. He laid it on top of some papers on the desk.

"Pavel Petrovich Dolinsky, the victim's receptionist, said this belongs to you," the Captain said.

Alexei opened his mouth to speak, but no sound would come out. He nodded.

"Some kind of train switch."

Again, Alexei nodded.

"Dolinsky said it was important to you." The Captain fingered the switch, but his eyes were on some papers in front of him.

Alexei didn't think he could control the shaking. For weeks now he'd imagined this moment, standing on the tip of a precipice, one side falling into the continuing abyss, the other into sweet redemption: arrest, trial, conviction, jail, even death. He had imagined the moment of his arrest feeling like ecstasy, an admission of guilt, the end of his nightmares. Sometimes he prayed for arrest; physical incarceration would give his soul freedom once more. But now that the moment of accusation was here, fear was getting the better of him, a fear far more terrifying than guilt. He could not open his mouth, certain he would betray himself with a sound.

"It was found on the floor not far from the body. Dolinsky was surprised to see it. He said Matyushin had thought it was lost. Dolinsky said you made it, some kind of invention." The Captain held out the switch to Alexei. "This is yours?"

The silence which followed reverberated, crushing about Alexei. He thought he was laughing, then crying, then screaming. He thought he was falling.

"Kalinin, Kalinin . . ." A hand was shaking him. "Here, Kalinin, take it. I don't have all day, and neither does the Captain."

Alexei opened his eyes. The Sergeant was standing in front of him, holding out the switch like an offering.

"No sense in us keeping this anymore," the Captain was saying. "Seeing as it's important to someone. Don't ever go into police work, young man, let me tell you. It's cases like this that make life unbearable. A man like Matyushin, with more enemies than the devil himself, and we haven't got a lead. Well, thanks for coming down again. I don't suspect you'll be hearing from us again."

"I'm going away," Alexei told Tolya.

"What will you tell Mama? She cries for you as it is."

"As much of the truth as I can."

Again Tolya nodded. "I want you to take the money and the jewels."

Alexei looked surprised. "What am I supposed to do with them?"

"I don't know. But more than I'd do. I'd have it all wasted

on drinking and whoring before you could wink an eye, and the necklace too. I'd bring the police right to me, I would, not that I'd mean to, but you know me once I get drinking. No, now the safest thing is for you to take the money and the jewels with you. You'll need expenses.''

"I can work."

"Can't be sure of finding work. A man can starve without work. Take the money with you, but don't go flashing it around. Don't make no friends, or talk to no one. Play deaf and dumb, you understand. You're a loner. And don't write us neither. Ain't no one here who can read, so it won't make no difference.''

"I need to talk to you, Mama," Alexei told his mother that night after her prayers. She was already in her bedclothes and her braids were down. He thought she looked beautiful. "I have to go away."

"You have done something?" she questioned sadly.

"It would be better if you didn't know."

"I feel your pain in my heart, Alyosha." Her voice quivered and tears streamed down her face. "A mother can feel her child's pain as if it is her own. And for you, I feel there is a terrible prison that tortures my soul." She rose to her feet and put her arms around him. "When you were a little boy, you told me all your secrets. Do you remember what fun we had? How we laughed and sang." She held him still tighter and he could feel her body quivering in misery.

"I'm not a little boy anymore, Mama." He turned and pushed her gently away. "I have to go, tonight, on the midnight train. This is for you." He dug into his pockets and handed her a roll of rubles. "It's all the money I've saved since Papa died. But don't worry, Tolya has promised me he will never leave you."

"But you'll be back." She pulled on him.

"I don't know, Mama. I don't know." He kissed her and held her tightly in his arms. There were no tears and that was good. Untangling himself from her, he grabbed his bag by the door and hurried into the night.

CHAPTER EIGHTEEN

Alexei bought a third-class ticket to Moscow and from there walked north, quickly leaving the promised spring of Yaroslavl behind; the chilling air of the northern nights reminded him he needed a warmer jacket. More and more often he chose to sleep in cheap inns rather than to spend the nights shivering in a farmer's barn. He walked for days, and spoke to no one. Should someone speak to him, a farmer or a peddler offer him a ride on his wagon, Alexei held tightly his sack stuffed with his money, diamonds and his switch and stared dumbly through his heavyset eyes.

"A deaf-mute, God be praised," would be the response. "And such a fair lad, too." Sometimes a man or woman would give him a few kopecks out of pity.

After eight days of walking, he took a coach for two days. He never asked where the coach was going, only that it was going north. The air grew still colder. He needed a warmer jacket and was grateful that the coach was filled. The bodies kept him warm. He talked to no one on the journey, and met no one's eyes.

In the middle of the second day, just after lunch, the coach passed a group of prisoners. The passengers leaned out the window and peered at the hapless band of men and women tied together, their clothes worn, their boots tattered. Some of them were singing.

The moment the coach slowed down, Alexei grabbed his sack and jumped out. He sat by the side of the road and watched the prisoners passing. He listened to their mournful song about star-crossed lovers, and there was an unnerving tugging at his heart. He stared into their faces, trying to individualize them, as if their eyes or the way they held their jaw might tell him something of their stories, but they seemed muted in their misery. He wondered if he simply walked beside them if he would be like them. Perhaps the guards wouldn't notice him, and when they reached their destination, he'd be sucked up into some pitiless mine or prison cell.

"What are you doing?" a tall, rough-looking guard with quick dark eyes and a scar across the bridge of his nose demanded. He wore heavy, warm boots, a wild-looking fur hat and an oily sheepskin vest over his fraying green greatcoat.

Alexei stared without speaking.

"Cat got your tongue, lad?" The guard spoke more gruffly, pulling his chapped lips back over chipped, stained teeth.

Alexei shook his head. "Walking." He spoke, thinking deaf-mutes might not be allowed in Siberia.

"Following prisoners is more like it—gawking, eh!"

"Isn't the road free to any man?" Alexei hoped his revulsion at this guard, who merged in his mind with all guards, wasn't too evident.

"Most men don't like to walk with prisoners. Where you going?"

"Siberia."

The guard guffawed. "You think they'll hire you in one of the mines? No one who ain't sent goes to Siberia."

"Can I walk with you?"

"Ain't allowed. We're transporting criminals, murderers, thieves, and them that's antisocial, wanting to overthrow the Czar. Should never have let the serfs go free. Now they want the world, God knows."

"Can I walk behind you?"

The guard shrugged. "Guess I can't stop you."

"I like the singing." Alexei smiled, and his eyes half-closed.

"You done something that they chased you from the fields for, lad?"

"No, my father's dead. Killed himself."

"Leastways you knew him." The guard's voice was still gruff, but his eyes were softening. "Can't get far up here in a jacket like that. Once we cross the Urals, it's hell's heaven. Even the prisoners have better wrapping than you. What you got in that sack? Anything to make me like you better?"

"I got a railroad switch."

"A railroad switch! God knows I got no use for a railroad switch."

"I made it with my father before he died, God grant him peace."

"Ah, come on, you can walk beside me if you can keep up. No telling what would happen to someone like you alone on these roads. Sasha Sabinsky's the name."

"Alexei—Alexei Pirogov." He hadn't planned to lie.

* * *

Alexei walked with the prisoner band for the next seven weeks, falling somewhere between the convicts and the guards, although of the guards, only Sasha Sabinsky spoke to him. The others, like some of the prisoners, peered disdainfully, seeming to say they tolerated his presence only because Sasha Sabinsky was their lieutenant. Sasha and Alexei drank together at night, and talked of Siberia, the prisoners and women.

Sasha had been leading prisoners to Siberia for twenty years. He told fascinating stories of prisoners and prisons, of snow, death, jewels and strange Siberians. He talked of the spirits guarding the great inland lake, Baikal, and of the mysterious Siberian tribes like the reindeer-riding Chukchi, the Tungus, who sewed their dead in bags of reindeer skin and hanged them in trees because the ground never thawed, and the Mongol Buriats, who worshiped the bear. Alexei clung to these moments of camaraderie with Sasha that seemed fleeting compared to the strain of endless days walking through frigid air, snow and frozen rain, of nights sleeping in cramped farmhouses or on barn floors, of poor food and frozen limbs wrapping each of them, guards and prisoners alike, in private worlds of agony. If not for the uniforms, the guns and the whips, Alexei would have been unable to tell the freemen from the prisoners by their gait or the blankness of their faces. Occasionally bickering broke out, usually at night, over an inch of space, a clump of warming hay or a crumb of bread. Then a guard would lash out with a whip or a fist.

They walked along the Great Siberian Post Road on which generations of convicts and political exiles had trudged and sometimes died. The road itself was often undecipherable from the desolate snow-swept expanses. Then they would fall into the grooves left by sleds, more snow, and hug the side of the road to let the coaches and caravans pass.

"Let me flag the next one down for you." the guard Sasha would say to Alexei. "There's not sense for you, this misery."

"Please, I want to walk with you." Alexei always met the guard Sasha's eyes, and inside, his heart skipped a beat, thinking Sasha had discovered his secret.

During the second week after Alexei joined the march, one of the women, a tiny wisp of a girl with burning black eyes and horribly scarred face, collapsed, and the guard Nikita ordered a convicted murderer named Rodchenko to carry her.

"Aye, and it's enough to carry meself," Rodchenko, the strongest of the men, complained. "Let him lift her. . . ." Rodchenko's surly lips curled over his jagged, cigarette-stained teeth as he warily eyed Alexei. "He looks fit enough, fitter than the rest of us."

With a flick of his wrist, the guard Nikita slashed his whip across Rodchenko's broad chest. "Pick her up, you miserable bastard. Pick her up or you'll be left to die and rot where ya stand!"

Cursing, Rodchenko hoisted the girl and heaved her across his back.

Rodchenko and a few of the other men prisoners frightened Alexei. They hated him. He could tell by their cold, hard stares. Rodchenko spit whenever his glance met Alexei's; and sometimes, before falling asleep, Alexei checked to see that Rodchenko was still in his chains.

He'd known such men all his life, seen them at the railroad yards, in the taverns and along the riverfront. With better luck and different clothes, Rodchenko might have been the foreman, or one of the guards brutalizing Alexei's father, or, ironically, the very guard who whipped Rodchenko. Such men battered at the boundaries of Alexei's existence, alternately threatening and beckoning. At times, he feared Tolya was one of them, or he himself, all of them little more than frightened boys grown into vicious men, deadened by the void of life.

There were sixteen prisoners in all. Rodchenko and his group made four. There was the Jew, Avram Shakarsky, the oldest, close to sixty. He'd been convicted of stealing from a wealthy Russian, of knocking him down as the wealthy Russian walked to church. Avram swore he was innocent, a poor beggar asking only for alms, and that he'd done nothing more than throw himself at the man's feet; but the jury convicted him and the judge sentenced him to five years of hard labor.

Avram was sick and bent and kept to himself. Only the thick overcoat which the old Jew's son had bought him seemed to hold bones and skin together. "Sold all his possessions to buy his father a new coat for the journey to Siberia. Why, only his God knows. The old man won't make it another week." The guard Sasha shrugged and picked his teeth with his knife. "But what does it matter? He's only a Jew. We've more of them than we need, God knows."

Of the six women on the march, the two who interested Alexei most were the young girl with the scarred face who collapsed and Polina Arbuzova. The young girl was a factory worker named Eugenie, sentenced to twenty years of hard labor for killing a man who she said raped her. Polina Arbuzova, sentenced to life for murdering her husband, said the reason Eugenie kept on collapsing was that she was pregnant with her victim's child.

Polina herself had borne ten children; she was haggard and shapeless like so many woman Alexei had seen in his neighborhood; her skin was leathery and colorless even in the biting wind. Her hands were swollen from a lifetime of hard work. Her teeth had all but rotted in her head. Polina claimed she was forty-one, but she looked more like sixty. Still, there was a manic excitement about her; at the moment when the cold or the hunger seemed to numb the body beyond exhaustion, Polina would burst into song, the wrinkles on her face softening and her dull eyes growing bright. She was an avid storyteller, and laughed heartily at her own jokes, her infectious laughter making even the most stoic crack a smile. Prisoners and guards alike took care of Polina. The prisoners allowed her the softest place to sleep. No one argued with her. The guards gave Polina extra rations and often let her walk without her chains. In return, Polina cradled the pathetic band of prisoners in some bizarre yet tangible warmth of family. To the guards, she gave her body.

Alexei walked and sat next to her whenever he could. They rarely spoke. The air seemed gentler about her, and Alexei thought to pour out the memories and fears knocking at his sanity. He needed to tell someone. Once, when drunk, he'd almost confessed everything to the guards Sasha and Nikita, but a quarrel among some of the prisoners distracted them, and Alexei fell into a fitful sleep.

It was on the third week of the journey that Polina settled beside him late one night. The farmhouse where they were resting was damp and cold. Alexei sat huddled under some hay to keep warm. Polina knelt and wrapped an arm around him. With his eyes closed, Alexei could pretend she was his mother.

"You make me sad, Alyosha, my pretty." She nodded as she peered into his eyes. "You're too young and handsome to be so miserable."

"We're all miserable here."

"We must get you a new coat. I'll speak to Sasha Sabinsky. He'll find you something warm to wear. In the morning, stick some of this hay inside your jacket. It may scratch, but it'll pad you." She took his hand in hers and kissed it softly. "How come you never sing with me anymore? Yours is the only voice that might make God take notice of this miserable lot."

Alexei shrugged.

Polina crooned, "I've a son your age, I think. What is your age?"

"Seventeen."

"Yes, Kolya is seventeen. He joined the army. He shall be killed in battle one day, but he'll die a hero, praise God. I see his death sometimes. It's glorious. His body'll rest covered with medals. Rather a hero's death than my lot, God knows. Kolya would have killed his father if I hadn't. That's why I did it. To save my son." She laughed then, an eerie, haunting laugh which frightened Alexei. He wanted her to love him as her son, and suddenly, she was frightening him. "I killed him with a knife. I stabbed him in the chest. I told the judge I did it. I was drunk, but I remember. How can one not remember such a thing? The scar on my soul is my punishment. But God is good. He holds my hand in the darkness, and I'm not afraid. What do you remember, Alyosha? Tell me of your scar. I see its misery in the darkness of your eyes that hang so heavy, as if you dare not look at a man or woman. Tell me, I told you mine." She kissed his hand again, and when he would not answer, she began to sing. She held Alexei's hand, singing to him until one of the guards motioned that he wanted her.

That night the Jew, Avram Shakarsky, died. He never woke from his sleep. Everyone knew he was dying, and wondered that he'd held on to life as long as he had. Rodchenko had carried him for the last three days. Polina was the first to discover the old man's cold body. She was peeling off his coat when Grigory Oblensky, one of Rodchenko's cohorts convicted of running a black market in meat, shoved her aside, claiming Avram had willed him the coat just the day before. A battle ensued, leaving Oblensky with the marks of Polina's fingernails across his cheek, and Polina with a bloody nose and blackened eye. In the end, the guard Sasha took Avram's coat and gave it to Alexei.

"I don't want it," Alexei insisted, ashamed at the present in the face of so much suffering. He wanted Polina to have it.

"You need it. Tomorrow we're reaching the Urals and have to climb the slopes of Mount Altai. That in itself is enough to suck the life out of some. If the Jew hadn't died already, he would certainly have been killed by Altai. Beyond is the wilderness and still worse cold. More shall die, my young friend. Those who live can have what the next to die leave behind."

"Why are you being so kind to me?" Alexei asked as the warmth of Avram's coat settled about his body.

"Ach, don't talk to me about kindness. I've no kindness. None of us who do this job knows kindness. It'd kill us. We trick ourselves, Vassily, Nikita and the other guards. Together we believe we're better than the tortured souls we herd into hell. But we're little better, eh, Alexei Pirogov. Otherwise we'd be doing something else.''

The snow stretched endlessly over the expanse from the horizon of the Urals. Dense snow clouds continually darkened the eastern sky. The Siberian wind was more biting than any Alexei had experienced; his feet, hands and face rarely seemed connected to him. He knew that if it were not for Avram's coat, he would be dead. Mountains, hills, villages, and occasional cities rose from the blinding white landscape like a mirage. A surge of energy quickened Alexei's step as they neared each village and town. The snow became packed; the air itself steamed with life. Alexei felt graced as the eyes of citizens of Perm and Ekaterinburg lighted on him. Surely, he supposed they were thinking, he must be a son of one of the convicts to march untethered. He thought they took pity on him.

"Stay here, leave us here," the guard Sasha suggested as they entered Ekaterinburg. "Here there's life and opportunity, great wealth from the mines. Leave us and go to the markets. You'll see jewels that find their way to the palms of the rich, to the Czar himself. Go to the markets, Alexei Pirogov. The merchants are as rich as the court in St. Petersburg. Amethysts, opals, topazes, emeralds, malachite doors like those in the Winter Palace, bought for a pittance.''

"I've no desire to be a merchant.''

"Tell me, then, what do you want with us?'' Sasha demanded in a threatening voice he used with the prisoners.

Alexei lowered his eyes and said nothing.

"Ach, never mind. I don't want to know your secrets. I don't know why I even care. You are meshuggah in the head, like the old Jew used to say. I'm done with you, you hear. You'll stay here in Ekaterinburg, and when I turn my back on you, I'll never think of you again.''

"You think I care what you think?'' Alexei shot angrily back. "You think I need anything from you—least of all you! A guard—you're scum, Sasha Sabinsky, you and all those like you. You killed my father!'' Alexei bellowed, a rage exploding as if from nowhere, and he lashed out at Sasha.

Sasha easily blocked the blow and felled Alexei with one punch.

Alexei struggled to get up, but Sasha pinned him to the snow.

The prisoners, guards and passersby encircled them, hooting and cheering.

"I'll kill you! I'll kill you!" Alexei struggled wildly to strike back.

"Yes, do!" Sasha taunted, baring his stained teeth as he slammed his fist into Alexei's jaw. "Then you'll get your wish to be one of us." He took a handful of snow and rubbed it in Alexei's face. Hoisting himself to his feet, he kicked Alexei brutally in the thigh. "Leave him," he snapped to the other guards. "You, Rodchenko, Latcky—stop gaping or I'll do worse to you."

Alexei held himself in a ball, moaning from the pain of Sasha's beating. Worse was the humiliation. A hand reached out to help, and Alexei pushed it away. Groping for his sack, he finally staggered to his feet.

Sasha was glaring at him, Sasha with his guard's cruel eyes, his arms folded confidently, Sasha with his gun and his whip.

Alexei stumbled past Sasha and through the crowd. He thought he heard Polina's voice, but didn't stop. "I hate them. I hate them all!" he kept repeating as his broken walk quickened to a limping run. He pressed his hand on the place where Sasha had kicked him. The pain radiated down his entire leg. *The pain*, he thought. *It's the pain that's making me cry.* Tears froze on his cheeks. He ran like a cripple, one leg bent, the other stiff. He ran until he reached the marketplace, covered and protected by huge tents. Once inside, the shadowy lights, foreign buzzings of language and the smells of spices, incense, fish and leather assaulted him. His stomach heaved, and he fell against the frame of the nearest stall.

A startled leather merchant dressed in a sable-edged caftan and peaked leather hat went to shoo him away.

Still clutching his sack, Alexei shrank back into the shadows. "Please . . ."

"I have a gun. If you try to steal from me, I'll shoot your head off."

"I won't. I . . . I'm not a thief."

"Why are you out of breath, then? Who is after you?"

"No one. No one. . . ." A sob cut his words, and he buried his head in his sack. The crying, if only he could stop the crying.

"Ach, youth! Crazy!" The merchant went back to his work.

Alexei felt so ashamed. He wanted to run still further, from Sasha, Polina, this merchant, the market of this foreign town, run to a tavern, find a whore. Yes, that's what Tolya would tell him to do. Find a woman. Dear God, if only the shaking and the tears would stop. He wiped his eyes and nose with the sleeve of Avram's coat, and feelings of hatred for Sasha fueled his rage. *Go!* he silently screamed. *I don't need you, and I don't care about you. I'll stay in this place and make my fortune. I'll show you, Sasha Sabinsky—I'll be rich someday, and you'll beg me for a warm place to sleep. I won't even know you then, Sasha Sabinsky—guard, torturer, devil's soldier. I won't even know you!*

Slowly, calm began to return. The shaking stopped, and with it the tears. Alexei pulled himself to his feet.

"Yes?" the merchant asked. "You want something? Ask me what you want and then go. You're no good for business."

Alexei stared blankly and walked away. Outside the market, the sky was rapidly growing dark. He wondered how long he'd been in there. A long time. His stomach was making hungry noises. He'd have to get something to eat, some good, decent meat and fresh bread. His feet began to move. His leg where Sasha had kicked him throbbed, but soon he was running. He ran until he saw the worn green greatcoats of the guards and Rodchenko's head bobbing in his ratty fur cap.

No one said anything when Alexei rejoined the group about two miles outside of Ekaterinburg, and the prisoner procession marched slowly toward Tobolsk, the capital of western Siberia, which wasn't, Sasha assured him time and again, even halfway to their destination. The snows grew worse, and the prisoners more lethargic, almost indifferent to the guards' beatings. Two more died, a woman with a hacking cough and swollen eyes, and the young girl, Eugenie. She began to hemorrhage one night. Polina tried to stop the bleeding. She padded in between the girl's legs with clothes from her own back, but the blood seeped through, and Polina began a mournful chanting. Alexei stole a look into the stall where Eugenie lay. Her face was as white as the snow outside. She looked so small, like a child. Polina was holding her in her arms, rocking her as she sang.

They buried Eugenie in the snow and marched on through snowfields of land, frozen lakes and streams which had no beginning and no end, through great primeval forests where the only sound was the silence settling like the breath of death itself.

Sometime in the sixth week, Rodchenko went mad, breaking from his chains and not stopping when the guards threatened to shoot. What seemed like hours later, Rodchenko's arms flew up against the muted, gray-white air stinging with the exploding of gunshot. Rodchenko stood grotesquely poised for a moment, his arms spread, his fingers clawing, his knees straight; then he teeterd backward, finally forward, and landed facedown in the snow. The guards stripped his corpse, kicked it covered with snow, and gave out his clothes and boots according to choice.

Seven weeks into the march, Polina Arbuzova killed herself and the guard Sasha. No one knew for certain what happened. They were on the outskirts of the city of Krasnoyarsk, sleeping in a well-kept barn where there was more than enough hay for everyone to rest in comfort, when Sasha motioned to Polina that he wanted her. They disappeared for a long time, longer than was necessary, and the guard Nikita found them lying in a stall. Sasha, still half-dressed, lay beside Polina, a gaping gash in his chest. The knife was in Polina's heart. Her eyes gaped as if staring; her mouth opened wide as if laughing.

The panic Alexei knew too well gripped him. The shaking made his head reel and his feet and hands turn icy. Without hesitating, he grabbed his sack and ran into the night. The moon was bright, but a heavy snow was falling and Alexei soon lost the road. He ran because there was no place to stop, only snow and scraggly trees. He thought he would run until he collapsed and sometime in the night he would simply freeze to death. Then he saw the shadow of a hut in the moonlight. There was no path through the snow or smoke from the chimney. Still Alexei knocked. "Anyone home?" he called, the shivering returning worse than before.

No answer.

He pushed. The door swung open. The room was pitch black. "Hello?" he called, feeling ahead with his arms. He tripped over a chair. Reaching into his pocket, he found some matches and cautiously circled the small room. There were a stove, some wood and a bed, a real bed with a mattress and blankets.

The firewood was well-aged and caught immediately. Alexei pushed the rickety bed closer to the heat and took off his shoes, holding his feet to the warming stove until they actually felt hot. Then he wrapped Avram's coat tightly about him, crawled under the blanket, and slept.

CHAPTER NINETEEN

The morning broke brilliantly. The sky was a flawless blue, royal against the white landscape. Alexei searched the cabin, inside and out, looking for signs of life, but could find none. Thick layers of dust covered all surfaces. The little remains of food were dried or molded and then frozen. There were no footprints in the snow except his own, and he began to explore the immediate area; his sack was cradled under his arm and he never lost sight of the hut. It was hard to tell direction when landmarks were blanketed white.

The neighing of horses, the jumbling of wheels and the sounds of men's voices urged him to explore further. To his surprise, the Great Siberian Post Road along which he'd walked with the prisoner band for so long was just over the horizon. A long, heavily laden caravan was passing by, traveling west.

Alexei flagged down the first coach. "How close is the nearest town?" he called.

The reply came from a slight Oriental man whose face was obscured in the recesses of his fur hat. He spoke in broken Russian. "Krasnoyarsk that way." He pointed in the direction from which he'd come. "Not far. Maybe two miles. Go straight."

Alexei watched the caravan until the last wagon disappeared over the horizon, then turned quickly away, filled with a sickening fear that the band of prisoners would appear in its place. He didn't want to see them, not then, not ever. There was no place among them without Sasha. Yet, oddly, he could conjure up little sadness over Polina's and Sasha's deaths, which felt more like a beginning than an ending.

Putting the convicts out of his mind, Alexei concentrated on traveling to Krasnoyarsk. One or two miles, the Oriental had said. Sasha had told him about Krasnoyarsk, one of the major trading points on the caravan route traveling east to the Orient. It was a city to anticipate: good food, drink and easy women, a real town, not some Siberian wasteland.

Before starting, Alexei looked about for a sign to mark the

cutoff to the hut, and decided on the large crooked fir almost opposite from where he stood. That would be good enough, he thought. He would find his way back. He liked the hut. He wanted to return.

He had walked little more than half an hour when Krasnoyarsk burst onto the horizon, its gold-domed churches sparkling against the brilliant blue sky and filling Alexei with childish excitement; he started to run. Sasha had been right; Krasnoyarsk was large and opulent. The streets were clearly marked, laid at right angles, and lined with well-kept wooden houses. There was an endless array of shops, bazaars, decent-looking hotels and restaurants. Beautiful horses pranced by and sleds loaded with furs were drawn by muscular, thick-coated dogs, even a team of stub-nosed, antlered reindeer. Unlike the market at Ekaterinburg, the bazaars in Krasnoyarsk were light and airy and smelled enticingly of spiced cooking, incense, roasting nuts, oils and perfumes. Or perhaps the difference was in Alexei's mood.

He felt elated as he entered Krasnoyarsk that morning, his senses excited by the colors, sounds and scents. The neatly laid-out streets reminded him of St. Petersburg, especially of Nevsky Prospect, where every nationality might be seen. There in Krasnoyarsk, rich, bearded Russian merchants mingled easily with European hunters and trappers, Oriental Tatars and swarthy Mongols in turbans. There were Chinese with pigtails and the dark, heavyset, broad-faced men and women of the Siberian tribes with their black hair, beaded headdresses, and animal-skin robes. Local fishermen dragged their nets. Inside the markets there were racks of Oriental silks and dazzling arrays of gem- and ore-filled stalls demanding his attention. The chatter, the bartering and haggling, filled the air with a cacophony of strange yet melodic sounds. The profusion of exotic sights made him forget his hunger.

He wandered about the town for hours, gradually feeding his stomach. He feasted on more food than he'd eaten in the last two months altogether: reindeer meat and Oriental pies, rich cakes and honeyed yogurt, caviar and chunks of goat-milk cheese on thick black bread. He ate until he thought he would burst, and then sought out the baths. Looking in a mirror, he was surprised to see his hair was well below his ears; he had more than a shadow of a beard. For the first time in his life he had a shave, and tipped the barber heavily, asking where he might buy good clothes.

He picked out his purchases with an excited energy, recalling his shopping spree in St. Petersburg with his father. He bought everything he wanted, regardless of price, and emerged newly clothed in fine woolen pants and shirt, a handsome sheepskin coat he'd seen on some of the more rugged men, heavily furred boots and a bearskin hat. Then he went to a tavern and drank vodka. He sat for over an hour listening to conversations, watching people talking and laughing, absorbing the vibrations of life. Finally, he left to buy blankets and provisions: coffee, sugar, bread, cheese and yogurt. Soap, too. He wanted to scrub the hut, which seemed to have been abandoned for years, clean it as his mother would clean, make himself a home. There was a stream, still frozen, which ran behind nearby. The water would be plentiful, and once the air grew warmer, he would take the shutters off the window.

For days Alexei followed the same routine. He awoke early, made himself strong coffee and ate chunks of bread and cheese for breakfast, sometimes smoked fish or caviar, then went to the rock he'd chosen carefully to hide his sack of diamonds, rubles, and his switch. After taking what money he thought he'd need for the day, he hurried into Krasnoyarsk, where he spent hours wandering about the bazaars, often making frivolous purchases, fine linen tablecloths for his mother, lace, and porcelain miniatures of animals and birds. He bought her a set of beautiful cut glasses, and for Tolya he bought a sable hat and a new sheepskin coat. He bought gifts for Katerina, too, necklaces, earrings and yards of brilliantly dyed silk for a new gown. He imagined carrying his purchases home on a sled drawn by a team of handsome dogs. He imagined reaching Yaroslavl in the dead of the following winter, surprising the whole neighborhood with his dogs, his gifts, not to mention his beard. For he no longer went for a shave after the baths. He decided to let his beard grow.

On bitter afternoons he went to the tavern, but when the wind was quiet, he watched the fishermen pulling their fabulous catches of seventy-pound sturgeon and other huge fish in nets from the holes cut in the ice of the Enisei River. It was said the Enisei was fathomless, and the local fishermen were artists at tapping the deepest pools and ringing them with their nets.

The sledded ferry crossing the frozen river, three miles wide at Krasnoyarsk, was Alexei's favorite pastime. No matter when the crossing, the boat was always brimming with passengers, merchants, travelers, sometimes prisoner bands, and always with the Buriat tribesmen and their beasts. The rapid outbursts of strange tongues filled Alexei's brain along with the spectacle of the great primeval river cutting through steep purple cliffs rising still further into towering pink granite. They passed the islands, the "holy lands" on water, little more than outposts of rock and birch trees where shamans and priestly sorcerers were said to dwell. Finally, as the ferry wound its way toward the eastern shore, a chain of blue mountains appeared on the distant horizon—the mountains of Transbaikalia. Beyond them lay the great inland sea of which everyone spoke, Lake Baikal. It was there, Alexei knew, in a mining camp near the lake, that the guard Sasha had been taking his prisoners.

The first two weeks in Krasnoyarsk swept by Alexei with all the reality of a man sleepwalking in dreams of the promised land. He thought little, and at night he fell into a heavy alcoholic sleep. Everything was surfaces: smells, sights, sounds. He approached a church several times, but never went in. The shimmer of his mother always touched him, and he'd run from the house of God to the shops, rapt in a frenzy of buying. The little hut was overladen with gifts for his mother. Upon his return to Yaroslavl, he would buy her a new house too. He would give her everything she deserved, but not with Matyushin's money. He would only use those rubles until he could start making his own. Then he would burn Matyushin's or throw them out to sea. Soon he would start making his own money. Soon, when it was safe to return to the west, he would show the right people his switch, and then he would be rich. Until then, he thought he would stay in Krasnoyarsk.

Alexei awoke to find a stern-looking woman with a large, angular face and piercing blue eyes sitting at his table. A ten-inch hunting knife lay by her hand. His sack lay by her feet. Alexei opened and closed his eyes, thinking he was still dreaming, but the woman did not go away. He remained perfectly still, afraid if he so much as moved, the hunting knife would be plunged into his chest. He tried to keep his eyes closed too, but they kept flitting open, drawn to the horrific woman. Her age was indeterminable. Long black hair hung in braids from a hunter's hat. She wore a coarse brown fur coat which reached below her knees, and worn reindeer-skin boots. At first he thought her a tribeswoman, but on closer look, her nose was more thin and pointed than broad, her cheekbones high, and her slanted eyes a Nordic blue. Her skin was white underneath its wind-chafed redness.

"Is this your hut?" she demanded in a husky voice. Her eyes never left his.

"Well, no, not exactly . . ." he stammered, wondering whether he dared yet move. "I mean, I've come across it. I mean, well, perhaps it is your house. If so . . ."

"How did you come here?"

"In the night." He lifted his head slightly. "I lost my way, and saw the hut in the moonlight."

"What was your way?"

"I . . . I'm not certain." Alexei's eyes moved to the knife.

"Siberia has many ways for those who have none. You come from Russia."

"Yaroslavl, a bit northeast of Moscow," he said, and then thought he should not have told her the truth.

"Your family is in Siberia?"

"Yes, my father. He's making his fortune."

"He is lucky, then. More men die here than make their fortune." She stood up, unfolding to a surprising height. She was almost as tall as Alexei. She nodded toward the stove. "You've almost let the fire die out."

"Yes, I do that sometimes. I forget."

"Such forgetfulness leads to death in Siberia." Then, as if noticing Alexei's preoccupation with the knife, she laughed carelessly, balanced it in her palm a moment, and shoved it into her boot. Her laughter quieted into a smile, showing remarkably white and straight teeth. "You may get up if you like." She watched him dress and then asked. "What is your name?"

"Alexei Sementov," he lied again.

"Well, Alexei Sementov, you are living in my house," she said matter-of-factly.

"Your house—I'm sorry, truly. I shall pay you, of course. I have enough."

"Yes, I know." Her eyes lowered to the sack. "I've been watching you almost since you arrived. I could have taken your secret anytime."

Alexei's body tightened with fear and he paled. "You can have it all—"

She laughed a deep, guttural laugh. "I want none of it. I have no use for money like that. It would only induce some poor soul to rob and perhaps kill me. You've been traveling from Moscow with all that?"

"Yes," he answered uncertainly.

"You're lucky, then. God watches over you." She kicked the sack toward him. "You may stay here if you like, Alexei Sementov. You've fixed it up for me, that's payment enough." She turned to leave.

"But wait—your name, you never told me your name."

"Kira Yurovna."

"Where will you live?"

"Not here, I promise you. I've another home." She shrugged and her expression grew serious. "I should tell you . . . the spirits of the dead live here."

Not knowing how to respond, Alexei said nothing.

"Many have died here. The shaman says he can cleanse the place of the spirits, but I think that is wrong. The spirits are my ancestors. They need a place." She looked at him as if wanting him to agree. "My great-grandfather, Rolf Svenson, was killed here by a robber, one who came to steal his furs. The robber slit his throat. Great-grandfather came from Norway to hunt the sable. He was a famous trapper, so famous he married the daughter of the leader of the Chukchi."

"The reindeer riders!"

"Yes." She paused thoughtfully a moment and went on. "My great-grandmother died here twenty years later, in that bed. Her son, my grandfather, died in the river when the spring came. He, too, was married to a Chukchi."

"And she died here?"

"In childbirth."

"I see." Alexei was smiling, his eyes exploring this woman, Kira Yurovna. She seemed to be growing younger as they spoke, although not more attractive. Still, he could feel her looking at him as a woman eyes a man. The longer their glances lingered, the more in control he felt. "You are Chukchi, too, then," he said easily.

"More than not. My mother married a prisoner—or one who had been a prisoner—from St. Petersburg. Once my father had been very rich, a soldier in the Czar's Imperial Guard. His mother and father, my grandmother and grandfather, dressed in satins and silks and danced in the Czar's palaces. They have my picture in St. Petersburg, from when I was very young. Father sent it to them. I never met them, of course. I never will. Probably they are dead. You see, my father tried to kill the Czar," she added matter-of-factly. "He was sent to Siberia, near Lake Baikal. Many years later, when his face and body were still older than his years, the Czar let him free, but he could never return to Russia. He married my mother; they had four children, my three brothers and me."

"I see." Alexei smiled seductively. Surely he'd known more beautiful women, but there was something undeniably arousing about this Amazon with the hunting knife in her boots.

"My brothers have all been drafted by the Czar's army. My mother and father are dead. I trap. Is your father a trapper?"

"My father?" he echoed questioningly.

"Yes, you said he is here to make his fortune. Men come to Siberia for three reasons, either because they are prisoners like my father or because they hunt the sable or dig the jewels from the earth. Your father is not a prisoner."

"No, no, he, ah . . . he's digging for jewels."

"Where?"

"Well, not far from here. But far enough so I don't see him."

"And those are his jewels in your sack?"

"Why, yes. Yes!"

"Hmm, I see. He's most clever, then, to dig the diamonds and cut and set them too."

"Oh, yes, he's very clever. And I'm just like him, you'll see." He stepped toward her.

"You have lied to me, Alexei Sementov." She flicked back her head.

"Lied, about what?"

"Your father." She flashed him a smile showing her startling white teeth. "And your thoughts." She eyed him intently. "How easily they surface in one so young and so self-centered. Truthfully, you are not so irresistible as you think you are." Without another word, she turned and left.

For a moment Alexei was too startled to respond. Then he was hurrying to the door. "Wait!" he cried, just as she disappeared behind some trees. He ran after her, following her tracks awhile and then losing them in his own circles.

Alexei was haunted by the strange Chukchi woman with the piercing blue eyes. He stalked the streets of Krasnoyarsk looking for her, questioning the merchants and shopkeepers. "Ah, yes, Kira Yurovna. She comes and goes," was always the response.

"When will she return?"

"When her traps are full."

Alexei checked the markets and bazaars daily. He walked the roads and lost his way in the woods. He imagined he would wake one morning to find her sitting on the chair beside the bed. He watched the passengers leaving and arriving on the ferry. Then he grew angry at himself for wasting his energy over such a woman and spent the afternoon drinking in a riverfront tavern where any of the women might be bought.

He slept the night in a cheap hotel, calmed only by his resolve to leave Kira Yurovna's hut and Krasnoyarsk in the morning. He'd buy a dog sled for his presents, and book passage on the ferry across the Enisei, this time not to return. He'd travel east to Lake Baikal, where the spirits of the lake might take a man as quickly as the mines. It was the place for him to go, he thought, but he awoke the next morning with such a fiery hangover, he considered not leaving the bed. All that got him to his feet was the need to find a full bottle of vodka, and he was on the way to the tavern when he spied Kira Yurovna crossing the marketplace. He'd know her long, loping gait anyplace, and without hesitation he broke into a run and called, "Wait, Kira Yurovna! I beg you, wait!"

She swerved just as he was about to touch her arm. "Alexei Sementov. You are sick?" Her concern was genuine.

"Kalinin!" he burst out. "Alexei Yakovlevich Kalinin. I lied to you about my name."

She laughed then, her face brightening. "You lie about many things."

"Nothing else, I swear!" he insisted, wondering that he'd remembered her as homely. She wasn't homely in the least. On the contrary, the fair Norwegian and swarthy Chukchi mingled irresistibly. Then he was laughing with her. The laughter felt good, almost like coming home.

"Maybe yes, you lie more—maybe no. Siberia is a place for secrets. Still, tell me, you look sick. Too much vodka?"

"Yes, probably!" Alexei exclaimed, then blushed deeply.

"So, it is not good, too much vodka. Some is good. Some more lets loose the evil spirits." She started walking briskly.

He walked beside her, almost needing to run to keep up with her.

"You have been looking for me," she said matter-of-factly.

"How do you know?"

"I have been told. They say there is a lovesick puppy wandering about calling my name." She flashed him a grin. And when he slowed down almost to a stop, she fell back beside him and tugged at his arm. "I've hurt your feelings, I fear. You are very young, Alexei Yakovlevich. How young?"

His face grew red with embarrassment. He thought he hated this woman, and wanted to run from her.

"Come, tell me your age," she insisted gently.

"Twenty!" he boldly replied, forcing his eyes to meet hers.

She laughed uproariously. "More like fifteen."

"No, I swear. Seventeen. That's the truth."

"Yes, I think so."

"Now you, tell me your age."

"Twenty-five. Too old."

"For what?"

"For you." She was smiling, her eyes seeming to caress him.

Instinctively, he leaned to kiss her.

She elbowed him fiercely, and her long strides quickly took her ahead of him.

"What did I do? Why must you always hurt me?" He ran after her, unaware of the passersby watching.

"You are too fresh, Alexei Yakovlevich. I don't like fresh men. I like fresh boys even less. Go bathe," she ordered, holding him at arm's length. "You smell like a tavern and you look worse."

He grabbed her hand and pulled her to a stop. "I'm no boy!" he burst out angrily. "And you would not think so. Yes, I think I see in your eyes, the way you look at me, the way a woman who wants a man looks!"

Again she laughed, her laughter seeming to explode in his head and shatter his body. "I suspect you are more like the jackrabbit. Up and down, always hurrying, never stopping for pleasure. Go bathe, Alexei Yakovlevich, and stop all this drinking." She slipped her arm free of his hold. "I have work I must do."

Alexei's lungs were aching from the cold as he tore into the hut, grabbing whatever was in his reach. He threw chairs, pots, dishes. He heaved the mattress from the bed and onto the floor. He ripped blankets, threw food, destroyed everything he could, except the presents he'd bought for his mother, Tolya and Katerina. Then he stoked the stove until the room was steaming, and settled on the floor with a bottle of vodka.

In the days that followed, he rarely left the hut, thinking all the time he would, thinking he would buy himself that dog sled and travel east to the Orient, China, Japan, then sign onto a freighter and travel to California. From there he'd board the Union Pacific Railroad and travel across all of America. He lay on the mattress dreaming of his travels, and sometimes music would find a way into his mind. He heard melodies and his fingers itched to play. Occasionally he tried to write down what he heard, but no sooner had he begun to write than a rage would overcome him. He'd break the pen, send the inkwell flying across the room, and begin to drink again.

Often he drank more than he ate; the haze of drunkenness choked him, and through it he saw Matyushin, arms held high in looming shadows of claws, coming toward him, wrapping him in chains studded with diamonds. He heard Matyushin laughing, and saw his gold teeth shimmering. He screamed and fought off Matyushin, killing him again and again, sometimes with his hands, sometimes with a knife; always the man came back. There was no escape. Thoughts of suicide obsessed him. He tied one end of a rope to the rafters and the other around his neck. He stood on a chair, but could not kick it over. Instead, he cried and prayed. He needed an icon, and saw the one from his mother's house on the wall above his bed.

When Kira appeared, he thought she was another of his mirages, except she was kind. None of his other mirages was kind. She cleaned up the hut about him and made the bed,

pulled off his boots, and held him when he pleaded for more
vodka. He fought with her to get from the bed, to get the
vodka, but she was stronger than he was.

"You are looking better, Alexei Yakovlevich." She smiled
at him from the stove.

Alexei pulled himself up in the bed. Despite his weakness,
he felt stirrings of wanting her, and turned, ashamed.

"I think you must be hungry. You have not eaten for days,
more than I know. Perhaps now your stomach will want
something other than vodka."

He ate the meat and eggs she brought to him in silence,
and drank several cups of coffee. "Why have you done this
for me?" he finally asked, sopping up the last bit of eggs
with the thick bread.

"I had a vision of your death. I did not want you dying in my
ancestors' house. You have some demons cursing you. This man
named Matyushin. He is a powerful man?" Kira questioned.

"He's dead."

"Death does not take away a man's power. Sometimes it
makes him stronger."

He wanted to tell her that he'd killed Matyushin, but he
dared not, afraid she would go away again.

"Is this man Matyushin, is he why you tried to kill
yourself?" Her eyes settled sadly on him.

He shuddered, pulled himself from the chair and lay facedown on the bed.

"Alexei." Her hand touched his shoulder. "You are in
such pain." Her strong hands massaged his back. "So young
to be in such pain."

"Go away, please. Please leave me alone. . . ."

Kira stayed on the chair by his bed. He did not tell her to
go again. Every time he looked, she was there.

"What do you want of me?" he demanded angrily.

"For you to live. You came to my ancestors' house. It is
my fate to care for you."

"Come . . ." She woke him, nudging him gently. "It is
time to wake up. Put on these clothes. I shan't dress you."

"No one asked you to dress me!" he snapped. The clothes
had been washed and ironed. He looked about for someplace to
change in private, but there was none. Kira was standing by the
stove, a cup of coffee in her hand. She was watching him.

Defiantly he tore off his clothes, and stood naked a moment before redressing. She never took her eyes off him.

"Where are we going?" he demanded.

"Dress warmly," was all she said.

She led him for almost a half-hour through trails in the woods. Spring was finally coming to Siberia, and halfway along the journey, Alexei had to open his coat. The snow was wet, but his feet, covered in boots Kira gave him, never grew cold. Finally they came upon a wooden house in a clearing. Smoke curled from the chimney and the windows were steaming. There were a barn and several smaller buildings by the house. A herd of reindeer perked their ears and galloped to the far end of the fenced enclosure.

"This is Keema!" Kira exclaimed, bending to greet a huge white dog who bounded from the barn, yelping excitedly as it leapt on Kira. "Keema—Alexei. . . ." She laughed, trying to calm the dog, who was standing on its hind legs, practically hugging Kira while its furry tail wagged, streaking the snow. "Down, now, Keema. Down, girl." She kissed the massive head as she led Alexei inside.

The house was larger than it appeared from the outside, with several rooms, including separate eating, living, and sleeping areas. Animal skins and thick woven rugs covered the floors and walls along with both primitive and modern paintings and beautifully crafted vases. There were books in both Russian and French, an ornate music box, and, to Alexei's amazement, a small piano. A withered old woman was cooking by the stove. Kira said something to her in a language Alexei could not understand. The woman turned to Alexei and nodded, smiling happily.

"This is Oni, my great-aunt. She lives with me, and keeps the house and the animals."

"This is yours, then?"

"Yes, my father built it. Some of what you see was brought from St. Petersburg. Here, this is my father." She showed him a picture of a tall, very old and sick-looking man. His shoulders were bent, his eyes were dull. "This is my mother." Kira smiled. "She hated to have her picture taken, but my father insisted."

Alexei looked at the cracking photograph. The woman was small and round, her leathery face so rigid she seemed frightened. Her eyes stared straight ahead. Her lips were pursed. Alexei looked from the pictures to Kira, wondering whom she looked like. Perhaps her father, before he had been broken by prison.

"Well, Oni says the bathhouse is steaming. That is what you must do next, Alexei, relax in the heat, regain your strength. My father built the bathhouse himself. It's quite wonderful and steaming, better than any you'd find in Krasnoyarsk. Oni has left towels and soap. Come, I shall show

you—but watch out for Keema. She shall attack us again once
we open the door!''

Kira threw off her fur cap and coat, urging Alexei to do the
same. Then, with Keema bounding at her heels, she led him
through the melting snow to a nearby building by the river.
Its large windows were fogged. She led him to a small room,
perfectly neat; its wooden floors were scrubbed. Large towels
lined the lindenwood shelves. The air smelled of moist cedar.
''The bath is through that door. Take as long as you want.
Oni will have breakfast when you are ready.''

CHAPTER TWENTY

Kira never invited Alexei to stay with her and old Aunt Oni,
rather he fell easily into their daily routine, as if he'd always
shared their lives. There were the morning chores, feeding
the reindeer, dogs and horses, cleaning the stalls, and chopping wood. Alexei was amazed by the speed with which Kira
split logs, and a competition soon arose between them. Alexei
sawed and chopped until he thought the bones in his arms
would splinter.

''Good.'' Kira smiled. ''Soon you will catch me.''

Each time he thought he had, each time he saw his wood-
pile rising to match hers, she put on a burst of speed which
left him still swinging the ax after she went inside for hot tea
and some of Oni's sweet rolls.

The afternoons they spent cleaning and oiling powerful
hunting rifles and the traps which had rusted over winter.
They sharpened knives and Kira talked of skinning prey. He
liked the mesmerizing droning of her husky voice which
drifted finally into an easy silence. Then Alexei's mind shifted
to other worlds, imagined places he hadn't visited for months.
He wasn't sure when his thoughts spilled into words, his tone
growing more and more excited as he chattered about his
switch, talking as he used to, before Matyushin, spurred on
by the power of his invention and how it would someday
revolutionize the railroads.

Kira listened intently and his talk of railroads spun into dreams

of wealth, and of the day when he would live in a great villa
and work in an office with a sunny window, high ceilings and
a polished mahogany desk. He imagined all the greatest men
in Russia coming to his office, even the Czar himself. With
Kira, these visions at the edges of his consciousness took on
shapes larger than life. It was only her gently mocking smile
that brought him fluttering back to earth.

"You shouldn't let me go on like this," he implored.

"Men must have dreams. Otherwise nothing good would
ever come about."

"My dreams are foolish."

"Some of them will come true, if you believe in them and
fight for them. That's the key, Alyosha, to fight for your
dreams. Nobody is going to come here to Krasnoyarsk and
hand them to you."

"I *will* be very rich one day, and I shall buy you everything
you want, Kira. You and Mama and Tolya. I want you to
meet them. Mama would like you so much."

She laughed softly and sometimes rubbed his hand or arm,
warming Alexei, wrapping him in a cord of connectedness
making each passing day more powerful than the one which
went before. He slept without nightmares, and no longer felt
the need to numb himself with vodka. The sun's warmth was
intoxicating, and his appetite boundless. The dinners with
Kira and Oni were feasts, and Oni, who spoke no Russian,
smiled and laughed as if she understood the conversation. He
caught the old woman staring at him, smiling approvingly,
and he bent to kiss her. She held his hand lovingly, catching
Alexei in a memory he could not place.

He read Kira's father's poetry books at night and played
the piano, which was badly out of tune, but no more so than
Kira's voice.

"My father tried to teach me, but I had no ear," Kira
explained. "He would play for hours, the most beautiful music anyone could imagine. He told me to keep the piano in
tune, but it is hard to find one to tune a piano here. Besides,
it didn't matter to me. I sing little better than I read. Still,
now, I wish I had it tuned."

"Well, it doesn't sound too bad," Alexei insisted as the
pitch grated in his ear. Yet he enjoyed playing the melodies
Oni hummed, and he taught the two women songs popular in
the taverns of Yaroslavl and Moscow.

Spring came quickly to Siberia. One day, or so it seemed,
the snow melted to brown earth. Ice roared as it cracked and
broke, rumbling like stampeding herds of underground de-

mons rushing water into crystalline streams. Forests grew
lush. Meadows blanketed green, bursting with brilliant strokes
of colored flowers.

"It is as if the earth knows the warmth will not last long,"
Kira told Alexei. "All life must soak up the earth's richness
now, so that the barrenness of winter will not empty us. We
must travel far to trap in summer. North and then east. Still,
there is no snow, and we will ride horses. Some use reindeer in
all seasons, but I like the pride of the horse." She beamed,
stroking the neck of her sleek bay stallion. "Oso is the son of a
horse given to my father. He rides with the breath of thunder."

Alexei, who had done little horseback riding, preferred
racing on the reindeer-drawn sled. The awkward-appearing
animal flew at a gallop across icy ground where other beasts
stumbled and fell.

"It is why we use the reindeer," Kira explained. "He
needs no roads and moves swiftly over hills and icy ruts,
barely touching the ground beneath. The earth here is fragile.
Even the dogs can injure the soil. But the reindeer is good.
Still, I like Oso. You will ride Fi."

Alexei looked dubiously at the broad, slope-backed nag.

Kira laughed. "I know she's not much to look at, but with
her gait she'll cause you the least pain. When you get better
in the saddle, perhaps you can ride Oso—but not for a while.
Oso is very proud. And he does not like men much."

They began their trip on a sunny May morning and traveled
northeast to lay the traps, sometimes riding on muddy roads
which had no beginning and no end, other times winding
through forests so tall the treetops seemed but pinpoints in
the sky. The forests were always cool, even cold at night.
They gathered mysterious mushrooms in the darkest recesses
and then broke into sunlit fields where warm, plump berries
crowded vines and rabbits and delectable birds could be had
for the taking. Kira was an unerring marksman, and spent
hours teaching Alexei patience and aim. They feasted daily
on pheasant, rabbit or fish. At night they lay under the stars,
and the quiet of the vast Siberian landscape, gone unnoticed
all day for their constant chatter and bantering, settled about
them as if the earth itself were their cradle. The sky was a
fathomless black, cushioning stars which seemed so close
they might be plucked. Their voices seemed unholy then.

Nights they slept under fur-skinned blankets, but during the
day Alexei rode bare-chested for hours. His skin browned.
He blushed delightedly at Kira's admiring glances and lifted the
heaviest rocks he could to build their campfires. He did whatever
she asked of him, worked to perfect his hunting and fishing,

tried to second-guess her wishes, needing to impress and delight her. He sang as they rode, and chided her for singing off-key. He raced her across lakes, dove off tree limbs.

One morning, Alexei spied Kira bathing by the stream. Her black hair was down, falling almost to her waist, and a shard of morning sun caressed her alabaster skin. Her breasts were small but firm. Her narrow waist rounded into womanly hips and buttocks slimming into long, perfectly shaped legs. Muscles rippled as she bent and swayed, smoothing soap, splashing water. There was not an inch of fat on the sleek body. Alexei watched for only a few moments before he turned and hurried away, feeling awed by her nakedness. He ran, and Oso trotted beside him. When Kira returned to the campsite, fully clothed, her hair tightly braided once more, her skin sparkling from the scrubbing, Alexei dared not look at her.

"What's wrong?" she asked as he busied himself with the fire.

"Nothing." He stared at the ground.

"Something bothers you."

". . . I think we should get an early start. Didn't you say we needed to start doubling back to check the traps?"

"Yes."

"Then I'll get us ready."

During the days that followed, the real work of trapping began. Alexei concentrated on the movements of Kira's large, strong hands as she gutted and skinned the fox and sable. He watched as if memorizing the mechanics of the movements; and by the afternoon of the second day, he was working on his own. After several days, one of the packhorses was laden with skins.

"You are a quick learner, Alyosha," Kira said as they traveled to find a camp late in the afternoon. "Skinning is not easy, especially for a city boy. You do well."

He nodded silently.

"Tomorrow we will sleep in a bed and have someone else cook our meal."

"Where are we going?"

"There's an outpost a day's travel away. I'll sell what we have to some trappers who transport the furs east. The money is not so good as what we can get in Krasnoyarsk, but the woods and fields are full this season. We shall have no trouble finding again what we have sold. I always stop there at this time of year. I have friends. You'll like them."

"Are there women?" The question fell from his mouth.

"Not often. Mostly men, trappers."

Alexei nodded, ashamed he'd asked, and thought he should apologize or explain. What, he wasn't sure. Except as the day

began to draw to an end, he became more and more agitated.
"Perhaps we should camp here," he suggested as they
crossed a stream. "And go in the morning."

"No, we're not far now. Only some ten minutes. I look
forward to a bed and the companionship of the men. It will
be good to have someone besides each other to talk to."

"Why?" he demanded, his face blushing hot.

She laughed heartily and slowed Oso to walk beside Alexei
on Fi. "Not that you aren't like talking to twenty men! I've
never known one to talk as you. Still, we shall go. I have
business, and I think you will enjoy yourself. Tonight, we
will get drunk. You'll like that." She tightened her legs about
Oso, and the horse began to trot. "Come!" she called as
Alexei lingered. "My throat is very thirsty."

The outpost was little more than an opening in the woods
with a few trappers' huts and a tavern selling vodka and supplies. There were some ten or twelve men in the dark, ill-kept
tavern, which smelled of beer and sweat. The men were older,
rough-looking, and although they spoke in strange accents, Alexei
thought he knew them, men like the prisoner Rodchenko, and
those in the taverns at home in Yaroslavl. He wanted to leave as
soon as they arrived, to be alone again with Kira; he wanted to
take her, save her. It angered him that she seemed not to know
her danger. In fact, she fell in easily with the men, laughing and
talking as they drank. Alexei had never seen Kira drink so heavily before, glasses and glasses of vodka. He drank to keep up
with her, silently competing.

"Kira Yurovna!" a husky voice called as the door swung
open.

Alexei turned with the others to see a tall, ruggedly handsome
man with a mass of blond curls and an imposing yellow beard
and mustache practically leap into the room. He opened his
arms, and Kira ran to him, swallowed by his embrace. They
kissed hello, a kiss that sent shudders down Alexei's spine, and
then they fell into rapid, intimate talk and laughter.

"Come, Karl, you must meet my friend." She pulled the
newcomer toward the table where Alexei sat. "Karl Gruen—
Alexei Yakovlevich."

Karl ran his broad hand along the curves of Kira's hip as
he extended his other to shake Alexei's.

"Vodka, eh!" Karl fell into a seat, pulling Kira after him.

She poured him a glassful, which he quickly downed, and
another and another.

"Andrei Soproka! Is that you I see?" Karl leaned back on
his chair and called out.

"Aye, it's me, Karl."

''Then why aren't you playing your mouth organ? Come, man, we need some merriment here!'' He leapt to his feet and Kira followed, the two of them breaking into a dance as Soproka began playing. Although Kira was light on her feet, Karl was clumsy.

Almost immediately, Alexei felt better. He waited a few minutes, then stood, his head woozy from the vodka. Steadying himself, he marched to the center of the floor and tapped Karl's shoulder.

''May I?'' Karl was swimming before his eyes. Still, even drunk, Alexei knew he could put this oaf to shame on the dance floor.

''Oh, hey, yes, my fine lad. Give Kira a spin or two if you like! I've never been one to keep her flying.''

Alexei took Kira in his arms as Karl stepped back, and guided her in a wild dance. She followed his every movement while the other men, Karl included, clapped and cheered. Alexei spun free of her, dancing around her, kicking high his legs, then reaching for her. He would have gone on tirelessly if Kira hadn't finally begged off.

''The boy has a way, my girl!'' Karl put a proprietary arm about her, kissing her as they went back to drinking.

More mortified than before, Alexei slipped into a far corner, and an angry brooding sobered him. Hours passed and finally Kira and Karl, without so much as a glance about the room, left the tavern arm in arm.

Heart pounding, Alexei followed after them, just in time to see them disappear into one of the huts. It was all he could do not to burst in and tear Kira from the brute; but he dared not, more afraid of Kira's wrath than of Karl's strength. Instead, he ran to the barn where Oso was stabled, and amid the confusion of embarrassment, anger and shame stinging his senses, he threw on some tack and pulled Oso into the yard.

The horse reared before Alexei could attempt to mount and, knocking Alexei to the ground, tore into the night.

Alexei ran after him, stumbling over rocks until he collapsed in a panic, and sometime in the night fell asleep. He woke shivering with the frigid dawn, and no sooner did he open his eyes to the graying sky than he remembered the nightmare: Oso was gone, run off, never to be found. Kira would never forgive him. Kira . . . He burned with shame to remember her with Karl, and his own drunken madness. Surely she had seen him following. . . .

Dragging himself to his feet, he began to run. He couldn't return to the outpost. He could never face Kira again.

* * *

As he walked, he searched for Oso, calling out his name, but the flatness of the land stretched endlessly, and no horse could be seen. He walked for several days, keeping to the road, catching fish as Kira had taught him, with spears made from saplings. His mind wandered often to his sack of money and jewels stashed in the house with Oni. He couldn't go back there, not even for his switch. It was just as well. With all that money, Kira could buy herself many horses as fine as Oso, and Alexei could build another switch, if he wanted. He wasn't sure he did. The switch had only caused him trouble. He would find a job, perhaps even become a trapper. He liked the quiet of the land, and the mechanical butchering, cutting at something already dead, killing without remorse.

On the evening of his third day alone, he was sitting by his campfire waiting for his fish to finish cooking when he heard what sounded like horses; he jumped into the shadows, grabbing his knife for protection. To his amazement, Kira appeared in the clearing, riding Oso, with Fi and the two other packhorses in tow. She slipped down from the saddle, tethered the horses to a tree and walked silently about the camp. Then she began eating Alexei's dinner.

"Hey, that's mine!" he burst out. "I worked hard catching them!"

She nodded and held out the pan.

Alexei grabbed it and crouched on the opposite side of the fire. He wasn't in the least bit hungry anymore, but he ate every morsel, methodically picking clean the bones. Then he went to the bed he'd chosen under some pines and lay on his back looking at the stars. He awoke in the morning to the smell of coffee and bacon. Blankets were covering him.

He determined to wait for her to speak first. When she didn't, he demanded, "How did you find me?"

"Oh, I've been following you for days. You were but an hour from the outpost when I spotted you."

"You mock me by following me." He glared.

"I'm sorry if you think that. It wasn't my intention. I supposed you wanted to be alone."

"Why did you think I wanted your company last night?"

"I wanted yours. But now I ask myself why. The spoiled child takes away from the man."

He blushed deeply, thinking of Karl with his massive shoulders and arms, the full beard and hair curling up from out of the neck of his shirt. Kira wouldn't talk to Karl as she spoke to Alexei. She wouldn't follow Karl; he wouldn't allow it. He'd probably box her ears as Tolya would. Alexei thought that was what he should do. Grab Kira, show her who was boss. Except she'd surely grab him back, fell him as easily as the guard Sasha Sabinsky had. No wonder Kira chose Karl over Alexei.

"Will you never talk to me again?" she questioned.

"I almost lost Oso!" he snapped, his words more of a dare than an apology. "It was because of me he broke loose."

"Oso always finds his way back to me. You were very drunk. Is that why you tried to ride him?"

Alexei closed his eyes, refusing to answer.

Then Kira was sitting beside him, holding his hand in hers. "Listen to me, Alexei Yakovlevich. This is not a place for someone inexperienced in the ways of the wild to strike out on his own. This road you are taking goes on for hundreds of miles with no sign of other men. Winter could return before you realize you are lost, and then with your clothes and shoes, you would die. I don't want you to die, not because of me."

"You!" His voice cracked as he tried to laugh. "You think I left because of you?"

"Alexei, the boy in you is very young and very angry. The man in you is strong, but too often not strong enough to calm the boy. It's what you have to learn to do, what we all have to do, calm the child inside us that cries out in fear."

"I am tired of you calling me a boy!" He yanked his arm away. "If you knew my life, you wouldn't call me a boy. If you knew anything about me . . . But you don't. Besides, it makes no difference whether I am boy or man! What do you care? You don't want the man!" he bellowed, swallowing hard, fighting tears that surfaced too easily with Kira. "Go back to your Karl! He's all man!" He turned and ran.

"Alexei, stop!"

He pushed on, needing to outrun her. He ran beyond her reach for almost a mile, until his chest began to ache. He ran until he could not take another step, and when he stopped, falling to the ground, she was only moments behind him. They lay breathlessly on their backs.

Kira finally spoke. "You are jealous. Ah, no, you are angry. You would like to hit me, I think."

He turned quickly, grabbing her and pressing his lips against hers.

"Alexei, no. . . ." She pushed him away, but held his arm tightly. "Not like this. Not in anger or because you must compete with another man. Someday," she promised, "the time will be right between us."

"It has *always* been right!"

"There is more to making love than just two bodies."

"I know about making love! I know more than you think."

"Yes, I'm sure, a handsome young man like yourself. Yet,

I think this time we've shared together is more important than all your hours with other women.''

"Don't be so sure of yourself.''

She smiled softly. "Tell me, then. If you had a choice, these months together for all your women, which would you take?''

The women! he wanted to shout in her face, except it wasn't true. "And have you spent such time with Karl as you spend with me?''

"No.''

"I don't understand you, Kira!'' He pressed his hands to his face. "I don't understand you at all!''

"It is easy with a man like Karl, as it was with the women you have known. It costs nothing and I take nothing from it. Once over, it is over. But loving someone beyond the moment is to take that person into yourself and hold him forever, no matter the distances, even in death. Then lovemaking flows like the breath of God, for the love and friendship are one and the same.''

"But we are friends.'' He was more confused than ever. "So what's wrong, then? I don't understand what's wrong.''

"Nothing, don't you see, there's nothing wrong between us.''

"Then why?''

"Because . . .'' She slipped her hand about his, pressing it to her lips. "Because you do not understand. When you understand, nothing need be explained. Come now, we have work to do. If we don't clean our traps, scavengers will.''

The sun was just setting and Alexei was singing softly, tunes Kira liked to hear. He broke off, and the air seemed very still. The first shadows of the moon cast a whiteness on the ground where Kira lay. He watched her until she looked back at him, and then he said softly, "I killed a man with my hands.''

There was a silence, as if the night had swallowed his words.

"Matyushin.''

"Yes.''

"What kind of a man was he?''

"Greedy, bad. He stole from me. . . .'' Alexei told his tale, explaining about his switch, and, days later, when he and Kira had finished their trapping and were on their way back to Krasnoyarsk, he talked to her about his father. It was a hot afternoon. The horses moved slowly with the weight of so many furs, and they stopped to let them drink and graze.

"Sometimes men have to kill. We have no choice. I don't think your father had to kill.''

"You don't know my father!" He jumped to his feet and grabbed at the tall grass. "He wasn't a murderer!"

"Any more than you. The difference is, he wanted to die. I don't think you do."

"No." He shuddered, afraid to look at her. "Sometimes I hate him for what he did. I try not to hate him, but I can't help it. I hate him for going away from me. I hate him because I love him." He fought to hold back the tears. "I love him so much. He was my father. He had no right to kill himself!" He turned to her then. "Hold me, Kira, please hold me. Sometimes I get so scared. . . ."

When they returned to Krasnoyarsk, Kira gave Alexei the task of selling the furs. "You have grown much this summer. Thickened, and your beard is all filled in," she told him. "The traders will respect you. But remember to start higher than you think they're worth, then you must haggle as if every coin counts."

To Alexei's surprise, the selling of the furs came easily. He enjoyed the bargaining with the scar-faced merchant in Krasnoyarsk, and ended up with more gold than even Kira had foretold.

"I want to celebrate!" he exclaimed as he handed her the heavy purse. "I want to take you to the finest restaurant in Krasnoyarsk. But first I want to go to your home and bathe. I want to stay in the baths for hours, then feast with Oni. And I want to sleep in a real bed!"

Oni wept with joy at seeing Kira and Alexei, and immediately set to work preparing food. Kira worked beside the old woman awhile. They spoke excitedly in their native tongue, words that made Oni grin at Alexei and nod her head up and down.

"What did you tell her?" he asked.

"That you need a bath. I shall go prepare the bathhouse. Oni said she hasn't used it for days. The stones must be heated. It will take a while. I'll come get you when it's ready. You feed Oso and the other horses. Then we can forget them for the rest of the day."

Alexei was done with the horses long before Kira was ready with the bath. He returned to the house and sat in the kitchen watching Oni, who kept turning and smiling at him. She gave him wine to drink and fruit and sweet honey cakes to eat. He was just about to refill his wineglass when Oni grabbed him by the arm, and muttering excitedly, urged him from his chair and out the back door. Pointing in the direction of the bathhouse, she repeated Kira's name.

"Okay, all right, I'm on my way." Alexei smiled, thinking

the old woman might beat him on the head if he didn't do exactly what he was told.

"Kira!" he called as he walked into the quiet changing room. He undressed quickly and reached for a towel from the scrubbed lindenwood shelves. Only then did he notice Kira's neatly folded clothes. A wave of nervous anticipation made him shiver as he wrapped a towel around his waist, bending his head as he walked into the low-ceilinged bathroom fogged with steam.

"Alyosha," she called softly. "Hurry in. The water is just right."

Dropping his towel, he slipped into the water, his shoulders rubbing against Kira's. Her hair was loose and the steam settled about it, causing it to curl in a spiderweb haze. "Welcome, my sun god." She smiled warmly and spread her hands across the water, making little waves rise and fall against the swell of her breasts.

For the first time since his first time with Katerina, Alexei felt scared, uncertain what was expected of him; he sank into the water as far from Kira as he could.

She swam to him and began scrubbing his back and shoulders with sweet-smelling soap. She lathered his face, then hers, laughing as their skin touched, sliding like silk.

He watched her.

"Come. . . ." She lifted herself from the bath, the clouds of steam drifting about her hips and legs. "This is the best part, even better when the snow returns." She extended her hand toward him and helped him climb from the bath. "Hmmm . . ." she breathed contentedly, her eyes traveling over his entire body. Then she switched her body with a birch-twig broom until she was shining with sweat and flushed to a rosy hue.

Alexei did the same, all the time unable to take his eyes off the gentle upturn of her breasts, their hard, pointed nipples and the sweat running down the curves of her waist, thighs and slightly rounded belly. Just as he was about to embrace her, she grabbed his hand and dashed into the yard, plunging the two of them into the racing stream, screaming as the frigid water attacked their bodies. Alexei felt as though his skin was on fire. His heart seemed almost to stop.

Kira was laughing and splashing him with water.

"It's freezing!" he yelped.

"You'll get used to it!" She splashed him some more.

Slowly his breath as well as feeling in his body came back to him.

"Like it now?" she asked, smiling as she swam close to him.

"I like you!" he exclaimed, reaching to grab her.

She dove under the water and emerged near the bank. "Now it is time to go back. Come, Alyosha!" She climbed from the river and turned to face him, hands on her hips as the water dripped from her sun-drenched skin.

He scrambled after her, following her into the bathhouse, where a rush of steam gripped him with a delicious light-headedness. Every muscle, every pore seemed permeated with pleasure; he was delirious with an energy which felt like flying. Grasping her in his arms, he kissed her face again and again, her cheeks, her nose, her eyes, her lips. His hands caressed her wet skin, smoothing frenetically over her breasts and buttocks, wanting to hold and touch all of her in the same instant. Never had he known such wanting, spreading in a rush of joy promising almost unbearable fulfillment.

"I want you very much, Alyosha," she whispered as her mouth closed on his and her strong arms pressed with their own insistence. "Oh, yes . . ." She shuddered, her breasts pressing maddeningly into his chest. "I want to soar with you as the falcons soar. I want to burrow deep into the darkness of the earth and swim the great oceans like a single streak of light. I want our love to flow like the breath of God. . . ."

CHAPTER TWENTY-ONE

"Kira!" he called as he woke to see Kira sitting in the same chair in which she'd sat, hunting knife in hand, blue eyes intent, twenty-three years before. "Kira?" he questioned, needing to touch her reality. Perhaps then his dreams would end. Anna and the ghosts would go away. Perhaps they were one and the same. "Kira!" He thought he was screaming, but there was no sound to his voice.

"It's all right, Alyosha. It is me," she assured as the bed settled under her weight. Her cool hand smoothed his brow. She was smiling. "You are better. You will live."

"How long have I been here?" he asked, his eyes gradually taking in the hut. It was as it always had been.

"I don't know for certain. I found you close to death five days ago. I was frightened, very frightened. I felt my ances-

tors struggling for your spirit as they never dared in the past.
I thought for a while they would win, but God has answered
my prayers.''

He smiled weakly and lifted his hand, so thin he barely
recognized it as his own, and rested it on hers. For a woman
so firmly grounded in the harsh realities of survival, Kira's
belief in the spirits never ceased to amaze him. Kira was
Kira. She hadn't changed.

The second day after his fever broke, Kira had Alexei up
and walking about the hut. On the third day, she wrapped
him in his coat, fur hat, and boots and took him for a walk.
Each day they walked further. On the fifth day, they reached
the Great Siberian Post Road. It was a frigid but sunny January morning, the kind of cold which constricted the lungs
with each breath. Still, it was good to be out again. All too
soon, his exhilaration turned to exhaustion.

''I feel like an old man,'' he gasped, battling the air for
breath; he leaned heavily on Kira's arm.

''But you look younger every day. I think I will shave you
today, and soon, perhaps tomorrow, I will get the reindeer
sled and take you to the big house. You will be more comfortable there. The baths will help sweat the sickness from
you. And Oni waits for your return.''

''Oni!'' He smiled. ''She's still alive?''

''Her body is a constant trial. She is blind and almost deaf,
but her mind is still strong. She prays all day for you. It will
be good for you to be with her again.''

''And Onan?'' he asked cautiously, and felt a moment's hesitation in Kira's step. She hadn't mentioned her husband once.
Usually she did, but Alexei did not pressure her. It wasn't until
they had returned to the hut and were sitting at the table drinking
strong tea that Kira said, ''Onan is dead. Four years now.''

''I'm sorry. . . .'' He faltered, feeling sadness and confusion. ''But the children—they are well?''

''Aliana has gone off to Irkutsk with a trapper. I do not
like him. I think he abuses her. But what can I do? She is
past sixteen.''

''And Dobrui?''

''He is with his father's family. A boy needs a father. With
the Chukchi he has many. I think he will be a fine man, one to
make his own father proud. Hurry now, finish the tea, then you
must sleep. Tomorrow I will get the sled and bring you to Oni.''

That night they made love. Kira's body was still firm, like a
young girl's; her loving was passionate and tender. He allowed
her to guide him as she always did, making him her plaything,

and he delighted in her delight. There was no frenzy of performing, ending in disdain, the urgency to be done, to smoke a cigarette and hurry away. Another night, another woman, hopeful young girls awed by his power, his wealth, perhaps his aging beauty. He counted on that still, often wondering if he'd know when it vanished, that power to attract women as if he gave off a scent. He was no better than poor Tatyana Rantzau; he'd never been any better, a whore in his own right, except with Kira. She never changed. Her loving sweetness calmed him; the magical touch of her fingers and lips, the press of her hips, the crush of her arms, the low, deep moans and cries, aroused him. He'd been asleep for years. The passion lingered as embers through the night, mellowing into sleep, their bodies intertwined, the touch of her silken skin as much a part of him as breathing. For the first time since he could remember, he had no nightmares and he did not think of Anna.

He tried to remember why he'd left Kira that first time, almost twenty-three years before. Or he tried to remember why he'd let her convince him to go, to see the lawyer in St. Petersburg, Yuri Dobrinsky. It was her idea to write to Dobrinsky just before leaving Krasnoyarsk for their second summer of trapping together.

Yuri Dobrinsky, or Dmitri Mayakovsky as Alexei came to know him, was the son of a co-conspirator of Kira's father, one of the four young officers in the Imperial Guards who'd been accused of plotting to assassinate the Czar.

"This Yuri Dobrinsky is a fine lawyer, the finest," she told Alexei, showing him the paper with Dobrinsky's name and address. "I met him when I was thirteen. He came to visit my father and stayed and talked with him for days. I remember I thought Yuri very plain when he arrived, too soft for a young man, and already balding—but then, I had expected some kind of hero in the son of my father's comrade, Andrei Mayakovsky. My father spoke of his comrades as if they were all heroes. Once Yuri began to talk, though, he changed. He became so fiery. Everything about him strengthened. My father called it the inner strength of a true revolutionary. It frightened me, for I was only a girl. Or perhaps I was like my mother. I did not want to know the hard side of my father. I wanted only the father who spoke softly and sang songs and made me laugh. But that was half the man. I saw the other half when Yuri came to visit. It was in 1868, not long after Karakozov was executed for attempting to kill the Czar. Yuri brought news of all kinds of revolutionary activity in Petersburg, the news you never read in the papers, my father said.

"It was springtime, I remember, and they went on long

walks. We children, my three brothers and I, were encouraged to walk behind them, even though my mother feared our hearing such things as my father and Yuri spoke about. I remember, we were all sitting under a tree just beginning to burst with buds, and my father hugged Yuri and kissed him on each cheek. Then he said, 'Yuri Nikolaievich, you have your father's soul. It is alive and strong and good.' 'Have I?' Yuri asked, excitement creeping into his smile. I remember that clearly, for I had not seen Yuri smile before that moment. It was sad to see such a serious young man. But he smiled then. Yes, he looked almost handsome, and tears filled his eyes. They sat in silence. It was a very powerful silence, even my brothers and I sat very still. It seemed as if the gods had stilled the moment. Finally Yuri said with great pride, 'From now on, I shall have two names, Yuri Nikolaievich Dobrinsky and Dmitri Andreievich Mayakovsky.' '' Kira pulled her long black braid. ''Dmitri was his father's father's name.''

She seemed to grow distant then and finally she went on, ''My father came to love Yuri very much during that short visit. He could talk to Yuri the way he wasn't able to talk to his own sons, even Leon, the oldest, who was far more interested in hunting and trapping than politics. I think none of us wanted to hear about politics because of what it had done to my father.'' She grew stiff and her eyes hardened with a vacantness. ''My father died not long after Yuri's visit, less than a year. I have Yuri's address. He told me I should write to him if I ever needed help. I think you should write to him.''

''Me! What would I say?''

''That you have this invention you want to protect. I think there are laws which can protect your switch, so anyone who uses it knows it is yours and has to pay you for it. You need a lawyer to help you now.''

''I'll think about it.''

''There is no time to think. Oni and I have discussed it. You will write Yuri Nikolaievich a wonderful letter, filled with all your excitement about your switch and its success. If you write now, perhaps when we return in August, your reply will be waiting.''

July 15, 1879

Dear Alexei Yakovlevich,

    I am pleased that Kira Yurovna suggested you write to me. It is my fondest duty to help to the utmost anyone who is connected with my father. Your switch seems very interesting and not without promise. I have already begun

working on the papers for patenting, and look forward to
meeting you in person. I am certain I can be a support.
My fondest regards to Kira Yurovna.
                                    Sincerely yours,
                                    Yuri Nikolaievich Dobrinsky

Dobrinsky's letter on the heavy white paper with its fine
embossed letterhead had been waiting for them when they'd
returned from that second summer of trapping. Just the sight
of the envelope had filled Alexei with more excitement than
he'd anticipated, expanding his mind with visions of all Russia, the Czar himself, coming to see his switch. He saw himself dressed in a white, gold-braided uniform, bowing to kiss
the Imperial hand, the glitter of the Czar's rings flooding
Alexei with warmth greater than the sun.

"You will go," Kira had said as soon as Alexei had finished
reading the letter. "I am sure Yuri Nikolaievich can help you."

"I'll be back, though, soon."

She smiled, taking his hands and holding them in her own.
"Make no promises, Alyosha. For I think life holds many
wonderful promises for you. But know this: I will never forget you, just as you will never forget me—my boy who grew
into such a man." She caressed his cheek and then her eyes
rested intently on his. "Always remember you have a home
here, Alyosha. It is more than just the will of my ancestors. We
have shared life together. Always, I will hold you in my heart."

Alexei arrived in Petersburg sporting a thick, full beard,
wide blue Cossack trousers, a jaunty black Tatar hat and high,
brightly decorated boots of the Chukchi tribe. He wore a
black blouse with a wide belt, and over it a long sable-lined
leather vest embroidered with semiprecious stones and silken
threads which he'd bought for a small fortune in the marketplace at Ekaterinburg, the same marketplace where he'd fled
from the guard Sasha two years before. He needed to appear
prosperous to meet the famed Yuri Dobrinsky, whom he expected to be living in one of the lavish palaces along the Neva
that he recalled from his Petersburg trip with his father.

To his dismay, the lawyer was living hardly better than
Tolya and his mother lived back in Yaroslavl. The neighborhood was perhaps better, but inside, the house was in worse
shambles. The walls were chipped, cracked and streaked with
gray as if they had been painted that way. Piles of newspapers
and boxes were everywhere. Curtains were mismatched, rugs
spotted and furniture heavy with dust. Alexei would have
taken his switch and looked elsewhere for a lawyer, if he'd
known where to look, and if the specter of Kira's wrath,

should he turn away from the son of one of her father's hallowed conspirators, hadn't terrified him.

Yuri Dobrinsky was thirty-six at the time, seventeen years Alexei's senior, but his shabbiness and stoutness made him appear far older. He was a plain-suited, humorless man, his thick lips set to bar merriment; his eyes behind the rimless eyeglasses met Alexei's with glaring superiority.

"Your trip went well, Kalinin?" Yuri Dobrinsky asked blandly. He seemed unimpressed with Alexei's vest, if he noticed it at all.

"Fine." Alexei nodded, his gaze fixed on the lawyer, thinking he would not give this man who had deceived him with a facade of wealth and influence an inch of control.

"We have papers to sign," Yuri announced. "Come into my office."

"What kind of papers?" Alexei demanded, gripping his black Tatar hat in one hand and his sack in the other.

Dobrinsky didn't answer, but started from the entranceway. Alexei watched the lawyer fade into the shadows of the long hallway, and thought he should simply slip out the front door while he had the chance. This Yuri Dobrinsky might well be setting a trap; perhaps he knew what Alexei carried in his sack; perhaps Dobrinsky was going to herd him into a dark place, take out a knife, kill him and steal the switch and all Matyushin's jewels and rubles.

"Kalinin!" Yuri Dobrinsky called impatiently.

Alexei thought of Kira and what he would tell her if he ran into the street. He could think of nothing, and taking a deep breath, he clutched his sack to his chest and started down the hall. His muscles were taut, his eyes alert, taking in everything. This time, he would be ready.

Dobrinsky led Alexei into the dimly lit, cluttered study. The air was heavy with cigarette smoke and the walls were lined with bookshelves, yet books and magazines spilled out onto the floor and chairs. Alexei had never seen so many books.

"I do nothing without a business contract—a rule of thumb you yourself must learn to live by," Yuri solemnly stated. "Sit," he urged.

Alexei stayed close to the door, blocking the entrance. "Don't you even want to see my switch?" he demanded.

"All in due time, young man." Dobrinsky settled into a large leather chair behind his enormous desk layered with papers. The chair creaked under his weight. "First we complete our business so it doesn't contaminate whatever comes next. It's very clear-cut as far as I'm concerned. If I succeed in patenting and selling your switch, I get twenty-five percent of whatever we make. You wrote in your letter that you have reason to believe your switch has enormous potential. Can you be more explicit?''

Alexei shrugged uncomfortably. "I . . . I once showed it to someone important in the railroad. He was very much taken with it.''

"I see. Who was this someone important?''

Alexei swallowed hard, and fought to keep his gaze focused on Yuri Dobrinsky. It was a trick Kira had taught him when bargaining with the fur traders: never take your eyes off the opponent; but despite Alexei's best efforts, the shabby round man seemed to be gaining the upper hand. There was such assurance in Dobrinsky's voice, and calculated control in his eyes. "Matyushin.'' Alexei's voice cracked on the name.

"Ah, yes, Konstantin Apollonovich. Murdered, wasn't he? When did you see him?''

"Just before he was killed. He said my switch was quite ingenious, and offered to do business with me—at fifteen percent, I might add. I was ready to agree when the terrible accident occurred, so I went to Siberia to seek my fortune instead.'' Alexei's breathing became more relaxed as he felt his lies spin out like well-oiled gears.

"And did you?'' Dobrinsky asked, eyeing Alexei's vest.

Alexei thrust back his shoulders, making himself tower even more over the round man. "Not all that I'd like to make, not nearly enough.''

"How did you meet Kira Yurovna?''

"I came upon her hut. I might have frozen to death without her. I have been hunting with her two seasons.''

"Kira is a fine woman.''

"Yes,'' Alexei agreed. In the tone he used when haggling over the price of skins, he added, "I think twenty-five percent is too much, Dobrinsky. Matyushin was willing to go for fifteen.''

"Matyushin is dead.'' Yuri inhaled deeply. "My offer stands firm. If I help you make a fortune, fifty percent would be a fair cut. For without my help, your switch would make you nothing. If I make you only a little money or none at all, then twenty-five percent would be too much. It's a gamble, Kalinin, but I promise you this: I'm a fair man. I'll never cheat you, and perhaps I can help you. You intrigued me with the letter you sent me. You see, I too would like to make my fortune.''

"Lawyers always make fortunes.''

"To boys like yourself it seems a fortune, and to me, well, right now I surely would not turn up my nose at a lawyer's income. But Kira Yurovna told you of my father.''

"Yes.''

"It's not easy for the son of a man who's been convicted of conspiring to kill a Czar to make a fortune in the law."

"Kira said you've changed your name," Alexei said, wanting Dobrinsky to know his life was not a blank page. "Dobrinsky is your maternal grandfather's."

"Kira told you everything, then."

"Everything she knew."

Yuri Dobrinsky's eyes flitted back and forth like a snake's tongue. "You don't trust me, do you?"

"You have given me no reason to trust me. You invite me here, and the first thing you ask is for twenty-five percent of my invention."

"If we're to work well together, there must be no business misunderstandings between us. I tell you straight out, this switch of yours is a long shot. But I'm in the business of risk and long shots. Besides, a man must eat. I could tell by your letter you're a smart young man, Kalinin, a little rough at the edges but smart. I'm smart too, and less rough than I appear, believe me. I have connections through my family that will open doors for you, and I'm an excellent lawyer, the best you'll come upon. I'll serve you well for my twenty-five percent. But perhaps you need time to think about the arrangement. Do you have a place to stay?"

"No."

"You can stay here. It's only me in this mausoleum. My wife is dead, you see, and my daughter is off to boarding school. She wants to become a doctor and tend the peasants. I've taught her well. Come, I'll show you to your room."

"Excuse me, Dobrinsky . . ." He made his voice sound churlish. "What if I decide not to sign your contract?"

"Then you'll have to find your own place to live," he replied humorlessly.

"Can I show you my switch first?"

"I'm not your mother or father, Kalinin, eager to tap you on your head and tell you it's a job well done."

Alexei blushed deeply. "I'm not asking for that."

"Besides, if I saw your switch, I might become greedy. Then again, I might become totally uninterested. Come now." Dobrinsky rose from his chair.

Alexei stared at Dobrinsky, thinking he hated the fat, pasty-skinned man. Twenty-five percent, indeed! Hardly better than Matyushin himself. Alexei wished Tolya were with him, or Kira. They would tell him what to do. Yes, Tolya would tell Dobrinsky to go to hell with his twenty-five percent. Kira would tell him to follow his instincts. "I'll sign your damn contract!" he blurted out suddenly.

"Good," Dobrinsky replied disinterestedly. "Come, sit down. The papers are here on my desk. Then I'd like to see this invention of yours."

Alexei saw Yuri Dobrinsky drunk only once, three months after Alexei arrived in Petersburg; it was the night they signed their first contract with the Glazunov Railroads for five hundred switches. In an unexpected burst of enthusiasm, Yuri took Alexei to dinner at Donan's and on the way home stopped to purchase five bottles of the finest French champagne. Alexei was amazed at the change in Yuri, who urged Alexei to play the dust-covered piano and clapped his hands, practically doing a jig to the tunes. It was almost three in the morning when they settled around the kitchen table with the last bottle of champagne.

"Is there a bit of your brain left that isn't pickled, young Alexei Yakovlevich?" Yuri demanded.

"Ha, me!" Alexei chortled. "I could drink this bottle alone and still walk a straight line."

Yuri scratched his almost bald head, leaving the few hairs to curve like a canopy. He frowned and breathed deeply, expanding his chest. "Money, young Alexei Yakovlevich. We've a definite cash problem."

Alexei wasn't certain what Yuri meant.

"Here we've signed a contract to produce five hundred of your switches, and I doubt we've the rubles to produce ten. There's my yearly stipend from my grandfather, which, after living expenses these days, barely leaves me anything. What about Kira Yurovna? She's a frugal woman. Surely she has some stash from her trapping. Ah, but would it amount to nearly enough to start manufacturing?" Yuri despaired and plopped his head on his folded arms.

Alexei feared Yuri might cry. "Yuri Nikolaievich," he whispered, slipping his arm about Yuri in drunken camaraderie. "What if I told you I've a necklace in my possession which is worth thousands of rubles, perhaps more than I know?"

Yuri looked up and tried to steady his bleary-eyed gaze on Alexei. He was quiet for a long time, as if trying hard to gather his thoughts. "Would I, young Alexei Yakovlevich, be correct in assuming then that this necklace would be dangerous to sell on the open market?"

Drunken tears welled in Alexei's eyes. "Am I a fool to trust you, Yuri Nikolaievich?"

"As Christ himself said, my boy, let him who is without sin cast the first stone."

They embraced, kissed each other's cheeks, and Alexei pushed himself away and stumbled to his room, hurrying back downstairs with his sack. He cleared the center of the table of the champagne bottles and dumped out Matyushin's money and the diamond necklace.

Yuri gasped in amazement. "Praise God, praise God!" he repeated, and crossed himself. He picked up the necklace and fingered it, holding it to the candlelight. "Don't ever tell me where you got all this from, Alexei, my boy, ever—I don't want to know."

Alexei flopped down into his chair before he fell. "What do you think, Yuri Nikolaievich, can we start manufacturing the switches with this?"

"Yes, yes, absolutely! First I must, like the alchemist, change these stones into cash." He eyed Alexei cautiously. "How careful must I be?"

"Extremely."

"All right. I know some people in Geneva. We'll leave tomorrow. How much cash is here?"

"I never counted it."

Yuri studied him a moment and his drunken gaze seemed to steady. "That surprises me, almost as much as your showing me this does."

"Why?"

"It's rare to come upon such complexities in one so young. This stash"—Yuri nodded to the jewels and money in front of them—"fills you with pain and guilt."

Alexei looked away, feeling his face flush hotly.

"Shall I tell you something about myself, then? Something to balance the scale?"

"It doesn't matter."

"Yes, I think it does. I know a terrible secret about you. Now you must know one about me." Yuri's voice was suddenly very sober. He refilled both their glasses. Then, leaning back in his chair, he thought awhile. "I will tell you about my grandfather," he began. "For all the world to see, he was the perfect gentleman, but hate and brutality ran his life. He despised my father and he despised my mother for loving my father. He took us into his house when my father was sent to Siberia, but he treated my mother little better than a servant. She lived in mortal fear of him, not so much for herself as for me. He was a soldier, you see, and his discipline was swift and strong. He punished me for the slightest infraction of a rule, but the most important rule was that I forget I ever had a father." Yuri paused then; his lips quivered; tears fogged his glasses and spilled helplessly down his round cheeks.

Alexei sat very still, mesmerized, even frightened by the flood of emotion in this heretofore stoic.

"The bastard told me if I ever mentioned my father or used the name Mayakovsky he would whip me. I didn't, not for years. I was terrified of my grandfather, especially after my mother died. Then his control over me was complete. I was a private in his obscene little army." Yuri fumbled for his handkerchief, not even trying to stem the flow of drunken tears. "When I was about twelve, I found a box my mother had given me. I'd quite forgotten about it, you see. It was filled with pictures of my father—there were newspaper clippings of his arrest and trial, even love letters he'd sent to my mother." Yuri's voice broke again and again.

"I read them over and over, and the more I did, the more of a hero my father became to me. I told my teachers in school that I was to be called Yuri Andreievich Mayakovsky . . ." He swallowed hard, as if pained by the memory. "My grandfather heard of it and he whipped me terribly. I remember his face when he'd finished. He was sweating and red from the exertion, but he seemed happy, happier than I could ever remember, as if he'd been waiting for the chance to whip my father out of me. I defied him several times after that, but he was a brutal man. I wasn't strong enough to face his beatings long. Do you know what it is . . . ?" He paused. "Do you know what it is to be so completely dominated by another human being that terror becomes your shadow?"

Matyushin, Alexei thought, but he said nothing.

"For years, I did everything my grandfather wanted of me. I even agreed to go into training for the Imperial Guards. My grandfather got me an audience before the Czar. I impressed the Czar. Following my grandfather's script, I knelt before the Czar and kissed his murdering hand, swearing eternal allegiance. I told him I forsook my father's name and abhorred his wretched memory. I pleaded with the Czar to allow me to prove my loyalty. I played the part assigned to me well. When I was finished, the Czar actually had a tear in his eye. He said my place in training for the Imperial Guards was assured. My grandfather was ecstatic. I think he believed in that moment I was truly his creation, perhaps even his son. I did not even recoil when he kissed me. I wanted him to believe he'd won, for in my heart I knew he would never change me or even bend me. Thankfully, he died shortly before I was to go into training for the Guards. Most of his money went to my uncle, but I received a yearly stipend, enough for me to go to law school."

"So you never entered the Imperial Guards?"

"No. I paid off a doctor who wrote a letter saying I had a weak heart and could not complete any military service. I went to law school thinking I would help men like my father. I did brilliantly in law school. The law is one of my callings, but . . . I have another, Alexei Yakovlevich, as dangerous to me in these times as this necklace and these rubles are to you. All I have told you is background to this: have you ever heard of the People's Will?''

"Of course, everyone has. They're the terrorists who killed Alexander II.''

"As they were the progeny of my father and his heroic conspirators, I am the progeny of the People's Will.''

"You were part of the assassination squad?'' Alexei's eyes were open wide.

"Unfortunately not. I never knew them personally. But in my heart and my mind they live still. You see, the police think that with the execution of Zhelyabov, Sophie Perovskaya, and the others, the People's Will was destroyed, buried. That isn't true. Terrorism will never die in the Russian soul until we are all free. The People's Will will rise again someday—I will personally see to that, and the money which I shall make from your invention will make it possible. I shall avenge my father's death. I shall finish what he started.''

"This is very dangerous, Yuri Nikolaievich. People who even speak of such things are thrown into prison.''

"Not prison, torture or death has ever stopped a true Russian in his fight for freedom. The revolution will rise again, I promise you. And your switch, the child of your mind, will help make it possible. How does that sound to you?''

"I'm not a revolutionary. I don't care in the least about politics.''

"You will learn that a man has many faces to show the world. There isn't any absolute single path he must or even should follow. Those who do, become obsessed, fanatical, ultimately doing disservice to those about them. Perspective is vital in life, even more so in revolution—or one runs the risk of being caught up by his own dreams and rhetoric. My father did that. It was his downfall. Yes, there are many roles a man can play in life; he must, to keep an edge up on the enemy and stay on an even keel with reality. Take you, for example—I believed you were an honest young man with an agile mind, and you bring me this!'' He eyed the money and the jewels.

"I have found few truly honest men.''

Yuri laughed in delight. "Morality weakens, for the opponent is never moral.''

"And your revolution?''

"Our enemies would shoot us in the back if given half the

chance. We must stand ready to do the same. We must create our own morality, our own definition of 'criminal.' "

"Then you believe the end justifies the means."

"Absolutely."

"No matter who gets hurt."

"Survival is meaningless if it isn't successful, my young friend. Now, we should get to bed. We'll have to rise early in the morning to set our plans for Geneva. Here . . ." He picked up Alexei's sack and swept the jewels and money back into it. "Will you sleep well tonight?"

"I'm not sure."

"I will not kill you for your treasure, if that's what you're thinking! No, we've far too interesting a future together."

"Who is Anna?" Kira asked one morning as they sat drinking tea. They'd been in the big house a week.

Alexei's heart fluttered at the sound of Anna's name. "Did I talk of her in my fever?" he asked cautiously.

"Often you raved of her. And sometimes in your sleep still, you hold me and murmur her name."

"She's just a girl."

"A very powerful girl. She has some hold on you, not only on your heart but on your soul."

"Do you ever stop to question that crystal ball inside your head?" he snapped, feeling suddenly annoyed.

"It is no crystal ball, only my feelings. And they tell me this fever which brought you to me is no sickness, but the fire of Anna. There is something maddening which keeps her from you. Yes, I can see it now as we speak. Your face grows fierce and your fingers want to crush something."

Alexei felt the fight slip from him. Kira was right. Kira was always right. Perhaps that's why he kept returning to her. When the rush of life became too confused or exhausting or simply meaningless, he escaped to Kira. She always seemed to expect him; she always had time for him, and he always left her renewed. Leaning across the table toward her, he smoothed back some flyaway hairs and gazed lovingly into her face, stroking the paper-thin creases of her skin. Her aging was a comfort. "It's all too complicated. Besides, her family forbids her seeing me. They've taken her someplace. I don't know where."

"And you love her?"

"It's madness, but I do. Yet, at the same moment I feel my love for her carrying me beyond the constraints of anything I've known as love before, I feel coarse, like a toad, as if my very touch would mar her."

"Oh, my poor Alyosha." Kira held his hand to her lips. "All your life you have waited to truly love someone."

"It can't be Anna," he insisted, his voice tight, his tone cold. "Besides, I love you!" he burst out, feeling suddenly the truth of those words. "I do love you, Kira. You must know that."

"Oh, yes, we love, Alexei, but it is not a love that binds forever. Like birds that come and go with the passing seasons, the returning is no less joyous for its leaving. Yet the leaving is inevitable."

"Not this time." He reached into his pocket for some envelopes. "Here, I've written to Yuri Dobrinsky giving him the power of attorney in most matters. Also to my friends Alexander Ryabushinsky and Andre Bobrinsky in the Symposium, and to my mother and Misha. I'm never returning to Petersburg or Moscow again, Kira. Never."

The snows and bitter, howling winds of late February and early March were relentless. Snow piled high, reaching above the windows. Even Kira no longer braved the cold. It was almost two months before they could make the trip to Krasnoyarsk, and Alexei pored over the newspapers he and Kira brought home. He spread them on the floor chronologically, so as not to miss any events, and glanced from headline to headline.

WAR WITH JAPAN!

BATTLESHIPS CZAREVICH, RETVIZAN AND PALLADA TORPEDOED AT PORT ARTHUR

ALL RUSSIA SUPPORTS OUR BELOVED MONARCH!
Students Mass in Front of Winter Palace Singing "God Save the Czar" and "Holy Russia"

30th January 1904, St. Petersburg. The Czar was greeted with the cheers of countless throngs of well-wishers as he and his Empress stepped from the state dining room to a porch facing the square. Chants of "Hail to the Russian Army and Fleet!" "Long Live Russia!" and "Hail to the Czar!" rose to the heavens from the crowd of mostly students, who then marched down Nevsky Prospect, picking up new recruits as they went. Everyone was soon mixed together—generals and tramps marched side by side, students with banners, and ladies, their arms filled with shopping. Everyone was united in a feeling of unity and sacrifice. Everyone sang our national hymns. Patriotism has returned to Russia. A spokesman for the Czar said his generals promise a speedy defeat of Japan.

INDUSTRIALISTS THROW PRODUCTION INTO THE WAR
EFFORT
Millions Donated to the Red Cross and Defense Funds

JAPAN'S SHIPS SWEEP SEA
DEFENSE OF PORT ARTHUR HELD IN DOUBT
Completion of the Trans-Siberian Railroad is a
National Priority

MINISTER OF FINANCE, SERGEI WITTE, THREATENS
RESIGNATION

"What do you think?" Kira solemnly asked Alexei as she
knelt beside him.

"I think Sergei Witte is a damned fool if he resigns!" He
pounded the papers with his fist and rose to his feet.

"You know this man, Sergei Witte?"

"Yes, I know him. He's the only one who can bring a
semblance of sanity to this whole insane affair."

"This is bad for the revolution, then. So many people are
supporting the Czar now. This is not what men like you and
Yuri Dobrinsky want."

"Want?" he asked, looking at her curiously, and as suddenly
as the pounding adrenaline had exploded within him, it quieted.
What the hell did he care about the Czar's war or what Sergei
Witte did with his life? He, Alexei, was at peace—for the first
time in years—and he was not about to give it up.

"Ah, Alyosha, you are too important to be hiding up here
when Russia needs you."

"Russia gets along just fine without me."

"Sure—you come to see me and we are at war!"

"And it all happened because I am here with you?" he teased.

"Be serious. You know what I mean. And you know where
your place is now."

"You're wrong this time, Kira. I'm not a politician, nor am
I a fighter. I'm simply a man who came up with an invention
that made him a lot of money. I spent my youth making that
money make more money, and now I want to enjoy life."

"You dream, Alyosha, you always were such a dreamer."

"My dreams these days are better than ever, wiser."

"I think not." She smiled sadly.

"Listen to me, Kira. This rash of support for the Czar is
only temporary. Soon, as more and more sons and husbands
die and people stand in longer and longer lines for bread, the
people will turn their backs on the Czar and take to the streets
again in defiance. It's impossible for Russia to win this war.

Our only line of connection to Port Arthur is the ten thousand miles of single-track of the Trans-Siberian Railroad—which isn't even complete.''

''You will be needed to help complete them, then.''

''Let them need me, let them need me all they want. I won't help this war effort, not a bit.''

''So many will die. Perhaps with your help . . .'' Kira was confused.

''The war can only hurt the Russian people. I will not support it.''

''Like your friend Sergei Witte. Perhaps that is why he wants to resign. For the same reason you will not return. Perhaps you and Sergei Witte are together on this. You both hope that without you the Czar will be defeated.''

''The Czar *will* be defeated, Kira. That is his destiny. Mine is to have nothing more to do with that world.''

PART THREE

THE PEDDLERS

CHAPTER TWENTY-TWO

Irina and Misha lived together in the house on Zhukovskaya Street under their real names. Stepan lived with them, playing the role of the valet, Lev. Olga was the housekeeper, and Josef was introduced to Agafia Markovna, the busybody land-lady, as Josef Grekov, cousin of Master Misha come to stay with the young couple while in mourning for his young wife, recently died of a fever. Josef's bereavement explained his shocking appearance. Always thin, he had grown bony and pale in the month since Katya's and Vera's deaths. His di-sheveled clothes hung scarecrowlike on his body, and deep circles blackened his eyes, giving him the appearance of a wild man.

"You're catching your death!" Agafia Markovna would shout as Josef took his gangling strides down the hall and out the front door. "Your hat, Grekov. You'll catch your death without your hat and scarf!"

Josef never so much as acknowledged the landlady's exis-tence.

"Poor boy," Irina despaired to Agafia Markovna. "And he was once the image of social grace. Can you imagine?"

It was Olga who insisted it was necessary to keep Agafia Markovna apprised of any odd movements or changes in their lives. For the landlady watched the comings and goings of her tenants with an eagle's eye, and loved nothing better than an invitation from Olga Gambarova for tea. Agafia Markovna wandered about the young couple's front rooms oohing and aahing over everything from their furniture to their curtains, their ornate silver samovar, their fine linens and Oriental rugs. She noticed anything new, and gazed as if transfixed at the silver- and porcelain-framed photographs of the Rantzau and Kalinin families on the piano, always careful to wipe any smudges with the edge of her apron. Then she sat down to tea with the arthritic Olga Gambarova and bemoaned the sin-ful union of the young couple.

"The young master is out, then, is he, Irina Ilyanovna?"

Agafia Markovna questioned as she delivered the mail one afternoon, craning her neck to see beyond Irina into the apartment.

"You know he is, Agafia Markovna. It's Thursday. Misha always has tea with his grandmother on Thursdays."

"And leaves an angel like yourself alone."

"Not that I mind, Agafia Markovna. Everyone needs time alone. Would you like to come in for some tea? I'm sure Olga Fyodorovna could fix some."

"No, no, I wouldn't want to impose. I was just wondering . . . oh, you know it's my old worry—has Mikhail Anatolyevich made his intentions clear yet?"

"Not yet, Agafia Markovna." Irina smiled demurely. "If he does, you shall be the first to know."

"Oh, no, not me, praise God. Your parents should know first, for surely it is a union devoutly prayed for. Has he given you any indications . . . ?"

"Misha and I live for our passion. There is nothing else that matters." She smiled sweetly, and lowered her eyes modestly.

Agafia Markovna blushed and crossed herself three times. "I pray for you, Irina Ilyanovna. I want you to know I pray for your marriage."

"Thank you, Agafia Markovna. And I thank God I have you as my voice to heaven. God will reward you. Now, come in for some tea. Please, I insist. . . ."

Misha and Irina always left the house on Zhukovskaya Street dressed in their aristocratic finery. They stopped to chat with Agafia Markovna while Stepan as the valet scurried about, busily loading the carriage with his master's belongings; he held doors, bowed and smiled deferentially, but no sooner was the carriage several blocks from Zhukovskaya Street than Stepan jumped down from beside Kiril in the driver's seat and disappeared for the day, often late into the night. Misha and Irina drove on to one of the several "safe shops" that Savva had identified, stores of sympathetic merchants on Nevsky Prospect whose establishments had back exits into open-ended alleyways. There they exchanged their fine clothes for the ragged dress of the peddlers Timofey and Lukyera from Kiev. At Stepan's insistence, they had retired the disguises of Sonya Mikhailovna, peddler of religious and bridal goods, and of Igor, the idiot leather man.

"It's amazing you two weren't arrested and tossed for good into the Fortress!" Stepan barked when he heard of Irina's near miss with the police. "Peddlers *never* talk to police un-

less they need something. And then they *have* something to
sell in return, something other than their gamy, insect-ridden
bodies,'' he said pointedly to Irina. ''If a cop wants a whore,
he goes to a whore, not a peddler. It's *information* that buys
information. Remember that next time, Irina!''

Misha bristled at Stepan's dictatorial overbearance, but he
never voiced his feelings, not even to Irina. Fanaticism notwithstanding, Stepan Ostravsky had a mesmerizing energy
about him. In truth, Misha thought Stepan somewhere between a hero and a madman. He was amoral, the perfect
facade of a man, a beguiling Trojan horse knowing neither
guilt nor remorse. His guts seemed made of bullets and steel;
his brain perked constantly; he was an instinctive political
beast, and Misha felt naked in his presence. He understood
why Irina both loved and hated the man.

What made living with Stepan in the house on Zhukovskaya Street bearable was that he was away more often than
not. Even present, he seemed absent. He rarely spoke, and
listened without comment to daily reports from Irina, Misha,
and Josef. He ate alone usually, holing up in his room with
his cigarettes, vodka, his books, and his manifestos. He left
Irina lists of chores, pages and pages of his writings to be
edited and copied.

There were also the times when Stepan inexplicably exploded with the aggressiveness of an untamed tiger, stomping
about the apartment, turning off the music without asking
who was listening, slamming doors, shooting off orders to
Irina in particular, criticizing work she, Misha, and Josef had
done, ranting about selflessness, dedication to the workers
and peasants, and finally disappearing into the streets or into
his room for hours.

Then even Olga, who was constantly challenging Stepan's
headstrong leadership with her own forty years of experience,
dared not cross him. ''Whatever's eating him, leave him be.
It will pass. I've known men like Stepan Stepanovich. They
have furies inside their heads that have nothing to do with the
revolution. No one can help them. The furies must sleep of
their own accord.

Misha looked forward to the moment when Stepan left their
company each day; only then could he fully gear up for the
role of the peddler Timofey from Kiev. He could feel himself
relaxing as soon as Stepan was gone. The constrained distance between Irina and himself melted as they began talking
to each other in the vernacular of the street. Misha's shoulders

rounded, affecting the look of a man bent from carrying a heavy pack through frigid streets for too long. He stood on corners selling his children's wind-up toys, while Irina as Lukyera hawked linens and petticoats.

Misha's friendly manner was welcomed readily among the street people, but it was Irina with her colorful brashness and slatternly ways who won their hearts. She was always good for a raunchy story or joke about her many famous lovers from her glory days, most especially a man most hated amongst the peddlers, chief of the Okhrana, Leonti Yermolov. At Stepan's suggestion, Irina carried a cheap bottle of vodka to pass around each night. Also, at Stepan's suggestion, Irina and Misha spent several nights in the street. They told Agafia Markovna they were going to Moscow for a few days.

The homeless band of peddlers slept in makeshift tents about roaring bonfires behind the Hay Market on Sadovaya Street. Fortifying their insides with as much vodka, wine or beer as could be found, and padding their skin with countless layers of castaway clothing and newspapers, the little band huddled closely to keep away the cold of the Petersburg nights. Misha slept near Irina, but held a Browning pistol tight in one hand; Irina clutched a knife. Misha slept so close to her, he could hear her restless breathing. It was the nearest he'd come to Irina since they'd moved into the flat on Zhukovskaya Street. There Misha slept on the green leather couch in the living room; Olga and Stepan slept in the servants' quarters, and Josef on a cot in the dining room. Irina had the master bedroom, which she shared with no one.

After four nights in the streets, Misha and Irina could barely walk from stiffness, and they yearned for hot baths and decent food. On the evening of the fifth day, Irina proudly announced to the compatriots of their shadowy counterworld that she and Misha had found a home with four walls and a stove. None of the other peddlers questioned or asked for an address; they were used to migration, a run of good luck, a run of bad, and the next morning Misha and Irina were welcomed back to the streets to peddle their wares. Their acceptance in the society of the streets was complete.

In the weeks that followed, they learned much about the undercover police and could, with a glance, tell a true peddler from a cop; the latter was stonefaced, never hawked his wares, rarely walked far from his appointed position, and was almost always eating. At the end of a long, cold day, the true peddlers, even those with "homes" to go back to, congregated behind the Hay Market, sitting about bonfires, nibbling on day-old cakes and gingerbread and drinking the strong dregs from the tea sellers' steaming copper samovars spiked with Irina's spirits. They drank from tin cups while holding a lump of sugar in their teeth and talked of everything from the weather to family feuds, aches and pains and the cost of living. It was easy, even natural, for Irina and Misha to turn the discussion finally to the police for an exchange of information. The peddlers were obsessed by the police infiltration of their trade, which they insisted was not only usurping needed territory but also scaring off the buying public. An undercover policeman, having little or no interest in selling his brass, linens, leather, tin or wooden goods, ignored prospective buyers, and if that didn't work, he snarled—worse, ordered them to be on their way.

"Aye, and we've left the land for this misery," a woman named Dunia wailed, wiping her nose with the corner of one of the many woolen scarves tied about her head. " 'Twas better to be sipping potato-skin soup than walking yer feet to the bone, and for this!" She held up her stale cake, then stuffed it into her coat. "It's all me husband will have to eat tonight, laid up as he is with a rotting foot."

" 'Twill be no better for them on the land, if it ever was. It's dreams of sleeping in yer mama's arms and guzzling her warm milk rather than potato-skin soup that brings you back to better times!" Ignatich, who sold tin goods, guffawed.

" 'Twas never better times, truly." A nameless old woman crossed herself.

"I'd still rather be walking in the fresh air than digging up rocky soil for another or slaving in them dark factories, praise God!" a pimply-faced young man who recently joined the group insisted as he wiped the top of the vodka bottle with his sleeve before downing a gulp. "Give me the roaming life anytime."

There were nods and mutterings of agreement.

"I'll tell you what I heard, talking as we are of the land," a tall, thin, gray-bearded man named Feofan spoke up. Feofan sold smooth colorful stones he claimed he dug from the Siberian ground himself, although rumor had it he'd never set foot outside of Petersburg in all his sixty years. Still, quiet settled about the group whenever Feofan spoke. The little he said was always of interest. "I hear the police are moving to the countryside, not alls of them, mind ya, but the mucky-mucks. There's to be war with the yellow devils, I tell ya, and any day, too. The police be needing to drum up support for the Czar, hanging them peasants who refuse to fight. Hanging them who burns the masters' fields, too. Me cousin from the steppe comes to Petersburg to work last week—to starve, I tell him. Anyway, he says more fields were black last harvest than gold with wheat. Says the peasants would rather burn the fields than have their sweat stolen.''

The nameless old woman laughed raucously. ''They'll pay, they will. The poor always pay—if not by their sweat, then by their useless necks. The Czar will break them with the hangman's noose and leave their hearts and bellies to the buzzards.''

''Why do they send Petersburg police to hang peasants, eh, Feofan?'' Irina spit as she spoke. ''Where'd you hear such lies?''

''Ain't no lies, Lukyera, may God grant me peace. It's rumored more than once. I heard it in the air, you see, flying the way words do. That friend of yours, the pox-marked fiend, Yermolov. He's leaving town, he is. Maybe not to hang peasants, though. Who knows? Maybe he's got a tryst with the devil, he has, deep in the Caucasian woods. Yermolov, the Czar, and the devil. Planning to sell the soul of Russia, they are!'' Feofan scratched his head under his furry cap and chuckled, showing a gaping hole where teeth once were.

The conversation quickly turned, and it was too dark and cold to question Feofan more on his news, but the next day Irina and Misha spotted him selling his wares along the Moika Canal. Buying his time with a pint of beer and some salted fish, Irina plied Feofan for more information.

''Knowed you be after me, Lukyera. I did. I told Mushka, I did. I said to Mushka last night that Lukyera will be picking after me brain, she would, wanting to know more of her torturer.''

''You're a smart fella, Feofan. That's why you do so well, eh?'' She nudged him with her elbow. ''But come now, ya beetle dung. I bought ya the pint. When are ya gonna tell me what I need to know?''

''Afraid you'll be disappointed, love, and won't want to spend no time with old Feofan.'' His merry smile vanished. ''Don't have much more to tell ya, love. Just words on the air is all I heard, that your Yermolov is thinking of leaving Petersburg for a time. Be good for us wanderers, eh, maybe his coppers won't be hanging around so.''

''When's he leaving? Did you find that out?'' Irina's voice sweetened.

Feofan scratched his beard and downed his beer. ''Couple of weeks, I hear.''

''For how long?''

Feofan shrugged. "Long as it takes for a man to hang peasants, I suppose. And maybe to do a thing or t'other."

"Aye, and so you do have something else to tell me, love?"

Feofan took another swig, wiped his mouth on his sleeve, and shrugged. He stared down at his rag-wrapped feet, then at Irina and Misha. There was a seriousness in his eyes that had never been there before. He both mellowed and seemed to gain more authority at the same moment. Then he shuffled close to Misha and Irina, so close their faces were almost touching. "Ya ain't peddlers, are ya?" he whispered hoarsely, more merriment in his tone than threat.

"And what ya be meaning by that?" Irina shoved him roughly with both her arms.

"I seen you, I been watching ya. Ya almost true, almost to thems that don't think, that is. But Feofan thinks." He patted his finger on his head. "That's why Feofan's got what he gots. I ain't no fool. Ya be revolutionaries, don't ya?" His eyes opened wide and the wrinkles of his skin seemed to dance. "Sure as I can smell Satan, I figured you ain't no cops, but ya ain't no peddlers neither. I'm right, ain't I?" he gleefully demanded, jumping from one foot to another.

Misha looked about to see if anyone was listening while Irina herded old Feofan nearer to the canal.

"No, no, now don't be doing an old man no harm!" he pleaded fearfully.

"I'm not, don't worry," Irina promised as she slipped her arm around the old man. "Just keep your voice down and don't look so scared. Have you told anyone else your thoughts about us?"

"Just Mushka, me cat, and he won't talk, praise God. But there's them amongst us that'd sell their soul to the Czar if the price be right, but not me, not old Feofan, hee-hee. I'm with ya, always been." He looked about and whispered, "I hate the Czar, believe me. He's no friend to the likes of a wanderer. What he ever done to make me life happier, eh? He wouldn't give half a kopeck for me leg, much less me miserable life, God knows. No, not him nor the likes of him. I'll work for ya, I will. I read the wind. Ya can use me." He winked.

Irina looked at Misha, and he nodded. "I think you speak the truth, old man. What do we pay you?"

"Whatever strikes ya fancy, like ya did today. Ain't much I need in life that costs even a poor man's fortune. I'll tell ya now, I'll tell ya why they say Yermolov's taking off. Seems he's got trouble in his own home."

"His wife?"

"No, Lukyera, don't ya listen? The Okhrana. There's another one wanting his job, a rival. I hears Yermolov's scareder than if the devil himself barred his way. His rival's smart, and well-connected to God."

"God?" Irina asked cautiously. "What do you mean, Feofan?"

"A friend of the priest, he is. Hee-hee, an unlikely match, some say, police and priests. Not me, not Feofan. I'd as soon confess me sins to a rag picker as a priest. Hee-hee!"

"Who's the priest, Feofan—the one with the police?" Misha urged.

"Georgi Gapon, it's what the wind says. A poor fool, aye, a lad off the land, he was, good of heart but tricked by the devil hisself." Feofan's lips turned downward as if he might cry.

Irina hesitated a moment, trying to remember the name of the Okhrana agent in the papers stolen from Paris. "Akimov!" she exclaimed suddenly. "Feofan, did you ever hear of a man named Akimov?"

Feofan stared thoughtfully, the name Akimov forming again and again on his silent lips. "Sorry, Lukyera, love. I ain't never heard no one called Akimov."

"That's all right," she promised. "But tell me, who told you about all this?"

"I listen here and I listen there. Who worries about an old man who keeps lice as his bedmates? Glad to know ya now. I got a reason for listenin' now." He smiled happily.

"Thanks, Feofan, truly." Irina grasped his hand warmly. "You find out any dates or names for me, and I'll have more than just a pint and some salted fish."

Feofan stared at the salted fish in his hand, took a bite and put the rest in his pocket. "Savin' it for Mushka, I am." He nodded happily and turned.

"Do you think we can trust him?" Misha asked uncertainly once Feofan was out of earshot.

"Yes, I think so, but don't tell any of the comrades that he figured out who we are as easily as he did, especially Stepan."

Misha rolled his eyes. "I was thinking of asking you the same! But say, who's this Akimov? And what's this business about a priest?"

Irina looked about to make sure no one was listening. "Come, I'm frozen. Buy me some tea, and I'll tell you."

"Yermolov's leaving Petersburg on February 26. That's the date the peddler Feofan told us," Irina announced to the squad as they sat about a table in the elegant dusty-rose and midnight-blue parlor in the apartment on Zhukovskaya Street. A silver samovar steamed on a lace-covered cabinet. Several bottles of vodka dotted the round mahogany-inlaid table along with dishes of herring, whitefish, caviar, breads, and fruit. Decks of cards and chips were in the center, untouched. Irina had told Agafia Markovna that Misha's friends were coming for an evening of cards.

Vladimir, the newest member of the squad, sat on the windowsill, every now and again parting the curtains to look into the well-lit street.

"You think we can count on the date?" Josef asked doubtfully.

"I'd count on the word of a peddler for life itself," Misha said. "Especially Feofan's."

"If he's good, yes," Stepan agreed. "The good ones breathe gossip from the air and winnow out that which comes to be. They're rarely wrong, the good ones. But the bad ones . . ." He grunted in disdain. "They'd as soon sell a revolutionary to the police as fart."

"Feofan's good," Irina insisted. "Besides, he said something else very interesting. Remember in the papers that were sent to Vera in Paris—remember that fellow Akimov, the one connected to the police unions—"

"Alleged police unions," Stepan corrected her.

"All right, alleged, whatever. Anyway, Feofan said Yermolov's rival in the Okhrana had connections to the priest, Gapon, the same priest mentioned in the Yermolov papers."

"Did he use the name Akimov?" Dmitri asked.

"No, I pressed him. But they must be one and the same."

"There are no 'must bes' yet, Irina. Possibilities, only. We can take nothing for granted," Dmitri said thoughtfully. "Did Feofan say anything else?"

Irina glanced toward Misha, who shook his head. "I can't think of anything else."

"Well, I say what we need to verify more than the connection of this Akimov to the priest is when Yermolov's leaving Petersburg," Olga protested. "If the peddler's dates are right, we may well abandon plans of hitting Yermolov until he returns. We don't have enough information to successfully move on him within a few weeks."

"Then we must make it enough, comrade," Dmitri said with quiet authority. "I don't like all these loose ends that keep appearing. Yermolov must not be allowed to leave Petersburg alive. Savva, you've pulled together all the information we have thus far."

Savva nodded. "I've made some maps. And these are the dossiers on Yermolov's captains." He pointed to a stack of brown folders in the middle of the table. "You can all look at them afterward. In fact, given the short time we have, we should all study them carefully. There are sketches Vladimir made as well as comments on the scum's personalities, characteristics, preferences for violence, torture, and so on. Thanks to Josef's and Stepan's sleuthing, we're beginning to get a pretty fair picture of Yermolov's life," Savva went on excitedly, his pale cheeks flushed with color. His eyes seemed to focus on everyone at once and on no one. "Happily, Olga, our friend is not so elusive as he once seemed. We know the house where he lives on Apetarsky Island. We know he leaves there precisely at nine-thirty every weekday morning except Tuesdays and Thursdays, when he spends the night with one of his mistresses in his flat on the Fontanka Canal. We know he travels every Wednesday to Tsarkeyo Selo for his briefings with the Czar, and now we know he is often in attendance at cabinet meetings at the Marinisky Palace."

"We also know he doesn't move without his battalion of spies and special agents," Vladimir interjected. "Our first problem is to find a place where it isn't so easy for the guards to protect him."

"The more public, the better, then," Irina said.

"Public is certainly safer for us, but such safety brings with it the problem of innocent people being killed," Olga said. "Stepan, how powerful are your bombs?"

"If we could be assured of a clear target, I could make them less powerful. I'm thinking of his carriage."

"Then I'm afraid the bomb must be strong. All the ministers' carriages are reinforced with steel, and it is rumored that Yermolov's is stronger than the one built for the Czar himself."

"Excuse me, comrades, but I've gone over Yermolov's route countless times," Savva broke in. "Given the circumstances, it seems to me that the only way we shall ever kill him is by throwing ourselves under the wheels of his carriage with a bomb. I am most ready to die, and would be honored to carry out my duty." The intensity of Savva's voice quieted the room for a moment.

"We're not reduced to a suicide mission yet, Savva, although I thank you for your dedication," Dmitri spoke.

"The proper way is the simplest." Olga Gambarova spoke authoritatively. "It is a time-tested way. Lord knows it was good enough to kill at least one Czar. Four terrorists walk forty paces apart. The first cuts off Yermolov's retreat. The second throws the bomb. The third is backup if the bomb thrower fails, and the fourth uses his bomb only in the case of most dire necessity. With any luck, the first and the fourth will surely survive the explosions, and in the chaos that follows, can come to the aid of both the second and third. Then, as quickly as possible, we all leave Petersburg, separately, to meet in a predetermined place."

"You make it all seem so easy, Comrade Gambarova." Stepan's eyes fluttered.

"In all deference, Comrade Ostravsky, in the past you have acted on your own," Olga retorted. "Your assassinations have been successful, but not coordinated. Neither have they had the sweeping political effect we expect from the death of Yermolov. It would be impossible for you to simply walk up to our target when he leaves a restaurant or while he watches the ballet and put a bullet in his gut."

"I appreciate your advice, comrade," Stepan replied with a hint of sarcasm. He leaned back on the chair and fumbled in his pocket for his cigarettes. "Savva," he said, lighting a match, "let's see your maps."

Savva reached for a large rolled paper and, clearing a section of the table, he spread open a map of Petersburg. Different-colored ink marked Yermolov's routes on different days. "He takes the train to Tsarkeyo Selo from the Baltic Station every Wednesday."

"The morning train," Kiril added.

Stepan tapped his finger on the red mark of the Baltic Station.

"But in the morning the streets will be most crowded," Irina advised.

"I doubt we can approach the carriage if it's not in some sort of traffic," Kiril said. "When the streets are clear, Yermolov's driver goes like the wind. He would run down anyone who didn't move out of his way."

"There are risks that cannot be avoided," Stepan said impatiently. He tapped the table with his fingertips. "When Czar Alexander was assassinated, twenty people lay dying in the snow and many others wounded. Comrade Gambarova can attest to that. The deaths of innocents are regrettable, and we must be as careful as we can be, but the unavoidable is unavoidable. Dmitri Andreievich, do you agree with me?"

Dmitri nodded. "We try. We are as cautious as we can humanly be. But in the end, think of how many people will be saved not only death but also torture once the butcher Yermolov is dead."

The others who had surrounded Savva sat down too. Ste-

pan passed about a bottle of vodka and Dmitri threw a pack
of cigarettes into the middle of the table. Olga Gambarova
cut off a thick piece of bread, spread it with butter, and passed
it to Kiril.

"The date?" Kiril asked anxiously. "When does the dog
die?"

"February 24," Dmitri announced.

"Are you sure, Dmitri Andreievich?" Olga asked.
"Shouldn't we wait? Surely when Yermolov returns . . ."

"I appreciate your concern over the pressure of time, Olga
Fyodorovna, but we can't wait. Think about it: we can't wait.
Leonti Yermolov will die on February 24, 1904. And remember, comrades, that when this happens, he who is not with
us is against us."

Two days later, the peddler Feofan was found frozen to
death under a bridge across the Moika Canal. There were no
marks on his body, but he reeked of vodka. The police said
he had fallen into a drunken stupor under the bridge and
frozen to death. The case was closed.

CHAPTER TWENTY-THREE

"You might bring Irina to tea," Zhenya Kirilovna suggested
as she sat with Misha in Myedved's having tea. "That would
be all right with me, despite what your mother and father
think. I'd like to see this love of yours."

"She hates tea," Misha grumbled. Irritability seemed the
only way to hide the sadness. For even if the assassination
were successful, even if he weren't killed or arrested, he
wouldn't see his grandmother for a very long time, perhaps
ever again. The squad was planning to regroup in Geneva.

"What's causing you to pout so, my dove?" His grandmother squeezed his hand.

"Nothing really. I suppose I'm bored." He shrugged. He
desperately wanted to tell her the truth. She would be so hurt
when she discovered his secret; besides, he needed to talk to
someone about Feofan's death. *Cause of death, drunkenness*

leading to exposure, case closed. Feofan came to Misha in his dreams, his skinless finger accusing, his rasping breath heavy, and, alone in the dark on the green couch in the drawing room, Misha would wake shivering and praying for understanding and forgiveness. For somehow Misha knew as Irina knew—yes, knew but dared not speak—that Feofan's death was no accident.

"Ach, I was afraid you were too rash with your little Duchess," his grandmother was going on. "Why not call it off if you're already bored? Unless, of course, there's something else trying you," she said pointedly.

"No, Grandma, it's nothing like that. Have you heard from Uncle Alexei yet?"

"No, but I spoke to Yuri Dobrinsky just yesterday."

Misha stiffened at the name: *Yuri Dobrinsky*. It was hard to think of Dmitri as Yuri Dobrinsky anymore.

"He says Alexei's probably taken off to see that woman in Siberia. God be praised. . . ." She crossed herself. "Children! What can a mother do? Just when you think you understand your children, you find you know nothing."

Misha smiled. He always found it amusing to hear Uncle Alexei spoken of as a child.

"Yuri Dobrinsky says it's time Alexei would be returning to Siberia. Yuri Dobrinsky told me, he said, 'You know Alexei Yakovlevich, he has an itch to go back there every now and again.' I asked Yuri Dobrinsky if he understood such an itch. Poor Yuri. I should never have insisted. He was so embarrassed with my questioning. Still, I complained . . ." She sighed wearily, and sipped her tea. "A woman needs someone to complain to once in a while—and who have I got? Tolya and Helena. God knows they're your parents, my dove, but they are a sorry pair. . . ." She reached for Misha's strawberry tart, which he hadn't touched, and began to eat it. "You're more like Alexei than either of your parents. . . ." She was staring intently at Misha as if enjoying what she saw. Suddenly her face darkened and her eyes brightened angrily. Stabbing the last piece of the tart with her fork, she blurted out, "Yes, you've got Alexei's blood in you— what with you and the young Duchess living as you are and Alexei traipsing off to Siberia to visit some Mongolian lady trapper!"

"Chukchi, Grandma. They're a tribe. I don't think they're Mongols. Besides, her father was a gentleman from Petersburg."

"Oh, whatever. I never did understand Alexei's fascination with that woman. But tell me, my sweet . . ." Her voice softened, the irritation passing as quickly as it had come. "What hold does this Irina Ilyanovna have over you? She's making you unhappy, that much I'll wager. I can see it in your eyes. And your skin, it's sallow. You don't get enough sleep. And food—is she feeding you enough?"

"I love you, Grandma, you know that." He reached across the table, took both her gnarled hands in his, and bent to kiss them. "I love Mama too—you tell her that, don't you? Poor Mama, and Mousia and the boys. And the baby. You'll tell them all I think of them often, won't you?" A sadness swept over him, and he had to look away.

"Oh, my heart, I fear you are lost to loving this girl. Whatever happened to your interest in the revolution? You were so hot on that when you came out of the hospital. I say, take the revolution over love anytime. It's less complicated."

"And what would you know about revolution, Grandma?" he teased, smiling despite himself.

"When you get to be my age, you know everything, believe me. Old age is like being a poet. You don't have to experience to know. Now come, kiss me, my sweetest soul." She lifted her face toward his. "Let's finish our tea. Then you can take this old body for a walk. The only exercise I get is when I meet you for tea."

Early Tuesday morning, February 23, Misha and Irina went to a chemist shop on Nevsky Prospect to purchase a two-pint bottle of common acid.

"For cleaning purposes, mademoiselle?" the chemist asked, smiling politely at the pleasantly dressed young couple.

"Oh, it's terrible. Mama gave me the most beautiful linen cloth, and I was quite the pig and spilled grease on it. I wanted to surprise my Misha with my own cooking, but to no avail. Now Mama shall be furious at me, and I'm afraid to tell anyone. Do you think Misha and I will be able to get the grease out with this before Mama comes?"

"Absolutely. But be careful to lay some thick clean cloth you have no use for underneath, and scrub from the outside of the stain in."

"You see, my love, it won't be so bad after all," Misha assured Irina as he paid the chemist. With the bottle of acid under his arm, he led Irina from the chemist's to a waiting cab.

Vladimir quickly jumped from the driver's seat and held the door for Irina. "Any problems?" he asked.

"None in the least." Irina couldn't suppress a grin. "Where to now?"

"There's a chemist shop on Znamenskaya Square. You'll get another two pints of the same there. Then we'll go over to Vasilievsky Island and buy the other acid. Stepan's bringing the glycerin and the rods."

After buying the other two pints of acid, Misha drew the curtains of the cab and he and Irina wriggled out of their fashionable dress and into their workers' garb. They folded their fine clothes neatly and hid them under the false bottom of Vladimir's cab.

Vladimir knocked on the roof three times when it was safe, and they slipped outside onto Vasilievsky Island, not far from the university.

"Ready?" Irina asked, tucking some flyaway hairs into her woolen scarf.

Holding his bottles of acid tightly under his arm, Misha took a deep breath and nodded.

Irina smiled expectantly, seeming pale and tired in her drab worker's clothes. The gray woolen scarf matched the threadbare coat which hung like a sack on her tall, thin frame. One of her gloves had a hole in the thumb. No one would recognize her as the reckless young Duchess who sparkled in jewels and gossamer gowns, or even as the bawdy peddler Lukyera of Kiev padded against the cold. "Come, let's hurry." She rubbed her hands up and down her arms. "Stepan hates to wait." Irina secured her packages under her arms and shoved her hands in her pockets. She walked quickly, stiffly, with the air of someone on an important mission.

Misha had to take long strides to keep up with her. He pulled his cap down his forehead, pushed up his collar, and held his head low against the chill wind blowing off the river, whipping icy snow up his sleeves and down his collar, into his eyes, against his nose, and stinging his cheeks. Perhaps if he could touch Irina, slip his arm intimately through hers, he would be warmer. Then the shaking might stop. Probably not. Nothing stopped the shaking lately. It was with him constantly, sometimes vague like a night noise beyond a dream; other times it racked his body like a ghostly rattle of the peddler Feofan.

Are you afraid? he wanted to ask Irina as they walked through the icy, windblown streets of Vasilievsky Island. He wanted to ask someone. He wanted someone else in the squad beside himself to be afraid. They all seemed so caught up in the details, strategies, timing, and movements. None of them but Irina and Misha had known Feofan: *cause of death, drunkenness leading to exposure, case closed.* None of them cared that somehow the insignificant old peddler's death was connected to them too. None of them wanted to hear. All that interested them was Leonti Yermolov. The people's will be done. Within twenty-four hours the butcher Yermolov would be dead.

Misha was so engrossed in his thoughts, he barely noticed the streets of the university district giving way to the dreary, regular, numbered streets of Vasilievsky Island, where the soot from the factory chimneys layered with the snow, making the fading greens, blues, pinks and yellows of the workers' small, wooden houses seem still duller. Gradually odors assaulted his senses: rotting herring and ship ropes fetid from years in the sea; stale tobacco seeped from cracked windowpanes. Rats crawled over garbage heaps. A cat leapt in front of them.

Irina let out a frightened cry. "I'm sorry," she said.

They stared at a miserably dressed young woman, the stringy hair of her uncovered head blowing in the bitter wind as she stood by a mound of frozen garbage, methodically picking through its contents. Occasionally she stuffed something inside her coat. A screaming infant wrapped in rags was strapped to her side.

"Afterward, when it's safe to return to Petersburg," Irina whispered, slipping her arm through his to steady her step on the ice-covered streets, "I'll live with the people in places such as this. I hate the apartment on Zhukovskaya Street. Living there is like being in a safe cocoon. Afterward, when we return," she repeated, "I'll get a job in a factory. I'd like to lead study groups for women. I want to talk to the women," she said intensely. The biting wind gave color to her cheeks. Her nose was running, her eyes tearing as she pushed with him against the wind.

"I think women would listen to you."

"Do you?"

"Yes."

"Stepan thinks not. He thinks I belong in the streets, not in the factories. But come, let's hurry before we freeze to death. We still have another two pints of acid to buy."

They were mixing the nitroglycerin in Kiril's flat. He lived at the end of a long hall, on the top of a three-story house deep in the back streets of Vasilievsky Island. The main room was small and dimly lit, just large enough to hold a table and a bed. The walls were bare, and what little clothes Kiril had were tossed in a heap in the corner. The solitary window was boarded up against the chill of winter. Pamphlets and news-papers were strewn across the bed. The apartment's main claim to fame was a huge kitchen sink, far larger than the one in the apartment on Zhukovskaya Street and perfect for mixing nitroglycerin.

"No smoking," Stepan announced, nodding a brusque hello to Misha and Irina. His shirt sleeves were rolled up and his collar open. Neither he nor Kiril wore a jacket. The room was stiflingly hot.

"I'll take those." Kiril reached with his long, thin fingers for Misha's and Irina's packages and carried them into the kitchen, which was little more than an extension of the main room partitioned by a thin piece of wood. There was the rustling of paper being unwrapped.

Stepan shoved his hands into the pockets of his pants, and held the pose as if he were an actor waiting for a cue.

Misha fumbled to take off his overcoat, and threw it with his hat and scarf on the bed. Unconsciously he felt for his cigarettes, but remembered Stepan's warning and started to help Irina off with her coat instead. He could feel Stepan's eyes mocking. Stepan never helped a woman on and off with her coat, never held a door, never offered a hand.

"So, Stepan, the hour draws near." Irina's smile was rigid.

Stepan flicked her a look, so quick, uncaring, yet posses-sive at the same time. He was a man content with his power.

Misha glanced away. The moment seemed too intimate for a bystander.

Irina coughed and fumbled nervously with the top button of her blouse.

"Everything's in order, Stepan Stepanovich," Kiril an-nounced, gratefully breaking the silence. "We can begin as soon as you're ready."

Stepan turned to Misha, his whole demeanor changed. The comfortable slouch was gone. He seemed larger, almost fill-ing the empty space. His voice took command. "Comrade, you're here because Dmitri Andreievich has determined it's important for you to be here so you can learn. If you survive tomorrow, you'll probably be doing this yourself someday. 'Caution' is the key word. Be clean, go slow, and do every-thing according to the book. *Everything*. There are no short-cuts when you're mixing nitroglycerin. You got that? It's twenty times more powerful than dynamite. It doesn't need a detonator. It can be set off by a match or something so innocuous as the heat of your body. That means you don't do something so stupid as carrying it around in your pocket too long. Also, if you drop it, if you so much as jerk it the wrong way, it explodes and you and everyone around you go with it.''

''I understand.''

Without another word, Stepan walked into the kitchen. He washed his hands slowly and thoroughly, then patted them dry with a clean towel. He reached for a large bowl and placed it in the sink. ''This is the easy part,'' he smirked. ''You and Irina bought two different kinds of acid.'' He pointed to the large blue bottles Kiril had lined up on a shelf above the sink. ''You bought twice as much of one as the other. That's exactly the proportions we need.''

Stepan poured the liquids from the blue bottles into the bowl, waited for them to cool, and rebottled the new mixture. ''Still not dangerous,'' he said, taking the bowl from the sink and resetting the drain plug sideways. ''See this.'' He motioned to Misha. ''Once the sink's full, I'm going to set the flow so the water drains out only as fast as it's coming in.''

Misha nodded. The air was getting very close. The stench of the acid was burning the hairs in his nose.

''It's the next step that can leave you a faceless mess of skin and bones.''

''This is where Stepan's genius comes in,'' Irina said.

Misha wasn't sure whether she was being sarcastic or approving.

Stepan wiped his hands on the towel again. ''A man who wants to live has nothing but the greatest respect for the power we are about to unleash.'' He poured the glycerin into the bowl and slowly, almost timidly, began to stir. He stirred, his fingers clasped tightly about a glass rod, his arm moving rhythmically, at a steady pace.

Misha watched as beads of sweat broke out on Stepan's forehead. Wet circles spread from his armpits.

Irina dabbed Stepan's forehead with a cloth, then wiped the sweat from her own lips.

Misha considered moving away from Kiril, who was chewing anxiously on his lower lip. The heat in the room seemed to ferment his sweat. His eyes stared from the sunken sockets of his bony face.

Misha tried not to breathe; he coughed. A wisp of dark orange smoke was rising from the bowl.

''Shit!'' Stepan quickly handed the bottle of acid to Irina. His face was very red. The sweat was matting his hair. ''Damn shit,'' he cursed, all the time keeping the rod stirring at a constant pace.

''That smoke is a bad sign,'' Irina explained, her eyes never leaving the basin. ''It means the chemicals are heating too fast, but don't worry—the flow of water will cool the bowl. . . ."

Misha felt like a palsied demon had burrowed inside him. Seconds jerked by with unbearable slowness. Stepan's arm never ceased making its circles. Misha never took his eyes from the surface of the bowl. Unbidden, he assumed the task of watching for rising fumes. His legs ached. His mouth was dry. His throat felt like sandpaper. Acid fumes were sucking up all the air in the tiny room.

"Don't," Irina warned as he began to rub his eyes. "It'll make them burn worse."

Misha nodded, and blew his breath up onto his face.

Stepan began pouring the acid again.

Misha lost track of time. He wanted to look at his watch, but dared not. He couldn't seem impatient. God, it was hot. He licked his dry lips. They tasted of sweat and bitterness. A second passed, a minute, an hour; it seemed they were being pulled back in time. Sweat blurred his vision. He needed to see if the dark orange smoke were rising. He needed to watch for danger. Better to watch the smoke than to watch Irina, who was watching Stepan as if there were a straight line between them, an invisible cord. Perhaps it had always been there. And could he blame her? Any woman would want a man like Stepan Ostravsky. Any woman would pick such a man—yes, he was a real man—over a boy like Misha, a boy playing with life, as his grandmother had said. His grandmother was right. He was playing, he'd been playing all along, and suddenly, desperately, he wanted to stop. He hadn't thought it through enough. He hadn't realized what killing meant. He hadn't realized an innocent old peddler would die.

He looked about. What was he doing here in this filthy little flat? What was he doing with these people? Kiril stank like a gymnasium and looked like a derelict with his ragged beard, hunched shoulders, and sunken eyes ringed with sickly black circles. Kiril was watching Stepan. Irina was watching Stepan. What was Misha doing here? He certainly wasn't learning. He could never do what Stepan was doing. Why had he been brought here? He might as well not exist. Perhaps he never had. Only his name, his uncle's name, Kalinin. That's what they'd wanted. A name to match to Irina's name, a name to give them cover, to give Stepan Ostravsky, the revolutionary hero, cover.

It was funny, all of it—at any moment he could die, be blown to bits, and all he could feel was the jealousy tugging at his gut each time Irina reached to wipe Stepan's brow; he saw them lying on the bed; he saw her naked in his brawny arms. He blinked, as if to wash away the image. Burning sweat ran into his eyes. He coughed. Someone else coughed.

"Not much longer," Stepan said. Immeasurable moments later, he added, "This is good. See, the mixture in the bowl stays clear. Come, Misha, look."

Misha thought he took several steps forward. He thought he looked, but he couldn't remember seeing anything.

"He's turning pale. Get him some air, Kiril." It was Irina's voice.

"I'm all right."

"You look awful—"

"The man said he's all right, for God's sake!" Stepan snapped. "Let him be!"

Irina fell silent.

Misha wanted to thank her for her concern. He wanted to thank Stepan, too, but Stepan was still stirring. He poured the second bottle of acid into the glycerin and stirred. He poured the third.

Irina increased the flow of water from the tap.

Stepan stirred.

Irina wiped his brow. She was so close to him.

Stepan stirred.

Time passed and stopped.

Irina loved Stepan.

"Finished," came the dull announcement. There was no triumph in Stepan's voice. He was exhausted. He looked exhausted, sweaty and disheveled, as human as the rest of them. "Misha, you can finish."

"How's that?"

"Those bottles there are clean. Slowly, I mean *slowly*, dip them one at a time into the bowl. Let them fill slowly. That's explosives we've got now. Fill them all up. There shouldn't be anything left."

Stepan left the kitchen. Misha could hear the bed squeak under his weight. Irina followed. The bed squeaked again. There was the hum of low voices. Kiril stayed with Misha. He watched Misha closely. *That's explosives we've got now,* Stepan's voice echoed. He wouldn't think of Irina and Stepan or of Feofan. He wouldn't think. That was the answer. Blindly, he'd do his job.

That's explosives we've got now.

On Tuesday night the squad met for one last time at the apartment on Zhukovskaya Street. Dmitri Mayakovsky was not in attendance; he'd gone over the details with Stepan, who painstakingly reviewed them with the others. Everyone had walked the route from Yermolov's flat on the Fontanka Canal to the Baltic Station countless times. It wasn't a long distance, and it was agreed the best time to throw the bomb was as the carriage came off the Chernyshev Bridge.

Timing was of the utmost importance. Kiril would be driving his carriage just as Yermolov's was crossing the bridge. Irina, who would be walking with Misha, would slip on the icy pavement as Kiril's carriage approached, and Kiril would have to bring his horse and carriage to a screaming halt, coincidentally blocking the bridge and forcing Yermolov's carriage to a stop.

"It's the next few seconds that are most crucial." Stepan breathed deeply as he spoke. His fingers gripped and ungripped a glass of vodka. "Yermolov is like a human timepiece. He moves in the exactitude of seconds. He will leave his apartment on the canal at precisely eight-fifty in the morning. Savva followed him last week and he himself has timed the ride many times. Barring an unforeseen circumstance, it takes ten minutes to reach the Chernyshev Bridge. Vladimir will be standing on the rail of the bridge so he can see Yermolov's carriage approach and, at the same time, drop a red scarf into the canal, which will be Kiril's, Misha's and Irina's signal to move. They will have approximately one minute, if that, to get clear of the bridge before Josef throws the bomb. Savva and I will be backup. We've made the bombs powerful, so you'll have to get away fast. There is no room for mistakes. And if you are captured, if any of us are taken alive, we reveal nothing to the police, *nothing*, not even our names."

"Just as important," Olga added, "we believe nothing the police tell us. Do you understand that? *Nothing*. The police are masters at extracting confessions. And believe me, we have more to fear from their lies than from their whips, fists and guns. They would just as soon tell you lies about your comrades, destroy your morale, your belief in your own people, destroy your heart and your soul, as scar your body. Remember, comrades, *nothing* the police tell you about any of us if you are captured will be true. No matter what they do to you, no matter how hungry or thirsty you are, remember: the police will only tell you lies."

Misha carefully laid out his clothes for the next day, everything down to his underwear and socks. He picked a new suit, not that anyone would see it under his greatcoat. Still, just as with Timofey the peddler, he needed to feel the part. His tie matched the burgundy dress Irina said she was wearing. Misha liked the dress. Irina would wear her sable coat, Misha his sable hat. They would be quite elegant together. Surely attention would be paid to such a fine lady when she slipped. Even the police would come to her aid. The plan was a good one.

Misha crushed out his cigarette, thinking it was his last for the night, kicked off his shoes and thought to change into his nightshirt, but lay fully clothed on the green leather couch instead. He pulled the blankets over himself and rested his head on his arm. His eyes wouldn't close. His mind wouldn't quiet. The details of the strategy repeated like the footfalls of soldiers on parade. Precision was important; it steadied the nerves. He got up to smoke another cigarette and sat by the window. The streetlight cast a dim shadow fogged by his smoke; he tried to imagine a body blown to bits, head and limbs severed, skin and bones scattered like so much dirt in a blustery wind. He couldn't. Instead he saw the girl on the steps of Kazan Cathedral, the girl with hair like snow, the girl with half a face, the girl who had started Misha on this course. Somehow he had forgotten about her, and he closed his eyes, remembering the blood flowing from her hanging white flesh, remembering her triumphant cry; he felt her voice caress him like a kiss. He felt strong. He would think of the girl with hair like snow tomorrow. Tomorrow would be his gift to her and to Feofan. Tomorrow would be the beginning of their revenge. Tomorrow Misha would be brave. He would. And if he died, his uncle, his grandmother, his brothers and sisters, perhaps even his mother, would know in their hearts that he had died bravely.

There was a soft knocking and then a whisper. "Irina . . . It's me, Josef. Can I come in?"

"Of course." Irina laid down her pen and rose from the desk where she was answering a desperate letter she'd received from Anna the week before. Josef's face was flushed, his eyes wild. She thought of what Olga had said when Irina privately had questioned the wisdom of Josef throwing the bomb. "He has nothing to lose, absolutely nothing. His life is intent on one thing only, revenge. He will be the most exact."

Irina wasn't so sure of that as she watched Josef nervously trying to find a place for himself in her bedroom. "Sit down, please." She pointed to a chair and pulled her own close to his.

"I'm sorry to barge in on you like this." His eyes twitched as they avoided hers. "I've been meaning to talk to you for days. There never seems to be the time. And someone's always around. It's the problem with communal living." He smiled uncertainly, then added without emotion, "I will not live past tomorrow."

"Don't say that, Josef." She reached to touch his hand reassuringly.

"It's the truth. But have no pity. I have no fear. I imagine Katya will be with me, waiting for me. When I throw the bomb, her hand shall be in mine." He paused then as if struggling for the right words. "It's hard for me without Katya." His lips quivered then as if he might cry. "I'm such an outsider. I've always been an outsider, you know, all my life, until I met Katya. She brought me into life. She did. It's hard to grow up a Jew in this country, unless you want to stay in the ghetto. Even then . . ." He shrugged. "And I couldn't stand that. Living in the ghetto is like living in jail, breathing in human waste every day, watching young men and women grow old from the fear and poverty." He paused then and fumbled in his pocket for an envelope. "If I die—here, this is a letter to my mother and father. You'll mail it?"

"Of course."

Josef pressed his outstretched fingers tightly together. "You're the only one I trust anymore, Irina, and you must trust only me."

"Josef—"

"Listen to me!" His voice grew low and hoarse. His eyes twitched and darted about the room. He was coiled; each muscle and nerve only needed the slightest touch to spring. "Yermolov didn't kill Vera and Katya. You remember the priest, Gapon, the one mentioned in the Yermolov documents and the one the dead peddler told you about."

"Of course."

"Well, he recently set up one of those *alleged* police unions, as Stepan likes to call them. He's called it the Society of Russian Factory and Plant Workers."

"Here in Petersburg?"

"Yes."

"You're certain it's run by the police?"

"I have no proof, but it's been set up awfully fast, with its own meeting halls and all. A lot for a simple parish priest to do on his own. Anyway, Vera was working on getting the proof when she was murdered. She'd joined Gapon's Society—not as Vera Martova, of course, but as the cotton worker Ilena Rzhevskaya. Katya and I went to a meeting with her. It was quite impressive. This priest has a following. It isn't large yet, but it is devoted. And as Akimov said, Gapon has a certain charisma."

His words buzzed like gnats on a summer night. "But wait, I'm confused, what has all this got to do with Vera's and Katya's deaths?"

"Don't you see, there was no reason for Yermolov to kill Katya and Vera in their beds! It never made sense to me that he was responsible for the thefts in Paris either. If he had been, he would have kidnapped Vera and brought her back to Russia to stand trial. It would have been quite a feather in his cap, don't you see, capturing Vera Martova. Besides, if Yermolov knew where Vera was, he could have found Stepan, possibly even Dmitri. He could have smashed the whole Paris squad in one swoop."

"But if Yermolov didn't steal the documents and have Katya and Vera killed, who did?"

"Father Gapon. It had to be him. He's a driven man. You can see it in his eyes. He wants power. He wants men to fall at his feet. The same madness can drive a priest as easily as a politician or a revolutionary."

"But how could he have known about the Paris documents? And why would he kill Vera and Katya?"

"The why is easy. He didn't want any exposé of the police-organized unions—which would lead directly to him. The how, well . . ." Josef's fingers clenched and unclenched on the arm of the chair. His eyes seemed to bulge, and Irina knew what he was going to say before he spoke. She wanted to block out his words. She wanted to tell him he was mad, but she sat waiting, listening, feeling tied to the death already claiming Josef, pulsating like the nervous thumping in the hollow of his neck. "Only the comrades knew about the documents in Paris. They were stolen too quickly—within a week of Vera's receiving them. Just enough time for someone to get word from Paris to Gapon in Petersburg and have Gapon send his thugs to Paris. And . . ." He paused, closing his eyes and slipping as if exhausted into the cushioned back of the chair. "And only the comrades knew Vera and Katya had returned to Petersburg. The answer is horribly clear, Irina. There's a leak in the squad, a traitor."

Irina paced after Josef left. *Traitor, traitor.* . . . The word assaulted her. If Josef were right, if . . . Time and again her mind recalled Stepan's behavior after the announcement of Vera's and Katya's deaths. The memory of his coldness touched like the finger of death, and she hugged herself, shaking her head as if to shake out the thoughts. Yes, Stepan could be cruel, but a traitor, no. . . . She explored what she knew about each member of the squad, searching for signs, weaknesses, character flaws—searching for a traitor. It seemed impossible. She knew her comrades. She loved them. And Josef, he had made it all seem so plausible, but he had no proof. Josef, poor Josef, his grief was distorting reality. He had only words, supposition. Perhaps . . . Damn, why had he come to her tonight of all nights? She needed a good sleep. She needed to be sharp tomorrow. She needed to trust her comrades implicitly.

Nervously, wanting something to do with her hands, she checked the clothes she had laid out for the morning, her burgundy dress and new boots. Her pearl-cluster earrings were on her dressing table near her hairbrush. She fingered the mother-of-pearl handle inlaid with the pink violets. It was her mother's hairbrush. Irina had stolen it years before, the first summer of her exile, when her parents had taken her to Italy for a holiday. Her mother had gone into a tizzy looking for the brush, and for the moment, Irina had felt guilty, and had almost returned it. The hairbrush was but the beginning of a treasure horde she'd stolen from her mother on her parents' yearly visits: pearl earrings, a slip, a sweater, a bracelet, a pocket mirror, nothing terribly expensive, nothing her mother might call the police over, items her mother usually didn't even notice were missing.

Irina slowly brushed her hair and then rubbed the smooth handle across her lips. What would her mother say after tomorrow? Would she cry if Irina were killed? Would she offer help if Irina were arrested? Would she even come to see her, acknowledge her existence? Her father would visit Irina in jail. He wouldn't have much to say, but he would come, hire her the best lawyer in Petersburg, and make a plea to the Czar, his cousin. It would be futile. The Czar would show no mercy. She wanted none.

Absently she undressed, slipped into her nightgown, and then sat down at her writing table, thinking she should finish her letter to Anna. Irina's mother had verified Anna's contention that she'd been stolen from Petersburg in the middle of the night by Aunt Marya and the dreadful Zinaida Golovnina, dragged to the Crimea, where she was now betrothed to the horrible old goat Prince Tairov.

"Pray for me, my beloved Irina," Anna had written. "And if you can, write back. But write in understatements, as my mother and Zinaida read all my mail. This letter to you has been secretly mailed. Oh, Irina, I dream of our summers here and of the naughty antics of our 'Club.' They were the happiest, freest times of my life, and except for the recent kindnesses of Alexei Yakovlevich, the last happinesses I shall ever know. Love seems a most enviable treasure to me now, forever locked beyond my grasp. Think of me sometimes, Irinushka, when you laugh with your Misha. Imagine your joy echoing all the way to my prison. . . .''

Joy. Irina shuddered. *Laughter.* . . . She was no better off than Anna, poor, dear Anna. Betrayal was as much a prison as the marital web spun around Anna by Aunt Marya and Zinaida Golovnina. It seemed futile to write to Anna. What could she say anyway? What words of hope? Looking back, it seemed Anna had been doomed her entire life. Aunt Marya was no better a mother than was Irina's, perhaps even worse. At least Irina's mother had let Irina go, but Aunt Marya held Anna in a death grasp. *Poor, lovely Anna.* . . . Her marriage to Prince Tairov seemed suddenly overwhelming. Irina crumpled the note in which she'd tried to offer consolation. She could not think about Anna now. A yearning beyond tomorrow was pulling at her.

Without searching for her robe or slippers, she hurried from her room. The hall carpet was soft, crushing in between her toes. She paused gently at the drawing-room door. The moonlight cast a shadow through the window over the couch where Misha lay sleeping. Dear God, she thought. Let Misha live free. She tiptoed past the couch and toward Stepan's room. A shaft of light shone from under his door. He was still awake. Quietly she turned the knob and slipped in.

Stepan was lying in his bed, smoking a cigarette. One knee was bent. A blanket covered him only to his waist.

Her eyes lingered on the dark swirls of hair spreading across his chest.

"What the hell took you so long?" he whispered.

She looked up uncertainly.

He held out one hand. His smile radiated a happiness which drew her back into lush memories.

She hesitated only a moment before pulling her nightgown over her head. Stepan threw off the covers and Irina slipped into his arms. "Jesus, I missed you," he murmured as his mouth hungrily engulfed hers.

CHAPTER TWENTY-FOUR

Misha and Irina left the apartment on Zhukovskaya Street at precisely eight-fifteen the next morning, followed by the valet, Lev, who carried a package in the crook of his arm. They were "so finely dressed, so elegant!" Agafia Markovna exclaimed as they passed the porter's station. The landlady's wide eyes hungrily caressed the dark, rich fur of Irina's sable coat. She followed them to the front door and watched as the unusually thin coachman leapt from his perch to greet his passengers. Taking off his wing-tipped hat, he bowed as he opened the door, helping Irina in first, then Misha. Josef, the bereaved cousin, followed. He and Lev, the valet, each carried similar bundles wrapped in brown paper in their arms. The valet walked particularly slowly, as if not to disturb his bundle; he eased himself onto the seat beside the coachman.

"Move on, fella, there's a good boy!" the coachman clucked, and the horse with its flowing braided mane began a slow walk, the harness bells barely making a sound as the sledded carriage glided on the freshly fallen snow.

It was a brisk, clear morning, and the streets were filling with people making their way to work; but as Misha gazed out the carriage window, his eyes ferreted out the now commonplace black-clad militiamen, the red-coated Cossacks and the undercover police; the latter Misha spied with the accuracy of a hawk sweeping a forest floor for prey. There were police dressed as peddlers; still others were disguised as beggars, and some wore plain gray coats and ordinary fur hats. Misha wondered if he'd ever be able to see people as people again, ordinary people going about their business.

Irina reached over suddenly and touched his hand. She smiled hopefully and then peered out the window again.

Misha watched her, wondering if she could be the same woman with whom he'd trekked through the streets of Vasilievsky Island just yesterday and stood beside in that sweltering room mixing nitroglycerin. It all seemed a dream as he looked at her now, the lovely young duchess. He couldn't remember the last time he'd seen her quite so radiant. Her skin seemed almost translucent and softly colored with hues of pink. Her gray almond eyes sparkled with glints of blue. Her smooth lips glistened with a rosy gloss. The memory of her gliding past him in the night, vanishing into Stepan's room, stabbed his reverie.

Kiril let Stepan off first, several blocks from the Chernyshev Bridge.

"You're next," Irina said to Josef, who was sitting very still and cradling the bomb in his arm. "Good luck." She touched him. He felt like a steel spring.

The carriage stopped. Kiril pounded on the roof. Without a word, Josef was gone. Misha and Irina got out on the far side of the bridge and walked arm in arm toward the Fontanka Canal, a young couple out for an early-morning stroll. It was Misha who caught sight of Savva's long loping stride coming toward them. Dressed as a railway porter with his brass buttons shining, his blue pants sharply pressed, his peaked cap a little to one side, he walked quickly, forever making little dancing steps as if to avoid being jostled by passersby. A brown-wrapped package, identical to the ones carried by Stepan and Josef, was held in the crook of his elbow, and when he passed Misha and Irina, he seemed to look right through them.

Misha and Irina walked slowly. Misha kept tapping her arm in a sign of intimacy. It was only eight-forty. They still had twenty minutes. The morning crowd was growing bigger, and police were more and more in evidence.

"Come, we must look casual," Irina said. "There's a tea seller. Buy me some tea." She nodded toward a table on the corner spread with teakettles of all shapes and sizes, glasses, sweet cakes and mounds of lemons. The copper samovar was furiously boiling, its steam seeming to melt the air.

Misha fumbled with his change while Irina ordered two glasses of tea and chatted easily with the burly tea seller, who constantly jumped from one foot to the other to keep warm.

"A pleasant day for February in Petersburg." Irina smiled, holding the hot glass to her lips.

"It's a terrible time, a terrible time," the tea seller replied, and shook his head as several workers stopped and laid some kopecks on the table, chose some sweet cakes and hurried on.

Misha and Irina slowly sipped their tea.

"Oh, come on now, why so bleak when you have the best spot in all Petersburg?" Irina questioned.

"None is a good spot if yer dead, miss." The tea seller grew serious. He took the padded cover off one of the tea-kettles and stirred the steaming brew. "Too many of the Czar's police around these days, I swear. Half of them you see out there today is coppers." The man's voice lowered.

"Is that so?" Irina looked around, seeming surprised. "Is today any different from any other day, then?"

"No different from some days, different from others. Depends on who's taking the train from Baltic Station, you see. Wednesdays there's always someone who needs the police, you see. The coppers come on Wednesdays, and even check me out, looking inside my samovar they do, as if a fella could hide a bomb there."

Irina and Misha put down their half-emptied glasses and started on. It was eight-fifty-four. Six more minutes. They started toward the bridge. "Well, I feel better, knowing it's like this with the police here every Wednesday," Irina said, and she nudged him. "Look, there's Josef."

Josef was on the far end of the bridge. He was walking stiffly, and his head kept jerking. His skin was very pale.

"He doesn't look good," Irina worried. "Come." They were within five feet of Josef when he disappeared suddenly, swallowed by the crowd.

Irina looked about for signs of Stepan. Her eyes locked on Vladimir instead, who was beginning his walk.

There was a moment's recognition, then Vladimir turned.

She looked at her watch. Three minutes of nine. "There's no more time," she said with calm authority.

Misha nodded and they turned, crossing back to their side of the bridge. The streets were crowded; sledded carriages seemed to form a caravan. There were so many people. Irina's eyes widened as if needing to grow to see. Too many people. Too many people for bombs. She searched for Josef, Savva or Stepan. Vladimir was climbing up on the stone railing. She wanted to warn him, to stop him. There were too many people to drop his red handkerchief.

Irina blinked. She looked at Misha, whose skin was pasty. He shuddered. His lips stretched like bands across his teeth.

"Are you all right?"

"Fine. Just fine." His lips parted in a grotesque smile.

"Too many people."

"What?"

Misha giggled. Or was the absurd sound coming from her?"

"Look." Misha's arm pressed hers tightly. He didn't know how hard he pressed.

Vladimir was on the rock siding of the bridge.

Too many people, too many police.

Vladimir skipped like a schoolboy, more like a dimwit.

Why didn't the police stop him? The police didn't see him. The police were busy, crowding in, making a line, barring all traffic, pedestrians and carriages, holding them up on both sides of the bridge.

Vladimir was skipping, weaving like an acrobat on a tight-rope. Vladimir was alone on the bridge.

A policeman shouted at him to move on.

Vladimir waved like an idiot. He was funny, very funny. Irina had never known Vladimir could be funny. He pulled a red handkerchief from his pocket and tossed it onto the fro-zen canal.

The policeman shouted louder.

Vladimir skipped on.

Seconds passed like hours. Nothing moved except the red handkerchief. It floated like a leaf swept on the current of a bonfire, a swan dance in the face of the inferno.

A black carriage appeared like a ghostly mirage at the far end of the bridge. It was large and heavy but moved quickly. Faster and faster. Police saluted smartly. Another sleigh filled with secret police followed closely behind.

The red handkerchief was gone. The air was very still. Eyes opened. Mouths gaped.

"Now!" Irina whispered.

Misha looked to see Kiril's carriage making its way toward them. Police were waving Kiril to stop. Kiril drove his horses, picking up speed. Police shouted. People pressed forward, necks strained, frenzied to see. Irina and Misha pressed hard-est. The police were concentrating on Kiril's cab. They forgot about the crowd. Misha and Irina broke free.

A policeman shouted, "Go back! Go back!" as if the finely dressed couple hadn't seen the speeding carriage.

Misha's head jerked. He was looking for Josef. He thought he saw Savva's peaked railroad porter's hat.

"Watch out! Watch out!" a woman from the crowd screeched in horror.

He wanted to tell the woman that he was all right, but she was not. Her very life was in danger. He wanted to tell the woman and all the others to run, run for their lives. Instead, he whispered, "Now! Now!"

Irina slipped.

Misha reached to stop her.

Still she slipped.

"Get her up! Get her up!" a militiaman commanded.

Misha pulled at her arm. "Get up, Irina!" He dragged her.

The crowd buzzed in frenzied curiosity. Police shouted, motioned with guns drawn. Two sledded carriages were rushing toward them. Horses whinnied. The carriages swung out, runners skidding. Shouts. A shot. Screams mushroomed. People pushed and shoved. Irina was on her feet. No bomb, no explosion—a shot. Who was shooting? A minute, Stepan had said, a minute to get clear. When did their minute begin?

Misha was running, his chest on fire. Talons of frozen breath tore at his throat. Shouts and gunfire! Where was the explosion? He was running faster inside than out, trying to outrun himself. He looked at her, afraid he'd lost her, and felt her hand in his. Then it came, the explosion. Terror seeped like poisonous gas snuffing out time. Bodies froze in flight. Screams faded on tongues.

"Irina!" He yanked her and they stumbled, tripped, steadied themselves. People were swarming. Misha looked back toward the bridge. A black carriage sped through a roadway cleared by an army. Behind it floated a thin sulfur-yellow cloud, ringed black at the edges.

"That's Yermolov's carriage!" Irina gasped.

"Let's get out of here."

"No, I want to see. I want to find out! Josef, Stepan—"

"We're too far away. They'll never let us through. We were told to meet at the Morskaya Gardens. Orders, we must follow orders." He held her tighter.

"Let me go!" She pounded him, her eyes wild, seeing nothing.

A cab pulled up beside them.

"Kiril!"

"Get in!" The door flew open.

Misha shoved Irina inside. Vladimir was already there; his face was sick with fear.

"What happened?" Misha's voice was too loud. He was shaking. It was dark inside the carriage, the curtains drawn. The world was shadowy. He was shaking, damn. His teeth were chattering.

"Josef's dead."

"What?"

"They shot him before he could get off the bomb."

"But it went off!"

"That was Stepan's. After the shooting, Stepan got his off. It missed Yermolov's carriage and blew up the sleigh with his bodyguards."

"Is Stepan alive?" Irina clutched Misha.

"I don't know. There was so much commotion about Josef and getting Yermolov safely on his way."

"But Josef—how do you know he's dead?"

"They got him at almost point-blank range. They shot him in the head." Vladimir's eyes were wide.

"Oh, God. . . ."

Misha pulled her closer, and reached out for Vladimir; the three of them huddled, breathing as one as the cab raced through the streets.

Olga was waiting at the appointed place in Morskaya Gardens. Fifteen minutes after Misha, Irina, Vladimir and Kiril arrived, Savva came, followed almost immediately by Stepan. Savva carried his bomb, wrapped in his scarf.

"We've failed!" Stepan thundered, his eyes wide with rage and accusation. "We've failed miserably!"

"Josef's dead." Irina's voice was soft. "Why?"

"He should have gotten the damned bomb off. I saw him. I saw it all. He had time, but he hesitated. I saw it. He could have gotten the damned bomb off if he hadn't hesitated. Timing! It's all in the timing. He knew that!"

"Why is he dead, Stepan?" Irina demanded again, her eyes riveted accusingly on him.

"Why? Why? Because he waited too goddamned long! Savva, what the hell are you still doing with your bomb?"

"I couldn't get it off. I couldn't get close enough," he offered apologetically.

"Oh, give it to me." Stepan held out his hands. "With everything else, I have to find a way to get rid of this nitro."

"You don't care that Josef's dead," Irina said flatly.

"First I care that Yermolov still breathes, do you understand that?" Stepan demanded, his stare ice cold. "It's what Josef would have cared about most."

"This is no time to argue!" Olga scolded. "We're all of us under too much stress. None of you should go back to your homes. I have the address of a safe place. Here, Kiril, you take everyone there. I'll contact Dmitri, and then I'll tell you what you're to do."

"I'm going with you, Olga," Stepan insisted, tucking Savva's bomb under his arm.

"Whatever you like. Misha, do you have money?"

"Yes."

"As soon as everyone's settled, give it to Kiril. It may be a while before we get back to you. Buy some vodka and food and cigarettes."

* * *

The house was a two-room run-down shamble on an alley in a slum district of Vyborg. The windows were boarded with rotting pieces of wood; what little light there was leaked in with the wind through cracks and loose boards. There were a few chairs, a wobbly table, a moth-eaten couch, and a stripped mattress.

"Wait here," Kiril said to the shivering group, and he returned moments later with blankets from the carriage and a kerosene lamp.

"Keep the light low," Vladimir warned as Savva lit the lantern. "The place is abandoned. Don't want to draw attention."

Savva handed Irina a blanket. "I have my coat," she said dully. "Misha, you have the money for Kiril?"

He nodded and gave Kiril his billfold.

Twenty minutes later, Kiril returned with the food, drink, and candles. Nobody ate, but the vodka was passed around and around. Slowly the day crept into afternoon and then night; it was impossible to tell the hours in the dank dark of the hovel. Conversations that started as whispers built into a frenzy of talk, sometimes even laughter, only to break off suddenly.

Vladimir paced. "When is someone coming?" he demanded. "Kiril, are you sure this is the right place?"

"Relax."

"Relax? I'm going mad. Each time I hear a noise, I think it's the police. It could be the police. We could be set up the way Josef was set up."

"Nobody said Josef was set up!" Savva protested righteously.

"First Vera and Katya—now Josef. There were too many cops today. It was a setup for sure."

"This is dangerous talk," Kiril advised.

"Dangerous to say what I feel! First Katya and Vera, now Josef."

"And Feofan," Misha added evenly. "He was murdered."

"He was getting too close," Irina added.

"You see!" Vladimir insisted. "Even the peddler. It's clear as the nose on your face. One of us hears the plans and runs and tells Yermolov."

"Maybe not Yermolov," Irina said.

"No one here is a traitor!" Savva nearly shouted, his voice lost of that calm that was his trademark.

"Can you be so certain, my friend?" Vladimir demanded

bitterly. "Would you lay your life on the line for such a belief anymore? Once I would have. Once I thought there were none so true as those who sit in this room. But now—"

"You, then, Vladimir!" Kiril spit. "All your protestations could be a device to make us trust you, when—"

"Liar!" Vladimir lunged at Kiril, but before he made contact, Misha grappled him to the floor.

"Don't!" Misha insisted to a struggling Vladimir. "Don't do this." He pulled Vladimir to a sitting position and shook him. "And for God's sake, man, don't drink any more!"

'We need Dmitri Andreievich," Vladimir blubbered. "Where the hell is Dmitri Andreievich?" He looked pleadingly toward Irina.

She wanted to be kind to Vladimir, but she couldn't. An anger mixed with fear bubbled to control her. "Dmitri Andreievich isn't God. He can't fix everything, any more than Stepan can. We're all of us competent, Vladimir. Pull yourself together. Think of Josef, if you need help. Think of Josef!" Her voice was becoming shrill.

"Where are Olga and Stepan?" Vladimir whimpered. "Where's someone to free us? Maybe they were set up too. Maybe they're dead and Dmitri Andreievich with them."

"I can't stand this anymore!" Kiril shoved the bottle at Vladimir. "Drink yourself into a stupor, then you'll shut up."

"Sitting ducks," Vladimir mumbled as he put the bottle to his lips.

"Then leave!" Kiril shot back. "Leave now and take your miserable pessimism with you."

Vladimir hugged the bottle and pulled himself into a corner.

There was a soft pounding at the door. The pounding grew louder. Kiril got up and hurried to the door, pressing an ear against it. "Who's there?"

"Stepan Stepanovich."

Kiril opened the door and Stepan slipped in. No light followed. It was nighttime.

"God, it's freezing in here. Well, you'll by happy to hear you're going to a safe place, safer than you'd dare imagine. I won't tell you where, don't want to ruin the surprise."

"I won't go without knowing!" Vladimir insisted.

"Damn, man, this day has feebled your brain. You think you can't trust me now?" Stepan questioned.

"I want to know where he's taking us," Vladimir insisted. "I'm not a sheep being led to the slaughter."

"We're comrades," Savva soothed.

"So were Josef and Katya and Vera."

"Damn fool," Stepan muttered, and said louder, "The truth is this—I can't tell you until we're there. I've got my orders. If you don't want to come, anyone who doesn't want to come, doesn't have to. But you're on your own."

"Come on," Irina urged, rising from the couch. Her body ached from sitting so long. "Come on, Vladimir. You stay with me. We're going to Dmitri Andreievich, aren't we, Stepan?"

"Jesus, where else?" Stepan led the others outside, climbing up onto the driver's seat beside Kiril.

Misha peered out the curtains of the carriage, watching the night streets of Petersburg slowly pass; Kiril was driving the horses at a gentle clip to avoid any suspicion. They crossed the Alexandrovsky Bridge and turned left onto the Gagarin Embankment, passing by Misha's house and on toward the Winter Palace. More guards than usual protected the Winter Palace that night. The carriage moved quietly along the English Embankment, past more fashionable houses, the home of Irina's parents, and turned finally into the drive of Alexander Ryabushinsky and stopped at the back of the house, by the servants' entrance.

A young woman in her early twenties, clearly not a servant, welcomed them with smiles and kisses on the cheek. "We are honored," she told each one as they passed.

"Charlotte Alexandrovna!" Misha exclaimed when he saw it was Ryabushinsky's daughter.

"Welcome, Mikhail Anatolyevich." She embraced him.

"Do you know?" he gasped.

"Of course," she said with an authority Misha had never noticed in her before. He'd known Charlotte Alexandrovna for years, and though older and not unattractive, she'd always seemed shallow, doomed to an ordinary life. "Hurry. Papa and the others are waiting."

With a sweep of her skirts, she led them through the kitchen and the pantry and into a large storage closet. Moving a bushel of turnips, she reached in her pocket for a letter opener and slowly slipped it under a floorboard. The floorboard moved and there was the sound of a lock unlatching. A part of the wall opened into a door which led into a large, pleasantly warm and comfortably furnished room. The floor was covered with a thick crimson-and-blue Oriental carpet. Huge vases of flowers gave a fresh scent to the air. Dmitri, Olga and Alexander Ryabushinsky were waiting. They rose to greet the newcomers, welcoming them with warm embraces and kisses on each cheek.

"Mikhail Anatolyevich, you look surprised!" Alexander Ryabushinsky smiled as he clapped Misha on the back. "Come, sit down, it will all be explained."

"Comrades . . ." Dmitri began after everyone was settled in the comfortable couches and chairs. "I know you are all exhausted. I know you are all questioning. I know you all did the best you could. And I know you all mourn, as I mourn, our fallen comrade. Josef was a true warrior. He died a warrior's death. His presence, his courage, his love, and his commitment shall always be with us." Dmitri paused a moment, and heads bowed. "But we must go on. Today was far from a catastrophe, and I implore you all to see it with objectivity. Our plans were not wrong. All that could have been done, was done. No one is to blame. Five out of six of you in the street survived. Josef Kidarsky's death will not be in vain, I promise."

Irina felt stiff as she listened. Dmitri's words seemed vacant, and she ached for the emotion, the blind faith she'd known.

"But something went wrong," Vladimir pressed. His eyes were bloodshot, his face gray from the strain and the drink.

"It seems that someone noticed Josef uncover the bomb before he had a chance to throw it."

"What if somebody already knew he had the bomb? What if someone was there waiting for him, waiting for us all? What if we were all sitting ducks?"

"That's possible, of course. It's been a consideration since the Yermolov papers were stolen in Paris. What's confusing, then, is why only Josef was killed. If they knew you were all there, why didn't they at the very least arrest you?" Dmitri calmly questioned.

Vladimir shifted uncomfortably.

Dmitri went on, "However, to still the fears of any of our young comrades, I make you all a promise. If Vladimir is right, if the police knew Josef was carrying that bomb, then one of us told them. If such a person exists, if such a traitor is here in our midst, then I swear to you all I shall personally discover him and he shall die at my hands. And in order to protect ourselves, it is imperative that none of you go back to the apartment on Zhukovskaya Street for any reason."

"Then there is reason to believe there was a conspiracy?" Irina asked.

Dmitri shook his head. "Actually, no. From all the reports I've garnered, it seems someone happened to see Josef with his bomb and alerted the police before he could get it off. But since Stepan managed to lob his bomb squarely on a carriage of Yermolov's bodyguards, the police are looking for at least one other assassin. However, before we go any further, I'd like to introduce our host to you, Alexander Ilyitch, and his daughter, Charlotte Alexandrovna.''

Alexander Ryabushinsky rose slowly to his full height of six feet. He was a trim, fine-featured man of about fifty. His light hair was graying at the temples, yet he seemed still in the prime of his life and content with himself. His smile was welcoming. ''Comrades, I am honored to be able to share my home with you, the vanguard of our revolution. I am humble in your presence, awed by your courage and your dedication. Perhaps . . .'' His gaze rested quizzically on Misha. ''Some of you are wondering what a man of my position is doing aiding and abetting those who strive to violently overthrow the Czar. Well, let me say there are more of us who are on your side, believe me.'' He seemed to be speaking directly to Misha. ''The reason we do not openly support you is that such support would only lead to our being watched by the Czar more closely than we already are, and would strongly hinder our ability to work. We offer you and others like you money and safety insomuch as we can. We help smuggle arms and other contraband, including''—he grinned—''those like your own Stepan Stepanovich, in and out of the country. This little apartment you're in has three other rooms. There's another exit to the outside and one that leads upstairs to my study. No one except Charlotte and I know of its existence. You're welcome to stay here as my honored guests for as long as you need.''

Dmitri called Misha and Irina into one of the back rooms. ''I want the two of you out of Petersburg tonight,'' he said, the words offering no space for argument. ''If it's true there's a traitor among us, the leak must be plugged before we can go after Yermolov again.''

''Dmitri Andreievich, I must tell you something . . .'' Irina hesitated. ''Josef came to my room late last night. He said . . . he was certain there was a traitor amongst us. And he thought the traitor worked not for Yermolov, but for Father Gapon.''

''The priest?''

Irina nodded. ''Remember in the documents we received in Paris—there were memoranda from the Okhrana agent Akimov that he was organizing false unions run by the police?''

"Yes, of course, and now there are rumors afoot that that is so."

Irina's eyes opened wide with surprise. She looked from Misha to Dmitri. "What do they say?"

"That Gapon is trusted only by the police and the most ignorant of the workers and those unemployed."

"Josef said that Vera was investigating Gapon before she was killed."

"Yes, that's so," Dmitri admitted quietly.

"You knew!" Irina gasped.

Dmitri stared thoughtfully down at his hands a moment; then he looked directly, determinedly at Irina and Misha. "What I am about to tell you is in the strictest of confidence, and I tell you because of what you already suspect. I sanctioned Vera's investigation of Gapon, not because I thought Gapon a threat to us, but because Vera was so keen on the matter. And it's possible that Gapon had her murdered, but I'm not in the least bit convinced of it. From everything we've found out about the priest, he seems more naive than manipulating. Murder doesn't appear to be part of his repertoire. Also, Vera covered her tracks well. There was no reason for anyone in Gapon's circle to believe she wasn't the worker Ilena Rzhevskaya. I think Yermolov might still be our man."

"What about that fellow Akimov?" Misha asked. "How does he fit into all this?"

"Uncertainly, if at all. Because of his possible connection to Gapon, the Brigade instigated an investigation of him after Vera's and Katya's deaths. We've gotten absolutely no place. The man lives in the shadows. In fact, that's about all we've discovered about him, his pseudonym, the Shadow." Dmitri shook his head slowly. "Nothing, as you can see, is clear; everything is in flux; anything is possible. There are countless intrigues afoot these days, some overt threats to the revolution, some not. What is important for us in the Brigade to remember is that we are *not* the watchdog of the revolution. We have our job to do. Right now that job is assassinating Yermolov. If and when Gapon or Akimov becomes a threat to us, we shall act accordingly. Until then, their fates are in others' hands."

"Then you don't think the priest had anything to do with the Paris theft or Katya's or Vera's death."

"With all due respect to Josef, I don't. Unless you have some proof, something Josef gave you . . ."

"No." Irina shook his head.

"All right, then!" Dmitri sighed, and almost smiled. His body seemed to lighten. "Right now, my priority is to get the two of you out of Petersburg. According to my sources, there's no indication the police are looking for you yet, but I don't want to take any chances. You two are the most well-known. Your pictures have been in all the society pages of late. I've arranged with Olga Fyodorovna to accompany you. Is there someplace you might go for a month, perhaps?"

"The Crimea," Irina suggested. "Misha, doesn't your uncle own the old Serebrov villa in Yalta?"

Misha nodded and looked toward Dmitri, who seemed lost in thought. "What do you think, Dmitri Andreievich?" he asked. "I'm sure we could stay at Uncle Alexei's villa."

"It's a possibility, I think. Yes, I rather like the idea of the Crimea at this time of year . . . it's practically empty of society who would know the two of you . . ." He was muttering more to himself than to Misha or Irina. Without another word, he wandered from the room.

Irina pressed her hand into her brow as if she had a headache.

"Are you all right?"

"Yes. I . . . I was just thinking. I mean, would it be particularly awkward for you to be with me in the Crimea?"

Misha felt suddenly prickly, but his voice was even. "I don't see why it should be. We've managed well together over the past months. Actually, I think we're quite a good team."

"Well, yes, we have been. I didn't mean that. I only meant, well . . ." She bit her lip. "I'll admit to you, I have ulterior motives in suggesting the Crimea."

"What?"

"First of all . . ." She smiled girlishly. "It's my favorite place in the world. I haven't been there since I was a child. And second . . . well, my cousin Anna Petrovna is there, and she's in desperate straits. She's been betrothed to Prince Tairov."

"That old goat! But what can you do about it?"

"I don't know. Maybe nothing. I would like to see her, though."

"You'd better tell Dmitri Andreievich."

"I'd rather not. I'll be careful. I'm not going to walk into my aunt's house and announce myself. You won't tell him, Misha, will you?"

"Not if you don't want me to."

"Thank you!" she exclaimed, hugging him effusively.

He thought she would pull away, but she didn't.

She lingered, letting her head fall against his chest. Then she looked up at him. "I want to thank you, Misha."

"For what?"

"For saving my life this morning."

"I didn't do that."

"Yes, you did. I was losing control. I felt myself losing control. If you hadn't hung on to me I don't know what I would have done."

Gently he disentangled himself, and smiling self-consciously, murmured, "It's the least Timofey could do for Lukyera—"

The sound of footsteps made them step further apart. Moments later Dmitri entered with Ryabushinsky and announced, "Alexander Ilyitch has been kind enough to offer you his villa in Yalta. He quite rightly remembered that Alexei's is rented out, and besides, his is even more isolated. Now, there are some details Alexander Ilyitch would like to discuss with Misha—and, Irina, I'd like to talk with you and Olga Fyodorovna awhile."

"Of course," she agreed, following Dmitri from the room.

"I'm sure you're wondering how your uncle and the Symposium fit into all this," Ryabushinsky said when he and Misha were alone. "Well, let me begin by making a clear distinction between the work your uncle and I do with a group such as the Brigade and the work we do on the Symposium. They are two very different animals, you know. There are many in the Symposium who would be shocked to know we support violence—your uncle's dear friend Count Bobrinsky among them. So you see, you must be very careful with whom you discuss these matters."

"Uncle Alexei is with us, then?"

"Most definitely. But you must swear never to let him know you know, not unless he chooses to tell you himself. He's spoken to me about his fears of your joining the Brigade. I told him he should be proud, but he's too afraid for you to be proud. And he's very upset now. I'm not sure I know why. I received a note from him saying he'll be away from Petersburg indefinitely. It's so unlike Alexei Yakovlevich. He's dedicated to the revolution, Misha."

"Then why does he want to stop me?"

"He doesn't know you've actually joined the Brigade. I'm the only outsider who knows, and even I didn't know until tonight. I didn't know any of the names other than Dmitri Andreievich's, of course. Charlotte and I do what we can. Charlotte travels back and forth a great deal between Petersburg and the Continent, even Turkey. She's quite a pampered young lady, you know." The gaiety returned to his eyes. "She never travels without many, many trunks. Of course, no one would stop her or inspect her luggage. Wouldn't they be shocked to find inflammatory pamphlets written by the exiles, not to mention rifles and explosives.''

"You let your daughter do such things?''

"I encourage her. None of us are exempt, you see. There are those who hide their heads in the sand and pretend the violence will never touch their emerald walls. But it does, willy-nilly. Your uncle knows that. I'm sure when he hears of your heroism today, he'll be filled with pride.''

"I don't think so.'' Misha looked worried.

"Well, we'll cross that bridge when we come to it, eh? But first, let me tell you what Dmitri Andreievich and I have come up with. You and Irina will be traveling as brother and sister, Marie and Anton Thibaut from Paris. It's as Anton that you're going to the Crimea. He's been weakened by a bout with pneumonia which the doctors fear will turn into tuberculosis. He'll be visiting a Dr. Kavelarov at the Tatlin Sanatorium. Kavelarov is one of us, and you'll see him once a week, more if necessary. All messages to Dmitri will be sent through him. Olga will be traveling with you as your great-aunt Fedora Ivanovna. You'll leave as soon as we can get you some papers, but you must be cautious. No one is to recognize you, and you must be certain you keep a low visibility once you arrive. Oh, by the way, here's a letter for you from your uncle. Dmitri Andreievich asked me to give it to you.'' Ryabushinsky handed Misha an envelope. "We'll have more time to talk. For now, I'll let you read in privacy.''

February 10, 1904

My darling Misha,

I write to you with a peace of mind I have not known for many years. Forgive me for leaving Petersburg in such a rush, not even a quick good-bye, but my mind was in a thousand pieces. Someday, perhaps as we talk man to man, I shall tell you of some of it. Your grandmother was right. Tolya and Helena have kept you a child, and I am as much to blame. I have held you too closely, thinking I only wanted your happiness. To that end, I laid out your life. How presumptuous of me to pretend to know another's happiness. It has taken me forty-two years to discover my own.

I shall not be returning to Petersburg for a while. I don't know when. I am with my dearest friend, Kira Yurovna, in Krasnoyarsk. Someday, yes, I very much want the two of you to meet. I first knew her when I was just a bit younger than you. I wonder if she would see any resemblance?

I know you've never wanted to travel with me this sum-

mer to find out about the business. So, my dearest Misha,
you are off the hook. You needn't come with me, because
I won't be there. Your life is your own. Twenty! It seems a
miracle you are a man already, but that you are.

Ask Yuri for the funds. He shall see to your allowance
and anything else you need. He's been in touch with me
over the progress of your case. It seems it will not be coming to trial for a while. I know you are in the best of hands.

God grant you peace, Misha. I am ever your adoring
uncle,

Alexei

PART FOUR

THE CRIMEA

CHAPTER TWENTY-FIVE

Anna liked to think the ring of sweat on the pillow around Konstantin Novy's head was the portent of a halo. Poor Konstantin was in the last stages of tuberculosis, and his suffering tugged at Anna's heart. Konstantin was scarcely twenty. Anna spent as much time as she could with him at the sanatorium, mostly reading, which was less trying on the boy than conversation. His words were too quickly stolen by coughing fits; his words, his very breath, seemed like the feeble flickering of a dying candle. So Anna spent the afternoons reading to him. Konstantin particularly liked the books by James Fenimore Cooper. His eyes seemed less feverish as he listened to the fast-paced tales of Indians, soldiers and settlers in that strange and exotic America. He smiled at her whenever she paused, and Anna felt encompassed by his love. Secretly, silently, she sent him hers, at the same time preparing herself for his death.

Anna prayed for Konstantin every night, and often cried at the thought of his death. Anna cried easily of late. Sometimes for no apparent reason, she threw herself on her bed, or on the grass or in the woods and sobbed desperately, her chest tightening until she thought she would suffocate. She wanted to, but she couldn't, not while Konstantin lived. Once he was gone, she would run away. She imagined dying in sepia shadows; she imagined drowning in a warm bath, the water filling her lungs, death caressing like the kiss of Konstantin Novy. She tried drowning once in the ocean, but just when she thought her head would explode from lack of air, she bobbed to the surface and the waves brought her safely back to the shore, where her brother, Boris, played happily, digging in the sand, and her mother and Zinaida Golovnina sat chatting under the brightly striped umbrella with Prince Tairov.

Anna shuddered as she walked to where they sat. Prince Tairov's hawk eyes followed, watching her from under the shadowy hairs of his peppery eyebrows. He wore a broad-brimmed hat to shield his stern face from the sun, leaving his

skin yellowed like the pages of an old book. Prince Tairov
was a tall man, as tall as Alexei Yakovlevich, and although
not unfit for his fifty years, his thickening waistline pressed
against the buttons of his shirts and vests. His thinning gray
hair was shortly cropped, and since he never swam, he
sweated profusely in the heat of the Crimean sun. His clean-
shaven face seemed always damp.

Anna reached quickly for a towel to cover her bathing
dress, which was sticking hopelessly to her skin; she felt horribly undressed in front of this man who was to be her husband. His gaze left her clammy like unwanted death.
Sometimes the thought of their marriage made her laugh hysterically, her laughter reverberating senselessly about in her
head. Other times she screamed, pounding her fists on the
walls or the beds. Even Boris had stopped worrying about
her when she stomped about her room pounding and crying.

"We had a little fit, did we, Anna Petrovna?" Zinaida
would glare when she and Anna crossed paths again. "Well,
we'll see what the Prince will allow once you're safely in his
care. He'll not tolerate your insolent ways, I'll wager."

"Better to be with the Prince than you," Anna spit back.
"Better a man than a witch."

Zinaida crossed herself and began furiously mumbling
prayers.

"God does not hear you any longer." Anna's laughter echoed mirthlessly. "God hears none of us." She sneered, but
her newfound power over the woman who'd once seemed her
guard had, like yesterday's ball gown, lost its allure. Anna
wearied of Zinaida as she wearied of life, and continued her
defiance toward Zinaida more for the sake of pride than anything else. Pride, it seemed, was all Anna had left. She wondered if it would be enough to carry her on to her wedding
day.

"Mama, you can't ask me to do this, you can't!" Anna
had implored when her mother told her of her betrothal to
the Prince, the father of poor Mitya Tairov, who had died of
typhoid six years before. It wasn't Mitya's death that Anna
thought of when her mother suggested the engagement, but
the horrible, red welts rising off Mitya's back the day of the
Club's first swim at the hidden pond, and of Petya's words,
His father is a brute. . . .

"I'll do anything you like, Mama—anything, I swear—just
don't ask me this, to marry the Prince. He's so old, Mama,
too old."

"Hardly a decade older than your beloved Alexei Kalinin."

"But Alexei was my friend, Mama—only my friend!" She gasped, horrified that her mother could speak of Alexei and Prince Tairov in the same breath.

"He'll take care of you, and tame you, Anna. He'll be both a husband and a father. You need a real father. You need someone to harness that wicked will of yours or God will turn his face from you in eternity."

"Please, Mama—I'll be good. I promise, I won't cause you or Zinaida Ivanovna any more trouble. I'll do whatever you want for the rest of my life. Please, Mama, please!" She shuddered violently, tormented by the memory of Mitya's whiplashed back. "He's too old. . . ." She sobbed, covering her face with her hands. "Please, Mama, he's too old. And I don't love him. I could never love such a man. . . ."

"Listen to me, Anna." Her mother grabbed Anna's hands and pulled her close so Anna could not avoid the pinched, threatening lips and slitlike eyes. "A man's touch is a man's touch whether he is young or old, handsome or not. The marital bed belongs to him. For you there's only endurance. Why does it matter, then, his age or his looks?" Marya Dmitreyevna's anger pulsated through her paling skin, throbbed about her darkly circled eyes, causing her fingertips to spike Anna's arm.

"I can't, Mama. I'll die first!" The words burst agonizingly from her. She wanted to run from the hatred distorting her mother's face, as if an angel of mercy had suddenly shed its light to reveal a ghoulish core.

Marya Dmitreyevna continued to grasp Anna's arms. "All right, then, I'll tell you the truth. You want to know the truth, what a fiend of a man your father is? We have nothing left, Anna, do you hear me? Nothing. That's why I fled Petersburg when Boris was born. I couldn't even pay the doctor's bill. There wasn't a merchant who would give me another kopeck of credit. I could barely afford to feed and clothe my children, much less buy new gowns for the season or host a dinner party!"

"No!" Anna cried, trying to break free of her mother's hold.

"Say no all you want, Anna." Marya Dmitreyevna tightened her hold. "But it's the truth. I sold most of my mother's jewels just so I could send you to Smolny and Zinaida Ivanovna and Boris and I could continue to live a moderately comfortable life here. Ah, but it's my penance for my sins. Lord knows, I've sinned. And you know what my greatest

sin was, Anna? Do you?'' She was shaking Anna fiercely.
"Marrying your father. Yes, my mother begged me not to.
My father threatened to beat me, but I had to have your father—just as you have to have this Alexei Kalinin! But God
has punished me for willfulness. I have suffered. You cannot
imagine the many ways. Your father's a beast. He spun his
web about me just as this Kalinin is spinning his web about
you—''

"No, Mama, it's not that way!''

"Don't tell me how it is, Anna! I can see. I have eyes in
my head. The only thing differentiating your great Alexei
Kalinin from your father is that Kalinin still has his money.
But do you know the worst of it—ah, it is too ironic, really,
Anna. Even you will see the irony. Do you know who owns
all your father's debts now? Do you?'' Marya Dmitreyevna
was screaming at her. "The whoremonger friend of yours,
Alexei Kalinin.''

"No, that's not true!'' Anna broke free, covering her ears
with her hands.

"Oh, isn't it?'' Marya Dmitreyevna demanded, an ugly
sneer distorting her face. "Ask your father, then. He's coming to Ravens Head next week for the announcement of your
marriage. It was he who approached Prince Tairov. Talk to
your father if you want a reprieve. But there'll be none, I
promise you. Prince Tairov has promised too much. He has
no living son. His daughter is barren. The Prince wants an
heir, and he wants someone young and strong to produce
one, two, as many as he needs to feel secure from the Angel
of Death. So!'' Marya Dmitreyevna snorted, her eyes widening, their blueness suddenly alive. "Talk to your haloed
father if you shudder at your marriage bed. What do you think
it will get you?''

Anna never talked to her father. She dared not. But something hardened inside of her after her engagement. The hot
shroud of fear and confusion turned icy as the Prince pressed
his thin lips on her cheek and grazed his jeweled hand across
her shoulders as he clasped her engagement gift, a priceless
necklace of emeralds and diamonds, around her neck. It was
a small party. February was the beginning of the rainy season, and the best families had left the Crimea for more pleasant climates. Prince Tairov led Anna in a quiet waltz. They
sat together at the table. He touched her hand every now and
again, but barely spoke a word to her. Occasionally she felt
him looking at her. Involuntarily she glanced up, only to look
quickly away. There was something so bleak about the man,

the old man. Yes, he was old. Ten years or not, he seemed more like a lifetime older than Alexei. His smile was joyless, his eyes flat graves. A sick feeling dripped from her heart and stomach. She could not eat, and she left the party early, complaining of a headache.

"I want you to stay, Anna." Marya Dmitreyevna caught her on the stairs.

"I'm marrying him, Mama. I'm doing that for you and Papa. There's nothing else you can ask of me ever again—do you understand, Mama—*nothing*," Anna said coldly.

Marya Dmitreyevna's body tensed. Her long, thin fingers gripped the railing. Her lips pinched.

Anna wasn't frightened. For the first time in her life she felt no fear of her mother, and no love. She felt nothing. "I'm going to bed now."

"Anna!" Mary Dmitreyevna demanded.

Anna lifted the skirt of her gown and kept walking. When she got to her room, she tore off the Prince's necklace and hurled it onto the floor. Then she went to her closet, and deep in the back, behind a pair of shoes, was a small velvet box. She carried the box to her bed and lovingly opened it, lifting out the ruby brooch that Alexei had sent her. She pressed it gently to her lips and smoothed its deep, richly colored stones across her face. Then she lay down on the bed, holding it to her heart.

February was a bleak month. The rain seemed never to cease. Fog hung heavily, creeping across the world like mold, leaving the sky muted with the gray sea. Konstantin Novy grew weaker and weaker. Marya Dmitreyevna told Anna she shouldn't spend so much time with the boy. There were others at the sanatorium who needed her charity. Anna ignored her mother and sat for sweet, silent hours by Konstantin's bed, touching his hand now and again, watching him sleep. It seemed important that she be there when he awoke. Even more important that she be there when he died.

"Anna Petrovna." A nurse nudged her.

Anna jerked into awaking. Her heart pounded fearfully as she looked from the nurse to Konstantin.

"We have to bathe him now," the nurse said. "You'll have to leave."

"Oh, yes, of course." Anna rose to her feet; *The Last of the Mohicans*, by James Fenimore Cooper, fell to the floor. As she bent to pick it up, she stole another glance at Konstantin, at the gentle rise and fall of his chest, and thanked God for not taking him yet. "Can I return?"

"As you wish. You can wait in the hall or get yourself something to eat. All the men in the ward must be bathed. Yes, do get yourself something to eat. You're wasting away to nothing, Anna Petrovna."

So long as Konstantin Novy was alive, there was still hope, Anna thought as she hurried from the ward. She paused outside the door, and brushing some hairs from her face, leaned against the wall, feeling light-headed. Perhaps she'd gotten up too quickly from sleeping. She hadn't meant to sleep.

"Good afternoon, Anna Petrovna." A doctor smiled at her as he passed.

Anna quickly straightened up and stood away from the wall. "Good afternoon, Dr. Yurovsky." She smiled back, delighted the doctor remembered her name.

So many of the nurses and doctors knew her name; some even stopped to chat with her. She loved coming to the sanatorium. It was the only place she felt peace anymore. Perhaps she would start spending more time here. Her mother was right. There were other patients who could benefit from her attention. She had a way with the sick and dying. Even Dr. Kavelarov said so. He'd commented more than once that Konstantin's continued life came surely from the hope Anna had instilled in the poor boy. Well, she couldn't take any time from Konstantin to give to the other patients, that much was certain, but she could spend more time caring for the ill.

She didn't have to arrange her schedule by her mother's, either. She was eighteen years old, and betrothed. Besides, Yalta wasn't Petersburg. There was no harm in her having Emil drive her down from Ravens Head alone. What more placid place could there be on earth than the Crimea? Even the Empress when she was here traveled with only her companion. Anna had seen the Empress walking in and out of the shops, just like anyone else. If the Empress could do that, so could she. She'd come early, perhaps early enough to help feed the patients breakfast. And she'd come every day, not only Monday, Wednesday and Thursday afternoons. Then they'd let her wear a uniform, one of those crisp white dresses. She could learn to bathe the patients and tend to them. She could become a nurse. Yes, that would be lovely, to be a nurse, to give selflessly. Certainly, Prince Tairov wouldn't disapprove of his wife devoting her life to those less fortunate. Perhaps she'd mention it to the Prince the next time he came to dinner. It would give them something to talk about. Yes, most certainly she'd tell him. Anna smiled, a calm setting about her as she started down the hall to the nurses' station.

"Pardon, pardon!" a Frenchman cried as two strong hands grasped Anna.

"Oh, excuse me!" she apologized, flustered as she realized she'd walked right into a bearded young man.

He opened his mouth to speak, but a look of shock seemed to whisk away his words.

For a moment Anna stared back. There was something so recognizable about the young man, but she couldn't place the face. "It was my fault, truly," Anna went on, afraid she'd hurt him in some way.

The bearded young man stared dumbfounded. His hands fell to his sides.

"You will excuse me. . . ." Anna hurried on. "Nurse Strukova!" she called.

A tall matronly woman just leaving the nurses' station turned to Anna. She smiled pleasantly. "Yes, Anna Petrovna, what can I do for you?"

"Are you certain it was Anna?" Irina asked, straining to sit up in the wicker chaise, but the blanket in which she'd wrapped herself was binding. Despite the fine mist of rain falling, she'd been lying on the veranda staring out to the Black Sea for hours.

"At first I wasn't absolutely sure. I'd only seen her that one evening, you recall, at Uncle Alexei's dinner party. And she's different, somehow. Well, I suppose it's because she's not dressed up, but she seemed older . . . no, thinner, definitely thinner. At first I wasn't certain, but then I heard her being called by her name, Anna Petrovna."

"And she didn't recognize you?"

"I'm quite certain she didn't." Misha settled into a seat across from Irina and laid his wide-brimmed hat on the table. "Why do you sit out here in such weather? It's depressing, not to mention wet."

"Not at all. Ryabushinsky has the best view in all the Crimea. Certainly better than Mama's and Papa's. Oh, they've grand grounds and a quite marvelous house, but Ryabushinsky has the view, no matter the weather. You're certain Anna didn't recognize you?"

"I was closer to her than I am to you. She practically fell into my arms. I stared right at her and there was nothing, no recognition whatsoever."

"Oh, dear, I ought to go see her. Next time you go to see Kavelarov, I'll go with you. Perhaps I'll run into her."

"Perhaps Kavelarov knows her and he could arrange a meeting."

"He wouldn't, any more than Dmitri would. He's strictly by-the-book. Oh, it's awful being so close to Anna and not being able to see her."

"We'll figure something out."

'That's what you keep on saying. And then . . ." She sighed despondently. "Sometimes I think I haven't seen Anna because I'm afraid to see her. The thought of her marriage to the Prince is so awful and I feel so helpless. What good would it do for me to see her now?" She reached for his hand and pressed it gently to her lips. "Or am I just being horribly selfish?"

"How's that?"

"I don't want anyone or anything to take away from this time we have together. It's so short, and I feel it will never come again."

He leaned to kiss her; and she laughed softly, stroking his cheek and luxuriating like a well-fed cat in his closeness, his smile and his caresses; the air about them seemed always fragrant and clear. Irina hungrily guarded their solitude which spawned, it seemed, their love, memorized moments, the shadow of an afternoon sun dappling Misha's cheeks, the strong lines of his fingers and the depth of his eyes when she caught him unaware. She held their happiness as a child grasps a parent's hand, knowing the impression has to last a lifetime. Misha, for all his gentleness, was strong; she was not. She felt ancient, as if life had worn her insides into sand. And then Misha would smile, or touch her, or say something to make her laugh.

"Do you want to throw the bomb that kills Yermolov?" Irina asked as she cuddled against Misha in the contented aftermath of lovemaking.

"I want whoever throws the bomb not to miss this time, and not to die." He lay on his back, his hands behind his head, and stared up at the ceiling. "I think someone with more experience would have a better chance at success."

"Forget practicality for a moment." She rested her head on his chest and pulled at the hairs. "Just as a matter of simple desire, do you *want* to be the one who blows a dog like Yermolov to eternal damnation?"

Misha turned on his side and propped his head. A curious smile creased his lips.

"You're laughing!" she protested. "You're laughing at me!" She shoved him.

He grabbed her as he fell back. "I love you!" he exclaimed, and his lips sought hers; his hand smoothed down the curve of her back and along the rise of her buttocks. "You are the most wonderful thing that's ever happened to me!"

She smiled happily and brushed the hair from his forehead. Then her expression turned serious. "Tell me seriously, Misha—do you dream of throwing the next bomb?"

"I dream of making love to you. I dream of you always being as you've been these last weeks." He cupped a warm, full breast in his hand and kneaded its softness.

"I dream of Yermolov's body exploding, an arm here, a foot there, head bashed in, eyes bloody."

"God grant you never hate me with such passion." He nibbled at her breasts and turned to caress her entire body, suddenly needing to pleasure her again. Here in this Crimean hideaway, far from bombs, death and Stepan Ostravsky, she was obsessively his; sometimes she clung to him, a different Irina than he had known before, quieter, older and younger at the same time. They played together, rising early to catch the sun and ride the morning waves. Irina showed him, as if she were unfolding a treasure, beaches where the surf was gentle as baby's breath and breezes cooled even the hottest midday sun; she led him on a journey through orchards and foggy meadows to a hidden pool where they swam naked and made love in a clearing padded with pine needles.

They visited her parents' villa, long closed up, the furniture covered with sheets, the gardens wild and untended. Irina dressed in a lacy white gown from her childhood that hung forgotten in a cedar closet of her old room of pink-flowered walls and pink satin sheets. She and Misha spent hours in her old room in the house that echoed with a forgotten loneliness. Misha watched Irina pore over memories; they danced on the veranda to music from her old gramophone and drank fine wines from her father's cellar. She showed him where her mother had discovered her with her tutor, Apollon, and they climbed to the woods above Ravens Head, Irina looking for glimpses of her cousin Anna; they walked endlessly on paths edging the cliffs of the Black Sea, meandering through the back trails of the imperial villa and along paths close to Prince Tairov's famed vineyards.

"Funny to think Anna will be mistress of all this soon, my little Anna . . ." Irina said, a sadness in her voice that left Misha uneasy. At any moment she might flit from him, caught up in thoughts, a world that shut her from him as surely as if a cocoon were wrapped round her mind.

Misha held Irina as he slept, crying out if she moved or tried to separate. The heat of his body, the rhythmic rise and fall of his chest, the drumming of his heartbeat called up feelings, lingering images she could not identify. Her mind drifted, catching scents and sounds of summer, children's laughter, berries heated in the midday sun, creamy ices and ladies' perfumes wafting through windows like lilacs and the salty sea air. Here, high on this cliff in Yalta, nestled on thick pillows behind lacy curtains enclosing Alexander Ryabushinsky's bed, Irina knew she could love Misha so well. Her body had a soul. Misha was both lover and brother, family, someone who would die for her. She'd never known anyone who would die for her, with the possible exception of Anna when they were children together here in Yalta. Anna mattered as Misha mattered, and life was very fragile.

CHAPTER TWENTY-SIX

The last week in March, the green-blue waters of the Black Sea broke free of the pervasive fog, sending a swirl of colors and warm sea breezes up over the beaches and the gently rising cliffs. From the mountains came the fresh, cool air of the pine forests. Delicate scents wafted through windows, around street corners, and through the leaves of the cypress, apple, peach, and cherry trees. Lilacs, wisteria, violets, and white acacias bloomed with the meadows of wildflowers. Wild strawberries crisscrossed slopes and grapes hung on huge vines along the roadsides. The windows of the sanatorium were thrown wide open, and Anna thought she saw the color return to Konstantin Novy's cheeks. He sat up in bed, propped by many pillows, and took real interest in Anna's reading once more.

"Mama, I think I'll be going to the sanatorium every day now," Anna announced at breakfast one morning. Her eyes steadied on Zinaida Golovnina as if to ricochet the spikes of her disapproval.

"I don't think that's wise, Anna, now that the nice weather has returned," her mother said with her controlled composure. "I'm sure Prince Vaslav will want to spend more time with you. He'll be returning to Petersburg soon. And there are so many details about the wedding—''

"You work out the details, Mama. Whatever you decide is fine with me." Anna added another lump of sugar to her tea. "And if you would be so kind, you might express my apologies to the Prince and explain that the patients at the sanatorium need me. Konstantin is so much better—and after the nurses said he would not live to see spring. I think I've a way with the dying, Mama, I truly do. It's a calling, I believe.''

"Your only calling is your husband and the children you shall bear him," Zinaida reminded her.

"He's not my husband yet!" Anna shot her a withering glance.

"Really, Marya Dmitreyevna, if Anna wants to decline invitations from the Prince, she should be the one to tell him, not you. I daresay—''

"You daresay nothing, Zinaida Ivanovna!" Anna spit. "I've already arranged it, Mama, with Nurse Strukova. I told her I'd be there this afternoon, in time to give the patients lunch. And I've spoken to Emil. He said he would bring me right to the door and pick me up at five. I don't see what the big to-do is about.''

"Not today, Anna! I told you the Prince is coming to play tennis and then stay for tea.''

"I'm terrible at tennis. I hate the game. I always have and I always will. Besides, it will be too hot for the Prince to do anything but sit and sip his tea. Certainly too hot for such a one to play tennis. Why, if he did, he'd be the next patient.''

"Anna!" Marya Dmitreyevna paled.

"It's the truth, Mama, and you know it. Besides, the whole afternoon will be spent with you talking to the Prince and me sitting there being bored. I'll end up with a headache, for certain, and have to go to my room, so I might as well go to the sanatorium as I promised Nurse Strukova and be useful,'' Anna said with calm assurance as she carefully folded her napkin.

"I don't like this, Anna, not at all. And I shall tell the Prince the truth when he arrives. I shall tell him of your insolence. I haven't yet. But this time I shall.''

"Do what you want, Mama," Anna said evenly as she placed her napkin by her untouched plate. "I told Nurse Strukova I'd be there by ten. I have to hurry and dress or I'll be late.''

"Anna, your breakfast!" Marya Dmitreyevna called anxiously.

"I'm not hungry, not in the least." Without another word, she hurried from the room.

Try as Anna might, she could not leave Konstantin Novy's bedside the entire day. She watched the fluttering of his eyelids and the beads of sweat forming on his brow and seeping into the fine strands of his hair, darkening the blond. She watched his skin rising and falling with each heartbeat, and saw the streams of blood coursing through the delicate veins, pumping life through a web of springs flowing from the breath of the earth itself. She traced the outlines of his pale fingers lying gracefully against the white sheets, and was mesmerized by the beauty of their design, a man's hands surely created by an artist. She savored each moment with Konstantin, and concentrated on the passing of seconds, hearing moments tick slower and slower until she and the boy were bound together, their closeness, their love captured in a frame of time, stopped forever. She was exhausted when Nurse Strukova told her it was almost five, time to leave.

"You've done enough, Anna Petrovna. Look how peacefully our Konstantin sleeps."

"I have done well, haven't I? Well enough for a uniform?"

"Very well, yes. We're all pleased," Nurse Strukova assured her. "The uniform is all wrapped up for you and waiting at my desk. You may pick it up on the way out." Nurse Strukova slipped an arm under Anna's as if to help her up.

"Oh, thank you, thank you!" Anna felt like embracing Nurse Strukova.

"Now, Anna Petrovna," Nurse Strukova went on, guiding her from the ward. "I want you to promise me you'll eat a good dinner. A nurse must be strong herself if she is to aid the sick. I worry about you."

"Oh, I'm fine. I eat like a horse, I promise you!" Anna laughed giddily. "But I shall eat even more tonight. I'll eat enough for Konstantin and myself. Through me he shall become stronger and stronger, you'll see."

Nurse Strukova smiled kindly, and brushed the hairs from Anna's face. "You're a sweet girl, Anna Petrovna," she said, and then she was gone.

The exhaustion of the day's work felt more like exhilaration as Anna skipped down the front steps of the sanatorium into the cool green afternoon. Green, green, she thought as she clutched her package with her crisp new white nurse's aide's dress closely to her. How grand God was to create such a lovely green as the trees and grass. Odd, she had never been particularly taken with the color green before, but suddenly all she could see was green, God's green, feeling cool and pure like the splash of a mountain stream. Nurse Strukova had been pleased with her work that afternoon, "very pleased" were her exact words. Anna beamed with the praise, smiling so hard she thought her mouth might crack. She would tell Emil as soon as she saw him, she thought, still smiling as she glanced about for the coachman; instead, her eyes lighted on Prince Vaslav climbing from his carriage.

"Anna, my dear." He waved, his lumbering body draped in a white suit, white hat, white shoes, yellow skin. He hurried toward her, his presence marring God's landscape. Then he was before her, bowing as he offered her his arm.

She blanched, unable to move or speak. The air through her eyes grayed.

"Come, Anna, I've a surprise."

"But . . . but . . ." She looked anxiously about. "Emil is coming for me. I'm sure he's just a few minutes late."

"Quite the contrary, my dear. I've come myself to pick you up from your hard day's work." A hint of condescension edged his voice. His suit was crumpled; there were specks of dandruff on his monocle. "Come along, now." He engaged Anna's arm in a proprietary manner.

She followed like a sleepwalker, and slipped into the furthest corner of the handsome open carriage.

"May I?" Prince Vaslav asked, reaching for her package.

"No!" she cried, grasping the nurse's aide's uniform to her. "It's fine, I can hold it."

"Nonsense. It's cumbersome." Prince Vaslav took the package from her and ordered the driver to start. Then he slipped closer to Anna. "You look very pale, my dear."

"No, no, I'm fine." She stared straight ahead.

"Your mother's quite worried about you, you know. She tells me you never eat anymore. And look at you. . . ." He wrapped his thick fingers around her arm. "You're thin as a rail, Anna," he chided, patting her arm. "Even those lovely hands of yours." He held her fingers to his lips. "You must play for me tonight."

Anna pulled away, the touch of his lips feeling like electric shocks. "I've stopped playing the piano, Vaslav Igorovich. Surely Mama has told you that too."

"Ah, but, Anna, you wouldn't deprive me of your music. Your mother tells me you once played for the Czar. And that you wanted to go to the Conservatory."

"Yes, but I don't play anymore."

"I will not accept no for an answer, Anna. I implore you to consider it."

"All right." Her voice was barely audible.

"Good, now turn to me so I can see your lovely face."

Obediently she turned, looking past him.

"That's better." He smoothed his hand across her cheek, and his voice lowered. "How I look forward to our union, Anna—"

"We're not man and wife yet!" she burst out, shocked at her own vehemence. Clasping her hands tightly together, she pressed them into her lap. Her breathing was too fast, coming in short, rapid gasps. She felt as if the air were cutting itself off from her.

"Anna . . ." The Prince took her hand.

"I feel . . ." Her hand shot back into her lap with a will of its own. "I feel . . ." She turned to face him, certain for a moment she would scream: his face cracked like shattered glass; his skin crumbled into ashes; his lips were sucked into blackened teeth falling into empty eye sockets. She blinked and looked again. He was the Prince once more and she said, "I feel I must tell you something, Vaslav Igorovich." Her words were whisked away in the fine mist of dust kicked up by the horse as they trotted along the quiet winding road. "I . . . I feel it is my duty to tell you . . . I don't love you."

The echo of the Prince's laughter closed upon her soul like the cold night of a coffin. "I didn't expect that, my dear, no, not in the least. How could you love someone you don't even know?"

"I can never love you." Each word felt like an explosion being forced back down her throat.

"Anna." He took her hand again, holding it tightly so she could not pull away. "I know this is difficult for you—a beautiful young girl like yourself, you must have visions of a husband far different from me."

Hot tears pressed against the inside of her eyes.

"But I'm not a bad sort, really. You'll see, I'm rather generous." He pushed some flyaway hairs from her neck and kissed her lightly there.

"Please don't!" Her voice was very meek.

He kissed her again.

Her skin rippled in revulsion.

His fingers smoothed against her neck and shoulder. "You're very lovely, Anna. So very lovely," he whispered, his breath hot in her ear. "I promise you there are advantages to our union you never dreamed of."

"The road!" Anna cried suddenly. "You've missed the turnoff to Ravens Head."

"I forgot to tell you, we're not going to Ravens Head, my dear. Your mother and I both thought a quiet evening alone, some time for you and me to get to know each other, might do you a world of good."

"But where? I've no clothes to change into."

"Your mother packed a little trunk. She says you have everything you need. She told me what a duel you and Zinaida Ivanovna are in. I suggested a few days in different environs might be all you need. I'm sure you'll find my home quite delightful. The surf is much calmer than below Ravens Head—"

"A few days!"

"Oh, don't look so horrified, Anna. We'll be well-chaperoned, I promise. Both of my aunts live with me. They're old and a bit dotty, but I'm sure you'll find them amusing. And I've a houseguest, Colonel Kurakin. He's rather raw at the edges, but quite entertaining. He loves music. I promised him you'd play for us."

"But . . . but, I can't stay with you a few days. I promised Nurse Strukova I'd be back to help the patients tomorrow."

"I'll send her a message. She'll understand."

"No, you can't!" There was something terrible about the complacency of Prince Vaslav's smile, settled, fixed like the folds of his yellow skin. She searched for kindness in his eyes and found only impatience as he watched her over the bridge of his beaked nose. Dark hairs fringed his nostrils. "I won't stay! I won't! I'm not your wife yet. You can't make me stay with you!"

A hollow laughter seemed to come from outside the Prince. "I like your spunk, Anna, I do. Your mother insists your hotheadedness is trying, but I find it quite entrancing. Yes, I rather like it. It brings the color to your cheeks and makes your eyes burn with a fire that is arousing. A bit of fight is well-placed in anyone, man or woman, and most certainly in the mother of Tairov children. You knew my Mitya, if I recall. Yes, he would have made a fine soldier. Well, you and I shall produce children as fine as Mitya, I promise you." He pressed her hand to his lips once more.

"Please don't touch me." A low growl, like the plaintive threat of a cornered animal, seeped through her gritted teeth.

"I think you shall grow to like my touch, Anna." He was smoothing his thumb over her hand and chuckling softly to himself. "I rather thought I'd be bored with all the trimmings of yet another marriage. Yes, that's the truth. When your father first came to me with the proposal, I tired at his very words. But he's a persuasive man, your father, and I think this is a happy turn of events after all. I think, with you, I shan't be bored at all. . . ."

To Anna's relief, the Prince and the Colonel were the greatest of friends, and after some feeble attempts at including Anna in the conversation, they fell into the intimate talk of old friends, leaving Anna to the aunts, Marie and Aunty. Marie was stone-deaf and so round she waddled when she walked. Aunty talked constantly to invisible companions. Neither was pleasant company, nor suitable chaperones, and Anna turned her mind to plans for her escape the next day. Somehow she would get to the sanatorium as promised. She wouldn't let Nurse Strukova or Konstantin down. She'd walk all the way from the Prince's villa, even if it took her half the day.

"Anna, you've hardly touched a morsel on your plate," the Prince scolded.

Anna jumped at the sound of his voice. "I . . . I'm not very hungry."

"Well, you must eat. I've had Cook prepare this meal especially for you. Colonel Kurakin and I shan't leave the table until your plate is clean, will we, Fyodor?"

The Colonel peered at Anna through bloodshot eyes and said, "Skinny, Vaslav, my old friend. Skinny as a chicken, she is."

"You see that!" The Prince roared with laughter. "I shan't have my oldest friend complaining about my wife. Now, eat, Anna—eat!" The last word came out more as a command than an urging. There was an angry edge to the Prince's voice, which made Anna push and pick at the piles of food before her. In the end she felt quite pleased with her deceit. Each time the Prince looked at her, she was chewing. She chewed each piece of food fifty times.

Then the Prince seemed to forget about her eating; he took the decanter of wine in one hand and two glasses in the other. "Come, Fyodor, to the parlor. Anna will play for us. She's quite talented, you know. Was even sought after by the famous Rimsky-Korsakov."

The Colonel belched, then excused himself, calling back over his shoulder, "I'll be back in a jiff. Don't start some happy ditty without me!"

The plush parlor was dimly lit by a tiered candle chandelier which threw shadows of blue on the couches and rugs. Anna quickly found her way to the piano, relieved by its familiarity, but she no sooner sat than Prince Vaslav was by her side. His breath reeked of wine. His skin looked leathery in the shadows. "Ignore my friend Fyodor's comments, my dear." His face was very close. "The truth is, he thinks you're ravishing, and is mad with jealousy at my good fortune. Yes, after such misfortune . . . Ah, Anna, you cannot know the pain of a man losing his only two sons, and a wife to boot. But I think good fortune has blessed me at last. I think you shall bear me many strong and handsome boys, sons to carry a man contentedly into his old age. But now, Anna, now I'm not so very old, I promise you. . . ." He held her face with both his hands. "Not so very old at all. . . ." He pressed his lips on hers.

She struggled to break free, nauseated by the smell of his closeness and the wetness of his mouth. She felt imprisoned in his arms, invaded by the horrible forcefulness of his tongue, and would have screamed if she could have drawn a breath. Only the sound of the Colonel's drunken step in the hall caused the Prince to cease his amorous advances. "Ah, Anna . . ." He breathed heavily. "If only we were married already." And then he leaned closer, until his lips were almost touching her ear. "Have you ever been touched by a man before?"

"Please, the Colonel is coming." Anna pushed away, rubbing her hand furiously into her ear to erase the lingering irritation of the Prince's breath. She wanted to spit, to throw acid where the Prince's mouth had touched her.

"I'm the first, aren't I? Those lips are as pure as the rest of you, I'll wager."

The Colonel's singing of a popular tune urged the Prince to his feet. "I'll steal only kisses from you now and again, Anna. For now you would kill me if you could, yes, I see that in your eyes. You are a plucky one. But when you're my wife, we shall make a romp of it, I promise."

Just before dawn, Anna slipped from her bed and pulled the brown package which Nurse Strukova had given her from under the sheets and lovingly unwrapped it, slipping into the white uniform as if it were her bridal gown. She fit the headdress about her head, tucking in loose hairs, then stepped back to admire herself. She liked the crisp white vision and imagined herself a warrior, like Joan of Arc. The purity of her uniform was her armor. No one would dare touch or stop her. Carrying her shoes, she tiptoed down the hall; the thick carpets cushioned her footsteps. She ran down the stairs and out the parlor door, across the wide veranda, through the rose garden, and into the grove of cypress trees.

The air of dawn was sweetly warm and thick with the scent of lilacs and dew. Sea gulls swooped against the graying sky. Small waves rippled the sheen of the sea. Anna hurried. Soon the drive to the main road came into view, but she decided to stay on the path along the cliffs; she was used to walking in the narrow, sandy trails. Her toes dug into the cool morning sand, and she sang as she began to skip. The Prince, his touch, his house, his unpleasant Colonel, her mother and Zinaida Golovnina seemed distant dots, candles flickering helplessly in the cave from which she had taken flight. The sanatorium was her haven. Someone there would help her. Konstantin Novy grew stronger day by day. Perhaps he'd be strong enough soon; perhaps they'd soar into life together.

Anna reached the sanatorium just before eight o'clock. The halls were quiet. Nurse Strukova was not at her station. Anna hurried to the ward where Konstantin Novy slept. She was early, she'd never been this early before, early enough to feed Konstantin breakfast. She'd taken only a step into the room when she saw his bed empty, the sheets stripped, the mattress bare.

"Anna has disappeared," Misha told Irina.

"What do you mean 'disappeared'?"

"It's the talk of the village, and of the hospital too. Even Dr. Kavelarov mentioned it to me. He knew Anna. Said she was lovely, but he worried about her. She'd grown so thin of late, and was abnormally obsessed with this one patient. The nurses couldn't get her away from him. Apparently she spent an entire day sitting by his bedside, reading even though the boy was practically comatose. And then she begged the head nurse for an aide's uniform. Anyway, the boy died two days ago. Nobody at the hospital saw Anna to tell her of his death, but they think somehow she found out and that the shock sent her into a desperate mourning. A Tatar said he saw a young girl with long blond hair, dressed in a white nurse's gown, wandering along a beach. They've been checking all the beaches and the waters. Oh, Irina . . ." He sighed uneasily. "I hate to tell you this, but they fear Anna's drowned."

After the third day of Anna's disappearance the search was called off, yet Anna's disappearance remained the talk of the tiny seaside town. Rumors of spottings of Anna wandering about the cliffs and through the forests were commonplace. A Tatar woman claimed she saw Anna flying over her village, her white nurse's uniform floating in the moonlight. An article appeared in the local newspaper, quoting Prince Vaslav Igorovich's coachman, recently relieved of his duties, as saying he overheard a conversation between the Prince and the unfortunate young lady, in which the Prince was far from gallant in pressing his affections. Gossip spread that Anna had run from her marriage rather than from Konstantin Novy's death, preferring a briny coffin to a marriage bed with a man more than thirty years her senior. Rumor had it that Prince Vaslav Igorovich had left the Crimea, and that the Countess Marya Dmitreyevna was in seclusion waiting for her husband, the Count, to arrive from Petersburg.

"Anna's alive," Irina announced to Misha and Olga after returning from an afternoon walk.

"You saw her?" Misha questioned.

"I saw signs of her by the pond where we went as children—a shoe and the impression of a body on a bed of pines."

"But a shoe and the impression of a body—it could be anyone, a Gypsy, a Tatar."

"This was neither a Gypsy's nor a Tatar's shoe. I daresay if I showed it to my Aunt Marya, she would collapse in a faint."

"Why don't you send it to her?" Olga asked.

"It's Aunt Marya's fault Anna is so desperate. I would never betray Anna to the witch. She was always acting better than the rest of us, God knows why. Mama said Aunt Marya's blood runs like ice and her passion shriveled long ago. Only such a woman could think of marrying someone so beautiful and alive as Anna to a smelly old fart like Prince Tairov. No woman should ever be forced to marry against her will. It's one of the things we'll change with the revolution. We will! But now . . . well . . ." Her jaw set determinedly. "I'm going to find her."

"It's been over a week," Olga warned. "How could a young, innocent girl like Anna Petrovna survive in the woods alone all that time?"

"I don't know," Irina said thoughtfully. "That's what scares me. I thought I would go and watch the pond awhile, maybe even camp out the night—if you'd come with me, Misha."

"Of course. It will be an adventure, an old-fashioned adventure without guns and bombs."

"Just do it quietly—don't let on to the servants. You know how word travels here." Olga lowered her voice. "Misha, you and Irina fix some bedrolls. I'll fix you food. Ah, if only I were twenty, even ten years younger, I'd go with you. I thought some weeks in a villa by the shore would be a relaxation, but I'm itching to get on with something.'' Olga hobbled off, muttering to herself.

Anna heard the footsteps before she saw the people. She heard everything lately; the sounds of life invaded her brain, keeping her awake, even in the night. She heard the heartbeat of the forest and the sweet siren call of the rising moon; there were the tinkling bells of the underground streams, and the pulsating drumbeats of the sun swallowing up the night. She watched a praying mantis devour a butterfly, and was paralyzed by the beauty of the butterfly's mournful death song. She tried to memorize the melody, and went over it many times in her mind, thinking one day she might play it for Alexei. She heard a tiny bluebird suck nectar from a large pink flower, and listened as its wings fluttered in the whirring of spinning wheels. She thought this strange new perception of life was a message from God, that the world was her comfort and she should not fear her loneliness.

Here, safe in nature, no harm would come to her. The sun was warm. The night air tender. The pond refused to take her life. She dove to its dark, muddy depths every day, thinking she heard the soul of the water calling her, promising to caress her as did the angel in her dreams. But a frantic screaming always called her to the surface, only to find the air silent and the sun streaming through leaves as if God were smiling on her. She thought life was good, and she picked berries and mushrooms, chewing each morsel fifty times, to take in all the nourishment. When her stomach felt as if it might burst from so much food, she lay in the sun and held her arm above her eyes, imagining her thin, smooth fingers playing a song of thanks and praise of God, who through Konstantin Novy's death had given her life.

Anna was lying in a bed of tall ferns when she heard the footsteps and knew it was the foul creature returned, the mirage of her beloved Irina, sent by her mother and the Prince. Anna listened closely, hearing two sets of footsteps, one light, barely breaking twigs, the other heavy, those of a man. Her fingernails dug into the earth. The pounding of her heart made the ground shake. She closed her eyes, willing her heart to quiet. If she lay very still, the foul creature and the Prince would never find her.

Misha rose early. The morning light was just streaming through the trees and his body was cramped from sleeping on the forest floor; his bladder ached for relief. He unwound himself from Irina and started for the woods surrounding the pond. On his return, he stopped to pick some berries and was carefully carrying back handfuls as a treat for Irina when his foot caught against something soft and he tripped, sending the berries flying and leaving him sprawled on the ferns.

"Oh, my God!" he shrieked, fumbling to escape the body with which he was entangled. He sat, then knelt, horrified at the specter of a human being that stared back at him. Her sunken blue eyes were surrounded by dark circles. Her dirt-streaked face was pale, its skin almost translucent. She wore a nurse's uniform, torn and stained with mud and berry juice. Her long, blond hair hung limp and straight. She looked so small, so frail. Her wrists were the size of a child's. Her collarbones protruded horribly.

"Irina!" he bellowed, afraid to move.

The girl jerked to her feet.

"No!" He grabbed her. "Irina!"

"What? What is it?" Irina was running through the brush.

The girl was struggling feebly. She had little strength. "Go away! Don't touch me! Go away!" Anna's terrified voice splintered the isolation of the place; her wild eyes darted miserably.

"Anna, it's you, isn't it?" Irina gently questioned, motioning Misha to let go of his hold as Irina's own hands touched Anna.

"I am no one."

"Annochka, I know it's you. It's me, Irina. Your cousin Irina."

"You can't fool me," she snarled as she reached for Irina's hair, pulling it with a newfound strength, pulling Irina to her knees.

"No, leave her alone!" Irina gasped as Misha tried to help.

"I will not harm you if you go away," Anna growled, her pull tugging painfully at the roots of Irina's hair.

"All right, all right." Irina dropped hold of Anna's arm.

Immediately Anna darted into the woods.

Misha quickly followed.

Grabbing her skirt, Irina ran, the twigs, rocks, and sticks cutting her bare feet.

"She's over there, behind that large rock," Misha whispered when Irina reached him. "What should we do? She's crazed."

Irina shrugged and shook her head. Tears wet her eyes. "Listen to me, Annochka," she called softly. "I know you're here. I know you can hear me. This is Misha with me. You remember Misha, Alexei Yakovlevich's nephew. Remember how you told me you were so happy for our love? Well, we're here to help you, Annochka, not to harm you. I promise. Please let us help you.''

There was a long silence and finally Anna walked from behind the rock. ''Can you take me to Alexei?'' she pleaded.

''Yes, yes, if you want!'' Irina promised, pressing her hands to her lips to hold back her cry of pain.

''Not to Mama or the Prince.''

''Never, if you don't want.''

''Promise?''

''On my life, Anna.''

Anna nodded, and Irina ran to her, embracing her, yet afraid to hold too tightly. Anna felt like a small child, her bones soft as a bird's.

''Irina . . .''

''Yes.''

''I'm very tired. I'm so tired. I just need to sit awhile.'' Anna slipped through Irina's hold.

Irina sat with her and motioned Misha over.

Anna stared at him for a long time. Then she smiled. ''Yes, you are Misha. I see Alexei Yakovlevich in your face.''

CHAPTER TWENTY-SEVEN

March 20, 1904

Dear Uncle Alexei,

I hope all goes well with you. I write to you from Alexander Ilyitch's house in Yalta, where I am on holiday with Irina Ilyanova. Alexander Ilyitch has been too kind in offering us his house. Papa has barred me from ours because of my love for Irina. It was, for many reasons, time for us both to leave Petersburg. Irina and I are fine here. We have been having a much-needed rest.

I write to you for a particular reason, though. It is about Anna Petrovna. I know you have such great admiration for her talent and once wanted to help her in whatever way you could. Well, I'm afraid she's fallen onto some bad times. It is a long story, but she is here with Irina and myself and a friend. She was gravely ill, and most certainly would have died, Dr. K. said. He is a fine doctor and comes highly recommended by both Yuri Nikolaievich and Alexander Ilyitch.

Dr. K. said Anna was starving to death. I know that sounds hard to believe, but if you had seen her when we found her, you would have known it was true. I have never seen anyone so thin. Dr. K. said he has read much of the work of Dr. Freud and others, and he believes that Anna's starving herself is due to her emotions. That is odd, don't you think, that a person could willingly starve himself? You see, Anna was betrothed to Prince Vaslav Igorovich Tairov, a man she detested. Dr. K. says perhaps that is why her mind went mad. Only an insane person would starve himself. Poor Anna, she is a shadow of the beautiful young girl you knew only four months ago. Dr. K. says he will know more when he can talk to her at length, which may be a while. For even though she is safe here with us, she eats little. It takes Irina sometimes an hour to feed her half a bowl of soup.

I write to you, Uncle Alexei, because we don't know what to do with Anna. We cannot tell her parents of her whereabouts—they think, in fact all the Crimea thinks, that Anna has drowned by now—we promised Anna we wouldn't tell anyone that she was safe with us. But she speaks of you often, and you know so much, you always know what to do, Uncle Alexei.

I hate to suggest this to you when you seem so happy in Siberia. I hate to disturb your comfort, but I know no one else to turn to who cares in the least about Anna Petrovna. If you could help her even in the smallest way, she would be forever in your debt.

> *With greatest of love and respect,*
> *Misha*

"What do you think of it?" Misha asked Irina when she finished reading the letter.

"You're not going to send it?" she demanded, her face a disturbing ashen color.

"Why not?" Misha questioned uncertainly, taken aback by the severity of her tone. He'd thought she'd be excited by the cleverness of his plan. After all, someone had to take care of Anna. He and Irina and Olga couldn't do it forever. Uncle Alexei seemed the perfect solution.

"Why not? You have to ask me 'why not,' when it was

you who warned me against mailing Josef's letter to his parents from here!''

"Uncle Alexei is different. The police don't suspect him. They're not reading his mail. Hardly anyone knows he's in Siberia.''

"For God's sake, I don't believe you're so naive. He's the head of the damn Symposium!''

"He's in Siberia,'' Misha said by way of an explanation. "He's been there for months. He might as well be at the ends of the earth.''

"That's not the point, Misha. You've broken discipline. My God, your uncle is hardly a fool. And it would take one not to read between the lines with all your references to Dmitri Andreievich and Ryabushinsky.''

"There's nothing wrong with my using the name Yuri Nikolaievich. The police, if they read this, which I doubt they will, know he's my uncle's business partner. I've known Yuri Nikolaievich all my life.''

"The police may also know that you're a member of the Terrorist Brigade! Quite possibly your uncle will read that into the letter too.''

"I want him to. Uncle Alexei is one of us, and he should be with us, not in Siberia. The revolution needs him.''

"Well . . .'' She snorted and handed him back the letter. "Show it to Olga Fyodorovna and Dr. Kavelarov. They'll convince you not to send it.''

"I can't. I mailed the original three days ago.''

"You mailed it!'' she echoed stridently. "How could you? All the lives you've risked. God knows what Dmitri Andreievich will do when he finds out. With all this vacationing, have you forgotten you're a comrade? You're committed to the good of the revolution, not to some selfish, bourgeois ideal.''

Nausea swept over him; he couldn't bear fighting with Irina. He wanted to silence her, to soften her eyes with kisses and cause her lips to smile with his touch. Breathing deeply, he looked past her so as not to see the biting cold of her stare. "I swear to you, Irina,'' he said calmly, "I thought I had no choice. If I'd showed the letter to Olga and Kavelarov, they would have had to consult Dmitri. That could take weeks, and yet another two weeks for the letter to reach Uncle Alexei. We can't wait that long.''

"Why not?''

"What if Dmitri calls us back to Petersburg? We can't bring Anna.''

"Why not? I'll teach her the way Stepan taught me, the

way I taught you—the way we all of us in the Brigade help one another.''

"My God, Irina, you're not seriously thinking Anna can become one of us! She's led the most sheltered life imaginable. Most likely she hardly knows there's a revolution going on. And if she doesn't agree with you?''

"She will. All she needs is to have her eyes opened. Look at yourself, look at most of us. One day we were just ordinary people, then we met someone, or experienced an atrocity of the Czar's, and we were different, we were revolutionaries. It happens all the time.''

"What about her parents? No matter how cruelly they treated her, we can't let them go on thinking she's dead. It isn't right.''

"Right!" she mimicked with disgust. "Uncle Petya and Aunt Marya are as much the enemy as Yermolov. We're not only fighting for people to eat better and have decent food and work—we're also fighting for respect—for workers, peasants, both men *and* women. Think about your own mother, why don't you. Think if she had been able to choose a husband out of love—or for any reason other than her father's convenience—do you think she would have chosen one who beats her? Do you think she would have chosen a man who eats away a little more of her soul each time he takes her to his bed?''

"Shut up, damn you! Shut up! Shut up for once in your life!'' He pushed past her and out to the veranda.

Irina shuddered, knowing she had gone too far, and she ran after him, pulling him to a stop as he bounded down the stairs to the garden. "I'm sorry—that was unfair, what I said, and cruel. Forgive me. . . .'' Her touch on his arms was soft; her voice had lost its bitterness, her face its tight edge. "Truly, I'm sorry.'' She slipped her arms about his waist and pressed her face to his heart. "I love you, Misha, but I love Anna too. I just don't want her hurt anymore.''

"I don't either, nor would Uncle Alexei.''

She tightened at the name of Alexei Kalinin, then said, "Let's forget it for now, all right? The letter's sent. There's nothing we can do.''

"What about telling Olga and Dr. Kavelarov?''

"I don't see the point. Besides, it's such a lovely day. Why don't we see if Anna wants to go for a walk on the beach?''

"Why don't we go alone?'' he asked, smiling playfully. "It seems we're hardly alone anymore.''

"Yes, you're right.'' Her arm slipped about his and she led him through the gardens and across the wide lawn to the cliffs and the beach below. The sea was perfectly calm and glittering in the noonday sun. "Shall we go for a swim?"

"It's a long way back for our swimsuits."

"Who said anything about swimsuits?" She smiled teasingly, and began unbuttoning the front of her dress. Eyeing him deliciously, she slipped the dress over her head, followed by her chemise and finally her bloomers. "Are you just going to sit there and gawk?" she demanded, hands on hips.

Misha was sitting fully dressed on the beach, watching her. "I was considering it. The view is simply breathtaking."

"Oh, no, you're not!" She began tugging at his arm.

With one quick pull he had her in his arms. His face nestled in her breasts, and he smacked her buttocks playfully. "You are the naughtiest girl I have ever known. You know that."

"Yes—it's one of my many goals in life!"

He smothered her laughter with the fullness of his mouth, and laid her down on the beach. Kneeling beside her, he scooped up handfuls of sand and dribbled it down her dark, erect nipples and full breasts. Taking off his shirt, he stretched beside her and began gently rubbing the grains slowly, softly, on her skin. "Turn over," he whispered, and massaged her shoulders, back, buttocks, and thighs with a flat rock warmed by the sun. She moaned and rocked, turning to him as her legs parted and her hands reached for his belt.

"Do you think it's all right here?" he asked as she began to undress him.

"Who ever comes? Olga can hardly make it down the stairs and Anna's asleep," she promised, sitting up to stroke his chest; she kissed each shoulder as her hands deftly unbuttoned his trousers and slipped them off. When he was fully undressed, she covered his sun-hot skin with kisses and they rolled together across the sand until the water lapped against them. With wet sand covering his side, Misha knelt and then stood, pulling Irina to her feet. Tightening her arms about his neck, she raised herself to his hips, and as he slipped inside her, she locked her legs about him. "Take me into the water," she murmured as they rocked.

"Is this possible?" He laughed softly.

"Where there's a will, there's a way, my dearest heart." She nibbled his lips and wriggled against him.

It was a lazy, late-April afternoon. Irina had drunk too much wine at lunch and had stayed up from the beach with a headache. She was dozing on the couch in the drawing room when a sharp knocking woke her. There was an opening and closing of a door and the sound of heavy boots on the entry-hall floor. Jumping to her feet, she looked about for a weapon, and grabbed a bronzed statue.

"Hello! Hello! Is anyone home?" a man called as she tiptoed across the room.

Irina pressed against the wall, grasping the statue tightly in her hand before stealing a look into the hall. To her horror, Alexei Kalinin was standing not four feet from her, looking about.

"Hello! Misha!" he called. "Is anyone here?"

Irina left the statue on a nearby table, fluffed her hair, smoothed her skirts, took a deep breath and walked from the drawing room, smiling as she extended her arm. "Alexei Yakovlevich. Welcome." She held her smile, doing her best to keep her composure.

"Irina Ilyanovna!"

There was a moment's awkwardness, and Alexei took her hand in greeting.

"I'm sorry you caught us so unprepared, Alexei Yakovlevich. I wish you had let us know you were coming."

"I wasn't sure it was wise to send a telegraph boy up here."

"Well, of course, you're right. In any case, you're always welcome." Her jaws were beginning to ache from the burden of the smile. Inside, a fury was growing at Alexei Kalinin's presence. Damn Misha, she thought irritably. Damn him for sending that letter. To Alexei she said, "I'm afraid Misha isn't here."

"Oh . . ."

"He's not far—just down at the beach with Anna Petrovna and our friend who's staying with us, Olga Fyodorovna."

Alexei's eyes widened happily at the mention of Anna. "She's better, then."

"Anna, yes, quite. Although she's still frail. She loves to walk by the shore, and the sun has put the color back in her cheeks. Can I get you something, Alexei Yakovlevich?" She eyed his suitcase by the front door. "I'm afraid we have no servants to help you. We let them all go when Anna came to stay. Everyone gossips so. We've just an old woman who comes to clean, and then we make sure Anna stays in her room. Would you like something to drink? Some wine?"

"Yes, that would be nice." Alexei smiled uneasily, feeling suddenly awkward standing in Ryabushinsky's house with this haughty daughter of Tatyana Rantzau. She had her mother's authority, for certain, and something else. She was far less the woman than the warrior. Oh, yes, Alexei thought, this

Irina did well with Dmitri Mayakovsky. She would throw a bomb remorselessly.

"Sit down, please, Alexei Yakovlevich." Irina ushered him into the drawing room. "You must be tired from your journey. I shan't be a moment."

Alexei did as he was bidden, settling with great relief into one of the overstuffed chairs upholstered in fabric covered with huge pink flowers. The frenzied journey of the past ten days was catching up with him. Perhaps he had been foolish to rush from Kira; but a force feeling like fear had pushed him on. He'd been so certain Anna would be dead before he could reach her. How foolish! Anna was fine, perfectly fine, romping on the beach.

His eyes took in the familiar furnishings of Ryabushinsky's seaside drawing room, and suddenly he was certain Kira was right: he had no choice in coming here. But as much as he loved Anna, this mad journey from Krasnoyarsk to Yalta had been motived by one thing: to save her from that marriage. Prince Tairov, indeed! Anna's father was a cockroach to conceive of such a travesty. Alexei had to be certain Anna was safe, settled in the Conservatory and with a companion. Then he would go about his life again.

"If you don't mind the mess out there, we might move onto the veranda. I've not cleaned up from lunch," Irina announced as she returned carrying a tray with two glasses. "There's some lovely Crimean wine already open."

"Of course." Alexei was on his feet, offering to carry the tray.

"It's no bother, Alexei Yakovlevich," Irina insisted, bustling ahead of him. Taking the wine from the table, she led him to some chairs underneath a shady linden tree.

"Ah, it is lovely out here," Alexei mused, staring at the cloudless blue horizon of sea and sky.

"Quite a change from Siberia."

"Oh, yes, quite!" He gazed down over the cliffs, his heart skipping at the sight of three people. They were too distant for him to see clearly. "Is that them?" he questioned, hoping not to seem overly excited.

"Yes. Olga Fyodorovna has a hard time walking with her arthritis, and they don't wander away from our beach. We've never had anyone walking here. We're quite secluded," Irina assured him as she offered him a glass of wine. "Are you sure I can't get you something to eat?"

"No, no, this is fine. We had lunch on the boat."

"You took the ferry from Sevastopol. It's the only bearable way. Overland, it's twelve hours from Sevastopol."

"It seemed that on the ferry. . . ."

The pleasantries continued for a while, both Alexei and Irina straining for innocuous commonplaces to exchange. Every so often, laughter or a happy cry was carried up from the beach on a warm sea breeze, and Alexei turned to look as if he could not help himself.

"We could go down and meet them," Irina suggested. "I'm sure they'd be delighted. Sometimes, if Anna is feeling strong, we stay down there the afternoon. Dr. Kavelarov says the sun and salt air are good for her."

"I'd just as soon wait here," Alexei assured. It wasn't his plan to greet Anna on a beach with three other people. He wasn't sure what his plan was. He'd hoped to come on her quietly, alone. He'd envisioned her lying gracefully in a giant bed, propped by lacy pillows, or lying on a shaded chaise, velvet ribbons holding back her hair. He'd imagined her joy in seeing him, and felt his own. Sometimes he thought it was the anticipation of their meeting that beckoned him from the moment he'd received Misha's letter and seen Anna's name written there. The rush of feelings and images swept him, hurtling him like dust in a squall toward this moment.

Anna had beckoned like a sorceress. Even as he sat beside Irina Ilyanovna, he felt Anna's nearness. Loving her was giddy like the enchanted seascape before him, alive in crystal blues, sun whites, yellows and newborn greens. Loving Anna brought him to the threshold of life, where stolen kisses tasted of immortality and greatness took flight on winged steeds. Loving Anna was touching a part of him he'd long left behind. Loving her was an innocence he'd never known.

"Actually," he began, smiling cordially at Irina, "I enjoy it up here. I'm quite content to wait, now that I know Anna grows stronger. Besides, all these years I've been such friends with your mama, I've never known you. She's told me much about you."

"None of it good, I'm sure." Irina laughed bitterly; then her face grew tense. "You didn't tell Mama I was here?"

"No, rest assured, no. The letter from Misha was a bit cryptic, but clear enough. Then I met a mutual friend in Moscow before coming here. Yuri Nikolaievich. Or perhaps you know him better as Dmitri Andreievich. We had quite an interesting chat."

Irina stared silently into her wine.

"Dmitri Andreievich has quite assured me Anna has no part in the Brigade."

"Misha never should have sent you that letter, Alexei Yakovlevich," Irina responded haughtily. "He did it without consulting me. Anna is my concern. She's my cousin. She trusts me implicitly."

"I'm sure she does, and with good reason." He poured himself some more wine and, leaning back on his chair, crossed his legs. This girl was truly annoying him.

"Please, Alexei Yakovlevich." Irina rose to her feet. "Let me get you something to eat. I'm not much of a cook, but I can put some meat and cheese and bread on a plate."

"I'm fine. Stay and talk with me awhile."

"You will excuse my rudeness, but I feel extremely uncomfortable talking with you now. I fear you're set on picking my brain."

Alexei laughed heartily. "You're very astute, Irina Ilyanovna! Tell me this, are you in love with my Misha, or is that too just part of your facade? Yuri—excuse me, Dmitri Andreievich—was uncertain about the affair."

"I'm very fond of Misha," she said coldly.

"I hope so. From what I know, he's very fond of you."

"And Anna of you."

"What's that?"

"Anna raved of you when she was most gravely ill. She called your name in her sleep and prayed for you to come save her. Misha wrote for you to come save her. No man is a savior, Alexei Yakovlevich."

"I have no argument with you on that."

"I'm not sure a man can understand the thirst for freedom inside a woman. It's easier for men. Even the poorest man is born freer than the richest woman. Anna has already been sold once. I love her. We grew up together. We're like sisters. I won't let her be sold again."

"I see, yes, and you think I've come to enslave her."

"You take my words too lightly, Alexei Yakovlevich. Perhaps you should wait until you see her. Yes, I daresay you'll be shocked—even after a month, she's still so frail. Yet she's a hundred times better than she was. Her fear, her uncertainty of what her life will be, eat at her like maggots. She admires you above all men. I won't let you use her innocence to your advantage."

"Truthfully, Irina Ilyanovna, I feel better knowing Anna has such a protector in you."

"What is it you want with her?"

Alexei's face grew quiet. "I'm not certain. That's the God's truth. I only know she's a very special person and no harm should ever come to her."

"But it has."

"I want to see that never happens again."

"So do I."

CHAPTER TWENTY-EIGHT

Anna raced up the slope ahead of Misha, who walked slowly with Olga Fyodorovna on his arm. It was a glorious day. Even after a long swim, Anna felt not the least bit tired. She was even hungry. Yes, she was certain she was. She was thinking a lot about food. Dr. Kavelarov told her it was the only way she would become totally well again. He said she had to nourish her body. Here with Irina, Misha and Olga Fyodorovna, she felt safe, and was beginning to sleep without the nightmares. If only she knew for certain she was safe forever from the Prince and any other man. She wanted never to marry. She would remain pure forever. Irina said it was possible. Irina promised when Anna was fully recovered, she would show her ways to be free of men without joining a convent, although sometimes Anna thought she would like to do that, to devote her life to God and the sick and the dying. There were so many lovely, helpless young men, victims of the disease and the horror of war. She could attend to them all. She would be a Sister of Mercy.

She ran faster, stumbling as she did and pulling at some tall beach grass. Irina would be pleased to find out how hungry Anna was. She could eat a horse, she thought, racing across the green lawn toward the veranda, stopping as the vision of a man rose before her. She grasped herself tightly, afraid she had gone mad again. Yes, surely she had. Why else would that man beside Irina look so much like Alexei Yakovlevich? She blinked, and looked again. The vision of Alexei would not go away.

"Anna," the man called out.

She pressed her hands to her ears and turned to run the other way.

"Anna!"

The man was running after her. His long legs carried him

easily. There was no way she could escape him, and she stopped.

He was by her side, smiling so happily, looking so like Alexei.

Mother of God, blessed Virgin, she prayed. *Take me now, take me to your bosom. Don't let me live in madness again.* . . .

"Anna, it's me, Alexei. Don't you remember me?" He was smiling his beautiful smile, smiling it as he did only for her. "Misha wrote and told me of your illness. That's why I came, to see you. How are you?"

"Is it really you?"

"Yes, it's me!" He took her hand in his.

She pressed her face into his broad, warm hand. "Alexei, Alexei," she repeated, half-crying, half-laughing, and then embraced him, burying her face in his shoulder, smelling his scent, luxuriating in the strength of his closeness. His arms were about her, protecting her. She wanted the moment to never end. She wanted him to never release her. "Come, come with me a moment," she pleaded, tugging at his hand.

"But the others . . ." He looked toward where Anna had just come from, to see Irina hurrying across the lawn.

"See, Irina has gone to tell Misha. Please, before he comes, just let me show you something." Her eyes locked in his, and she could not stop smiling.

"All right. Come!"

Still holding his hand, she began to run, and he ran beside her, following her through trees to a clearing by the cliffs.

Anna urged him down next to her. "This is my place, Alexei Yakovlevich. It's so quiet and cool. Even in the hottest part of the day, a breeze blows. And you can see no other house, no other people. I come here often, to be alone. And I always think of you. I do! Is that silly?" She wound her fingers absently through his and without thinking pressed them to her lips. "Oh, you are my friend after all. I knew you were. I knew you didn't believe I would run from you and the audition for the Conservatory. I wanted it, Alexei, more than I wanted anything in my life. You have to believe me. It was my mother, and the awful Zinaida Golovnina. I shall never go back to my mother or father. I'd rather beg in the streets for food. Irina says I don't have to return. She says she'll help me."

"I've come here to help you, Anna. I've traveled all the way from Siberia for the purpose of helping you. I'll always be here for you, I promise. You are so special, you know that, Anna—a gift from God to the world." His smile faded, his face saddened. "I want to make you well again. I think I can, if you want me to."

"But . . . but . . ." She looked away, afraid of the feelings his beauty, softness, and closeness were stirring. She'd fought the feelings ever since the day, almost a month before, when she saw Irina and Misha on the beach. First there'd been a terrible argument; Misha and Irina were shouting as Anna's parents used to shout, and she tiptoed down the stairs, overwhelmed with relief when she saw them embrace. She followed them. It was foolish and wrong to spy. She just needed to be certain they were still happy. Anna needed them to be happy. And she curled up behind some sand dunes. She could watch Misha and Irina endlessly. Their love radiated, binding them without touching.

They kicked off their shoes and started barefoot down to the water. Suddenly Irina stopped and began undressing. Anna thought it was a dream, or a moment of madness. She was back again at the pond so many years before, Irina undressing, smiling that smile; Irina standing naked, white against the white sand, golden on the sun. Then Misha grabbed her to him, his hands smoothing over her body as his face nestled against her, kissing every part of her, even that place between her legs that burned so hotly on Anna.

Anna knew she should go, but the touching was mesmerizing. Irina was undressing Misha, her hands slipping down his trousers. They were gods entwined; arms, legs, mouths, bodies rocking, swaying, naked bodies loving. Slowly, sweetly, Alexei came to her in shadows. She tried to imagine herself with him on the beach. She tried to imagine his arms holding her, his lips kissing her. She tried to imagine his hands on her breasts, and when she looked again, Misha and Irina were in the water together, Irina's arms and legs wrapped about him. Irina threw back her head and they tumbled laughing into the sea. Their laughter brought tears to Anna's eyes.

Night after night Anna lay in bed, her mind reliving the lovemaking even though she swore she would not think of it again. She was so confused. Her mother spoke of physical love between a man and a woman as if it were a duty to be borne. With the Prince, it would have been far worse than eternal damnation. But with Misha and Irina, the exuberance, the glorious melting of their bodies, flowed like the heated scent of grapes hanging thick and purple in the summer sun.

Bodies, bodies, she could not stop seeing them. Irina's body. Misha's body. Anna looked at her own. It was true she was too thin. Her bones protruded, but her breasts, although smaller, still swelled. She spied them sideways in the mirror and bent over, pressing them into a cleavage with her arms. She would eat more, she determined, and remembered those afternoons with the Club. Odd how bodies could be so ugly or so beautiful. It was all too confusing. Most confusing of all was the obsessive longing that smoldered within her, bursting into the strangest dreams that she never quite remembered; rather she felt touched by the lingering memory of Alexei, his smile, his eyes, his hands, his laughter, his presence waking her, spreading warmly from within. In the dark of night, she felt a flower press to open, glorious in shades of red, its petals spreading row upon velvety row. She held and touched herself and cried in whimpers that sometimes gushed. The glorious madness passed and she slept again, thinking life was good; but in the morning, memories of the night horrified and repelled her. She swore she'd never touch herself or allow a man to touch her. Love was all right for Irina; it had always been all right for Irina; Anna would find beauty and contentment in serving others.

"What's wrong?" Alexei asked, nudging her.

She jumped at his touch, desperately afraid he could see into her mind. "Nothing. I . . . I'm just tired. Yes, suddenly I'm very tired."

"Of course, I understand. Come." He stood up, offering her his arm. "Come, we'd better get back to the others. We have plenty of time to talk. We've all the time in the world now."

"Dmitri Andreievich told you just about everything, then," Misha said as he and Alexei walked the grounds of Ryabushinsky's villa together. "Are you angry with me?"

"At first I was. I don't think I could bear your being hurt or put in jail. I don't think I could bear your death. That's a possibility, you know, in this line of work you've chosen."

"Yes." He looked hard at Alexei as they walked. "I feel strong for the first time in my life. Even Irina, loving her—it's different. I care about her. I would die for her. She's difficult, oh, yes, very difficult. Sometimes I feel it would be better to walk away from loving her. But I can't. It's like the revolution—it doesn't come easy, but it's important. It's worth fighting for, and at times I'm not even sure why. But it seems—this is going to sound odd, but . . ." He hesitated, blushing slightly. "Ever since I joined the Brigade and met Irina, it's as if I never before had smelled clean air or known the warmth of the sun or a woman's touch. It's as if I've lived asleep for twenty years, and now I'm awake, and despite everything, even despite Josef's death, I feel alive, my heart bursts with life.''

"I'm happy for you, although I don't envy you your love.''

"You'll grow to like Irina, I promise.''

"All right, I'll tell you, then. I tire of women who are too much in command. But you, I think they fire you. So be it!'' Alexei wrapped an arm tightly about Misha. "I think you are in love with the revolution too.''

"I see it as the great pattern of my life, as if that day at Kazan Cathedral, it was the path on which God started me the day I was born.''

"Ach, don't tell me you were born to be a terrorist.''

"In this life, yes. I believe that. In another time, a time of peace and equality, I might be something else, a politician, even the poet you've always seen me as being. But now, here, today in Russia in 1904, I am what I should be. And it's not that I'm not afraid, Uncle Alexei. I am. I don't want to die like Josef and the others. But I couldn't go on living the way I was. I can't go back. I believe in what we fight for. It's in my blood. In your blood. We're fighters, the way Grandma always said. The streets are far more my home than palaces and villas. As much as I love it here, treasure these weeks with Irina, I can't wait to return to Petersburg. This time we shan't miss when Yermolov passes in front of us.''

"Ah, Misha, you've long been my conscience as well as my hope for the future.''

"That's because we're so much alike,'' he said proudly.

"How's that?''

"I used to think you were a god, the most powerful being in the world. But I don't anymore. I see you as a man, and what's nice about that is you're closer to me. I look at who you are, and I say: I can be like Uncle Alexei too. I can be strong, and wise. I can make change, my kind of change.''

"Violent change.'' Alexei frowned.

"My life has been violent.''

Alexei looked surprised.

"Oh, not with you and Grandma and Mama, but with Papa. Do you think a Cossack's whip could hurt me any more than he has?''

Alexei's voice saddened. "I tried to protect you.''

"I know. I don't blame you. I'm not even sorry. Worse things happen to people than having drunken brutes for fathers, far worse. You've only to walk through the slums. Even poor Anna Petrovna. She was ready to choose death over her fate. I've never been brought to such desperate straits.''

"Tell me, how ill is she really?"

"I'm not sure. You should speak to Dr. Kavelarov about that. But I can tell you this, she's much improved. She was like a starved, wild bird when we found her. Do you think you can do anything to help her, Uncle Alexei?"

"I'll speak to her father first, in Petersburg. As soon as Anna's strong enough, I'll take her with me. My plan is to find her a companion. She must be allowed to practice her music as soon as she can. I'll talk to Kavelarov. Music is her soul. I'm certain it's what she needs to grow strong. I'm glad you wrote to me, Misha. I'll take care of Anna. I daresay I'm the only one who can."

"Why are you smiling so, Uncle Alexei? You're grinning like a giddy fool."

Alexei's face grew stern, and his pace quickened. "Shall we go to the beach or back?" he questioned suddenly.

"Oh, the beach." Misha hurried to keep to his uncle's stride. They walked silently down the cliff and across the dunes. It was hot, and Alexei took off his jacket and undid his tie. Misha sat staring out at the sea, calm and shining with an even gloss. "You're in love with Anna Petrovna," he said, reaching for a handful of sand.

"I love her. Yes, I'll admit that. I wouldn't have traveled thousands of miles if I didn't. But I'm not in love with her. There's a difference. I'm forty-two years old. Do you think a man of forty-two, a man who's lived the life I've lived, can fall victim to some silly passion such as grips you?"

Nodding, Misha said, "Yes."

"Absurd! And, I might add, none of your goddamned business. You may be a terrorist, but you're still a boy." Alexei rose to his feet and started walking in long, deliberate strides. He kicked the sand off his shoes a few times, then kicked off his shoes and tore off his socks. He paced to the water's edge and stood so the water gently lapped his feet.

"Anna loves you, Uncle Alexei, you know she does. You love her, she loves you—what's the problem?"

"She's a child!" Alexei roared back. "For God's sake, Misha, she's more than twenty years my junior!"

"She's thirty years younger than Prince Tairov."

"Would you stop this nonsensical gibber!" Alexei turned and started back up the beach.

"I've a question for you, then." Misha trotted in the sand beside him. "What brought you here to Yalta? Anna Petrovna or my involvement with the Brigade?"

"I won't answer such a question, Misha. It's impudent beyond endurance."

"You're blushing, Uncle Alexei!" Misha exclaimed, running backward just out of Alexei's reach. "I've never seen you blush before, never in my life!"

"Oh, now you're asking for it—now you truly are!" Alexei caught Misha in a bear hug, and no sooner did Misha break free than Alexei was after him, chasing him down the beach. They ran about a hundred yards before Alexei tackled him to the ground, where, to Alexei's surprise, Misha pinned him after a serious match. "I swear, but you've grown stronger!" Alexei laughed breathlessly.

"Or you've grown weaker."

"Please, don't accuse a man my age of such a thing—not when you're talking of my loving an eighteen-year-old girl." Alexei struggled to break free.

Misha released his uncle and, shaking his head, laughed softly. "You love Anna Petrovna and, personally, I think it's grand. But I warn you, Irina shall battle you. She thinks Anna should fight the revolution." Misha finally jumped off Alexei and helped him to his feet.

"Anna in the Brigade! I won't have such a thing." He wiped his face with the sleeve of his shirt.

"Try to tell Irina that. Once she's got her mind set on something, there's no stopping her." Misha grabbed Alexei's arm. "Marry Anna, Uncle Alexei. I know she'd say yes if you asked her. She loves you. She told me she did. She talks of you constantly when Irina's not around. She told me you were the most wonderful, perfect man in the world. Marry her and she'll be strong again. It's not her music that is her soul, Uncle Alexei, but you."

PART FIVE

BLOODY SUNDAY

CHAPTER TWENTY-NINE

Anna and Alexei were married on the morning of June 7, in a church in the bustling Black Sea port of Sevastopol. At Dr. Kavelarov's suggestion, Alexei tried to keep the wedding a quiet affair, but Anna's father, Count Orlov, waxed poetic on the marriage contract he had exacted from the great Alexei Yakovlevich Kalinin, who would, the Count drunkenly bragged, have given his fortune for the hand of the beautiful Anna Petrovna. The Count was also heard to mark his blessings that his high-strung daughter was another man's burden. The Countess, Marya Dmitreyevna, described by a reporter as "a tight, grim-faced devotee of the old religion," refused to comment on the marriage, and when pressed as she left a sanatorium in Yalta where she prayed for the dying, snarled, "I have no daughter."

Flocks of curious townspeople and tourists, as well as newspaper reporters, thronged the gold onion-domed church in Sevastopol to catch a glimpse of the near-legendary couple as they arrived on their wedding day. Police and private bodyguards held back the curiosity seekers, who bulged like swells of waves as the carriage stopped and Alexei, dressed in a simple white linen suit, emerged. He held out his arm and a bent, arthritic old woman stepped out, followed by a handsome, bearded young man, a tall, slim woman whose face was shadowed by an enormous feathered hat and dark veil, and finally Anna Petrovna. Beaming, she took Alexei Yakovlevich's hand. With her other hand, she gathered the richly embroidered skirt of her wedding gown, flowing yards painstakingly woven with silk, pearls, emeralds and rubies. She streamed in movements of fluid grace toward her betrothed.

A hush of silence settled, and onlookers shielded their eyes from the sun glaring off the brilliant gold of the bridal headdress studded with clusters of diamonds and rubies; Anna's yellow hair was thickly braided and gracefully edged her neck, encircled by a glittering diamond choker; but as every curiosity seeker and eager well-wisher knew, the luminous glow of Anna Petrovna's smile far outshone the brilliance of her jewels. Anna's radiance was the triumph of romantic love in a time when life was pitifully bereft of fairy-tale endings; it was the victory of the heart over lecherousness, betrayal and deceit. The whole Crimea knew that Anna's journey from the clutches of the hawk-nosed Prince into the arms of the rich, handsome Alexei Yakovlevich had not been an easy one. Beneath the bridal flush, telltale signs of strain shadowed her eyes, and there was an unhealthy angularity to her fragile face. She was almost too tiny to be real; her arms, wrists and waist were wisps; Anna Petrovna was the embodiment of the suffering heroine. Love and purity encircled her as she slipped onto her true love's arm; her eyes fixed lovingly on his; her radiance was beguiling. Sighs, oohs and aahs rose quietly from the sated onlookers, awed in the presence of such happiness. Alexei Yakovlevich was surely a man who had everything life offered.

Anna felt touched by the love of God. His blessing lighted the purified air of the church; his smile emanated from the serenity of the icons painted on resplendent frescoes, the great screen of the altar, and the sides of the many columns reaching to the vaulted ceiling, where halos, lighted by golden chandeliers, shone in heavenly splendor. Unmixed hues of blue, yellow, green and vermilion colored the benign presence of the saints and the apostles; the icononstasis soared in gilded tiers, ornately decorated with breastplates of gold and silver and halos of precious stones. God, Christ, the Virgin and their entourage had, it seemed, gathered for the celebration. Misha and Irina knelt behind the bridal couple and held the gold-and-velvet wedding crowns above their heads. The priest stood before them, arms outstretched in an embroidered crimson robe of gold threads, velvet, pearls and colored stones. His voice rose melodiously.

"Be happy for me, Irina, please," Anna begged in a stolen moment before the wedding supper.

"I am." Irina forced a smile.

"You think Alexei isn't good for me, but he is. I know. Please don't think I forsake you in my love for him." Anna squeezed Irina's hands.

Irina kissed Anna's jeweled fingers and smiled sadly. Smoothing Anna's pale cheek, she said, "I don't want to steal a moment of your happiness. I just want you to know, I shall never be far from you. When you return to Petersburg, I'll find you, I promise."

Anna grew serious. "I'm not sure I want to know the details of all you and Misha and Olga Fyodorovna do, not even if you wanted to tell me—but I want you to know I shall pray for you every night. God will watch over you as surely as he has watched over Alexei and me."

They hugged each other tightly.

"Oh, Irina, I feel you are my friend after all."

Irina held her a moment longer. "You'll be all right tonight?"

Anna blushed softly.

"No last-minute questions?"

"No last-minute questions." She shuddered as she smiled.

"Misha, Olga and I are taking the late train."

"I love you, Irina."

"I love you too." They hugged once more, falling apart as they heard Misha and Alexei approaching.

"Anna," Alexei said, sitting beside her on the velvet couch.

The light of the full moon shone through the window, casting pearly shadows on his face. The air was warm and sweet with the scent of the lilies and roses filling vases and hanging from baskets in the bridal suite. They were alone for the first time all day. *Monsieur Alexei Yakovlevich Kalinin* and *Madame Anna Petrovna Kalinina*—she repeated the names again and again, imagining how it would look on a calling card. *Anna Petrovna Kalinina*. . . . The very thought of her new name sent quivers of anticipation through her. Alexei's wife. She was alone with him for the first time as his wife.

They'd spent hours, mornings, afternoons and evenings alone over the past weeks, wandering arm in arm through Ryabushinsky's villa and along the beach. Anna had led him to her favorite Crimean haunts, and they'd sat for hours by the pond where Misha and Irina had found her. He'd always come in to wish her good night, kissing her forehead softly, and they'd talked for hours more sometimes, Alexei holding her hand, gazing at her as she gazed at him, smiling when words were no longer necessary. This aloneness was different, charged. Anna felt breathless, beautiful. She thought of the nightgown Irina had helped her pick out. It was long with white lace and the skinniest of shoulder straps. She wondered how she could stand before Alexei in such a negligee; she tried to see herself as he would see her, and visions of Irina standing on the rock in her white lace chemise, reciting Pushkin's poem *"The Nereids"* so many summers before, flooded her senses, leaving her prickly. Irina had been so beautiful then; Anna dared hope she would be so beautiful for Alexei.

"Anna . . ."

The softness of his voice made her jump. He caught her like an alchemist in the dark intensity of his gaze. He brushed the hair from her face and wrapped an arm about her, holding her close . She felt his heart pounding, and the playful touch of his fingers on her neck was maddening.

"I love you," he whispered, his tone edged with a haunting desperation.

She felt crushed in his arms, and for a moment she was afraid. The moment passed. His breath was warm and moist on her cheek. "I love you too. . . ." Her happiness felt beyond endurance. Alexei would be kind, gentle. She had nothing to fear. Her hand touched his cheek. "I love to look at you. I love your eyes, your nose, your lips. . . ." Her fingers smoothed his mouth.

He grasped them tightly. "How do you feel?"

"Fine, wonderful! I've never felt better."

He put her hand in her lap and stood up. He paced the room and poured two glasses of champagne. She shook her head when he offered her one. He downed his and hers, then stared out the window. "Look how lovely the sea looks in the moonlight."

She was beside him, slipping her arm about his waist. "You can see the whole harbor. Do you think there's anyone down there who's as happy as we are right now?"

He rocked her slowly. "You are my wife now," he said after a long, sweet silence, and then slipped free of her and filled his glass again. Without looking at her, he said, "I shall sleep on the couch in the other room tonight. Dr. Kavelarov said it would be best."

A bolt like a burning spear shot through her. She waited for him to say more.

"Good night, my love." He kissed her cheek, and taking the bottle of champagne with him, disappeared, leaving her alone.

When she awoke in the morning, he was sitting on her bed, bathed and cleanly shaven, dressed in a crisply pressed white suit, white shirt, and pale blue tie. "You slept well, Madame Kalinina?" He smiled eagerly when she opened her eyes, and took her hand, holding it to his lips.

"Oh, Alexei!" She pushed herself to a sitting position. "I can't believe it's real. I can't believe I'm truly your wife!"

"I hate to be the bearer of bad news, Madame Kalinina,

but you must get up soon. We've a steamship to catch in less than two hours." He started to stand.

"Alexei." She held him a moment. "I . . . I'm confused about something. About Dr. Kavelarov. You said, last night— I don't understand why—but you said Dr. Kavelarov said you should sleep on the couch." Her chest ached as she forced out the words. Her face burned with shame. She dared not look at Alexei.

He was quiet for a painfully long time, and then he said, "You were very sick, Anna. You're fragile, still. Dr. Kavelarov likened you to the finest crystal."

She stared at his hand wrapped about hers. Her gaze fixed on the lovely dark swirl of hair on his knuckles. His hands were so large, they totally enclosed hers. "I'm not so fragile," she insisted. "I don't break easily. If I did, I would be long dead by now!"

He chuckled softly. "Yes, I daresay your spirit isn't worse for the wear. Still, Dr. Kavelarov said, well. . . ." He paused awkwardly. "We have our whole lives together, my love. The important thing is for you to grow strong in body as well as mind. Nothing else matters." He stood and kissed her forehead. "Come now, I shall send Lidia in to help you dress."

"Lidia?"

"A little maid I hired for the trip. She will see to your every need. You are to do nothing but grow strong. You'll do that for me, won't you?"

"Alexei!" She grabbed his hand and kissed it. His skin was exquisitely warm. "I love you!"

He tapped her head. "I shall send Lidia right in."

Anna and Alexei sailed on a steamship from Sevastopol, across the Black Sea, through the Bosporus Strait to Istanbul, and on to an island in the Aegean Sea. Blue skies and warm sun followed; and if Alexei was sometimes distant, preoccupied, even bleak, the happiness of their shared moments, the anticipation of the next, bolstered Anna, blotting out jagged edges of uncertainty. Alexei showered her with gifts. He had a small piano and a gramophone with boxes of records taken wherever they went. Whether in their stateroom on the ship, or their suite in the hotel in Istanbul or their villa in Greece, Anna spent hours playing for Alexei, or sitting beside him, her head on his shoulder, her hand in his as they listened to Mozart, Brahms and Tchaikovsky on the gramophone. They walked through loud, colorful bazaars and along bustling docks; they sat on deck chairs and luxuriated in the sun; they danced in ballrooms and under the stars. They talked incessantly; even the commonplace seemed elevated to philosophy on Alexei's tongue.

Anna loved best the moments of brimming silence which unexpectedly connected them, bringing them so close, their love igniting the air; she thought he would take her in his arms as a lover then and kiss her as a woman; she waited breathlessly for him to teach her the wonders and the secrets of love. Instead, when she felt the moment threatening to burst and sweep them away, Alexei vanished, sometimes with an excuse and sometimes with none, leaving Anna more desperately alone and afraid than she'd ever felt. There was something wrong with her, something dreadfully wrong with her. Perhaps she was dying, and Alexei had married her out of pity. It was no wonder, she thought; a man would not want to make love to a dying woman. And if she weren't dying, then Alexei knew some other dreadful secret about her, something which Dr. Kavelarov most likely had confided. Alexei's words from their wedding night battered the peace their closeness promised. *Better isn't well. You're fragile, still. Dr. Kavelarov likened you to the finest crystal.*

"Finest crystal, indeed!" she fretted, feeling the edges of her mind curl like smoldering paper.

"What is it? Is something wrong?" Anna asked, finding Alexei on the terrace of their Aegean villa one morning. He was poring over a newspaper; his face was pinched with worry and concern.

"Nothing, my dove." He quickly folded the paper and put it down. "Nothing to worry your pretty little head about."

"But you worry. I see it on your brow, here. . . ." She ran her finger across his furrowed forehead. "And here." She took her hands and forced his lips into a smile. "Tell me now, what awful news did you read?"

"Just about the war with Japan. It goes worse every day."

"Oh." She feigned interest and took the paper as she sat beside him. It was a Russian-language paper that followed him wherever he went, usually some two weeks behind the times. Her eyes scanned the late-July headlines.

JAPANESE WIN ON THE YALU

ASSASSIN'S BOMB KILLS
CZAR'S CHIEF MINISTER
IN ST. PETERSBURG

FIVE THOUSAND SENTENCED TO EXILE
FROM ST. PETERSBURG IN JUNE

She lingered on the article about the assassinated Minister of the Interior, M. Plehve:

. . . with great force and precision a bomb was hurled on the cobblestones under Plehve's carriage. The detonation was terrible and the concussion was such that all the windows of the houses were broken within a hundred yards. Out of the dense smoke could be seen black objects being hurled upward.

When the smoke cleared nothing remained but the wheels, springs, frame, pole, and a few fragments of the woodwork of the carriage. Plehve was literally blown to bits. His entire face had disappeared. The coachman and likewise the horse were dead. Lying on the ground was the assassin, identified as Yegor Sazonov, member of the Fighting Section of the Social Revolutionary Party, who was wounded in the stomach by pieces of the bomb. . . .

Anna grimaced. "How awful, to be blown to bits." She shuddered. "Irina spoke to me of the people's fight for freedom. Of people starving. Of workers choosing to be shot rather than living like animals. What do you think of revolution, Alexei?"

"Why clutter your mind with politics, Anna? Music is your soul."

"But tell me what you think of that minister, Plehve or whoever, who had his face blown to pieces. Do you think he was an evil man? Do you think the people who blew him to pieces were murderers or heroes?"

Alexei thought carefully before answering. "I think he was more evil than good."

"Then you think the assassin was right—you think he was a hero."

"You have a wicked mind, Anna!" He laughed, and reached across the table for her hand. Kissing her fingers, he smiled happily. "You look better this morning."

"I slept quite well," she said stiffly, staring into her coffee.

"Oh, my, what did I say now to put you into a tiff?"

"You laughed at me when I was being serious!" She shot him a withering glance.

"Not at you. It was a laughter of enchantment. I love that I can't get away with anything with you. You catch me at every turn, squirreling around in my mind. How did you and I ever get into a discussion about assassins and revolution, anyway?''

"Isn't everyone talking about assassins and revolution these days? Irina says no Russian is free so long as—''

"Irina, Irina!'' Alexei gasped impatiently. "You talk of her as if she were some kind of goddess.''

"She saved my life!'' Anna admonished, startled that Alexei could harbor even the slightest ill feeling toward Irina.

"Why, yes, that she did,'' he admitted begrudgingly. "I'm sorry. Forgive my slander.'' He cocked his head and took her hand again. "I shouldn't be short with you either. It's just that I tire so of political talk, Annochka. It's not something I expect from you. Actually, it's unbecoming in a woman.''

"Quite the contrary. I think revolution has made Irina even more ravishing. Even in your newspapers, there's talk of women in the streets.''

"Revolution isn't child's play, I warn you. It's a drug, like opium or morphine. Once you get a taste of it, it consumes you.'' He sounded worried.

Now it was Anna's turn to laugh. "Oh, Alexei, you've quite fallen for my game, haven't you! I just want to tease you. I don't care for revolution, not in the least. In truth, I read your newspapers for word of Russia. I get homesick sometimes—oh, it's not that I'm not having fun. I'm having the grandest time. Still, I miss Petersburg—the White Nights . . .'' She sighed wistfully. "They're over by now, gone for another whole year. Sometimes I think the White Nights are what I love best about the city.''

"Ach, those dreadful eternal days.''

"Dreadful! How can you say such a thing? The White Nights are magical. They're what heaven must be. Of course . . .'' She frowned. "At school, come May, they made us draw the shades and curtains at nine every night, so we shouldn't think about the White Nights. I believe Lydia Karlovna considered them sinful, filled with romance, you know. And of course, we were never to think about romance—only about our studies and about becoming young ladies—whatever that means.'' Her cheeks flushed with color, and she stirred her coffee until it splashed over the edge. "I never closed my shades, not for long, that is. I'd sit by my window for hours, sometimes all night, watching the light. It changes, you know, if you watch closely. And it's not like daylight, not at all. I used to imagine the sun enveloping the city in a transparent blanket. I used to imagine so many things, Alexei, things that would have quite shocked Lydia Karlovna and Miss Heidlemann.''

A shadow of despair grayed her face and she burst out, ''Never mind that the White Nights are the grandest time of the whole year! We were the young ladies of Smolny—oh, how I hated that place, Alexei.'' Her eyes narrowed. ''I despised it almost as much as I despised Zinaida Golovnina!''

Alexei began to chuckle, but the bright glare in Anna's eyes quickly cut him off.

''Can you image what it is to spend your childhood in a prison? That's what it was for me. Just when I felt freedom, I was sent to that horrid place. And you laugh!'' She threw her napkin on the table and ran to her room.

Alexei followed, and sitting on the bed, pulled at her arm.

''Go away. You laugh at me all the time—you treat me like a child!'' She refused to look at him. Her lower lip quivered and the words burst forth. ''I'm your wife, and you treat me like a child! I'm not a child and I'm not sick—if you'd make me your wife, you'd see!''

He glanced at Anna, thinking to take her in his arms and devour her with his love. Damn Kavelarov, damn him and his advice. *Handle Anna as you would the finest crystal. Nothing must upset her. The marriage bed is a trauma for young women like Anna. If you can wait awhile . . .*

Damn Kavelarov, damn the man. Alexei should never have listened to him. Alexei knew more about women than the toad-faced doctor could ever hope to know. Anna was not one of those frightened, frigid little virgins. There was desire in the way she watched him, and in the unconscious rhythm of her body. She was ready for love. What had the sorceress Tatyana called Anna? Ripe. Yes, she was. All Alexei had to do was reach out and her petal-soft body would open to him. She was a woman like any other woman, like the countless women he had taken to his bed. More than that, she was his wife. He had a right to her. And he wanted her. God knows, he wanted her. Then why couldn't he touch her? Why did a sickening fear swamp him whenever he thought of possessing Anna?

CHAPTER THIRTY

It wasn't until the train bringing Irina, Misha, and Olga home from the Crimea pulled into the Baltic Station that Olga Fyodorovna announced Dmitri wanted to see them. "You are to go to his house immediately. He's waiting for you."

"Something's wrong," Irina said cautiously.

"It's not for me to say," Olga replied dryly, putting on her bonnet.

Irina glanced at Misha and rolled her eyes despairingly. Relations had been strained between Olga and Irina and Misha ever since Alexei had arrived in the Crimea.

Irina knew the meeting with Dmitri would not be pleasant as soon as he opened the door. There was no smile, no word of greeting, no pleasant chitchat. He led them wordlessly to his office and abruptly closed the door.

"How dare you send such a letter to Alexei Yakovlevich without clearing it with anyone first!" Dmitri exploded. "Do you think this is a school play we're acting in?" His face was red and blustery. He pointed an accusing finger first at Misha and then at Irina. "If you want to risk your own lives, fine, then leave the Brigade now. I will not have your sophomoric little whimsies put the rest of us in danger."

"Irina had nothing to do with sending the letter—" Misha tried to explain.

"She knew of it!"

"But after the fact, Dmitri Andreievich. I had already mailed it to Uncle Alexei when I told Irina."

"Why didn't you warn Olga Fyodorovna or Dr. Kavelarov after the fact then?"

"I didn't see much point," Irina said stiffly. "I wasn't certain the letter would bring Alexei Yakovlevich."

"*If* it even reached him. Did it occur to you that the letter might have been siphoned by the police before it ever reached Alexei Yakovlevich?"

"It occurred to Irina, but not to me. I'm sorry—"

"Sorry!" Dmitri thundered. He wiped his hand again and

330

again across his sweating bald head. It was a very warm June day. The office was stifling. Dmitri poured himself a glass of water and downed it. " 'Sorry' means only one thing to me—that you've broken discipline. And to tell you the truth, Irina, I'd expected more levelheadedness from you." Dmitri was pacing his little office by now. "Ach, I should have you both tossed out of the Brigade! I would if you'd broken discipline with anyone but Alexei Yakovlevich. And damn, I need the two of you. But so help me God, we can be ready to blow Yermolov to smithereens, and if either of you dares to give me even suspicion of breach of discipline, you're out. From now on you're to clear anything you suspect *might* be out of the ordinary with me personally. Is that understood?"

"Yes, sir," Misha readily agreed.

Irina nodded, but her demeanor grew still more severe. Her eyes fixed stonily on her hands. Her lips pursed. Her jaw set as her cheeks colored.

"All right, then. Sit." Dmitri lumbered over to his desk and pulled back his chair. He sat, and when he looked up again, he seemed more composed. He reached for a cigarette and offered one to Irina and Misha. The reprimand was clearly at an end. "There are some things we need to go over, a few changes since you've been away. To begin with, Vladimir Ropshin has left us."

"That's not surprising," Irina muttered. She was sitting very tall and straight. Her eyes glared immutably down at her hands. "Vladimir was on the verge of a breakdown after Josef's death. In his weakness, he might have been the traitor. Have you investigated him, then?" Her voice was strong with the challenge of the question.

Dmitri hesitated a moment; his response was straightforward. "Unfortunately, Vladimir Ropshin simply disappeared."

"But you investigated people he knew," she continued sharply.

"Perhaps I should have called you back from the Crimea, Irina Ilyanovna, to lead the investigating squad." His tone was disparaging.

Irina blushed deeply. "I'm sorry. I didn't mean—"

"Good then." His smile was sugary. "We can move on. Rest assured, the Brigade did a thorough investigation not only of Vladimir Ropshin but also of everyone else in the squad since Josef's death. From all we can put together, it appears Vladimir was as loyal as the rest of you. I tell you this with confidence. I don't think we're dealing with a traitor here."

"And the connection between Vera's death and the thefts of the documents in Paris?" Misha asked, feeling very confused.

"I'm not in the least convinced there is a direct one. Vera Martova was very high on the Okhrana's list of wanted criminals. Someone may have independently recognized her, or she might have spoken with someone once she returned who talked to someone who talked to the Okhrana."

"Yes, I see . . ." Misha nodded. "Then you think there may not be a traitor?"

"It's certainly a possibility at this juncture. And we must proceed accordingly. To do otherwise would bring unwarranted suspicion and mistrust among the comrades, something we can't afford. Discipline must be kept. Trust among comrades is of the essence if we are to carry out our mission. We must keep our sights steady and fixed on Yermolov."

"I understand," Misha said.

"And you, Irina?"

"Yes, I too understand."

"Good, then to get on to the next business at hand. To begin with, we've some additions to your squad. Charlotte Ryabushinskaya has joined us, along with a young man from Moscow, Kolya Susanin, and an acquaintance of Savva's, Aksinia Moroskaya."

"Aksinia!" Irina exclaimed. "She led the strikes at the Putilov Iron Works. Savva introduced her to us—you remember her, Misha. She wears men's trousers and a Browning revolver strapped under her arm."

"Yes, and she shot a foreman when he threatened to call the police during a strike this summer. She's quite bold. We're fortunate Savva has recruited her. Now, Misha," Dmitri went on, "your trial for the attack on the Cossack at Kazan will be coming up in a few weeks. It won't be a trial actually. You'll be exiled, I'm certain, and the terms of exile being meted out for others arrested on that day are stronger than were expected. I don't want you showing up for the trial. You'll be sentenced in absentia, and so be it. I want both you and Irina to live in disguise from now on. I would suggest you don the garb of the workers and find yourself rooms in some workers' district. I don't want either of you to contact your families, or anyone who might know you in your former lives. Does that cause you any hardships?" He glanced from Misha to Irina.

"None for me," Irina quickly assured Dmitri. "There's none in my family who would mourn my loss for long."

"Can I contact Uncle Alexei?" Misha asked uncertainly.

"When he returns from his honeymoon, which won't be

till fall, I understand. And then, I should put him in contact
with you. We must all be very careful from here on. When
we strike against Yermolov again, we are not to fail.''

"I'm going to one of Gapon's meetings tonight,'' Irina told
Misha. They had been back in Petersburg three weeks, and
were living in a room in a boarding house in a working-class
district on the Petersburg side of the Neva River. It was within
easy walking distance to Alexander Ryabushinsky's house,
where the printing press was running full time now. *The People's Will* was published weekly. Savva, under the pseudonym
N. V. Siskin, was editor.

"Gapon's meeting! Whatever for?''

"I just have to go, is all.'' She hesitated. "I wasn't going
to tell you. I was just going to go, but I didn't want to lie to
you. I can't.''

"Did you tell Dmitri Andreievich?''

"No.''

"And you're not going to, I presume.''

She grimaced. "Something sticks in my craw, Misha,
something about this whole mess with Vera and Gapon and
the police unions, and what Josef said about a traitor.''

"Josef also told you he believed Gapon killed Vera. You
think there's truth to that?''

"I don't know what I believe anymore. I only know something's amiss. But it's all intuition, and you can imagine what
Dmitri Andreievich would say about that. I'll go to him when
I have proof he can't deny.''

"Proof about what?'' Misha sounded worried.

"I don't know—that Gapon had Vera and Katya killed . . .
the name of the traitor . . . or maybe something none of us
expects. Look, Misha, I know I'm not being very scientific
and I don't expect you to agree with me or even go along
with me. I just needed to tell you what I'm doing. And one
day I may need you to cover for me with Dmitri I need to
know if you're willing to do that.''

Misha's brow furrowed. "This is wrong, Irina. We made
Dmitri Andreievich a promise, and in joining the Brigade we
agreed to adhere to the discipline. If you feel so strongly, we
should talk to him. I'm willing to go with you.''

"No. This is between you and me, Misha. If you don't
want to join me, that's fine. But I swear, if you tell Dmitri
Andreievich or anyone what I'm doing, I'll never talk to you
again. In fact, you'll never see me again. I'll be out of the
Brigade before Dmitri can even kick me out.''

Misha knew he had no choice. His love for Irina was deeper

than any love he'd known. Deeper than his devotion to his family, deeper than his regard for Dmitri and his dedication to the revolution. "I'll go with you tonight," he said simply.

She was momentarily silenced by his announcement; then her eyes softened in confusion.

"I love you, Irina," he murmured, taking her in his arms and pressing her tightly to him. "You mean more to me than anyone or anything in the world. If that makes me less of a revolutionary, then so be it."

In the summer of 1904, Father Georgi Gapon's followers were a small but devoted group of largely middle-aged, illiterate factory workers. Much of the meeting time of the Society of Factory and Plant Workers was spent reading articles from the conservative press. "Halls" had been set up in various parts of town. There were monthly dues, insurance and vacation plans, self-help projects, as well as dances and musicales for the workers and their wives. Plainclothes police, immediately evident to Irina and Misha, were unobtrusively present at every meeting and function, some seeming to enjoy the goings-on.

For the first few meetings, Irina and Misha sat quietly in the back of the hall, listening attentively. Gapon had an intriguing way about him. He was ephemeral and of the earth at the same time. Slight of stature and weakly handsome, his wiry body took on dimension clothed in the simple black priest cassock. His face was marked more by youth than manhood; his most attractive feature was his large, deep brown eyes, which lighted his face with a feverish intensity. There was a sporadic and endearing uncertainty to his voice as he roamed about his followers, touching men and women alike as he read and spoke; his reedy voice was mesmerizing. His language was simple and of the people. Irina often found herself hanging on his every word.

"Though the Czar is far away and God is high in the heavens, there is much we shall bring to the attention of the factory owners and the bureaucrats. It is the bureaucrats and capitalists who slowly siphon our lifeblood; they must be made to hear our pleas—not our beloved father, the holy Czar. The Czar is our protector on earth. Good night, dear brothers and sisters. Godspeed, citizens of Holy Russia."

Gapon's closing words were spoken like a benediction. Men lined up to shake his hand. Women carried their babies to him to be blessed. His followers bought his portraits, put them on the walls of the meeting halls and in their homes.

The poor priest, son of Ukrainian peasants, understood their pain and would defend their interests to the death.

Misha and Irina lingered in the meeting hall, waiting for the others to leave. Irina suspected Gapon knew they were there. She'd caught his eye more than once during the evening. She hesitated as he neared her. The few men still by the door were plainclothes police. "Father." She smiled. "A few words, if you have the time."

"Of course." He nodded to Misha, who shuffled awkwardly. "I see you have been steady visitors to our meetings of late, but you have not joined."

"Aye, Father. We need to speak to you first. My name is Kuksina Ivanovna Polonskaya and this here is Izaak Ilyitch Belzac," she began by way of introduction. "Izaak comes from Yaroslavl, where he worked on the railroads until he was fired after the strike. Myself, I come from Kharkov, and I tell you humbly, although Izaak loves his family, mine was a lot that never came together. I grant that. My father never could make my mother an honest woman." She crossed herself and rambled on. "Had another family, he did, and he just a low-level accountant. But he loved my mama and me, if we were the deepest secret of his heart. Praise God, He will forgive such a sinner as Papa." She crossed herself again. "It's because of Papa that I can read and write like any university student." She paused expectantly, her eyes fixed radiantly on Father Gapon.

"God forgives, my child," he said, unable to return her gaze.

"I feel so free to tell you all this, Father. I feel, after listening to you all these nights, that you understand."

"The lot of the common man on this earth is never easy, Kuksina Ivanovna."

"Well, my mother, God bless her soul"—she crossed herself reverently and her eyes filled with tears—"she slaved in the wretched steel mills to put food on the table. When she died from exhaustion, I decided to come to Petersburg. My father, God bless, had enough of his own problems with his other children and wife. He gave me a kiss and twenty rubles and wished me luck. The only good luck I've had since I've come here is meeting up with Izaak. Someday, praise God, you shall marry us, Father, but not till we've enough between us to take pride in the roof above our heads. My money's all but gone, and Izaak arrived with barely a handful of kopecks. We do what we can to keep body and soul together, and then we heard of you, Father."

"Your name is holy among some, those we respect." Misha spoke for the first time. "We're not for violence or revolution, Father, and we're no Czar haters."

"The Czar is our father on earth, praise God. It's the rich who take from the poor. Father," Irina concluded, "we'd like to work with you. I'm educated. I can write your thoughts for you, if need be. Izaak is quiet, but honest and true. I've a way with women. My dream has always been to have a reading circle of women, you know, even teach them who don't know how to read. I've had a thought, too, as I've been sitting here. It is for us to create a lending library for the workers. Your society's own lending library."

Gapon's face piqued with interest.

"We'd be honored to help your cause, Father, and the cause of Holy Russia."

Gapon was much taken with Irina's idea of the lending library and quickly made funds available to her to get the project started. She should, he suggested, make a list of the books she thought most virtuous for the workers and he would review the final list. She was careful to make the list as pleasing to Gapon as she could, including Gorky's radical play *The Lower Depths* as the only possible work that could arouse Gapon's displeasure. The play was set in the slums of Nizhni Novgorod, in the lowest kind of den, where murder was commonplace, ten-year-old girls were sold for half a ruble and prostitutes auctioned their children to professional beggars, often horribly mutilated men and women with pus-oozing sores and stumps for arms and legs. The play ran to well-attended audiences in the large cities, but had been banned in the provinces.

"You've read Gorky, then?" the priest questioned as his eyes scanned the library list.

It was almost midnight. The meeting had run late. Misha, Irina, and Gapon had walked home together; they lived only a few blocks apart; and as was quickly becoming a custom, Gapon had invited them in for a late-night cup of tea.

Father Gapon's house was small and dark and squeezed in between similar nondescript workers' houses on the narrow back street. He had to bend as he entered the front door. Irina and Misha waited in the shadows of the street until he lit the lamp, and then followed him through the familiar pathway in between piles of books, magazines, and boxes of paper on the floor. The desk was barely visible under the mounds of papers and books. Even the couch, which served as a bed, was always strewn with newspapers. Gapon cleared a chair and then shoved everything off the small table near the stove.

"Yes, I adore Gorky, everything he writes. I would gladly go see his play if I had money for such entertainment."

Gapon looked at her thoughtfully. "I tell you, Maxim Gorky is a friend of mine. Yes, that's true. If you like, I should have you meet him one day. He is truly a man of the people. He has lived their hardships. He writes from life. Still, I'd hardly call his new play entertainment, Kuksina Ivanovna. The Czar himself said it was harmful to the state. Gorky has been called a dangerous man, a revolutionary malcontent."

"Gorky is an artist, Father. Artists speak the souls of the people before the people know what is in their souls themselves."

"Well said, Kuksina Ivanovna."

"But those are not my words, Father. You said them yourself last week at the Putilov Hall."

"Did I?"

"Is it a sin to read Gorky, then, Father?" Misha asked.

"No, no, not a sin." Gapon began thoughtfully, absently stroking his bear as Stepan often did. "The horrific places he describes in his play exist. I have seen them myself. Sometimes, in my heart, I fear even God has turned in horror from those lost souls."

"Shall we take it from the list, then, Father?"

"No. In honor of my friendship with Gorky and of the truth he writes, let it stay."

"Will the Czar and his ministers be angry?"

"The Czar and his ministers surely will not see our humble library."

Irina was fast winning Gapon's confidence. For all his godliness and expansiveness with his followers, the priest was an easy mark: he was exceedingly vain, and if Irina knew anything, she knew how to feed into a man's vanity. As the weeks passed, she saw herself becoming indispensable to Gapon. He sought her out before and after meetings, and slowly but surely she was pushing him politically further to the left.

"Gapon's vain and power-hungry," Irina said to Misha one night as they lay in bed. "He's dangerous, I believe. He leads the workers down the rosy path to destruction with his devotion to the Czar. But I agree with Dmitri, Gapon's not a murderer. I doubt he had anything to do with Josef's, Katya's and Vera's deaths. I don't think he has the least connection to the Brigade."

"Yes, I've been thinking the same. I've also been thinking

that if all this is true, there's not much reason for us to continue playing these roles of Izaak and Kuksina."

Irina looked shocked. "How could you even suggest such a thing when Gapon has taken us so much into his confidence? Just because Gapon didn't kill Vera and Katya doesn't mean he doesn't know who did. There's that fellow Akimov. We had proof in the stolen Yermolov papers that Akimov and Gapon are connected. It was Akimov who set him up and is probably still funding him. Just look at all the money Gapon gave us to start the library. You don't think he's getting money like that from workers' donations!"

"All right, let's say this Akimov is backing Gapon. How has that got anything to do with you and me and the Brigade and Yermolov?"

Irina sat up and pulled the covers about her. After a few moments of thinking, she said, "Akimov and Yermolov are both in the Okhrana. I just know there's a connection to Vera's murder. She was getting close to something about Akimov."

"Oh, so now you think Akimov killed Vera?"

"By process of elimination, it certainly seems possible. I agree with Dmitri that Yermolov wouldn't have murdered her. He would have arrested her. Her capture would have been quite a feather in his cap. And we can reasonably rule out Gapon. That leaves only Akimov."

"And countless unknown men. Who knows who and what Vera was involved with?"

"Somebody wanted her dead to shut her up, of that I'm certain. Akimov's a logical suspect when you put the pieces together. He was mentioned in the stolen Yermolov papers as being the police connection with Gapon, and Vera was investigating Gapon."

"So you think it was Akimov who had the Yermolov papers stolen? How did he know we had them?"

"The only thing I can imagine is that the traitor in the Brigade is connected to Akimov and not Yermolov."

Misha sighed and shook his head. "I hate to say it, but now I think you're really grasping at straws. More important, I think you're too involved with Father Gapon. I think it's Gapon himself who's holding you. I think you're very much taken with him!" he burst out, his face reddening.

"You're not jealous!" she gasped, her eyes wide in disbelief.

"What am I supposed to think?" He threw off the covers and reached for his cigarettes, lying on a rickety end table. "You're spending more time with him than with me. I'm always making excuses for you with the comrades. And he's fascinated by you, any fool can see that!''

The anguish in his voice saddened Irina and she kissed his hair as she slipped her arms about him. ''Misha, my truest love, I swear to you, there's nothing romantic in the least between Gapon and me. I don't think he even thinks of me as a woman.''

''He's a man, an attractive man—filled with charisma,'' he petulantly reminded her. ''It wouldn't be the first time a priest took advantage—''

''When have you ever known any man to take advantage of me?'' She laughed softly and kissed him from the top of his head to his neck and shoulders. Then she reached for his hand and pulled him toward her. ''I want to tell you something.'' She took his cigarette and put it on an ashtray. ''I love only you.'' She wrapped herself about him and pressed her face to his. ''Sometimes I can't believe it myself. I never thought I should feel such love for a man. I'm true to you, Misha. I shall always be true to you.'' She caressed his face. ''Loving you has freed me to be more of a woman than I ever dreamed of being. Praise God, I feel so strong with Gapon. As if he's the puppet and I'm the puppet master. I feel I can really influence him and the growth of his Society. And it's because of you, Misha. It's because I have you to come home to and love.''

He did not answer.

''Misha, what are you thinking? What lie has someone told you?''

Painfully, uncertainly, he told her that he'd seen her go to Stepan's room, the night before the assassination attempt on Yermolov.

''Yes, I went to him,'' she said flatly. ''I shouldn't have. I should have gone to you, but I was so confused then. You have to understand, I'd felt such passion for Stepan once, and he was my teacher.''

''And you were mine,'' he said, as if belittling himself.

''That doesn't make you any less, Misha.'' She rested her face on his chest. ''Perhaps what was confusing me even more then were my feelings for you. They were quieter, more complicated. With Stepan, it was just abandon that always pulled me into an abyss. But with you, I feel alive and so happy. I think that's what scared me at first, that you could make me so happy. I wasn't used to being loved and not hurting for it.''

''I'll never hurt you, Irina.''

''I know.''

"And I'll kill anyone who does."

"You needn't do that, my love." She kissed him tenderly.
"So long as I have you to come home to, no one can ever
hurt me so deeply that I can't be patched up again."

CHAPTER THIRTY-ONE

Anna and Alexei returned from their honeymoon trip in late
September. They had been back in Petersburg two weeks
when Alexei announced he had invited Rimsky-Korsakov for
dinner. "He's most anxious to hear you play. Of course, with
all the turmoil, your taking classes at the Conservatory is out
of the question, but if Rimsky is impressed—which I'm certain he will be—he'll do everything he can to further your
musical education."

Anna nodded absently, and went on with her reading.

"I thought you'd be happy, my love."

"I am," she said, staring at him blankly. A dank October
rain was falling relentlessly and she pulled her shawl more
tightly about her. "When are your brother and his family
returning?"

"Oh, didn't I tell you? They're not. Helena was insistent
they stay in Peterhof. I've hired tutors for the children. She's
terrified for their lives here."

"And your mother?"

"She'll stay with them, to help with the children."

"I see. I should like to meet Misha's mother and father
and brothers and sisters someday."

"I'm sure you will. For now, it's just as well they're not
here."

"The house is so big. Sometimes I hear my echo."

"Which is why I've invited Rimsky."

"Have you contacted Misha and Irina?"

"Not yet."

"What about Aunt Tatyana's invitation?"

He sat down beside her and took her hand. "I don't really
think you're strong enough to go to one of her fetes, my dove.
Neither does Dr. Teffi."

"I despise Teffi."

"He's the finest physician in Petersburg."

"He makes my skin crawl. And his powders! I'll never take them! They drug me, that's all. And then I have fearful dreams."

"Then you needn't take them." He kissed her hand and stood.

"Where are you going?"

"I've an appointment, but I promise I won't be long. Madame Brissac is coming for a fitting this afternoon. She and I have already discussed the design of the gown. I want you to look ravishing for Rimsky."

"When did you say he was coming?"

"Thursday next. You'll practice when I'm gone, won't you?"

"What time is Madame Brissac coming?"

"At four. I'll be back way before then. I'll tell you what— I'll send Lidia up. She can draw you a bath. Wash your hair." He smoothed her head. "I think Dr. Teffi would feel better if you were more concerned about your appearance, Anna."

"I go nowhere. I see no one. Why should I care how I look?"

"You see me, my love. And once Rimsky takes you under his wing, there won't be enough hours in the day for you to worry about parties and balls. They're all so tiresome. You know that, Anna. Society is for the aimless, empty-headed shells of people to mark time while they live. But you can experience life as few people can. You're an artist, Anna."

She looked blandly up at him. She'd heard Alexei's vision of her life too many times. It was his vision. Hers was far different. Hers had no concert halls strewn with roses. Hers had no audience wildly applauding "Bravo! Bravo!" Hers was quieter, simpler. It had to do with loving Alexei, dancing through the night in his arms, leaving society spellbound with the radiance of their union and of their children.

"It will be different once Rimsky comes," he assured. "Once he hears your playing, everything will be different."

"Alexei Yakovlevich, welcome!" Sergei Witte expansively greeted.

Alexei had not seen Witte since the Grand Duke Ilya Mikhailovich's name-day ball over a year before. He was horrified at the change in his old friend. His large face was gray and carved with heavy lines. He had lost weight, something which had seemed an impossibility over the years; dark shadows wore at his eyes.

The two men embraced.

"Sergei Yurievich, it is good to see you. You look fine, just fine."

"Don't lie to me, Alexei Yakovlevich. I look like hell. I feel like hell. But come, we've much to discuss." Witte took Alexei's overcoat, scarf, and hat, laid them on a table in the front hall, and led Alexei to his office, where he locked the doors behind them. He poured two large glasses of vodka and they sat in chairs near the window, which was already boarded against winter. "I will tell you, Alexei Yakovlevich . . ." Witte's voice was lowered. "I trust very few people anymore. You are one, and the Czar's Uncle Nikolasha is another. Spies and traitors are everywhere in the court and the government." Witte rubbed his eyes warily. "Russia has never been so volatile. The war with Japan grows more unpopular with each passing day. I tell you, the papers give a tenth of what's truly going on in Manchuria. The Japanese are grinding us into little bits and feeding us to the fish—but the Czar refuses to admit defeat. At home, we're paralyzed by strikes. And now, Plehve's murder."

"Yes, yes . . . So tell me, Sergei, what do you want of me this time? What's so urgent?"

Witte reached for his cigar and handed one to Alexei. "Plehve's death has truly unbalanced everything. It's created a void someone must—will—fill. Plehve was a powerful man. For better or worse, the Czar relied mightily on him. And, as you know," he added as an afterthought, "the Czar's son was born only two weeks after Plehve's death."

"Surely that softened the blow for Nicholas. A son has been long awaited."

"You haven't heard, then? The Czarevich is a bleeder. Hemophiliac. He probably won't live out his first year. It's all hush-hush, of course. Nobody, not even the doctors, dares mention the word around the Czar or the Czarina. The court is shrouded by despair and dark forces." Witte frowned and lit a match. He inhaled until satisfied his cigar was lit, then went on. "I'm a politician, Alexei Yakovlevich. I can cope with court intrigue, sunken ships, lost battles, bombs, strikes, even outright rebellion. I believe I can preserve the House of Romanov against everything except this defect in this tiny little human being. In my heart of hearts, I fear the Czarevich's illness will topple Russia."

"Strange how I feel so little pity." Alexei got up to refill his drink.

"I ask not for your pity. Just that you understand the totality of the picture. The Czar is so lost in despair, he is probably the only man in Russia who doesn't see the hand-writing on the wall. He will not accept the inevitability of defeat in the war, and he won't listen to talk of a constitution. His sense of reality is somewhere . . . oh, good God, the man simply doesn't see reality."

"When was he ever otherwise?"

"As distracted as he used to be, the illness of his son has left him helpless. Worse, it leaves him and hence Russia more open to the treachery of men who would follow in Plehve's shoes. Men like Leonti Yermolov and his cohorts General Annekov and Prince Dubensky."

"I'm not sure I understand."

Witte flicked the ashes off his cigar and settled his large body comfortably back in his seat. He inhaled deeply, as if lost in thought, and then announced in a professorial tone, "History, Alexei Yakovlevich—to influence history you've got to see the events growing about you as history." He sat up and leaned toward Alexei. "Nothing happens in society for fifty, a hundred years, and then, in a matter of days, the world is changed upside down, or as some would argue, right-side-up, forever. Is this not so, Alexei Yakovlevich?" He was nodding even as he asked the question.

"So far you'll get no disagreement." Alexei could not help smiling. As much of an exacting strategist as Witte was, he loved nothing better than to sit back and map out the world in broad strokes.

"Every man, woman, and child in Russia will be either a participant or victim," Witte said emphatically. He reached for a paper and pen and began to draw. He drew a triangle, writing "Landowners/Church" in one corner, "Workers" in another, and "Industrialists" in the third. He held it up for Alexei to see. "These are the major forces in Russia today, these are the currents pulling against one another. It's rather crude, but will fit my argument well enough. The hard core of the nobility is, always has been and always will be basically reactionary. Even those who toy with liberal thoughts, like your friend Count Bobrinsky, will, if threatened, revert to their history. They need old Russia. They're wedded to the dark side of the church and the land. Holy Russia and the Czar are synonymous. The nobility and the church will fight to preserve as much of the imperial ways as possible. And they'll wipe out anyone who tries to stop them with the same vengeance Plehve unleashed on the Jews last year in Kishinev."

"Why do I feel this is being all directed at me?"

"Ah!" Witte smiled expansively. He went back to his diagram and circled the corner of the triangle marked "Industrialists." "This is you, Alexei Yakovlevich, the new class of industrialists and bankers—you and your friends."

"And how do you classify us, Professor?"

"I'd say you're basically a rather progressive bunch. Your social conscience is heartfelt. It can't help but be. There's a bit of guilt in you that the nobility never feels. For your roots are often in the very class you oppress in your factories and mills. You can't believe your good fortune. Rags-to-riches stories are not uncommon amongst you, am I right?"

"You should know, Sergei. Had you chosen to work in the private sector rather than government, you would be one of us."

"Touché! Yes! But, fortunately for you, I haven't. It gives me the perspective you lack. I see you all scurrying around, trying to find ways to spend this incredible wealth, which dazzles even old Russia, but except for a few mavericks like yourself and Ryabushinsky, your industrial brethren are considered social upstarts, nouveaux riches. They're not welcomed by Petersburg society and not consulted by the Czar."

"Unless he needs them to support a war."

Witte shrugged. "They could always refuse to help. Paradoxically, your brother industrialists keep thinking if they give the Czar what he wants, the Czar will love them and make them counts and dukes. But he won't. He can't. The Czar and his court must despise you."

Witte tapped his pen on his paper. "The only group we've not considered are the workers, the proletariat, that gray mass of the downtrodden swarming into the cities to fill your factories. They're largely illiterate and superstitious, one foot still on the land, the other in the squalor of the slums. Like many of your industrial brethren, they are straddling the fence between Holy Russia and the revolution. It's Holy Russia that keeps them in bondage, yet they remain faithful believers in the Orthodox church and loyal suffering children of the Czar."

"And where do the peasants work into your little scheme?"

"The peasants will go with whatever order takes hold," Witte said, writing the word "peasants" in the middle of his triangle. "But to move on to the crux of our discussion, Alexei, the reason I asked you here today. I began by saying the death of Plehve has unhinged everything." He madly circled the "nobility" on his diagram, and looking Alexei squarely in the eye, said, his voice filled with portent, "The right has been basically biding its time up until now. But I warn you, they will not take the death of Plehve lying down.

He was their helmsman. They're already rallying around Leonti Yermolov.''

"Yes, you said that before. I thought Yermolov was touring the provinces, rounding up peasants for the Czar's pathetic army." Alexei sneered.

Witte sipped at his drink before speaking again. "What if I told you we have evidence that Yermolov is one of the founders of the Black Hundreds?''

"I'd say your evidence had better be pretty damn indisputable.''

"Yermolov's name is on the founding charter. We're absolutely certain the signature is real.''

"How did such a document fall into your hands?''

"Suffice to say, an associate of mine with great influence in the Okhrana came upon it.''

"Why haven't you used it to expose Yermolov?''

"The timing must be absolutely right. We must be certain the Czar can in no way suppress it. Yermolov's been back in Petersburg only a few weeks, and there are rumors—and I must emphasize at this time that these are rumors only—that he's plotting to use the Black Hundreds as a gun to the head of the Czar.''

"How so?'' Alexei was incredulous.

"As vicious as the Black Hundreds have been in attacking workers and students, I'm certain we've seen only the tip of the iceberg. At Yermolov's bidding and with the tacit approval of men like General Annekov and Prince Dubensky, not to mention the Archbishop himself, the Black Hundreds stand ready to unleash a bloodletting that would make Plehve's pogroms against the Jews look like child's play. That's Yermolov's ace in the hole with the Czar. Right now it's the workers and the students fighting in the streets against the police. If it's Russian against Russian, it's civil war. Yermolov, controlling the Black Hundreds, would be given the helm, and would step in and ruthlessly crush the disorder.''

"And the left with it.''

"Certainly that would be the intent. God knows what would happen then.''

"Outright revolution.''

"You know as well as I do, Alexei, the left isn't organized enough to hold power for more than a day. Not even the workers have a true leader.''

"What about this priest—Gapon? He seems to have their ear.''

"From what I hear, he's little more than a pawn of the police.''

"Well, yes, I've read that too. Still, the workers seem to flock to his side."

"The workers are a superstitious lot. I wouldn't put it past Yermolov to try to manipulate them through a priest."

"You think Gapon is the tool of Yermolov, then?"

"I have no proof as yet. My sources have come up with nothing more than what the newspapers tell us. But the very idea of police-controlled unions is so appalling, it could only be the workings of a mind like Yermolov's. They're doomed to failure, don't you see. Either the police in their abominable disdain for the common man will alienate the workers from the beginning, or with their blundering ways, they'll lose control of their creation as soon as it begins to take on steam. This priest, Gapon, seems quite charismatic. If he is a police pawn, I daresay the day will come when he'll leave the police in the dust."

"Then the workers will have their leader."

Witte shook his head. "Then Gapon will have outlived his use to Yermolov and he will be crushed along with his followers—along with us all."

"You paint such a bleak picture, Sergei." Alexei grinned, a glint of mockery in his eyes.

"It behooves you to take this more seriously, my friend. If Yermolov isn't stopped, all Russia will be thrown back into the Dark Ages. There'll be no place for men like you or me in such a world. The resurrection of the past will be our grave."

Alexei thought before speaking. "What makes you so certain Yermolov has a following?"

"The Okhrana is firmly split. Yermolov has his spies. I have mine."

"You?"

"Yes. I tell you outright—my man in the Okhrana is the spearhead of our attack against Yermolov. Victory of his forces within the Okhrana is essential."

"Who is this man of yours?"

"Believe me, it's in your interest to know as little as possible about the Okhrana right now."

"It rather seems it is in my interest to do as little as possible right now, Sergei Yurievich. I can't see what my aiding your little palace revolution will do except put me and Anna at risk. Something I'm not willing to do."

"Christ, man! I don't know how to make myself any plainer. You're at risk whether you want to be or not. The forces are gathering. The battle is brewing. It's Yermolov and his Black Hundreds against the rest of us—the new culture of the individual, if you will.''

"And your man in the Okhrana?''

Witte sighed despairingly. He inhaled on a dying cigar and vehemently crushed it out. "All right, Alexei, let me put it another way. Let me ask you this: where do you think your beloved Rimsky-Korsakov and his Conservatory will be if the reaction takes hold? Where do you think your schools of modern painting and poetry will be? Do you think you'll have poetry readings all over Petersburg calling for the heart of man to step forth?'' Witte was pacing the room by now. "You know what really perturbs me, Alexei? It's these young people racing through the streets demanding justice and freedom as if they have some kind of patent on liberty. Yes, dissenters are arrested. Yes, there's repression, but there's more open exchange of thought in Russia today than there has been in years! Nobody's been mowed down by gun volleys. People aren't dragged from their beds in the night and tortured for information. But I'm telling you, Alexei, the new Russia, all that causes you to breathe freely, will be swept away in one fell swoop should Yermolov and his forces take hold. They will grind everything that even hints of the new into the dirt. Modern Russia will be buried before she has a chance to really live!''

"You're so certain of this?'' Alexei's question was more of a dare.

"I've never been more certain of anything in my entire life.''

"And this man of yours in the Okhrana—you know he's any better than Yermolov?''

"If the world were a different place, Alexei, I would have to reserve judgment on that. In better times, I would probably disdain the man. He's not above treachery, I tell you that outright—but he's the best we have right now. He hates Yermolov.''

"And he wants Yermolov's power.''

Witte nodded.

"It seems to me we're shooting dice with the devil.''

"It seems to me we haven't much choice. That's why I need you, Alexei. I trust you. I'm beginning to think you're the only man in Russia I trust anymore.''

"Damn you . . .'' Alexei grumbled, knowing Witte had finally found his vulnerability. "What is it you want me to do?''

Witte sat down and pulled his chair closer to Alexei. "I'm forming a broad-based coalition, everyone from moderates to reformists to radicals, from the Peasant Congress to the Symposium—demanding the Czar declare a popularly elected National Senate.''

"Not a constitution?''

"There's not a one among the Czar's chief advisers who isn't in agreement over open elections. It's the foot in the door we need. A constitutional government will necessarily follow—so long as we can keep Yermolov and company at bay. That's my job. Yours is to help me solidify this coalition, then write up the petition to the Czar. Today is October 15. I'll arrange a formal presentation to the Czar with a sampling of representatives, those who would impress the Czar most, on November 15, if I can, the twentieth at the latest.''

Alexei nodded slowly. "I'm certain I can get the Symposium behind you.''

"Us.'' Witte eyed him carefully. "It must be us, Alexei.''

Alexei nodded. "What else would you want of me?''

"To go to Moscow and talk to the liberal industrial leaders, men like Morozov, Guchkov, and Chelnokov. They're already beginning to organize in support of the Peasant Congress and are rallying the intelligentsia around a call for a constitutional government. They won't be against us on principle, but I need you to convince them of the absolute necessity of presenting a united front to the Czar. It can't be Petersburg against Moscow anymore.''

"All right . . .''

"I'm asking for your nights and your days, for awhile anyway. How will that sit with your wife?''

"You needn't worry yourself about that. But I warn you of this, Sergei . . .'' Alexei rose to his feet. "Our coalition is only temporary.''

"Ah, Alexei!'' Witte embraced him heartily. "Thank you, my friend!'' He kissed both cheeks. "Russia thanks you!''

"Russia has given me little choice.''

"Russia, yes, Russia—it's all for the future of Russia! For you shall see—once we have a working constitution, then nothing will stop us. A constitutional monarchy will pave the way for Russia's becoming the greatest industrial nation the world has ever seen. Greater than England. Greater than America. We have the manpower, the natural resources, the ingenuity. All we need is a constitution so men like you and Ryabushinsky can help lead the people legally.''

"Ah, Sergei Yurievich, you are a politician to the last. Perhaps when we depose the Czar and set up a republic, you shall be our first President.''

Witte laughed heartily. "I shall, Alexei Yakovlevich, for

this one time, allow you the last word. Come now, sit down. I'll ring for lunch.''

''I'm afraid I promised Anna—''

''A little bit longer of your time, I beg of you. There are some matters we must get started on right away.''

CHAPTER THIRTY-TWO

Anna felt strangely at ease, even unconcerned the night Rimsky-Korsakov came to dinner. Perhaps it was Alexei's nervousness that left her so laconic. He bustled about, rustling and smoothing her velvet gown of deep sea blue, deciding on one necklace, only to insist she try another and another.

''It's settled,'' Anna finally announced, reaching for a simple pair of ruby earrings Alexei had bought her in Rome. ''I shall wear these and the brooch you first sent me. Monsieur Rimsky-Korsakov is not coming to see my jewels, after all.''

''Yes, yes, you're absolutely right, my love.'' He watched as Anna fixed the earrings on her ears.

''Here, you put it on.'' She stood and handed him the brooch.

Alexei, who had pinned jewelry on the bodices of countless women's gowns, felt all thumbs with Anna.

''Oh, come, put it here.'' She held her head high and took his hand.

He fumbled nervously to pin the brooch on her shoulder.

''Here, you must slip your hand under the fabric or you'll stick me!''

''I'm afraid you must do it yourself, Anna.'' He placed the brooch on the dressing table. ''Rimsky shall be here in twenty minutes. I have to finish dressing myself.'' He hurried through the door to his rooms.

Rimsky-Korsakov was a tall, aging man, far older than Anna had expected; his shoulders were bent, and he peered at her through thick blue-tinted glasses. He was abrupt in his manner, but not unkind, and made sure to include her in all the conversation. He talked of the mayhem at the Conservatory, of his enemies who were out to sell his domain, and of the revolution which more and more called his students into the streets. He talked of the Evenings of Contemporary Music and of the newest Russian and French composers; he spoke of one student in particular, a young man by the name of Igor Stravinsky. "He shall take the world by storm soon, I promise you." Rimsky smiled in self-satisfaction. "He has the most revolutionary ideas about composing, and filtered through his mind, his ideas shall find a home. But, Anna Petrovna, your husband tells me you will take the world by storm one day yourself."

"I fear Alexei is influenced by his affections. I played before the Czar once, but Alexei has convinced me that is of little merit." Her voice was piqued. She hadn't meant to sound bitter. She'd all but forgotten the horrid note that Alexei had sent along with the brooch, and suddenly the remembering annoyed her.

"Would you like to hear Anna now?" Alexei said.

"I thought we should wait until after dinner." She stiffened.

"Better to play on an empty stomach than a full one," Rimsky insisted. "Food dulls the senses. Unless you're quite set on later, my dear, I would like to hear you now."

"As you wish." Anna smiled rigidly at the old composer, and when she looked at Alexei, she felt the same flush of anger that had caught her in her Uncle Ilya's greenhouse nearly a year before. Alexei had angered her a lot then; and as she stepped toward the piano, she remembered his haughty abuse of the Czar in Lydia Karlovna's office. Her anger was melting any fear which she might have had of playing before the great Rimsky-Korsakov. Who did Alexei think he was? Keeping her pampered to show her off! Keeping her like some little doll, dressing her up, winding her up, showing her off! "Alexei suggested I play some Mozart, but I've been quite taken by the work of d'Indy lately. I haven't polished it as much as the Mozart, but it's quite taken hold in my mind."

"By all means, then." Rimsky-Korsakov nodded approvingly.

"Anna, if it's the piece you were practicing yesterday—"

"It is, my love." She cut him off.

"It's hardly perfected."

"Aren't you always telling me it's passion that matters, not perfection?" She threw up the top of the keyboard.

Anna was sitting on her bed, the lights low, when Alexei knocked. It was a little past ten. "Come in."

"You're awake, then. I was worried about you, my dove."
He reached for her hand.

She slipped it from him under the covers. "Well, you see
that there is no reason. I just needed to rest. You still might
be enjoying yourself with your friend."

"Rimsky himself was distressed when you had to leave
dinner."

"I shall write him my regrets."

"Something is bothering you, Anna."

"Nothing."

"Come now, give me your hand and tell me it's nothing,"
he cajoled, reaching for her.

She pushed him away. "Well, to tell you the truth, my
head still hurts. It's quite horrid, Alexei. I wish you would
leave now."

"Can't I stay long enough to tell you what Rimsky said
about your playing?"

"I'm sure it's nothing good!" she snapped, feeling herself
coiling madly.

"On the contrary, my love. Rimsky was quite taken with
your playing. I can tell when the old man is affected, and he
was, I promise. He was listening to every note you played.
Not even your mistakes bothered him. He said d'Indy is quite
difficult, especially to teach oneself. He's offered to come
here and teach you himself."

Anna nodded, scarcely listening, not caring.

"I would expect you to be happier."

"It's my head."

He sat for a moment in silence and slowly pushed himself
up from the bed. Staring at her, he finally questioned, "You're
not angry with me?"

"Whatever for?"

"I don't know." His voice was painfully uncertain.

"Well, then, how would I? Now, you must go. I'm very
tired." She sank into her covers.

He bent over to kiss her forehead good night.

She pushed him away, muttering something about her head.

"You're going out again tonight?" Anna questioned when
Alexei came to her after dinner dressed to go out. It was
several weeks after their engagement with Rimsky-Korsakov.
She was in the parlor, reading a magazine.

"I'll only be at Ryabushinsky's, my love. It's all politics
and dreadfully boring."

"You promised me we would have the evening together."

"Something's just come up."

She felt her body tighten and a shrewish voice take hold of her brain. She knew the voice. It was her mother's, the echo of her mother's nagging rage from years before; Anna remembered it as a child lying terrified in her bed, listening or trying not to listen, blotting out the words but never the angry tones. Her mother screeched; her father was silent; then there was the slamming of the door. Now her mother's wrath spilled like foul-tasting venom. "You spend half your time in Moscow, and when you're home, you're out almost every night!"

"Anna, I've told you about the importance of the negotiations."

"You tell me nothing of substance. You talk in riddles, as if you're on some secret mission."

"It's not that at all. I just don't think you'd be interested in the details."

She pulled anxiously at a thread in her sweater. "But you see Misha and Irina."

"No."

"I think you lie."

"I know you do." His voice was maddeningly calm. "We've been through this so many times."

"I must see Irina. I must. I've no way to get in touch with her. She promised she would see me when I returned. But she hasn't."

"Perhaps she's not in Petersburg."

"Or perhaps . . ." Anna's cheeks colored. Her eyes glared accusingly. "Or perhaps you told her not to see me."

"Anna, I truly do not have time for your hysterics tonight."

"I'm not hysterical!" She breathed hard and bit her lips to hold back the tears. "I'm lonely, Alexei. I have no friends. We go to no parties. I never see you."

"We do see each other. We went to the ballet twice last week and to the Evening of Contemporary Music."

"Yes, and afterward you went out to see your dear friend Ryabushinsky or Bobrinsky or Sergei Witte or whomever."

He glanced at the clock on the mantel, and said with a hint of impatience, "You have your music—"

"My music, my music!" She threw down the magazine and began stomping about the room. "You know what I think, Alexei? I think it's *your* music, not *my* music. If it were *my* music, it would make *me* happy, but it doesn't. I feel it's a chore, a terrible, enormous chore that I do to please you!"

He didn't answer right away, but his face grew grimmer

and grimmer. "I talked to Rimsky this afternoon." He eyed
her carefully. "He says you're not practicing."

"I am."

"Don't lie to me, Anna!"

"Fine!" she shrieked. "All right! Then go, why don't you!
Go to your meetings!" She turned and ran from the parlor
and up the stairs, thinking Alexei would follow her, but the
front door slammed with a reverberating bang.

"Go!" she shouted over the banister. "Go!" She ran to
her room and threw herself on the bed, tearing at the pillows
and the bedsheets, gnashing her teeth to hold back the screams
that, she was afraid, once let loose, would never stop. She
wasn't crazed again, she knew she wasn't. She was angry,
infuriated, and sitting up, she tore at her wedding ring, dash-
ing it to the floor.

Bounding from the bed, she raced from her room and down
the stairs to the drawing room. Throwing open the piano, she
began pounding at the keys, the chords ringing in a cacophony of sounds like terrified animals banging from wall to
wall. She pounded and pounded with her fists, then kicked
over the piano stool and, reaching for a vase, hurled it at the
piano. She tore open the piano and yanked at the wires. When
they would not break, she pushed the piano, trying to knock
it over, and when she couldn't, she raced about the room,
reaching for anything she could throw—statues, books, bric-
a-brac. Anything movable was hurled at the piano.

"Madame!"

She swerved to find the servant, old Volodia, staring wide-
eyed in the doorway. He was dressed in a nightshirt and
woolen robe. Behind him stood the cook, Matryona, and the
servants Lidia and Grigory.

"What do you want?" Anna demanded. "Did I call for
you? Did I call for any of you?"

"Madame . . ." Grigory, started into the room.

She reached for a book and threatened to hurl it.

Grigory stepped back, pushing the other servants with him.

Anna followed them from the drawing room and ran to the
closet for her coat, boots, and scarf.

"Madame?" Lidia uncertainly questioned.

"I'm going out!" Anna announced.

"Alone, madame?"

"Yes, alone."

"What should I tell the master?"

"Tell him I went out!" She stomped to the front door,
pulled it open and hurried down the steps.

* * *

The Kalinin Palace was on the fashionable English Embankment, diagonally across the river from the university district on Vasilievsky Island. Anna stood on the palace steps, gasping for breath. She huddled her arms about herself, trying to regain her composure. She'd had temper tantrums in her life, but never anything like that. The tumult still racked her. She was shaking. A tear trickled down her cheek. What would Alexei say? Would he ever forgive her? Why was loving him so hard now, when it had seemed so easy, so wonderfully calm as he'd settled about her in the Crimea, soothing like the gentlest of summer breezes? He'd made her laugh then. He'd made her want to reach out and grab life again. What had made it change? Why did she always feel like a seething wildcat with him, watching, waiting?

A wind salted with an early-November snow was whipping off the Neva, and in the distance she could see the students' torches burning. She often watched them from her bedroom window. Every night students congregated at the university. Anna imagined Irina and Misha there; she tried to imagine herself with them, dressed in shabby student garb, heavy boots, marching, waving a red flag and shouting obscenities at the police, but such imagining was difficult, even frightening. It was the violence that scared her. She read about heads being smashed and people being shot.

A carriage noisily passed and Anna drew into the shadows, and listened to the shouts and cheers intermittently echoing from across the river. She walked a few steps from the house and stopped to look about; seeing no one, she took a few more steps then began to run down the palace drive, through the gates and out into the street. She shivered, holding herself tightly. She'd never been alone in the streets of Petersburg during the day, much less the night.

Anna had no intention of actually crossing over the river to the university. She might, however, take a casual stroll to the Winter Palace, which was always so beautiful at night. A walk to the Winter Palace would calm her nerves, and then she'd hurry home and plead with the servants, bribe them, if she had to, not to tell Alexei of her tantrum.

She walked quickly against the wind blowing biting snow off the Neva. She walked faster and faster, a strange exhilaration driving her on; it was a small feeling at first, like the silent ripples of the tiniest of pebbles in water. She breathed deeply to steady herself. Ahead, the brilliant lights of the Winter Palace were beginning to make the night like day. Across the river, the torches grew brighter. The students were chanting; she couldn't understand their words, but the chanting sounded beautiful, like singing.

She slowed as she neared the bridge. Police were everywhere: fierce-faced Cossacks carried whips; lines of armed Imperial Guards made a human barricade in front of the Palace Square, and black-suited gendarmes fingered their guns. Anna shivered with fearful anticipation; her attention was on an ever-growing group of young people milling about the bridge. No one, she noticed, was on the bridge itself.

She slowly edged her way past a line of Cossacks to the other side of the street. "Excuse me." She tapped the shoulder of a tall, pleasant-looking girl whose eyes were fixed across the river. "Is something going on?"

"I'll say so! The entire university has been closed again. This time they say indefinitely, but they've said that before. The students will be marching here soon."

"What will happen then?" Anna asked.

"Rumor is the police have word to let the march cross the bridge. That's when I'll pick it up. We'll go all the way down Nevsky Prospect to gain numbers and then back to the Winter Palace."

"To the Czar?"

"If the murderer will listen to us, which I doubt. Hush now." The girl began edging her way through the crowd to get closer to the bridge.

Anna edged with her.

A roar went up from the people around her as the crowd at the other side of the bridge began swelling noticeably. A huge banner waved in the wind. Anna strained to see. The banner read, "Freedom of Thought Is the Right of All People!" Red flags and countless other banners bobbed and waved along with the torches.

"Let them pass! Let them pass!" the crowd around Anna began chanting.

She was afraid to chant with them.

"Let them pass! Let them pass!" The cry became more urgent.

Anna slipped away from the girl and looked at the police in front of the Winter Palace. They hadn't moved. She looked back across the bridge in time to see the flank of Cossacks suddenly split and fall aside. With a warwhoop, a crush of students pressed onto the bridge. The chanting about Anna broke into wild cheering and applause, and as the marchers with the banner stepped off the bridge, strains of "The Marseillaise" rose triumphantly into the night air. The energy of the song gripped Anna, and she could not stop herself from singing along, but as the crowd about her fell into step with the marchers, she slipped into the shadows again, certain Misha and Irina would pass soon.

An endless stream of marchers, faces glorious in the glow of the torches, drew Anna near. "Petya! Petya, is that you?" she cried, spying a young man in a fur hat and fur-trimmed coat. She ran into the throng. It was her brother. She hadn't seen him for almost a year.

"Anna! What the hell are you doing here?" He embraced her and grabbed her hand to keep her by his side.

"What are you doing?"

"Marching, of course. This is going to be the grandest march Petersburg's ever seen. We're going to wake up the whole town and bring them with us."

"Can I march with you?"

"Of course! But your husband—Alexei Kalinin. Surely he doesn't approve of your being here."

"He doesn't know. You won't tell him, will you?"

"Not if you don't want me to."

"Or Papa."

"I haven't seen the old man in months." Petya began introducing Anna to his friends, a happy group of finely dressed young men and women who eagerly welcomed Anna into their midst.

Anna had so many questions. She wanted to ask Petya if he'd seen Irina; she wanted to ask about her mother and her brother, Boris; she wanted to know why Petya had taken to the streets. The last Anna remembered, he thought revolution was a waste of effort, but there was no time for talk. Chants swelled through the ranks as they started on Nevsky Prospect, and "The Marseillaise" burst forth again. The triumphant surge of the song bonded the marchers one to the other, and the words brought tears to Anna's eyes. She held Petya tightly, hardly able to believe she was walking by his side in such open camaraderie. They hadn't been civil to each other for years. He'd scarcely deigned to talk to her the little bit she saw him, and now, each time their eyes met, he grinned happily. Dear God, she thought, if this was what revolution was all about, then she was for it!

They marched for what seemed hours, but Anna never tired or grew cold. They marched and people poured from buildings to join their ranks. The numbers swelled until they filled the wide expanse of Nevsky Prospect, singing, chanting, linking arms. "Free University!" "Peace!" "Constitution!" "Justice!" filled her brain. She never once gave a thought to the police until the crowd about her began falling apart; panic replaced camaraderie. People were running madly.

"What is it?"

"Police! Hold my hand, Anna. Whatever you do, don't let go!"

An arm caught her from behind, gagging her. "Petya!" she screamed as she was pulled to the ground.

CHAPTER THIRTY-THREE

Anna's hat was lost and her coat torn as she was dragged through the street and thrown into a police wagon; the numbing fear vanished as she saw the wagon filled with smiling, welcoming faces. A few were bloodied, but most were merely cramped in the close quarters. Two more marchers were quickly tossed in after Anna, and the doors were locked. The wagon took off with a jolt, throwing bodies one against the other in the darkness. Anna felt hands reach for hers, and as she nestled against unknown comforters, she joined the singing, which continued all the way to the police station.

Rough police pushed and shoved, yanking the arrested from the wagon if they didn't move fast enough, then leading them to a basement room alive with the excited talk of countless other marchers, who cheered with the arrival of the new contingent. Strangers hugged and kissed Anna as if she were a long-lost friend. Cigarettes were passed about. Anna listened, entranced by the talk about her. "Anna Petrovna," she answered when asked her name.

People cursed the Czar with more vehemence than she'd ever heard from Alexei, and she wasn't affronted. Hadn't she been knocked down, dragged in the street and arrested? And she was one of the lucky ones. Many of those about her had dried blood matting their faces. Bruises were already swelling and turning purple. What did curses matter in the face of all that?

She thought fleetingly of Alexei, who was, she was certain, still at Ryabushinsky's. She walked about the crowded room looking for Irina, Misha, or Petya, but there was no sign of them. She asked people if they knew them; no one did. She wandered from group to group, listening, smiling, holding a cigarette to her lips before she passed it on to someone else. Every time the police entered, the room exploded in a wild stomping, jeers, and whistling as a new group was cordoned off to be processed. They returned and another group took its place.

Finally it was Anna's turn. She lined up between a short, stocky young man named Andrey and an exotic young woman named Dora, with straight black hair and a black enamel cigarette holder. Dora let off a steady stream of curses. Anna decided to stand close to Andrey, who told her he was a philosophy student, and talked endlessly about the differences between anarchism, socialism and Marxism. Anna merely nodded, grateful he was not interested in finding out anything about her.

The waiting was interminable, and Andrey's monologue didn't make it any easier. When she finally caught view of a clock in the hallway, she was aghast to find it was four in the morning. "The time!" She pointed to the clock. "It can't be four in the morning!"

"Why not?"

"My husband!" she panicked. Never had she imagined it was so late. Alexei would be frantic looking for her. She stared ahead at the line in front of her. She was still only halfway to the processing room. She had to reach Alexei. Somehow she had to get him a message. "My husband doesn't know where I am. I mean, he wasn't on the march."

"He'll find out soon enough. Don't worry," Andrey said blandly, and went on with his monologue.

"Name," a burly sergeant demanded flatly.

"Anna."

"Anna what?"

"Anna Petrovna . . ." She hesitated only a moment before adding, "Kalinina."

The burly sergeant stopped chomping on his cigar. "Kalinina, huh. Spell that."

"K-a-l-i-n-i-n-a."

"That's what I thought. You ain't any relation to the Kalinin family?"

She nodded and, holding her hand so he could not see her ringless finger, she pulled herself as tall as she could. "I'm Alexei Yakovlevich's wife."

"Kalinin's wife! What the hell you doing here? Out with

your husband for a late-night dinner and got separated?'' The sergeant sounded concerned.

"I was marching."

"Praise God." He groaned, and took Anna's arm. "Come with me."

As Anna was whisked away from the line, she caught Dora's astonished glance.

Kalinina? Dora mouthed, and stared disbelievingly. "Sure," she muttered. "And I'm the Czarina."

Anna was quickly ushered into a quiet office where a tall mustached man in a trim black uniform sat writing. The burly sergeant whispered something in his ear and the man at the desk put down his pen and stared at Anna. "I'm Captain Bruyevich. Please sit down, Madame Kalinina." He waved his arm.

Dutifully Anna sat.

"Do you have any papers?"

"No. I . . . I must have lost my purse in the fray."

"Yes, Sergeant Nikulin tells me you were marching. Does your husband know?"

"No."

"You realize you're under arrest."

"Yes."

"We'll have to get in touch with your husband immediately, Madame Kalinina."

Anna sighed a breath of relief. "Thank you, Captain Bruyevich."

"You're sure you want us to do this?"

"Yes, absolutely, he must be frantic with worry."

"He'll have no problem recognizing you, then."

"Of course not. I'm his wife."

"Yes, well, I doubt he'll be much relieved to discover where you are. Nikulin!" he shouted.

"Yes, sir!" The burly sergeant stepped back inside the door.

"Get all the necessary information on Madame Kalinina. Then take her to Strelnikov's office and get her some tea. And before you do any of that, dispatch someone to the Kalinin Palace immediately and tell Alexei Yakovlevich his wife is here, under arrest."

Anna heard Alexei's footsteps before the door opened. Quickly she tried to fix her hair, but her hairpins had been lost along with her hat. She smoothed her stained skirt and rubbed her cheeks. She was standing when the burly sergeant walked in, followed by Alexei.

The fear Anna had been holding back rushed over her when she saw his face. He was ashen. His eyes were barely more than slits. His lips were pressed like pincers.

"Alexei—"

"Nothing, Anna. Don't say a word." His voice was coldly in control. "Come." He held out his hand. "The sergeant says you're free to go."

It was seven in the morning when they walked from the police station, but the Petersburg night still hung heavily over the city. Alexei grasped her arm tightly as he led her to the carriage. Once inside, they sat as far from each other as possible and rode the entire way home in silence.

Lidia and Matryona were waiting in the hallway when they arrived. Lidia took their coats.

"Is there anything you need, sir?" Matryona asked.

"No, nothing. We do not wish to be disturbed, Matryona, for any reason." Taking Anna's arm again, he led her up the stairs to her room. He turned the knob and pushed open the door. "We'll discuss this later,' was all he said, and turned to leave.

"Alexei!"

"Yes." He turned back.

She knew he was more in pain than he was angry, and she wanted to run to him and beg his forgiveness. All she could say was, "I . . . I'm sorry about the piano."

"It can be repaired." He started again to leave.

"Alexei!"

"What is it now?"

"I . . . I don't want to be alone now."

"I do," he said, and he went to his room.

Anna followed, and stood before his closed door a few minutes before getting up the courage to knock.

"What is it?" He sounded very tired.

"Can I come in?"

"I'd rather you didn't. I haven't slept all night."

"Neither have I."

There was a silence, and the door opened. Alexei was in his shirt sleeves. He stood back as she walked in. She looked about the masculine furnishings. She was so infrequently in his rooms. Usually he came to her. "May I sit?"

"Look, Anna . . ." He reached for her.

She gasped and pulled back, afraid in that instant he was going to strike her.

His hand fell limply to his side. Slowly he walked to his bed and sat on the edge. Suddenly he covered his face with his hands and began to sob uncontrollably.

"Alexei!" She hurried to him, sitting beside him and wrapping a comforting arm about him. "What's wrong?"

For a while he couldn't speak. He sagged like a rag doll, his broad shoulders heaving. Then he wrapped his arms about her and buried his head in her lap. "I was so terrified," he moaned. "I was so scared you'd left me."

"Left you! Where would I go?"

"Oh, Anna, Anna, don't ever leave me." He was pleading. His arms were holding her still tighter. His head nestled against her waist and as his face worked its way to hers, she realized he was kissing her. He stared so long, so hard, so silently into her eyes, she became frightened, and then his mouth closed on hers, hungrily taking her into him. The moment, like the kiss itself, slipped into timelessness. She was a heated grain of sand. She was white sun. She was rushing, a drop of water crashing through a mountain glen. He was the sweet cover of night curving above her. He laid her on the bed beneath him. Slowly, his lips never leaving her skin, he began unbuttoning her dress. He undressed her slowly, his fingertips lightly grazing her neck and shoulders. He was sitting back, gazing at her nakedness. He was smiling. "My God, you're beautiful."

"Alexei . . ." She drank in his joy. The anger, misery were gone, and she felt free, freer than she had marching through the streets with Petya, more exuberant, or perhaps it was just an explosion of the same feeling. There was no awkwardness or uncertainty. His wide-eyed wonder caressed her. His hands reached out, gently covering each breast.

She shuddered as if a ball of fire were spinning through her.

His mouth engulfed first one breast and then the other, released a slow, streaming mellowness she needed suddenly to share.

"Can I do that to you now?" she asked uncertainly.

He smiled happily and lay down as she reached tentatively to his shirt. Her hands fumbled with the buttons, growing steadily more certain. She sat back on her feet, staring in wonder at the broad expanse of his shoulders and the thick muscles straining at the skin of his arms. Dense black hair curled about his chest. He seemed, as he lay there, more the perfection of a marble statue than a man. She kissed him as he'd kissed her, rubbing her face against the warm tightness of his skin. She stopped when she reached his waist, staring at the bulge in his pants.

"Don't be afraid," he said softly, taking her hand and holding it to him.

His hardness filled her with an urgency, a flowing connected desperately to him. She rubbed and pressed the mysterious thing, still hidden, and looking at him, said, "I'm not afraid. Is that awful?"

"There's not a thing about you which can be awful."

"Not even what I did tonight?"

"Not even that."

"Then you forgive me?"

"There's nothing to forgive. It was my fault, my love." He turned and pulled open the drawer to his bedside table, taking out her wedding ring. "Don't ever take this off again. Promise me." He slipped it on her finger. "And I'll never give you cause." He took her in his arms, but she pulled away, waiting to finish what she had begun. Her heart was thudding, mixing with a delicious excitement as she finished undressing him. "Oh, my!" she gasped as his penis stood out straight. She thought of the tiny penises of the boys in the Club. "Oh, my . . ." she repeated, reaching out. The silky smoothness surprised her, as well as the power her touch commanded. Alexei's breathing became deep and irregular. He thrust himself against her, his penis seeming almost to have a life of its own.

"Oh, Anna . . ." he moaned, and reached for her, rolling on top of her; his powerful arms encased her; his body was soft and hard, hot and moist; his hips rotated in gentle curves and she moved to meet him. The rhythm between them built; chords played madly inside her; she wanted the movements never to cease.

"I don't want to hurt you," he murmured as he pressed to enter her.

Her legs fell wider part. "Just do it, Alexei. Irina told me about it. She said the pleasure is so much greater than the pain."

His hands smoothed between her legs once more; his fingers probed, seeming to draw the burning, silky smoothness from her; her hips rose and she pressed against him.

"Do it, please . . ." It was a desperate madness driving her. All life was focused on the moment, on his pressing to break through. The work of it seemed enormous and then suddenly she cried, the pain forgotten in the merging, like swimming. She felt him and felt nothing. The darkness in her mind grew light. He was inside her. She was inside him. She felt lost, as if his body were devouring her.

"Oh, God, Anna!" he was moaning, rising and falling against her.

"Anna, yes, Anna!" He drove on with a madness she'd

never expected, and suddenly it was over. He collapsed, hot and sweating, his skin sliding against hers as he gasped for breath. "Oh, God, you're so beautiful. Oh God, I love you," he repeated again and again. His arms were under and around her, holding her, and he was smiling, laughing softly. Then he slipped out of her and away, lying beside her on his back. "Just a few moments," he promised. When his breathing became more regular, he asked, "Did I hurt you?"

"I don't know. It doesn't matter."

"Oh, my sweet . . ." He was smiling. She was smiling. He lit a cigarette, and laughed as she climbed about him, continuing to explore his body with a childish intensity. "Oh, look, he's gone all small!" She seemed both surprised and uneasy.

"A temporary setback, I assure you!"

She sat pensively beside him, her hand on his thigh.

"What are you thinking, Annochka, my love?"

"How odd this all is. I don't understand it, not at all."

"Don't try," he assured her. "Lovemaking is for pleasure, not understanding."

"But there's something else I feel," she insisted, needing to have him inside her once more. "Something else is pulling me."

"Yes, I know." He nibbled at her fingers. "There's much more. We've only just begun." He sat up and put out his cigarette. Kissing her lightly as he eased down on the bed, he said, "Now I shall really make you a woman." Kneeling beside her, he whispered, "There's no place on your body or inside you, no place that I can touch that I won't. Every inch of you will be mine. Doesn't that frighten you?"

"I think so, yes, a little." She laughed nervously.

"But it will be all for the sweetest of moments this time, Annochka, my heart. I will give you pleasure such as you never imagined, I promise."

Her eyes closed as his fingers smoothed her mouth and cheeks, slipping to her neck and shoulders in movements that ignited the burning again. His hands and lips neared but did not touch her breasts. For endless, taut moments he caressed, kissed, and licked each part of her except those which ached for his caresses. She cried and moaned as the hotness spread, and she remembered the sun-drenched moments of Misha and Irina on the beach. She was there with Alexei now; her body had no will except to open and open for him. His touch drew her into the exquisite spans of time; she was soaring into crystal light, refracted colors bursting with the brilliance of stained-glass windows in the sun. His hands massaged and

molded about her, inside her, and when she felt his head
press between her legs, small cries escaped her. He drew her
into his mouth, his tongue licked and smoothed the soft folds
until the ecstasy broke loose and her whimpering grew to
cries, then screams, building and building. Her hands gripped
his head, pushing him deeper inside her; she thrust herself
against him again and again; the pleasure rolled in waves,
revealing a part of her feeling like an unknown soul. Peace
settled like the glow of dawning. He lay beside her, cuddling
her, and they slept.

When she awoke, Alexei had a feast spread about her:
duck, caviar, fruit, champagne, cakes. She pointed to the
chocolate layer first and he fed her with his fingers; she sucked
each one clean. Then he held a crystal goblet to her lips. The
champagne dribbled down her chin and she laughed, dipping
her fingers into the caviar, scooping it into his mouth. He
tore off a piece of duck and smothered it with gravy, which
dripped down to her belly. He licked her clean, swearing to
devour her. Her laughter streamed like wind off wings, and
they fed each other until they could hardly move. She lay in
his arms. He worked her hair around his fingers and breathed
in its scent. She lay on him and he played with her body once
more. They were on the bed, the floor, in her rooms, on the
couch, and back to his rooms. Love embraced them finally
in a completeness which left them entwined in dreamless
sleep.

The playful innocence and exuberance of Anna's lovemaking both startled and seduced Alexei. He, who was the older
and experienced, found himself caught up in her game that
hurled each moment recklessly into the next. He was breathless with the newness; years were shed like useless cocoons,
old, painful memories vanished like prison doors swung open
into daylight. He was giddy, ravenous, awed; her body seemed
an expression of the perfection of her soul. The dewy whiteness of her skin, her flaxen hair streaming onto breasts so
round and full, so soft with all which was a woman, the
golden mound between her legs rising eagerly, opening before him, glistening like a treasure no man had ever known,
drugged him with a frenzy flowing into peace. Loving Anna
seemed as holy as it had once seemed forbidden. She beckoned and he followed.

Anna was sitting at her writing desk, going over the list
for the dinner party; the date had changed twice due to the
Czar's postponements of the meeting on which Alexei was so

vigorously working with Sergei Witte, Alexander Ryabush-insky, and Count Bobrinsky. Alexei often talked of the Coalition now and of its planned petition; he described how different life would be if the country were run by constitution rather than the whims and wills of the Czar. The concept made sense when he explained it, and she rather liked the picture he painted of himself as a statesman sitting in the Duma. She thought he would look very dignified, and everyone would listen to him because he was so smart. The more Alexei spoke to her about the state of the world, the more she was impressed by how much he knew. Still, she was anxious to have her dinner party, more like a Christmas party, as it was turning out. Well, that was all right. She'd decorate the house gaily, even have the living room, dining room and front parlors redone in deep tones of winter. She never had liked Helena Kalinina's whites and beiges. Alexei promised that Helena, should she ever return to Petersburg, which he strongly doubted, wouldn't mind Anna's changes. Anna was, after all, mistress of the house.

Anna looked over her list. What had started as a small affair of thirty was burgeoning closer to a hundred. Each day Alexei added a new name, another important person of whom Anna had never heard. There were quite a few invitations sent to Moscow, to people who would have to stay over as houseguests. Anna didn't mind having the houseguests; she was already planning the next day's menus; she just wasn't certain of having the guest list so weighted with Muscovites, and wondered what Aunt Tatyana and her friends would think. Alexei insisted it didn't matter what Tatyana and her friends thought. Anna wasn't certain. Too many Muscovites, and Anna and Alexei might be excluded from the most fashionable of Petersburg fetes just as the winter season was beginning. She'd tried to explain that to Alexei, but he'd become impatient.

"I've never had my friends dictated by Petersburg society and I won't start now! If you don't think my friends and your friends mix, then cancel the damned dinner!"

"But they're all your friends—Petersburg and Moscow alike. There's hardly any of them I know except Monsieur Rimsky-Korsakov, Aunt Tatyana and Uncle Ilya, and Petya."

"Then why are you taking it into your head to worry?" he demanded, and then his face burst into a smile. "Come here." He held out his arms.

Eagerly she hurried to him.

He embraced her and kissed first her hair, then her nose,

then her mouth. "Forgive me if I snap. My bark is far worse than my bite, I promise."

"I know." She wrapped both arms about him. "I love you."

"I love you."

"That's all that matters, isn't it?" She looked up at him.

"Certainly more than who's sitting next to whom at some dinner party."

"Yes, yes, you're right. Oh Alexei . . ." Her body fluttered. She closed her eyes, slipping her hand inside his shirt and wondering if this hunger she had for him would ever go away. She hoped not, but sometimes she wished it would give her some peace.

"Anna, I do have work to do."

"I know, I know. We needn't be all morning. Let me just steal you a little while. Please. . . ."

She set aside the guest list and leaned back in her chair, closing her eyes as a rush of Alexei memories flooded her. They often did, several times an hour when they were apart, making his return seem the most wonderful of gifts. She smiled to think that life could be so good. She remembered an intimacy between them. Moments plucked at her brain. Even when she was practicing, even as poor old Rimsky-Korsakov was sitting by her side, Anna was thinking of making love with Alexei and the memory would drive her music on.

A knock at the door brought Anna from her reveries.

"There's a young lady downstairs to see you, madame," Lidia announced. "She has no card, but she said to tell you her name is Valia Vaslavna."

"Valia!" Anna was flustered. What would Valia be doing here without warning? Anna had sent her an invitation to the party, of course, but Valia, living with her father in Moscow, had been one of the first to decline. "Send her up . . . no, I shall go myself." Anna hurried past Lidia, down the hall and the steps. The visitor was standing with her back to Anna, staring at an arrangement of flowers, but Anna knew in an instant that the tall, slim woman was not Valia.

It wasn't until they were alone in Anna's room that Anna and Irina felt free to embrace.

"Oh, it's wonderful to see you!" Irina hugged her again and again. "And you look wonderful, Anna, ravishing. Marriage has been good, I see. Look at you!" She pinched at her waist. "You've positively got some flesh on you."

"I eat like a pig now, just as I used to when we were little. Did you read that I was arrested?"

"Oh, yes, I read all about it in the papers."

"But it's all cleared up. Alexei's lawyer, Yuri Nikolaievich, has quite fixed it. Uncle Ilya, you see, wrote a letter to the Czar, begging him to forgive me. Oh, it was quite a letter. I saw it. He made me appear like a saint. So, between Yuri Nikolaievich and your papa, Alexei says there isn't even a hint of my arrest on any police records anymore."

"You're lucky, then. Whatever made you go on a march? Or were you mistakenly arrested?"

"I was marching." She blushed. "I was very angry at Alexei, you see. Not because I don't love him. I do. Sometimes, though, he can make me very angry. Or he used to. He doesn't anymore. Actually, the episode was quite foolish and I ran out. You want to hear something? I kept hoping to see you or Misha. How is Misha?"

"Fine, just fine. But tell me, what do you think of Yuri Nikolaievich?"

"Not terribly much. I mean, he's a good lawyer. Alexei said he's the best. He made me dreadfully nervous, asking me all these questions over and over and looking at me with those eyes of his!" Anna laughed, making her own face bug out. "But I don't want to talk about Yuri Nikolaievich. Tell me about you, Irina." Anna was smiling very hard, delighted with Irina's return. Her presence filled an emptiness Anna hadn't known was there. "What have you been doing all these months? I've been desperate to see you."

"I've thought of you often. I ask about you. Hasn't Alexei told you?"

Anna paled.

"Oh, dear. Look, Anna, don't be angry at him. I suppose if I try, even I can understand his motivation. I'm not a very safe person to know right now. It's why I've stayed away."

"Were you exiled too?"

"No, just Misha. I've done nothing the police know about yet. But it's a dangerous world. There are so few one can trust."

"I don't want to think about it. It will only make me sick with worry over Alexei and the Coalition. He's working quite hard on the Coalition, you know. Alexei says that if there's a constitution, then people will have all kinds of freedoms, rich and poor alike, and I'm sure you and Misha wouldn't have to be in hiding anymore."

"It's all very complicated these days. Nothing's straightforward."

Anna nodded, feeling that gray heaviness settling as it did when Alexei talked about politics too long. "Oh, by the way, did you hear I'm giving a dinner party?"

Irina seemed momentarily startled by the question. "Of course!"

"It's been changed to December 15," Anna went on. "Phillipe Sedov, you know, he writes the society page in *Our Days*—well, I told him I wasn't at all certain of December 1, which was why I wasn't even sending out the invitations yet, but he went and printed the date anyway. He's an awful man, truly, quite a dandy, if you ask me. I didn't want to talk to him, but he just invited himself to tea. I'm not even certain how he knew I was planning a dinner party. I'd hardly told anyone but—" Anna stopped herself short. "I don't suppose you read the society columns anymore."

"Actually, I do sometimes. Old habits die hard. I just find myself turning to the pages. Are Mama and Papa coming to your dinner party?"

"Of course!"

"You've seen them?" Irina asked casually.

"Only once, actually, since we've been back. Aunt Tatyana invited us for tea. She wouldn't talk of you at all."

"I'm not surprised. How is she?"

"All right, I suppose. I mean, she's fine. She looks fine. She was just terribly . . . well, the tea was awkward." Anna sat beside Irina. "Yes, I've never felt awkward with your mother. I felt as if she didn't like me, or Alexei. I don't know. She kept on making these cutting little remarks to Alexei which made no sense at all to me, but I was a bundle of nerves. Alexei said it was nothing."

"She's jealous that you've married Alexei, of course." Irina sat down on the bed and began untying her boots. "She's been mad for him for years."

"But she was the one who originally brought us together."

"Don't expect any semblance of sanity from my mother when it comes to men, Anna." Irina kicked off her boots. "And don't expect her to be the loving aunt at your dinner party either."

"I wish you could be there. I'd feel so much better if someone who was really my friend was there."

Irina smiled sympathetically. "You'll do fine on your own, I can tell. But you mustn't tell anyone, not even Alexei, I've been here."

"Of course not."

Irina yanked at her skirt and sat cross-legged on the bed the way they used to when they were girls. "Tell me, Anna, tell me everything that happened when you were arrested. I want to know every detail.''

"Haven't you ever been arrested?"

"No."

"Really!" Anna felt suddenly proud. She talked endlessly about the march and all that followed, describing feelings, people, surroundings, smells. She talked about the girl Dora with the long black hair and black enamel cigarette holder. She talked of all the curses the marchers used. She talked of the camaraderie, and sharing the events with Irina made her relive the moments again. "Most exciting were the people. They were all so friendly. This is going to sound foolish, but I actually felt the most beautiful sense of love when I walked into the basement room in the police station and everyone cheered. And Petya and I have become friends since then. I see him at least once a week. He's coming to my dinner. Can you imagine?"

"No! Any more than I can imagine him marching against the Czar."

"Alexei says once the Czar grants the constitution—"

"*If* the Czar grants the constitution."

"He will. Alexei's writing a petition. He can convince anyone of anything! Oh, Irina, I'm so happy you've come to see me at last. Now it can be just as it used to be. You can come to visit and pretend to be Valia. You could come as much as you like. We'll have a grand time. I'll order the best lunches and teas for us." Anna hugged Irina very tightly.

CHAPTER THIRTY-FOUR

"An insult to one is an insult to all! Yes, I say, the day is near when we shall stand as *one* . . ." Father Gapon's voice crescendoed on the word and shimmered into an awesome silence. His outstretched arms flowed from the black, priestly cassock; his dark eyes widened into gleaming pools as he gazed about the sharply attentive audience of drably clothed men, women, and children crowded into the Putilov Hall of the Society of Factory and Plant Workers. They'd come about the firings of four Putilov ironworkers: Segunin, Subbotin, Ukolev, and Fyodorov.

Irina was sitting in the front row; she was watching Father Gapon closely, and felt his glance sweep the audience and return finally to her. She nodded ever so slightly as their eyes momentarily locked. He was doing well, very well. His passion was contagious. The electricity in the hall was tangible. Irina could see it not only on the faces of the workers but also in the attentiveness of the newspaper reporters come to cover the meeting. All Petersburg was awaiting the outcome, for the firings of the workers Segunin, Subbotin, Ukolev, and Fyodorov, all vocal Gapon supporters, had been a clear-cut attack on Gapon specifically and the workers' movement in general.

"*One*, I say—each and every worker in Petersburg, nay in all Russia, shall move as *one*!" Gapon's word rumbled with an inspired foreboding. "For this insult to our brothers Segunin, Subbotin, Ukolev, and Fyodorov is an insult to every worker, every man, woman, and child who has felt the whip of oppression, starvation, and poverty. It is time to let the bosses and bureaucrats know that if they fire one of us, they fire us all. This is what we shall tell Director Smirnov of the Putilov plant, and our voice shall be strong. For it will be hundreds, nay thousands speaking as one. Our voice shall be heard not only by Director Smirnov, but by our father, the holy Czar, and by God in his heavens!"

"What do we ask for, citizens?" Kostya Sergeievich Savich, Gapon's closest aide, called as he jumped to his feet, his arm thrust into the air.

"An eight-hour day!" another called out.

"Rule of law that protects all of us, not only the rich!" A woman rose.

"Freedom to talk our minds!"

"Freedom to meet without having our heads bashed in!"

"Freedom to strike for a decent wage!"

"Schools!"

"Praise God, the Czar will protect us!"

"The Czar is our holy father!"

Irina watched and listened as the words burst religiously from faces grimy with dirt and alive with the holiness of their cause. Each day their demands grew stronger, more defiant, their passion more turbulent. She felt like a midwife in the rush of birth, and she was on her feet with the others. "A constitution is what we need, Father!" she shouted.

"Constitution! Constitution!" came the chant.

"We will support Segunin, Subbotin, Ukolev, and Fyodo-rov to the death!" Misha as Izaak rose to his feet next.

"Segunin, Subbotin, Ukolev, and Fyodorov! Segunin, Subbotin, Ukolev, and Fyodorov!" The hall rocked with the pounding of feet, the clapping of hands and the thunder of exultant voices.

Irina lingered as always when the meeting broke up, talk-ing to the women workers, who were more and more coming to her with their grievances about their husbands as well as their jobs. Irina's weekly women's reading group was turning into an organizing session. Tonight, though, the women were talking only about Father Gapon.

"Father sounded so fiery, don't you think, Kuksina Iva-novna?" a middle-aged cotton worker named Felia asked.

"He grows more fiery each day, I think."

"Surely the Czar, much less the puny little Director Smirnov, cannot deny such a one as Father Gapon," Za-bela, a young woman with a sleeping infant in her arms, cooed. "Segunin, Subbotin, Ukolev, and Fyodorov will have their jobs back in no time once Director Smirnov hears from Father . . ."

Irina was listening with only half an ear. She was gazing about the room looking for Misha when she caught a glimpse of a tall, square, brutish man in an ill-fitting gray suit stand-ing against a far wall. His round, red, clean-shaven face gleamed with perspiration. His sparse hair was closely cropped. His eyes were small, the black appearing like pin-heads. She recognized him instantly and her body shrank in terror. Instinctively she tugged at the worn babushka about her head, pulling it down further on her face.

"Kuksina Ivanovna, are you all right?" Zabela asked, nudging her gently.

"Yes, yes, you'll excuse me, though . . ." She hurried away from the women, pressing through the crowd with her head bent and her shoulders hunched. "Izaak." She tugged at his sleeve.

Misha was deeply engrossed in a conversation, but he ex-cused himself as soon as Irina appeared and followed her to the back of the small raised stage from where Gapon spoke. "What's wrong?"

"I want you to turn slowly. There's a tall, ugly brute in a gray suit leaning against the wall, on the far side of the po-dium. He has beady little eyes."

Misha did as she told him.

"Can you see him?" she whispered.

"Yes. He's a cop for sure."

"More than that." She leaned forward and quickly peeked. Again her stomach churned. "Do you know him?"

"No."

"Think, Misha, it's important."

"Perhaps he's been at one of the meetings before. I can't be sure. Why?"

She pulled him closer. "Remember the break-in at Vera Martova's flat in Paris, the men who beat us up and stole the Yermolov papers last summer?" she whispered breathlessly. "That's him, that's one of the men!"

"Are you certain?"

"I was as close to him as I am to you. Closer. He nearly broke my arm. He held a knife to my face."

"Did he see you?"

"I don't know, but he's from Yermolov, Misha. I don't understand. What is he doing here? Oh, God, Misha . . ." She held his arm tightly, trying to keep the panic at bay. "I'm scared. That man is an animal." Irina grasped ferociously on to Misha as they watched the pin-eyed man make his way through the crowd toward the door. "He's leaving!" she gasped. "Come on. You get our coats, and hurry . . . hurry!"

Irina pushed frantically through the crush of people in the meeting hall, and burst out on to the stairs. Many people were milling about outside the building. Irina stood staring into the gaslighted streets. There was no sign of the pin-eyed man.

Alexei's gaze was fixed on the crudely written note lying on his desktop. *Your life and those of the ones you love aren't worth the paper your petition is written on.* He'd been staring at the words for twenty minutes, ever since Volodia had brought it to him, trying to gain control of the storm whipping round in his mind. His only thought was of Anna, of getting her to leave Petersburg without him. He would have to maneuver her. Threats or no threats, she would not, he knew, leave willingly.

There was a knocking at his door.

"Yes."

"Minister Witte is here to see you, sir," Volodia announced.

Alexei was on his feet, note in hand, as Witte walked into the room.

"You got one too, then?" Witte's face was grave with worry.

Alexei handed it to him.

"It's identical to mine."

"Has anyone else received them?"

"I don't know. I came here first. Ryabushinsky surely, and probably the whole damn Coalition. We'll have to send messengers to Moscow."

"Yermolov sent them."

"I'm certain, but I have no proof. Not that proof would do any good these days. Come, sit, there's more I must fill you in on now." They settled on the leather couch. "It's not only the work we're doing on the petition that's prompted these threats, I fear. Yermolov's in a death struggle for control of the Okhrana. One of Akimov's men was found murdered in his bed yesterday."

"Akimov?"

"Arkady Akimov, my man in the Okhrana." Witte reached into his jacket pocket, taking out a half-smoked cigar, and began to light it.

"I don't understand. How does the struggle between Yermolov and this Akimov affect the Coalition?"

"The Coalition and those who support us represent a movement toward liberalization. Yermolov represents extreme reaction. The scales are weighted such that if the Coalition threw its support behind Akimov, even the Czar might be forced to take away his support of Yermolov."

"Why don't we, then?"

"I'm afraid such a move would force Yermolov to dig in his heels even more deeply, and a bloodbath would follow. In fact, pressure by Yermolov and the right may be one of the reasons the Czar still refuses to meet with the Coalition. Besides . . ." He sighed uneasily "To tell you the truth, I'm not certain about Akimov anymore."

"Not certain?"

"The man's an egomaniac. I knew that from the first. But he's bright and determined. I thought I could use him if I trod lightly. More and more I feel I'm in his service rather than the other way around."

"How so?"

Witte seemed embarrassed. "You remember we talked of this Father Gapon's police unions and their connection to Yermolov?"

"Yes."

Witte grimaced. "I've discovered these police unions are not the brainchild of Yermolov at all, but of Akimov."

"You're certain?"

"I confronted him, and he told me I was treading waters out of my depth."

"Cut him loose, then."

"And leave the Okhrana to Yermolov? I can't. There's too much at stake. We need Yermolov out of the picture. Akimov's hell-bent on that."

"It seems to me this Akimov isn't much better than Yermolov. There must be a way to get rid of Akimov, or at least get him more under your control."

"My instinct says to tread lightly with him now. I've learned to follow my instincts. Besides, we need Akimov's protection." He ruffled the threat note he held in his hand. "I'm meeting with him in a few hours. He'll be giving you, Ryabushinsky, everyone in the Coalition round-the-clock protection."

"We could hire our own bodyguards if it came to that."

"Akimov's men know the workings of the enemy. For this I trust him. Still, if I were you, I'd get Anna out of Petersburg as soon as possible. Tonight."

"Come, sit, we've much to talk about," Father Gapon urged excitedly as he took off his coat and hat and tossed them onto a pile of newspapers in the small, crowded front room of his flat. It was past midnight. The meeting hall had taken hours to clear out, and then Gapon had invited Irina, Misha and Kostya Savich back to his house for tea and talk. Kostya Savich was Gapon's closest aide and in charge of the "Life Guards," a small group of workers dedicated to Gapon's security. It was, Irina thought, Kostya's dogged devotion to the priest, not the acuity of his advice, which had won him a place by Gapon's side. There was something sluggish about Kostya. His eyes were flat. His face rarely showed expression. He was short and muscular, the grayness of his thinning hair reflecting the shadows of his skin. Irina didn't dislike him; rather, as she and Misha had grown closer to Gapon, she tended to forget Kostya's existence. He was usually at these late-night talks with Irina, Misha, and Gapon, but said little.

"Kostya, get the brandy to add to the tea. We owe ourselves some celebration. It went well tonight, I think!"

"You were inspired, Father," Kostya said solemnly as he fixed the tea.

"The women talked of nothing but your fire, Father," Irina added.

"Yes, I felt on fire tonight, Kuksina, just as you said I would." The priest smiled expansively from his desk. "As if the words flowed from the heavenly Father himself. But tell me, Izaak, what you thought of our meeting tonight."

"I thought it was wonderful, Father. I thought you were wonderful. We are on the brink of making history." Misha nodded as Kostya handed him his tea.

"History . . ." Gapon crooned as he settled into his seat. "Yes, I believe you're right, Izaak. History is a marvel, don't you think, crafted by God. Yet . . ." He dropped three lumps of sugar in his tea and motioned Kostya to sit. "God is the architect but people are the builders. People are history."

"Oh, yes, Father," Kostya agreed.

"The relentless march of history," Gapon went on. "Nay, we are more than its builders—we are its footsoldiers."

"You are its leader, Father. Surely, without you, the course of our history would be different," Irina insisted.

Gapon thought a moment and began to smile; he placed his teacup on the edge of his cluttered desk and leaned forward. "I'll tell you my dream, Kuksina, Izaak, and Kostya. You are the first to hear it. For it's only come to me lately— but it comes like the passion tonight, on the breath of God. I believe . . ." His eyes opened wide and he pressed his hands fervently together in childlike excitement. "I believe it is my mission to unify all revolutionaries under my banner."

"Revolutionaries, Father? I don't understand."

"Was not our Lord, Jesus Christ, a revolutionary in his own time?"

"Yes, but surely today's revolutionaries do not carry the banner of Christ. Whereas Christ offered love and forgiveness, they throw bombs and curse our Czar," Irina dutifully reminded him.

"No, no, my child, you misunderstand me. I don't mean the terrorists. For every terrorist there are a hundred revolutionaries. For every conscious revolutionary, there are a thousand more who will tomorrow or the next day rise to the call. That, Kuksina, my child, is the way of history."

"But the revolutionaries hate the Czar," Misha reminded him.

"They know not whom they hate, but I shall teach them. It is my mission. God has spoken." Gapon pressed his finger to his smooth, thin lips a moment. "Trust is what carries men's hearts, and I trust you, Kuksina and Izaak. No one who follows me gives me truer advice. Kostya and I have discussed this. For so long, he and I alone have been the heartbeat of our humble flock, but as we grow, we must become more organized. Our leadership must be infallible. For history will someday demand to know, and we must not disappoint those who will carry on in our name. Therefore, with Kostya's help, I have drawn up proper papers, making you,

Kuksina, and you, Izaak, along with Kostya, my advisers, my ministers. You will walk by my side with God. You will be first before all others. You, Izaak, shall be a general in my Life Guards, and you, Kuksina, you will lead the women. They flock to you already. Like myself, your magnetism flows from God. You will be my chief aide. It was Kostya's suggestion. You are wiser than most men, Kuksina Ivanovna. Wherever I go, you will march by my side and God will protect us.''

Irina didn't know what to say. Higher visibility in Gapon's organization was out of the question for either Misha or herself. Not only had she Dmitri to worry about, but now there was the pin-eyed man. Perhaps he'd already recognized her. ''Father,'' she began, knowing she had to say something, ''I . . . I am honored beyond words that you have chosen me as one of your ministers, but first, there are things I must ask you. Perhaps it would be better for us to speak in private.''

''My ministers can have no secrets from one another.''

She nodded, and her voice quivered with uncertainty. ''There are those, good men and true, who say you are little more than a pawn of the police. Forgive me, Father,'' she quickly added, bowing her head as she crossed herself. ''But it's what I have heard.''

''It's what the revolutionaries and the intellectuals say, Kuksina Ivanovna.'' Kostya Savich sneered, his words almost a reprimand. ''And they say it as if it's something to hide. Father has no secrets.''

''Then it's true?'' Kuksina directed her question to Gapon.

He eyed Irina thoughtfully as he sipped his tea, and finally said, ''I will tell you a story, Kuksina and Izaak, one which Kostya knows all too well. Three years ago, I was far younger than I am now, not only chronologically but also in terms of my understanding of human nature. I was innocent as a babe, even though at the seminary I was considered a renegade. You see, I have always believed it is the role of the priest not only to protect his flock but also to lead them, nourish them, educate them. How can we talk of a better life in heaven, how can we ask people to wait until death for happiness when the sun rises and sets each day on this earth? God is good, he is merciful. He never meant his children to suffer so cruelly. I believe that in my heart and my soul. I believe, I have always believed, that God has put me on this earth to lead his Russian children out of misery just as Moses led the Jews.''

Gapon paused breathlessly and went on, ''Three years ago I was approached by a man whom I knew was the messenger

I'd been long awaiting. He said he was sent by the Czar, but I knew he was sent by God. He said the Czar needed a man of the people and a man of God by his side. I said, 'There are many men of God in Russia,' and he said, 'Yes, this is true, but the church is painfully bereft of men of the people.' Those were his exact words. I remember them. He told me it was God's will to preserve the House of Romanov. He said I alone could carry the holy sword by organizing workers into unions who speak not against the Czar but against the factory owners and the bureaucrats. Truly, it is they who are responsible for the people's misery. This man promised the forces of the Czar would protect me and all my followers.''

''This man was from the police, then?'' Misha asked ingenuously.

''The police wield the sword of the Czar, who rules through God's love, Izaak.''

''But what of this man who came to you in the seminary? What is his name?'' Irina asked innocently.

''Father . . .'' Kostya Savich warned.

''I understand, Kostya.'' Gapon held up his hand. ''But if Kuksina and Izaak are to be one with us, there can be no secrets. God will protect us.'' He crossed himself and looked at Irina and Misha. ''The man's name is Arkady Akimov.''

Irina held her hands tightly together to keep her body from noticeably trembling. She dared not look at Misha, and staring directly at Gapon, she asked. ''And is this Arkady Akimov a good man?''

''Gapon considered the question. ''He is a powerful man.''

''You trust him?''

''Kostya, would you say we trust Akimov?''

''In my heart, you know I could never trust the man.''

''Kostya worked for Akimov before he came to me,'' Gapon explained.

''Akimov still thinks I do,'' Kostya added proudly. ''I run errands for the dog, but my allegiance is to Father!''

''Why don't you trust Akimov, Kostya?'' Irina asked.

''I saw too much. Akimov uses people for his own ends.''

''I don't understand—I thought you said he was sent by God, Father.''

''God tests us in many ways, Kuksina Ivanovna. The fact that God's messenger is not at peace with God makes him no less a messenger. What is important is my peace with God. It's why the people follow me. Akimov thinks he gives me power, but it has always been mine to take.''

''Does this Akimov know how you feel?'' Misha asked.

"It doesn't matter. Soon I will be beyond his touch. The people will protect me as Akimov's police do now."

"Praise God, the shield of heaven cannot protect you against Akimov's guns, Father." Kostya crossed himself.

"Ach, such a worrier is our Kostya. Kuksina, have we satisfied your curiosity about the rumors you have heard? For you see, they are true, but nothing to worry about."

"There is one more thing, if you will forgive my boldness, Father."

"Yes."

"Some of the police who you say protect us are so fearful-looking. There was one tonight in particular." She lowered her eyes. "A tall, brawny man with little eyes. He wasn't wearing workers' clothing. He seemed evil. In my heart I felt that."

"Did he wear a gray suit?" Kostya asked.

"Yes."

"You must be most careful of him," Kostya warned.

"You know him, then?" Misha asked.

Kostya eyed Gapon uncertainly.

Gapon nodded.

"His name is Kolesnikov," Kostya went on. "And you're right when you sense his evil, Kuksina Ivanovna. Truly, he speaks the will of the devil. I have seen him cut a man for the sheer joy of it. He kills with the same relish a normal man loves."

"What is he doing at one of our meetings, then?"

"He was bringing a message to me," Gapon said flatly.

"To you!" Irina gasped in wide-eyed wonder. "But, Father, I don't understand."

"Kuksina, do you trust me?"

"You know I do, Father."

"Then trust that I know what I'm doing with a man like Kolesnikov. Just as important, my child, take Kostya's warning to heart. Stay away from Kolesnikov, the two of you."

She nodded dutifully and said, "There's just one more question I must ask, Father."

"Yes," he said patiently.

"This Kolesnikov—surely he's not from Akimov."

"But, of course, he is. Now, Kuksina, enough questions. Are you and Izaak to walk by my side?"

"Father, we are honored beyond words," Irina began. "And I, of course, cannot speak for Izaak, but for myself I can say in spirit I will be your most faithful aide and supporter. But I cannot stand on the stage before you or talk to many people at one time. By my nature, I am not a speaker to the masses, or a leader—''

"Ah, but, Kuksina, you are."

"Thank you, Father, but I know what I can do. Let me remain like a quiet mouse, always by your side but in a way that no one but you, Kostya, and Izaak truly know. I can do no more."

"And you, Izaak? Will you be a general in my Life Guards?"

"It would be an honor such as I never dreamed possible, Father."

"Well, then, everything is fine." Gapon smiled happily. "Kuksina shall speak like a mouse but carry the thunder of a lion. And you, Izaak, with Kostya, shall carry my sword."

"I'm not going!" Anna said flatly.

Alexei tried hard to contain his anger. That Anna should defy him at such a moment seemed beyond comprehension. "There's no time to argue and nothing to argue about. I'm sending you to Peterhof tonight."

"I'll not go. You can drug me as my mother and Zinaida did, and I'll still not go."

"Anna!" He held up the note to her face. "This is not child's play. This is serious. I know men like this. They won't go after Witte or Ryabushinsky or me. They'll go after our families."

"Then they shall find me in Peterhof and I shall die alone. I'd rather die here by your side."

"Don't even talk to me of dying! And as for Peterhof, you'll be quite safe there with my mother and Tolya. I'm hiring men to guard the house twenty-four hours a day."

"Hire them to guard this palace, why don't you? Then I'll be safer than I'd be in Peterhof because I'll still be with you."

"Five days, Anna—I'll join you in Peterhof as soon as we present the petition. We'll go away for awhile, to Paris or London."

"But my dinner party—I've my dinner party in two weeks, and the decorators are in the middle—"

"There'll be plenty of time for dinner parties, I promise. If not this one, another."

"We can't put it off again, Alexei. You promised we wouldn't. I shall be the laughingstock of all Petersburg."

"So long as you're alive."

"You're being overly dramatic."

"I'm not."

She frowned. "What about my piano lessons?"

"Something can be arranged. Peterhof is less than an hour away. Now, please, get ready."

"No, Alexei. I'll not leave you." Her voice was filled with determination. "You can't make me—"

"Dammit!" he thundered, grabbing her arms. "I can make you do whatever I want! Do you understand that, Anna? You'll do precisely what I tell you to do, when I tell you to do it!" He let her go with such force, she fell back onto a chair.

Fear paled her face. She bit her lip to keep back the swell of tears.

He breathed deeply. "I'm sorry . . ." He began pacing. "But what do you expect? You block me at every turn! If you act like a child, you'll be treated like a child."

"You hurt me," she managed to say.

"Yermolov and his Black Hundreds will hurt you a lot more, believe me. Now, please, pack whatever you need. You can buy the rest in Peterhof or have it shipped."

"Where are you going?"

"To send a messenger ahead so my mother and brother will be expecting you."

As he started from the room, she felt the last shreds of her defiance slip away. The thought of the night without Alexei was too terrible, and she ran after him. "Please, Alexei, not today. Tomorrow I'll go. Just let me sleep home tonight." She reached for him and pressed against him; his body was stiff, distant, the way she had not felt it for weeks. "I'm so afraid to be separate from you. Something terrible will happen, I know it."

"Something terrible will happen if you don't do as I say." He untangled himself.

"Alexei . . ."

"Just get ready." The words came out as an order, and he was gone.

CHAPTER THIRTY-FIVE

December 15, 1904

My darling Annochka,

It is with the deepest regret that I must again postpone my coming to Peterhof. Witte has once more changed the date of the meeting of the Coalition with the Czar, for he is certain he will soon have all the Czar's advisers behind us. I know how miserable you must feel today, what should have been your first grand dinner. I, too, am sad, alone in this empty palace which might be ringing with all your happiness and preparations. The little calm there is in my heart comes from knowing you are safe with Mama and Tolya in Peterhof. I am delighted to hear how well your music is going and that the young Igor Stravinsky is a suitable replacement for Rimsky-Korsakov. The trip to Peterhof would be trying on Rimsky's old bones for just a few hours of lessons. I send you my enduring love, Annochka, and count the hours until I hold you in my arms again. Kiss Mama for me. I knew you and she would become great friends. She is a great fan of music and anything of the heart.

Ever your adoring Alexei

December 19, 1904

My beloved Annochka,

I was about to leave for Peterhof, to steal even a day and a night with you, when the news came. General Stossel has surrendered Port Arthur to Japan! Although many of us have known defeat was coming, there is not a Russian alive who is not stunned by the surrender. Never have we been so humiliated. All Petersburg is in mourning. The streets are so packed, one can hardly move a block in a half-hour. People are confused. Some cry. The police are cautious. Ironically, this may be the Czar's undoing. I promise I shall see you within days. Give Mama my love.

You are in my thoughts always.

Alexei

December 21, 1904

My darling Alyosha,

I cannot bear another day without you. If it were not for your mother, I would be mad by now. Helena hasn't talked to me in days, and Tolya, well, I stay away from him. He quite frightens me, my darling, but thankfully, he mostly stays in his rooms. The boys say he is drunk all the time and Nikita told me he beats them, even little Mousia, who is such a precious little soul. I didn't believe Nikita's tale at first, until I heard it one afternoon. Poor Sasha was crying pitifully and Tolya was screaming horrible curses. I begged your mother to do something to stop Tolya, but she said you are the only one who can. If that is so, we need you here more than ever.

The news about Port Arthur is truly a nightmare. Your mother and I were in town shopping for Christmas when the news broke. People here were in shock too, and as in Petersburg, there were tears. It was so awful to feel such unhappiness in the middle of the Christmas season. And now Nikita told me he heard the surrender doesn't mean defeat. He says the war goes on. It is all too confusing, Alexei. I wish you were here. You make everything make sense.

In truth, I expect you any moment. Every noise at the window or door makes my heart soar, thinking it is you. I would pine away mourning our separation if we weren't so busy preparing for Christmas. Your mother and the boys and Mousia and I have so many surprises for you. We've the tallest, widest tree in all Peterhof, and the grandest of decorations. But the best is my present for you—oh, I do hope you like it, my darling. Your mother has been encouraging me. I could never have done it without her support.

I also promised Mousia and the boys we will build an ice slide in the courtyard once you arrive. The Sulimovs have a grand one, but ours will be still grander, I know. I want to ornament it just as they do in Petersburg, and edge the course with gaily decorated fir trees. Your mother, Mousia, the boys and I go to the Sulimovs' every day to slide. Can you imagine, even your mother slides! I worry about her, for the slide is very tall and fast. We have to climb all the way to the roof of the house, but Sasha guides her down, and I have told him I will never speak with him again if he takes her too fast. He is a good boy, in truth, Alexei, if he is a bit rough. At first he fought bitterly with

*Nikita to see who would take me down the slide, for I was
quite nervous. It had been so long since I'd been on such
an enormous one. We had one at Smolny, but it was all
quite calm and ladylike. Ugh! But soon I grew brave and
am now quite the expert sledsman I once was. I can slide
all day, my darling, and never tire, for the exhilaration of
the flight makes me think of you. Just when I think I shall
never catch my breath, I start to laugh and scream deliriously—what fun, what fun!*

*Please, please, if you have not already left Petersburg
when you receive this letter, leave immediately. My heart
cannot stand another day without you.*

I love you more than words could ever express.

Annochka

It was almost ten o'clock on the night of December 23
when Alexei's carriage pulled up before the Anetzov Hospital on Morskaya Street in Petersburg. It was a private
hospital appearing more like a palace with its marble en-
tryway and gilt-columned front. An ominous detachment
of armed police guarded the entrance. They stepped to attention as Alexei threw open the carriage door and bounded
out.

"It's Kalinin, for God's sake!" he heard Witte cry, and
moments later saw Witte pushing his way through the detachment of police. "Thank God you're all right, Alexei Yakovlevich," he murmured as he embraced him, then stepped
back. "Where the hell are your bodyguards?"

"I dismissed them when I left for Peterhof. I've my own
private guards there."

"Did it never occur to you that you'd need protection on
the way?" Witte went on, herding Alexei through the police
and inside the hospital lobby. He was painfully pale and
dressed in an old smoking jacket. He wore no tie and his
boots were half undone. "Thank God my messenger reached
you."

"Halfway to Peterhof. How's Ryabushinsky?"

"I've just come from the doctor. They've removed the bullet. It went into his chest several inches above his heart. He'll
survive, thank God. The doctors said he will be fine."

Without realizing it, Alexei crossed himself. His breathing
became lighter. "How did it happen?"

Witte eyed one of the policemen standing inside the main
door. "We'll be in there." He nodded to a side door. "I
don't want to be disturbed."

The room was small but comfortable. A samovar steamed

on a table. There was a tray of sweet cakes and dishes of cigarettes and cigars.

"Tea?" Witte asked, sitting down. "I'm afraid I've nothing to give it body, though. As you can see"—he pointed to his informal dress—"I was expecting a quiet night at home when I got the message."

"How did it happen?"

"Ryabushinsky was about to enter the theater for the ballet. Someone called his name. He turned and the man fired. The assassin wasn't more than a few feet away."

"Was he captured?"

"Ryabushinsky's bodyguards immediately tackled him. Then, if you can believe it, a crowd of balletgoers dressed in furs and jewels proceeded to tear the man from the bodyguards and practically beat him to death. It's madness, I tell you, but I don't blame them. I think people grow tired of these wanton acts of violence."

"A terrorist trying to assassinate Ryabushinsky? Why?"

"He wasn't a terrorist. He wore the armband of the Black Hundreds. But the worst is yet to come. He was taken to the police station and whisked away almost immediately. There's not a trace of him."

"Yermolov."

"Yes, I'm afraid he's gotten his man free and clear."

"Damn." Alexei reached for his cigarettes. "What about Akimov? What does your man have to say?"

"He's unavailable for comment."

"What the hell does that mean?"

"It means I sent him a message and he hasn't responded."

"Isn't that odd, considering it was Akimov's men who were supposed to be protecting Ryabushinsky? Then they take the assassin to the police station and he disappears."

"I'm sure I'll hear from Akimov soon," Witte said in a tone of bold assurance, but his eyes gave away his uncertainty. "He probably already knows the details and is after the assassin."

"My, how you blow like the wind with this fellow Akimov," Alexei said sadly. "One day he is your savior, the next a hangman, and then he's back to savior again."

"Akimov has been neither savior nor hangman!" Witte shot back, clearly affronted. "He's useful."

"I see," Alexei said calmly. "The last I spoke to you, you complained that he was using you."

"I was wrong!"

Alexei leaned forward to touch Witte's arm. "This man Akimov—he makes you desperate, Sergei, and that frightens me. I've known you for a long time. I've never seen anyone unnerve you so. Tell me about him. Who is he? Where did he come from? What are his credentials?''

Witte smoothed the massive palm of his hand over his balding head. His face relaxed a bit and he shrugged his wide shoulders. ''The truth is, I know very little about Akimov, except for his record, which is startling. His star began rising in 1889. Before that, I know nothing. He was a policeman in the Okhrana perhaps. Anyway, in 1884 he arrested two men plotting to assassinate Alexander III. It was a major coup, needless to say. Almost every arrest Akimov has made is like that. At the last minute he foils a terrorist plot or exposes the workings of the extreme left.''

''He has a network of agents, then, working amongst the revolutionaries and terrorists.''

''It would appear so. No one questions his means, I'm told. His record of success is such that he owes no one any explanations. He lives in the shadows of life, which is how he got his nickname—the Shadow.''

''Any arrests lately?''

''Not exactly an arrest, but a coup of sorts. You remember Vera Martova?''

''The name is familiar.''

''A few years ago she walked into the police chief's office in Minsk, pulled a gun out of her pocket and killed the police chief in cold blood. Unfortunately, the chief was uniformly despised, and when Martova was being taken to court, her supporters surrounded her and whisked her away to safety.''

''Now I remember.''

''Word was she was very involved with the Terrorist Brigade in Paris. Stepan Ostravsky.''

Alexei paled.

''What's wrong?''

''Nothing. Go on.''

''You know something about this Ostravsky?''

''I've heard the name is all. He's quite notorious. Go on, Sergei Yurievich, tell me, how does Akimov relate to Martova and Ostravsky?''

''He had Martova killed. You may remember she was found dead in her apartment with another member of her group. Of course, he never publicly took credit for the matter. He never does.''

''The 'matter'! That's quite a euphemism. He had the girl murdered.'' Alexei's eyes riveted on Witte; his fist opened and closed about the arm of the couch.

''She was a murderer herself. And would have killed many

more if given the chance. Come now, Alexei, this is disturbing you, I can tell."

Using all his self-control, Alexei asked calmly, "How is Akimov related to Stepan Ostravsky?"

"He's after him. It would be quite a coup to get him, too, alive. Ostravsky probably knows as much about the terrorist networks as anyone."

"Is Akimov close to getting him?"

"I don't know, actually. He doesn't talk in detail about his cases with me."

"How did you get to Akimov?"

"He came to me about a year and a half ago. It was just a few months before I saw you at the Grand Duke Ilya Mikhailovich's birthday ball. He said we could be helpful to each other. He's a great supporter of the Czar. I think his only true feelings are for the Czar—" Witte cut himself off and angrily crushed out his cigarette. "Damn! That's a fool's dream. It would be more accurate to say he knows I'm a great supporter of the Czar."

"This is not the type of man you usually align yourself with."

Witte snickered. "You know the old saying: if a man lives with wolves, he must learn how to howl."

"That has never been your way before."

"The times, Alexei Yakovlevich. History. You remember our little discussion about history. One must be pliable, eh!"

"This Akimov is a spy, little more than a traitor."

"Traitor! How so? Really, Alexei, you confound me at times."

"You yourself said it: He has a network of agents. He wins the confidence of young people like Vera Martova and Stepan Ostravsky only to murder them."

"Terrorists." Witte snorted. "Since when have you become a supporter of terrorism?"

"I despise spies and traitors."

"What do you expect of the Okhrana? Spying, treachery, are what turn its wheels."

"I expected better of you, Sergei!"

"Oh, please, don't mark the boundaries of my morality. A man does not rise from the slums of Yaroslavl to the pinnacle of Petersburg society without blackening his own hands a bit. Oh, no, my friend, save your little morality play for someone else. I want to survive! I've given my whole goddamned life to Russia. I'd sleep with the devil himself to preserve her!"

"To preserve the House of Romanov, you mean."

"I will not get on this merry-go-round with you again."

"And I'll not work with traitors and spies."

"My spies, your traitors."

"Yes, there's a difference," Alexei said bitterly, and crushing his cigarette forcefully in the ashtray, he rose to his feet. "I think we are on far too different sides of the fence after all."

"Where are you going?" Witte was standing beside him.

"To Peterhof. To my wife—to a life with my wife."

"And the Coalition—"

"Damn the Coalition!"

Witte grabbed his arm. His tone was ominous. "What happened to Ryabushinsky can happen to any of us, Alexei Yakovlevich, and to our families."

"Yes, and there seems little we can do to stop it—your Akimov notwithstanding."

"We'll get Yermolov."

"And then what? I see little difference between your man and Yermolov."

"It's important, Alexei Yakovlevich, to have a foothold in the police. Better to control it than to have it controlled by one's enemy."

"Then I see little difference between your man, Yermolov, and yourself. More's the pity, Sergei."

"Don't be a fool. You don't believe what you're saying for a minute. We're so close . . ." Witte was squeezing Alexei's arm still tighter. "We're so close to a constitution. You know we are. It's what you want. It's what Russia wants. If it takes the goddamned Okhrana to do it . . . well, there's irony in that, isn't there? Even you might enjoy the irony if you'd step down from your sparkling clean ivory tower a moment."

Alexei eyed Witte's hand, still firmly grasping his arm.

In embarrassment, Witte dropped his hold.

"I see no irony in a secret police force, Sergei Yurievich. Whoever runs it, runs scum. But I'll tell you what, I'll stay in the Coalition on one condition."

"What?"

"Get me an introduction to Akimov."

"Impossible."

"All right, then—" Alexei reached for his coat, and started to stand.

"It's Misha, isn't it?" Witte asked, his tone friendly, but the question stabbed Alexei.

"Misha—what do you mean?"

"Sit down. Please," Witte encouraged, taking Alexei's coat. "Yes, I think you'd better sit."

"This had better be substantive."

"Oh, it is—and serious." Witte leaned back and crossed his legs. He frowned as if remembering an unpleasant thought, and began. "Mikhail Anatolyevich Kalinin. Twenty-one years old. Son of Anatole Yakovlevich Kalinin, nephew of the wealthy and influential industrialist Alexei Yakovlevich Kalinin. Young Misha has been exiled in absentia for his attack on a Cossack at Kazan Cathedral. He was last known to be living with Irina Ilyanovna, daughter of the Grand Duke Ilya Mikhailovich, in a house on Zhukovskaya Street with one Josef Kidarsky, a lover of a young woman who was killed along with the terrorist Vera Martova. Olga Gambarova, an old-timer to terrorist activities—she was once a member of the People's Will, the group who assassinated Alexander II—was also living in this house on Zhukovskaya Street, itself thought to be a front for terrorist activity, the Terrorist Brigade to be exact. Josef Kidarksy, a Jew with a radical history, was killed at the scene of the attempted assassination of Leonti Yermolov last February. Kidarsky was carrying a bomb at the time. It's thought that the notorious Stepan Ostravsky was also involved in the plot on Yermolov and might have been living in the house on Zhukovskaya Street too. At the very least, Ostravsky was back in Russia at the time, and he, along with young Misha and his beautiful mistress, Irina Ilyanovna, have not been heard of or seen since February."

"You realize your accusations are absurd! Irina Ilyanovna is the daughter of the Czar's own cousin."

"She's spoiled, wild, out for whatever risk comes her way. Terrorism quite fits her makeup."

"Tell me, is it through Akimov that you've gotten this absurd information on Misha and Irina Ilyanovna?"

"Yes, and you should be relieved it's not through Yermolov. Akimov's a reasonable man. When the time comes, and it will, Alexei—Akimov always gets his man—I'm sure he could be persuaded to ignore Misha's record."

"It's useless—Misha is not a terrorist. He doesn't need the support of you or Akimov."

"Still, think about it over the holidays, my friend. The Coalition can do little until the new year."

"This is blackmail, plain and simple." Alexei reached for his coat.

"I rather like to think of it as survival." Witte rose with Alexei. "The survival of your interests as well as mine. We need you in the Coalition. Stay, and I promise you your efforts will not be forgotten."

Alexei half-nodded. "I will, of course, give it serious consideration."

Witte held out his hand. "I'm working in your interest, my friend. Young Misha has embarked on a dangerous journey."

"Haven't we all?" Alexei said with disdain. Without another word, he turned to leave.

Alexei paced about Yuri Dobrinsky's tiny kitchen, describing the night's events as Yuri shuffled in his slippers and robe, making tea. It was after midnight. Yuri's eyes were puffy from sleep.

Alexei closed his own a moment, then reached for a glass and the bottle of vodka from above a kitchen cabinet. He settled in a chair which wobbled under his weight, and sipped his vodka while listening to Yuri tinker about the kitchen. Slowly Alexei began to unwind. It was good to be here, in the close familiarity of Yuri's house. Alexei could almost feel the balance of his life evening out again. That balance was important. He'd spent the last twenty-two years building it, digging its pilings so deeply, they could not be toppled—or so he'd thought. "Odd," he mused. "Do you realize, Yuri, that I've never before needed you to be Dmitri Mayakovsky."

"Times change."

"You sound like Witte."

"You know, I believe Witte was doing you a favor warning you about Misha."

"He used it as a threat. He's scared."

"Perhaps, but then, he's not alone. Russia's farmlands are in cinders. Our cities are paralyzed by strikes. Our only ice-free port had just been handed over to our enemy. Our children lie bleeding in the snow. Have you no fear, Alexei?"

"You know I do. That's why I'm here. Witte has me over a barrel with his information on Misha, and he knows it."

"You haven't told any of this to Misha yet."

"No."

"Good, don't."

"He should know."

"Not yet." Yuri stood against the sink, watching Alexei intently. "It would dilute Misha's energy, and Irina's. Rumors would fly again. Young people think spies are everywhere."

"And what if they are?"

"Revolutionary organizations must learn to survive in spite of them. Witte himself said that Akimov has his suspicions only. If he had infiltrated the Brigade, do you think any of us would be standing here talking right now?"

Alexei thought for a moment, and then blurted out, "What if he's using you?"

"How's that?"

"To kill Yermolov—Witte says Akimov is dedicated to destroying Yermolov."

"Yes."

"He killed Vera Martova and he knows Misha and Irina are involved not only with Stepan Ostravsky but also with the attempt on Yermolov's life. I'll wager my fortune Akimov knows where Stepan is and where Misha and Irina are right now. I'll wager he's using them, using the Brigade, don't you see, to do his dirty work for him, to get Yermolov killed, and then he'll kill Misha, Irina, Stepan, even you—he's already tried to kill Ryabushinsky."

"I thought you said it was a Black Hundred who shot Ryabushinsky."

"Anyone can wear the armband of the Black Hundreds. Perhaps Akimov is beginning to kill off the squad."

"Think about it for a moment, Alexei. Akimov has made his reputation, or so Witte told you, on these sensational arrests or killings of revolutionaries. Stepan Ostravsky is one of the most wanted men in Russia today. You really think if Akimov knew where he was, he wouldn't bring his head on a silver platter to the Czar?"

"Not if he wants Yermolov more."

"But with the arrest of Stepan, even of me—with the destruction of the Brigade, the Czar would hand over the Okhrana to Akimov. He would probably make him a count."

Alexei pressed his hand to his head. He was feeling suddenly very confused.

"My friend, you're overwrought. You've been working day and night on the Coalition, spending your life traveling between Petersburg and Moscow. I want you to listen to me. Go to Anna, relax for a few days. You never think well when you're overwrought."

"Tell me this, are you close to finding Yermolov?"

Yuri shook his head. "Unfortunately, no. Yermolov guards himself tightly. But that can change in a moment. We've all our feelers out, and we've brought some more comrades into the squad. Something will break soon. It always does."

"If you found Yermolov and assassinated him—you'd go after Akimov next?"

"That's not a decision I alone can make. It would have to come before the organizing committee of the Brigade. It would surely be discussed."

"Discussed! Akimov has a network of agents infiltrating

the revolutionary movement! He's already murdered several of your comrades.''

"Listen to me, Alexei.'' Yuri settled into a chair at the table. He touched Alexei's arm sympathetically. ''The information you've gotten from Witte is of enormous importance, but it will have to be verified. For all we know, Witte could have purposely passed it on to you, knowing you would pass it on to at least Misha, and then imagine the confusion it would create. I need more proof than just Witte's say-so.''

"You think Witte is so Machiavellian?''

"Don't you?''

"I don't know.'' Alexei shrugged, feeling defeated. Yuri was right, he was tired and he was overwrought.

"I promise you this, Alexei, the Brigade will intensify its investigation of Akimov, but I warn you, it won't be easy. We've tried. He's as difficult to pinpoint as is Yermolov.''

"Is there anything I can do?''

"Let me discuss it with some people first. After the holidays, we'll talk again. But now, perhaps you'd like to spend the night here and go to Peterhof in the morning.''

"Thank you, but I really must get on.'' Alexei downed his drink, then stood and reached for his coat. ''This Akimov is an enemy worthy of death, Yuri. I feel it.''

"If you're right, he will die. I promise you.''

The two men embraced.

Alexei kissed Yuri's cheeks. ''Merry Christmas, my friend''

"Merry Christmas to you too. And my best to Anna and your mother.'' Yuri chuckled and warmly clasped Alexei's hand. ''You know, after all these years, it's hard for me to think of you as a married man. Be off with you now. I'm sure your wife awaits you!''

CHAPTER THIRTY-SIX

"Aunt Anna! Aunt Anna! Wake up now!'' Mousia pulled at Anna's arm. ''Come quick, Aunt Anna, you must see the surprise!''

Anna groggily lifted her head from the pillow, and smiled. Of all Misha's brothers and sisters, including the baby Nadezhda, she liked eight-year-old Mousia the best. They were becoming fast friends. Anna was teaching the child to play the piano, and Mousia often crawled into bed next to Anna before the rest of the house was awake. "It's far too early to get up, and far too cold. Matryona hasn't even stoked the fires. Now, come into bed with me and I shall warm your icy feet and maybe we'll both—"

"But you must come with me!" Mousia was smiling excitedly as she began yanking on Anna again. Her blond curls were bobbing. "There's a surprise downstairs."

"No presents yet, not until tonight."

Mousia's eyes opened wide and she said in a loud whisper, "It's Uncle Alexei."

Anna bolted up in bed. "Alexei!"

"Yes, I went downstairs to get some cookies and I stopped in to look at the Christmas tree and Uncle Alexei is asleep on the couch in the drawing room. I saw him!"

Anna was already out of bed. She grabbed her bathrobe and went to her dressing table to throw water on her face and comb her hair. She crept down the darkened stairs with Mousia and motioned her to be quiet as they neared the drawing room. The door was ajar and Anna slipped in first. In the dim light she could barely make out the large figure sleeping half on, half off the couch, a blanket wrapped haphazardly about him. She inched closer and saw Alexei was still in his clothes. Tiptoeing across the room, she knelt beside him and placed her hands over his eyes. He moaned sleepily; she looked at Mousia and they both giggled noiselessly. "Alexei!" she whispered in his ear.

He turned and groaned, pushing her away.

"Shall I tickle his feet?" Mousia whispered, her hand pressed to her lips to hold back the giggles.

Anna nodded. "But turn on a light first. Then be careful—he kicks!"

Alexei flung his arm over his eyes as the lamp went on.

Mousia was just about to lift up the blanket to tickle his feet, when Alexei sat up with a roar, terrifying both Anna and Mousia. Then he held out his arms and pulled Anna to him. Mousia shrieked with delight and clambered onto the couch, wrapping her arms about his neck.

"So you were going to tickle me, eh!" Alexei reached up and flipped the child over his shoulder onto the floor. Then he wrapped both arms about Anna, and holding his face very close to hers, smiled giddily. "Hello, Madame Kalinina."

* * *

"I'm sorry, Anna," Alexei said despairingly as he lay in the bed beside her. "I'm very tired. This has been a terrible couple of weeks, and last night with Ryabushinsky—I suppose it's all undone me. It's nothing to do with you, though, you understand that."

Anna wasn't sure she understood. She couldn't imagine not being able to make love.

"You're so lovely, my sweet." He smoothed her cheek. "I missed you so. Come, just lie with me awhile."

She stretched out beside him, lying half-across him, hoping he would touch her, but his body felt limp beneath her. "Does this happen often?" she asked uncertainly.

"Well, not to me. I'm sure it won't last very long."

"Perhaps that's why you didn't come to me when you arrived."

"Yes, perhaps."

They lay together awhile, until Anna thought she could not stand it anymore. Her eyes took in the seductive expanse of his body, the thick waist and round rise of his buttocks beneath her knee. She wanted to caress him and kiss him until he grew hard. He would. He always did. She needed him. Slowly she pressed with her hips, rubbing against him as she kissed his neck.

"Don't, Anna, please! If you want to make me feel better, have Volodia run me a bath, why don't you, and then go get me some coffee, and add some brandy to it."

"Brandy—it's only eight o'clock in the morning."

"Just do it, Anna!" he snapped, pulling the covers about him.

"Mousia told me Alexei is here!" Zhenya happily greeted Anna as she came into the kitchen for the coffee. The old woman was wrapped in her thick plaid robe. Her long gray braids were still down and she wore several layers of socks on her feet. She was sitting at the table drinking her morning tea with Matryona, the cook.

"Yes, he's here. Isn't that wonderful?" Anna tried to smile as she leaned to kiss her mother-in-law good morning. "He's rather tired. He arrived in the middle of the night. Mousia and I found him asleep in the drawing room."

"In front of the Christmas tree!" Matryona exclaimed, her round red cheeks seeming to lighten in her merriment. "Aye, and for sure he must have loved the tree, Anna Petrovna, for it's the grandest one I've ever seen. Praise God, it's as glorious as any of the trees in Petersburg." Matryona rose from the table, her ample body teetering as always when she stood.

"Tell the master I'm up to fixing his favorite foods. Now we shall have a merry Christmas for sure, Zhenya Kirilovna!" She nodded happily at Alexei's mother.

"Like the old days, Matryona Alexandrovna," Zhenya told Cook. "We were once a happy family. Oh, yes, we were." A shadow of sadness clouded her eyes. "If only Misha were here—I'd even welcome him with his Duchess—if I could only lay eyes on my Misha again." Barely a day went by without Zhenya mourning Misha's absence.

Matryona clucked and shook her head. "Master Tolya and Misha's mother would certainly have a fit should the young Duchess step foot into this house on such a holy day as Christmas."

"To think of my Misha alone at Christmas again."

Anna wanted to say he wasn't alone. Anna wanted to tell Zhenya that Misha was quite happy with Irina, but that was a fact she knew Zhenya didn't want to hear. Instead she announced, "I'm here for some coffee for Alexei."

Sophie, the skittish, pimply young girl who followed Matryona about like a slave, jumped from her spot near the stove and began fixing the coffee.

"And some tea for you, Anna Petrovna?" Matryona asked, nodding toward the steaming samovar.

"Yes, thank you," Anna said, and thought to sit at the table opposite Zhenya, but couldn't. She knew if she did, Matryona would take it as her cue to join her. Anna always drank her morning tea in the kitchen with Zhenya and Cook. It had become her favorite part of the day, sitting in the warm country kitchen, huddled over steaming tea and nibbling hot buns while chatting with the two women, listening greedily to their tales of marriage and men and babies and children. Matryona had had three husbands, all dead, and six children, long grown; Zhenya loved to talk of Alexei's growing-up years and of her daughter, Mousia, who'd died when she was only ten years old. Occasionally Zhenya spoke of her husband, Yakov, too, but most of her stories were of Alexei, of his beauty and charm, his singing and dancing, his excellence in school, and of the model train he'd built with his father, the train that all the neighborhood had come to see. There was the gossip Matryona picked up at the market about the other families in Peterhof, too. She loved a spicy, rowdy tale, which often made Anna blush; yet she was mesmerized by the ease with which Matryona and Zhenya spoke of men and women, of secret affairs, and the fun they poked at men's heated passion. It was the golden kitchen talk that Anna had loved, but never fully understood, as a child sitting in the darkness of the back stairs. She was in no mood for such chatter now.

"So Alexei is fine, then?" Zhenya went on as Anna stood nervously smoothing her hands along the back of a chair.

"Oh, yes, quite fine!" Anna's smile quivered at the edges, and she turned away, pressing her fists into her stomach. The silence about her was accusing, as if Zhenya, Matryona, and even the insipid little Sophie knew her shame, and she wanted to run. Then Zhenya was by her side, her arms pressing through Anna's.

"Come with me a moment, my dear. I want to show you something." Zhenya herded Anna from the kitchen. They didn't speak until they were seated on the couch in the drawing room. Still caressing Anna's hand, Zhenya gently probed, "Something's wrong? Is it Alexei?"

Anna turned from her mother-in-law, and her burning eyes settled on the enormous tree laden with candles and the Christmas decorations she and Zhenya, Mousia and the boys had lovingly made over the past weeks. The glistening angels and strands of berries, the painted balls and the tiny wreaths with brightly colored bows blurred in a streak of watery color. She remembered the pride she'd taken in decorating the mantel with candles ordered especially from Petersburg. She'd worked so hard to make the house festive for Alexei, and he hadn't noticed a thing. Anna burst into tears.

Zhenya wrapped an arm about her and rocked her. "It is Alexei. He's done something. Come, you can tell me."

"I fear he doesn't love me anymore. . . ."

"Of course he does. He traveled all night to be here with you!" Zhenya brushed the tearstained hair from Anna's cheeks and grasped her hands. "Now listen to me, Anna Petrovna, and you listen well. Alexei is forty-three years old and was probably the most sought after bachelor in all Petersburg. Isn't that right? Well, isn't it?"

Anna nodded reluctantly.

"He chose you, didn't he? He came all the way from Siberia to the Crimea to take care of you. Do you think a love like that goes away in a matter of months?"

"I don't know." Her lips trembled against the tears.

"Well, I do. I also know you. Yes, in these weeks together I've grown to know you well, Anna, and I know why Alexei loves you and needs you. Are you listening to me?"

Anna nodded and pressed the old woman's gnarled hands to her face as if they were a lifeline.

"You are his soul, Anna . . ." The old woman's voice snagged and her dark eyes edged in wrinkled skin became watery. "You are the soul my Alexei lost when his father died so miserably. You are the happiness that once filled him, the music and the laughter. You've brought more happiness to this miserable house in the few weeks you've been here than we've known in years. Look around you—just look around you at the decorations. We look like Christmas, praise God! You should see the miserable trees Tolya usually brings home, and there's always an argument about the decorating—always, but not this year. Mousia flies like a carefree bird through the house. The boys laugh instead of knocking each other and bellowing all the time. That's you, Anna, your happiness, your spirit. That's why Alexei loves you."

"No, no . . ." She pushed Zhenya away.

Zhenya held her hand tightly. "Something terrible is going on between you and Alexei. I can see it in your face."

"If only I could make Alexei happy. It seems everything I do makes him cross."

"It's not you, believe me, child. A husband will find a million ways to be cross with his wife, no matter what an angel she is. If you spend your life trying to make Alexei happy with you, you'll be a sorry wife, indeed. Tell me, what is it that you could possibly have done to make him cross in such a short time?"

Tears welled in Anna's eyes again, and she shook her head. "I don't know."

"There, you see, I'll wager you've done nothing. I'll wager he woke up cross for some reason that has nothing whatever to do with you. Ach, men, they're all babies. They think they want us under their whip when it's us they really want to hold the whip. I tell you, Anna, worry more about your own happiness than Alexei's black moods. He has them with or without you, and he'll use them to break you. Alexei is my son, God knows, and a prince among men, but he's a man nonetheless, no different from the others. Be strong, Anna. He needs a woman to stand by his side, not quivering at his feet. Now, I can smell the coffee is done by now. Bring some to the brooding beast, why don't you, and if he's still licking his wounds, then go about your own business. In truth, we've much to do today. It's Christmas Eve, praise God— Alexei can't be cross long on Christmas Eve. He'll soon be wanting to be part of all the festive doings."

Alexei felt like a bewildered giant staring down over the tiny, imperial village of Peterhof fortified within the walls of yesterday. Smiles abounded with Christmas cheer; sleds flew down slickened ice followed by the careless, happy shrieks

of joyful fear; skaters wrapped in lush fur hats and warmed
by thick muffs whirled on placid ponds; the bells of gaily
decorated sleds pulled by fancy, prancing horses echoed in
the crystal air, and Alexander Ryabushinsky lay wounded in
a hospital bed. Private guards followed Alexei and his family
wherever they went; Misha and Irina lived in a dreary little
room on the outskirts of a slum, while Yermolov and the
Shadow, Akimov, circled vulturelike around them all.

He gazed at Anna, who smiled sweetly, eager to please.
She pulled at him like an excited child, urging him into
Christmas, an ice slide, a troika ride with Sasha, Nikita and
Mousia. Anna's laughter exploded in billows of smoke and
he wanted to grab her and run. Tomorrow had no connection
to today. Tomorrow edged into today. Tomorrow would
wound, scare, kill, and he would stand helpless.

He helped Anna on with her skates and urged her onto the
ice, watching from the sidelines as her face grew red with
cold; her brilliant blue eyes teared, she tossed him a childish
smile. *Watch me! Watch me!* she seemed to say as she spun
in reckless circles. Hers was the only face he saw, a lone
dancer, the theater empty except for the two of them. He
wanted to applaud; he wanted to apologize, and didn't know
how. She waved, skated to him, embraced him, pulling him
into the moment before speeding away. Wordlessly he was
forgiven. How long would she go on forgiving him? She
begged him to fly with her. He had forgotten how. And when
she wasn't looking, he took the flask from his pocket, and as
the fiery vodka smoothed down his throat, streaming through
his veins, he felt warm.

It was well past midnight before Anna was ready to give
Alexei his present. Helena, the children, Zhenya and the servants were gathered about the tree. Mousia hugged her new
china doll. Matryona wore her new fur hat. Grigory and Volodia puffed on their new pipes, Lidia and Sophie sat with
their hands wrapped in their new fur muffs. Even Helena
seemed content. Alexei had bought her a tea set ordered from
Paris, and Anna had given her a pair of ruby-and-diamond
earrings. Helena sat on the couch with Mousia cuddled beside
her while the boys tinkered with the new engine Alexei had
bought them for their train sets.

"You two are the only ones left," Zhenya said. She was
wrapped in the pink silk dressing gown Anna had given her,
and on her feet were deerskin slippers. The diamond tiara
from Alexei was perched at an angle atop her thick braids.
She was giddy from all the champagne at dinner. "Come

now, we've all been waiting. We know what Anna has for you, Alexei, so you give her yours first.''

"First, another toast!" he insisted, opening a fresh bottle of champagne. Volodia hurried to help him pour, but Alexei reminded him, "It's Christmas, my faithful friend. Christ was a poor man and the three Wise Men knelt before Him.''

"Thank you, sir, thank you!" Volodia exclaimed, and bowed as Alexei filled the goblet to the brim.

"A toast!" Alexei began when the last glass had been filled. "A toast to peace and goodwill toward all men!''

"Amen!" Everyone but Alexei crossed himself.

Alexei quickly downed his champagne and refilled his glass before reaching for his gift, which was sitting wrapped on the piano. "For you, my dearest heart.'' He lifted his glass to toast her, and quickly downed the champagne.

Sitting on the piano stool, Anna carefully unwrapped the silver-and-white package. The others looked on in hushed anticipation. On the gold box inside was imprinted "House of Fabergé" and everyone drew closer. Fabergé was goldsmith and jeweler to the Czar.

"Oh, Alexei, I'm so excited, see—my hand shakes!" Anna held up a trembling hand.

"I'll open it, Aunt Anna!" Mousia piped.

"No, you won't!" Helena reprimanded, and held the child firmly on her lap.

Breathing deeply, Anna slowly lifted up the top of the box, which was lined inside with crimson velvet. Sitting on the velvet was a miniature gold-and-enamel figure of a young blond-haired woman seated at a piano. By gently pushing the woman's fragile arm, a device was set in motion that moved the miniature piano keys, and the suite from *Swan Lake*, which Anna had been playing when Alexei first saw her, streamed forth as if from the piano itself.

"Oh, Alexei! It's exquisite!" she cried as she gently placed the figure on the piano. She hugged him tightly.

"Raise the arm again, Aunt Anna. Oh, do!" Mousia scrambled from her mother's lap. "Oh, can I do it? Can I?''

"All right," Anna agreed, lifting Mousia onto the piano stool. "But you must be careful. It's very, very fragile.''

As the music from the tiny figurine faded, Alexei took Anna's hand. "Now it's time for my present!''

As if on cue, the household gathered around the piano.

"Come." She sat him down on the piano bench.

"Here?''

"Yes, but you must move over to make room for me, and close your eyes.''

He did as he was told and silence settled on the room.

"Are you ready?"

"I can't be readier!"

"Eyes closed?"

"Tight as a drum!"

Anna reached into her pocket for a piece of paper, and unfolding it, she propped it on the piano. It kept falling over, and Zhenya came to hold it for her. Taking a deep breath, Anna began to play.

She'd barely played the first few chords when a shock of realization spread through Alexei. It was no music he knew, and yet he knew it intimately. He knew the piece was Anna's, that she had written it for him, and that it was good; in places there were even hints of brilliance. He sat very still, listening, and his heart beat furiously.

"Play it again" was all he said when she finished.

Anna played the piece again.

This time when she finished, Alexei was on his feet. "Bravo! Bravo!" He clapped, then pulled some roses from a nearby vase and tossed them at Anna. "Bravo! Bravo!"

Amid shouts and laughter, the boys and Mousia imitated Alexei, until the flowers were scattered about the piano.

"You liked it, then?" Anna asked breathlessly. Her smile was radiant, her cheeks flushed.

"It's wonderful!"

"Well, not wonderful, it's only my first piece. Oh, but I worked so hard on it, Alexei. Igor Stravinsky helped me, of course, but it's you who inspired me."

Alexei bent to kiss her. "It's the best present anyone's ever given me."

Alexei refilled champagne glasses and sent Volodia to the cellar to get a few more bottles. "Grigory, get your hand organ—we'll have some dance music! Nikita, Sasha, push back the furniture. A mazurka first, Grigory—Anna and I are quite the champions of Petersburg at the mazurka!"

There was a heated madness to Alexei's dancing as he swirled and leapt first with Anna and then with Helena. He danced with little Mousia and the maids Sophie and Lidia; he danced with his mother and Matryona and urged the boys to choose partners. The more he danced, the more he drank, insisting everyone drink with him. He was particularly insistent about Anna's keeping up with him, and grew almost annoyed when she said she'd had enough.

"A party is only happy when everyone is drunk, my love!" He urged champagne on Anna, holding the glass to her lips

until it spilled down her dress. Alexei stumbled back onto
the couch, tumbling into Lidia and Nikita, laughing uproariously.

"Alexei, look what you've done!" Anna burst forth, more
angry than she'd thought.

Matryona was by her side, wiping her gown with a handkerchief.

"Here, here, let me do that!" Alexei took out his own
handkerchief and rubbed it up and down the front of Anna's
dress, his hand pressing against her breast as he did.

"Alexei!" she chided, and tried to push him away, but he
grasped her in his arms and began whirling in a drunken
zigzag around the room, crashing himself and Anna onto a
chair.

"There's my girl!" He playfully smacked her behind and
began nibbling at the low-swept neckline of her gown.

"Stop it!"

"It's a party, my love." His voice sounded coarse. "More
music, Grigory!"

Grigory nervously started a lively number.

Alexei stumbled to his feet, only to sprawl with a thud
across the floor.

Anna cried out.

The music stopped. The room fell silent.

Alexei reached for the hem of Anna's skirt and began to
laugh. He lay on his back, his arms outstretched, staring up
at her. "What's wrong, my love?"

"You're drunk." She glared back.

"Drunk! Me?" He bolted upright. "You confuse me with
my brother—right, Helena Ivanovna?" He turned toward Helena, who looked quickly away. "Come, my love, a little
Christmas merriment . . ." He reached for Anna again.

"Alexei, stop it." It was Zhenya who spoke.

"Mother, you scold!" He chorted. "Like I was a schoolboy again."

"You act like one. And it's late. The party is quite over
now. It's almost two in the morning."

"Ah, but, Mama . . ." He stood, twirling her about the
room. "The night is young."

Zhenya punched him to break loose. "Nikita, Sasha, up to
bed with you now. Sophie, take Mousia upstairs."

"Wise, Mama, very wise, as always." Alexei bowed as
he watched Helena, the children, and the servants scurry to
obey his mother. Leaning toward Anna, he whispered. "My
mother's the wisest woman there is. Praise God, Anna, you
will be so wise with only half the bite. Now, Mama, are you

going to send me up to bed with Anna?'' He laughed raucously.

Zhenya closed her eyes in exasperation. ''I would advise you to take yourself up to bed. A man in your condition is no help for a wife.''

''Ah!'' He turned to Anna, swaying as his eyes opened wide. ''Wise to the end, didn't I tell you? She knows all life's mysteries. Come now, my sweet.'' He tried to take her in his arms, but Anna easily stepped aside.

''Go to bed, Alexei!'' Zhenya scolded. ''Go to bed before you say or do something you truly regret.''

Standing at attention, he saluted his mother, bowed abruptly to Anna and started marching across the room. ''Never fear, my sweet. I shall be waiting for you! Don't stay talking about me long with Mama.'' He marched from the room.

To Anna's surprise, Alexei wasn't in the bedroom when she went upstairs. She checked in all the guest rooms, and then went downstairs. He was in the dining room, his jacket off, his shirt half-unbuttoned; he was sitting alone at the head of the table, drinking champagne from the bottle. When he saw Anna, he swept the table clear of his ashtray and glass and pounded his fist. ''Up here, my girl! Up here and dance for me in all your wild abandon! Dance like a little showgirl. It will delight me, I promise, and then I shall ravish you. Yes, it's what you want.'' His laughter was biting. ''Well, isn't it?''

''Alexei, please don't drink any more. Just come upstairs with me.''

''Ah, but no . . .'' He stumbled to his feet. ''I can't do that. What if I disappoint my lovely bride again? Eh, Annochka . . .'' He grabbed her in his arms and twirled about, his hips rolling in a hideous dance.

''Just come to sleep, Alexei, that's all.'' Tears wet her eyes.

''Oh, my dove, I make you sad, and that was never my intention. Perhaps if you sat and drank with me! Yes, come, my dove, come sit and drink with me. A party is never happy unless everyone is drunk! It was my father's favorite saying. In fact, it was the law he lived by. The problem was, each day was a party for him.'' Alexei started to laugh, then lifted the champagne bottled to his lips. When he looked, she was gone. ''Anna!'' he called. ''Anna!'' He went after her, tripping over a chair and crashing to the floor. ''Anna . . .'' he moaned, and rolled on his back, finishing the bottle before drifting into sleep.

* * *

A spray of water wakened Alexei, and he looked up to see his mother staring down at him. Her braids hung halfway to her waist; she wore her old thick plaid robe and was holding a pitcher full of water, poised threateningly.

"Get up or the rest of this will be on your own pathetic face," she promised.

"Have you gone mad?" Alexei tried to sit. His mouth was dry and cottony. His head throbbed. The glare of the lights hurt his eyes.

She grimaced as if disgusted and snapped, "Get up and come into the kitchen. I've made a pot of coffee for you."

"What time is it?"

"Six-thirty in the morning, you idiot. I couldn't sleep—I didn't think there was any reason for you to sleep, considering it was worry over you that's kept me up all night. Now, come on." She stomped ahead into the kitchen.

Alexei followed. "Oh, come, Mama—because I had a bit too much to drink. Since when is it a crime for a man to drink on Christmas Eve?"

"So much so that you pass out on the dining-room floor!" Her voice was churning. The veins in her neck and forehead pulsated.

Alexei couldn't remember seeing her this enraged since before his father died.

"A man who has the love of a beautiful young wife like Anna doesn't choose to sleep with the bottle unless he has no choice."

Alexei stiffened noticeably. He felt his own anger surfacing and he warned her, "You're interfering where you have no business, Mama."

"Anna is every bit my business." She placed a cup of steaming coffee before him. "She's the best thing that's happened not only to you but to this whole wretched family in more years than I can remember. She's the first really smart thing you've done since you first took off to Siberia. How such an angel agreed to marry a lout like you is beyond me—but if I were you I would bow down before God and thank him for the wife he has allowed you."

"God had nothing to do with it." He stood.

"Where are you going?"

"To get some brandy for the coffee."

"No!" She was on her feet, her hand grabbing his arm.

"Let go of me, Mama. Let go of me and go back to bed. This is *my* house, do you hear me!"

The echo of his anger reverberated with the slap of her hand across his face.

He closed his eyes and said nothing.

Zhenya fell back into the chair and buried her head in her arms. ''Blessed Virgin . . .'' she moaned. ''What is happening? There is no sanity left in the world, blessed Virgin, Mother of God . . .'' she prayed.

They sat for a long time in silence. Alexei stared at the patterns of the frost on the window. His mind raced but he could not remember his thoughts. His mother's prayers clattered in his mind. He wanted a drink, some brandy—a bit of brandy wouldn't hurt—but he dared not. He tried to remember if his mother had ever struck him before, sometime when he was a child. He could not remember her ever having done so. He could not remember his ever enraging her before. Damn, why was she doing this to him? Why wouldn't she leave him alone? Why wouldn't they all leave him alone, even Anna? He thought to put on his coat, harness the horse, and ride back to Petersburg. There was so much pressing work to do in Petersburg. Perhaps he would stop in on Misha and Irina, then on Yuri Dobrinsky. He had to decide how to act with Witte. Or perhaps he would simply go home, have a few drinks and go to bed, alone.

''Alexei . . .'' Zhenya picked up her head from the table. Her eyes were dry. Her mouth was set. ''What are you afraid of?''

He did not answer. Her question made no sense. He averted his eyes and waited for her to speak again.

''It's fear that sends a man to the bottle. What fear is so great within you, Alexei, that you would sacrifice the best part of your life when it is only just beginning?''

Again he didn't answer.

''Do you want to destroy Anna the way your father destroyed us, the way Tolya has destroyed his family?''

''I'm not my father.'' His voice was dull, without conviction.

''Do you really remember him, your father? What was he like?''

''Filthy, drunk, brutal.''

''No . . .'' She shook her head slowly. ''That wasn't your father, but the monster who grew from the bottle. Yakov was a good man, a kind man with a gentle soul. Don't you remember the hours he spent with you, talking with you, teaching you, encouraging you? He wanted the best for you always. If you could only remember that father, Alexei. He's inside you. He helped make you strong and kind and clever.''

His mother was close. The familiar touch of her hands was soothing the pain his head.

"Papa has nothing to do with this."

"Everything, Alexei. A father is everything to his sons. Tolya hated him, so hate was all he had of him. Tolya is the worst of your father, and for that I have shed so many tears, there are no more left to cry. But you are the best."

"Oh, Mama, there's so much you don't know. So much." He sighed and started to pick up his coffee cup; then his hand fell limp as if he had no strength.

"Anna's your wife. You'd be a fool among men if you threw her love away."

"Let me ask you something, Mama. You talk always of God, but what of the devil?"

"What of the devil?"

"You asked me what scares me. The devil's what scares me. He's a patient fiend. He can wait a man's lifetime."

"I don't understand."

"Don't you see how everything, everything I want, has come my way? It's as if my life is blessed. That's what people think. There was even a newspaper article about my marriage to Anna, and the reporter wrote that with Anna, the great Alexei Yakovlevich had everything a man could want, that my life was as rich as even the Czar's. Except for one thing— in the end, everyone pays up. If not on earth, then one must stand before God or the devil."

"God is forgiving."

He stared at her vacantly and said, "Inside I still live in that terrible little house in Yaroslavl. It follows me, infecting all my fine palaces and villas, and I wonder that no one notices. They must, they will someday. They'll see me for the impostor I am, and drag me away, throw me in a prison. I know the prison, though. It's that dark little house where Papa went mad and our precious little Mousia died. And I laugh at my guards because they don't know the prison can't hurt me. They don't know that it's really my home." He laughed bitterly and stared at the frosted window again. "You know what, Mama? Sometimes I just wish my turn would come. That the devil would stop toying with me and call me home."

"Stop talking like that! The devil will never touch your soul."

"A man must pay somehow. Everyone does. I've never paid."

Zhenya grew still. The color drained from her face and she uttered the word, "Matyushin."

Alexei felt his body grow cold. He shuddered and closed

his eyes. For a moment the fat, angry, red face and the gold tooth between the woolly sideburns flashed before him.

"Tolya told me, just weeks after you left home. It was a secret he could not bear to keep alone."

"You never told me."

"I didn't see any reason to—it was years later when I saw you again. You were so vibrant with life. I saw no reason to dredge up the past."

He nodded as if agreeing, and said, "Everything I am, everything I own, even Anna, is based on the filth that was Matyushin. It was his money that started it all. Do you think Anna would have looked twice at me if I were some poor wretch?"

"Ach, self-pity! It will drive a man to the bottle faster than anything. I have no patience for it, and you should have none either. You've not only yourself to think of now, but Anna too. You're all she has, after all. Forget Matyushin. He's long rotted. That was his fate. Yours is a wife and family. Have children fast, Alexei, before you're too old to enjoy them. Take Anna away from Russia before Russia consumes you. This is no place for happiness anymore."

"I can't do that. I can't just walk away. You wouldn't want me to. I could never face my children if I did."

"For a while, anyway. The pressure of what you do is taking its toll. Anna's your life now."

"I find that hard to believe coming from you, Mama. You who urged Misha into the revolution."

"As I urge you to your wife. Everything has a time, Alexei. Misha is young."

He thought to tell her of Misha then. He thought to ask her if it were possible to leave Russia knowing Misha was in such danger, but all he said was, "Thank you for loving Anna."

"How could I not?"

"I just want you to know it makes my being away easier."

"But surely you'll be staying—especially after last night. You owe her the best of you after your behavior last night."

"I must return to Petersburg in a few days, but I'll be back for New Year's Eve."

"Praise God, Alexei, you'll break Anna's heart! She's counting on the week with you."

"But she has you, Mama." He smiled hopefully. "I feel she's safe with you. You're of the same heart. Besides . . ." He stood slowly. "I have no choice. I must be back to work with Witte on the Coalition, and there are other pressing matters."

"Where are you going now?"

"For a walk."

"It's pitch black out."

"The air will clear my head."

"Go to Anna first."

"I will soon. I promise. I shall be devoted to her these next days, but just now I need to be alone awhile."

"Love Anna, my heart. Be a good husband. Open your soul to her and I know she will return the trust and love tenfold. She will grow into a strong woman, a fine mother for your children, and a comfort to you in your darkest moments."

CHAPTER THIRTY-SEVEN

On December 27, a delegation of the Gapon Society was sent to the Putilov Iron Works to discuss the firing of the workers with Director Smirnov. The delegation was made up of Kostya Savich, two of the fired workers, Segunin and Ukolev, and Irina as Kuksina. Misha tried to convince Irina not to go. Everyone was talking about the delegation. Someone would surely recognize her, but Irina, who had volunteered for the assignment, was insistent.

"I know men like Director Smirnov," she said. "They're arrogant bastards who assume workers have less feeling than a flea. Kostya, Segunin, and Ukolev will get nowhere without me."

"It's too risky."

"Any more risky than assassinating Leonti Yermolov?"

The delegation's send-off was triumphant. More than two hundred workers jammed the Putilov meeting hall, which was decorated with fir and balsam boughs, wreaths, and brightly colored Christmas balls and ribbons. The writer Gorky and some of his literary friends stood beside Father Gapon and the delegation. Gorky, of medium height and wiry, with long dark hair and a mustache, wore the workers' belted black linen blouse, dark pants and high boots. His eyes were large, deep, brimming with the portent of the moment.

"My brother and dearest friend, Alexei Maximovich, known more readily to all of you as Maxim Gorky, will say a few words before we depart," Gapon announced.

There was an air of hushed expectation as the famous writer, Gorky, stepped forward. Many of the humblest workers crossed themselves. A few knelt. Gorky smiled a quick, quirkish, friendly smile and said in a soft yet resonant voice, "Go with open hearts, my comrades, for the love of God and the will of the people are with you. The righteousness of your cause shall triumph. If it pleases God in his heavens, Segunin, Subbotin, Ukelev, and Fyodorov will be the last to suffer in silence under the whip of injustice. Men and women of Russia, we must be beggars no longer, but stand determined and pure before God!"

"Peace be with you," Gapon added, making the sign of the cross over the crowd. "In the name of the Father, the Son and the Holy Ghost. Amen."

There was a swelling murmur of "amen, amen," and then a cheer rang out. The workers massed about Irina, Kostya, Segunin, and Ukolev and practically carried them from the hall into the street. It was a clear, brisk December day. Misha and his Life Guards stayed close by Father Gapon, Gorky, and the delegates; police followed, but calmly and at a distance; the crowd sang as they marched, "Save Us, O Lord, Thy People." They walked en masse to within half a block of the Putilov plant.

"We shall win, brothers! The time for us to stand as men is now!" Worker after worker clasped Irina's, Kostya's, Segunin's, and Ukolev's hands, embraced them, kissed them, wished them well. Buoyed by the energetic defiance of their supporters, the four started forward toward the gray, foreboding Putilov Iron Works.

"Names!" demanded a fat, yellow skinned watchman, stopping them at the gates. A gun was noticeably strapped about his waist. Four other large armed guards stood behind them.

"Savich, Segunin and Ukelev, and Polonskaya," Kostya announced. "We've come to see Director Smirnov."

"Have an appointment?" The guard spit to one side.

"Ah, you know we do, you pompous fart, Simeon Simeonevich!" Segunin snorted. He knew the guard well.

"Be watchful of your tongue, Segunin, or you'll never get past me."

"You think that gun you're carrying makes you more the man?" Segunin shot back. "Looks to me like it makes up for what you're naturally lacking, Simeon Simeonevich!'' Segunin and Ukolev chortled.

The guard grew swollen with anger. His hand went to his gun. The guards behind him stepped closer.

"Simeon Simeonevich, I'm sure if you'll look on your calendar, you'll see we've an appointment.'' Irina spoke calmly, smiling as she steadied her gaze on the unnerved guard. "After all, all Petersburg knows we've this appointment, so why not just let us in?'' The playfulness of her tone eased the tension a bit, and the guard grumbled a few words to himself and motioned for them to follow. The four armed guards flanked the delegation as Simeon Simeonevich led them on the circuitous route through the Iron Works, finally depositing them in a tiny, hot, empty back room of the plant.

"Wait here!'' Simeon Simeonevich snapped. "The Director will arrive shortly.'' Without a word, he turned on his heel, motioned the other guards out before him, and slammed the heavy door in his wake.

Kostya, Segunin and Ukolev began immediately to make fun of Simeon Simeonevich. Their pride swelled as they noted again and again how many armed guards had been ordered to greet them.

"We've got Director Smirnov shaking in his boots already.'' Ukolev grinned.

"I only wish that Father could have seen how well we done,'' Segunin added. "And my wife, praise God. She wanted to come, but I made her stay home, afraid there'd be violence. Now I wished she'd been there like your wife, Kostya Sergeievich. Wouldn't she have been proud, though, eh? I feel a victory brewing. What you say, Kuksina Ivanovna?''

"I say Director Smirnov is ten minutes late already, and they're treating us like dogs. Not even a chair to sit on or a glass of water to drink.'' She unbuttoned her coat and leaned against the wall. Five minutes later, she yanked open the door. Simeon Simeonevich was there, as if he'd been waiting.

"Where's Director Smirnov?''

"Busy, I assume.''

"We had a two o'clock appointment. It's two-fifteen already.''

"I'll see what I can do.''

"It would be appreciated.''

Fifteen minutes later, Irina opened the door again.

Simeon Simeonevich was standing in the exact same place.

"Well!'' Irina demanded. She'd taken off her coat and scarf.

Simeon Simeonevich eyed her carefully.

"Where's Director Smirnov?"

"Busy, like I said. If you want to leave, no one's stopping you, though."

"Tell Director Smirnov we have no intention of leaving until he keeps his appointment with us. And we'd like some chairs and some water. It's like hell itself in there."

"I'll see what I can do."

Fifteen minutes later, Irina tore open the door. Segunin was right behind her. The hall was empty.

"What do we do?" Segunin asked.

"Wait. We'll wait all night if we have to."

A little after three, Director Smirnov and an aide walked in. Smirnov was a tall, immaculate man in his early fifties. He smelled of expensive cologne and used the same tailor as Irina's father. She could tell by the cut of the suit and the cloth. He wore gold cufflinks and tie stud. There was not a wrinkle about him. His boots shone like black glass. His face was thin, his nose pointed. He moved as if oiled, and Irina could feel Kostya, Segunin, and Ukolev sink like sludge in his presence.

"We have been waiting an hour, Director Smirnov, in the most unpleasant of circumstances." She steadied her gaze.

"You must be Kuksina Polonskaya." His smile was sterile.

Irina wiped her sweating hands on her soiled skirt and held one out to him. "Aye, that's me." She forced him to shake it.

His hand seemed to pull away before they'd touched.

"And this is Kostya Savich. Anton Segunin and Georgi Ukolev you know."

"By name only." Director Smirnov nodded at the men, and held his hand to his aide, who immediately placed in it a cigarette. "My apologies for any inconveniences," Smirnov went on, and turned to his aide for a light. Inhaling deeply, he said, "Igor, I am surprised there are no chairs for our visitors."

"We thought the meeting would be brief, sir."

"Yes, and so it will be. You're right, Igor Petrovich. Yes, now I recall the purpose of this meeting. It was to discuss the rehiring of Segunin and Ukolev." Smirnov turned back to Irina and the others, the coldness of his eyes immobile like a river in winter. "The meeting, therefore, is useless. The Putilov Iron Works will never negotiate with a bunch of godless hooligans, and as for the firings—there are thousands more like Segunin and Ukolev crawling the streets, eager to work at half the pay."

"You're certain of that, Director Smirnov."

"If you think you can pressure me with threat of a strike, you're mistaken, woman. Take this back to your little priest. Tell Gapon he's a water bug compared to the Putilov Iron Works. Tell him he will be crushed under the heel of Holy Russia."

"*We* are Holy Russia!" Irina shot back.

"You are power-hungry fanatics who represent no one but yourselves."

"You're wrong, Director Smirnov."

"There is nothing more for us to discuss. There was nothing for us to discuss in the first place." He tossed his cigarette on the floor. His aide crushed it and followed the Director from the room.

"Ah, you were wonderful, wonderful, Kuksina Ivanovna!" Segunin practically danced before her as they left the iron plant. "I feel so strong—yes, I can't tell if we've had a victory or a defeat. Does anyone else feel as I do?"

Kostya and Ukolev nodded in agreement, and waited for Irina to speak as they hurried along the street. A bitter wind was blowing now and dusk was quickly falling. The streets were nearly empty.

"Why do you see it as a victory?" Irina asked.

"It's what's jumping around inside me, praise God, Kuksina Ivanovna. It matters little that we haven't our jobs back"—he eyed Ukolev, who again nodded in agreement—"but that we didn't bow down to the lying dog, Smirnov. To the day I die, I shall never forget the way you said, '*We* are Holy Russia!' I almost cried then and there, Kuksina Ivanovna. I did. Let's hurry. I can't wait to tell Father and the others. We'll show Smirnov who's a water bug!"

Their pace quickened in their excitement, and as they passed a side street, Irina noticed some men in black jackets watching them from around a corner. She scanned the empty streets and saw shadows in doorways. One twirled what looked to be a chain, others thumped sticks in their hands. From the frozen expressions on her comrades' faces, Irina knew they had seen them too. But there wasn't time to react. As if on cue, thugs converged on them from all sides and, covering their mouths with their hands, dragged Irina, Kostya, Segunin, and Ukolev into an alleyway.

There were moans and groans as fists and sticks fell on bodies. Irina struggled to break free, but two men carried her further, shoving her into a basement apartment. A light switched on and a hulking form emerged. In an instant she recognized the pin-eyed man, Kolesnikov, and with the recognition, fear surged, almost causing her to double over.

"You remember me, I see!" His face shone with sweat despite the cold, and his thick lips pressed like putty over yellow teeth. His laughter echoed mirthlessly, and he edged closer.

"Don't touch me! Leave me alone!" she shrieked.

His fist lashed out, smacking the side of her head and knocking her to the floor. He knelt beside her, and holding the back of her scarf with one hand, he drew his knife from his pocket and held it to her neck. With a flick of his wrist, he cut through the knot of her scarf.

Fear gagged in her throat.

His hand tightened on her hair and as he twisted back her head, he pressed his face with his stinking breath very close to hers. "It's all my pleasure seeing you again, milady. But where are your friends now, that simpering little Jew?" He chortled.

She spit in his face. It landed on his cheek.

He slapped her face so hard her ears rang.

Tears swelled.

"That wasn't very smart, milady." Grinning, he held the blade of his knife to her cheek. "As I recall, I let you off easy the first time, didn't I? This time, I don't think I will." He turned the blade until she felt it cutting her skin. Immediately his hand fell back and he pressed his finger where the knife had been. "Only a drop. See?" He held up his blood-smeared finger. "Only a beginning."

"Please, please, no more," she begged. "What do you want? Just tell me what you want."

His laughter terrified her. "I want to put you where I put your girlfriends, but I can't. I got me orders, milady, you see."

"Orders . . ." She swallowed hard, trying to keep a semblance of control. "Orders from whom?"

"I ask any questions, milady." He grinned, his tongue smoothing over his fat lips. "How come?" he asked, running the blade of his knife down her cheek. "How come if you're such a fine lady, you dress like this?" He popped each button on her coat with his knife, then pushed open the coat.

"Please, God, please! Please don't do this. I can pay you. I'll pay you whatever you want."

"Yes, I'm sure you can, what with your being the daughter of a Grand Duke and all, but I got more than I need as it is." His knife sliced the top buttons of her blouse, then slipped under her chemise, the tip pressing her breast.

"Please, please . . ." She groaned. The weight of his body pressing her into the stone floor was sending waves of pain from her back down her legs. She could barely see him anymore behind the blur of her tears.

Suddenly he straddled her, knees pressing into her sides. With the knife to her neck, he shoved his hand under her chemise and grabbed hold of her breast. "Nice, milady. Never felt the flesh of one so fine as you before."

"Please don't. Please don't do this." She was whimpering.

"Ah, but I think I will, you see. That's my payment, to frig a lovely, fine Duchess like yerself. Or would you rather I cut you up a bit more? Eh? Either one is fine with me." He pressed the full weight of his body down on her hips.

She tried to speak, but could not make a sound.

"What is it, then? A little frigging or a little cutting?" His one hand lunged inside her coat and pressed between her legs while with the other he held the tip of the knife inside her nose, pressing the blade above the upper edge. He laughed and took his hand from her legs and pressed it against her shoulder. "Well, then, milady. I see the choice is mine. But I give you fair warning, and if you're smart, you'll take it. Next time, I'll have my way with you every way, and when I'm done, you'll be thanking me for death. You understand?"

She nodded ever so slightly, her eyes riveted on the length of the knife.

"Forget Akimov. That's what I'm here to tell you. Just forget him." He flicked his wrist, and the most searing pain she'd ever known shot from her nose into her brain. Warm blood spurted over and into her mouth as she screamed. She tried to move and the pain grew worse. A black numbness was swirling around her. She coughed on the blood and then there was nothing.

Irina opened her eyes to the edge of white blocking her sight. She blinked and the memory of the pin-eyed man in the basement came surging back. She clutched her waist and tears swelled, making her face ache, and she remembered the knife. Gently, fearfully, she lifted her hand to feel her face. It was covered by bandages. She was on a bed. Slowly she moved her head and the room came into focus. She was in Father Gapon's house, in his bed. She lay still and heard voices in the other room. She recognized Misha's and was about to cry out his name, when she remembered he was Izaak to Gapon, just as she was Kuksina. "Izaak," she called weakly, and the movement of her mouth sent a spasm of pain through her nose and her skull.

Within moments Misha was by her side.

Her hand fumbled for his and squeezed it tightly. Tears escaped. "You're safe now, you're all right."

"What about the others?" She spoke softly, barely moving her lips.

"They're beat up, but all right. Segunin found you. The fiend, whoever did this to you—"

"Kolesnikov."

"Kolesnikov!" He gasped. "Are you sure?"

She nodded. "Tell me, Misha, tell me what he did to me," she pleaded softly.

"Your nose—the fiend cut your nose."

"That's all?" she asked fearfully, closing her eyes. She squeezed his hand very hard.

"A small cut on your cheek."

"That's all?" She was afraid to look at him as the memory of the pin-eyed man's body on hers gripped her.

"That's enough, my God." Misha seemed confused. He held her hand to his lips and kissed her.

Involuntarily she pulled away.

"Kuksina, my child." Father Gapon was standing beside Misha. "How are you?"

Misha stood to make room for Gapon. Sitting beside Irina, the priest took her hand and gazed softly into her eyes. "You were so brave. Segunin, Ukolev, and Kostya speak only of your bravery. You are a saint, my child."

"I want to go home," she said, swallowing hard. "Please, I just want to go home."

"As soon as you're strong enough. For now, the doctor said you shouldn't be moved. He said you should be taken to the hospital, but Izaak insisted it wasn't wise. It would be hard to guard you there, and I agreed. Still, the bleeding was difficult to stop. You must stay as quiet as possible or the bleeding will start again. You've lost a lot of blood already, so promise me you won't try to move."

She nodded. Suddenly she was too exhausted to even speak.

"The doctor will be back in a few hours, and Izaak promises he'll never leave your side. I have four men standing guard outside, although I myself have to go. There's a meeting in the Vyborg Hall tonight. Kostya, Segunin, and Ukolev will sing your praise. I must go now." Tapping her hand gently, he stood. "Already the hall is overflowing and many stand in the street. News of Smirnov's brutality is spreading like wildfire."

"It wasn't Smirnov," she said.

"What?"

"Kolesnikov."

Gapon's faced paled. "Kolesnikov!"

"Yes. He said Akimov sent him."

"But why? I don't understand. Why would Akimov do this to you?"

"I don't know . . ." Tears filled Irina's eyes again as she gazed pleadingly at Gapon. "Put me in touch with Akimov."

Gapon looked frightened.

"Please." She pressed his hand tightly. "Help me, Father, please. Help me revenge what was done to me."

He pulled his hand free and stood. Making the sign of the cross, he murmured, "God protect you, Kuksina Ivanovna. Surely you carry his sword."

Gapon came into the bedroom as soon as Irina stirred the next morning. Misha followed behind.

"You look better, Kuksina."

"I feel better." She pushed to a sitting position, and although there was a throbbing in her nose, her head was clear.

"Some tea?" Gapon asked.

"Yes, I'd like that."

"Anything else? Dr. Litvinov said you can eat whenever you're hungry."

"I'm famished."

"Wonderful! I shall bring in a tray. Izaak, stay with our heroine. Then I shall tell you all about the meeting last night!" Gapon's eyes were bright with excitement. "Our flock is ready, Kuksina Ivanovna. I kept on wishing you and Izaak had been beside me to see the glory in their tired faces. Smirnov's rude response to the delegation may be the key we need!" He left in a flurry.

"What's he talking about?" Irina asked when she and Misha were alone.

"The Putilov plant will surely walk out after New Year's Day. Apparently the Society's halls all over Petersburg were overflowing last night. There's talk of a general strike."

"Really!" Her expression became despairing. "And I'm stuck in this bed."

"You'll be better soon, I can tell." He sat beside her. "You look a hundred times better than yesterday."

"I feel it. But tell me—has Gapon said anything about Akimov?"

"No."

"Did you talk to Kostya?"

"Yes, I've already questioned him. He swears he told Akimov nothing, but I think he's lying. He's very frightened."

"The only thing that confuses me is that Kolesnikov knows my real identity. Kostya doesn't."

"I don't know," Misha said, his tone subdued.

Irina reached for his hand. "To think Kolesnikov and this Akimov know so much about me, and I know nothing about them. I'm scared, Misha," she murmured. "Can you bring Kostya to me?"

"I don't think he'll come. He's terrified. He was very badly beaten, far worse than Segunin and Ukolev."

There was a noise in the kitchen from Gapon's preparations. Irina frowned. "I have to get out of here today, Misha. There's so much we need to talk about. I feel like every word we speak is going directly to Gapon."

"Yes, I know. Dr. Litvinov is coming at noon. Eat, get up your strength. If you can convince the doctor you're strong enough, Gapon won't try to hold you."

Alexei sat in a chair in the small, dark one-room flat, slowly nursing a glass of vodka as he listened to Misha's and Irina's story. He tried not to stare visibly at Irina, who was sitting in the bed devouring the food he'd brought. He could not bear looking at her once-beautiful face swollen, cut, most assuredly scarred, and he could not stop looking at her. The sight of her mutilation against the backdrop of this shabby little room filled him with an enormous sense of futility. His love for Misha ached.

He couldn't imagine any child he and Anna might have tugging at his heart more than Misha. From the first moment Alexei had seen the tiny human being who was Tolya's firstborn, he had sworn to be the father he knew Tolya could never be, to give the boy everything that he and Tolya had never had growing up. Misha would move unthwarted toward his destiny, which seemed as the years passed to mirror that part of Alexei which had never been allowed to flower. Misha was sensitive, a poet, Alexei was certain. He would live the life of the mind and soul, unburdened by practicality and necessity. It's what Alexei had always wanted for Misha. How, then, had the boy ended up a terrorist in this miserable, drafty one-room flat with cheap second-, even third-hand furniture and a bed that sagged?

Alexei despaired for Irina too. Perhaps he and she had never been on the best of terms, but Misha adored her, that was clear enough, and the sight of the butchery done to her face both nauseated and enraged Alexei.

"The point of it is, Uncle Alexei, it wasn't Smirnov or anyone from the Putilov plant who did this to Irina."

"It was set up to make it appear that way," Irina explained.

"It's why we called you, Uncle Alexei. We don't know anyone else. You see, we've been working with Gapon without telling Dmitri Andreievich."

"Why is that?" Alexei asked with concern.

Misha opened his mouth to speak, but Irina raised her arm to silence him and began, "Dmitri Andreievich has different priorities, Alexei Yakovlevich." Her voice was filled with authority and she fixed her eyes on Alexei. "He thinks Gapon is beside the point. Misha and I think—rather we're certain— that there's a link between the deaths of our comrades Vera Martova and Katya Kazen and associates of Gapon's at the very least. Perhaps the connection goes deeper, to Yermolov himself."

"Have you presented your ideas to Dmitri?"

"No. It's not easy to differ with Dmitri Andreievich. In fact, he's made it clear that he will tolerate no initiative other than his own."

"But surely he's interested in finding out who murdered your comrades."

"He's more interested in finding Yermolov," Misha said. "Besides, he wasn't particularly happy that I wrote to you in Krasnoyarsk without consulting him first. He as much as told us if we break discipline again, we're out of the Brigade."

"Yet you did."

"We thought it was important, Uncle Alexei. We still do. In fact, this attack on Irina has only confirmed our suspicions. We're just not certain what to do next. It's why we've called you. You see, there's this man, an Okhrana agent. It was his thug who attacked Irina and who led the attack on the squad in Paris. The agent is also connected to Father Gapon. He originally funded Gapon's Society, and we think it was he who had Vera Martova and Katya Kazen killed. We don't know for certain. We know very little about the man, except that he's very powerful. His name is Arkady Akimov."

"It's as I said—Akimov knows about Irina and he most surely knows about the rest of you!" Alexei exploded as he slammed the door of Dmitri Mayakovsky's house.

"What are you talking about?"

In as calm a way as he could, Alexei described what had happened to Irina the night before.

Dmitri listened without comment or expression, quizzically raising an eyebrow when Alexei finished and asking innocently, "Why? Do you understand why they did this, Alexei Yakovlevich? Does it make sense to you why they disguised themselves as workers in Gapon's Society? Do you understand their rationale?"

Alexei knew all too well Yuri's game of disarming the opponent with apparently guileless questions calculated to reveal weaknesses and inconsistencies, and ultimately to disarm. He tried to outthink Yuri, but was too emotionally taut. Images of Irina's battered face and that miserable little one-room flat spat at his composure like sizzling fat. "Apparently . . ." He breathed deeply. "They felt there was a connection between Gapon and Vera Martova's death."

"Ah, yes, the infernal police unions. I should have realized." Dmitri puckered his lips. "And did they find anything out, anything to help us in our efforts to locate Yermolov?" His eyebrows furrowed.

"I'm not here to defend them or to play word games with you, Yuri."

"Excuse me, Alexei Yakovlevich. I don't mean to upset you, I'm just trying to find out the facts, you see." He inhaled deeply on his cigarette. "Why didn't Misha and Irina tell me what they were doing with Gapon weeks ago?"

"I think they were hoping to come up with indisputable evidence about Martova's murder. Now, look, Yuri. I know your game, and I will tell you straight out. I came to speak for them because they're afraid of displeasing you."

Dmitri nodded thoughtfully. "Their fears are well-grounded. I am intensely displeased." He leveled his focus on Alexei. His voice never lost its unsettling calm.

"Still, I think you'll admit what they've found out is more important than their violating the Brigade's discipline. Perhaps even more important than killing Yermolov."

"Really? How so?" Dmitri asked cynically.

"This man who attacked her—Kolesnikov—he was the same man who stole the Yermolov documents in Paris. He knew Irina wasn't the worker Kuksina Ivanovna. He knew her true identity. Don't you see, Yuri, this Kolesnikov was sent by *Akimov*, not Yermolov. Yermolov had nothing to do with the theft of the Paris documents, any more than he had anything to do with the deaths of Vera Martova and Katya Kazen. *Akimov* is the enemy. *Akimov* knows about Irina—he probably knows about the rest of you!"

"But Akimov isn't our target."

"I don't understand." Alexei pressed his hand against the

bridge of his nose. "This Akimov, one of the Okhrana's top agents, knows who Irina is, maybe who you are."

"Listen to me, Alexei Yakovlevich. I will tell you what I told Misha and Irina, what every successful revolutionary must not only know but also understand in his gut. There will always be infiltrations, leaks, and traitors in revolutionary organizations. There's nothing we can do to prevent it. But we can combat it through discipline and absolute dedication to our end of overthrowing the Czar."

"And if you're killed doing it?"

"A risk we all must be willing to take. You see, we're not assassinating Yermolov out of some sense of revenge for what he did to Vera Martova or anyone else. Nor do we care if by assassinating him we aid or hinder someone like Akimov. Our motives are and must remain purely political. By assassinating Yermolov, we strike at the heart of the monarchy, and for that reason the people will be emboldened in their struggles against the Czar. They hate Yermolov as they hated Plehve. By assassinating Yermolov, we further the revolution, but by going after Gapon or this Akimov, we dilute our efforts. Our energies become counterproductive, and then, only then, are the risks unacceptable. Quite simply, neither Gapon nor Akimov is a political target."

"And if the squad is destroyed?"

"That's a risk, as always, and that's why the Brigade is broken down into separate squads, no one knowing anything about the others. We do our best to minimize the risks. This harebrained adventure of Misha's and Irina's of getting close to Gapon is totally beyond what I consider acceptable risk. And look where it's ended. With Irina almost being killed. Damn the girl!" Yuri's voice was suddenly filled with emotion. His face colored. "If I could only bridle her will, she could be a leader. Tell me, Alexei Yakovlevich, is she badly hurt?"

"I think she's more frightened of your expelling her from the Brigade than she is of her wounds."

"I should do that, you know. This is the second time I know of that they've broken discipline," Yuri insisted, but the bite was gone from his voice.

Alexei knew the crisis had passed. For the moment, Yuri was more the man than the political machine; he would act as much from his heart as his reason.

"This attack on Irina has changed matters." Dmitri nodded. "And I suspect you're right. We are caught up in the politics of the Okhrana, in this feud between Yermolov and Akimov."

"Then they've got you cornered."

"Not necessarily. Assuming that in some bizarre way Akimov is using us—then he's also protecting us. Yes . . ." Dmitri was ruminating out loud. "I think we can make use of Irina's and Misha's position with Gapon after all."

"How's that?"

"As soon as Irina's feeling better, she and Misha must ply the priest for more information about Akimov. If someone's passing on information about us to Akimov, then we must find a way to intercept it. Perhaps the priest will be the way. Still, we must act carefully, very carefully. The next time, this thug of Akimov's won't stop at some fancy knifework."

CHAPTER THIRTY-EIGHT

"Go on, now, Anna, read it all," Zhenya encouraged as she sat with Anna, Mousia, Nikita, Sasha, and the servants Matryona, Lidia, Sophie and old Volodia around the large kitchen table in Peterhof. The samovar steamed and plates of cookies and sweet breads were within everyone's reach.

Anna spread the newspaper before her and began. "This article is dated yesterday, January 5, 1905, Petersburg. And it says, 'The 12,500 striking Putilov Iron Plant workers were joined today by one thousand men and women from the Franco-Russian Machine Shop. Sixteen thousand quit work at the Neva Machine and Ship Building Works, and another two thousand at the Neva Textile Factory, and yet another seven hundred at the Yekaterinhof Textile Plant. Countless other small shops are closing daily.

" 'Workers' delegations march freely, stopping in front of work places crying, "Strike! Strike! Get dressed, comrades, we are marching with the men of Putilov in search of true faith!

" 'Within minutes, workers don their outer clothes and begin streaming into the streets to the joyous shouts of those already marching. Blacksmiths join clockmakers. Stablehands march with stonecutters. As they parade through the streets, even some coachmen have joined the ranks. Gas workers are expected to strike by midnight tonight, thus forcing the minority of workers who still refuse to strike out of their jobs. Without the gas to light the shops and homes, much of Petersburg will then come to a standstill.' ''

"Oh, my!" cried the kitchen maid, Sophie. "Imagine Petersburg without lights!"

"Sure and we lived without gas to light the cities once," old Volodia grumbled.

"Go on," Zhenya urgently ordered.

" 'The police, although everywhere in evidence, are keeping an easy distance from the workers,' '' Anna read on. " 'Some have even been seen to cheer on the marchers and tip their hats—' ''

"Isn't that nice now?" It was Matryona who interrupted this time. She was dipping a sweet roll into her tea. "My cousin is a policeman in Petersburg, you know."

"It shows the righteousness of the people's cause," Zhenya said.

"Tell me, Anna Petrovna," Matryona went on. "Is there any more news of that brave priest, Father Gapon?"

"Oh, yes. There are always articles on him."

"I was talking to Isabella Vaslavna at the market. You know, she works for the Burdenkos. Anyway, she's got a brother who's been to the meetings the Father holds. She told me her brother said Father Gapon is the holiest man he has ever met. She said her brother said he would take her to one of the Father's meetings on her day off. I would so like to go myself." Matryona eyed Zhenya uneasily. "We are to see if we can arrange it."

"Make sure you keep me informed, Matryona, or I shan't give you the day off," Zhenya scolded. "Now, go on, Anna, read what the newspaper says about the priest."

Anna scanned the page for his name, and quickly found it in one of the headlines. "Yes, here it is. The article is called 'Membership in the Gapon Society Grows Daily. Father Gapon Plans to Petition the Czar.' ''

"A petition to the Czar!" Matryona exclaimed. "Isn't that exciting, Zhenya Kirilovna—a petition just like the master does."

"Hush, now." Zhenya nodded to Anna to continue.

" 'The Gapon Society's meeting halls are never closed these days, and reports are that membership in the Society doubles daily. An official count has not been issued, but at a meeting in Vyborg early this morning, the speakers had to move into the streets so everyone could hear. Huge bonfires were started for warmth as well as light, and about dawn, a

Gapon orator took to the makeshift stage and cried, "Our lives are beyond endurance. We will live like dogs no more!" Although this cry has often been heard lately, this time the audience echoed with an ominous, "No more, no more!" The orator then cried, "Far better the grave than hell on earth!" and the response this time seemed to rise from the earth itself, sounding like a chant of the dead, "The grave, the grave—" ' "

Lidia, Anna's maid, giggled nervously. "Oh, my, I don't think I would have liked to be there."

"Ach, you have no heart, Lidia, except for your fancy men!" Matryona snapped. "Please go on, Anna Petrovna."

"It says that 'Another orator took to the stage then and cried, "Brothers and sisters, our only hope is the Czar! We must petition the Czar as the rich do! We must throw ourselves on the Czar's mercy!" "And if the Czar won't receive us?" came the cry. "If he is truly our Czar, he will listen to his people," called another. "And if he don't, then we have no Czar!" "No Czar! No Czar!" the crowd mourned, arms reached to the heavens—' "

"Oh, no, no, I don't like that." Old Volodia shook his graying head as he chomped on his cigarette. "I don't take to blaspheming our Czar, praise God." Volodia crossed himself.

"Don't be an idiot, Volodia," Zhenya reprimanded. "Since when has the Czar ever done anything for you?"

"Yes, Zhenya Kirilovna." Volodia nodded. "Still, the Czar is our Czar."

"Read on, Anna." Zhenya sighed despairingly.

Anna scanned the article. "There's not much more. The reporter said he tried to reach Father Gapon to comment on the report of a workers' petition to the Czar, but could not."

Mousia leaned across the table and tapped Volodia, who seemed lost in thought. She tugged at his scraggly, peppered beard. "Grandma doesn't like the Czar, Volodia," she announced. "I don't either."

"Ah, you see, Zhenya Kirilovna, the fruits of blasphemy!" Volodia crossed himself more vigorously, and started to stand.

"Sit, Volodia," Zhenya insisted. "Perhaps if you open your frozen mind, you can get some sense. Our Mousia has good reason not to like the Czar."

"Oh, yes, he wants to send my brother Misha to jail."

"If I were bigger, I'd march," Nikita said.

"Do you think we'll ever see Misha again?" Sasha asked.

"Of course we will. Now, go on, Nikita, it's your turn to read an article."

"What shall I read?" Nikita asked, taking the newspaper from Anna.

"Look for mention of the Coalition and Alexei," Anna said.

"Yes." Zhenya pursed her lips. "We get more news of Alexei from the newspaper than anyplace else these days."

"It will be a Resurrection!" Gapon's voice echoed through the crowded hall. "Every worker, every wife, sister, brother, child, even those of you who are old and bent, shall walk as one, and truly, I tell you, it will be as if the dead have arisen and a new dawn begun! We shall go before our Father, the Czar, and tell him in a voice that he cannot ignore how sorely we have suffered. We shall march to the gates of his mighty palace and fall to our knees and beg the Czar to hear our pleas—or we shall die in the square!" The roar of Gapon's voice quieted into the sweet tension of a violin bow drawn across the taut string.

"When, Father?" A tall, broad worker rose to his feet. "When shall we march?"

"Sunday, Donevsky. We shall march on the Lord's day!"

"Sunday, Sunday!" came the chant.

"Kuksina Ivanovna, do you have a minute?"

Irina felt a tapping on her shoulder and she turned to find Kostya Savich, who had been avoiding her ever since Kolesnikov's attack, standing uncertainly by her side. It was almost two in the morning of January 6. The meeting hall was just clearing out, although the excitement of the proposed petition and march to the Winter Palace lingered like the aftermath of a great shock.

"Of course." Irina smiled wearily.

Kostya nodded and sat beside her. The bruises on his face were almost healed. "The march Sunday is good, I think." His eyes twitched, afraid to rest on her. "Do you think the Czar will hear us?"

"I don't see how he cannot."

"Yes, yes, that's what I think. Kuksina Ivanovna, Father asked me to tell you we meet tonight at his house to draft the petition. He said you are to go home now and get some rest. He said I am to drive you." He spoke without looking at her.

"I have been hoping to talk to you for a while, Kostya Sergeievich."

"We prayed for you every meeting while you were gone."

He nodded furiously. "Wherever Father spoke, he mentioned you in his prayers. Everyone is so happy you're back with us. May I take you home now, Kuksina Ivanovna? My carriage is just outside." He started to stand.

Irina held his arm. "We must talk, Kostya Sergeievich. Surely that's why Father has asked you to drive me home. Even Father knows we must talk."

"Not here." Kostya lowered his voice. "On the way home."

"We'll wait for Izaak."

"Of course."

"You must believe me, Kuksina Ivanovna, I meant you no harm. It is my job to keep Akimov informed. To do otherwise would mean my own death. As true as I am to Father and our cause, I must also be true to Akimov. Father understands that. I beg of you to do the same and to forgive me. I never meant you no harm," Kostya begged as he drove the carriage; he stared straight ahead into the night, his eyes fixed on the horse's harness.

"What did you tell him, Kostya Sergeievich, about me?" Irina asked gently.

"Only that you are a true follower of Father, you and Izaak, and that you have Father's utmost confidence. I swear, that's all. I don't know why he chose to have Kolesnikov treat you so miserably, or the rest of us for that matter."

"Did you ask him?" Misha questioned.

"One does not ask Akimov anything. One only follows his orders. The man is a devil." Kostya's voice was low, almost a growl. He paused then, swallowing hard, and said, "Father told me you want to take revenge on Kolesnikov, Kuksina Ivanovna. What would you do if you found him?"

"Kill him."

"He's not an easy man to kill. Still, if I could, I would help you. It's the only way my family or I will be free. Tomorrow Akimov will command a meeting with Father in the Summer Gardens, in the path along the pond. He'll be there at two in the afternoon."

"How do you know this?" Misha demanded, leaning across Irina to grab Kostya's arm.

"I was sent a message. It is my job to arrange all matters between Father and Akimov."

"How do we know you're telling the truth? How do we know you aren't deliberately placing Kuksina in danger?"

"I swear on the lives of my mother and my children." Kostya crossed himself. "You know where I live."

"What good would that do if we're dead? Tell us something about Akimov, something that would compromise the cur."

"I can tell you this. He always meets people in public places, outside. It's never the same place. Kolesnikov is always in the shadows."

"How do you know Father is to meet him tomorrow?"

"I received the message."

"How?"

"A man came to my house in the middle of the night. He just walked in and dragged me from my bed. Akimov has the key to my house, you see."

"What if Father needs to get in touch with Akimov? How does he do that?"

Kostya was silent awhile, then shook his head.

"You don't know or you won't tell me?"

"Please, I can say no more."

"Why, Kostya? What scares you so?"

Kostya closed his eyes and bowed his head. "Akimov told me . . . he said if I ever betrayed him, he would set Kolesnikov on my wife. She's a good woman . . ." Kostya's body shook involuntarily. "I can't—don't ask me to do this, please."

"Why don't you just leave Akimov's service if you're so frightened?" Irina asked.

"Nobody leaves Akimov's service alive. Even Father. I try to tell him that. He doesn't understand. He's a man of peace. He's never seen Akimov's evil side. I think a part of him doesn't believe Akimov ordered Kolesnikov to do what he did to you, Kuksina Ivanovna. Akimov's a chameleon. He changes with whoever he's near. I've seen it. Yes, I used to think it was his power. I wondered how he could be ready to stab a man in the back and appear to be the man's greatest friend. I think it is a sickness now, the work of the devil."

"Do you trust what this man Savich tells you?" Alexei asked.

"I think so, yes. His fear wasn't pretended. Besides, he was badly beaten during the attack. He seems honest in his desire to help us, even to kill Kolesnikov."

"What do you think, Uncle Alexei?" Misha asked.

"I think none of us are experts on such matters. I think we should talk to Dmitri before we do a thing."

Misha eyed Irina as if to say: Yes, that's what I think too.

Irina pursed her lips. "You know what Dmitri will say. He'll say Akimov is not a political target. He'll say killing

Kolesnikov is motivated by revenge, and I say yes. I dream of revenge, not only for myself but also for Katya and Vera. If that makes me less of a revolutionary, then so be it!'' she exclaimed, her cheeks burning brightly.

"The Chinese have a saying, Irina Ilyanovna: when revenge drives a man, he must be willing to dig two graves.''

"You sound like Misha!''

"That I take as a compliment.'' Alexei smiled. "Besides, I could not in good faith move forward on anything concerning Akimov or Kolesnikov without discussing it with Dmitri Andreievich first. He has most generously overlooked your and Misha's excesses twice—''

"Excesses!''

"Irina, Dmitri Andreievich is a brilliant strategist. There's much you can learn from him.''

"I never said otherwise. But sometimes I feel he's too cautious. Sometimes if one doesn't seize the moment, the moment is lost forever. I say we follow Gapon to his meeting. We might never get this close to Akimov again.''

"I understand your passion for Akimov, truly I do. It burns in my own heart too. But Dmitri's right. We must separate our passion from our reason. It's the only way to survive.''

Misha nodded. "We must talk to Dmitri Andreievich.''

"Then I suppose I'm outvoted!'' she snapped angrily. "You go, Alexei Yakovlevich. You talk to Dmitri. Misha and I have work to do for Gapon's meeting tonight.''

"Yes, all right. Perhaps it's better if I discuss this with Dmitri alone.''

"This Akimov keeps popping up like some unwanted growth.'' Dmitri was impatient. "What is it you want me to do about this meeting between the priest and Akimov?''

"I'm not sure, but the opportunity arose, at least to get a view of this Shadow.''

"And kill him?'' Dmitri's question was more of a demand.

Alexei colored and shifted uncomfortably in his seat.

"You seem uneasy with talk of assassination,'' Dmitri said as he refilled Alexei's glass.

"You know I am.''

"Yet you came to me for precisely that purpose.''

Alexei closed his eyes a moment, and Irina appeared, urging him on. Yes, dammit, it was assassination that had driven him to Yuri, but now it all seemed like a tempest in a teapot. He was tired. God, he was missing Anna. He had never thought he would miss her so. "Surely, Yuri, we can make something of this meeting between Gapon and Akimov. Even you must admit your curiosity is piqued by the man. If only to store away for another day, it would behoove us to see what he looks like. Perhaps follow him, find out where he lives.''

Dmitri nodded. ''I'll go along with that.''

''I don't think it's wise to have Irina and Misha do it.''

''Yes, I'll arrange it.''

''But be careful.''

''We always are.''

Anna knocked uncertainly on Zhenya's door. ''It's me, Anna.''

''Come in, come in,'' Zhenya murmured, and Anna knew the old woman was saying her prayers.

Anna tiptoed in and knelt beside Zhenya before the icon. It seemed that the only time she could feel close to God anymore was when she prayed with Zhenya Kirilovna. Alone, Anna's thoughts turned to Alexei, to her impatience with his absence and her longing for his love, neither of which was appropriate to think about before God.

When prayers were over, Anna helped Zhenya to her feet and they sat on the edge of the bed. ''Mother, is it true you're going with Matryona and Isabella Vaslavna and her brother to a Gapon Society meeting in Petersburg Sunday?''

''It's not a meeting, exactly, from what Isabella's brother said. It's a great assembly of people. There'll be processions from all parts of the city, converging on the Winter Palace. There Father Gapon shall present his petition to the Czar himself.''

''And the Czar has said he will meet the priest?''

''Well, I don't know. But he'd better, is all I can say. How can the Czar refuse to meet such an outpouring of his people? For these will not be just workers and students, but all his people, young and old, mothers with children—''

''Can I go?''

''Alexei wouldn't approve, you know that.''

''Alexei isn't here to approve or disapprove.''

''Yes . . .'' Zhenya smoothed her hand on Anna's. ''I don't blame you for being impatient with his absence, but you must think hard about going, Anna. You promised Alexei you wouldn't march again.''

''I know, but this is different, Mother, you said so yourself. It's a holy procession led by a priest. It will have the blessings of God. Surely no one will be hurt or arrested. The Czar will not shoot or arrest women and children. Besides, I feel I must go. I shall go mad if I stay cooped up here much longer. I detest those bodyguards! I mean . . ." She bit her lip and burst out, "Alexei needn't even know we went. We can go and be back here by nightfall."

Zhenya could not repress a smile. "I can't stop you, Anna, if it's what you want."

"Oh, thank you, Mother. Thank you!" Anna hugged Zhenya tightly.

Irina, Misha, Father Gapon, Segunin, and a worker named Golitsyn spent the night of January 6 drafting the petition paper to the Czar. The writer Gorky appeared for a while, not to help write the petition but to arrange to meet Father Gapon at the march the next day. Kostya Savich was supposed to be there, but he never appeared. Gapon sent a messenger to Savich's house, and his wife said he hadn't been home in over twenty-four hours. Just before dawn on January 7, a group of workers came rushing into Gapon's house.

"Kostya Sergeievich is dead!" their leader cried.

"Dead! How?" Irina gasped.

"He was run over by a carriage on Vasilievsky Island. The police said it was an accident."

"Did anyone else see it?" Misha asked.

"No one's come forth. It was dark, the street was narrow."

Gapon lifted his hands in the air and intoned, "Let us pray for the soul of our brother Kostya Sergeievich. . . ."

"Kostya Savich is dead," Alexei somberly announced as he walked into Yuri's house that morning. "Run over by a carriage last night on Vasilievsky Island."

"My God." Yuri paled.

"Yuri, did you tell anyone about Savich, about his being the informant?"

"No, no one. There was no reason to."

"How the hell did Akimov find out, then?"

"Perhaps the leak came from Savich himself. Perhaps he told someone, even Gapon. And perhaps his death had nothing to do with the meeting between Akimov and Gapon today."

"Do you believe that?"

"No."

"Dammit!" Alexei forced his fingers through his hair. "I can't stand living in the shadow of this Akimov another day. He's everywhere, and we can't see him!" Alexei paced. "Do you think he'll show up at the meeting this afternoon?"

"Would you if you were he?"

"No."

"Still, I'll dispatch some people, just in case."

"Yuri, what's the best way to draw this Akimov out into the open?"

"Eh?"

"Yermolov—once he's dead, Akimov takes over the Okhrana."

"It's what he wants."

"And if he did get control of the Okhrana, he'd have to surface in some official capacity. Then the Brigade, if it's ready, can strike at him before he can strike at you. If we draw out Yermolov, we'll be killing two birds with one stone."

"Still, our problem is in locating Yermolov."

"There must be people in court who know where Yermolov lives. The Grand Duke Nikolai Nikolaievich, for example. He's closest to the Czar. He would have to be able to make contact with Yermolov on a moment's notice. If we could get someone like Nikolai Nikolaievich to confide Yermolov's whereabouts . . ."

"What are you thinking, Alexei?" Dmitri was interested.

"Andre Bobrinsky—he's very close to Nikolai Nikolaievich."

"What are you going to do? Ask him to get you the address of Leonti Yermolov?"

"Yes," Alexei replied matter-of-factly.

"It's insanity. Why would he help you with such a thing? He's in the Symposium, but he's a dyed-in-the-wool moderate. He'll have nothing to do with anything which smacks of violence."

"He despises Yermolov. Besides . . ." The hint of a smile creased Alexei's lips. "He owes me a rather sizable debt, one I think it's time to call in."

Count Andre Andreievich Bobrinsky was of noble birth and had vast wealth and family holdings as well as imperial connections. Alexei had known him for more than fifteen years, and their friendship went far beyond their membership in the Symposium. They'd met in the days when Alexei believed the ballet the highest form of art, ballerinas the most desirable mistresses, and card playing the only form of relaxation. Bobrinsky was as wild with women and as flagrant a spender as Alexei had ever been. They threw extravagant week-long parties in Bobrinsky's villa in Tsarkeyo Selo, took their mistresses on vacations to London, Paris, and Vienna, and won and lost fortunes in a night of playing cards. Bobrinsky, however, was more than just a dilettante or a Don Juan. He was highly intelligent and quirkish by nature, often more of an introvert than an extrovert. His passion was engineering, in particular, the newly invented automobile. He was one of the first in Petersburg to own and drive a car, and he'd spent a year in America studying engine mechanics and American automobile plants. When he returned to Russia in 1900, his dream of building an automobile factory in Petersburg had flowered into an obsession. The car of his design was called the Marissa, after his young wife, and it would be, he said, the most luxuriously outfitted and mechanically advanced automobile the world had seen.

If Andre Bobrinsky was an engineering genius, he was a totally impractical businessman, and by 1901, he had lost most of his ancestral fortune to his faltering factory. It was a frigid February night when Alexei received a frantic message from Bobrinsky's wife, insisting that Andre had gone to the plant to kill himself. Alexei found his friend sitting in his office, a gun to his head.

"Everything, I've lost everything!" Bobrinsky cried when he saw Alexei. "The creditors are hovering like vultures. Even the villa at Tsarkeyo Selo is tainted, yes, even that! I can't stand another minute, Alyosha, my dearest friend. Tomorrow my family will be begging in the streets. . . ."

Alexei hurtled himself at Bobrinsky as he pulled the trigger, and the gun went flying, the bullet ricocheting as it exploded. Miraculously, no one was hurt. Alexei stayed with the distraught Bobrinsky throughout the night, and by morning they'd come up with a plan of salvation. Alexei would refinance the factory, find a trustworthy business manager and keep the creditors at bay while Andre went to America to hire some automobile mechanics and a plant manager who knew what they were doing. By 1903 the first Marissa was delivered to Alexei's palace, and Bobrinsky was now having difficulties keeping up with the orders.

Count Bobrinsky smiled expansively when Alexei found him eating lunch in his factory office. "Ah, my dearest friend! It's been too long!" He jumped from his seat to embrace Alexei, kissing both cheeks several times. "Much too long. Come, have some wine, a bite to eat." He herded Alexei to the table and filled his glass. "It's a Crimean wine, quite distinguished, as good as, if not better than any of the French, I think. And this sturgeon is marvelous." Bobrinsky began piling high a plate of food for Alexei who, in fact, found himself hungry.

They talked aimlessly as they ate, Alexei allowing himself some careless time with Andre before tightening the noose that he knew would constrain their friendship forever. It was Bobrinsky who brought the conversation to business. "Well, Alyosha, as much as I adore your company, I know it's not friendship alone that brings you to see me today—not with the priest threatening his march tomorrow. Do you think it will be the beginning of the revolution? There are many in the court who are talking of leaving Petersburg before they're murdered in their beds."

"I doubt it's come to that." Alexei leaned forward to take a light for his cigarette from Bobrinsky.

"Do you think the Czar will greet them at the Winter Palace?"

"I think he should if he wants to keep his head."

"Yes, my thoughts exactly. Just a few words from the Czar would be so easy, and make the people so happy that they would forget this priest Gapon and tramp happily back to work on Monday. Tell me, what news of our friend Ryabushinsky?"

"He's recovering nicely."

"Thank God. It was awful, just awful."

An uneasy silence followed, and finally Alexei said, "Andre, I've a favor to ask you."

Bobrinsky smiled expectantly.

"I need an address."

"Yes."

"Leonti Yermolov."

Bobrinsky's face grew grim. "He's a dangerous man to pay a visit on these days, and one not likely to accept an invitation from the likes of you."

"Yes." Alexei nodded. "Still, Andre, I need the address."

"May I ask you why?"

"Suffice to say it affects my family."

Bobrinsky looked peevish. "How would Yermolov affect your family."

"Please, Andre, I can tell you no more. You know I wouldn't ask you for something like this if it weren't vital."

"Yermolov means politics, Alyosha, one area you and I have never agreed on." Bobrinsky stood then and stared at a car design pinned to his wall. He explored the design for a long time and turned slowly to Alexei. "I owe you my life—more than that, the lives of my wife and children as well."

"This will wipe out the debt, Andre. I swear, do this for me, and we're even."

"When do you need it?"

"Tomorrow."

Bobrinsky closed his eyes and drew a deep breath. "Stop by around ten. I'll see what I can do."

CHAPTER THIRTY-NINE

"Anna, Anna . . ." Zhenya nudged her gently. "Anna, it's time."

The instant Zhenya's hands touched her, Anna shot up in bed. She searched for her mother-in-law's shadowy form in the predawn darkness and embraced her. "Can you feel my heart beat, Mother?" she whispered excitedly. "Oh, I hardly slept a wink."

"Neither did I." Zhenya kissed each cheek. "But hurry, we must get ready quickly if we're to slip out unnoticed."

"Is Matryona awake?"

"I'm going to wake her now. Dress warmly. It's frigid outside."

Anna had to sit for a moment, taking deep breaths to contain herself. She could not believe the daring of their plans. Lighting the candles about the icon, she knelt to pray, and this time her prayers gushed forth. "Heavenly Father, forgive me if I sin against my husband. I know I have given him my word, but, in faith, I do no less than he does. And it is in your name, Father, that we march. Surely a march led by a priest is not a sin. I fear if I did not go today with Zhenya Kirilovna and Matryona I would do something even more rash. You above all know that rashness is one of my greatest undoings. I couldn't bear being left here in Peterhof while Alexei and all of Petersburg seem to be moving the heavens and the earth. Zhenya Kirilovna has explained that in such a struggle we are all soldiers of God. For the struggle of the people is a holy struggle, as the good priest Father Gapon says. Heavenly Father . . ." She held her hands tightly together and gazed reverently into the understanding eyes of the Virgin. "I thank you for my marriage and for Zhenya Kirilovna. Sometimes I think my meeting her is nothing short

of a miracle. Truly, she feels like a mother and a friend. She
is the kindest woman I have ever known, and if, at the age
of sixty-seven, she can march behind the priest, I can too.
Protect us, Father. Protect Alexei and Irina and Misha. Stand
by Father Gapon. We march in your footsteps. Freedom is
God's love.'' She crossed herself and hurried to dress.

Sometime during the night of Saturday, January 8, the
howling wind quieted, leaving the brittle coldness of Petersburg still. Without gas for lights, darkness smothered the city,
poising it on the edge of a precipice. Rushing footsteps echoed. Hushed voices exchanged strategies, conspiracies, and
rumors. The Gapon Society's meeting halls were shadowy
with candlelight and workers who waited for morning and
leadership.

Gapon and his closest cadre, including Irina, Misha, Segunin, Ukolev, and Golitsyn, slipped secretively into the flat
of a Putilov worker named Sinelovsky about midnight. Gapon's face was pale and drawn; his eyes gleamed dark and
wild. His voice was hoarse. He smoked incessantly, drank
tea and would not eat.

Irina sat with Gapon and listened to his talk about the glory
of God and the Czar. He raved of how the Czar would meet
the march, the holy pilgrimage, and as he spoke, tears filled
his eyes. He became breathless when he described his vision
of the Czar rushing to greet him, to receive Gapon's blessings. Irina grew uneasy as Gapon talked on and on. He was
fired, coiled, ready to snap. She urged him to sleep. None of
them had slept for more than a few hours for days. ''You
need your rest, Father, for tomorrow. We all do.''

He stood, walked to the window, and opened the shutters.
Moonbeams lighted up milky patterns on the frosted panes.
Gapon was still; his slim black-clad figure was straight like
the edge of a razor. His fists were balled. His stillness echoed
like the cocking of a gun.

''Odd.'' He finally spoke. ''That Akimov never showed
up today. Do you think it had anything to do with poor dear
Kostya's death?'' His voice was low, innocent.

''I did not know you were to meet Akimov today, Father,''
Irina replied.

''Oh, yes, surely I told you.'' His eyes were fixed on the
frosted panes.

''No.''

''Well . . .'' he said as if it did not matter.

''Are you worried, Father?''

"I thought perhaps he would have word of a permit from the police."

"Perhaps you could still meet Akimov. Perhaps there's still time."

"In the end a permit doesn't matter. God will protect me. Tomorrow will be glorious." He quieted then.

Irina thought he was praying. Sometime in the night she laid her head on her arms on the table and fell asleep.

At three in the morning Misha and ten well-chosen scouts began fanning throughout the city. The stillness reeked with restlessness. More than once they fell into the shadows to avoid a roving gang of Black Hundreds. At five-thirty in the morning they watched the Eighty-ninth Belomorsky regiment detrain at the Baltic Station. At six o'clock the thirteenth Irkutsk regiment arrived from Pskov. Squadrons of mounted Cossacks guarded bridges across the Neva. Their horses pawed the frozen snow and snorted. The Palace Square was lit with torches and lined with detachments of the Czar's Life Guard Grenadiers and Preobrazhensky Guards. Under the tense spell of darkness, guns were held in readiness. A cannon was strategically mounted, pointing out over the square.

"It is all for show. They will not shoot on a holy pilgrimage of the people," Vasily Shavitsky, a blacksmith, murmured to Misha.

At six-thirty Misha and his scouts met up with the first massive contingent of workers, a group of one thousand Kolpino workers just finishing a ten-mile march. They carried torches and banners which praised the Czar and called for peace, food and jobs.

"Greetings from Father Gapon and all the workingmen and women of Petersburg!" Misha greeted them.

Cheers went up and Misha and his men were swallowed for the moment in the embraces of the marchers. It was still pitch black. The sun would not rise in St. Petersburg for another two hours.

Alexei awoke early that Sunday and lay in bed listening to the frost cracking on the windowpanes. The night was unbearably dark; the only light was the low glow of his cigarette. The bed felt cavernous without Anna. Life felt cavernous without her. That was the fear, being without Anna. The madness wasn't in their loving, but in the world about them. Akimov, Yermolov, Witte, the revolution. Alexei would end the madness, bring the scales into balance once more. He would order his life, and love Anna, never leave her. They would have children, as his mother said. He would love his children, hold them, teach them. Their world would be safe. He would make it safe.

Anna scraped the frost and peered excitedly out the window as Isabella's brother's carriage stopped and started along the dark road already clogged with countless other carriages, wagons, open sleighs and walking bands of men, women and children. There was religious singing and solemn talk as torches blazed. People plodded through the icy night. Every now and again a cry erupted. "We are going to the Czar! We are going to the Czar!"

"Let's offer some a ride," Anna suggested. "We've room for several more in here."

"Ah, but they're a ragged bunch out there, Zhenya Kirilovna," Matryona warned.

"Yes, but look at the little ones, and it's so cold and the way is so long. Surely today we're all brothers and sisters before God. Isn't that what the march is all about?" Anna eyed Zhenya for agreement.

"Anna's right." Zhenya's voice was filled with command. "Ivan! Ivan!" She pounded on the roof. "Stop a minute."

"What's the problem?" Ivan roared back. "The going's so slow, I can't be stopping just when we're finally moving."

"Stop a moment only to offer someone a ride. We've room for two or three more, if we squeeze."

"There's none out there you'd like to ride with, madame," Ivan called back.

Zhenya pounded harder. "Stop, you idiot! There's a tired family. Invite them in."

The carriage came to a halt and they heard Ivan call, "Come on, then! You're lucky my mistress has a kindly heart. And mind your manners, now. You're sitting with the mother and wife of the great Alexei Yakovlevich Kalinin."

Zhenya opened the door and the dumbfounded family dressed in shabby workers' clothes stood huddled before them.

"Come in, come in now!" Zhenya ordered fussily, and she poked out her head.

The family—a wife, two small boys, and the father carrying an infant—fell to their knees before Zhenya.

"Come now, we won't bite. We march as one today," Zhenya implored the family, but they would not move or even raise their eyes to her.

After some encouraging, Anna and Isabella descended to usher the family inside.

The mother slapped the hand of the smallest boy as he

reached to touch the soft, lush warmth of the blanket. She shoved the child along with his brother onto the floor and ordered them not to utter a word.

The father handed the infant to his wife and snapped, "Make sure she don't make a cry in the presence of such fine people." He crossed himself and his wife did the same.

"Here, then, it's cold," Anna insisted, spreading the blanket across the terrified children.

The mother crossed herself.

The father stiffened.

"It's all right," Anna gently prodded. "And, Isabella, share your warm blanket with our guests. There's more than enough."

Isabella looked put upon.

Anna frowned at the silly girl and reached across the carriage, spreading the blanket on the legs of the mother and father. "There, now." She smiled happily and felt quite righteous. "We're all warm and toasty. And we might as well introduce ourselves. I'm Anna Petrovna. This is my mother-in-law, Zhenya Kirilovna, and Matryona and Isabella. What are your names, then?"

"I'm Maxim Igorovich Kashirin. And this good woman is my wife, Natalya Grigorevna, praise God," the husband said with great deference.

"And the children?" Anna asked.

"Maxim, Leonid and the infant Varvara."

"Matryona, break out the cookies and sweet breads for the Kashirin family!"

Matryona hesitated, grimaced, and looked toward Zhenya to counter Anna's command.

"Do as Anna says, Matryona. Lord, but my blood runs hot with shame for you, woman! There was a time when either you or I could have been walking like the Kashirins. Natalya Grigorevna . . ." Zhenya smiled to the wife, who was cringing in the corner of the carriage. "Although my son is Alexei Yakovlevich, I myself was born a poor peasant, and my husband, Alexei's father, fared no better. I enjoy your company and that's the truth. Come, we shall have a party today and march together. Yes, it would please my heart for the Kalinins to march beside the Kashirins."

Maxim Kashirin crossed himself several times. "Please God, it would be an honor worth dying for, madame."

"Don't be an idiot, man!" Zhenya snapped. "I'd as soon kick the seat of your pants with an iron shoe as have you die for me. Come, Anna, Isabella, the Kashirins need some livening. Let's have a happy tune. Maxim, Leonid—" She reached for the smallest of the two brothers and pulled him onto her lap and wrapped the warm blanket about him. "Now, then, my fine little friend, what's your favorite song? My daughter, Anna Petrovna, has the fairest of voices and can pick up any melody."

"Leonid!" the father snapped. "Speak up. And stop fidgeting. That's a fine lady's lap you sit on!"

Gapon opened the shutters again and stared through the frosted panes of the worker Sinelovsky's flat to the street below. Dawn was only beginning to seep through the night; a crowd was gathering with torches. "Kuksina, why did you let me sleep so late?"

"I thought it would be best, Father. I heard you stirring until almost three in the morning. You need your strength."

"Some food, a bite to eat, Father?" the wife of Sinelovsky begged.

"Just some tea, good woman. Izaak, what word have you on the gatherings?"

"I've scouts reporting to me hourly, Father, and I myself have been checking the streets all night. Already tens of thousands are massed."

"Police, troops?"

"Oh, yes, they're in great numbers everywhere, but the police are very friendly."

"Kuksina, any word from the police prefect?"

"No, not yet."

"We can't wait for the permit any longer." Gapon absently took his tea from Sinelovsky's wife and stared back out the window. "I worry. Just because the police and foot soldiers are friendly doesn't mean their officers will be. Praise God, I am not leading my people to the slaughter."

"Truly, Father, this march is their desire. They lead you as much as you lead them."

"You have a wise way about you, Kuksina Ivanovna." He sat beside her at the table. "Still, I had a vision of blood last night. I don't think it's wise for the women and children to march first, as planned." He set down his tea, and pressing Irina's hand, gazed at the handful of workers standing awkwardly about him. "Come, brothers, we will pray together one last time. Then I shall dress and we will move into the streets."

Shouts outside the palace windows urged Alexei from bed. He opened the curtains and shutters and threw open the glass. A group of students was forming along the embankment. Cossacks on horseback lined the river and stood rigid as stone. It's time, Alexei thought, almost nine. He could go to Bobrinsky.

Without calling for his valet, he dressed in a doorman's uniform he'd bought for the occasion, thinking it would be easier to walk about town dressed as a common man on such a day. Besides, he wasn't certain he wanted to be readily recognized as he went about his business. He downed a glass of brandy, and minutes later was walking the streets, which were unusually crowded for such an early Sunday hour. The clear sky and low winds had urged out the curiosity seekers. Skaters were gliding up and down the frozen Neva. Nurses pushed carriages and children played in the parks. Tea sellers quickly sold out their steaming brew and honey cakes.

"Brother, we're off to see the Czar," more than one worker called to Alexei, dressed as he was in his doorman's uniform. "We go in search of truth, brother." They waved their white flags. "Join us!"

"In time, brothers," Alexei called back. "I've some business to attend to."

"So long as it's God's business."

Alexei nodded and smiled. He passed several acquaintances, who did not give him a second look. He was pleased with his easy anonymity and broke into a fast walk as he neared Bobrinsky's palace.

Bobrinsky's servant, who knew Alexei well, was flustered when he opened the door. "Master Kalinin, is that you?" he questioned, eyeing Alexei's dress.

"Yes, Boris." Alexei chuckled, handing the servant his hat and coat. "Tell your master I'm here. He's expecting me."

Moments later Bobrinsky appeared in a navy-blue silk dressing gown; he was smiling good-naturedly. "You've quite upset Boris, I'm afraid. He didn't think the priest's march was a costume affair! So, you're marching after all."

"I wouldn't miss it for the world. What about you, Andre?"

"I haven't your fortitude, I'm afraid. I shall watch from my windows. But come, I've some news for you. . . ."

At ten o'clock Gapon emerged from the apartment of the worker Sinelovsky dressed in his most ceremonial of raiments. He wore a gold-threaded cassock with a glittering jeweled cross about his neck. On his head was an embroidered fur-edged headdress. Irina, in her plain workman's coat, scarf, and boots, walked by his side, with Sugunin, Ukolev, Sinelovsky, his wife and several more of Gapon's closest followers. A contingent of Gapon's Life Guards led by Misha flanked the inner core.

People in the street fell down before the priest, and he stopped to bless them. They held out babies for him to kiss and murmured, "To the Czar! To the Czar!"

"It's a glorious day, my children. The sun is shining. The heavens are clear. God walks with us."

"Amen." The people crossed themselves. Some wept.

"Come!" Gapon urged them on in his most priestly tone. "We must walk to join the others. With each step we gain strength. With each step we are nearer to the holy wisdom and mercy of our glorious Czar!"

Anna clung tightly to Zhenya as she searched for the Kashirin family, who had literally vanished in the sea of faces gathered on Vasilievsky Island. Isabella and her brother were gone too, leaving Anna, Zhenya and Matryona on their own.

Matryona was busy cursing Isabella. "The no-good wench, leaving us to fend for ourselves. And after all the hours I've spent listening to her complaining and moaning."

"Well, we're here, and that's what's important. Come, let's hear what that group of people is about."

Anna followed Zhenya, her eyes fixed in wonder at the sheer number of poorly dressed souls. There were thousands upon thousands of men and women, children and old people. They carried icons and white flags on which were written the words "Peace" and "Brotherhood." Some seemed worse off than others, but even the finest were not close to the kind she'd invite to tea. The houses about them were shabby too. The narrow streets were lined with faded little wooden structures having no elegance. Here on Vasilievsky Island there were no broad sweeps of avenues, no fine shops. Garbage piled up outside the stoops; mangy dogs ran wild.

"Where are all the students?" Anna whispered in Zhenya's ear. "I thought they'd be here," she said, thinking back to the night she'd marched with Petya, when streams of students had funneled off Vasilievsky Island.

"The university is further over, dear," Zhenya explained, edging toward a group encircling a portly middle-aged man dressed in his Sunday best and standing on a crate.

"What do you think, citizen?" someone called to him. "Will we get beaten and arrested today?"

"Father Gapon would not lead us to such a fate. We go to see the Czar for truth!" he roared.

"And what if a policeman raises a gun, brother?" called a woman holding a child.

"We say: Brother, what about it? Is your lot much better than our own? And if the policeman is an honest sort, he'll answer no. Then he'll know he is one of us and will himself join us."

There were murmurs of assent and another man called out, "Rumor says a cannon has been set in front of the Winter Palace."

"Still, a cannon needs a man to light the fuse. Citizens, have no fear. We go with open hearts. I myself will march in the first rank. If I fall, as I am ready to do, those of you who follow will walk in my blood. I say this to you fearlessly, for I know it cannot be so. The Czar will not fire on his children!"

Speaker after speaker took the first man's place on the crate. They talked about the worker's life; they spoke of endurance; they hissed and booed at names of bureaucrats and hated factory bosses. Women, men, old and young, got up to speak. A student tried, but was shouted down, and a long debate ensued. Among the workers, some favored the students' support; others insisted the students had it too easy, and could not be allowed to march with Father Gapon's flock.

Anna listened intently, half-hidden behind Zhenya, as the long debate ensued. She hoped the students would be allowed to march; if they were expelled, she would be expelled with them.

"Brothers, sisters!" The first man took the crate again. "I say let the students walk with us, for surely they suffer under the regime as we do. They are the first to march against injustice and the first to be beaten. For this they are sent to the front lines of war to die. Their classes where they study are nailed shut and they have no places to learn, as we have no places to work. Father Gapon says we are one today. I say let the students march. I say let anyone who understands suffering and injustice march with us today!"

Cheers rang out and a chant of "We Are One! We Are One!" burst forth.

"Brothers and sisters, citizens of holy Russia, let us pray to our Father in heaven!" the man on the crate called as the chanting died. "Let us say the Twenty-third Psalm."

Silence settled and many in the crowd fell to their knees in the snow. Zhenya knelt with them, pulling Anna and Matryona down with her. They crossed themselves and a breathless silence rippled. Shoulders touched. A woman sobbed.

"The Lord is my shepherd, I shall not want . . ."

Slowly, voices joined.

"He leadeth me to lie down in green pastures . . ."

The voices swelled in a gentle power.

"He restoreth my soul . . . ."

Anna looked at Zhenya. Tears were streaming down her ancient face.

The Countess Montenegrina's Palace, Alexei kept repeating to himself as if he might forget the address. A nervous energy made him bounce as he walked. He had to restrain himself from running. The Countess Montenegrina's Palace . . . The Countess Montenegrina's Palace . . . How easy it all was. Why hadn't he thought of asking Bobrinsky to begin with? How absurdly easy. Alexei could hardly wait to see Yuri's face when he made the announcement. Yermolov is living in Countess Montenegrina's Palace on Voznesensky Prospect. . . . And it occurred to Alexei as he pushed toward the bridge leading to Vasilievsky Island that the Montenegrina Palace was only a block away from the Yusupovs', where he'd first heard Anna play.

When Alexei reached the Palace Bridge near the Winter Palace, it was blocked by a solid mass of Cossacks, and Alexei hurried to the Nikolaevsky Bridge; the crowds there made bridge traffic just as impossible. There was no way he could get to Yuri's house until the march was over, and shoving his hands in his pockets, he stood in the midst of the crowd, trying to decide where to go.

"Move on, move on, there," a guardsman urged from atop his horse. "This is no time for daydreamers." His tone was coarse, and Alexei felt indignation rise, only to remember he was dressed as a doorman.

Nodding, Alexei started on, stopping to ask an ill-clad worker, "Do you know where Father Gapon himself starts his walk?"

"I hear it's over near Znamenskaya Square."

"Thank you, citizen."

"To the Czar," the man said reverently, crossed himself and hurried on.

Father Gapon's contingent was, in actuality, amassing across town from Znamenskaya Square at the Nevsky Iron Works. At eleven o'clock precisely, Gapon raised his gilt cross high above his head. "Brothers and sisters, citizens of holy Russia, it is time to begin!" His voice boomed sonorously.

The streets and the thousands who had joined to march with him fell miraculously quiet. An enormous portrait of the Czar carried on a long rod by a bent, white-haired man bobbed behind the priest. Smaller pictures of the Czar and

Czarina swayed on either side. Excited young boys held religious torches. Weathered old women carried icons mounted on sticks. A large white flag blew in the gentle breeze. The day had turned glorious, almost warm. On the white flag were the words "Soldiers! Do not fire on the people!"

"We walk in God's name. Peace be with you!" Gapon smiled on his followers; his eyes glowed as if they were the source of life itself.

Irina felt Gapon's gaze rest on her as he turned. He smiled for her, with her, and she was awed by his radiance; an aura of holiness settled about the crowd. Irina shuddered. Perhaps this priest wasn't mad after all. Perhaps this truly was the beginning of a revolution.

Gapon clasped his gilt-edged cross in his bare, outstretched hands and began to walk at an even pace. His gold raiment glittered in the sun.

The crowd swayed behind him like billowing ripe wheat; the high, clear sweet voice of a woman rose and broke the silence. "Save Us, O Lord, Thy People," she sang, and voice after voice joined, flowing like a chorus of angels.

Police along the route took off their caps in reverence.

Irina turned to look about her. The procession filled the street from side to side and spread as far as the eye could see. There were thousands upon thousands—ten, twenty, thirty thousand marchers and more. Irina inched her way to Misha and linked her arm through his. "It's wonderful, isn't it?"

He nodded, smiling broadly. Then he began singing too.

The procession moved freely toward the Winter Palace. Gapon's eyes stared luminously ahead. His cassock grazed the ground as if he floated. The strength of the people felt like spring bursting through winter's ice. The crowd surged as the gates of the palace came into view.

"My God, I can't believe we've actually made it!" Irina cried.

Everyone stopped, the back of the march pressing breathlessly up against the front. Time seemed framed as in a photograph: the enormous green-and-white palace of the Czar was ringed by colorfully dressed squadrons of soldiers on sleek, shining horses. Brass buttons shone. Sabers sparkled in the sun. People gasped, awed, and crossed themselves.

"The Czar is our father! He shall hear us at last!" cried a man.

"To the Czar! To the Czar!" cried the people joyously. Icons, banners, portraits of the Czar and the Czarina bobbed.

A squadron of Life Grenadiers broke from the formation and charged from the gates of the palace like an army of gods. It was magnificent. Horse nostrils flared; manes flowed; hooves thundered as the soldiers spurred on their mounts. The people were delighted, as if the show were for them, and then horror set in, sweeping through the crowd in a paralysis. The horses were driving toward them. The gods were attacking.

"Father!" Irina shrieked as a line of cavalry split the march in two, tearing her from Gapon.

A regiment of foot soldiers appeared by a nearby bridge. The soldiers raised their rifles and took aim.

Voices broke out in song again. "Save Us, O Lord, Thy People." Many joined hands and tried to close ranks again.

A bugle sounded.

Gun bursts exploded.

People fell, bloodied, silent.

"What are you doing? How can you fire on a holy pilgrimage and the portrait of the Czar?" a policeman screamed. A moment later, his body jerked in the air and he collapsed, a bullet through his head.

There was a horrible relentlessness to the soldiers' gun volleys. They came and came like machines, pressing the people. Boom. Boom. Boom. The soldiers' faces were expressionless, their eyes void. People pleaded with them to stop. Boom. Boom. Boom. Again and again. The old men carrying the portraits of the Czar and Czarina died. The young boys carrying the holy torches died. The old women carrying the icons died. The wounded moaned and cried.

Irina watched as the body of Sinelovsky's wife arched suddenly; blood gushed from her mouth and she fell backward, her legs bent grotesquely. Then Irina saw Gapon's gilt cross shoot into the air. She ran, but a horse careened by her, knocking her to the ground, and as she fell, she saw Gapon's golden vestments crumple. His fur-edged hat rolled.

"Gapon's shot!" Irina screamed as Misha grabbed her and dragged her from the path of the storming horses. When they looked again, there was no sign of Gapon other than the fur-edged hat a soldier carried like a trophy on the tip of his saber.

The march on Vasilievsky Island had gone barely three blocks when it was met by the line of Finnish Life Guards standing with sabers drawn. Behind them were soldiers with rifles.

"Disperse back to where you came or be shot!" an officer called.

Anna cringed beside Zhenya. "They wouldn't shoot un-armed people, Mother."

"Hush," Zhenya warned, and wrapped a protective arm about her.

The portly man who'd first stood on the crate stepped forward from the front line of marchers waving a white handkerchief. "Brother!" he called to the officer. "I am a deputy of the people. There is no need to shoot. We come in peace."

"Disperse or be shot." the officer repeated.

"Soldiers, do not shoot your own!" the deputy called bravely.

A line of infantry climbed up from behind the embankment of the river with rifles raised and pointed.

Five more men came forth from the marchers, waving white handkerchiefs. "We come in peace! We are all brothers!" they cried. "Think of your own mothers and sisters and wives who sit home waiting for you."

"I tell you once more, disperse or be shot!"

The deputies of the people tore open their coats and bared their chests. "We are your brothers. You will not fire on your brothers!"

The officer raised his arm and lowered it.

Gunshots ripped the stilled air.

The deputies fell.

The officer raised and lowered his arm again. More shots rang out. People ran screaming. Horses charged. The crowd tore Anna from Zhenya and Matryona. Anna turned to see a soldier on horseback charging her. She ducked just as a saber sliced the air inches from her face. Her mouth opened but no sound came out. Someone pushed her. She tripped and slipped in a pool of blood staining the snow. A strong hand pulled her to her feet. She looked up to see Maxim Kashirin. He was alone.

"Where's your family?" Anna screamed.

"Lost!" he cried, and his face contorted.

"We must find them." They began running, looking as they ran. Bullets whistled. People fell. Suddenly Maxim dropped hold of Anna's hand and a terrible sound tore from him. Anna looked, to see Natalya Kashirin's limp body lying almost upright against a parked carriage. Her head fell limply on her chest. The two little boys were pulling at her, crying, "Mama, Mama!" The baby had rolled under the carriage and was screaming.

Maxim dove for his wife and grabbed her, shaking her as if he could bring her back to life.

Anna grabbed the boys and dragged them under the carriage, throwing herself on the infant. When she looked, a soldier on horseback was charging Maxim from behind. "Maxim Igorovich!" she screamed. "Look out!"

The little boys huddled against her in horror. Maxim turned and fell backward, letting go of his wife's body as he rolled to safety under the carriage. The soldier charged on, his horse trampling Natalya Kashirin. Anna and Maxim lay trembling under the carriage, the boys and the infant crushed between them.

Alexei never reached Vasilievsky Island, nor did he find Gapon's contingent, but he met up with the group marching up Nevsky Prospect. It was an odd mixture of workers and well-dressed strollers out on a fine Sunday afternoon. Some of the shops were open, hoping to pick up needed business from the crowds. Detachments of Cossacks wandered unobtrusively up and down the avenue. The occasional volleys of gunfire seemed far away.

The further along Nevsky Prospect he walked, the more unified the crowd became, until he found himself in the middle of a solemn contingent heading toward the end of Nevsky Prospect and the Winter Palace. Some carried banners, others white flags and still others marched with icons and portraits of the Czar and Czarina. Nervousness edged the crowd. The air was too still.

The Admiralty had just come into sight when a distraught worker began racing among the marchers crying, "Gapon is dead! Our holy Father has been murdered!" His words seemed to burst open a dam; hands flew amid excited talk; rumors raced: fifty men, women and children had been gunned down on the Troitsky Bridge, countless more wounded. Hundreds were dead on Vasilievsky Island. Thousands wounded. The snow on Vyborg ran red with the people's blood. Untrue! Untrue! No citizens had fallen, only a handful of hooligans opposing the march had been shot, and them deserving death. The Czar was standing on the balcony overlooking the Palace Square, smiling as he eagerly awaited the arrival of the holy pilgrimage.

The crowd swelled; footsteps pounded, pumping like heartbeats. Faces were animated. An irrepressible energy hurtled the marchers toward the gleaming Admiralty and the Winter Palace beyond. Many linked arms, workers with fine ladies and gentlemen. The city was bathed in the brilliant winter sun. Harmony and brotherhood, heaven on earth beckoned from the horizon. "To the Czar! To the Czar! The Czar and Father Gapon await us!"

The white and green of the Winter Palace came into view. All was peaceful. Children played in the nearby Alexander Gardens. Girls and boys ice-skated on the pond. Tea sellers were doing a bustling business as the curious filled the gardens to watch the handsome detachments of troops in their colorful, trim uniforms.

The march surged toward the Palace Square.

Two lines of Preobrazhensky Guards broke neatly from formation inside the square and marched outside, re-forming across from the Alexander Gardens.

The scene seemed a still life. Everything was so hushed.

A burst of childish laughter tickled the air.

The first line of Preobrazhensky Guards fell to one knee as if displaying their sharpness.

People seemed happy and perplexed at the same moment.

A bugle sounded. The Preobrazhensky Guards lifted their rifles.

A ripple of nervousness jolted marchers' shoulders against shoulders.

The bugle sounded again.

"Aim!" came the thundering voice of the colonel.

The first line of the Preobrazhensky Guards took aim away from the marchers and toward the Alexander Gardens. Bullets flew. Several skaters' bodies arched, then crumpled, their blood streaming onto the ice.

Expressions froze in confusion and horror. Hands reached for the heavens. Thousands made the sign of the cross. Small children, oblivious of the horror about them, laughed playfully as adults grabbed them.

The soldiers swerved like well-rehearsed dancers and took aim at the crowd before the Admiralty.

The bugle sounded.

More bullets. More dead and dying.

The soldiers pointed their guns at the Palace Bridge.

The bugle sounded.

More dead and dying.

The soldiers turned toward the General Staff Arch.

The bugle sounded.

Those who could, were running, tripping over fallen bodies.

The bugle sounded.

Alexei was mesmerized by the bloodletting. He stood as bodies pushed past him. He stumbled a few steps and a woman beside him fell against him. Her blood spurted on his face. He pushed her off and tried to keep her from falling at the same time. The back of her head seemed to dissolve in his hand. Nauseated, he pulled his hand away and gagged. She crumpled to the snow. His legs wouldn't hold him, and as he fell, his knees knocked the body of a little girl. She lay flat on her back, her eyes staring vacantly. Alexei lifted her gingerly. The back of her coat was saturated with blood. He pressed the fragile little body to him, and a woman attacked him, screaming, "My God, my God, my baby!"

Alexei tried to help her, but she beat him off, tearing the child from him as she did. Then she stood, burying her face against the child's, kissing it as she sobbed.

"Come." He tried to pull her to safety.

"My baby! My baby!" she wailed until the cut of a bullet silenced her and she fell. The child spilled from her arms and rolled in the snow.

Alexei bent, desperate to save her once more, but this time when he tried to lift her, she was too heavy. Finally he stood, his hand gloved with blood. The soldiers were taking aim once more.

"What's the matter with you, man!" Someone grabbed Alexei's arm. "You want to get yourself killed or what?"

CHAPTER FORTY

Alexei walked, vaguely aware of passing stunned, pale faces, vaguely aware of a silence, like life without air. A distant scream clawed through him. The day was hurtled into premature night; snow fell furiously, thick, heavy wet flakes to blanket the blood, the bodies, the madness. It was beyond madness. It was evil, a cesspool of nightmares. He paused to catch his breath. His eyes closed and he saw men kneel like machines, take aim, fire, kneel, take aim, fire. Bodies piled in garbage heaps spurting bright blood from eyes, heads, arms and chests, broken like the limbs of poor dead animals, debris littering the snow. He drew a breath and pressed his fists into his eyes and crushed the image into clotted mold.

"Murderers," he heard someone growl, and looked to find a short middle-aged man in a fine overcoat and fur hat standing next to him and staring across the canal at the shadows of Cossacks patrolling with guns and swords drawn.

"Murderers!" the man bellowed, and began to run toward a bridge.

A Cossack swerved and leveled his gun.

Alexei tackled the middle-aged man to the ground.

A bullet rang out.

The man struggled to break away, then collapsed against Alexei and started to cry like a desperate child. He grasped Alexei and kneaded his arms. "What's happening to us? Russian killing Russian. What's happening?"

Afraid to let the man go, afraid to stand, afraid to stay a target in the middle of the street, Alexei backed up into an alley, dragging the sobbing man with him through the snow.

"I was at the Winter Palace," the man said.

"Yes, me too."

"Did you lose anyone?"

"No."

"A neighbor, I was with a neighbor and now he's dead. We were just out walking and now he's dead. Why? Can you answer me that?"

Alexei leaned back against the building. He had no answer. He was very tired. He cradled the man in the fur hat in his arms.

"Come, wake up or we'll freeze to death here."

Alexei opened his eyes, surprised to find he'd been asleep. Night sucked round them like a tomb. The man was standing. Alexei was shivering.

"I'm Pavel Igorovich, accountant." The man held out his hand and helped Alexei to his feet. "There's a pub open a few blocks over. I saw candles lighting it up before. Will you let me buy you a drink? It's the least I can do for your saving my life."

They drank for a while, but talked little. Words withered in the empty hush of the bar.

"Do you know the time?" Alexei finally asked. He was thinking about Yermolov and the Montenegrina Palace. He was thinking he had to reach Dmitri and make Yermolov pay.

Pavel Igorovich took out a gold watch. "Ten past five."

"I must be going."

"In what direction?"

"Vasilievsky Island."

"I hear it's still closed off," said the barman. "The troops are letting no one on or off. There was horrible rioting, telegraph poles pulled down, a gun shop broken into. Many died,

I heard, many. They're not even letting the workers take their dead from the streets.''

"Pigs." Pavel Igorovich spat.

"I must be going," Alexei said, shook Pavel's hand and started to leave.

"Brother!" the barkeep called. "I heard the only way to get to Vasilievsky Island is across the ice. Your best bet is far down past the Nikolaevsky Bridge."

"Thank you, brother." Alexei tipped his hat.

Outside the wind cut like stalagmites and howled like a wounded wolf crawling in the forest. There were no streetlights, no moonlight. The snow coated death in anonymity. Alexei made his way slowly to the river, keeping close to the buildings. Cossacks patrolled the streets, lighting their way with lamps. Bands of workers roamed, hurtling wood, rocks, bricks, whatever they could find at the soldiers before vanishing into the night. Stores were looted. Single shots rang out. Curses. Moans. Wails. Alexei passed his palace, or what he thought was his palace. Without lights, it was hard to tell. He saw soldiers encamped at the bridges, their shadows looming, their guns like cannon against the glow of bonfires and torches. Alexei thought if he had a gun, he could pick them off, one by one. He raised a hand and pointed a finger, pulled an imaginary trigger. The shadows melted like molten lead. Bang, bang. He owned no gun. He would buy one tomorrow.

He walked until he found a dark strip along the embankment, unmarked by torches. He waited, listened. There were no signs of soldiers. He climbed up and over the railing and slid down to the frozen river. The new snow reached the middle of his calf. He walked bent in the darkness across the ice.

"Who goes there?" the edgy voice of a young soldier demanded. "Step forward or I'll shoot!"

Alexei pressed himself against the riverbank.

A shot rang out.

"Anything?" another soldier called.

"Don't see or hear nothing."

"Forget it. It was probably the wind or a dog."

Alexei waited. The soldiers' voices grew distant. He crept up the riverbank and waited until the silence was complete; then he hurtled himself over the railings and began to run. The university buildings were only a few hundred yards away.

"Halt! Who goes there? Halt or we'll shoot!" A bullet rang out.

Alexei pressed against the wall of a building and waited,

trying to control the rasping of his breath. He thought he heard a woman crying softly. He listened. The cries were small, pitiful. He crawled toward the sound.

"Don't shoot, please don't shoot!" the woman pleaded in terror.

"I'm not a soldier. I swear." He knocked into what felt like a half-frozen body lying on the ground. "Where are you?" he whispered, unable to see anything in the blackness.

The woman's breath rattled.

"Please, I won't hurt you. Maybe I can help."

"He's dead. My husband. The soldiers say I can't take him. They say we must leave our dead to the dogs. Help me, please!" The woman was close.

He could feel her breath on his face. "What can I do?"

"There's a building where they're tending to the wounded. It's got a large ice cellar. We were told if we could, we should bring our dead there. Tomorrow or the next day there'll be a procession of coffins. Yes, that's what they say." Her voice turned dull, apathetic; her fingers were clawing at his arm.

"Of course."

"Praise God, praise God!"

Alexei fell in front of him. "Is this your husband?"

"Yes."

He lifted the man, groaning under the weight. Alive the man would have been a load; dead he was a block of stone. "You're sure you know the way?"

"Yes." The woman slipped her arm through his, guiding him for what seemed hours.

"I can't go much further without a rest."

"We're almost there."

"Who goes there?" came a voice from the dark, and a gun cocked.

"Tamara Shulgina. I have the body of my husband, Eugene." Her voice trembled. "I was told to bring him here."

"You carry a dead man, woman?"

"No, a friend carries him."

"What is your name, friend?"

"Yakov Nuvel. I'm a doorman."

"Go on then, deposit the body." The man rapped three times on a door behind him and it opened. From inside, the hum of prayer and the wail of mourning buzzed and seethed.

"Another dead one saved," said the man, and he urged Alexei and the woman inside.

A small coal stove burned and black figures swayed rhythmically in the candlelight. An old woman, her face flattened with sagging skin, neared them, holding the candle first to

Alexei's face and then to the woman's. "Tamara Shulgina! Not your Eugene?"

The woman's tears flowed unchecked.

Two men took the body from Alexei.

"My name is Inessa Grigorievna," said the old woman. "Come have some tea, a little vodka. We thank you for your concern. Come, eat, say a prayer for the dead."

"Thank you, Inessa Grigorievna, but I must be going. If someone could only point me in the right direction. I'm going to—"

"Alexei!" a voice rang out, and a woman came running to him. "Alexei!"

"Anna, my God, is that you?"

"You know each other?" Inessa Grigorievna asked.

"This is my husband."

"Alexei Yakovlevich!" Inessa Grigorievna exclaimed, and crossed herself.

The room fell silent.

"Sonya Mikhailovna, go upstairs, go get the blessed mother of Alexei Yakovlevich. Hurry, girl. Run!"

The three of them sat in a dark corner, so dark they could barely see each other's faces. Alexei held both Anna's and his mother's hands. "So long as you're safe," he assured. "I saw too much horror today. All that matters is that you're safe." He kissed first his mother's hand and then Anna's.

"You're not angry we came?"

"I suppose when I think about it, I will understand. Or you, Mama, will make me understand. Besides, who knows if you're any safer in Peterhof anymore? With all that happened today, who knows who is safe anymore?"

"How did you get here, Alexei?" Zhenya asked.

"I was on my way to see Yuri Nikolaievich. I must reach him, and I found a woman trying to move her dead husband. I carried him here for her."

Zhenya crossed herself. "It was God's wish that you find us, Alexei."

"You can't leave now, Alexei," Anna pleaded. "I would die with fear. They say the soldiers shoot anything that moves."

"I'll be careful. I made my away across the river in one piece. I'll come back and get you, Anna, and Mama and Matryona. I think it's safer if we go home under the cover of night. It's not far across the river."

"Take Anna, Alexei. Matryona and I are staying here.

There are many wounded upstairs, and only one doctor. I know how to tend to sick people. I'm going to stay here.''

"But, Mama—"

"There is no discussion, Alexei. I haven't felt so useful in years. Besides, these are my people. I understand them. Go to Yuri Nikolaievich if you must, but take Anna with you. You may not find your way back here in the night. It will be easier crossing the river without two old women like Matryona and myself.'' She paused a moment, then grasped Alexei's hand and pulled him toward her. "I heard rumors,'' she said slowly. "Some say the priest is dead.''

Yuri Dobrinsky's house was dark, like every other house on Vasilievsky Island, and without sign of life. Alexei tried the doors. They were locked. The windows were nailed shut against the winter.

"I can get you inside if you want,'' the worker who guided them offered.

"Thank you, but there's no point,'' Alexei assured him. "I should have realized my friend wouldn't be here.''

The guide led them back through the maze of blackened streets and down to the embankment far from the soldiers' torches. "You and your wife will be safe crossing here, Alexei Yakovlevich.''

"Thank you. I owe you. Can I—''

"No, no money, please. Your mother is an angel. That is enough. God be with you, brother,'' the worker said, and he was gone.

Alexei thought to take Anna home and then go to Ryabushinsky's. Perhaps Yuri was there, and Misha too, but he could not leave Anna once they were home. Her nearness filled the hollowness. They talked softly; her breath heated the skin of his face; she quivered with fragility; if he let her go, she would crumble and fall. They talked of death and mangled limbs. She talked obsessively, insistently, and clung to him, squeezing his hand, nibbling on his finger. Her eyes opened like screaming mouths, luminous in the low light, chained in terror. He held her, stroked her, coaxed her from the thorny thickets of her mind with meaningless assurances of safety and peace, and they made desperate love. Each moment seemed the last; he tried to imprint her scent, her feel, the silky folds of warmth surrounding him before time closed its fist. Ecstasy spun into exhaustion; his body heaved against her and he cried, "I don't know, I don't know . . .''

She cradled him.

He remembered the woman falling on her dead child, and he grew still. "It could have been you," he said soberly. "Don't die, Anna. Promise me you won't let anything take you from me."

"I promise, my darling." She kissed him. "I'd never leave you. It's you who leave me."

"Never again, on my life. We'll always be together. You're my soul, Anna, my breath."

"Can we leave Petersburg, Alexei? Please. Take me away, far away. I'm not like your mother or Misha or Irina. I'm not a fighter."

"Where shall we go?"

"Anyplace, so long as there is no shooting."

"Vienna, Paris, London, New York."

"Yes, New York." She smiled. "I'd like to see America."

"Then you shall, my love." He took her hands and held them to his lips. "By tomorrow night we'll be out of Russia. I promise."

"Master, Master!" There was an urgent rapping on the door.

"What is it, Yashka?" Alexei sat up in bed. Daylight was slinking through the shutters.

Without warning, the door was kicked in and two large armed soldiers of the Okhrana pushed past the quivering valet. "Alexei Yakovlevich Kalinin!" the taller of the two demanded.

"Yes."

"You're under arrest."

Anna woke and pulled the blankets to her neck, swallowing a shriek.

Alexei wrapped his arm about her. "By whose order?" he demanded.

"The Czar. I have the arrest order here." The soldier shoved it at the valet, who carried it to Alexei, holding his lamp so Alexei and Anna could read.

Alexei was charged with subversive activities against the throne. Below the signature of the Czar was the signature of Leonti Yurievich Yermolov.

"Can you wait outside while I dress and say good-bye to my wife?"

"Ten minutes, Kalinin, that's all."

"You can't go, Alexei, I won't let them take you. You haven't done anything!" Anna's eyes were wild. She was clutching him.

He held her, allowing himself a moment to drift on the warmth of her skin. He held his face against her hair and felt ravenous. "Listen to me, Anna," he began softly, calmly, even matter-of-factly. "I'll need you to do something for me. It's very, very important. Only you can do it. You were so brave yesterday. I need you to be just as brave today. All right?"

She nodded, swallowing as she wiped her tears.

"You have to find Yuri Nikolaievich. First I want you to go to Ryabushinsky's house. Ask for Charlotte. Is that clear? When you're alone, tell her you need to see Dmitri Mayakovsky. Yuri Nikolaievich is also known as Dmitri Mayakovsky."

"I don't understand!" She panicked.

"It's very simple, Anna, my love." He smiled reassuringly. "Yuri goes under two names, and with each name, he lives a different life. Now, if you find Charlotte, tell her you must see Dmitri Mayakovsky. Tell her it's very, very important. Perhaps Yuri will be there, at Charlotte's, and if he's not there, perhaps Misha or Irina will be."

"Misha and Irina?" she echoed.

"Do you have that so far? Whom are you going to ask for?"

"Dmitri Mayakovsky."

"Good. Now, this is the message. Tell him I've been arrested by the Okhrana. Tell him Yermolov is living at the Countess Montenegrina's Palace. This is very important. You're to tell only Misha, Irina, or Yuri Nikolaievich what I told you. Yermolov is living at the Countess Montenegrina's Palace. Say it, Anna."

"Yermolov is living at the Countess Montenegrina's Palace."

"Good. And one more thing. Tell them the information is from the Grand Duke Nikolai Nikolaievich via Count Bobrinsky."

She nodded, wondering if she could remember so many names, so much confusion. "Oh, Alexei . . ." Her lips trembled.

There was a harsh knocking at the door. "Five minutes, Kalinin!" the soldier called.

"Hush now, my darling. Hush." He rocked her. "It will all be over soon. You'll see. We'll be together again. Now we must get dressed. You must be brave in front of the soldiers. You will be brave."

"Yes." She nodded and wiped her tears. "And I'll find Yuri Nikolaievich, I promise. I'll get him the message."

"That's my girl." He stroked her face a moment longer, his eyes drinking her like a bee drinks nectar. "You are so beautiful. I love you so very much."

"I love you."

"Can you forgive me—?"

"Hush." She covered his mouth. "There's nothing to forgive."

"Three minutes, Kalinin!" came the soldier's voice.

Anna stood at the door and watched Alexei disappear into the soldiers' carriage. She watched the carriage pull away down the wide boulevard, empty except for the soldiers. She stared at the soldiers patrolling the embankment. Their bonfires danced against the raw bleakness of the day. A fog was rolling in, blotting out the other side of the river. She thought of Zhenya and Matryona and stood listening for the voices from Vasilievsky Island.

"Madame," Yashka, the valet, broke her reverie. "Can I get you anything? Anything at all?"

"My coat, Yashka, and my hat and muff. The ones I wore yesterday. And the warmest boots you can find."

Anna went to Ryabushinsky's house, but the doors were locked tight. She banged. There was no answer, not even from a servant. She turned and started back down the drive, and saw two soldiers with guns watching her.

"Looking for someone, miss?"

"Yes, Monsieur Ryabushinsky and his daughter."

The soldier chuckled. "Yes, so is the Czar. I'd be on my way if I was you, miss. The Ryabushinskys aren't ones to be partying with anymore. And the streets aren't safe for one like yourself, miss."

"What have the Ryabushinskys done?" she questioned innocently.

"Subversives."

"No, that's impossible! I've known the Ryabushinskys all my life. They give the grandest balls."

"Can't tell about no one today, not after yesterday, miss."

"Oh, it was awful, wasn't it? I never saw such rowdiness. And imagine, a ragged priest demanding an audience with our beloved Czar! The gall of the man. Well, I don't blame the Czar for what he did. Those workers deserved what they got, I'd say."

"Good to hear one like you," the soldier replied. "Seems all of Petersburg hates us today."

"Not all, I warrant. But I tell you, I live with my uncle on Vasilievsky Island. I was out for a stroll yesterday, it was such a lovely day, and I became quite stranded on this side. And, dear me . . ." She glanced past the soldiers to the embankment. "It still looks as if they're not letting anyone in

or out of Vasilievsky Island. My uncle's a professor in the
Academy of Economics. We live near the university on Les-
kov Street. I stayed with my friend Anna Petrovna Kalinina
last night, and oh, it was awful. Her husband was arrested
this morning, and she's all in hysterics. Subversion too. God
knows I don't want to be found with a subversive. I only want
to be home with my dear Uncle Yuri. He must be mad with
worry that I'm dead. Which is why I went to the Ryabushinskys', to see if they could help me get home. Is there anything you might do to help me?'' She smiled sweetly.

"I don't know, what do you think, Samsonov?'' the soldier
asked his comrade.

"We can speak to the sergeant.''

"I only need to get across the bridge.''

"Come.'' The first soldier took her arm.

Anna was surprised to find so many people milling about
the university district. They were mostly students who had
crossed the river under cover of night. They stood in groups
about their own bonfires, and talked of fighting back. Some
carried guns, sabers, sticks, and chains. They eyed the troops,
who eyed them in an uneasy truce. They talked of joining the
workers and making Vasilievsky Island a fighting commune.

Anna moved from group to group, stopping every so often
to ask about Misha and Irina, but no one had heard of them.
She was just leaving the university when she heard footsteps
and turned to see a slight, fair young man hurrying after her.

She started on and glanced over her shoulder to see him
only a few feet away. His face was grim behind its boyishness
and when he was close enough, he roughly grabbed her arm
and pulled her to a stop.

"Why do you want Mikhail Anatolyevich or Irina Ilyanovna?'' he demanded, and twisted her arm until it hurt.
His blue eyes pierced, and she looked away.

She sucked in her breath with the pain and blurted out, "I
have information for them.''

"Tell me your name then.''

"Anna Petrovna Kalinina.''

"Alexei Yakovlevich's wife? What are you doing here?''

"I told you, I've a message.''

"From whom?''

"Alexei Yakovlevich.''

"Why did he send you?''

She forced herself to meet the young man's gaze. "Alexei
Yakovlevich was arrested for subversion this morning.''

"My God.'' His hand slipped off her arm.

The pressure of the release made her groan.

"I'm sorry if I hurt you. One can trust no one these days." He stood at attention and bowed ever so slightly. "My name is Savva Safanov. I'm a comrade of Misha and Irina's. If you like, I can take you to them."

CHAPTER FORTY-ONE

Savva kept looking over his shoulder to see if they were being followed. They ducked into alleyways and wandered up and around streets. Anna wondered how he knew where he was going. All the streets and houses seemed alike. Red-faced, runny-nosed, ragged children played happily in the snow as if the horror of yesterday had never happened. Men and women stood about bonfires arguing hotly. Father Gapon's name flew like summer's dust.

"Is he dead?" Anna asked Savva as she hurried to keep up with his strides. "Father Gapon, I mean."

"At first they thought he was, but last I heard he's staying with the writer Gorky, of all people. At least that's the rumor. Some say the priest spoke before the Free Economic Society last night, calling for armed revolution."

"I see." Anna was almost running to keep up with Savva's strides; she stopped abruptly when two men emerged from an alleyway carrying a simple wooden coffin. Then two more appeared and two more. Anna watched the procession. Clearly the coffins were empty, for the men carried them easily.

"Later, can you bring me back here?" Anna asked, hurrying to catch up with Savva. "I think Alexei's mother must be around here, and Matryona."

"Yes, yes."

The run-down workers' district turned into slums which grew more desolate as the blocks passed. Wind wailed through windowless buildings and whipped the snow off mounds of frozen garbage, spreading it like shifting sand dunes against buildings and walls and inside burned-out shacks.

"Is it much further?" Anna was gasping for breath. Her

toes were so numb she could scarcely feel them. She was exhausted.

Without answering, he held up his arm to brake her. "Wait here," he snapped, and disappeared down an alley.

She stood on the empty street corner, her hands clasped, her eyes tearing from the cold. The poverty and gloom howled as oppressively as the wind. Dear God, what if this boy, Savva, had simply left her? She waited, rubbing her arms and jumping up and down as she peered over her shoulder and peeked down the alleyway. She bit her lip to hold back the tears. Somebody, anybody, might come and attack her, kill her, then she could never get her message to Yuri Nikolaievich and no one would ever know that Alexei had been arrested.

A hand touched her and a fearful scream escaped; she swerved to find Irina standing behind her. "Oh, God!" Anna gasped, suddenly not certain the woman was Irina. The smile was hers, the shape of the body, but the clothes were so ragged and there was a horrible scabbed gash on her nose. The gash was deep, as if the nose had been cut clear through; the cheek was swollen, the skin discolored. Anna gaped at the cut on the woman's nose and thought she might vomit.

"Don't you know who I am?"

"Irina! What happened to you?" Anna gritted her teeth, thinking each step Irina took must cause her nose to hurt fearfully. "Oh, Irina, what happened to your face?"

"It's nothing. It will heal. Come inside. Misha's here, and everyone. Savva said Alexei's been arrested . . ."

"Yes, that's why I've come. He gave me a message. He . . . he said I can give it only to you or Misha or Dmitri Mayakovsky, who he told me is also Yuri Nikolaievich Dobrinsky." Now that she was finally with Irina, the terror which she'd been holding in since the soldiers first walked into her bedroom threatened to spill over. She could feel hysteria edging into her voice, and she was clawing at Irina's arm.

"Come, it's too cold here to talk."

They made their way through a dark, half-burnt building, climbing over rubble and garbage and then up a stairway that had lost its railing. The slime-covered walls were frozen in streaks. Water dripped. Rats scurried. "Wait . . ." Anna begged, afraid she could not breathe.

"We're almost there," Irina urged. "I know you can't tell it from the entrance, but it's quite nice inside. A little work and it could be homey. Be careful here, you have to bend or you'll knock your head."

They had to practically crawl the next few feet, and then

the ceiling rose again to a hallway. They passed the first door, the second. Irina knocked two times, paused, and knocked twice again. The door opened and Misha welcomed them.

"Anna." He embraced her, kissing each cheek.

Her eyes scanned the miserable room lit by a single oil lamp, and she wondered if Irina were going mad—this place could never be "homey." The walls were filthy, the floor deeply scarred and stained. There were several chairs and an old leather couch. Miraculously, a samovar was bubbling and a small coal stove heated the place comfortably. Rifles lay against a wall, and a tall, dark, handsome young man with a beard was cleaning a handgun. Anna scanned the many faces, recognizing the boy, Savva, Olga Fyodorovna, and Charlotte Alexandrovna, who, like Irina, was wearing ragged working-women's clothes.

Olga rose and Anna hurried to greet her. Then Irina introduced her to the others, but the names flew so fast, she could not keep track of them.

"Savva said Uncle Alexei was arrested," Misha began as he ushered Anna to a seat near the stove.

"Yes, early this morning. We were sleeping and the soldiers burst into our room. The Czar himself ordered Alexei's arrest."

"For what?" Misha asked.

"Subversion."

"Did they mention any other names? Or say where he was being taken?" Olga asked.

Anna shook her head and began to unlace her boots. She needed to thaw her feet; more, she needed to hide her face. Tears kept threatening to overwhelm her. If only she were alone with Irina, or even Misha and Olga. It wouldn't do to cry in front of the others, these blank, hard faces with their guns. She pressed her forehead a moment, hoping when she looked again, she'd be in bed with Alexei, the last hours a miserable dream.

"Anna, are you all right?" Irina's voice was near; her hand was rubbing Anna's back reassuringly.

"Yes." She nodded, slipping off one boot and starting on the other. "There was another name on the arrest order. They showed it to us. A man named Yermolov."

"Shit!" muttered the young man cleaning the gun. "Dammit to hell!" He pounded his fist. "It's happened, then."

His words attacked Anna like bullets. She looked imploringly at Irina. "I . . . I have to talk to you alone. Please."

"Of course. Come." She led Anna to a small back room.

"The message Alexei gave me . . ." She was shaking away from the warmth of the stove. She was terrified.

"It's all right, Anna. I promise." Irina embraced her. "There's nothing to be frightened of. You're all right now."

"I'm frightened for Alexei. Oh, Irina, it was terrible. What if I never see him again?"

Irina held her and soothed her, and when Anna had calmed down, Irina asked quietly, "Now tell me the message from Alexei. You said it was important."

"Yes." Anna sniffled and reached inside her pocket for a handkerchief. "Alexei said to tell you this—that Yermolov is staying in the palace of the Countess Montenegrina. He said the message is from the Grand Duke Nikolai Nikolaievich through Count Bobrinsky."

It was early on the morning of Friday, January 14, four days after Alexei had been arrested. Anna was sleeping next to Zhenya Kirilovna on a thin straw mattress in the flat of the old woman Inessa Grigorievna when a gentle nudging awakened her. Anna looked up to see Inessa Grigorievna.

"What is it?" Zhenya stirred.

"Your grandson is here, Zhenya Kirilovna."

Zhenya got up before Anna and hurried into the other room. "What's so urgent that you wake us in the middle of the night?" she demanded, kissing Misha on both cheeks.

"Anna's needed. Dmitri Andreievich."

"What about me? I'll come."

"No, Grandma, just Anna," Misha assured her.

"You think I'm too old to carry a gun!"

"Never." He chuckled and kissed her, nodding to Anna as she walked into the room. "But I think you're too old to walk as far as we need to walk in the dark."

"I could surprise you." Zhenya hugged him and took his hand. She could not stop touching him when they were together. "You'll be careful, won't you, my heart?"

"I always am."

"Any news of Alexei?"

"No."

"Come, let's take a minute and pray." She tugged at Misha.

"Grandma, Dmitri Andreievich is waiting."

"So is God, right, Inessa Grigorievna?"

The old woman nodded. "Pray with your grandmother, Mikhail Anatolyevich. The revolution will never win without God. And don't forget that."

"A short prayer only, Grandma."

"Oh, yes." Zhenya slipped one arm through Anna's and

the other through Misha's and led them to the corner with the icon.

Inessa Grigorievna lit the candles.

Misha took Anna through the increasingly familiar back streets of Vasilievsky Island to a fourth-floor flat about ten blocks from Inessa Grigorievna's. Anna had never been there before; she'd met with Dmitri twice in the past few days, but never in the same place. The room was bare except for a mattress and a small table where Irina and Dmitri were waiting, drinking tea. An oil lamp shed soft light on their faces, muting Irina's scar and making Dmitri seem less foreboding. She hadn't liked him the few times he'd been introduced to her as Yuri Dobrinsky. She liked him less as the revered leader of a band of terrorists.

"Welcome, Anna Petrovna." Dmitri stood when she walked in. "I would offer to take your coat, but I think you would do well to keep it on in here. A cup of tea, though." He held the chair for her.

"Thank you," she murmured, smiling uncertainly to Irina, who leaned to kiss her.

"Your skin is like ice." Irina held a cup of tea to Anna's frozen cheeks. Anna looked more haggard than usual. Her eyes were bloodshot with lack of sleep. "Here, drink, you'll feel better."

When the tea was poured and Misha was sitting down, Dmitri leaned back in his chair and lit a cigarette. Inhaling slowly, he tipped forward the chair and pressed toward Anna. "Russia, the revolution, cannot thank you enough for the information you have brought us about Yermolov, Anna Petrovna."

She nodded. All that seemed so long ago.

"We've used your information well. Yermolov will not live to see the setting sun."

His words jolted her.

"You look frightened, Anna Petrovna."

"I'm not used to thinking about killing men, Dmitri Andreievich."

He smiled sympathetically. "There is no man in Russia more deserving of death than Leonti Yurievich Yermolov, I assure you. He's a very, very evil man, responsible not only for Alexei's arrest but also for scores of others. Worse, he's ordered countless fighters for freedom tortured, even hanged. Peasants and Jews in particular he likes to hang." He reached out and touched her hand reassuringly.

"I can't help but worry about Alexei." She stared away

from Dmitri down at a stain on the table. "It terrifies me to think he might be tortured. Have you seen him, then?"

"No. I'm afraid not. Perhaps, though, with your help we can free him."

"Free Alexei!" Her eyes opened wide. "What can I do?"

Dmitri leaned back in his chair. "Do you know what we're about, Anna—Misha, Irina, myself and the other comrades?"

"Yes, Irina's told me."

"Good. Can you tell me, just so I'm certain there are no misunderstandings. We can't afford to have misunderstandings now."

"You're terrorists."

"I sense a note of disapproval. But you do believe in the revolution?"

"I wasn't sure until Sunday. Now I know it's the only way." She spoke softly.

"Yes, like so many. Brutality has one of two effects. It blinds seeing men or opens blind men's eyes. Do you know there are many kinds of revolutionaries, Anna? Some fight with guns, others with words. Some, like Alexei's mother, support others. We all have a job to do. No one can succeed without the other. We're all part of a whole, you not the least of us, I assure you."

Anna nodded, feeling complimented.

"We need your help, Anna." Dmitri's voice was melodic. His eyes seemed suddenly kind. "We need you to help draw Yermolov out."

"What can I do?"

"What I tell you can go no further than this room, Anna. We trust you, do you understand? Your decision to help us is your own, but you must swear to keep what we tell you confidential, even from Zhenya Kirilovna."

Her gaze shifted to Irina, who nodded slightly. "All right," Anna said.

"We've been watching Yermolov ever since you gave us the information on the Montenegrina Palace. He travels in triplicate. Whenever he leaves or arrives at the Montenegrina Palace, two other men who have the same physique as Yermolov, who dress exactly in his image, drive in a carriage exactly the same as his, leave in intervals of five minutes. There's no telling who the real Yermolov is."

"Why would he do that?"

"There have been many attempts on his life over the years," Misha explained.

"We ourselves tried to kill him once. That's why we came to the Crimea," Irina went on.

"Anna, we already know what a very brave and clever young woman you are," Dmitri went on. "Irina told me how you escaped from an unacceptable marriage and how you survived in the woods for almost a week alone. And then you came from Peterhof to march on Sunday. Although there were many who marched, there were few from your social class, Anna. You survived the mayhem, survived your husband's arrest, managed a little trickery with the soldiers to get you here when few people were allowed on or off the island. You've done all this and remained sound in body and mind. That's brave, Anna Petrovna, very brave."

She couldn't help smiling. She'd never viewed herself in such a perspective.

"We need your bravery again—and your cunning. There's nothing violent you need to do, I promise."

"Will it help free Alexei?"

"Alexei and all Russians."

She hesitated only a moment before nodding. "All right."

"Good." Dmitri smiled broadly. He clapped both hands on Anna's. "Now, the plan has been carefully laid out. People have been working on it around the clock for the past four days. We have uniforms, forged documents—everything has been done with the utmost care and to assure maximum safety. It's six A.M. now. Yermolov leaves the house at nine-thirty promptly. That only gives us three and a half hours. Irina, will you and Misha fill Anna Petrovna in on the details? I have to meet with Stepan."

At nine-ten, Kiril stopped the carriage at Marie Square, in front of the monument to Nicholas I, and Irina and Kolya Susanin, the new comrade from Moscow, stepped out into the morning rush. They were dressed in fine coats, hats, and boots. Irina clutched a large pocketbook to her. Inside was one of Stepan's most powerful bombs. She and Kolya would walk slowly to the bridge over the Ekaterininsky Canal, where they would stand ready should Yermolov's carriage make it out of the driveway and speed toward the river. Then Irina would throw her bomb.

At nine-fifteen, Kiril slowed the carriage as it passed by the Montenegrina Palace on Voznesensky Prospect, a quiet street of fine houses not far from the Yusupovs', where Anna had first met Alexei. Anna, Misha, Olga and Charlotte stared out the windows: only one guard stood at the end of the curving driveway, another at the front door.

"They don't want to draw attention to the house, so there aren't many guards in evidence," Misha explained. "But I'll wager there's an army inside the palace,'' he went on. Then he squeezed Anna's arm. "How are you doing?''

"All right, I guess.'' Her heart was beating very fast. Her hands inside her sable muff were stiff with cold.

"Scared?''

"Terrified.''

"So am I.''

"Fear isn't bad,'' Olga said. "It keeps the wits sharp.''

"Oh, look, there's Stepan and Dmitri Andreievich!'' Charlotte exclaimed. "And Stepan's shaved his beard.''

Two soldiers, one young, tall, and slim, another middle-aged and portly, were walking stiffly back and forth across the street.

"I heard Dmitri Andreievich has never actually participated in an action before,'' Charlotte went on.

"Not for a long time,'' Olga advised. "But today is crucial. Nothing can go wrong.''

Dmitri and Stepan vanished from sight as the carriage pulled to a stop. It was Misha's and Charlotte's turn to get out, leaving Anna alone with Olga.

Anna watched as they walked arm in arm, appearing before the world like the finest of couples. Charlotte wore a long red-fox coat and Misha wore one of Alexei's best great-coats. The shoulders were a little broad and Irina had stuffed them with felt padding. Misha's shoulders appeared massive.

"Have you seen Savva and Aksinia?'' Anna asked.

"I believe that's them,'' Olga said as the carriage turned and headed back toward the Montenegrina Palace. She pointed to two street cleaners shoveling snow.

"Where are they carrying their bomb?''

"No doubt they've buried it in the snow for safekeeping. Those things go off with the slightest bump.''

Anna shuddered despite the warmth of her sable coat. She wished her stomach felt better. She stared out the window as the carriage neared the Montenegrina Palace again. A large black carriage was pulling up to the main entrance. Moments later, a tall thin man flanked by two footmen hurried out the door and into the carriage.

"That's the first Yermolov,'' Olga said.

"You're sure it's not the real one?'' Anna asked.

"Very unlikely, my dear.''

Kiril continued down Voznesensky Prospect to the bridge near where Irina and Kolya Susanin were strolling, then turned the carriage for one last time, stopping some fifty feet from the Montenegrina Palace.

"Godspeed, my dear." Olga embraced her, and Anna stepped outside.

"Good luck." Kiril bowed quickly, as a regular coachman would, and climbed back to the driver's seat.

Anna threw back her shoulders and held her head high. She imagined Alexei was watching her, and she smiled. She felt strong. She felt her heart beating. She thought of bursting from the waters of the pond in the Crimea. She remembered how it had felt, breathing in fresh air, shrieking as she did. The shriek from that time swelled in her throat. It seemed a battle cry.

"Begin now," she heard Kiril say, and she started the short walk to the driveway of the Montenegrina Palace just as another carriage, exactly the same as the one which had picked up the first Yermolov, pulled up at the front door. The guard at the end of the driveway was turned, his back to Anna, and she slipped past.

"Stop!" he shouted.

Anna began screaming. "Leonti Yurievich! Please help me, Leonti Yurievich!"

The commotion made one of the horses rear and whinny. The Yermolov who was about to enter the carriage turned and ran back inside, followed by three guards who surrounded him like a wall.

Anna was left, pursued by one lone guard. "Leonti Yurievich! Leonti Yurievich, please!" she pleaded, and threw herself against the carriage, tearing at the door.

The guard roughly grabbed her.

"What's going on here, miss?" he growled in her face. "Who are you, barging in like this?"

"Please, please," she begged, not having to force the tears. They flowed naturally. "Please." She clawed at the guard. "Please take me to Leonti Yurievich. I must speak to him. I must!"

"Calm yourself, miss. No Leonti Yurievich lives here."

"But this is the Montenegrina Palace, he must be here. Leonti Yurievich Yermolov. I was told he lives here . . ." The tears wet her cheeks and she began to open her purse.

The guard grabbed it, tore it open, and tossed her gold-edged mirror, pearl-handled comb, silk money holder, and linen handkerchief onto the ground piece by piece.

"What goes on here?" Another guard approached them.

"This lady here wants to see Yermolov."

"Ain't no one by that name here."

"But I know he is. The Czar's uncle, the Grand Duke

Nikolai Nikolaievich, told me I could find Leonti Yurievich here.''

"Nikolai Nikolaievich, huh? And who are you, might I ask?''

"Anna Petrovna Kalinina, wife of Alexei Yakovlevich Kalinin.''

The second guard grunted. "Do you have a note of introduction from Nikolai Nikolaievich?''

"Why, yes, it's here.'' She reached into her pocket, producing the letter that Savva had spent painstaking hours making perfect. Stepan had broken into the Grand Duke Nikolai Nikolaievich's palace two nights earlier and stolen some of his stationery and an example of his handwriting.

The guard read the forged note. "Wait here.''

He was gone an endless amount of time. Anna bent to pick up the strewn contents of her purse. Finally the guard reappeared. "Come this way.''

Flanked by the two guards, Anna entered the Montenegrina Palace. As Misha had suspected, guards were everywhere inside. She was led to a side parlor.

"Commander.'' The guard stood at attention. "Anna Petrovna Kalinina.''

Yermolov was a thoroughly unpleasant man to look at. Tall, skinny, with terribly pockmarked skin, he wore a monocle over one of his flat, vacuous eyes; his lips twitched under a pencil-thin mustache. The reddish hair on his head was clearly a toupee. He leaned toward Anna, his head seeming to balance precariously on his long, pitifully thin neck. "I haven't much time,'' he said coldly. "I suppose you have barged in here on behalf of your husband. It's useless, I assure you.''

"But I haven't even been able to see him, nor has his lawyer. If only I could see him. It's been four days.''

"All in good time, Anna Petrovna. Your husband is but one of thousands.''

Anna lowered her eyes, knowing she needed to conceal her revulsion. Yermolov was nothing more than a self-important insect like Zinaida Golovnina, but one with considerably more power. "If only you could let me see Alexei, I would be forever in your debt, Leonti Yurievich,'' she pleaded, feeling strengthened by his disdain. "The Grand Duke assured me—''

"The Grand Duke had no right assuring you anything, madame!'' Yermolov bellowed, his sickly skin turning bright red. "Now, if you will excuse me . . .''

"Please, sir!'' She reached for his arm.

He stiffened. "Do not touch me and do not embarrass me with the commonness of your plea. Your husband will be formally charged and tried in due time. Until then, I warn you not to try my goodwill by barging into my home again. Is that clear, Anna Petrovna?" His eyes narrowed, and he dropped his monocle; a cruel grin crept across his thin lips. "I've all Russia to worry about, not the plight of some filthy son of a murderer."

This time Yermolov won her attention. Anna was so startled by his words, she didn't know what he was talking about for a moment.

"You seem surprised, Anna Petrovna. Or didn't your husband tell you his father was a miserable little accountant who hanged himself in a prison for the criminally insane? He was sent there for a brutal, senseless murder. The father of Alexei Kalinin beat a helpless old man to death. So you see, Anna Petrovna, the Czar is all-powerful. He knows all there is to know."

"Quite the contrary, Leonti Yurievich," she said, regaining her composure. "My husband has never hidden the circumstances of his father's death. Good or ill, a man must never forswear those who gave him life. Is that not one of God's commandments?"

"I have no more time for this nonsensical chitchat. Take the woman home!" Yermolov snapped to one of his guards.

As the guard took her arm, Anna said, "I've my own carriage waiting outside."

"All right then . . . ." Yermolov coughed to clear his throat. He anxiously wiped a finger across his pencil-thin mustache and said, "Madame, I'll look into your husband's case, but I make no promises. But should you ever return here again, I will see your husband is punished to the fullest extent of the law. Is that clear?"

"Yes, sir." Anna nodded, feeling smug despite Yermolov's threat. Her mission was accomplished. Clearly, she had perturbed him far more than he'd perturbed her, and as the guard opened the front door for her, she turned to Yermolov once more. He was only a few feet away; a servant was helping him on with his coat. In his preoccupation, Yermolov didn't even notice her. She walked by slowly.

He followed closely behind, then pushed past her and hurried into the waiting carriage.

"Be quick, be quick!" a guard ordered Anna.

She hurried down the driveway, her eyes scanning the street ahead. Everything was in order: Kiril was waiting for her by the carriage door; Misha and Charlotte were strolling arm in arm; Aksinia and Savva were shoveling snow; Stepan and Dmitri were marching at a brisk soldier's pace.

"It's him," Anna said as Kiril helped her in.

Kiril quickly closed the carriage door and leapt into the driver's seat.

"Be off, be quick!" The guard shot out the order. "You're blocking the way."

"Yes, sir." Kiril threw his hat high into the air and rapped his horses with the reins. "God speed the devil to hell!" he shouted as the carriage tore down the snowy roadway.

"It's him. It's right," Misha whispered. Kiril's hat in the air was the signal. Squeezing Charlotte's arm tightly, he quickened their pace. Aksinia and Savva were about a half-block past the palace. They'd stopped shoveling. Savva was digging something out of a mound of snow. Stepan and Dmitri were on the other side of the street, almost directly opposite the Montenegrina driveway.

"Now," Misha said, urging Charlotte in front of the driveway. Yermolov's carriage was hurtling toward them. The guard screamed at them to move on.

Charlotte smiled and waved at the guard.

"You fools, they'll run you down!"

"Oh!" Charlotte nudged Misha as if just noticing the on-coming horses.

"Make way! Make way!" called Yermolov's coachman.

At the final moment, Misha pulled Charlotte clear and they began to run.

The horses tore into Voznesensky Prospect, sending the heavy sledded carriage careening at a dangerously wide angle, sweeping almost to the other side of the street. Stepan's arm shot high in the air. The bomb flew. The explosion was so powerful, it knocked Misha and Charlotte to the ground. When they looked, there was an enormous cloud of yellow smoke. Black-and-white snow spit into the air along with chunks of the carriage and flesh.

"Come on, come on!" Savva and Aksinia were pulling Misha and Charlotte to their feet.

They ran.

Shots were fired.

Charlotte screamed and fell to the ground. Aksinia turned to pick her up.

More shots rang out.

Aksinia fell. "Run!" she shouted to Savva and Misha as they started toward her. "Get the hell out of here! Go!"

There was such vengeance and authority in Aksinia's voice that Savva and Misha ran as if swept by a great wind.

"I can't!" Savva cried as Kiril's carriage came into view at the end of the street. "I can't leave Aksinia!"

"We can't help them, Savva!" Misha reached for him, but Savva was already running back. Soldiers were surrounding Aksinia and Charlotte, pulling them to their feet.

An inhuman cry tore from Savva and he leapt. Shots rang out. His body stiffened like a dancer caught in midair, and he crumpled to the ground.

"Misha!" Anna called. "Misha, come!"

He swerved. The carriage door was open. Anna's arms were outstretched. He ran. Bullets followed him. He dove into the carriage as it took off, hurtling down Sadovaya Street.

PART SIX

ON THE TRAIL
OF AKIMOV

CHAPTER FORTY-TWO

The cell door deep in the back quarters of Spassky Prison was thrown open, casting a shock of light on Alexei's sleeping face.

"Come on, Kalinin. You're free to go." A guard hurled out the words as he kicked Alexei's bunk.

Groggily Alexei pushed himself up on his elbow and shielded his eyes from the glare. He stared uncomprehendingly at the looming guard.

"I said you're free to go, Kalinin. Come on. Come on." The guard yanked him to his feet. "I don't have all day."

"Free?" Alexei questioned, the word having an empty sound. He looked about the tiny space with the worried frown of a man who thinks he's forgotten something, and spied his shoes in a corner. He dumped them upside down and a large water bug came scurrying out. He shook them a few more times, stuck his hand inside each, and sat back on the bunk. As he began lacing the shoes, a shadowy pain fluttered through him. What if this were a ploy, a trick to get him to follow the guard to some place? Perhaps they were planning to kill him.

"Come on, Kalinin," the guard called impatiently from the door. "What the hell's taking you so long? Not used to tying your own shoes?"

"I'm not going," Alexei answered, his hands gripping the edges of the bunk.

"Are you daft?" The guard bounded toward him and grabbed him by the shoulder, tore him from the bunk and tossed him, stumbling, outside the cell. He crashed into a wall before steadying himself.

"Go on, Kalinin. Go on!" the guard ordered with disgust. "Go on or so help me God, I'll beat this over your goddamned head." He held up the butt of his gun.

The futility of resistance seemed suddenly pitifully clear; feeling his body grow limp, Alexei went where he was told. The guard led him from the cellblock up the stairs to the

471

entrance of the prison. Daylight poured through tall frosted windows. "What date is it?" Alexei asked, gazing at a clock on the wall. It was ten-fifteen.

"Ask him." The guard pointed Alexei toward a sergeant at the front desk.

Alexei watched in amazement as his jailer turned and walked away, leaving Alexei totally unfettered.

"You!" the sergeant at the desk called. He was a fat, rough man with an uneven mustache and a bald head. The sergeant motioned Alexei over.

Alexei stood uncertainly, staring about the lobby of the police station; it was steamy with people sitting lumped on benches, crowded on the floor; many more stood. They were waiting. They were tired. There was that defeated, vacant look about them that comes from senseless hours of waiting; old and young people, men and women, a few children, some finely dressed, others in rags, it seemed they all were watching Alexei. He was the sideshow, something to break the monotony.

He felt his chin covered with a heavy growth of beard. He looked at his hands, the fingernails ragged and dirty. His suit was stained, wrinkled. He hadn't bathed or changed since he'd been arrested. The stench of his own body repulsed him. His voice seemed scratchy too. He hadn't spoken to anyone other than the recent interchange with the guard since the morning of his arrest. He'd never been formally charged. He'd been allowed varying lengths of light each day, with nothing to do with the light but stare at the four walls about him, at the bugs caught in huge spiderwebs, at the rats and large roaches. He knew each crack in the stone walls about him. Some cracks seemed carved, the patient etching of previous hapless tenants.

His food had been shoved under the door. Hands had reached in once a day for his slop pail. He'd heard other men's moans and screams, listened to keys turning in locks and recited poetry to himself, written imagined letters to Anna, read hers back, relived favorite journeys and played music in his mind. His longings for Anna had felt romantic, heroic; he'd imagined her life without him. She was in mourning, her blond hair streaming against black cloth. She wrote his funeral dirge and played it on the piano as his mother, Misha, Tolya, Helena, the children, Yuri Dobrinsky, Alexander Ryabushinsky, Kira, Witte, and others of his closest friends followed the casket to the cemetery. Even Andre Bobrinsky was there. The grandeur of Anna's music ignited forgiveness, and Alexei knew Anna was free. With his death, she returned to life with all that had been his, all he'd struggled for and more. She was beyond the flames. She would succeed where he had failed, and that was a comfort. His solitude was a comfort. His only fear was that, like his father, he was losing his mind. And then, at times, as the hours wound their way with the torturous slowness of flesh freezing in snow, he thought madness had been his father's salvation.

"Name?" the sergeant demanded.

Alexei looked up. He was standing in front of the sergeant's desk. "Alexei Yakovlevich Kalinin."

The sergeant shoved a box at him. "Look inside."

Alexei opened it curiously and found his wallet, watch, and other valuables.

"Sign this." The sergeant handed him a paper. "Don't waste time reading it. Says you've been properly treated and all your personal belongings have been accounted for. Sign. You can't leave if you don't."

Alexei signed and stared, his hooded eyes heavy, and almost smiled at the burly sergeant.

The sergeant grunted. "Go on, go on, Kalinin. You're free to leave."

Alexei thought to shake the sergeant's hand and say thank you. Instead, he asked, "Can you tell me the date?"

"February 10."

"Nineteen-five?"

" 'Course 1905."

"It's almost a month to the day since I was arrested."

"So what do you want? A medal?" The sergeant went back to his papers.

Alexei turned and hurried outside, certain Anna would be there waiting for him. He balked as if assaulted by the brilliant light of the sun reflecting off the snow.

"Alexei! Alexei Yakovlevich!" a voice he recognized as Sergei Witte's called.

He shielded his eyes to see Witte hurrying toward him.

"Alexei, my friend!" Witte stopped a few feet away.

Alexei looked about in confusion. A sluggishness like the stirring of muddy waters was weighing down his brain. "Where's Anna?"

"Come." Witte took his arm and started for the carriage.

"Something's happened to Anna!" Alexei pulled away.

"No, nonsense. Come inside the carriage, Alexei. You need to clean up, something good to eat. You look like they've hardly fed you—or bathed you."

"Anna's alive?"

"Oh, yes, quite. You'll see her shortly, I promise. Now come." Witte took Alexei directly to the baths, and stayed by him every moment. Men whom Alexei had known for years avoided him. Even Igor, the gossipy attendant, averted his eyes when Alexei passed.

"I'm a marked man." Alexei laughed bitterly.

"Not true, Alexei Yakovlevich. They just don't know what to say. You look rather odd, you know."

Alexei stared in the mirror at the thickness of his black beard. His body was gaunt. His hair was matted. His skin sagged. "How could all this happen in only four weeks?"

"What did they do to you?"

"Nothing. Absolutely nothing. It felt like death." And he added, "I know why my father went mad."

"What's that?"

"Nothing."

Witte wrapped a towel around himself and handed one to Alexei. "Go, stand under the hottest shower you can. Igor gave me some special soap for you. Then you can relax in the baths. It will do you good."

Alexei followed Witte's orders. He floated for a long time in the pool of warm water, relishing the buoyancy and the cleanliness. He started to think about Witte, wondered why he'd come to the prison, why Witte was caring for him, but the answers to the questions were too hard in coming. Instead, he lay on the water, listening to the echoes of voices bouncing off the vaulted ceilings. Then he had a shave and haircut.

"Take me home now," Alexei said.

"Come to my house first. We'll have something to eat, and talk."

"All of them, then?" Alexei asked, the numbness of fear making it hard to swallow.

Witte nodded warily. His eyes seemed shrouded. His thick fingers wrapped awkwardly about the fork piled high with food.

Alexei fought back an urge to reach across the table and throttle the man.

"There were soldiers waiting for them not far from Yermolov's house, just at Pokrov Square. They shot the coachman, Kiril, and arrested Anna, Misha and the old woman, Olga Gambarova. Stepan Ostravsky and Dmitri Mayakovsky were killed in the explosion, blown to bloody bits like Yermolov, his bodyguards, and his horses. Who knows who's really buried in the graves, you see what I mean." Witte raised an eyebrow. "From what Misha told me—I've seen him; I thought you would want me to—anyway, he said Ostravsky had expected to get off the bomb before the carriage turned into the street. But then he couldn't, and the carriage swerved out at such a wide angle—well, it was suicide to throw the bomb as Ostravsky did. There was no room for them to escape, you see. Damn terrorists. Don't understand what drives them to suicide missions like that. Even a man like Dmitri Mayakovsky." Witte stuffed the fork filled with salmon into his mouth and chewed thoughtfully. He swallowed and wiped his mouth with the linen napkin. "Anyway, Safanov was shot trying to escape. He died before they could get him to the hospital. The woman, Aksinia, died several days later from her wounds. Charlotte Ryabushinskaya has only a superficial wound."

"What of Irina? You didn't say." Alexei's heart was beating painfully; there was an edgy crackling to his voice.

"She was arrested with Kolya Susanin the next day. They were in a teahouse in Vyborg. Someone turned them in."

"Traitors and spies." A low growl gurgled from deep in his throat. He stared at the plate of food, picked up a piece of smoked fish and put it down.

"Have you seen Anna?"

"Yes."

"Where is she?"

Witte looked worried. "I thought I told you . . ." He hesitated. "They were taken to the Fortress."

Alexei paled noticeably. He felt a wound opening up within him, draining out his lifeblood. For a moment he could neither speak nor breathe. The Fortress was something he hadn't counted on. His imprisonment in Spassky Prison was surely a summer holiday compared with the desperate deprivation there. Like everyone living in St. Petersburg, Alexei had heard stories of the daily torture; even in the best of times, the Peter and Paul Fortress loomed like a machine of terror and madness, ranking with the Bastille and the Tower of London as an expression of absolute monarchy's power to snuff out life with agonizing slowness.

The ugliness of its insides was all the more horrible for the beauty of its facade. The Fortress stood on a small island at the heart of the city, its grayish-pink walls looking like some fairy-tale fortress rising majestically above the Neva River. Inside was a small, ornate cathedral where Czars and Czarinas and all members of the House of Romanov had been buried for two hundred years. The golden spire of the cathedral soared with its delicate gilt, cross-bearing angel above

the eternal mists of the river. The cupola glittered in the
sunlight, giving an ethereal quality to the Fortress.

Once inside the Fortress, the grimness was unrelenting. A
Czar's son had died there under torture; royal princesses and
dukes had been incarcerated there, some gone mad; revolutionaries had been executed, worse, damned to oblivion. The
silence of the Fortress was absolute. The silence was the
Czar's greatest weapon of torture. It was said even the guards
wore felt boots. It was said that once inside the Fortress, a
man or woman became a nonperson. It was said that once
inside, a prisoner never saw daylight again.

"Alexei . . ." Witte nudged him gently. "They've done
nothing to harm her or any of the others, I promise."

The pain in his heart was almost unbearable, and he asked
tightly, "When can I see her?"

"I must advise you, she doesn't look well. She's got some
kind of stomach ailment. It comes and goes. She keeps little
down. But she told me to tell you she's not afraid. She told
me to tell you she's trying to eat. She said that's important
for you to know."

Alexei couldn't focus on Witte; he couldn't listen to him
either. Witte was babbling, and keeping secrets. Witte always
kept secrets, but these Alexei had a right to know. "Get me
in to see her," he said, the words twisting with the bile pressing up his throat, the pressure conjuring up maddening images of Anna, her lovely body misshapen, clothed in rags;
he saw her blind like the creatures who swam beneath the
sludge of the Fortress; he saw her being marched across the
ice, and digging her own grave with frozen fingers dropping
hunks of flesh.

"The Czar's out for revenge on this one, I'm afraid," Witte
was explaining. "They've full confessions from just about all
of them. The Czar wants to make an example of them. Except
for the old woman, Olga Gambarova, the survivors are all
young, well-to-do, intelligent people, the kind the Czar fears
most. I'm afraid he's pushing for hanging. Akimov's doing
what he can—"

"Akimov!" Alexei thundered, rising from his seat. He
slammed down his fist on the table, making the glasses and
plates clatter. "What the hell does Akimov have to do with
this?" He seized Witte, yanking the huge man from his chair
by the cloth of his collar.

"Let go! You're choking me!" Witte gasped, shoving at
Alexei. "Let go! Are you mad?"

"Tell me about Akimov." Alexei dropped hold of him and

slumped back into his seat, pressing his hands into his forehead.

Witte bristled, rearranged his tie and smoothed his jacket before sitting. "He's in control of the Okhrana now. Privately, he considers the survivors of the squad to be heroes, as does most of Russia. Yermolov is mourned by few. Believe me or not, Akimov's doing everything he can to persuade the Czar toward leniency."

"Exile."

"It's the best that can be hoped for."

The edges of Alexei's brain felt like so many kindled fuses racing to detonate. Witte was not the enemy, he had to remind himself, but Witte could lead him to the enemy. Witte could lead him to Akimov. Always Akimov. "Exile is out of the question. I've seen prisoners on the trek. I've seen them die. Get me in to see Akimov."

"He expected you would want to see him, and he told me to tell you that any meeting between the two of you would compromise his new position. It took him a while to gather his forces after Yermolov's death—which is why, I might add, you were in prison as long as you were. Akimov had you released as soon as he could. You and others like you, many prominent, outspoken citizens, were arrested after Bloody Sunday—"

"Bloody what?"

"Bloody Sunday. That's what they're calling Gapon's march on the Winter Palace. The Czar says thirty were killed. Real estimates run as high as a thousand and more. Much has happened in the month since you've been in jail. Not only was Yermolov killed, but the Czar's uncle, the Grand Duke Sergei Alexandrovich, was blown to hell a few days later in Moscow. Gapon, I heard, has fled Russia. There are rumors he's in Geneva talking with the likes of Vladimir Lenin and other radical revolutionaries in exile. There's no clear-cut leadership among the people, but conflagrations spread like wildfire—all over Russia there are riots, strikes, political assassinations; fields are burning. Many fear the cities will be next. Revolution is at hand, I tell you, and the right is urging the Czar to meet it with unmitigated force. It's what the Czar would like to do, but the threat is too great. All Russia might rise against him. In any case . . ." Witte sighed, seeming suddenly tired. "Although Akimov's gained control of the Okhrana, he holds far less power than Yermolov did. The Czar's brought in General Trepov from Moscow to take Yermolov's place within the government."

"All this doesn't explain why Akimov won't meet with me."

"What is this obsession you have with Akimov?" Witte cried in exasperation. "He's your bogeyman, Alexei. I implore you, let it rest. Akimov is truly not your enemy."

"Which is precisely what Akimov wants you to think. My God, Sergei, don't you see how Akimov's using you—just as the Czar uses you. They throw you into the gutter like so much garbage and pick you up and brush you off when it suits them."

"You try my patience . . ." Witte's face grew red. "But I forgive you. I know your anguish—"

"My anguish has nothing to do with it. It's the truth of my words that frightens you. It's as plain as day—Akimov knew every move the squad was making. He used them to assassinate Yermolov. Then he had the police waiting to ensnare the survivors. It was no accident that the carriage carrying Anna and Misha made it only to Pokrov Square!"

"You're wrong on this one, Alexei—Yermolov's men were blanketing the area. They had been for weeks. The squad knew what a risk they were taking."

"Then what of Irina and the boy Susanin? Tell me, why were they arrested twenty-four hours after the others?" Alexei probed.

"I told you, somebody turned them in."

"Who?"

"Not Akimov, if that's what you're getting at. I tell you, he's doing everything in his power to help your wife and her comrades."

"Then tell him to free them."

"He's not so powerful as you think."

"An escape, Sergei. Your Akimov is head of the secret police of all Russia. Surely an escape could be arranged."

"You're mad! You don't think Akimov would risk all he's done for you or Anna or Misha. They did commit a crime, you know. They murdered a man."

"At his bidding."

"You don't know that. You have no proof!" Witte cried indignantly.

"But I will."

"Fine, then, see if you can get such proof. If you do, I'm sure Akimov will see you."

"Yes, I'm sure he will."

Anna lay exhausted on her bunk. The vomiting had finally stopped, what little there was to vomit. She could barely eat the watery gruel they brought. The very smell made her nauseous. The bread was always stale, the tea weak, although she savored the prized sugar lumps, saving them for nibbling through the endless hours when even the dripping of water or the scurrying of rats seemed like company. The hours of light, when the guard lit the lamp hanging way above her reach, seemed like ecstasy. She talked endlessly to the expressionless guard during those few moments he was with her. It didn't matter what she said. She needed to hear her own voice. She tried speaking out loud alone, but was afraid it would make her lose her mind again. She couldn't lose her mind again. She wouldn't. She fought her terror, which led her to meaningless fits of hysteria. If anyone heard her screams, no one cared. No one came. She pulled at her hair, scratched endlessly at her skin, and sometimes thought Zinaida Golovnina was hovering in the shadows.

She lunged at her tormentor, crashed against the wall and banged her head so hard she once drew blood. Then peace came, a protective cover feeling like the skin of scalded milk. She huddled in the corner, her knees pressed to her chin. The dampness sucked up through her skirts. She closed her eyes and hummed music and slowly Alexei came to her. He warmed her and she laughed. He crawled inside her, wiping clean the bloodied, broken mirrors. Then she prayed. Other times she imagined Alexei in the cell next to hers. There were no sounds in the Fortress except her own.

"Prisoner Kalinina, you are to come with me."

She sat up in the bed, her heart beating. "Where?"

The guard held up his lamp and motioned her to follow. He led her through the darkened, vaulted corridor where gendarmes silently paced, and up the damp steps dripping with the nearness of the river. A huge iron door was unbolted and Anna found herself in a tiny room with wooden floors, painted walls, a chair and a table looking like a doctor's examining table.

"Wait here," the guard said, closing the door behind her.

The warmth of the room made her tremble at first. She remembered a similar room where she'd been brought shortly after her arrest. A terrifying policewoman with a whip and a gun ordered her to strip entirely of her clothes and then had hurled questions at her as she stood shivering. Anna had done her best to answer. The policewoman's cold stare threatened like the eyes of a sullen dog. She made Anna stand until nakedness seemed unimportant. Then the policewoman told her that besides Kiril—Dmitri, Stepan, Savva and Aksinia were also dead.

"Everyone else, even your precious Irina Ilyarovna, has been arrested, and they have confessed everything. You will sign this paper, prisoner Kalinina. It is a full confession of your crimes against the Czar. You will sign or your husband will be executed at dawn."

Without hesitation, without reading a word on the paper, Anna signed the confession. Then she was allowed to dress and led to the tiny damp cell in the belly of the Fortress. She'd been there ever since, except for the one visit from Sergei Witte, but that was so long ago, it seemed a dream.

There was a gentle knocking and the door opened; a pleasant-looking young man in a doctor's uniform walked in. He carried a doctor's bag and smiled at Anna. "My name is Dr. Stepaiak. They tell me you've been ill for a while."

Anna nodded, suddenly aware that the awful stench filling the room was coming from her own body. She looked down at her dress, which was terribly stained, and wanted to apologize to the pleasant young doctor for her appearance. Instead, she said, "What day is this?"

"February 24."

"Oh, goodness. I've been here a long time."

"Yes. Can you tell me something about your sickness, Anna Petrovna?"

"It comes on me mostly in the first part of the day, or what I think is the first part of the day. Sometimes it's hard to tell day from night, but once it begins, I dare eat nothing, for it only comes up again for hours."

"Anything else, any aches or pains otherwise?"

"My head hurts often."

"I see." He placed his bag on the table. "Would you mind sitting up there."

"Of course. I . . . I must apologize for my state. I'm normally a very clean person."

He smiled sadly. "No apologies, please." He proceeded to examine her, his thumb gently feeling the bruise on her forehead; then he looked into her eyes, nose, ears, and mouth.

"I itch terribly."

"Yes, I've no doubt. It's the lice."

"Lice?" The word burned her throat.

"You're covered with them. All prisoners are."

She nodded. Lice! God, lice. . . . She started to tremble.

"You're cold, Anna Petrovna."

"Lice." She swallowed. "Please." She shuddered. "Please get them off me."

"Well, we'll see what we can do. Now, if you would undress for me please, Anna Petrovna. Take everything off if you will.''

Feeling hot and confused, Anna nodded, fumbling with the buttons of her dress. It seemed to take forever to get everything off, and then she was afraid to look at her skin, afraid of what she'd see crawling there.

"Are your breasts normally this large?" the doctor asked.

"I . . . I don't know." Tears blurred her eyes. "I don't think so."

"Do they hurt at all?"

"Yes, at times."

"Have you had your monthly bleeding since you've been arrested?"

She shook her head, wishing the doctor would stop asking such questions.

"All right, if you'll lie down for me . . ." He eased her onto the hard table and covered the top part of her body with her dress. Then he guided her feet until they were resting on the edge of the table and her knees were bent. "There, that's a good girl. This will only take a minute. It shouldn't hurt . . ."

The examination seemed to go on for an eternity, like life itself in this horrible place, and Anna wondered if he found lice inside her too. When he finished he told her to get dressed, then announced, "You're pregnant, Anna Petrovna. That's why you're throwing up every morning. It's a very common occurrence among pregnant women. It's hard to say for sure, but I'd estimate you're about two and a half, maybe three months gone. That makes the baby due in August or September."

Irina anticipated her father's weekly visits; it was the only measure of time she had. They met in a tiny windowless room, bare except for a table and two chairs; the air was dry if not heated, almost invigoratingly crisp. The walls and floor were made of real wood that didn't drip with the all-pervasive dampness of the cellblocks. The light bulb was covered to shield the glare. He brought her cigarettes, fruit, cheese and sweets. She ate what she could when they were together. The guards stole everything when he left, and later, Irina's stomach rejected the rest. Still, she ate hungrily, hoping a little of the nourishment would stay with her.

The time with her father ached with life. He dressed in his best uniform. He wore his medals. He smelled of fragrant lotions; his touch was quick yet tender as his kisses in her childhood had been. She remembered how he'd come into her room at night, long after she'd been sent to bed. He'd come in when he thought she was asleep and bend over and kiss her head. Her father was an almost unbearably quiet man; as a child, that quietness had felt like indifference, but now, in prison, the quietness bathed her in the dearest love she thought she'd ever known.

The visits always began the same way. He shuffled into the room preoccupied with the basket he carried; wordlessly he laid it on the table. The contents were in disarray. The guards, she knew, had rummaged through them first. Methodically he began laying out the contents, cigarettes first, followed by fruit, cheese, bread, wine, sweets, glasses and plates. There was no silverware. Her father always took back the glasses and plates. "The guards insist," he explained.

"Hello, Papa." She leaned to kiss him, thinking how once he'd been so much taller than she. "How is Mama?"

"Fine." He took out a napkin from the bottom of the basket and sat.

"Does she speak of me?"

His eyes fluttered shut, and he stared down at his hands.

She lit a cigarette and inhaled deeply. The smoke rushed to her head, and she began to pace. "I know she hates me, Papa. She's always hated me. What I need to know is, does she hate me more?" She waited.

He never answered.

She dropped her cigarette on the floor and crushed it with her heel. She thought she must stop asking about her mother. She thought it wasn't fair to her father.

He sipped his wine and wiped his lips carefully with the linen napkin.

"The guards told me . . ." His eyes flitted uncomfortably about the bare, windowless room. "They told me just before they let me in to see you today that Anna Petrovna is with child. I thought I should tell her husband." He broke off some cheese, placed it on a piece of bread and handed it to her. "Eat," he insisted.

"Will they hang a pregnant woman?" was all Irina said.

The Grand Duke paled at the mention of hanging. He finished his wine and refilled his glass. "No one need be hanged, Irina. I've spoken to the Czar himself. He's not intransigent. He indicated to me that if you would just sign the confession, he would be moved to leniency."

"I told you, Papa, I'll never sign a confession. I committed no crime against the Russian people, and I committed no crime against God. God himself would spit in the face of a man like Yermolov and hurl him to hell if he dared tried entering heaven. You know that.''

"Your signature on a piece of meaningless paper, Irina. It will save your life.'' He tried to lift his wineglass, but his hand was shaking too badly.

"And you believe that, Papa? Well, I don't. Not for a moment. I'll not sign any confession. I'll not make it easy for Nicholas Romanov. Let him try to hang us. I'd rather die to the roar of the people, to their anger burning Petersburg to the ground, than crawl before Nicholas Romanov. I will not beg for mercy.''

"I have.'' Her father's puffy white lips quivered. His thin eyes grew watery and he looked away. "I would die in your place if I could.'' His voice was very soft. "Do it for me, Irinushka,'' he was pleading. He took out a lace-edged handkerchief and blew his nose. "I'm an old man. You're my only child. Do this thing for me, I beg of you. It's not groveling before Nicholas Romanov. No, I swear to God Almighty it isn't.''

"I can't, Papa.''

"The Czar has promised me, if you sign now, you'll be exiled to Siberia. He promised me, none of you shall die. They're waiting for you. All the others have signed the confessions.''

"I don't believe that. I know them, especially Misha and Olga. I know they would never sign. Don't you see? This is what they do. They make us believe lies. They pit one against the other. They manipulate us with our fathers!'' she was shouting. "The Czar wants a confession and then he'll hang us anyway.''

"There is some honor left in Nicholas Romanov. I don't believe he'd lie to me about my daughter's life. Please, Irinushka, do this for me. Live for me. I couldn't bear it if you didn't.''

A guard appeared and told Misha that Irina was dead, that she'd hanged herself with strips of cloth torn from her skirt. The guard vanished so fast, Misha wondered if he'd appeared at all. Most assuredly, he hadn't. Irina would not kill herself.

"Prisoner Kalinin!'' A guard banged on his door. "Prisoner Kalinin!''

"Yes.'' Misha jumped to his feet.

"Repent your crime against the Czar and all Russia!''

Misha didn't answer, knowing if he didn't, the guard would go away.

CHAPTER FORTY-THREE

Dawn was breaking, heavy with snow to hide the blood that night inevitably brought, making Petersburg appear a virgin again. If Alexei cocked his head, he could see the slender golden spire of the Peter and Paul Cathedral. He watched the pearly mist shift serenely about the gilt angel at its tip, and he smiled unconsciously. Pressing his head against the sloping roof, he wrapped the heavy blanket more tightly about himself. The attic was freezing, yet Alexei went there every day to watch the night pale. It was a moment of peace, a connection to Anna; at least it seemed that way, sitting, his knees pressed to his chin as morning broke over the city, over the Fortress where Anna lay in darkness, their child growing within her.

Alexei could not think of Anna for long. He could not think of the child at all. He could not imagine the unborn, only Anna, her reality too often lost to memories of madness, of his father's scabbed, rancid body feeling like an orphan in his arms, and of Anna wandering through a barren world, her sunken eyes frozen, empty in death that howled with the eternity of a Siberian winter. He remembered the young girl, Eugenie, a marble statue, perfection in death, blood-soaked padding between her legs, and saw Anna. Then it was all Alexei could do not to grab a gun and go running across the Troitsky Bridge, shooting at the gates of the Fortress, screaming Anna's name. Other times he thought he would kill Sergei Witte, who hadn't been able to arrange for him to see Anna after all.

"Unfortunately, it's the Czar, not Akimov, who determines the parameters of their imprisonment. However," Witte explained, "at his core, the Czar is a family man. It's a blessing, I tell you, that Anna's pregnant. The Czar will not hang a pregnant woman."

Alexei often thought these thoughts as he sat in Yuri Dobrinsky's attic. He'd all but taken up residence in the little house on Vasilievsky Island as an escape from the vastness of his own palace, empty except for a few servants. The dark, masculine

484

disorder of Yuri Dobrinsky's house was a comfort—damn, but he missed the man. He spent hours aimlessly poring over Yuri's records of their business investments and holdings, the neat columns of figures seeming far easier to consider than the plight of Anna and Misha, or even Yuri's death.

He left the attic and made his way to the kitchen, where he poured himself some cold coffee. He stood by the sink, cup in hand, and stared about the familiar room, almost expecting Yuri to shuffle in at any moment. Why did you let yourself get killed, Yuri Nikolaievich? he complained, trying not to blame the man for dying, but he couldn't help himself. There must have been a reason for him to have risked his life, to have risked Anna's life. And there must have been a mistake.

What had gone wrong? he pondered as he stood in the quiet, dimly lit kitchen, waiting, almost listening for Yuri to speak wisdom from the dead. Finally he sat at the rickety table and stared at the pad he'd left there the night before. *Why did Yuri risk everything to kill Yermolov?* he'd written.

Alexei could make no sense of it. Yuri Dobrinsky mapped out life too carefully; he was obsessed with covering his tracks, obsessed with never taking an unnecessary risk in the riskiest business a man could be in. What had changed? Alexei sipped his coffee, shaken, as always, with the feeling that not only Yuri but also all of them were caught in a conspiracy, dazzling, blinding in a brilliance named Akimov. Therein lay the answer, so simple he'd almost missed it: with Arkady Akimov, Dmitri Mayakovsky had met his match.

Alexei got up to pour himself a drink, but fought the urge. He needed his mind absolutely clear. He needed to work this out once and for all. He leaned back in his chair and closed his eyes a moment. The Trail of Akimov, he thought, and sitting forward, he crumpled the paper from last night and wrote on a clean sheet, *The Trail of Akimov.* Then he wrote:

Facts

1. Akimov was in a death struggle with Yermolov.
2. Akimov made an alliance with Witte.
3. Akimov made an alliance with Father Gapon.
4. Somehow (traitor?) Akimov manipulated the Brigade to assassinate Yermolov.
5. Akimov (the Shadow) had to suppress any leaks about himself—i.e., his connection to Gapon and the police unions and the Brigade.
    a. steals Paris documents
    b. kills Vera Martova when she gets close

    c. intimidates Irina through henchman when she gets
       close, kills Kostya Savich.
    d. kills: Yuri Dobrinsky/Dmitri Mayakovsky, Stepan
       Ostravsky, etc., and arrests Anna, Misha, Irina, etc.
       (If there was a traitor in the squad, he is now either
       dead or in jail.)

Alexei stared at his notes, wondering where they led him.
He dropped the pen and pressed his hands to his temples as
if the solution were in his mind's eye. What else do I know?
he questioned. "Think, man, think, what else do you know?"
he said out loud, and wrote:

What Is the Situation Now?

1. The Czar can seriously strike at forces of liberalization as
   represented by me and the Symposium by executing Anna,
   Misha, Irina, etc.
2. The right will bring pressure on the Czar to do this. Akimov has no motivation to intercede.
3. THEREFORE THE PROBABILITY IS HIGH THAT EXECUTIONS
   WILL TAKE PLACE.
4. The only answer is ESCAPE. HOW???

Alexei searched for a common chord, a springboard for
action. Who could help him? He thought of Witte, Andre
Bobrinsky, and of Irina's father, the Grand Duke Ilya Mikhailevich. He thought of many other rich and influential people he knew, but he discarded them as soon as he thought of
them. The answer was painfully clear: Arkady Akimov, Russia's chief policeman, the man who held the keys to every
prison, was the only man who could turn the locks. The problem was, Akimov had no reason to help. He had to be forced.
He had to be blackmailed.

Alexei glanced at his notes again. His evidence against
Akimov was circumstantial at best; he didn't need Yuri Dobrinsky to tell him that. Yet, Akimov's power was still unsta-
ble, and in such precarious times, circumstantial evidence
could be enough to propel a man like Akimov into action, if
only Alexei could reach him. Witte was a dead end. Alexei
would have to lure Akimov into a meeting. If only he could
meet this Shadow, this man who held his anonymity so dear,
if he could only meet Akimov face-to-face, he might indeed
convince him of the wisdom of their working together to free
Anna, Misha and the others. It was Alexei's only hope.

* * *

Alexei invited the Grand Duke Ilya Mikhailevich to lunch at his club on February 28, and reserved a small private dining room where they wouldn't be disturbed. The Grand Duke arrived precisely at twelve-thirty. He shuffled into the dark oak-paneled sitting room, his feet dragging on the thick carpet. His head bobbed with the look of a broken man; lines scoured his face. The once-broad shoulders, which had fit so finely in uniforms, slouched pitifully. Alexei quickly rose from his seat and hurried to greet the Grand Duke, but they did not converse until they were seated in the private dining room and lunch had been offered. Alexei poured the Grand Duke a glass of wine.

The old man's hand shook as he lifted his glass for a toast. "May God have mercy on their souls, Alexei Yakovlevich." His gray eyes became watery. His puffy lips quivered.

"I'll not leave their fate to God, Ilya Mikhailevich."

"It's God or the Czar, and save for your wife and her condition, the Czar will show no mercy, I warrant. He pities me, he told me, yes, he pities my father's grief, but he will do nothing for them without confessions, and Irina refuses to sign. As for the others, I don't know." The old man shook his head and slowly sipped his wine.

"I didn't invite you to lunch today to mourn our loved ones, Ilya Mikhailevich. I believe there's something we can do, or I can do. But I'll need your help. When do you see Irina again?"

"Tomorrow."

"Good. Are you relatively free to say whatever you want to her?"

"If I'm careful. No one is with us. I don't think they can hear us if we speak softly."

"Excellent. Now, what I need is some information from her . . ."

Irina thought her father looked more sprightly when he came into the tiny room where they met. His embrace was tighter; he kissed each cheek three times and set about his routine of setting their table with an eagerness she hadn't seen before.

"Papa, something has happened—you know something, some good news," she whispered.

"Come, sit, eat as we always do," he said softly. "Everything must be as it always is. I know they watch us through their little hatch out there, but they cannot hear us through these walls. I must be as I always am too. Here . . ." He handed her a glass of wine.

She started to sit.

"No, stand," he insisted. "You always stand and pace awhile when I arrive. And you smoke too many cigarettes, so smoke. Go on, Irina, smoke and pace and I will talk."

Irina did as she was told, although she paced in small circles about the table so as not to miss anything her father said.

"I saw Alexei Yakovlevich yesterday and we had the most interesting of conversations. He told me that you were friends with the priest, Father Gapon, the one who organized that march they now call Bloody Sunday. Oh, don't look worried. I'm not here to chastise you. He said to tell you that he needs information on contacting Gapon."

"Contacting Gapon? Whatever for?"

He motioned her to sit, and she sat, crushing out her cigarette and picking absently at the food he set before her.

"I don't know all the whys and wherefores, my dear. Alexei Yakovlevich most wisely didn't tell me. He said the less we all know, the better." The Grand Duke offered her a piece of smoked swan. "Now, tell me everything you can to help Alexei Yakovlevich locate this Father Gapon."

"Before I was arrested, I heard he'd fled Russia. Word was he was going to either Turkey or Switzerland, Geneva most likely. I think if anyone would know anything, it would be a worker named Anton Segunin. Also Maxim Gorky."

The Grand Duke slipped a pen and a piece of paper from his pocket. "Your back is to the door. You write their addresses, but don't look as if you're writing. Can you do that, Irinushka, my dearest?"

"I think so." She smiled, and did it slowly, intermittently as they ate, drank and pretended to be in conversation. Then she slipped the paper under the table.

"Alexei Yakovlevich has asked me one more thing. Should he get in touch with Gapon, he needs some information from you, something personal which would prove that in fact he is your emissary."

"I understand," she said thoughtfully. "Tell him to tell Gapon this: three years ago Gapon was approached by a messenger who said he was from the Czar, but Gapon knew the messenger was sent by God. The messenger's name was Arkady Akimov."

Alexei visited Maxim Gorky first, for he knew the writer through a mutual acquaintance, the millionaire Moscow industrialist Savva Morozov, son of a serf and backer of the avant-garde Moscow Art Theater; it was there, under the direction of Konstantin Stanislavsky, that the works of such playwrights as Gorky and Chekhov first had been produced successfully. Although Alexei was extremely fond of the large, slow-moving Morozov, he had never been comfortable with Gorky, the romantic revolutionary who seemed to covet the very ghosts of impoverished childhood that Alexei shunned.

Self-educated and decidedly a brilliant voice of the oppressed, Gorky still accented his O's in the manner of the people from the banks of the Volga. He was a great supporter of the Bolshevik Lenin, and wore the black shirt and high boots of the peasant; he wafted in and out of the Czar's jails, seemingly never the worse for wear. Gorky, too, had been arrested after Bloody Sunday, but while Alexei rotted unknown and uncelebrated in the depths of Spassky Prison, arrest of the proletarian writer was universally decried by the scientists and artists of the West. Savva Morozov personally gathered together Gorky's bail of almost ten thousand rubles over a weekend, with the banks closed.

"Alexei Yakovlevich," Gorky welcomed him into his Moscow flat. His smile was friendly. "My condolences about your wife. She's a true fighter of the people, as you yourself are. I'm honored to have you as my guest." Gorky embraced him and kissed each cheek, then led Alexei to a cluttered parlor and poured some vodka. They drank and smoked and chatted about Savva Morozov, who seemed on the edge of personal destruction. The workers in his plants had gone on strike, and when he advocated profit sharing, his mother, the matriarch of the family, took over control of the factories and tried to violently suppress the strike.

"Savva's gone to France, you know. He's in utmost despair," Gorky said. "I always told him his liberalism would end up in murky places, though. He means well, always, but he never would firmly take a stand, revolutionary or liberal, you know what I mean?"

Alexei nodded absently. He was in no mood for a political discussion with an avowed revolutionary and, as sorry as he felt for Savva Morozov, he had his own worries to tend to. "I was wondering, you knew Gapon."

"Georgi Apollonovich, of course. I had great hopes for his leadership."

"You know where he is?"

Gorky grimaced. "Gone. He came to my apartment after his march was bloodied. Savva Morozov was here then too. Gapon was on the edge of hysteria, but Savva calmed him and disguised him, personally shaving Georgi's beard and cutting his hair. By then rumors of his death were flying. Gapon had to make an appearance, you see, to stave off the people's mourning. Savva had Gapon's face made up by

someone from the theater. It was a happy disguise. Gapon
looked quite like a stylish young shop assistant. We all had a
good laugh. Gapon drank a lot of wine, and then he appeared
wild-eyed before the Free Economic Society. All of intellec-
tual Petersburg was there. We appeared on the balcony, and
I recalled Gapon's words. He shouted in that voice of his,
powerful even when excited. He said, 'Peaceful means have
failed. Now we must go over to other means.' '' He read a
letter which began, 'Dear blood-welded workers,' and called
down his 'pastor's curse' on the soldiers and 'the traitor Czar.'
He spoke well, our wild-eyed priest.''

''Where is he now?''

Gorky shrugged. ''To hell and back. Who knows? He disappeared the next day without so much as good-bye. We've
not heard of him since. Why are you looking for him?''

''I think he should return to Russia.''

Gorky chuckled. ''Impossible, I assure you. The man has
a voice which flows like nectar from the gods, but his politics
are those of a hick. He ran scared, and he's not coming back.''

''Do you know anyone who might know of him?''

''There are a group of workers from the Putilov Iron Works
about him. A feisty young woman named Kuksina Ivanovna
and her fellow, Izaak. Then there was Kostya Savich, but he's
dead, killed in an accident, all very mysterious. There was
Anton Segunin and a fellow named Sinelovsky. His wife was
killed at the march. Perhaps one of them can help you, but
be watchful. Rumors are that agents abound amongst Gapon's
old followers. Be careful whom you tell what.''

Even as Alexei was leaving Gorky's a plan was forming
in his mind. Upon returning to Petersburg he went immediately to his old friend Semyon Tatlin, a costume designer,
and borrowed from his wardrobe a priest's cassock and hat
as well as a large, wooden cross to wear about his neck and
a long, flowing, black beard. He bought an overcoat and boots
at a secondhand store and returned to Yuri's house to change
into his disguise before setting out once more.

Anton Segunin lived in a quiet working-class neighborhood in the Vyborg district. He had his own house, a neat,
faded pink two-story wooden structure, and Alexei knocked
at the door several times. No one answered.

As he was leaving, a rough-looking young man of about
twenty, dressed in black pants, boots and jacket and a furry
cap, accosted him. ''Looking for someone, Father?'' he demanded gruffly. His eyes were narrow, abusive in their stare,

and there was a scar across his upper lip. He was shorter than Alexei but just as broad.

"I'm Father Grigory Khitrovo, a friend of a friend of Segunin's. I was sent to see him."

"Yeah, and who's sendin' you, Father?" the youth demanded disparagingly. He crossed his arms in front of his chest. "You want Segunin, you got to get past me first."

Alexei smiled cordially. "Well, then, if you would, you might just give Segunin a message for me. Tell him that Kuksina Ivanovna and Izaak Belzac sent me. Tell him it's very important."

The youth stood, a bear on the verge of attack. Suddenly he snapped, "There's a teahouse the next street over. Wait there." He started down the street.

It was early afternoon, too early for workers who worked to be coming for tea, and those who didn't work didn't have the money to have their tea served. The teahouse was empty except for the proprietor, a round middle-aged woman with rough red skin. The room was steaming with heat and the tantalizing scents of honey and cinnamon. Alexei ordered tea and several cakes and ate them hungrily. He was about to order more, when a square man of medium height, with a worker's coat and cap and his arm in a sling came in and unhesitatingly sat at the table with Alexei.

"Are you Father Khitrovo?"

"Yes." Alexei nodded, looking around to see if anyone else was about. The man appeared to be alone.

"I'm Anton Segunin." He pulled his chair closer. "You were sent by Kuksina and Izaak. How are they?"

"They're in jail."

Segunin's face grew somber. "Yes, I thought that had happened. Either they were in jail or dead." He crossed himself. "Kuksina and Izaak were faithful followers of Father Gapon and true friends. How can I help you?"

"I need to get in touch with Father Gapon . . ." Alexei told a well-prepared story that as Kuksina's priest from Kiev he'd recently visited her in jail; although she hadn't actually seen Izaak, they'd been able to get messages back and forth. The jail was brimming with angry workers and Father Gapon's name was always on their lips. Alexei was searching out Gapon at Kuksina's bidding, to plead with him to return to Russia and take leadership of his flock once more. "This I think you'll find interesting," he concluded. "Prison has not broken Kuksina Ivanovna. Not in the least. She's as feisty as ever, and has somehow gotten a message to the great Alexei Yakovlevich Kalinin, whose wife and nephew are being held in the Fortress for the assassination of Leonti Yermolov. Kalinin was a great admirer of Gapon and is willing to finance Father's return to Russia as well as the reorganization of his Society." With that, Alexei produced an impressive roll of money as well as a note from Kalinin to Gapon detailing his intentions.

Segunin was impressed. "As always, Kuksina Ivanovna is right, Father. We need Father Gapon back to lead us, but only she would dare implore him. If you can get him back, the working people of Russia will be eternally in your debt."

"But can you help me find him?" Alexei asked cautiously.

"I've an address in Geneva of a man by the name of Stankevich, and I will write a letter of introduction."

"Can this Stankevich take me to Father Gapon?"

"Things change so quickly, Father. Father Gapon may not be there anymore, but if he is, Stankevich can help you. He's a good man and true."

Stankevich's mother, Sonya Ilyanovna, a petite, white-haired, old woman, led Alexei into a drawing room cluttered with fraying although once fine furniture, lace curtains and many books. The room was decidedly Russian in character. An icon of the Virgin was in one corner. A samovar steamed on the table. There were the remains of a breakfast of black bread and smoked fish. Alexei had to shout to make himself heard. Stankevich's mother was very hard of hearing. She read the letter from Segunin several times before she announced, "My son leaves the house at seven every morning and usually doesn't return until past midnight."

"Do you know where I could find him? As you can see, it's most urgent."

The old woman disappeared into another room and returned with a piece of paper. "This is the address of another Russian. He will put you up for so long as you are here. He is a friend."

Alexei looked at the paper. Valery Voyekiev. He didn't know the man, but he knew the address. It was one of the most expensive in Geneva.

Valery Voyekiev's skin reminded Alexei of the finest white parchment; he was pleasantly round and perfumed; his suit was made of the softest wool. Voyekiev was a jeweler, his specialty diamonds. He'd left Russia as a young man with his father, who had been peripherally involved with the revolutionary movement of the 1880's. Alexei knew Voyekiev's kind well. He was shrewd in business, but a dilettante in life; he collected interesting people the way some men collected art. Father Gapon was most surely his most recent treasure. Men such as Valery Voyekiev were useful, but not to be trusted. Alexei hoped Gapon understood that.

Voyekiev welcomed Alexei enthusiastically after reading Segunin's letter of introduction and led him to a lavishly appointed library of wall-to-wall books, where he asked him to wait. "I will be back as soon as I can," Voyekiev assured him. "Stankevich is not always an easy man to track down. Something to drink while you wait?"

"Tea would be fine," Alexei assured him, and Voyekiev was gone.

A few moments later a maid appeared with a tray of tea and rich cakes. Alexei drank the tea and scanned some magazines. He was impatient. He smoked. He walked about, taking books down from the shelves and putting them back. Voyekiev had an impressive library, but Alexei was in no mood to read. He stared out the window into what was most assuredly a lush garden in spring and summer. He looked at his watch again and again. Voyekiev had been gone almost an hour when Alexei heard footsteps followed by a knock on the door.

Valery Voyekiev entered first, smiling pleasantly. He was followed by two others, a rather short, chubby, nondescript man with closely cropped light brown hair and a slim, aesthetically handsome young man whose fashionable black suit seemed to drain the color from his fair skin, making his clean-shaven cheeks even more sunken and his black eyes voluminous.

Valery Voyekiev quickly introduced the short man as Emile Stankevich and the slim man simply as Apollon. No one made a movement to sit. Stankevich spoke first. "So, Father Grigory, it was Kuksina Ivanovna who introduced you to Segunin."

Alexei nodded.

"I unfortunately have never had the privilege of meeting Kuksina Ivanovna, but I've often heard Father Gapon sing her praise. It distresses Father deeply that she and Izaak are in prison."

"Yes, but they're both well, and still working with Father's flock. Kuksina asked me to pass that message on to Father Gapon." He found himself intuitively directing those comments to the slim man named Apollon, who had separated himself from the others and was standing, staring out the window. "I would appreciate it if you could introduce me to Father Gapon as quickly as possible. My business here must be of the most abbreviated nature."

"Yes." Stankevich nodded. Then he coughed. "Father, this is most awkward, but you understand, we must be careful about Father's Gapon's welfare. His enemies are many. I must be sure you carry no weapon."

"Of course." Alexei nodded and raised his arms to shoulder height as Stankevich expertly felt for any concealed weapons.

"He seems all right," Stankevich said to Voyekiev, who nodded and looked toward the slim man at the window.

Slowly the slim man turned and smiled on Stankevich and Voyekiev. "Thank you, my brothers." His face radiated an innocent pleasure. "Will you be so kind as to leave us now?"

"Of course." Voyekiev and Stankevich nearly bowed as they left, and Alexei knew this third man was Father Gapon.

"Father Grigory, I am pleased to meet you." Gapon extended his long, feminine fingers. His handshake was gentle. "I am Georgi Apollonovich Gapon. No longer Father, I am afraid. Or soon not to be. They are in the process of defrocking me, for my love of the people."

"I'm sorry."

Gapon smiled sweetly. "No need for that. Holiness cannot be ordained, nor can it be taken away. My people understand that. Kuksina Ivanovna—ah, my heart soars just to speak her name. I so feared for her life, hers and Izaak's. No one heard of them after our march. Come . . ." Gapon urged Alexei to sit on the velvet couch beside him. He settled with the grace of a dancer. "Shall I call for something to eat or drink perhaps?"

"Not for me. We have much to discuss, Father. First, I must tell you this. I'm not a priest. My name is Grigory Pirogov, a comrade of Kuksina and Izaak. I met Izaak in prison and we talked of nothing but you and Kuksina. I traveled as a priest at Kuksina's suggestion."

"Yes, wise, always wise. But how did you get out of jail?"

"It makes no sense. Without explanation I was released one day with some others, after never having been charged. But my time in prison changed my life, Father. I was a hanger-on before I met Izaak. There was a friendly guard, you see, and he carried letters back and forth between Izaak and Kuksina. Although I've never met her, I feel as if I know her and you, Father. They want you to return to Russia, Father. The people need you."

Gapon's cheeks flushed with color; his eyes deepened to a glowing black. His smile was radiant; his happiness seemed at the same time humble and proud. "Nothing would please me more, but I've work to do here first, you see, important work which will help me to truly lead my people once I return. I've issued an 'open letter' to all Russian revolutionaries. For the movement is torn with quarreling factions. Someone must lead the revolutionaries, someone must unite them and bring them back to Russia under one banner. Then the workers and revolutionaries will be so great, like a clan of bears sweeping down from the frozen lands. Then I can truly lead,'' he said with the simplicity of a Sunday-school teacher. ''Already I have spoken to Vladimir Lenin, who leads the Bolsheviks, and to others. And I am writing a book, the story of my life. It is my most devout hope to inspire those who read it, workers and revolutionaries alike. For truly it is the work of God we carry forth. Further, I am planning a great Congress of Russian Socialist Parties . . .'' Gapon went on. His voice flowed mellifluously. His eyes sparkled with a lovely, vibrant passion. There was an innocence about him. He seduced like a most wonderful actor, but he was a madman, and therein his danger lay. He was also, as Irina said, exceedingly vain. That was the hook.

''Father, it seemed to Kuksina that if you did not return to Russia soon, your movement would be crushed. There is no one whom the people trust and love more than you. In truth, how can those who leave Russia lead the workers? Kuksina and Izaak have devised a plan to get you back to Russia, and to protect you. Here, I even have this letter from the great Alexei Yakovlevich Kalinin. You know of the man?''

''Of course.'' Gapon's interest was piqued.

''His young wife and nephew are in the Fortress for the crime of assassinating the hated Leonti Yermolov.'' Alexei slowly reached into his pockets and pulled out the letter he'd written to Gapon, promising monetary support for Gapon's Society.

''This is an honor that such a man as Alexei Yakovlevich would wish to give me support.'' His eyes scanned the letter once more. ''And of course, he would garner the support of other businessmen.''

''I'm sure.''

''But still, what good is support, Grigory, if one is dead or in jail?''

''Yes, there are many who would like to see that,'' Alexei agreed gravely. ''We must find a way to steal you back to Russia and protect you even as the one they call the Shadow is protected.''

''The Shadow?'' Gapon questioned, his lips tightening ever so slightly.

''Yes, Kuksina said you know him, but perhaps only by his name Arkady Akimov.''

''Go on, what else did Kuksina tell you?''

''She said this man, Akimov, was once your benefactor, but now cannot be trusted. However, he has recently taken the place of the hated Leonti Yermolov as head of the Okhrana. Surely he could, if he wanted to, assure you safe passage.''

Gapon looked frightened. "As Kuksina said, Akimov is not to be trusted."

"Let me go to him, Father, as your emissary. Let me speak to him. I have had much experience in the ways of men. I sniff out a lying dog, I promise you. Let me talk to this Akimov for you. Perhaps he'll be useful for your return, perhaps not. Allow me to meet with him and make a report back to you. Then you and only you can decide what to do."

"Why would you do this?" Gapon sounded suspicious.

"Because you are our leader, Father. Russia needs a leader and a hero. The people are crying, bleeding, dying—only you can save them. You know that's true, Father. you know it's your mission in life, the greatest mission a man could have."

Gapon leaned back against the couch, crossed his legs, and stared straight ahead.

Alexei gazed at the swanlike profile.

"What is your experience that you think you can sniff out liars and traitors?"

"I grew up a poor boy, Father, in the slums of Yaroslavl. My father, my brother, and I worked on the railroads. My father killed a man, then went mad and hanged himself in prison. I got my schooling in the streets with thieves and whores. One must always have one's wits about him with thieves and whores, else one ends up a beggarman or dead. I am neither. I've had fortunes, Father. Yes, you wouldn't know it to look at me, but it's true. I've had many riches in life. They come and go like dust of the dead. Brotherhood and freedom are the best a man can hope for in this miserable life. Kuksina and Izaak convinced me of that. I'm willing to die for that. I am willing to die for you, Father, for without you, Russia is lost."

Gapon was quiet a few moments, then slowly sat up and folded his hands elegantly on his lap. "And do you know this man Akimov?"

"Not personally. I'd need you to introduce me."

Gapon nodded thoughtfully. "There's a woman, Marie Savich. Her husband was a faithful follower and a close friend of Kuksina's and Izaak's. She's my last contact with Akimov. But you must be clever with her, Grigory. She blames me for her husband's death, you see. Marie can put you in contact with Akimov."

CHAPTER FORTY-FOUR

Upon his return to Petersburg, Alexei went first to see his mother, who was living still with the old woman Inessa Grigorievna on Vasilievsky Island. Zhenya and Inessa had become inseparable, walking arm in arm down the snowy streets like two school chums, or sometimes, Alexei chuckled to think, like two Madame Defarges plotting revolution. In fact, he suspected that the makeshift hospital, funded almost entirely by Alexei through his mother, and dubbed by some in the neighborhood "The Hospital of the Holy Revolution," was a cover operation for covert workers' activities on Vasilievsky Island, if not in all of Petersburg. Zhenya spent most of her waking hours there, nursing the wounded and the sick.

"Alexei! What is a blasphemer like yourself doing dressed as a man of God!" Zhenya exclaimed as he walked into the hospital early in the morning of March 9, dressed as the bearded priest. The hospital was still. Zhenya was alone in the front room; Inessa was snoring on a sagging couch.

"You recognize me that easily, Mama." He frowned as he kissed her. "That worries me."

"A mother recognizes a child from a shadow even." She embraced him. "But where have you been? I've been trying to contact you for over a week."

"On a mission. Can we talk?"

"Of course. Come." Linking her arm through his, she led him into a small room used for storage. Boxes of medical goods as well as sheets and blankets were neatly lined against the wall. She offered him a seat on a box, and sat beside him, holding his hand still.

"Any news of Anna or Misha?" he asked.

"There was an article in the newspaper—it was read to me—it said they go to trial soon, by the end of the month. Oh, Alexei, they'll have to let you see Anna then."

"The Czar doesn't have to do anything, Mama. You know that. But listen, I need your help. I need you and your people

497

to start a rumor, and start it very quickly. Gapon is returning
to Russia."

"You know this for a fact?"

"The facts are meaningless. All you need say is that a
priest by the name of Grigory Khitrovo, a close associate of
Gapon's from Geneva, told you this. Say that Gapon will be
back in Russia within weeks." He could see the pained questions in his mother's eyes and he added sympathetically, "I
can tell you no more. To do so would put you in jeopardy."

"All right, then. I'll ask no more. But I promise you,
within hours news of Gapon's return will be throughout Vasilievsky Island."

"I need it all over Petersburg. I need it to reach important
people."

Zhenya smiled encouragingly and rubbed her hand along
his shoulder. "Vasilievsky Island within hours. The Admiralty, even the Winter Palace, by the end of the day."

Alexei took off his long beard and mustache before leaving
the workers' hospital and went directly to his palace to check
his mail. He hadn't been home in eight days. He leafed aimlessly through the pile of letters. There were several messages
marked "Urgent" from Sergei Witte. All were dated within
the last four days and all said the same thing: "Need to meet
with you. No one knows where you are."

Alexei smiled at the coincidence. Witte was the next person he wanted to see, but the meeting would have to wait
until tomorrow. It was critical that the rumor of Gapon's return reach Witte, and by necessity, Akimov, first.

They met for lunch in a fashionable restaurant not far from
Witte's office. Alexei was early. Witte was late, looking harried as he pushed past the maître d' and waved a frantic hello.

"Forgive me, Alexei Yakovlevich. Schedules mean nothing
these days. Ah, but it's good to see you. I was beginning to
worry you had done one of your vanishing acts." Witte sat down
and immediately poured himself a glass of wine. He took a long
sip and settled into his seat. "That's better." His smile was
tired. "Now, where have you been off to?"

"Business. It's all that keeps my mind ordered these days. I
read in the papers that a trial was imminent. I'm surprised I
wasn't informed."

"Which is why I've been trying to reach you. The Czar
asked me to personally acquaint you with the details. He's
not without heart, I promise."

Alexei decided to let the remark pass.

"The trial is set for March 21. They have confessions from all of them now. In any case, you'll be allowed to be there, and to see Anna and Misha afterward. I advise you to get them counsel, too, someone more experienced in criminal law than your Yuri Dobrinsky. The Grand Duke Ilya Mikhailevich has obtained Viktor Valentinov to represent Irina."

"Do me a favor, then. Talk to Valentinov for me, will you, Sergei? See if he'll carry out the details for all of them."

The waiter interrupted their conversation to take the order, and once he left, Witte continued, "As to the sentencing, the Czar has not made up his mind about the others, but Anna will be exiled to a labor camp on Lake Baikal—"

"Baikal! It's thousands of miles. Such a trek means death to a pregnant woman."

"We'll do everything we can to make sure Anna's exile is sufferable. We don't want your wife or child to die. You must believe that."

"We?" Alexei questioned.

"Akimov and myself."

"Akimov!" Alexei snorted.

"She'll not be mistreated—"

"There's no way you can promise me that! So don't, all right? You're cowards, the bunch of you, your Czar, Akimov, and you—how convenient exile is for you. It saves the monarchy the stigma of executing a pregnant woman."

Witte shifted uncomfortably in his seat and looked anxiously about. "Alexei, please, a scene here will accomplish nothing."

"Damn you all," he muttered, pressing his hand to his head. "Damn you to hell." He started to stand.

"Wait, Alexei, please. In all that has happened these past months, I fear we have lost the last shreds of our friendship. That saddens me. I want to help you in your pain."

"I told you how you can help me. Get me in to see Akimov."

"I can't. I've tried, believe me. Please sit. Let's at least have lunch."

Feigning reluctance, Alexei sat, and a long, awkward silence followed. The two men didn't speak until the entrée of smoked oysters was served.

"Have you heard the rumor?" Witte finally asked, smoothing his thumb about the rim of his wineglass.

"What rumor is that?"

"About Gapon."

"No."

"He's returning to Russia."

"Will Akimov kill him?"

"Whatever for?" Witte seemed genuinely surprised by the question.

"Perhaps for the sheer pleasure of the kill."

"It would do you well to moderate your feelings toward the man, Alexei. Not only is he in a position to make life easier for Anna in exile, but he's good for the country, he's good for industry, which makes him good for you. Each day he grows more ensconced in the court. He has a way about him. He's very diplomatic when he needs to be. He's charming the Czar."

"How very fortunate for you, Sergei."

Marie Savich lived in a first-floor flat of a run-down boardinghouse in the back of Vasilievsky Island. Alexei had to knock three times before there was an answer.

"Who is it?" came a timid woman's voice, followed by the cry of a child.

"Father Grigory Khitrovo. I'm a friend of a friend. Please let me in."

The door opened a crack and Alexei stepped back so Marie could see his priest's cassock. "Please let me in, my child. It's very important. It's about your husband, God rest his soul."

The door opened just enough for Alexei to slip in. Marie Savich quickly turned the lock behind them. She was a short, stout woman of indeterminable age, with large, dark, frightened eyes. Her skin was as sallow and sickly as that of her two children, a small skinny boy and an older skinny girl, who clung to her. The boy whimpered. The girl coughed miserably and pulled at her stringy brown hair. The flat, no more than a crowded room, was cold and smelled of fat and urine. There was a bed with rumpled blankets, more blankets on the floor, a rickety table, and some worn children's toys. Several icons surrounded by candles were the only adornment on the walls.

Marie Savich and her two children peered silently at Alexei.

"I was sorry to hear about your husband's death, Marie."

"Who sent you here?" she demanded hoarsely.

"A friend. Father Gapon."

"Gapon! You think he is every poor person's hero?"

"He was your husband's."

"And Kostya is dead." She eyed him warily, then asked, "Is it true what people say, that Gapon is returning?"

"With your help, praise God."

She spit. "He'll rot in hell before he gets my help."

"An address is all I need, Marie. Father said only you can help me. Only you know how to contact Akimov."

Marie shrank before him; fear seemed to suck out her blood. "Go now, Father, please, I beg you."

"Marie . . ." Alexei smiled and touched Marie's shoulder in a way he'd seen priests touch without touching. He was careful to show no signs of urgency. "Father Gapon told me you're the only one who can help me reach Arkady Akimov."

"That was Kostya's job!" she snapped back. "He's dead. If I die, who will watch my babies?"

"Surely, simply passing on one message wouldn't put your life in danger."

"Anything that has to do with Akimov is dangerous. I know. I lived with that danger for ten years. It's over. It died with Kostya."

"Marie, did you grow up in Petersburg?"

"No, praise God. I came from a small village on the Volga. It was where I met Kostya. It was he who brought me to Petersburg, and left me here. I was poor in my village, Father, but not alone."

"Would you like to go back?"

"Ha!" she snorted. "As if they'd welcome me with my two hungry children."

"I can help you, Marie. If you help me just get this message to Akimov, I'll see you have enough money to feed, clothe, and protect not only your children but also the rest of your family."

"With money like that, you think I'd return to them!" She snickered.

"You can do what you want with it. I'll see that you and your children are safely escorted to any place you want, even outside Russia, if you want. Just get this one message to Akimov and you'll have enough money so that you never have to worry for the rest of your life."

She laughed then, a high-pitched laugh that made the skin of her face stretch in wrinkles. Her mouth opened wide, showing two blackened teeth. "You think I believe you? A poor priest!"

"How much money do you need, Marie? Ten thousand rubles?"

Her mouth fell open. Her eyes widened in surprise.

"I can have it for you within the hour. Ten thousand rubles and passage to any place you want to go. All you have to do is get this message to Akimov and bring back a response. Or tell me how to contact him, and I'll do the rest."

"Are you daft? I'd be dead before I could spend a miserable kopeck."

"But you can get him a message. Father Gapon says you

can. That's all I need you to do. Tell Akimov I've been sent by Father Gapon to meet with him. Tell him it's urgent, and bring me back a place to meet with him, and you'll be a rich woman, Marie. You can take your children out of this damp, miserable city, into the fresh air where they can grow strong.''

"Sure, I'll believe you when I see the cold cash, not some holy note of wealth in the other world!''

"Fine.'' He extended his hand to hers. "I'll be back in an hour—with the cold cash. Ten thousand rubles.''

"Why would you give this to me?'' she asked furtively.

"Russia is giving this to you, Marie. Russia needs Father Gapon. Ten thousand rubles is nothing to end the suffering of so many millions.''

She pulled back her hand and stared beyond him, as if considering something. "I won't be here in an hour, Father. I've business, you see, an appointment I've had for a while. Can you be back here at three o'clock? I'll let you know about Akimov then.''

"Fine.''

"With the cash.''

"I promise.''

Before going to the bank, Alexei went home and took off the priest's beard and clothes and changed into a suit. He packed a bag with the doorman's uniform and coat he'd worn on Bloody Sunday, then went to a gun shop and bought himself a revolver and ammunition. Finally, he went to the bank and withdrew the cash for Marie Savich, and behind the closed curtains of his carriage, he changed into the doorman's clothes. He had his coachman leave him off at the Nikolaievsky Bridge and walked the rest of the way, arriving at Marie Savich's house twenty minutes early; he waited in an alleyway.

At a quarter to three Marie stepped from a carriage and hurried, eyes to the ground, to her house. What appeared to be the same carriage slowly passed the house twice in the next five minutes. Then the carriage disappeared and a tall, bullish man with a fur cap and a fur-trimmed coat appeared. His features were hard, his eyes small. The muscles of his body strained even against his heavy coat. Alexei watched him walk slowly down the block, past Marie Savich's house, and then back. It was a gray afternoon, bitter with a cold which keeps most people indoors. Alexei felt for his gun, and as he did, he glanced to Marie's window. She was peering out, her eyes fixed on the bullish man.

When he passed out of Alexei's view for the third time, Alexei slipped from the alleyway and walked at a brisk rate in the opposite direction. Even if Marie Savich saw him, she wouldn't recognize him, a doorman without the hint of a beard. He turned the corner and hurried into the front of a building and waited. Soon he could hear the bullish man's feet crunching in the snow.

"Pst—you!" Alexei called, stepping into the middle of the street.

The man looked up, his eyes instinctively scanning the area. He was fatter than he'd appeared, softer and meaner at the same time. The man scowled churlishly. His hands were pressed into fists.

Alexei knew this man was a professional thug, most assuredly one of Akimov's well-trained goons sent to get Marie Savich's priest. Alexei was glad he had taken the precaution of changing his clothes. When he met Akimov, it was going to be on his terms. Smiling casually, Alexei started forward. "I was wondering—"

"I'm busy. Find someone else to give you directions." The man's skin was an unhealthy yellow. His fat lips curled over even yellower teeth.

Alexei turned and slipped his hands into his pockets, appearing to walk away. He stopped after a few steps and fingered the gun in his pocket. The bullish man's footsteps crunched the snow; he had clearly dismissed Alexei, who pivoted and, after three long steps, had his arm squeezed around the unsuspecting man's neck, a gun in his back.

"What the hell!" the bullish man cursed, and jerked his arms to break free. His body arched and thudded like stone against Alexei, causing him to almost lose his hold.

"Come with me, or so help me God, this gun will blow you in half. There's no one here to care, not in a neighborhood like this." He pulled the hammer back. It echoed in the cold air.

The bullish man quieted. "All right. All right. If it's money you want—"

Alexei bent up the man's arm until he moaned in pain, and Alexei pushed him into an alley, shoving him to the icy ground. In an instant the man turned, grabbing Alexei's leg and sending him and the gun flying. He was on top of Alexei, pounding his head and face with his powerful fists. Then he pulled Alexei by his shoulders and slammed him into the side of the building.

"Who the hell are you, scum?" In a flash, the man had pulled out a knife and was pressing the blade against Alexei's throat. He reeked of garlic. "Tell me or I'll shove this into your fucking neck."

Alexei raised his leg, thrusting it forcefully into the man's groin; the yellow face and fat lips twisted in agony, but moments later, propelled by an agonized cry, the man was stabbing at Alexei again. Alexei swerved and the knife crashed into the building with such force the blade snapped. Alexei kicked and the man teetered and fell, moaning as he grasped his groin. Grabbing the man's head, Alexei pounded it on the ice. He reached for his gun, only inches away. "Now, you tell me: who the hell are *you*, scum? Or so help me God, I'll blow your fucking head off."

The man opened his mouth, but no sound came out.

Alexei tore open the fur-trimmed coat and reached into the man's inner pocket for his wallet. With his knee pressed into the man's neck and gun still pressed to his head, Alexei searched through the wallet, throwing out the ruble notes until he came across identification. It read, "Ignoty Ilyitch Kolesnikov."

"Kolesnikov! The knife wielder!" Alexei's eyes screwed wildly on the fat man, and as if jolted by an electric current, he began pounding Kolesnikov. The vengeance flowed like blood from a severed limb. "That's for Irina Ilyanovna, you pig! You remember Irina Ilyanovna, don't you?" When Kolesnikov didn't answer, Alexei slammed his cheek with the butt of the gun. "You remember Irina Ilyanovna, don't you?" He raised the gun once more.

"Yes, yes, I remember her!" Kolesnikov cried, holding up his arm to shield his face.

"And the rest of them?" Alexei lowered the butt of the gun on Kolesnikov's nose. Blood gushed and Kolesnikov writhed as he pleaded, "Yes, yes, whatever you say."

Alexei raised his hand again, but his own eyesight was blurred. Blood dripped from a gash in his forehead. He wiped it away and pressed the gun to Kolesnikov's neck. "You're lucky I need you or you'd pay right now. Get up!" Alexei thundered, yanking him to his feet. "Where's all your bravery without your knife, you scum!" Alexei laughed and shoved him forward. "Walk, you son of a bitch. Walk or you'll never breathe again." Alexei half-dragged, half-pulled Kolesnikov to Marie Savich's apartment. "Open the door, Marie. It's me, Father Grigory, with a friend of yours." He banged with the gun. He could hear whimpering. "Open the door or I'll break it down."

There was a fumbling of locks and the door sprung open. Alexei pushed Kolesnikov inside and the man crumpled to the floor. Alexei stepped over the body, dragged the rest of Kolesnikov inside, and kicked closed the door.

Marie was staring in confused horror from Alexei, whom she clearly didn't recognize without his beard and priestly garments, to Kolesnikov, his face bloodied almost beyond recognition. "Sweet Jesus, son of God!" she cried out, pulling both her children to her and then shoving them away. "Sweet Jesus!" she repeated, crossing herself again and again. Both her children were crying. "Who are you?" she pleaded.

"It doesn't matter who I am." He reached into his pocket and took out a packet of money. "I have the ten thousand rubles I promised." He shoved it into her hand.

"Praise God!" she gasped, pressing the money to her. "You are Father Grigory. Oh, forgive me, please. I never thought you'd bring the money, I swear. I was only doing what I thought I had to do to protect me and my children. You understand, Father. I was only doing what I had to. Please don't hurt us. We're just poor folk is all, and my husband's dead." The woman was hysterical.

Alexei couldn't bear her hysteria. "Take the money and your children and get out of here, Marie. Do you understand? Get a cab and go straight to the train station. Don't stop to see anyone or talk to anyone. Don't tell anyone where you're going. If you do, your life won't be worth a kopeck, you understand. Akimov will think you set up this thug, and he'll find you and kill you. You know he will."

She was nodding, her face white with terror.

"Go on, now. Get your children and get out of here and don't ever come back."

"Thank you, Father. Thank you." She grabbed his hands and kissed them.

"Go quickly before I change my mind."

Within minutes Marie and the children were gone.

Alexei pulled Kolesnikov to his feet and dumped him on the couch.

"She'll go straight to Akimov." Kolesnikov snorted, his voice stronger than Alexei expected.

"I doubt it. But even if she does, I don't lose, you see. I want to see Akimov. I welcome the man. Still, I'd rather meet him on my own terms. In fact, I don't think we'll be here very long. See, this is the way it is, Kolesnikov." Alexei sneered. "Either you tell me where I can find Akimov, or I'll kill you."

"I'm laying bets you won't. With the Savich woman gone, there's only me." His laughter was biting.

Alexei sat on the couch beside Kolesnikov. "Tell me where I can find Akimov."

Kolesnikov spit on him.

Alexei held the gun to Kolesnikov's thigh and pulled the trigger.

CHAPTER FORTY-FIVE

It was dark, almost five by the time Alexei ventured into the street again, and workers were beginning to congregate in groups. Soon they would march to the university, where there was, as usual, a rally. Torches and bonfires lit the streets. Alexei wound his way through the crowd, watchful for any signs of disorder. He couldn't afford to be caught up in mayhem now. If Kolesnikov had told the truth, he had to hurry. Akimov had instructed Kolesnikov to bring the emissary from Father Gapon to a storage room of the Finland Railroad Station in the Vyborg district—if he proved to be legitimate.

Alexei looked at his watch. It was five-fifteen. The meeting was set for six. He wanted to get there early, and as soon as he was clear of the massing students and workers, he began to run.

He arrived at Finland Station at five-forty. There was the normal crush of evening travelers as well as the now-all-too-common patrolling troops and police. Alexei knew, however, it was the porters, ticket sellers, floor sweepers, and even that drunk sitting slouched on a bench who posed the greater threat. Any of them might be part of Akimov's private force, waiting for Kolesnikov, perhaps, waiting to give Akimov the all-clear sign.

Following Kolesnikov's instructions, Alexei easily spied the storage room marked "Unclaimed Goods"; it was down a short hall at the far end of the huge waiting room. He stopped as soon as he noted the room, and hurried back to the waiting room. No one, it seemed, was watching him. He found a niche behind a flower seller's stall, lit a cigarette, and waited, recalling Kolesnikov's description of Akimov, an older man of middle height with white hair and beard. Odd, Alexei had always imagined Akimov as tall and virile.

He scanned the waiting room for the man Kolesnikov had described, but saw no one. He finished one cigarette and immediately lit another. His heart was pounding too fast. His nerves were too taut, his energy too high. The cut above his eye pulsated. He had to calm down. Minutes passed slowly.

Six o'clock came and went. Alexei smoked countless cigarettes. At six-fifteen he noticed a rather well-dressed man in a sable-collared coat. His face was shaded by a dark gray broad-brimmed hat, but Alexei thought he caught the hint of a white beard. A raucous group of students hurrying for a train raced in front of Alexei, and by the time they were gone, the man in the sable-collared coat had melded with the evening crowd. Alexei glanced back to the storage room. The door was still closed, the hallway empty. He scanned the waiting room again. People blurred like shadows on a speeding train. His head jerked. Damn the beating of his heart. Damn Akimov.

"Sir, can I help you?" the flower seller asked.

Alexei looked into the face of a strong young man who looked little like any wizened flower seller he'd ever seen.

"No . . . no thank you."

"Then if you don't mind, I'll have to ask you to move on. This is my place. There's plenty of other walls to lean on."

"Yes, all right." As Alexei looked for a place to move to, he noticed the man in the sable-collared coat heading in his direction again. This time his white beard was unmistakable. Unconsciously, protectively, Alexei fell back into a small crowd of businessmen and he focused on the white-bearded man. He had to calm himself. He was shaking inside and beginning to sweat. Perhaps this man was Akimov and perhaps he wasn't. There were countless white-bearded men in Petersburg.

Slowly, yet directly, the white-bearded man made his way to the flower seller's wagon and, fondling a bunch of flowers as if to buy them, he leaned closer to the flower seller, who shook his head in answer to a question. The bearded man turned, his eyes riveted for a moment on the storage room marked "Unclaimed Goods." Then he looked at the huge clock on the wall. The wide-brimmed hat still partially shadowed his face, but Alexei could see clearly not only the beard but also white hair curling at the neck. Akimov. Suddenly he was certain—he was within feet of Arkady Akimov.

Akimov left the flower seller and started back across the waiting room. A hitherto unnoticed worker, porter and soldier fell into step behind him. Alexei followed as they left the station, and Akimov climbed into a large, black waiting carriage. The soldier, porter and worker clambered into an open carriage behind.

Alexei looked about. There were several cabs waiting for fares, but he didn't trust any of the drivers to stay behind Akimov in the night. He spied one at the end of the line that was empty of its driver. Alexei raced to the cab, a fine new drozhki, and leapt in. "Make way! Make way!" he shouted, urging on the startled horse. The drozhki tore away from the station to the surprised cries and curses of a coachman.

Within moments Alexei spied the open carriage with the porter, worker and soldier following at a discreet pace behind the closed black carriage. Clearly, they were in no rush and had no suspicion of being followed. Alexei slowed his horse to an equally easy pace, grateful when he saw the carriages headed toward the Alexandrovsky Bridge and the center of Petersburg. The streets were more adequately lit there; he would not lose Akimov now.

From the Alexandrovsky Bridge, Akimov took Liteiny Prospect, turning near the Ciniselli Circus and pulling into a mansion on the Fontanka Canal. The drozhki with the soldier, porter and worker paused at the gates. Alexei stopped his horse in the shadows of the canal; the mansion was still visible in the streetlights; he could easily see Akimov climb from the carriage and walk to the house. Then the drozhki with the soldier, porter and worker started off down the street.

Alexei left his drozhki and walked toward the mansion, where armed guards stood in the shadows. He considered what to do, now that he had found Akimov. He had to confront him, convince him he had incriminating evidence about Yermolov's assassination. If Akimov remained unconvinced, Alexei need only point out that, in the hands of Akimov's enemies, such evidence was scandalous. A well-placed rumor could destroy an ambitious man. If Akimov doubted Alexei's connections with the court, Alexei would explain that it was he who had discovered Yermolov's whereabouts for the Brigade. If Akimov threatened Alexei with death or arrest, Alexei would assert he was not alone. Should he not leave Akimov's palace on time, the rumor-mongers would begin their work. Akimov would be a *persona non grata* in the court before he could issue one more command in the Okhrana.

A sudden light filtering through the shutters of a second-floor room of the mansion focused Alexei's attention on the moment and the numbing coldness already at work on his toes. He couldn't stand there any longer, and he began walking at a fast clip around the block. The mansion directly behind Akimov's was in total darkness; Alexei slipped along the side of it to find guards sitting around a bonfire in Akimov's backyard. They were talking loudly and laughing, so preoccupied in their storytelling, they never noticed the hunched shadow making its way along a far brick wall. Within minutes Alexei was by Akimov's house, feeling in the darkness for an entrance. The windows were low, probably leading to the basement; the middle one budged ever so slightly, then squeaked open with the pressure of Alexei's weight.

"What's that?" one of the guards cried out.

Alexei fell, kneeling in some leafless bushes. He reached for his gun.

A torch appeared at the back end of the house and there was the scurrying of an animal. "Jesus, it was only a cat," the guard said, and the torch followed him back to the bonfire.

Alexei waited until the laughter of the guards started up again, and he went back to the window. The opening was narrow. He had to take off his coat to slide in; he crawled gingerly through the pitch-black basement, pausing for what seemed like hours at each creak or bump. When he finally found the stairs, he sat against them, finding he was extraordinarily short of breath. He was tired, too, suddenly exhausted, and he leaned his head against a wooden stud and closed his eyes. He was back more than twenty-five years, back on the marble stairs of the railroad office in Yaroslavl, back with Tolya, back before killing Matyushin. The bearded figure of Akimov flashed in his mind, merging with Matyushin and his gold tooth, then with Kolesnikov. He heard Kolesnikov's cry as the bullet seared his flesh, saw the agony on Kolesnikov's bloodied face. *Help me, please, don't leave me to die,* Kolesnikov had pleaded, and Alexei had left him writhing on Marie Savich's greasy couch. *Akimov, Akimov*—the name echoed in the chambers of his mind. Alexei hoped he could terrorize Akimov half as well as he had terrorized Kolesnikov. He wanted revenge. He wanted to strip Akimov's life bare. He wanted Akimov to feel what he had felt, what Anna was feeling, Anna, Misha, Irina and the unborn child. If anything happened to Anna or their child, Alexei would kill Akimov.

Alexei wasn't sure how long he sat there, until he was cold and stiff; the gun in his hand was frigid, making his fingers numb. He pushed himself to his knees. Light was coming from under the door at the top of the stairs. He listened. There were women's voices. The kitchen was most surely beyond. He waited. Finally the light at the top of the stairs went out, and there were footsteps clunking on bare stairs, the back stairs to the servants' quarters. The servants were done for the night. He crawled up the stairs and listened. Holding his gun firmly in one hand, he turned the knob with the other and the door opened noiselessly. The kitchen was dark, save for a light coming from the hallway. Pressing his body against the wall, Alexei crept toward the light, pausing when he saw the shadow of an armed guard in the foyer.

In the flick of a moment, he rounded the staircase. The carpet absorbed his footsteps and he climbed quickly, slipping onto the second-floor landing. A light was coming from under only one door. He wondered if Akimov were alone. Perhaps a woman was with him. He couldn't burst in with a woman there. The woman would shout. The guards would come.

He stood by the door listening. There were only the sounds of papers rustling and an occasional masculine muttering to which there was no response. He thought of knocking, pretending he was a guard, but such a noise might call a guard, and grasping his gun, he reached for the knob, turned it and slipped inside.

Yuri Dobrinsky looked up from the desk.

Alexei didn't know what was more terrifying: the shock he felt or the horror on Yuri's face. Neither man spoke or moved for what seemed like a very long time. Alexei thought he would suffocate from the heaviness in his chest.

Yuri eyed the gun in Alexei's hand. "Sit, please, Alexei Yakovlevich," Yuri finally said, and stretched out his pudgy hand in offering.

Alexei looked about the elegant, finely furnished room, so unlike anything he could imagine surrounding Yuri. His eyes rested momentarily on a white wig and beard. "Why?" he asked, and thought he was pleading.

"A drink perhaps?" Without waiting for an answer, Yuri poured vodka into fine crystal glasses and handed one to Alexei, who shook his head. Then Yuri sat back at his desk. "I see I've disappointed you greatly," he said matter-of-factly.

Alexei could not speak.

"It's not the end, you know." Yuri smiled ingratiatingly. It was odd to see him smile. He so rarely did. "You knew me as Yuri Dobrinsky, Dmitri Mayakovsky, now I am Arkady Akimov."

"A murderer and a betrayer." Alexei's voice sounded oddly unlike his own. "I was your friend," he anguished, feeling an aching like mourning clutch at his chest. "You used me and my family. You used your comrades, even your Stepan."

Yuri shook his head. "Stepan's death was unavoidable, I'm afraid, as unavoidable as was bringing poor Anna into the bloody mess. I'd hoped she wouldn't be arrested, of course."

"Liar!" Alexei, his gun gripped in his hand, started from his seat.

"Don't be a fool. This house is loaded with guards. One cry is all they need and you'll be dead before you can reach me," Yuri snapped angrily.

As if for the first time, Alexei noticed the elegant blue silk dressing gown Yuri wore.

"Now, we can either be intelligent, grown men about this, or one of us can act like a child and end up dead. I beg of you, my friend, don't force me to kill you. Give me your gun, please." The hardness was gone from Yuri's voice. His sincerity was all the more confusing.

Holding the gun in one hand, Alexei pressed his other hand to his forehead, inadvertently touching the gash above his eye. The pain reminded him of Kolesnikov, a creature not of the fiend Arkady Akimov, but of a friend, once a friend, Yuri Nikolaievich. God, it was so hard to think. Reality slithered and shriveled, rank with the stench of decaying flesh.

"How did you find me? Kolesnikov? Yes, I knew something was amiss when he never showed. And the bruises on your face. They seem like Kolesnikov's handiwork." A sly grin crossed Akimov's lips. "Ah, yes, I'm beginning to see. It fits, most clearly, but then, I would expect nothing less from you. You are Gapon's emissary from Geneva, are you not, Alexei? That's where you've been, why Witte couldn't contact you."

"Does Witte know about all this?"

"About my many personae, you mean? Good God, no. Besides me, you're the only person on earth who knows." He frowned with displeasure. "I tell you, Alexei, as your hatred of Akimov grew, I had fears of something like this happening."

"Why?" Alexei demanded, his voice taking on authority as he gripped his gun more tightly. "What made you do this, Yuri—or should I call you Arkady?"

"Whatever makes you more comfortable."

"Were you always Akimov, even when I first met you?"

Akimov eyed the gun as he reached for a cigarette and offered one to Alexei. Lighting his, he said, "No. The irony of it all is that I was as true as my father before I met you. Dedicated to the revolution. It was you and all the incredible wealth and power you afforded me that made me rethink my values. Values!" He snorted. "Dedication!" He laughed vacantly. "To what? To poverty and heroic-sounding words about freedom and brotherhood. I had never known freedom until I had your money, our money, Alexei. Yes, for the first time in my life, I felt happy, and that was strange. It got me to thinking . . ." Akimov was talking in an easy manner, as if telling someone else's story. "My wife died because I couldn't get her proper medical care. I didn't have the money. Oh, I had the devotion to the revolution, but it wasn't enough to keep either my wife or my daughter alive."

"Laura died for what she believed in. What her father taught her to believe in."

"Well, her father was wrong." Akimov ran his hand across his head again in a decidedly Yuri habit. "Just like my father was wrong. Wait, I take that back. My father wasn't wrong, just unprepared. You see, I recognize that the revolution might well win one day. The reign of the House of Romanov might end. Who knows? I don't pretend to, and in actuality, I've done my bit to push the revolution along. Yes, I daresay I've done more to help than to hinder. I've masterminded some of the most progressive assassinations in Russia."

"And arrested or murdered some of the finest revolutionaries."

"I had to create credibility, you see, at the same time making sure the most vile reactionaries, those most deserving of death, got their just deserts," Akimov said righteously. "I'm far from having betrayed the revolution."

"You're mad."

"Hardly that. I'm a realist, my friend, something you've never been. For you see, if the monarchy wins, Akimov is firmly entrenched. If the revolution wins, I'll dispose of Akimov as easily as I appeared to kill off Dmitri."

"Appeared?"

"No one found Dmitri's body, did they? He can reappear quite easily."

"I can't believe this is you talking."

"Don't fool yourself, Alexei. You never knew me. No one has ever known me, nor shall they."

"The Shadow." Alexei's lips curled with the words.

Akimov grinned self-contentedly. "I rather like that. Although I've often thought Chameleon would have been a better *nom de plume*, or should I say *nom de guerre*? Oh, come on, Alexei, don't look so grim. We've always worked well as a team. I don't know why we can't now."

"With Anna in Siberia and Misha hanged."

"Lord, no. I've all but convinced the Czar not to hang the conspirators. In truth, such deaths would only add fuel to the fire of revolution. They're to be exiled, the lot of them. I think a rather easy escape can be managed somewhere between Petersburg and their final destination. I can't promise they'll all make it to freedom. No, that would be far too neat. A few will be recaptured, maybe one even killed in the escape. Credibility, you see. Misha, Anna, and Irina will make it though. It's what you want, isn't it? It's what you came here for. But the irony is, I would have arranged their escape regardless of your tracking me down. I hope you believe that."

Alexei steadied his glance. "Tell me how it felt to betray those who thought you were a leader, close to a god."

"Men are fools to make other men gods. They're bound to be manipulated and disappointed."

"Me, then, how did it feel to betray me?"

"I wouldn't have let them die. I promise you."

"Why wouldn't you let me in to see them?"

"I wanted to, of course. I knew your anguish, but I couldn't make it look as if I were coddling an enemy of the Czar."

"And when you discovered Anna was pregnant?"

"It was I who sent the doctor to see her in the first place, as soon as she was ill. He's a fine young physician, Dr. Stepaiak. I've seen his instructions were carefully followed. Anna's diet's been enriched. She's allowed to walk in the courtyard every day—"

"Am I supposed to be grateful?"

"No, not grateful. Ah, Alexei, in my heart I wish you could believe that I never would have let any harm come to Anna. I would have taken care of her and Misha."

"Like you took care of Irina?" He snorted. "Tell me how you could have had Kolesnikov disfigure her so."

"To keep her alive. She's like you, Alexei, too smart and pushy for her own good. I wanted to scare her away before she discovered anything which would have forced me to kill her, as Vera Martova unfortunately did. As a matter of fact, it was an unfortunate series of events from the beginning, one which never would have happened if that despicable little fly on the wall hadn't sent those documents to Vera in Paris. Unfortunately, I haven't been able to discover the slimy little culprit or how he got his hands on the memoranda from me to Gapon. But I shall, and then he'll pay. So, if you need to blame anyone, Alexei, blame that little mole in the Okhrana who started this house of cards toppling."

"You're mad to think that any of this makes sense or that you can get away with it. I've your handwriting on thousands of business deals, your handwriting as Yuri Dobrinsky. I'm sure we could find papers written by Dmitri Mayakovsky too. And they'll all match up with Arkady Akimov's."

"Yes, but you wouldn't do such a thing." Akimov shifted his plump body in his seat. His hand slipped down to his lap. "For if you did, I would have to push the Czar for hanging. And Anna wouldn't make it a hundred miles to Siberia. She'd be shot very quickly, trying to escape."

Alexei leapt to his feet.

"Sit down, my friend. Cool down. I'm just showing you the limits of your situation. I'm afraid you don't have many options."

"I could kill you before you could call for your guards."

"How foolish, really. Then Anna and Misha would lose their greatest support. Now, be easy. Sit. Let's talk about how we can solve this problem posed by your knowledge of my secret."

Alexei steadied the gun pointed at Akimov. The man's smugness was beyond bearing.

"I've a plan," Akimov was saying. "Why don't you sleep here tonight. Get a good night's rest. Your body must ache from your tangle with Kolesnikov. He's a nasty son of a bitch, I'll admit. Come, give me the gun." Akimov's hand was outstretched. "Have a few more drinks, a good night's rest, and tomorrow I'll arrange for you to see Anna and Misha. I promise—"

"Drop it!" came a voice from the doorway.

Alexei turned to see a stony-faced guard with a gun trained on him.

"You see, Alexei, you really have no choice," Akimov said, a hint of sadness to his voice.

It was the sadness that caught up Alexei, connecting him to Yuri once more and to the betrayal. A sick feeling gripped him and, gun still pointed, he jerked around toward Akimov and then back to the guard. Before he could pull the trigger, there was an explosion, a searing in his chest as the bullet hit. He was burning, the pain expanding into a terrifying blackness threatening to crush him. Suddenly the burning ceased; fear was slipping from him, seeming to swim down his arms and legs and fingertips. He was weightless, floating beyond the darkness toward a burst of light, golden like Anna's hair in the Crimean sun. The weightlessness was euphoric. Anna was near. He was streaming toward her, billowing down a long tunnel, and calling her name. *Anna! Anna!* He was smiling. The pain was over. Soon, very soon, she would embrace him.

CHAPTER FORTY-SIX

Anna almost laughed when the lawyer told her Alexei was dead. Olga had warned her against such machinations. Olga had said the Czar's greatest torture was lying to prisoners, making them believe they'd been betrayed and were alone in the world. What could make her more alone than Alexei's death? Oh, yes, Alexei had been right all along. The Czar was an evil man, but she wouldn't believe his lies. Besides, she'd signed the confession. They had promised that if she signed, nothing would happen to Alexei. And hadn't Uncle Ilya told her Alexei was out of prison and safe? Well, she'd show this lawyer, Viktor Valentinov; she was nobody's fool.

Not only wouldn't she believe Valentinov, but she wouldn't trust him or agree to anything he said. He'd barely looked at her since they'd met, but she watched him carefully, noting that his flat gray eyes were without emotion. His wide cheekbones made him look like a cardboard man. She wondered how Alexei could have asked him to be her lawyer, and decided Alexei hadn't. Valentinov was the Czar's lackey; in his arrogance, Valentinov thought he was good-looking when he was merely clean. His skin was clean, his clothes were clean, his boots were clean; his mousy hair and mustache were trimmed to perfection. She could be as perfectly clean and far more elegant if she weren't a prisoner. Then Valentinov would treat her, the wife of Alexei Yakovlevich Kalinin and the daughter of Count Pyotr Ivanovich Orlov, with the utmost deference.

"Excuse me," Viktor Valentinov was saying.

"My baby," Anna repeated. "What will happen to my baby? Will Alexei take it? Will Alexei care for it?"

Without looking up from his papers, Viktor Valentinov said, "I've explained this to you, Anna Petrovna. I know it's hard, but you must accept the fact, your husband is dead. He was shot by some adversary, a member of the Black Hundreds, they think. It's the fate of men such as your husband. Now, here, I have papers for you to sign. A major portion of his estate was left to you. A prisoner cannot own property."

She sat very straight in her chair and breathed deeply. "You're lying and I'm not signing anything."

"As your lawyer I must advise you to do so. Eventually you will sign."

"I won't, not without talking to Alexei."

"Your husband is dead."

"Liar!" she shouted, her cheeks fired.

"Anna Petrovna." Valentinov was becoming impatient. His flat eyes looked everywhere in the room but at her. He tapped his pen on the table. "Do you like your weekly showers and your daily walks in the garden about the cathedral?"

"Yes."

"Do you like the special food that's prepared for you and you alone?"

"Yes."

"Do you know why you are allowed such special treatment?"

"Because of Alexei. He—"

"No, because the Czar is a compassionate man. He has spared your life because of the child which grows within you. And he is helping to nourish that child with fresh air and food which prisoners such as yourself never see. Now, if you want all that to continue, I would sign these papers immediately."

"No."

"Have you ever seen children born of prisoners, Anna Petrovna? They're small, weak. They rarely live. The Czar is giving your child a chance. Sign the papers, Anna Petrovna. As your lawyer, I must tell you that you have no choice."

Anna wanted to say no again, but she couldn't. Her baby had to live. Her baby had to be strong. Alexei wasn't dead. One day they would be together again, all three of them. For the sake of that day, she reached for a pen and signed wherever Valentinov pointed.

Misha thought nothing could compare with the joy of his first shower in almost three months. Never mind that this might be the last shower of his life; he luxuriated in the beating of the hot water on his skin and held the bar of strong-smelling soap to his nose, its disinfectant odor smelling like perfume. He scrubbed his hair several times until his scalp actually stopped itching. He would have liked to shave, but the guard merely grunted when asked, and led Misha to a room where, to his amazement, a clean change of clothes was waiting for him, his own clothes, which had been left in his closet at the palace before he'd moved in with Irina. New boots had been sent too, strong, sturdy boots, as well as a heavy greatcoat, fur hat, and thick scarf and mittens. Perhaps it was true after all, he thought. Perhaps as Viktor Valentinov had said, they were not to be hanged, but sent into exile. Why else would they be afforded new clothes?

When he was all dressed, chains were clamped about his legs and then his wrists and he was led out of the prison for the first time in months. The brilliant daylight sparkling off the snow was blinding; he drank in the air and daylight as a parched man drinks water. He felt hungry for life, awed by the beauty of a glittering ice-coated branch. Then he saw Irina. She too was being led in chains from the prison. "Irina!" he cried.

A guard butted him with a gun. "No talking."

He tried to wave beyond the constraints of his chains.

The guard butted him again. "You want to be soiled for the court?" he growled.

"Irina!" Her name fell joyously from his lips. He was

breathless; life was revealing itself like the green of spring. He was buoyant; Irina was beautiful. Like himself, she was dressed in a fine hat and coat. She wore new boots. She was thin and pale, but alive and beautiful. She was looking at him; her smile was love.

The guard pushed him forward.

He turned to watch her walk.

The guard kept butting him and he tripped in the chains. Pushing himself to his feet, he glanced back at her and called, "I love you!"

The courtroom was small and hushed. At one end, on a raised platform, was a table covered by a velvet, crimson cloth. Behind the table were three heavy carved oak, high-backed chairs, and centered behind them was a full-length painting of the Czar in a white uniform and crimson sash; his chest was covered with medals and he held a glittering sword in his hand. In the corner to the left of the painting was an icon of Christ with a crown of thorns. His face was grotesquely anguished and blood seeped from a slash in his chest. There were no jury seats, only a hard bench for the accused, already convicted. In the back of the room was the gallery, tiered rows of benches crowded with bearded men in finely fitted uniforms and women in furs. It was a courtly audience.

Anna scanned the gallery for sight of Alexei, and spied Alexander Ryabushinsky and his wife and Uncle Ilya, but not Aunt Tatyana; Sergei Witte was standing in a corner talking with a man as tall and broad as Alexei. Anna's heart soared, but when the man turned, he was a stranger. She searched the room again, thinking perhaps Alexei was just late. She looked for Petya and her father, and for a fleeting moment had hopes of seeing her mother; it was foolish; they hadn't come. She was dead to them already. They'd thrown away her photographs and forbidden anyone to mention her name again. Then she saw Zhenya Kirilovna sitting very close to Matryona and the old woman Inessa Grigorievna. The women were holding hands. Zhenya Kirilovna and Matryona wore black. Zhenya seemed so much older than Anna had remembered.

Zhenya smiled when their eyes met, a somber smile, without energy or hope.

"Alexei?" Anna mouthed.

Zhenya stared back, her usually expressive eyes barren. She crossed herself and bowed her head.

Anna Petrovna Kalinina, you are sentenced to a life of exile for your role in the conspiracy to assassinate Leonti

*Yurievich Yermolov. You are hereby denied all rights as a
citizen of Russia and all your worldly possessions are hereby
remanded to the state. . . .*

*Mikhail Anatolyevich Kalinin, you are sentenced to a life
of exile for your role in the conspiracy to assassinate Leonti
Yurievich Yermolov. You are hereby denied all rights as a
citizen of Russia and all your worldly possessions are hereby
remanded to the state. . . .*

*Irina Ilyanovna Rantzau, you are sentenced to a life of
exile for your role in the conspiracy to assassinate Leonti
Yurievich Yermolov. You are hereby denied all rights as a
citizen of Russia and all your worldly possessions are hereby
remanded to the state. . . .*

All six of the defendants were condemned to the Gotcharny
Prison Camp, a remote Siberian colony on the shores of Lake
Baikal. Their journey was to begin immediately following
sentencing. Due to the compassion of the court, each prisoner
was allowed twenty minutes with his family before departure.

The families and prisoners met in one room, all but Olga
Gambarova, who had no family, and so she was kept in the
prisoners' box. The families were let in first and then there
was the shuffling of feet and clanging of chains as Misha,
Anna, Irina, Charlotte and Kolya filed in one after another.
After a terrible moment of silence, a woman's voice erupted
in sobs, and arms flew about each other. Zhenya didn't know
whom to embrace first, Misha or Anna, and she reached for
both of them, showering them with kisses.

"Where's Alexei?" Anna asked, her voice high-pitched
and painfully giddy.

"Didn't they tell you?" Zhenya's eyes filled with tears.
"They said they told you."

"Lies," Anna whispered hoarsely. "You can't believe their
lies, Mother."

"Oh, my darling, my sweetest soul. . . ."

Anna pulled away. "Lies," she repeated.

The hides of the cows steamed with the closeness of the swaying railroad car. The dust of the hay speckled the air, mixing
with the heavy damp odor of manure. Anna sat as far from the
mooing beasts as she could, near the end of the car, near a vent,
and tried not to breathe. Irina, Misha, Olga and Charlotte formed
a protective semicircle about her. Kolya Susanin stood. He was
mumbling to himself and sometimes he cried.

The other prisoners, six rough, ill-clad men and women
sentenced to exile for crimes ranging from robbery to black

marketing to murder, formed an opposing group. Their leader was a skinny, leathery-skinned, toothless woman named Varvara. "Politicals!" She glared at Misha, Anna, Irina and the others with vengeful disdain. "Little fancy asses." She spit, running her tongue across her toothless gums. Turning to her miserable band, she chortled, "Look at 'em in their fine clothes and warm boots, smelling like roses. Well, it won't be long till they stink and beg like the rest of us, eh!" She eyed Anna triumphantly. "Only the first day, and look at her. She'll not make it across the Urals." The toothless hag snorted. "And I'll get her coat and boots—you hear that! Every bit of clothing the wench wears is mine when she goes!"

"Shut up, hag!" Irina warned. "Shut your damn mouth." She pulled herself across the floor to where Anna lay. Pressing her head on Anna's shoulders, she wrapped her arms around her, and they lay together in silence. There was nothing to say, no words of comfort or hope. In her heart Irina agreed with the hag: Anna wouldn't make it to the Urals, much less the prison camp, at least not sane. Irina wondered what the guards did when someone went mad. She wondered what they did with a baby.

They spent the night in a shack in the Moscow train yards, and in the morning they were fed weak tea and hard black bread with rancid-smelling fish. Anna threw up at the smell, and Irina saved their bread for later. At seven o'clock they boarded another train. This time the prisoners were allowed in the back of a passenger car. An hour later, they were ordered off at a nameless stop along the tracks. Waiting for them was another, larger group of prisoners, who looked worn, beaten, as if they'd been marching a long time.

"You, you, and you . . ." One of the guards pointed to Charlotte, Kolya and Olga, then to the hag Varvara and a murderer named Nestor. "You all go over there with them." He waved them to the other prisoner band. The order to march was given, and without a chance to say good-bye, Charlotte, Kolya, and Olga started off. It was snowing very hard, and within minutes they had vanished in the storm.

"My God, we'll never see them again," Irina said to Misha.

"We're still together." He tried to sound hopeful.

"For the time being." She looked at Anna, who was staring into the falling snow.

Anna, Misha, Irina and others started off five minutes later; without the enmity of the hag, the group seemed more cohesive. The criminals no longer held themselves so stringently apart from the politicals. They walked together, not talking, but occasionally their shoulders touched, and no one cursed or shoved. Within half an hour they turned onto a road which seemed to have no beginning or end. The snow was merciless, accompanied by a bitter wind, leaving them no place to stop or rest. They walked for hours; the snow almost reached their knees; the sky was gray, at times almost black. They walked until a farm appeared like a mirage on the horizon.

"Come with me," a guard said to Anna as the others were led to the barn.

"Where are you taking her?" Irina demanded, grabbing hold of Anna's arm.

"You don't ask questions no more, missy," another guard shot back, smashing his gun into Irina's shoulder and hurtling her onto the ground.

Irina leapt to her feet as fast as she could, given the chains, but Misha held her steady. "You can't stop them," he pleaded. "They'll do what they want."

"Anna!" Irina called out, grasping onto Misha.

Anna never looked back. She marched stoically beside her captor, thinking perhaps he was going to shoot her. She didn't care for herself, but the child, the child was all there was left of Alexei. She would kill the guard before he hurt her child, somehow she would.

"Inside." The guard shoved her through the back door of the farmhouse. "This is the one I told you about, Pavlushka."

A fat old man with a kindly face looked up from where he sat whittling wood by a stove. He smiled at Anna as he stood. "Take off her chains," he told the guard. "She'll not be going anyplace in a storm like this."

The guard did as he was told.

"The soup's ready. It's there on the stove," the old man went on. "Enough for all of them. Go on, take it to the barn. The bread and bowls are already there."

The guard nodded, wrapping some rags about the hot pot before taking it with him.

The old man led Anna to his chair by the stove and urged her to sit. "Wait here, I'll get my wife. You'll be more comfortable with her."

Pavlushka returned moments later followed by a wife as round as he was. Her name was Natalya, and without talking she began taking off Anna's boots. Anna's toes were red with the cold and they burned as the old woman rubbed them. Pavlushka brought Anna hot cider, which she drank greedily. Then Natalya took off Anna's hat and scarf and unbuttoned her coat. She gave Anna sheepskin slippers to wear.

"Are you hungry?" Pavlushka asked excitedly, and seemed relieved when Anna said, "Yes, very."

Natalya gave her thick beet soup with fresh bread and then some light, moist poached fish.

"Who are you?" Anna asked.

"Just people. They pay us to feed and board the prisoners as they pass."

"But why are you doing this for me?"

"We have been asked," said Pavlushka.

"You are Alexei Yakovlevich Kalinin's wife," said Natalya proudly. Then she paused. "You have our deepest sympathy, my child." Taking Anna's arm, she led her to a small room off the kitchen. The bed was freshly made and heavy with blankets. Natalya gave her a warm nightgown and socks. "You must take care of yourself and the child." She smiled encouragingly. "Sleep now. You must be strong for tomorrow's trek." And she was gone.

Anna had the strangest feeling that she'd dreamt the night with Pavlushka and his wife, and said nothing of it to Misha and Irina as they set out the next morning. The wind that had howled all night had thankfully quieted, leaving the air brisk but tolerable. After only an hour of plowing through untouched snow, they passed a long, sledded caravan traveling in the opposite direction that left wide tracks on which to walk. For lunch, the guards handed out more bread and dried fish and told the prisoners to scoop up snow to wet their mouths. The guards urged them on relentlessly. They had to reach their destination by dark.

Their destination was a farmhouse not far from the road. This time the prisoners were all brought into the house and served hot soup and black bread before being ushered to their sleeping quarters on the third floor. There were blankets for all of them, but not enough floor space, and Anna, Misha and Irina were directed to follow a guard back downstairs. They were taken to a small room off the kitchen, which had one bed.

"You two take the bed," Misha said. "The floor's fine for me."

Anna sat on the edge of the bed staring in confusion at Misha and Irina. There was so much she wanted to say. She needed to talk about Alexei and the feeling, growing as assuredly as their child, that Alexei was still alive. But she said nothing and lay down on the bed facing the wall. Irina curled beside her.

"It's all right. It's all right," Irina soothed, and stroked her. "We're together, that's all that matters."

* * *

Irina heard the noise first. Her eyes sprang open. She couldn't see in the blackness, but she was certain the door-knob was turning. She nudged Anna, then shushed her. As she did, the door opened and the shadow of a guard entered.

He walked to the bed and put one of his hands over Irina's mouth and another over Anna's. "Don't move or call out. Don't make a sound. I'm not your enemy. Stay perfectly still, I'm going to unlock your chains." After freeing Anna and Irina, he bent to nudge Misha, who was still soundly sleeping. The guard woke him in the same way, urged them all to dress in their outer clothing and was soon leading them into the night. A full moon flooded the powdery snow. The sky hung low with stars.

"What's going on?" Irina demanded hoarsely.

"Just follow me. No harm will come to you."

The guard turned to her, his face visible in the moonlight. He was no one Irina had seen before. "Who are you?" she demanded.

"A friend. Now, come. This has all been carefully planned. Many have risked much to free you."

"Please," Anna begged. "Just do as he says."

The guard led them to the road, clearly delineated in the moonlight, and hurried them along until they were out of sight of the farmhouse. Then he said, "I have to leave, but you're to keep on walking along the road in this direction. Other comrades will meet you soon. Long live the revolution!" He kissed them each on both cheeks and was gone.

Irina started after the guard. "Wait!"

"Let's do as he says," Anna insisted, her voice on the edge of hysteria. "Please." She pulled at Irina. "We're free, please let's just go!"

Irina looked about for a place to walk in shadows, but the road before them stretched like a flat field. There were no trees, slopes or cliffs, nowhere to hide from the relentless light of the moon. Her gaze swept back to Anna and Misha, who were waiting expectantly for her leadership. "Come on," she whispered, grabbing each of their hands. They had no choice. The unknown stretched before them, the farmhouse behind.

They walked in long strides, bounded by a nervous excitement which soon made them run. In the distance a speck, a light, appeared. They all saw it, but no one questioned it until it began bobbing larger and larger, and then there was the sound of horses' hooves muffled on the packed snow. A sleigh appeared on the milky horizon.

"It's the others!" Anna cried joyously. "It's Alexei! I'm sure of it!" She broke free of Irina and began racing again.

"Anna!" Irina ran after her.

The light grew nearer, the horses' hooves louder.

"Anna, wait!" Misha tore ahead of Irina. Just as he reached Anna, shots rang out from behind them. He tackled her to the ground, rolling with her until they were off the road. "Stay down!" he ordered, and lifted his head to look for Irina.

More shots burst forth.

Anna screamed.

Misha covered her with his body, and wanted desperately to look for Irina.

The sound of horses' hooves came nearer, then stopped, followed by muffled men's voices and the crunch of boots running in the ice-coated snow. More shots rang out. Shots tore in all directions. Then a sudden eerie silence fell, broken by footsteps. The footsteps came closer and closer.

Anna pressed her face against Misha and waited for death.

"Are you all right, comrades?" came a concerned voice, and a man with a gun knelt beside them. He was prying Anna and Misha apart. "Come, we must hurry before they return with reinforcements. The other woman is wounded."

"Irina!" Misha was on his feet and bounding into the road. Irina lay limply on her back, her body washed by the moonlight. A man with a rifle slung over his shoulder was kneeling by her. "Irina!" Misha bellowed, and the man looked up. Misha stopped and gasped. The frigid air stung his lungs. For a moment he could not move.

The man reached out his hand. "She's hurt badly, Misha," he said in a voice Misha knew so well.

"Dmitri Andreievich, is that you?"

"Yes." He beckoned Misha to him.

"But I thought . . ." Misha looked in confusion from Irina to Dmitri.

"We've no time for explanations now. They'll be back with reinforcements." He looked down at Irina. "There's still life, but barely. Lift her carefully. Fedya!" he called to the driver. "Come help."

"Yes, yes," Misha said as he walked toward Dmitri, the ghostly god come to set the world right. Misha's body jerked in odd little motions. He slipped his hands under Irina's head and shoulders. Dmitri took her legs and feet. They lifted her. Misha walked backward to the sleigh. Blood dripped, leaving dark shadows in the moonlit snow. Irina's hand fell from her chest and dangled. Misha's knees buckled. Steely air cut the back of his neck. "Oh, God! Oh, God!" he cried as he stumbled.

Anna steadied him.

"I'm all right. I'm fine," Misha assured, and kept walking. Blood soaked through his gloves. He felt it pool, sticky and warm, between his fingers. Could it all be Irina's blood? Her head lolled to one side. Terror gushed in a rush of black tomorrows. He screamed, but there was no sound, and then his eyes were frantically trying to focus on the ghost, Dmitri. "She's dying, Dmitri Andreievich! Do something—I know you can do something!" he implored, his voice breaking.

"Fedya, take her." Dmitri snapped the order. "Anna, get Misha into the sleigh. Hurry! We must make speed. They've gone back for sleds, that's for sure."

Irina was lifted from him. Anna was pulling at him, tugging him to the floor of the well-worn sleigh. Anna whispered something he could not understand, and Irina was handed back to him.

"She'll be all right, Misha. She will," Anna insisted in an odd, birdlike voice.

He watched her wrapping a blanket about them, and she knelt, her hands clasped tightly in prayer. Her eyes were wide, charred like the inside of his heart.

Fedya slapped the horses' backs with the reins, and in a whirl of whinnies and flying snow, the sleigh turned, hurtling them into the night.

Misha engulfed Irina in his arms; he bent his head and kissed her cheeks, her lips, her eyes. The wind whipped and wailed. His tears froze. "Don't leave me now, please don't leave me. . . . Oh, God, Irina . . . Oh, God . . . Oh, God . . ."

Anna spread her arms across Irina, and buried her head in Irina's chest. A dull sound droned against her skull, and behind her eyes, the night stained blood. Death stole upon them like a scavenger. *Irina, Irina, Irina* . . . Anna intoned. The sound filling her head grew into a high-pitched whine. The sleigh sped on.

PART SEVEN

REVOLUTION

CHAPTER FORTY-SEVEN

*The air was so cold, it cut the breath. The moon lit a path
to the barn, and Anna walked slowly, her feet landing like
feathers on the flawless snow. A piano was playing, and a
harpsichord. Anna stopped, smiled and patted her belly reassuringly.*

*"Mama?" she called, and paused at a gaping barn door.
A soft light flickered.*

*"Mama?" The warmth of the barn beckoned. The music
was like bathwater. "Mama!" Her heart was pounding very
fast. Her mother had come all the way to Siberia. Her mother
would take the baby out.*

*Anna began to run. She ran faster and faster down long
hallways lined with gilt-edged mirrors and enormous tiered
crystal chandeliers. She ran barefoot into a meadow brilliant
with wildflowers. A girl in a white dress was swinging on a
swing. "Irina!" Anna called ecstatically. Irina wasn't dead
after all.*

*The ground gave way and she was falling into black, cob-
webbed air; huge, vile creatures scurried along slimy walls.
The baby streamed past her. Anna reached for it too late; it
landed with a thud, followed by a silence as if the baby had
never been. Anna looked down and saw blood where her
stomach had been. "Irina," she called to the shadows. She
switched on a light.*

*Irina was sitting in the middle of a crowded ballroom.
Everyone was there, Alexei, Anna's mother and father, Petya,
Aunt Tatyana and Uncle Ilya, Valia Vaslava, even the Czar
and Czarina. They were drinking champagne and laughing.
No one, not even Alexei, noticed Anna and the blood; no one
saw Irina in her black prisoner's dress. Irina was holding the
baby. The baby had no face. Irina and the baby sat perfectly
still.*

*Anna drew closer. "Irina." She touched the flawless cheek
and her fingers froze to the skin. She reached for the baby,*

whose head fell off. Irina's frozen body cracked like a shattered windowpane.

Anna woke up screaming.

Within moments, Misha was by her side. "It's all right, Anna. It's all right," he soothed. "Come now, it's just a dream."

"It's so horrible, always so horrible . . ." She searched for his face in the night, and then, like a frightened child, wrapped her arms about his neck. "I'm so scared, Misha. I'm scared to sleep."

"Hush, now. It'll be all right. I'm here . . ." He rocked her until her breathing became more regular. Then he eased her back down to the pillow and pressed the covers around her.

"Stay with me awhile longer," she pleaded, holding fiercely on to his hand.

"Of course," he promised in a voice which sounded so much like Alexei's.

"Dmitri Andreievich coming here, to Geneva, for a visit!" Misha exclaimed, rushing into the apartment waving a letter. His face was red and sweaty from the exertion of running up the three flights of stairs in the brutal August heat.

Anna looked up from the couch where she sat knitting. "When?"

"As soon as he can. But of course he can't be certain with all that's going on in Russia now." He handed her the letter, and she scanned it quickly. Dmitri wrote of the newly established Duma and the peace treaty that Sergei Witte had signed, not only ending the war with Japan but also prompting the Czar to make Witte a count. Dmitri wrote of the people's anger with the limited power of a Duma without a constitution, and the fear that the troops which had been fighting the Japanese would be brought home to crush the revolution.

Anna refolded the letter and handed it back to Misha. She put down her knitting, pushed herself up from the couch and walked to the window, staring out into the alleyway. Scarcely any light filtered between the congested buildings. She had to strain her neck to see the sky. Anna rarely went outside. She didn't want anyone to see her in her swollen condition, and it was becoming more and more difficult to navigate the three flights of stairs. Carrying a baby in her arms would be no less trying. She'd have to find another flat before Misha left or she'd be stranded inside forever. She'd have to find a means to earn some money, too. She had a little nest egg hidden, even from Misha. She hoarded a few francs each week from what Misha made from his tutoring and from the allowance Dmitri Andreievich sent. Once the baby came, she decided, she would teach piano. She'd buy herself a fine dress with some of the money, and run an advertisement in the Russian-language newspapers. *Talented young pianist from a well-known Petersburg family available to give piano lessons* . . . She'd bring the baby with her. The music would soothe the baby, who'd sleep while she taught.

"Anna, what's wrong? Can I get you something?"

"No." She turned to him. "Is there any word on your grandmother? You did write to Dmitri Andreievich and ask about her. What if she's dead? So many people are dead." She smiled absently. "The iceman came today. Isn't that grand? I've made some lovely lemonade. Wait here and I'll get it."

Anna and Misha hadn't seen Dmitri in five months, not since the morning after their escape. Fedya, the driver of the getaway sleigh and a comrade, had led them out of Russia to Paris and finally to Geneva, where a furnished apartment was waiting for Mikhail and Anna Marks, although within days everyone in the teeming Russian émigré neighborhood knew them by their real names. Everyone in the neighborhood was a revolutionary, it seemed, and everyone, even the Bolshevik Lenin, wanted to meet them. Anna would receive or visit no one. She had nothing to say to those people and despaired of Misha's running from meeting to meeting. She wasn't a revolutionary and she wasn't a Russian. The Czar had stripped her of her citizenship. The revolution had widowed and betrayed her.

"The revolution also saved you," Misha would say. "You're alive, and your baby will be born in freedom."

I'm alone, too, she thought, certain that one day Misha would leave her. What young man in his right mind would tie himself down with someone else's wife and child? What young man in his right mind would stay in a miserable apartment in Geneva when a revolution in Petersburg was calling? *Why?* she asked God every night. *Why did you save Dmitri Andreievich and take my beloved Alexei and Irina?*

"I wish he wasn't coming!" Anna flared when Misha announced that Dmitri would be arriving in Geneva on August 26. "I don't want him in my house!"

"I don't understand."

Anna hadn't meant to explode like that. The angry words had spewed from her, and once begun, she couldn't stop. "Am I supposed to thank him for the rest of my life for saving us? Am I supposed to grovel at his feet because he sends us some rubles every month?" she demanded, pacing back and forth across the tiny parlor. The blue of her eyes hardened; her arms waved wildly. "I don't thank him and I won't. I didn't care about Yermolov! I didn't care if he lived or died. If it weren't for your precious Dmitri Andreievich I never would have helped. Then I never would have been arrested, and Alexei never would have been forced to be without me . . ."

Misha listened without argument. He'd learned over the months that there was no rational dealing with Anna when she became this way. He wondered if all pregnant women were shrews. He tried to imagine Irina pregnant with his child. He couldn't. At times he couldn't remember anything about her except how she looked in death. How quickly she had frozen lying in that kindly stranger's barn overnight. How still she had looked, not peaceful, just still. He wished she had looked peaceful, but her body had been too rigid, her skin bloodless. He tried to think of her as Kuksina Ivanovna. Irina had never been more beautiful, more commanding than she'd been as Kuksina. How she had loved burrowing in and around Gapon. How Misha had loved her for it. He tried to think of those days, but the memories ached with longings. He could not forget Irina and he could not remember her. There was only the moment when he'd seen her frozen in the kindly stranger's barn, and the void where his own nightmares gathered.

"If you'd like me to meet with Dmitri Andreievich elsewhere, Anna, I can tell him you're not feeling well," Misha volunteered. "I'm sure he'll understand."

Anna looked shocked. She drew up stiffly. "Dmitri Andreievich will be a guest in my home. I shall be a gracious hostess. I am the wife of Alexei Yakovlevich. Always, I will behave as such."

Anna and Misha believed the story that Dmitri had told them about his miraculous reappearance. Dmitri had explained how he'd been badly wounded by the force of Stepan's bomb, which had hurled him through the air and landed him in some bushes across the street from the Montenegrina Palace. Soldiers who found him unconscious and dressed in a uniform assumed he was one of them and took him to a hospital, where he lay in a coma for almost two weeks. When he regained consciousness and found himself immobile with a severe chest wound, he feigned amnesia. In the midst of the constant flow of wounded clogging the hospital during the weeks following Bloody Sunday, the doctors didn't pay much attention to one forgetful soldier. When Dmitri was strong enough, he simply took an orderly's uniform and coat, walked out of the hospital and went straight to see Alexei, who was himself out of prison by then. It was Alexei and Dmitri who had planned the escape. Alexei, if he hadn't been so brutally murdered, was to have driven the getaway sleigh himself.

Yuri Dobrinsky, Dmitri had explained, was thought to be dead. Yuri Dobrinsky, Dmitri had insisted, was to remain dead. Too many rumors had mushroomed after Yermolov's assassination, connecting Yuri to the Kalinin family and Yermolov's assassins. No one knew for certain how Yuri had died, although the bloated, unrecognizable body of a man built like him had been found floating in the Neva when the ice melted. Some said Dobrinsky had been killed at the same time as his business partner, Alexei Kalinin, his body shoved down a hole in the ice. In any event, the case was closed. Too many bodies were found floating in the Neva. Too many people of uncertain sympathies were disappearing.

He thankfully brought news of Zhenya Kirilovna. Although her hospital had been raided by the police, she was alive and well. "Zhenya Kirilovna spent a night in jail, but was released the next day, none the worse for wear, I'm told," Dmitri explained. "There's no stopping the old woman. She reestablished her hospital deeper within the slums of Vasilievsky Island."

Misha was euphoric over Dmitri's visit. It was good to have firsthand information from home that he could trust. Rumors ran rampant in the Russian émigré population in Geneva, which was rife with political infighting and dissent. Misha counted no fewer than twenty socialist parties, factions and splinters among them; many had not been on Russian soil in years. Some, like Lenin, cultivated Misha's company for details of commonplace life in Russia.

"And what of the strikes?" Misha asked earnestly. He leaned toward Dmitri. "We hear they are getting worse again."

"Oh, yes, quite." Dmitri sipped his tea. "And the discontent within the army is terrifying the monarchy. Mark my words, the day is coming when the monarchy will quiver in abject terror before the very guns with which it has trained its army and navy. No one doubts the revolution is here. It's swelling like groundwater in spring."

"And what of the workers' councils? We hear they are truly being organized in the cities."

"The soviets, yes. They're no longer wishful thinking. And not a moment too soon. The workers need to have something of their own. The revolutionary parties are so painfully bereft with all their rhetoric and infighting, I think they do more harm than good. The workers need a place where they can speak their own language, be their own leaders, try their wings if you will. Strong soviets will give them that."

"And if the Czar grants a constitution, Dmitri Andreievich?" Anna asked with a prim, quiet defiance.

"Do you think the Czar will do that, Anna Petrovna?" Dmitri questioned, his bushy eyebrows raised, his tone vaguely condescending.

"I'm not the political expert. You are." She smiled with feigned deference.

"I, like so many others, my dear, believe that by now a constitution, even should it come, is too little too late. It's hard to grasp the scope of what's happening without being there . . ." He turned his attention fully to Misha. "You know, despite the strikes and the marches and the movement among the soldiers, I've sensed a relative calm this summer. Nothing definitive, you see. Calm only in comparison with the revolutionary fervor during the months following Bloody Sunday. It's almost an unnerving calm if one thinks about it, as if everyone is waiting, the government, the workers, the revolutionaries, the Czar. We've been waiting since Gapon's march for the other shoe to drop. . . ."

Anna sat still, poised, her eyes closed, but inside she was churning. For a moment she'd been insulted by Dmitri's unceremonious dismissal of her, but suddenly she didn't care. Suddenly it was all too clear. She knew why Dmitri was here, prattling on about soldiers and the calm before the storm and what anyone could read in the newspaper every day. He was priming Misha as he'd once primed Anna, getting him excited, circling around him, readying for the kill. A man like Dmitri Andreievich didn't make friendly visits. A man like Dmitri Andreievich didn't give anything without wanting something in return, and Anna knew what he wanted: he wanted Misha. Just as Dmitri had taken Alexei and Irina from her, now he'd take Misha, and Misha would go, willingly. His eagerness for battle reeked like musk. What was it about men and fighting? Dear God, she wished her baby was a girl. No . . . A sick feeling gripped her. Not a girl to grow into a woman, not a boy to grow into a man . . .

"Anna . . ." Misha was nudging her. "Anna, are you all right?"

She looked at him through glazed eyes. "It's the heat," she said. "It's making me very tired. Would you mind"—she smiled cordially at Dmitri—"if I lie down?"

"Of course not, my dear." Dmitri was already on his feet. Misha was helping her up.

"I'm fine," she assured, brushing him away. "If you'll just get me some water, Misha, I'll be fine." She turned abruptly and headed for her room.

"Perhaps it would be better if we went for a walk," Misha said as he returned from Anna's room. "She has dreadful dreams at night, but seems to be able to sleep quite well during the day. I'm afraid our voices will keep her up."

"Of course," Dmitri agreed.

The heat of the afternoon streets was oppressive and they walked only a few blocks before stepping into a dark, cool basement café for lunch. "You got my reports I sent on the meetings with Lenin?" Misha asked.

"Yes, they were very good, very thorough."

"Lenin's brilliant, quite as brilliant as anyone I've ever met. It's odd, though, how he questions me about the smallest details, down to where workers buy their bread."

"He's desperate to return. He's been away too long. He's afraid he's lost the pulse of the people."

"You spoke with him, then."

"All day yesterday."

Misha waited for Dmitri to tell him more; instead, Dmitri began fumbling in his pocket. He pulled out an envelope thick with cash. "This is for Anna, for her confinement and for the child, but I don't want you to tell her where it came from. I want to provide for her whenever I can. It may be sporadic. It's just something I want to do. And later, it can appear as if it's being sent by you."

"Me? I don't understand."

Dmitri's voice lowered. "The Bolsheviks are calling for armed insurrection, Misha. Lenin is planning to return soon. His people are smuggling arms into Petersburg and setting up workshops for the making of bombs for the street fighting, but he fears they're not proficient enough bomb makers to meet the task."

Misha was confused.

"If the workers do successfully organize and form themselves into soviets, the spearhead will be Petersburg. Everyone knows that. The soviets will have to protect themselves

and those they represent. And if that happens, the Czar will
not stand idly by. While our staunch liberal Witte strokes and
coaxes the workers, the Czar could well recall General Trepov and give him dictatorial powers. Troops will pour into
the city to crush the revolution. The workers will need to
fight back. Lenin wants to be ready. I've offered him the
assistance of the Brigade, of you, in particular. You became
an efficient bomb maker under Stepan's tutelage.''

"You mean here, in Geneva.''

"Lord, no, I'm rebuilding the Petersburg squad. I want
you to come back as one of its leaders. The papers are all
arranged. You'll have little problem getting back, and with
the proper disguise, I think you'll be able to get along quite
nicely. You know, Misha . . .'' His voice cracked with sudden emotion, and for an awful moment Misha feared Dmitri
might cry. "Stepan was like a son to me. His loss to the
revolution is immeasurable. But you can help retrieve the balance. Yes, I believe you can. I want you to take Stepan's
place. . . .''

Pride swelled through every fiber of Misha's being; it
seemed impossible that Dmitri Andreievich would be com-
paring him with Stepan Ostravsky, that Dmitri could even
consider Misha to be a leader. "I have not had all that much
experience.''

"In a way, you have potential for even greater leadership
than Stepan. For you've something Stepan never had. You had
the love of a man like Alexei Yakovlevich. Oh, I tried with
Stepan, but by the time he came to me, his experiences had
hardened him too much to life. He had the fire of injustice
within him, but he didn't know how to love. A true leader
must be capable of loving those who follow him.''

"But . . .'' Misha stammered, not knowing how to respond. "I've never made a bomb on my own. Always Stepan
and Irina were with me.''

"And they will be with you still. We carry our fallen comrades inside us. They give us courage to do what seems impossible. You want to return, don't you?''

"Oh, yes,'' Misha said with an almost hushed reverence.
"I want to fight until every one of them is dead!'' he added
fervently, imagining in that moment one of his bombs tearing
and burning the flesh of the men who had murdered Uncle
Alexei and Irina. He would get them one day, if it meant
killing every Black Hundred and prison guard in Russia.

"So, then, it's settled.'' Dmitri clapped him warmly on
the back. "There's a two-o'clock train leaving Geneva tomorrow. I'll meet you at the station no later than one-thirty.''

Misha hesitated as his eyes met Dmitri's, and unexpected words fell from his lips. "I can't, Dmitri Andreievich. I mean, not yet, not until the baby's born."

Dmitri leaned forward, his face very red; his thick lips tightened to white threads and his eyes narrowed darkly behind his thick lenses. "What do you think I gave you that money for?" There was a slow, threatening deliberation to his voice.

For a moment Dmitri loomed like his father, and it was all Misha could do not to pull back and cover his face as if to ward off blows. He blinked and breathed deeply, a semblance of calm returning. Dmitri wasn't his father, and Misha wasn't an impotent child anymore. "I want to return to fight, Dmitri Andreievich. I want nothing more than to destroy those who killed Uncle Alexei and Irina, Stepan, Savva and the rest. I know they will go on killing until we stop them, but I can't, I simply can't leave Anna until after the baby is born. It won't be much longer. Then I'll come, I promise."

"History demands dedication to the cause now. Personal desires must be put aside."

"I understand what you say, Dmitri Andreievich and I know in my mind it has much merit. But I can't leave Anna until the baby is born."

"You've fallen in love with her!" he exclaimed disdainfully.

Misha was horrified by the idea. "Dmitri Andreievich, I love her as I would love a sister! She's alone and she's Uncle Alexei's wife. I loved Uncle Alexei as a father. For him, I can't leave Anna now. You must understand that—"

"Ach, I understand that it's the pampered little rich boy who sits before me now. You want to have your cake and eat it too!"

"That's not fair, Dmitri Andreievich."

"Don't tell me about fair!" Dmitri grabbed Misha's arm as he leaned still closer. "Do you know how many women and children are dying in childbirth at this very moment because of the filth that surrounds them, because of starvation and disease? At least Anna will give birth in a clean bed with a doctor and a midwife to care for her. I've seen to that. Yes, and I've seen to much more, you idiot!" Dmitri tore his hand from Misha's arm and stood up. He threw some cash down on the table to pay for their food. "I'll expect you at the station at one-thirty tomorrow. No later," Dmitri ordered, and he was gone.

CHAPTER FORTY-EIGHT

Anna was vigorously polishing the parlor table when Misha returned.

"I see you're feeling better, then!" Misha greeted her cheerfully. "Did you nap well?"

Anna didn't so much as turn her head.

Misha walked by her to the kitchen and opened the icebox. The inside was warm. "I thought the iceman was coming," he said, returning to the parlor and chomping on some cheese.

"I can't beg, borrow or steal more ice until we pay him what we owe him," she coldly replied. Eyeing the crumbs of cheese dropping to the floor, she chided, "That was dinner." And she went back to her polishing.

Anna's abrupt admonishment pricked Misha's tenuous equanimity. It was all he could do not to take Dmitri's envelope from his pocket, throw it at her and tell her he was returning to Petersburg on tomorrow's afternoon train. Instead he said, "I left you more than half the cheese." Grabbing a newspaper, he lay down on the couch to read.

"You might take off your shoes," Anna snapped.

"And I might not," he muttered sullenly, eyeing his paper, but he couldn't read. Only moments before, he'd been so certain of his decision to stay. He'd even managed to ease the sting of Dmitri's tongue-lashing by stopping at Peytock's secondhand shop to put a down payment on the cradle which he'd seen the week before. Peytock said he could polish it until the wood looked brand new. He promised that Anna would never suspect it came from a secondhand store.

"It may not be elegant, but it's the only couch we have!" Anna's shrillness broke his recollecting. She was standing above him, frowning, and she swiped at his feet, pushing them off the couch.

"You sound like a fishmonger's wife, Anna!" he attacked. "I don't know how much longer I can stand being around a fishmonger's wife!"

Anna wanted to shout back at him to leave, but she dared

not. She was afraid he might go. Reaching for her knitting, she turned and hurried to her room.

Misha and Anna barely spoke for the next week. They didn't eat together; Misha didn't go into Anna's room when she woke up in the night crying. He gritted his teeth and burrowed his head under his pillow. He refused to comfort her and, determined to prove to Dmitri he could be as much use in Geneva as he could be in Petersburg, he immersed himself in meetings and article writing.

One night when he came home, Anna wasn't in her usual place, knitting on the couch. Her room was empty too. To his horror, he found her in the kitchen, on her hands and knees, scrubbing the floor.

"No!" he exploded, yanking the rag from her hand. "This is one thing I'll never allow you to do! Scrubbing like a scullery maid! Get up, Anna! Get up!"

"Give that to me!" She reached for the rag and fell backward with her weight, landing belly-up on her elbows.

Terror-stricken, Misha was beside her in a moment.

"I'm fine, just fine!" She allowed him to help her to her feet and then stormed into her room and slammed the door.

Misha was knocking almost immediately.

"Go away!"

He pushed open the door, holding out a box of chocolates he'd bought for her several days before. "Buttercrunch, your favorite," he said uncertainly.

She thought she could have refused anything at that moment but buttercrunch; it had been at least a month since she'd had chocolates, and a craving she couldn't control overcame her. Pushing her hair from her face, she hungrily ate two. Wordlessly she offered Misha some. Feeling contrite, she said, "This was very thoughtful. And, well . . ." She licked some chocolate from her finger. "Well, the truth is . . ." She blushed, feeling confused yet relieved at the same time. "I don't even know why we've been so angry at each other all week. I've quite forgotten what started it."

He shifted uneasily from foot to foot and shook his head. "I don't know either." The hint of a smile crossed his lips.

She wanted to say something witty and merry, but without warning, tears burned her eyes. She quickly wiped them away. "I hate this crying, I just hate it!" She fumbled for her handkerchief and blew her nose. "I don't know why I cry so much, Misha. I don't know why I do half the things I do. Sometimes I think I am going mad again. Alexei would hate that, and . . . and I'm so ugly, so horribly ugly."

"How can you say such a thing, Anna? You're beautiful. You grow more beautiful every day. You're pale is all, from being inside so much. I found a lovely café, and wait . . ." He hurried from the room, returning moments later with Dmitri's envelope.

"What is it?" Anna asked when Misha gave it to her. "Oh, where did you get it?" Her eyes opened wide as she began counting the bills. "There must be . . . well, in rubles, it must be over a thousand."

"My grandmother. Yes, she gave it to Dmitri for you and the baby. She said she'll send more when she can."

Anna thought she would burst with joy. "She does remember us still, then. Oh, Misha, I thought she'd forgotten us too." She smiled contentedly as she held the money tightly to her. "Misha, there's something I have to ask you. When are you going?" Her voice was soft and uncertain.

"Going where?"

"Into your own life—I mean, you can't stay about me and your uncle's baby forever."

"What am I going to do with you then?" He was confused.

"Do! You make it sound as if we're some kind of stray dogs." She stiffened then, and her voice turned hard. "You have no ties to us. I want you to know that. I don't expect you to stay with us forever, or even for a moment . . ." That awful, willful, accusing tone was back, when all she wanted was to thank Misha for being with her still. She wanted to hug him. She desperately wanted to hug someone. "I don't want charity and I'm not afraid of being poor either. My mother was poor. Oh, yes, she was, although no one knew. She was poor with dignity, just as I shall be. So you needn't worry. Besides, there are worse things than being poor. Well, I don't have to tell you . . ." She was standing now and beginning to pace. Her back ached horribly from having been on her hands and knees scrubbing the kitchen floor so long. Suddenly she gasped and the envelope fell from her hand. Her mouth contorted and her eyes widened in fear. She gripped her belly and her face grew white.

"What is it, Anna? What is it?"

She took deep breaths until finally the pain passed. "Oh, my God." She swallowed. "Oh, God, Misha, get Sophie, fast. I think it's starting!"

Sophie Nikitina was a pudgy, no-nonsense woman with an air of relaxed authority about her. After examining Anna, she announced the baby would not appear for another twelve to twenty hours, but that she would wait. Her presence had a

calming effect. Anna and Misha played cards. Misha read
poetry out loud. They chatted easily, as they hadn't for a long
time. Around midnight, Anna was pacing to ease a particularly distressful pain, when a gush of water rushed from her;
she gaped in horrified embarrassment at the pool lying at her
feet. Another pain, far worse than the previous, followed immediately. She turned a ghostly white and let out an awful cry.

By the time the pain had passed, Sophie was at her side,
nodding in approval. "Now we're in business!" she exclaimed, ushering Anna into the bedroom. She ordered Misha to boil water and barred him from entering the room
again.

For about an hour, terrible screams came from behind the
closed door every ten minutes or so. Then there was a seemingly endless silence. Misha feared Anna had died and Sophie was afraid to come out and tell him. Finally he knocked
on the door.

"She's fine, Mr. Marks. Why don't you just lie down or
go out for a walk. It doesn't help any, your knocking on
the door."

"I'm sorry," Misha meekly apologized. He lay on the
couch, listening to the quiet, and sometime in the night he
fell asleep. He awoke to a strong arm shaking him vigorously.
It was morning. Sophie was standing above him, her face
sweating, grim and gray with exhaustion.

"Anna! Is she all right?" Misha asked, bolting to a sitting
position.

The midwife sighed wearily. "I'm beginning to get concerned. Things should be moving faster, Mr. Marks. She's
rigid like a board in there and refuses to cry out even though
I know the pain is terrible. Her lips are bleeding from where
she's bitten herself. All she does is say his name over and
over."

"Who?"

"Alexei, her husband. You're Kalinin, yes, I know, Mr.
Marks. So I think Dr. Pitkin should see her."

Sophie gave him the address of Dr. Pitkin, a thin, stern,
elderly man who was not happy to be taken from his house
at seven-thirty on a Saturday morning. "Women," he snorted
to Misha. "They have no sense of timing when it comes to
such matters. I suppose this is your first, young man. Nothing's worse than the first."

Misha simply nodded.

"I see nothing wrong with the woman, Marks," Dr. Pitkin
explained after examining Anna. "Nothing physical, that is,

and I'm not one to use the knife indiscriminately. I told her
that. I told her I didn't want to take the child from her, but
she had to work harder with the midwife. Is the woman prone
to hysteria?''

"She's had a rough time of it lately."

"Yes, well . . . it's not good for the child, not good at all.
I told the woman she has to relax if this baby is going to be
born the natural way. Here's the address of my office. I advised Sophie that if things don't look any better by noon, to
call me. We may have to take the child. If I were you, I'd try
to catch some sleep yourself, young man. You look like hell.
Good day,'' said Dr. Pitkin, and he was gone.

Anna concentrated on a black inkstain on the faded, flowered wallpaper. If she concentrated hard enough, she could
control the pain. She couldn't allow it to defeat her; she
couldn't allow her baby to be born, she couldn't allow the
world to take all she had left of Alexei; the baby had been
safe inside her for so long; the baby had kept her whole. Let
the midwife grimace and the doctor threaten with the knife.
What could their threats be in comparison with the fierceness
of prison guards, in comparison with the heartlessness of
judges sentencing her to a life of exile, in comparison with
the brutality of the man who murdered Alexei?

"Push, Anna Petrovna. You must push down as hard as
you can,'' the midwife insisted, resting both hands on Anna's
belly as the next contraction came.

Anna stared at the inkstain and gasped for breath. The pain
was like riding a wave. If she caught it at just the right moment, it wouldn't sweep her under. That was the trick.

"Push, Anna Petrovna, push, if you want this baby to be
born. . . .''

Anna closed her eyes, thinking the pain was over, thinking
she had won again, but without warning another crashed
down, catching her unawares. "Alexei! Oh, God, Alexei!''
she screeched, her body rising.

"That's it, Anna Petrovna, that's it. Go with it, push,
push!''

The pain increased and the scream in her throat wouldn't
let her breathe. Then she was pushing at the midwife, swiping
at her fat hands. "Don't touch me!'' she bellowed as the pain
eased. "Go away, you witch!'' And as the midwife went to
wet her brow with a cloth, Anna clamped her teeth on the
woman's hand. The contraction grew stronger and Anna bit
harder.

"Let go of me! Ah, you're killing me!"

Finally Anna fell back on the pillow, exhausted.

"Little she-devil!" Sophie snapped, waving her bloodied hand up and down.

"What's going on in here?" The door flew open.

"Alexei!" Anna struggled to sit. She held out her arms.

"This woman's crazed is what it is!" The midwife dangled her dented, bloodied hand in front of Misha. "Bit me, she did! For sure, I'm not getting paid enough to be bitten. Go for the doctor again, Mr. Marks. Go for him straight away and tell him it's time to take the child from her or I'm leaving."

"What are you talking about?" He looked from the enraged Sophie to Anna, who lay in a pool of perspiration. Her skin was white as the sheets and her eyes burned with a madness he remembered from the early days in the Crimea.

Before Sophie could explain more, Anna let out another horrible cry and Misha ran to her.

"You must leave now, Mr. Marks!" Sophie pulled at him. "You must go get Dr. Pitkin. He'll cut the baby from her."

"Like hell he will!" he shouted, shoving Sophie away. "I'll not let him near Anna with a knife."

For one terrible moment Sophie and Misha were locked in a duel of wills, broken only by another cry from Anna.

"Do something, damn you!" Misha threatened.

"All right, then, Mr. Marks." Sophie threw back her shoulders proudly. "If you've the stomach for staying, I've seen a woman helped by her man a few times in my day. If you can just get her to push, she's got to push," the midwife ordered, authority back in her voice. "Lift her there, Mr. Marks. I'll bend her legs and you lift her back."

They tried, but Anna kicked and punched so, they finally left off until she lay trembling in an uneasy silence.

"You see what I mean, Mr. Marks," Sophie said, straightening herself at the foot of the bed. "If she'd only help like any normal woman, the baby would be born by now. She's holding it in. Ain't never seen the likes of it. She's killing her baby and herself."

Fearing the midwife was right, Misha turned to Anna to say good-bye, and she reached imploringly for him. "Don't, Misha, don't let them take my baby. Not ever. Promise me."

"Tell her we'll give her her baby if she just helps, Mr. Marks."

Misha knelt beside the bed and wiped Anna's forehead and cheeks with his hand. "Did you hear that, my sweet? Sophie can help you, and so can I, if you just let us."

"I can't. I can't." Anna was trembling. She pulled at his arm and suddenly her nails dug into him as her body arched.

"Push, Anna Petrovna!" the midwife urged.

"Come on, Anna, push!" Misha held out his arm for her to pull on.

She tossed her head from side to side. Her eyes rolled in a frenzy.

He wiped the perspiration-soaked hair from her forehead and kissed her. "Help your baby, please, Anna . . ."

Another contraction convulsed her and she grabbed on to him. "Push now, Anna," he urged. "Push for Alexei."

"No," she cried, but her defenses were weakening. The pain was too much. She only wanted it to be over. Misha was near. She thought he'd gone, but he was still there, holding her against the trembling, stroking her. He dripped water on her parched, swollen lips and cooed soft words.

"Another one's coming!" Sophie urged.

"Come on now, Anna, come on!" Misha shouted like a fan at a horse race. "We're going to do this one together. Now, push." He eyed the midwife, who was blowing very hard. He began blowing too, and Anna blew with him.

The pushing and blowing went on interminably, yet Misha was energized by the rhythm he felt building between Anna and himself. In between contractions she was quiet; at times he thought she slept, waking in a panic until she saw him. Suddenly the pains took on a new and different intensity.

"Wait now, my girl! Hold everything!" Sophie called excitedly as she crawled onto the bottom of the bed. She was practically hidden beneath Anna's bent legs. "Praise God, I see the head! Now, you stay put, Mr. Marks, but I promise you, the end is near . . . push now, that's it, push, push . . . I've got it! I've got the little head, gently now, here comes the shoulders—all right, Anna Petrovna, push—push one last time!"

Anna bore down with all her might, and within moments a wriggling, slimy red little body appeared.

"It's a girl!" Sophie exclaimed, holding the child upside down, and the room was filled with newborn screams. After quickly and efficiently cleaning the baby, she wrapped her in a soft blanket, placed her in Misha's arms, and began busily pressing on Anna's stomach again.

Misha turned his gaze to the tiny new person, who was sucking wildly with her pink lips. It seemed hard to imagine that only minutes before, she'd been inside Anna. "My God, she's beautiful!" he crooned, and turned to Anna, who was lying peacefully now.

"Let me see her." She reached out, an exhilarated smile enlivening her. "Look at all that black hair. Just like Alexei," Anna said, her voice barely audible. She was very tired.

Misha reached for her hand and squeezed it gently. "You did wonderfully," he said, and kissed her forehead. "She's so beautiful, Anna. I've never seen anything so perfect and beautiful. She looks just like you."

"What are you going to name her?" Sophie, who was smiling now too, brimming with pride, asked.

"Irina, of course. If it had been a boy, I would have named him Alexei. But I shall name her Irina Alexeiyevna. My own Irinushka."

CHAPTER FORTY-NINE

Anna was sitting on the couch, playing with month-old Irinushka. Playing consisted mainly of watching her, cuddling her, smelling her, and singing to her. Anna could hardly bear not touching her, and often stood over her, watching her sleep. She searched for Alexei in the constantly changing face, in the large, sky-blue eyes which lately followed Anna and Misha about the room, but it was difficult to find a grown man in a month-old girl. She thought she saw him sometimes, in a crooked smile or a quiet, sleeping pose. Anna trembled with the sweet likeness, fleeting like the shadow of a great bird sweeping the forest floor.

"Listen to this, Anna," Misha exclaimed. He was hunched over the parlor table with the newspaper, and without waiting for a response, he began to read, 'Street clashes in Moscow have been particularly violent since the bakers went on strike. The government, fearing the city would be left without bread, attempted to lock in the workers at the huge six-story Filipov bakery on the Tverskaya. Bakers hurled cast-iron pans, cake molds, and bricks at police. Finally two companies of the First Don Cossack Regiment attacked the plant. The students joined in on the side of the bakers and the result was more than one hundred casualties. . . .' Can you imagine?" He turned to her, his eyes bright. "Can you imagine how desperate the government must be to send in two whole companies of Cossacks?''

Anna's face was animated, but her excitement clearly did not stem from the news report. ''Come, look, Misha—she's smiling! Yes, I'm certain it's a smile. Larisa Filipovna said it was only gas, but I'm certain she's smiling at me!''

Misha stood, newspaper in hand, and hurried over to the couch, where he leaned over Anna and the infant. He cooed and Irinushka's eyes followed him. He dangled his fingers and grinned idiotically. A soft smile lighted the baby's face. ''Look at that—she did smile at me!'' He reached down, slipping his finger inside the warm little fist, and began cooing and clucking again. The more silly noises he made, the more she smiled, until finally Misha put down his paper and sat. ''Can I hold her?'' he begged, hands extended.

Reluctantly Anna gave the baby to him, and the two of them peered at her, smiling and talking baby talk in unison. Anna clutched Misha's arm. ''Isn't she beautiful? Have you ever seen anything so exquisite in your entire life?''

''Who would have believed this?'' Misha cried in astonishment. He was reading from *Figaro*, the French newspaper. ''Here's Uncle Alexei's friend, good old Sergei Witte—excuse me, Count Witte. And I'll be damned, but noble or not, he's sounding quite the revolutionary! Wouldn't Uncle Alexei get a chuckle, though?''

''Go on, read what Witte says.''

''All right. This is a quote from the great man. 'The basic slogan of the contemporary social movement in Russia is freedom. Its roots lie not in the events of the past turbulent year but deep in history, in the ancient freedom movements of Novgorod and Pskov, in the fierce independence of the Zaporozhye Cossacks, in the peasant revolts of the Volga, the rebellion in the Orthodox church, and even in the revolt against Peter's reforms.' ''

Anna's hands fell into her lap and she sat very still a moment. More to herself than to Misha, she added, ''Imagine Sergei Witte defending terrorists.'' She grimaced thoughtfully and repeated, ''Imagine that.''

Irina began to whimper.

Anna leaned forward to pick her up.

''Witte's sounding a bit like Grandma to me.'' Misha chuckled.

Irina's whimpers were turning to cries.

''Maybe she's hungry,'' Misha suggested.

''Larisa Filipovna says I should only feed her on schedule.'' Anna was standing now, bouncing Irina and pacing, all thoughts of Sergei Witte silenced by Irina's increasing wails.

''Don't you ever get cravings in between meals?'' Misha persisted.

''But Larisa Filipovna says—''

''Larisa Filipovna isn't here. And I promise I won't tell if you give Irinushka a snack.''

''Well, I guess you're right. I guess it won't hurt just once.'' Anna hurried to her room, and leaving the door half-open, she sat in the rocker Misha had bought her and unbuttoned her dress. ''Why don't you keep on reading about Witte,'' she called when Irina was nursing peacefully.

Misha started to read.

''I can't hear,'' she called.

He stood outside the door and read.

''Oh, come in, why don't you,'' Anna encouraged.

Slowly, silently, Misha appeared in the doorway. He thought not to look at Anna nursing the baby, but he couldn't help himself. His eyes hungrily sought out the scene, and he stood, scarcely breathing, gazing at the black curls and tiny fist pressed against Anna's fair skin. He watched the fist open and close in rhythm to the contented sucking, and the sweetness of joy caressed by time fluttered through him. He smiled.

''What?'' she chided. ''What's so funny?''

''Funny, nothing—I swear.'' He backed away, flustered, and slammed his head into the doorjamb.

In an effort to contain a laugh, Anna scolded him more severely. ''Well, are you going to come in and read or what? You see, what really interests me . . . Is anything written about the workers' hospital? I do worry, not hearing anything from your grandmother.''

''Nothing about the workers' hospital, but . . .'' Misha was rubbing his head; he tried to focus his eyes on the newspaper, and saw only a blur. What a jerk he was making of himself. Anna probably thought him an imbecile. Hopelessly he stole another glance, relieved to find Anna oblivious of his presence. She was rocking slowly, contentedly, the golden silk of her hair curving against the childlike delicacy of her smile. He had forgotten as Anna had swelled in her pregnancy just how slim and delicate she was, so unlike his Irina. Anna had none of his Irina's striking sensuality or her earthy majesty. Anna's beauty was ethereal; the bitterness that had encased her during the months after Uncle Alexei's death seemed gone; she rarely flew into an angry fit. Time with her was often so quiet, he sometimes had to look at her to make sure she hadn't simply vanished. He wondered what she was thinking about now. Surely not about him or the newspaper article. She was thinking about Uncle Alexei most likely.

What a poor replacement Misha made, yet how he was growing to love Anna and the baby . . . Irina. . . . Sometimes, still, the name pricked like the thorns of a rose. Other times, he cuddled the baby, repeating the name over and over as he nuzzled her, feeling she was his. She almost was, he thought, the memories of her birth still so vivid in his mind. He had practically brought her into the world. That counted for something he told himself, lying on his couch at night, listening to Anna sing to Irinushka, knowing they were snuggled together, a family, almost.

It was madness, but he wanted desperately to crawl into bed with them and sing and coo with them. He wanted to complete the circle, to be husband and father. He wanted someone to love, someone to fill the void left by Irina's death, someone to hold him through the night, someone to stop the aching.

"Aren't you going to read to me?" Anna asked, shifting the baby from one breast to the other. "Read to me about the railroads. Are they still not running?"

"Mostly. The strikers even threaten to stop supplies to and from the Far East."

"Goodness, imagine Russia without its railroads. What do you think Alexei would say about that?"

"What do you think?"

"I think," she began, fixing her eyes serenely on Misha, "I think he would say it's time for you to go back to Russia."

"What?" Misha shuddered, shocked by Anna's words. "I don't think he'd say that at all! I think he'd say it was my place to stay here."

"That's his place, Misha, not yours. I . . . we, Irinushka and I, we appreciate all you're doing for us. But we can tell, Misha, it's in your heart to return to Russia. That's your true place."

"Misha, Misha, wake up!" Anna nudged frantically as she turned on the lamp.

"What is it?" He pushed himself up on the couch, shielding his eyes as he did.

It was the middle of the night. Anna was holding Irina, wrapped in blankets, in her arms. "She has a fever. She's burning up!"

Misha reached for the infant, and holding her, slipped his hand across her forehead. "My God, she's on fire."

"Do you think you could get Larisa Filipovna? With all those children, she must know about such things."

Without another word, Misha handed Irina back to Anna and bounded from the couch, hurrying out the door in his nightclothes.

About five minutes later he appeared with a bleary-eyed Larisa Filipovna, her ample body tied up in a dull gray woolen robe. Anna, tears streaming down her face, handed Irina to the woman unbidden. "Oh, thank you, Larisa Filipovna, for coming, thank you!"

Wordlessly Larisa Filopovna pressed her lips to Irina's forehead, then unwrapped the blankets and felt her hands and feet. "It's hard to tell, Anna Petrovna, when they're so young. It could be the ears, or some infection set in. You'd best call a doctor as soon as you can. Dr. de Nery is who you want. I'll send my oldest, Gerald, to get him as soon as the sun rises. Now, you calm down, Anna Petrovna. We'll do our best." She patted Anna's hand.

Dr. de Nery was a compassionate, thorough doctor; but he couldn't identify the source of the fever. He prescribed rubdowns and careful watching. Anna and Misha never left Irina's side; Dr. de Nery visited twice a day; Larisa Filipovna came up more frequently, bringing Misha and Anna casseroles, bread and cheese. She hovered about them, insisting that they eat. Irina wasn't nursing. She never moved. Anna prayed. Misha paced, read newspapers and thanked God he hadn't left for Russia after all.

"It's broken!" Misha shouted, shaking Anna from her sleep on the chair near the cradle. "The fever's broken!" It was the morning of the fourth day.

"Are you sure?" Anna pushed past him.

Irina was awake, her blue eyes staring very wide. Her black hair was plastered with sweat. Her little feet kicked in the bunting. Anna lifted her carefully, laughing as she wiped her hand against the cool, wet skin. Irina started crying, her lips looking madly for the breast.

"Go tell Larisa Filipovna, Misha," Anna insisted as she sat down to nurse. "Hurry, she'll be so glad!"

By October 1905, a general strike across Russia was complete. The demands of the nation were straightforward: only a constitution and universal suffrage would start up the engines, telegraphs, electricity, and the wheels of industry again. Restaurants and taverns closed. Doctors marched beside plant workers, bank clerks beside bakers, coachmen beside stockbrokers.

"Look at this—the dancers at the Marinsky corps de ballet are marching too!" Misha chuckled, imagining his old girlfriend Mathilde in her ballet shoes waving a red flag.

In Petersburg the water workers were locked into the water plants to assure a continued water supply. There were no newspapers except for the revolutionary press. The streets were clogged with tens of thousands of citizens congregating nightly at the university and then fanning throughout the city. Those without red flags tore down the tricolors of the Czar and ripped off the white and the blue, leaving only the red.

The Czar dispatched his troops. They marched relentlessly, crushing resistance, bloodying the streets from Petersburg to Odessa to Yekaterinoslav. Cossacks charged with whips lashing and sabers drawn. Soldiers shot without warning. The ranks of the Black Hundreds swelled, unleashing their own lawless terror under the approving eyes of local officials.

The strikers built barricades and seized weapons from gun shops. Bombs were made, homemade weapons fashioned. Strike committees were organized into workers' councils called soviets, made up of elected deputies from hundreds of plants and factories. The strongest soviet rose in Petersburg, the nerve center for the revolution.

On October 12, 1905, the Czar handed over dictatorial powers to General Trepov, who ordered his troops to "Spare no cartridges and use no blanks!"

Anna couldn't sleep when Misha was out late, which was almost every night. She lay in her bed, worrying, until her fears became waking nightmares. They were always the same. She imagined soldiers like the ones who had arrested Alexei bursting into the flat and tearing her from Irinushka. She imagined Misha being arrested, kidnapped as he walked down a deserted Geneva street. She imagined them both being taken back to Russia in chains and hanged. Larisa Filipovna would find Irinushka in her cradle, screaming from hunger, her poor little bottom red from lying in wet diapers for so long. Larisa Filipovna would take Irinushka home and care for her as one of her own.

Anna was up to the part in her fantasy when she and Misha were long dead, and Irinushka was a beautiful young girl of seventeen, returning to Russia to claim her birthright; Zhenya Kirilovna was still alive, welcoming her favorite granddaughter with open arms when Anna heard Misha come in. It was later than usual, past two in the morning. She heard Misha tiptoeing about as he readied himself for bed. She wondered if he had eaten the herring she'd left for him. Probably not. He wasn't the least bit like Alexei when it came to food. Alexei was always hungry. . . . She smiled, remembering how Alexei loved to eat after making love, no matter what time of day or night it was. She turned on her side, pulled her knees to her chest to contain the memory, and tried to sleep. She tossed and turned, hoping Irinushka would wake soon for a night feeding. Finally Anna sat up, thinking she would read, and saw Misha's light still on.

"Hello," she called from the doorway.

"You're still up?" He seemed surprised, and quickly put down the pencil with which he'd been writing.

"I couldn't sleep. Maybe I'll have some hot milk. That helps, you know. Larisa Filipovna told me it's not just an old wives' tale. That hot milk helps calm the nerves. Do you want some?"

"I don't think so."

She knotted the sash of her robe tighter and went to the kitchen; she was standing at the stove stirring her heating milk when Misha came in. "Did the meeting go well?" She sipped a spoonful of milk. It was barely lukewarm. "What did you talk about so late?"

"The Czar has signed a constitution," he said soberly.

"A constitution—well, isn't that good? Isn't that what everyone wants?"

He shook his head. "How can anyone trust the Czar's signature on a piece of paper when people are still starving and troops are ordered to shoot to kill? No one is deceived. Petersburg and Moscow are up in arms. There are massive demonstrations against the constitution, and the Black Hundreds are retaliating viciously." Misha was staring down at his hands the whole time he spoke, nervously folding and unfolding a piece of paper. "Anna . . ." he began again hesitantly. "I have to talk to you. Can we go into the other room?" He waved his arm as if to say he needed more space than the tiny hole of a kitchen.

"Of course." She slipped the pot off the burner and followed him into the parlor. They stood awkwardly by the couch, and when she could bear the silence no longer, she blurted out, "You're going back, aren't you?"

"For a while," he said softly.

"Well, that's grand! I won't lie to you and say we won't miss you, Irinushka and I, but we're joyous for you. We know that's what you want. Besides, we've Larisa Filipovna and her family for friends now, so we're not all alone.'' She tried to sound excited. She wanted Misha to think she was excited, but her voice was too high and singsong. She was pacing back and forth across the small parlor. ''And I've been thinking, I'm feeling so much stronger now, absolutely one hundred percent healthy, I've been thinking I'll begin giving piano lessons. Larisa Filipovna says she knows—''

''Anna.'' His hands gripped her shoulders, forcing her to stop walking. Gently he turned her to him, and she blinked to erase the ghost of Alexei from his face. ''I'm not going back for good. I . . . I can't . . .''—leave you, he wanted to say, but couldn't.

''What are you going to do?'' She was quivering.

''I'm in charge of a group who's running arms to the Petersburg Soviet. I swear, that's all I'll be doing. I'll be back in a few weeks.''

She pushed away from him and turned, afraid she might cry from relief. She couldn't let him see her cry anymore. ''If you're thinking it matters to me, well, of course, I'd be worried to death if you stayed in Petersburg, but don't not return to your comrades on my account . . .''

''You're my comrade too.''

''But I'm one and they're many!'' she reminded him forcefully, and then he was holding her in his arms, his fingers smoothing away the few tears. His lips grazed her cheeks and pressed against her hair. His breath was sweet and she trembled as her mouth sought his.

''Oh, God, Anna . . .'' His arms tightened about her until she felt his strength penetrating the aching hollow, warming the blue coldness of her loneliness. His body was at once familiar and unknown. ''I can't leave you. I can't ever leave you. I love you. God, I love you . . .'' he murmured as he kissed her.

She hungered after his touch and his taste; their bodies intertwined; hands pressed on bare skin. She was a swimmer caught in a glorious rush; she was her music when no one else could hear, and then, without warning, the air darkened like snow in a moonless night, and she was standing alone.

''I'm sorry,'' he was saying, his voice low, far away.

She was shaking as she wrapped her robe tightly about her again. The imprint of his lips on hers burned.

He was so far from her, standing across the room.

She pressed her arm to her face and breathed the lingering scent of his muskiness; her wanting for Alexei washed over her like an impenetrable sea.

* * *

"I need to return to Petersburg now, today, tomorrow, as soon as you can arrange it!" Misha insisted to a startled Matthew Grigorievich. Misha was pacing across Matthew's small one-room flat, his mind set on one thing, spending as little time with Anna in that apartment as possible. He'd been up all night thinking about her, about them, about their relationship, which could never be the same anymore. He'd been mad to give in to his feelings. Anna must surely despise him—but not nearly as much as he despised himself. To think that he could ever have dreamed of taking Uncle Alexei's place! Her passion for him was only fleeting, a weakness of the flesh. Thank God he'd stopped the madness before he'd humiliated himself and, worse, brought Anna to despair.

"I thought you were going at the end of the week," Matthew was saying.

"I can't wait that long."

"Dmitri Andreievich will need to know why."

"Look, I can go back without you and without Dmitri Andreievich, you know!" he flared.

"Sure you can, kid. You'd also have a chance of being picked up by the first border guard."

"That's a chance I'll have to take. But pass this on to Dmitri Andreievich next time you contact him. Tell him I'm on my way back to Petersburg. I'm leaving tomorrow."

Matthew hesitated. "I shouldn't do this for you. But hell, you're some kind of a hero. Look, I'll get your message coded and sent off this morning. Here . . ." He scribbled down the name and address of a man named Alesander Volkov in Warsaw. "Memorize the address and get rid of the paper before you leave Geneva."

Misha nodded. "Thanks, Matthew. I owe you one."

"Just keep out of trouble, all right? Dmitri Andreievich will have me shot at dawn if anything happens to you."

"I was thinking, I might go away for a while," Misha said as he sat down with Anna at breakfast the next morning. They'd hardly spoken since their embrace two nights before. He stared down at his cereal growing cold.

"Yes." She could not look at him either.

"I just think it would be best. What do you think?"

I think I need you! I need you to hold me and love me! she wanted to cry out. She hadn't realized how empty the woman in her was until he'd held her and kissed her, but all she said was, "Yes, it would be best." Involuntarily her eyes met his, their deep blue-gray like an alchemist's wand, beckoning the warm stream from within her. She stared down at her plate of food and prayed, *Blessed Virgin, Mother of God, protect Misha in his struggle and help make me strong.* . . .

"I will return," he promised Anna, and kissed Irinushka's downy head once more.

The baby smiled, and her smile seemed like a golden cord to his heart.

"Be safe, Misha," Anna said fervently. "You have all your documents?"

"Everything's in order. Matthew Grigorievich made the arrangements. And once in Petersburg, I'll be fine. They say the Soviet controls much of the city." Misha took Irinushka in his arms. The pain of good-bye opened the wounds inside him again, a path feeling damp, lined with peat and broken lives. *I'm not brave, Anna. I'm not so brave at all,* he wanted to tell her. He wanted her to ask him to stay. He could stay and never touch her again. He wanted to tell her that.

"I . . ." She shook her head and reached for Irina, grasping Misha instead. She held him tightly. "I just want to thank you, Misha. I could never have survived without you."

"Nor I without you." He gave Irina back to her. "You'll be all right?"

"Yes. Larisa Filipovna has already invited me to dinner. We'll be fine. Go on, go now . . ." She tried to smile.

He thought to hug her one last time, but reached for his bag, turned, and hurried out the door.

CHAPTER FIFTY

Alesander Volkov was a member of the Polish underground. Although Poland was under Russian martial law, Misha was safely transported to the border, where Fedya, Dmitri's man who had led Misha and Anna to Geneva, was waiting. They passed through several roadblocks without the hint of a problem, and when they reached a roadblock just outside of Petersburg, Misha settled comfortably by a bonfire where a group of travelers, mostly workers and students, was hotly debating the effects of the constitution while waiting for their papers to be checked.

Misha noticed a man with a scar, as if a knife had been slashed across his cheeks and lips, standing silently at the edges of the group. He was more disheveled than most of the travelers; his jacket and ancient fur cap were peppered with moth holes; rags held together his boots and gloves. The man leveled a belligerent gaze at Misha, only to look quickly away when their eyes met. Misha felt instinctively in his coat for his gun and looked for Fedya, who was on the other side of the road, deep in a conversation with some peasants. He looked back toward the ragged man to see him slipping from his place and walking purposefully toward the roadblock.

Misha bolted after him, losing him in the tangle of horses, carriages and carts waiting to be inspected. Chalking up his foreboding to his overly anxious mind, he detoured into the woods to relieve himself. As he stood, he heard footsteps in the crusty snow and swerved in time to see the blur of a man leaping at him. Something cold and hard slammed into the side of his head, and the next thing he knew, he was lying on the ground staring at the black boots of three guards and a pair of rag-wrapped feet.

"Kalinin, aye, I knowed it's him from the first! Kalinin, him that killed Yermolov and escaped!" the ragged man yelped his accusation.

"What's the problem here, Captain?" came a softly important voice. It was Fedya.

Misha tried to sit. His head pounded fiercely.

Fedya bent down to him. "Be still, don't say a word," he warned as he reached in Misha's coat for his papers, then stood again. "Been a mistake, I think, Captain," Fedya went on congenially.

The Captain glanced at the papers for only a moment and handed them back to Fedya. "Arrest him!" the Captain snapped, and two guards immediately surrounded the ragged man. "His papers are not in order. They've been clearly forged."

The ragged man was dragged away screaming, "Not me— him! He's the criminal. He's Kalinin!"

"Sorry about the disorder," the Captain said as Fedya helped Misha to his feet. "You all right?"

"He's fine, fit as a fiddle," Fedya assured, linking his arm through Misha's.

"Well, as long as you're here, you might as well go on through," the Captain announced. "Your papers are in order."

"What the hell was that about?" Misha whispered as he sat beside Fedya in the sleigh, the roadblock swiftly slipping behind them.

"That ragpicker recognized you. I'm not surprised. Your picture was on the front page of every newspaper in Russia for weeks. But you'll be safe enough when you're in Petersburg, so long as you stay in the Soviet-controlled parts. You'll be able to walk about quite freely."

Misha nodded thoughtfully. "I don't understand why the ragpicker was arrested, though."

"Don't worry about such scum. He'd join up with a Black Hundred band in a moment. Come now, your grandmother is anxiously awaiting your arrival."

Survival, Anna thought as she sat at the parlor table, her cache of money carefully laid out. Survival was all that mattered, her survival, Irinushka's survival, and survival depended on money. She stared at her pathetic pile of francs and coins. Much of what had been sent by Zhenya Kirilovna had been spent to pay Dr. de Nery, Sophie, Dr. Pitkin, and to buy a layette. . . . Her heart ached at the memory of the day Misha had come home with the layette. Irinushka had been only a few days old, and Misha had gone out, saying he was going for groceries, only to return several hours later with a smiling Larisa Filipovna and armloads of boxes. Larisa Filipovna had helped him pick out everything necessary for a new baby, and a few things not necessary, such as an exquisite baptismal dress. Larisa Filipovna had offered to lend Anna her children's, but Misha had insisted on a new one—Anna hadn't dared guess at the price—as well as two of the tiniest dresses and the most delicate, minuscule lace hat Anna had ever seen.

Anna swallowed and wiped away a tear as she remembered how she'd scolded Misha for spending too much money, and then how she'd hugged him and together they'd dressed Irinushka in one of the dresses, which had been so big for her, they'd laughed. Now the dress fit her perfectly, and, Anna thought, Misha would never see her in it.

She fingered her pile of savings and tried to force Misha from her mind. Missing him was nothing compared with what she had felt after Alexei's death. Besides, it was best that Misha was gone. He belonged in Petersburg. It would have been selfish to keep him from the revolution any longer. Yet she couldn't help but remember the moment he'd held her, and his words, *I can't leave you, I can't ever leave you, Anna. Oh, God, I love you.* . . .

"Love," she said out loud. "Love," she repeated blandly, and thought of the many kinds of love. Love for a child, love for country, love for freedom, love for a man. Fleetingly she thought of remarriage. Someday, perhaps, she would remarry for Irinushka's sake, someone rich, of course, and not for love. She would never love anyone but Alexei . . .

"No!" she shouted, slamming her fist so hard the francs flew into the air and scattered on the floor. The coins jangled. She hadn't sold herself for her parents and she wouldn't sell herself for Irinushka. She would earn what money they needed. She would be poor but proud. Irinushka would respect her.

First she gathered up the fallen francs and tucked them safely under the mattress in Irinushka's cradle. Then she took a pen and paper and began to write: *Talented pianist, daughter of a well-known St. Petersburg family, offers piano lessons at reasonable rates. For interview, please write to A. P. Marks* . . . Anna paused as she wrote "Marks," thinking she couldn't say "well-known St. Petersburg family" if she used "Marks." But she couldn't use "Kalinina." What person in his right mind would want a convicted terrorist for a teacher? She thought to use the name Orlova and felt her hackles rise. Anna Orlova was dead. She had died the night her mother had told her about the engagement to the Prince. The only name to use was Marks.

She looked down at what she'd written and crossed out "well-known St. Petersburg family" and carefully penned in the phrase "student of Rimsky-Korsakov," and paused. If she used Rimsky-Korsakov's name, people might think she'd been to the Conservatory, and then they'd begin asking her about disturbances at the Conservatory and if she'd been a revolutionary.

Quickly she crossed out Rimsky-Korsakov's name and folded her paper and slipped it into her pocket. Then she lifted Irinushka from the couch. Larisa Filipovna would help her figure out what to say.

Fedya left Misha without further incident on the outskirts of Vasilievsky Island, and he wandered about, marveling at the changes in Petersburg since the last time he'd walked the streets as a free man. Barricades or remains of barricades were evident all over the island. Windows were cracked and broken and fences were blasted with bullet holes. People openly carried weapons, guns or homemade knives and chains. Proclamations from the Soviet and announcements of meetings were posted everywhere. People walked with purpose. The usually slouched, reticent workers looked Misha clearly in the eye as he passed, nodding, "Good day, comrade," and "Long live the revolution." Red flags hung from windows; doors, walls, fences, every coverable surface was papered with posters and fliers demanding "Strike!" "Amnesty!" and "An Eight-Hour Day and a Gun!" Many had headlines such as: "Brother Soldiers and Policemen! Lay Down Your Arms and Join the Righteous Struggle of the Workers!" Others proclaimed solidarity with the Polish workers and mutinying Kronstadt sailors. To Misha's surprise, he saw several men in army uniforms wearing armbands of the people's militia.

It was late afternoon before he arrived at the workers' hospital, which was more bustling than ever. He slipped in unnoticed and stood leaning against the wall watching his grandmother tend to a wounded man, then snap off orders military fashion to a young girl following her about.

"Anything I can do?" he whispered, slipping his arms about Zhenya Kirilovna's shoulders as she started for the supply closet.

"Misha!" Zhenya spun around. "Misha, my heart!" She stared in wonder, her gray eyes watery, her lips quivering between sadness and joy. Then she held his face in her hands and kissed his cheeks. "I expected you hours ago. Oh, what happened?" She smoothed her fingers across the swollen purple gash on the side of his head.

"Nothing, I'm fine." He kissed her.

"Come now, let me clean that up." She took him by the hand and marched him to a small side room, where she urged him onto a chair and began cleaning his wound.

Zhenya Kirilovna wanted to know all the details of Misha's return and told him what little that she knew. A messenger had come to her from the Brigade just the night before, informing her that Misha would be arriving in Petersburg the next day and that notice of his return should be given to the Soviets. "Of course, I would have done that anyway." Zhenya Kirilovna seemed miffed. "A hero such as yourself—of course, the Soviets will want your services. What does Dmitri Andreievich think? While he's off someplace, the revolution goes on quite well without him. As if I need to be told how to treat my own grandson." She was silently thoughtful a moment, then asked, "Have you seen Dmitri Andreievich at all?"

"Oh, yes. He was in Geneva about a month ago."

"Of course, we've heard rumors about his being alive. We heard that it was he who arranged your and Anna's escape.

But there was no word from him and no one actually saw him. There were rumors that he was dead, and then there were rumors—'' She cut herself off.

"What?"

"Nothing, rumors only." Her smile was stiff. "Rumors fly about Petersburg like insects about a corpse. One moment's truth becomes another moment's lie. Well . . .'' She smiled and took both of Misha's hands in hers and held them to her face. "My goodness!" she exclaimed. "In all this talk you haven't told me a word about Anna! Is she all right? Has she given me another grandchild?"

"Anna's fine, just fine. And you've a new granddaughter—Irinushka. She's beautiful, Grandma, the most beautiful creature I've ever seen in my entire life!"

At first Misha didn't recognize his brother. Nikita had grown at least three inches in the year since they'd last met. His face had lost its baby softness, replaced by the angularity and mismatched features of young adulthood. There were shadows of their father in Nikita's full lips and oddly in his smile. Misha couldn't remember his father ever smiling, yet when Nikita did, which was often, Misha felt touched by the likeness. Nikita was of medium height and broad, already broader than Misha; he wore the armband of the people's militia.

Nikita seemed giddy to be with his brother, and he talked endlessly of patrols and skirmishes with the Black Hundreds and Czar's troops. He already had a battle wound, a scar along his right cheek, where a thug's knife had swiped him.

"I'm proud of you," Misha said when Nikita finished his tales of his four months in the militia.

The boy beamed.

"What do Mama and Papa say of all this?"

"Nothing good, you can be certain. So I don't go home anymore. I still meet Sasha, though. He's dying to join us, but someone has to take care of Mama, Mousia, and Nadezhda."

"How is Mama?"

"I miss her, I do." A doleful expression shadowed Nikita's face, making him look very young.

"And Mousia and Nadezhda?"

"They're fine. Nadezhda's quite big. She's walking and talking. But, Misha, tell me, what was it like to throw a bomb? What did it feel like to blow the scum to death?"

"I didn't actually throw the bomb."

"But you've killed a man! I bet you've killed many men.

Oh, Misha, I'm so glad you've returned!" Nikita's hands were flying in excitement as he spoke. "I've already spoken to Benya Timofeievich—he's my squad leader. I told him you'd want to be with us. I hope that's all right. Benya was honored. Then nothing will stop us, Misha. We shall attack a whole squadron of Cossacks. We shall push them all back to hell!" He held up his arm and pointed his finger. "Die, scum!" he shouted. "Ready! Aim! Fire! Pow! Pow! Pow!"

Anna never advertised in the newspaper. Larisa Filipovna insisted it was a waste of good money, of which Anna had tolerably too little. Instead, Larisa Filipovna and her husband "passed the word around" for her, and within a week Anna had her first student, an asthmatic twelve-year old named Masha, who lived only two blocks away. Her mother, Anastasia Ivanovna Melgunova, was a friend of Larisa Filipovna's, and Anna was admonished against charging too much. "Her husband is not a rich man, you see. Oh, he's a talented watchmaker, but there are so many in Geneva, you see. He takes what he can get. You must be generous with my friend."

"Of course," Anna agreed. Since she had no idea what to charge, she went along with the arrangement Larisa Filipovna worked out, which was a few francs in exchange for two one-hour lessons a week and unlimited practice time at the Melgunovs' piano for Anna herself.

Anna was confused and excited at the same time. "You mean I can just use the Melgunovs' piano whenever I like?" The old upright wasn't impressive, but was well-tuned, and it was a piano.

"Well, of course, you'll have to work out some kind of scheduling, but Anastasia Ivanovna is in heaven ever since she heard you play. She says your practicing will be like having her own gramophone. So I'm certain you could arrange to go there almost every day. And I'll watch Irinushka. She's such an angel, I can never get enough of her."

Anna could hardly believe her good fortune. She opened her mouth to speak, but didn't know what to say.

"What's the matter?" Larisa Filipovna questioned.

"I . . . I . . . ." Anna bit her lip, and then, bursting with a happiness she hadn't felt since Misha had been with her, she leaned over to embrace her friend. "Thank you, Larisa Filipovna. I'm just so happy—to be able to play every day, you see!"

"Yes, yes . . ." Larisa Filipovna poured Anna more tea. "I thought it was a good arrangement."

Anna dropped sugar in her tea and stirred slowly. "Why?" she began hesitantly. "Why are you so good to me?"

The question seemed to surprise Larisa Filipovna. "Goodness, you're such an easy person to be good to, Anna. Imagine!" Larisa Filipovna poured milk into Anna's tea. "Imagine something so simple as playing a piano making you smile again."

After teaching Masha Melgunova for only a week, Anna received a letter from a young Swiss woman named Victoria Ghent, who wrote that she "always took her watches to Mr. Melgunov for repair." Apparently Mr. Melgunov had raved about Anna's talent as a pianist, and Victoria Ghent, who "loved piano playing more than life itself," was in particular need of a teacher at the moment. "Would you, my dear Mrs. Marks, think of coming to my flat so I could audition for you?" Victoria Ghent wrote. "Afterward we shall have a lovely tea with my grandmother, who is a great admirer of Rimsky-Korsakov and all the wonderful Russian masters."

"Well, of course, Marc Antonovich will have to go with you," Larisa Filipovna said, referring to her husband. She ran her fingers across the fine, scented writing paper of Victoria Ghent. "And look at this address. It's not the best in Geneva, but it's not the worst. Far from it. You shall be able to get a pretty penny from Victoria Ghent. When the time for discussing fees comes, let Marc Antonovich take the lead."

"All right," Anna agreed, feeling suddenly awkward under Larisa Filipovna's insistent stare. "Is something wrong?"

Larisa Filipovna picked and poked at Anna's dress, which, like the rest Anna owned, was taken in from her pregnancy. "Your fingers may know what to do with piano keys, Anna Petrovna, but when it comes to sewing . . . well, of course, you can't visit a fine lady like Victoria Ghent in something like that." She finished her tea and then stood up abruptly. "Wait here," she announced.

Anna could hear Larisa Filipovna rummaging about in her bedroom; finally she reappeared with a box and laid it carefully on the table.

"Go on, open it," she urged.

"What is it?"

"You'll see!" Larisa Filipovna was grinning.

Gingerly Anna opened the box, and under layers of tissue paper were yards of pale blue damask woven in a pattern of flowers. "I bought that five years ago from a neighbor who was moving. She was going to make curtains, you see, and I bought it to make curtains too. It was such a bargain, even

Marc Antonovich didn't complain, but with all the children, I never got around to it. I could easily make you a dress from it.''

''Oh, but I couldn't! What if you want to make the curtains?''

''I've had that material five years, Anna. What do you think the chances of making curtains are after five years? Now come!'' Larisa Filipovna swept the material from the box and draped it across Anna.

Anna found herself more nervous about the interview than she'd expected, despite the success of Larisa Filipovna's dress, designed in the height of fashion. She couldn't eat the entire day before going to Victoria Ghent's.

''It's you who are doing the interviewing,'' Marc Antonovich reminded Anna as they sat on the bus taking them across town. Marc Antonovich was sitting very tall and still. He looked almost like a mannequin in his best suit and scrubbed face. Larisa Filipovna had trimmed his hair and beard. ''The lady's the one wanting your expertise, remember that.''

The bus left them off several blocks from Victoria Ghent's apartment in a distinctly middle-class neighborhood, which impressed Marc Antonovich and calmed Anna. She had expected Victoria Ghent to be quite noble. To Anna's surprise, Victoria Ghent herself answered the door. There seemed to be no servants whatsoever in the apartment, which was decorated unremarkably in bland tones of greens and browns. The large, sunny windows in the parlor only accented the fading fabrics on the couches and chairs. The pictures on the walls were weary reproductions of old masterpieces or photographs of family members. The surface of every piece of wooden furniture was covered with lace doilies and porcelain knickknacks. Victoria Ghent and her grandmother were decidedly middle-class.

Victoria herself was a cheerful, attractive young woman in her mid-twenties. Her features were small and refined. Her brown eyes glimmered with nervous excitement and her smooth, thin lips parted in a smile designed to please. The elder Mrs. Ghent was unpleasantly wizened with curly white hair and watchful eyes embedded in folds of wrinkled skin. She came barely to Anna's shoulders, and shook hands weakly, but would not smile or speak. The elder Mrs. Ghent seated herself in an oversize brocaded wing chair, clasped her folded hands on her lap, pressed her knees together, and settled in to watch the proceedings.

Marc Antonovich sat silently erect on a small side chair.

Anna and Victoria Ghent stood by the highly polished grand piano, which, along with a large flowered diamond-and-ruby pin on the bodice of Victoria's dress, demanded Anna's attention. Anna was wondering if the stones were real, when Victoria, noticing her interest, pressed her hand to her pin. "It's lovely, isn't it? A dear, dear friend of mine gave it to me. Baron von Hindler, the younger Baron von Hindler. We were engaged," Victoria added thoughtfully. "This was my engagement gift."

"It's lovely."

Victoria's eyes clouded as if some painful inner thought were tugging at her; then she was smiling again. "Is it true you were a student of Rimsky-Korsakov?"

"For a while."

"Oh, how lucky for you, Anna—you don't mind if I call you Anna, do you? Formality quite takes away my creative urges, don't you think, and we're practically the same age. Mr. Melgunov tells me your husband was killed in the revolution, but that you come from the noblest of Russian stock, a true aristocrat, just like Baron von Hindler." Again Victoria's eyes clouded and Anna sensed the relationship between Miss Ghent and Baron von Hindler was not all that could be hoped for. "Baron von Hindler gave me the piano too. Oh, it's marvelous, I can assure you. Quite the best money can buy. He thinks I'm talented. Well, I'm afraid I'm not so talented as he thinks, but I do have a flair, I believe. And I do love playing so much. But first, Anna . . ." Victoria touched Anna's arm. "I would so like to hear you play."

Anna slipped her arm away. "Of course." She smiled courteously.

As Anna settled herself at the piano, she decided to play a Mozart concerto, one of Alexei's favorites, and as her fingers flew across the keys, the disdain she felt for the Ghents was swept away by a delirious happiness which no amount of playing on the Melgunovs' upright could produce. Victoria Ghent's piano was as magnificent as the one Alexei had bought her in Petersburg. Anna was unable to stop once she finished the concerto. Her fingers felt tied to the keyboard; her eyes closed; the music streamed like radiant heat.

"Bravo! Bravo!" Victoria shouted as Anna finished. Marc Antonovich rose to his feet, and even the wizened Mrs. Ghent broke into applause. "Oh, Anna!" Victoria was so close, Anna feared she might embrace her. "That was marvelous! Like a concert hall. See, it's put goose bumps on my skin." She pushed up her sleeve and held out her arm. "I must have

Freddy, the Baron, that is, hear you someday." She eyed her grandmother uncertainly, and added, "Not yet, you see, the pain is still too great, but soon. Baron von Hindler has such a passion for music. And such passion—" She broke herself off. "I'd be quite ashamed to play following you. But you must promise to give me lessons, Anna. I shall despair if you don't."

"On the matter of your fee," the elder Mrs. Ghent spoke up, her voice surprisingly strong. "Despite my granddaughter's enthusiasm, you must understand that we live on a fixed income. Victoria was engaged to Baron von Hindler, but the engagement's been broken off three months already." She seemed to be chiding Victoria.

Marc Antonovich cleared his throat to speak, but Anna preempted him. "What I'm in greater need of than money, Mademoiselle Ghent—"

"Victoria, please."

"Victoria." Anna smiled graciously. "Is a piano to practice on myself. If I could stay after the lessons and practice for an hour or so, I think a reduced payment can be arranged."

"Oh, of course, of course!" Victoria was giddy with the offer.

"And I'll need you to pay my cab fare here and back," Anna added as she rose to her feet.

"That's more than fair," Victoria agreed, eyeing her grandmother, who nodded a curt approval.

"I should like to come three times a week," Anna said authoritatively. "And if you don't mind, I should prefer if you addressed me as Anna Petrovna."

Anna threw herself into her lessons, modeling her teaching method on the patient, inspiring techniques of her former teacher, young Igor Stravinsky. Although neither Victoria Ghent nor little Masha was a brilliant musician, they had some talent, and they worked devotedly. Anna found herself particularly liking the time she spent with Victoria, not only teaching and playing on her piano, but also the chats they inevitably had over tea afterward. Victoria was younger than Anna had thought, just twenty-one, and she was still desperately in love with Baron von Hindler, Freddy, who was still in love with her. He wrote her letters, sometimes daily, and begged to come see her, but Victoria, despite the pain their separation caused, refused to see him.

"We'd planned to elope," she explained to Anna. "But his mother heard of our plans and threatened to cut Freddy off entirely. I couldn't let him suffer for me. Freddy so loves the finer things of life. He's presently engaged to a rather plain girl from a very well-to-do Munich family. Oh, Anna Petrovna, sometimes it's all too much to bear. Sometimes I feel like throwing my honor to the wind and agreeing to see him again. Have you ever been so tempted?''

Victoria's candor reminded Anna of Irina, and she smiled as the memory of her embrace with Misha caused her skin to tingle.

"Oh, you are wicked, Anna Petrovna!'' Victoria happily chided.

Anna shook her head and forced a serious expression. "The only man I ever loved was Alexei Yakovlevich.''

Victoria reached for another piece of chocolate cake. "You're so lucky to have experienced the fruition of true love, if only for a short time. And you have your baby. I have little left of Freddy except the pain in my heart. Oh, Anna, if I ever fear I'm faltering in my virtue, I'll come to you and you must keep me strong.'' She reached out for Anna's hand and squeezed it gently. "I feel, even though you are my teacher, that we are friends.''

"Oh, yes, I feel that too.''

"That helps heal, Anna. Your friendship and your teaching. When I play the piano, even though I shall never play like you . . . still, when I play, I almost feel everything that I felt for Freddy. Is that crazy?''

"No . . .'' Anna said thoughtfully, feeling an inexplicable sadness tugging at her. "Not at all.''

CHAPTER FIFTY-ONE

Zhenya Kirilovna arranged the meeting between Misha and the leaders of the Petersburg Soviet for November 6 at the university. Misha and Nikita arrived early and wandered about the buildings and grounds, swarming with more workers than students; peasants, soldiers and sailors, shopworkers, men and women from diverse walks of life filled the courtyards and corridors. Every union and organization imaginable was represented. Revolutionary newspapers and manifestos were handed out freely. Eager young agitators were urging people to attend this or that meeting. Crowd-filled rooms overflowed into smoke-filled halls. For all the current of talk and the rushing to and fro, there was a seriousness of purpose in the attentive expressions of the drably dressed workers. How far they had come from the religious awe that had led them like sheep to Father Gapon. None were leaders here, it seemed, and everybody was.

Nikita led Misha to the third floor of the Philosophy Building and knocked on a door marked 302. A slim, pale woman in her late twenties, her dark hair cropped short and severe, answered. "Ah, Nikita, we have been waiting for you." She rested her sharp eyes on Misha. "This is your brother?"

"Yes, Mikhail Anatolyevich . . . Marta Pavlovna." Nikita grasped his rifle to his chest so tightly his knuckles became white. He was bursting with pride.

"It is my pleasure, comrade." Her hand was small but her grip strong. "Come . . ." She stepped back so Misha could pass.

"I'll be waiting outside," Nikita assured. "I'll make sure no one disturbs you." He tapped his gun.

Closing the door, Marta led Misha to the small circle of men, all in their mid- to late twenties, sitting in the classroom chairs. They rose courteously. The first was comrade Yanovsky, introduced to Misha as the rapporteur of the Executive Committee of the Petersburg Soviet. The second was comrade Skobelov, deputy from the Railroad Workers Union, and Misha already had met his grandmother's friend comrade Romanchenko, deputy from the Obukhov plant.

"Comrade Kalinin!" Yanovsky smiled broadly. He was a man of medium height, with dark hair, mustache and goatee, intelligent face, and watchful eyes behind wire-rimmed glasses. "I consider it an honor to welcome you back to Petersburg on behalf of the Soviet. Comrade Romanchenko tells us you had something of an adventure getting back. But come, sit, we have much to talk about." He urged Misha into a seat in the circle between himself and Marta Pavlovna.

"I pray it's not imprudent of me to ask, comrade Yanovsky," Misha said tentatively. "But I have seen you someplace before, and given the circumstances in which we all live today, I can't continue our meeting until I place you."

Yanovsky's smile was obliging. "I don't think we've met in person. I don't know you, save by your reputation. I myself have been in exile for many years."

Misha tried to match Yanovsky's name with the face and

could not. "Still, I feel uncomfortable until we can work this out."

"Perhaps you've seen my photograph in the newspapers as I've seen yours," Yanovsky suggested. "My given name is Lev Bronstein. When I was in Siberia, I found it amusing to write under the name 'The Pen.' There have been others, but you might recognize me most readily as Leon Trotsky."

"Yes, that's it!" Misha exclaimed, relieved to have the mystery solved. He reached forward, hand extended, his smile sincere. "Now, it is my honor to meet you, comrade Trotsky. I have read much of your writings and was very impressed with how you turned around the *Russian Gazette*. It was quite a tepid little paper before you and Parvus took it over. Even in the hospital, I see it's read everywhere, that and *Izvestia*. I most enjoyed your series on the use of revolutionary violence and the forming of a people's militia."

Trotsky nodded contemplatively. "Times are very strange in Petersburg these days. We all teeter on the brink of victory or defeat. The workers teeter. The Romanovs teeter. The bourgeoisie teeters. Who will win?"

"Surely the Soviets are strong. It seems the law in many places."

Trotsky shrugged. "We're legal, yes. Even in the eyes of the Romanovs' law, we're legal. Our deputies are democratically elected. Our meetings are open to anyone. Our chairman, comrade Khrustalev, is received by the Petersburg City Governor himself, yet we hide from no one our intention of violently overthrowing the existing order. I myself was asked to the home of Baroness von Hildebrant just last week. I spoke to some sixty or seventy most elegantly dressed persons, including thirty or forty officers, some of them guardsmen. They asked me about the state of Russia. Isn't that odd, that they should turn for the truth to one who is sworn to strip them of their riches and their power?" Trotsky asked, a boyishly mischievous glint to his eyes.

All those listening seemed pulled into the circle of his storytelling, and Misha asked, "What did you tell them?"

"Well . . ." Trotsky shrugged, unable to repress a smile. "I told them what they wanted to hear and I told them the truth. I told them that at present liberty was unharmed, that the people were unarmed, that the keys to the arsenals and guns were in the hands of the officers, and that at the decisive moment they must be turned over to the people."

"And didn't they balk at that?"

"Amazingly, they applauded me and gave me a collection for the poor and starving!"

"Yet, when the time comes—when we do take over the arsenals—these very people shall be our enemies and we shall kill each other," Marta Pavlovna said, her seriousness a reprimand. She sat very still in her chair, her small rigid frame in stark contrast to Trotsky's expansiveness. She seemed suddenly old and matriarchal.

Comrades Romanchenko and Skobelov seemed to shrink under her watchful glare. Even Trotsky grew somber. "Yes, you see, comrade Kalinin . . ." He cleared his throat. "People like the Baroness and even our Prime Minister, Witte, support the revolution because they think it is in fact their revolution, the revolution that will bring Russia into the twentieth century."

"They believe in a republic but not in a workers' state—as I believe your uncle did." Marta Pavlovna eyed Misha warily. "Comrade Kalinin, are you fighting the bourgeois or the proletarian revolution?"

"I'm not sure I've ever made that distinction."

"I see. It all seems like one revolution." She did not hide her disdain.

"I would die for the revolution!" Misha shot back.

"That already is quite clear," Trotsky reassured, casting Marta Pavlovna a quick glance of disapproval.

"Excuse me, comrade Yanovsky," Marta Pavlovna said with lips pursed. "The lines are quite clear today."

"Quite the contrary, my dear comrade. Today the lines are less clear than ever. Many loyalties will twist and turn before the workers hold the reins of power. The victory will be neither easy nor quick. All too soon the bourgeoisie will see we are more their enemy than is the autocracy. Then they will stop inviting us to their parlors, stop giving us money, and turn their support to the Black Hundreds."

"My uncle would never have supported the Black Hundreds!" Misha said defensively.

"Your uncle would be surprised if he saw Russia today. Times make the man, my friend, and in such times a man may surprise himself. We don't always know which side we shall choose until forced to choose under pain of extinction."

More and more Misha felt the circle was tightening about him. "If you think I'll turn on the revolution and side with those of wealth when the time comes, you must know I have nothing left to me, nothing of my uncle's fortune. I am as penniless as the worst beggar in the streets. I haven't even a country."

"The workers' state would make you its hero!" Romanchenko said proudly, his head held high, his chest wide.

Misha thought Romanchenko might salute him, and for a moment he had to suppress a smile. Nodding to Romanchenko, he said soberly, "I thank you, comrade. I am honored the workers see me as such. But, in fact, you are the true heroes."

"You see, Mikhail Anatolyevich," Trotsky went on, quickly bringing the conversation away from personal matters. "I believe at this moment the revolution has the psychological edge. We gained a great victory with this newest strike. Only days after the October strike ended, before the workers could even lick their wounds and wash away their blood—on the call of the Soviets, the workers went out again, striking as one man. At exactly noon tomorrow, the workers will go back to work, not because the government begs or threatens, but because the Soviets, the voice of the workers, deem it strategically wise."

"Yes, yes." Romanchenko was nodding his head furiously. "We have attained our goals, comrade Kalinin—to free the mutinying Kronstadt sailors and to lift martial law in our long-suffering sister Poland. Ah, the power of a strike! My heart soars so at the thought, I can hardly contain my joy."

"Yet, a political strike is only a demonstration of force, not force itself," Trotsky went on to explain. "The government has backed down to reassess and it will strike out more forcefully. We must be ready to defend and to attack. We must fight to win in the streets or we'll be destroyed. We must"—he held his hand palm-up and drew his fingers into a fist"—hold the keys to the arsenals in our hands."

"Then you think it's truly possible that the army will someday turn on its officers?"

"In truth, the Czar's army is made up mostly of peasants dragged from the land and given bayonets to use against their brothers. Once the common soldier becomes politically conscious, as he has increasingly since Bloody Sunday, then he begins to see the conflict of his loyalties. He begins to see that his officers are asking him to shoot his brother. This"—Trotsky held up a finger for emphasis—"is the start of the moral process that allows the army to cross over to the camp of the revolution. A year ago it would have been unthinkable that there could have been any organizing within the army itself, yet every day representatives of the Soviets are doing just that. Already we have deputies from certain battalions and ships elected. That"—Trotsky smashed his fist into his palm for emphasis—"is what we must have. For you see, an insurrection is, in essence, not so much a struggle *against* the army as a struggle *for* the army."

"The *druzhinniki*," Skobelov announced, uttering his first words since Misha appeared.

For a moment everyone simply stared at the heretofore silent Skobelov as if to acknowledge his presence. Then Romanchenko said, "Thank you, comrade Skobelov. Yes, you are right. It is time to talk to Zhenya Kirilovna's grandson about the *druzhinniki*."

"The fighting arm of the Soviets," Trotsky said.

"Militarily organized armed detachments," Skobelov went on humorlessly. "Invulnerable because they are clad in the armor of the people's sympathy."

"Yes, you see, comrade," Romanchenko added, his voice rising with excitement again. He smoothed his finger repeatedly across his wide mustache. "The *druzhina* have something that the Czar and all his generals will never have. They have the millions of Russian people on their side, people who look just like them, people who will feed them, house them, and hide them."

"Guerrilla warfare," Misha almost whispered, feeling suddenly enveloped in a cocoon of conspiracy, feeling his heart beating faster.

"Precisely. We believe the people are ready. We have the fighters, what we need are leaders," Trotsky went on, an inscrutable Buddha smile on his face. "Men and women experienced in street fighting and bomb making. Leaders who will quickly earn the respect of their troops. Your and your comrades' bold assassination of Yermolov will long go down as one of the revolution's brightest moments, because it showed all of Russia that even so closely guarded a symbol of the Czar's power as Yermolov could be attacked successfully. We need your leadership, Mikhail Anatolyevich."

"I'm honored, comrade, but before I can commit to such work, I must talk with Dmitri Andreievich."

There was a silence and Trotsky asked, "What have you heard from Dmitri Andreievich since your return?"

"Nothing directly. Fedya Yurievich, who guided my return to Petersburg, said Dmitri Andreievich is out of town and isn't expected back imminently."

"Then how can you expect to talk to him?" Marta questioned.

"I will speak with Fedya Yurievich."

"If you see him again." She steadied her glance on him, then turned to Trotsky. "May I go on, comrade?"

Trotsky nodded.

"You worked with Stepan Ostravsky," Marta began. "So did I, several years ago. I knew Stepan well. He taught me to read the streets and make bombs. He was a genius when it came to strategy and leadership.''

Misha was surprised. ''You're in the Brigade, then?''

''I was with the Kiev squad. We carried out effective assassinations of local officials for over a year, then there were sudden arrests. A traitor was suspected, and mistrust spread like a plague. Word came that Dmitri Andreievich had been killed. Members of the squad turned one upon the other. The squad fell apart, and I came to Petersburg to fight with the Soviet. It was here that I heard Dmitri Andreievich was alive, that he had engineered your and Anna Petrovna's escape. I tried every channel I knew to make contact with him, but with each I found myself at a dead end. No one—other than you—has seen him.''

Misha looked to Trotsky as if in his wisdom he could lift the foreboding cloud of Marta's tone, but Trotsky's face was grim. ''What are you trying to tell me?'' Misha asked nervously.

Trotsky took off his spectacles and rubbed his eyes wearily. His gaze settled sadly on Misha and he said, ''We have reason to believe Dmitri Andreievich is a traitor.''

Misha gaped at the four intensely serious faces surrounding him, then laughed disbelievingly. ''That's insane! Dmitri Andreievich was fighting the revolution before most of us gave a thought to the oppressed!''

''God knows none of us would make such an accusation unless we had damaging proof.'' Trotsky offered Misha a cigarette. ''This man, Fedya Yurievich, who brought you to Petersburg—he is nowhere to be found. Nor can we find a trace of the Pole Alesander Volkov.''

''Matthew Grigorievich in Geneva, then. You can talk to him. He made my connections . . .''

Trotsky held out a match for Misha. ''Matthew Grigorievich is gone, vanished without a trace.''

''And do these facts make Dmitri Andreievich a traitor?'' Misha felt suddenly angry. ''Perhaps Fedya, Alesander, and Matthew have all been arrested. Perhaps Dmitri has been arrested too!''

''Rumors began about Mayakovsky's connection to the Okhrana shortly after his daring rescue of you and Anna Petrovna. At first we thought they were simply lies started by the Okhrana to undermine those in the revolution who were loyal to him. Then one of his most trusted men from Kharkov was exposed as an Okhrana spy. The evidence against this man was incontestable. The morning after revolutionary agents put him under house arrest, he was found hanging. Suicide or murder—we'll never know.''

"Did he implicate Dmitri?"

"He didn't have the time. And it didn't occur to us then that he might. As you said, Dmitri Andreievich's name had long been synonymous with the boldest upholding of the revolutionary banner. In fact, we didn't give the rumors much more thought until your grandmother came to us with your stories about the incident at the road check outside of Petersburg.''

"You remember when I borrowed your identification papers at the hospital the other night?" Romanchenko questioned.

"Yes."

"May I see them again?"

For a moment, Misha wanted to say no. He wanted to get up from this ridiculous conversation and flee. But then he was taking his papers from his pocket and giving them to Romanchenko, who laid them along with two other sets of identification papers on a desk. He motioned Misha to look. "These are your identification papers. These are mine and these are the ones taken from the Okhrana spy in Kharkov. What do you see?"

Misha looked, but all three seemed alike. "Nothing unusual."

"Precisely, unless you know what you're looking for. Look here, under the signature of the Prefect. You see there is an insignia of some sort on yours and the spy's from Kharkov. It is a stamp, actually. Mine has none. Nor does anyone else's that we know. If you look closely, you will see the stamp is actually in the shape of a lizard or perhaps a chameleon. We explored it under a microscope. Inside are the initials A.V.A.''

"Arkady Vladimirovich Akimov," Marta intoned.

"It is known within the Okhrana that Akimov considers himself a chameleon. This little stamp is somewhat idiosyncratic," Trotsky went on.

"I don't understand." Misha unbuttoned his sweater. He was growing very warm.

"The reason you were passed so quickly through the roadblocks, the reason the ragpicker was arrested instead of you, is that your papers are marked with the insignia of Akimov. You have, in fact, safe passage throughout Russia. You have the protection of the Okhrana." Trotsky paused, then asked, "Who had these papers made up for you, comrade?"

"Dmitri Andreievich."

"The facts speak for themselves." Marta bristled.

"You're telling me that Dmitri Andreievich is connected to the Okhrana because of this little insignia! Anyone can forge an insignia."

"We've had experts look at it, and they're convinced it's as real as the one on the papers of the agent who died in Kharkov. Our sources tell us that very few people are given this priority protection. It seems you've been accepted into a very exclusive club, Mikhail Anatolyevich."

"The inner sanctum of Arkady Akimov's protection," Skobelov said flatly.

"Dmitri and Akimov?" Misha asked in disbelief.

Trotsky nodded. "We think that's why Yermolov was targeted from the beginning. He was a most difficult man to kill. Akimov and Mayakovsky needed you and your squad to do their dirty work. With Yermolov neatly assassinated, Akimov easily stepped in."

"My God, that's what Irina thought," Misha gasped, his heart pounding very fast. In the way bizarre dreams so often have an aura of reality, Trotsky's scenario was beginning to make horrible sense. "But why? I don't understand why, if this is true, that he would save my life twice."

"There are two possibilities. The first is that Mayakovsky has some yet-unknown plans for you. Equally plausible is that he's acting out of some kind of loyalty to your uncle. Comrade Romanchenko tells me that Mayakovsky was a close friend of the family for years. He would have known of your uncle's fondness for you."

"Yes, he did. And of my love for Uncle Alexei. He was like a father to me."

"Then you'd like to avenge his death."

"Surely you don't think Dmitri had anything to do with Uncle Alexei's death?"

"We have heard a rumor that your uncle was not killed by a Black Hundred, but was shot to death in Akimov's own bedroom. Do you know what your uncle might have been doing in Akimov's bedroom?"

"He hated Akimov, desperately," Misha said softly, and he slumped down in his seat. "We all did."

Trotsky reached out and grasped Misha's arm. "I know this is hard for you. I know it's a lot to take in, but if this is true, if Dmitri Andreievich is the traitor we think he is, then he's truly a fiend and capable of anything. Mikhail Anatolyevich, we need you. We need your help in finding the truth."

CHAPTER FIFTY-TWO

"What do you think, Grandma?" Misha asked as they sat in his grandmother's closet-size room at the hospital. "Do you think Uncle Alexei could have worked with Dmitri Andreievich all those years and trusted him if he were a traitor? How can two men be so close as Uncle Alexei and Dmitri Andreievich and one hold such a horrible secret from the other?"

"They were business partners, Misha. I'm not sure Alexei ever considered Dmitri Andreievich his friend, not in the way a man loves a friend. You knew Dmitri Andreievich better than I. Was he the sort another man could befriend?"

"I don't know. He was my leader, Grandma. I never looked to him as a friend."

She nodded and refilled his teacup. "The truth is, I wouldn't be surprised if the evidence against him turned out to be true. Praise God, I wouldn't condemn a man before knowing all the facts, but should the facts find Dmitri Andreievich guilty, I would feel no regrets as he stood before a revolutionary firing squad."

The image of Dmitri before a firing squad caused Misha to tremble in horror. His mind shifted back to their first meeting together, when Misha had gone to Dmitri's house to talk about terrorism and the Brigade. He remembered Dmitri sitting like a great bear behind his cluttered desk, and he remembered the understanding that had flowed between them. It was Dmitri who had perceived Misha's struggle between violence and chaos, and had given him ways to channel the terrifying darkness within him. It was Dmitri who had shown Misha that his rage needn't debase him as it had debased his father. In some ways, Dmitri understood him better than even Uncle Alexei or his grandmother. Misha wanted to tell his grandmother that. He wanted to ask her: *Does not such understanding define friendship? Is not compassion for the inner turmoil of another the sign of a good man?* Instead, he asked her, "You think I should do as Trotsky wants, then? You think I should help set this trap for Dmitri?"

"It's nothing less than Alexei would have done."

"You think Uncle Alexei would have believed these rumors about Dmitri, then?"

"I think he would have done everything humanly possible to discover the truth, not only for personal reasons, but for the revolution."

Trotsky's plan was simple. On the surface, Misha was to organize *druzhinniki*; discreetly, however, word was leaked that Mikhail Kalinin had returned to Petersburg to organize an assassination squad whose target was Arkady Akimov. The assassination was rumored to be personally as well as politically motivated: Arkady Akimov was responsible for Alexei Yakovlevich's death. Misha was out for revenge.

Misha would have preferred to organize the squad without Marta Pavlovna, to whom he'd taken an intense dislike, but her knowledge of the Brigade was clearly advantageous. Besides, it was taken for granted by Trotsky and the others that she would participate. To balance Marta, Misha insisted that Nikita and Benya Timofeievich be included in the core squad. He liked Benya, a tall, lanky, energetic young man Misha's own age. Born and bred in the worst slums of Petersburg, he was a natural guerrilla warrior.

The first volunteer for the assassination squad was Boris Schmidt, an avowed anarchist, who, after spending five years in Siberia for disseminating incendiary literature, had joined the terrorist arm of the Social Revolutionary Party. During the last two years he'd been involved in three successful assassinations and had personally uncovered a spy network within the SR's. He was an experienced bomb maker and believed the only way the revolution would succeed was by blowing every monarchist, including the Czar and his entire family, to hell.

After Schmidt came Nadia Rachinskaya, recommended by Lev Antonovich, an old school friend of Misha's, once an anarchist, now a Bolshevik. Nadia had mousy brown hair and the small, pointed features of a bird. She wore round, tinted spectacles, and brought with her two Browning revolvers and a cache of ammunition. "I can mix nitro as well as any man," she said almost immediately upon presenting herself to Misha.

Misha felt at once inadequate to lead the squad and impatient with its work. In actuality, any of the members other than Nikita had more street experience than he, Schmidt in particular. If it weren't for Marta's dislike of the man, Misha might have left the workings of the assassination squad in

Schmidt's capable hands. Marta was certain Schmidt had been sent by Dmitri.

Misha didn't think so, and sometimes he thought he simply didn't care. In truth, he had no heart for this search that seemed almost incidental to the day-to-day movement of the revolution. The streets of Petersburg were electric with the workers' victories. The November strike had barely ended when the cry for "an eight-hour day!" sounded spontaneously in factories and plants. All over the city, workers carefully timed their hours and, precisely eight hours after work began, marched from the workplaces waving red flags and singing "The Marseillaise." For days the demonstrations were so strong that the plant owners and managers as well as the police and the Black Hundreds simply watched in astonishment.

While the workers were striking the army and navy were ripe for mutiny, with the strongest rebellion in the Black Sea port of Sevastopol where sailors on the battleship *Potemkin* had mutinied in July. By October thousands of soldiers and sailors were marching with the striking workers. The call for a soldiers' soviet mushroomed, and on November 11, 1905, a ban was placed on all political meetings within the military. As Rear Admiral Pisarevsky read the order to his men, a sailor named Petrov stepped forward and in sight of everyone shot and killed Major Stein of the Brest Regiment and with a second shot wounded the Rear Admiral.

" 'As soon as the sailor Petrov wounded Rear Admiral Pisarevsky, another officer immediately ordered, "Arrest him!" ' " Misha read from atop a table in a crowded, smoky workingmen's pub. He held the newspaper in one hand and a tall mug of beer that someone kept constantly filled in the other. " 'No one moved.' " Misha's voice was loud and dramatic.

His audience listened like mesmerized schoolchildren.

" 'Comrade Petrov threw down his rifle and called, "What are you waiting for? Take me!" Petrov was arrested and sailors came running from all sides, demanding his release. The excitement reached such a height that another officer stood forward and began questioning Petrov. "Petrov, did you fire accidentally?" the officer asked. "How can it be accidental, sir? I stepped forward. I charged my rifle. I took aim. What's accidental about that?" The officer looked very serious and said, "I must believe it was accidental, for everyone is demanding your release." ' And"—Misha closed the paper and raised his hand high in the air—"comrade Petrov was immediately released!"

The audience went wild with applause and Misha leapt from the table and was encircled by a group wanting to talk more about the mutiny. Misha obliged. He was always ready to talk, till dawn if the conversation kept going. For it was here in the pubs, at the meetings, and in the streets that Misha felt himself come alive. He loved these men and women who burned so fervently with the quest of revolution, most of them never having heard of Dmitri Mayakovsky, most of them never knowing nor caring whether they were fighting a proletarian or bourgeois revolution. Misha didn't have to worry about their loyalty. They fought as fiercely as they drank and argued. From them Misha handpicked his squad of *druzhinniki*, and sometimes in their midst he thought he saw Irina dressed as Kuksina.

He was missing Irina more and more, and felt cheated by her death. It was a mistake, a bad mistake, that the bullet had ripped through her instead of him. At times, he was desperate to have her by his side once more. The yearning was most intense at night as he lay in the snow, hand on gun, his senses alert for the slightest crunch of a boot on ice or the flare of a match, the signal that one of his men had seen the enemy. How Irina would have loved the surveillance. How clever she would have been. As much as Misha's men esteemed him, they would have adored Irina. Sometimes he talked to his men about her, told stories of their days with the peddlers and Gapon. The men listened, awed by the tales that spun out effortlessly.

Misha's men worked the back end of Vasilievsky Island with Benya's men, and Nikita went back and forth between the two squads. It was a dangerous zone, where the Czar's police and Black Hundreds infiltrated Soviet-controlled territory under cover of night. The Czar's forces were growing desperate, and the *druzhinniki* fought back relentlessly. More and more, Misha found himself living for the exchange of fists or gunfire; sometimes just the anticipation of action quieted his restlessness. He could actually feel himself relaxing as he dressed for patrol, checked his guns, snapped his pistol into his holster, and loaded his rifle.

The release of the sailor Petrov led to an uprising of the fleet at Sevastopol, which spread to the army barracks of the Brest Regiment and gathered the support of thousands of workers in the Black Sea port. The uprising lasted five days, and by the time it was repressed, the monarchy had begun digging in its heels across Russia. By the third week in November, martial law was extended from Kiev to the chief centers of rural rebellion. On November 24, 1905, "temporary" press regulations were introduced. Revolutionary presses were smashed, and the police descended in cities across the country, arresting anyone near the presses, handing out or reading revolutionary newspapers, or even suspected of having a revolutionary thought.

The revolution met the attack with renewed strength. In the countryside the night skies glowed with the flames of burning fields and landlords' mansions. In the cities meetings were held round the clock. Astonishingly, combat Cossacks, railway policemen, ordinary policemen and police officers, and even some repentant detectives began filtering into public assemblies. Petty officials, prison wardens, and army clerks could be seen waiting in the offices of revolutionary newspapers to have their turn to speak their mind against the government. As if the revolution had stirred some unknown substratum of society caught in the maelstrom of survival, old enemies became comrades. In Irkutsk a garrison of four thousand men voted to endorse a demand for a constituent assembly. Messages raced across the wires from the Far East that the entire Manchurian army would at any time turn its guns on its officers. Cossacks marched through the streets of Moscow singing "The Marseillaise."

Then, on November 26, Georgi Khrustalev, Chairman of the Petersburg Soviet, was arrested. A three-man presidium was elected in his place, with leadership of the Soviet passing to Leon Trotsky. One of the new leadership's first directives was to find new and immediate ways to arm the revolution.

"I've made contact with a man named Volk," Schmidt told Misha as they came off guard duty one night. "He's been quite successful running guns and ammunition from Germany as well as Turkey and the Balkans. He was a bit nervous at first. Said he likes to work alone, but he calmed down a bit when I mentioned your name. If he can help us, he'll be outside your grandmother's hospital at ten o'clock this morning."

Hermann Volk was in his late twenties, his face cleanly shaven, and he wore a once finely tailored greatcoat and wolf-skin hat. His handshake was firm and he seemed genuinely happy to meet Misha. "I can speak only to you, Mikhail Anatolyevich," he said in a lowered voice, and eyed Schmidt disapprovingly.

"Comrade Schmidt is one hundred percent trustworthy," Misha said.

"Such is the time, Mikhail Anatolyevich, that I can take

no man's word but that of the man whom I love beyond all others. He said I am to bring you and only you. I swear to you, there is no danger.''

"I don't like it," Schmidt snapped.

"You have no choice if you want the guns," Volk told him pleasantly. "There is someone invisible behind you. If he sees you following us, I shall be warned and immediately part ways with Mikhail Anatolyevich.''

"I'll be all right, Schmidt," Misha reassured.

"I'll kill you if he's not," Schmidt warned. "So help me God, if anything happens to Mikhail Anatolyevich, I'll not rest until I slit your throat, Volk.''

Volk wordlessly led Misha to a quiet artisan neighborhood of Vyborg lined with mildly neglected, small wood-frame houses. They stopped at the back door of a pale yellow house and knocked three times on the door, waited, and knocked twice more.

To Misha's amazement, the door was cautiously opened by an elderly man he immediately recognized as Semyon, Alexander Ryabushinsky's valet. Semyon's eyes widened in teary delight when he saw Misha. "Mikhail Anatolyevich!" He grasped Misha's hand as he pulled him inside. "The master will be so happy to see you.''

"Alexander Ilyitch! You mean he's here?''

"Yes, yes, and anxiously awaiting you, Mikhail Anatolyevich.''

Misha glanced at Volk, who nodded. "Yes, Alexander Ilyitch. You see why secrecy was of such importance. I will bid you adieu now, comrade.''

Semyon led Misha through the tiny kitchen down a dark hall and to a dimly lit parlor.

Ryabushinsky was living in the ground floor of the house. The rooms were small but neat and not without comfort; the furniture was graying and worn. There was little if anything from Ryabushinsky's grand palace except for some pictures of his wife and Charlotte, a few crystal glasses, china dishes and leather-bound books. Everything else was second- or third-hand and nondescript. Most shocking, however, was Ryabushinsky's appearance. He seemed to have aged twenty years since Misha last saw him only a year before. His handsome virility was gone. His shoulders were bent and his once-thick hair had thinned and grayed. Misha didn't think he would have recognized him if they'd passed in the street.

Ryabushinsky embraced him fervently and kissed each cheek, then embraced him again, holding him for a long time.

"I never thought I'd see you again, Misha, my boy." There were tears in his eyes.

"It's good to see you, too, sir. Tell me, have you heard anything from Charlotte? Is she well?"

Ryabushinsky's thin lips trembled and he asked weakly, "You haven't heard, then? Charlotte was killed." He took off his glasses and pressed his fingers against the bridge of his nose as if to ease the pain. "Some say they died of exhaustion. Others say they were killed trying to escape. Others say they were just killed. I fear we'll never know the truth."

"Olga and Kolya too?"

"I'm afraid so."

Misha's eyes closed. His fists clenched by his sides and his body knotted.

"Like your Irina . . ." Ryabushinsky's lips trembled more uncontrollably. "Ah, I cry too easily these days," he scolded himself. "I have no one to make me strong without my good friend Alexei Yakovlevich." His gaze steadied on Misha. "I miss him, my good old friend. I grow quite impatient with him for getting himself killed." He shook his head and his expression was forlorn. "So many good men and women have died. I sometimes fear that when it's all over, the best will be gone. It's the best who fight the hardest, isn't it, Misha?"

"We've many good men and women left in Russia today, Alexander Ilyitch," he said earnestly. "But tell me, what brings you to these straits? How do you happen to be here, and in what appears to be such secrecy?"

Ryabushinsky motioned Misha toward a tattered chair and settled himself onto the couch. "Volk's a good man, Misha. We talk, we make plans, I give him the money, and he does the work. Thank God, I was fortunate to have gotten hold of most of my money before they came after me."

"Came after you? Who?"

"The Okhrana. I knew I was suspect, and after the squad was arrested, after the assassination, I set about liquidating my assets. I was too closely connected with the Brigade." He paused a moment and smiled. "Can I offer you something? Some coffee, please. Semyon just brought me in a hot pot. I live on the brew. Semyon still manages to get to the teahouse on Nevsky where my wife always shopped." There was a silence as Ryabushinsky gathered the cups and poured the coffee. He took a while to settle in, and then he was quiet, seeming to gather his thoughts. "They tell me Anna Petrovna escaped with you."

"Yes."

"They tell me she was with child."

"She had a girl. She named her Irina."

"Ah, yes!" Ryabushinsky's face lit up. "And they are both safe and well?"

"Fine, very fine, and living in Geneva."

"Good. Good! Then there is still much of Alexei Yakovlevich and Irina Ilyanovna alive." Ryabushinsky sipped his coffee. "My wife, you know, went mad after Charlotte's death," he said matter-of-factly. "She was on the verge of it, living in hiding as we were. It was never her choice, the revolution. Not that she was opposed to it. She's no monarchist. She just wasn't a fighter, you understand. A fine woman, gentle and loving. I sometimes think it's better she lost touch with reality. Volk helped me get her to the country. She's in quite a nice sanatorium. God pray she dies in peace, is all I ask. Ah, Misha, sometimes I blame it on myself. My family is torn apart. I am alone, an old man in hiding."

"Why are you in hiding?"

"Have you heard anything from Dmitri Andreievich?" Ryabushinsky asked uncertainly.

Misha closed his eyes, his body seeming to deflate into the cushions. "I have heard the rumors. Nothing is proven."

"To me it is," Ryabushinsky said emphatically. "Dmitri Andreievich was the only one who knew where my wife and I were hiding. It was just after your sentencing. Volk came to me and said he had heard the police were in fact going to arrest me. Of course, my poor wife was so frail at that point—she'd just said good-bye to Charlotte—that I moved her immediately to the house of a cousin of Volk's not far from Novgorod. It was a small, out-of-the-way place. We were there for about a month, and I heard that it was Dmitri Andreievich who had arranged your and Anna's escape. I asked Volk to see if we could make some kind of contact with Dmitri. It was my madness to see if he could help Charlotte too. Anyway, it was in late May when Volk got word Dmitri wanted to meet me. We arranged for him to come to the house. He never showed up. The police came instead. I swear God was watching over us that day. It was lovely and warm and Dmitri was not to come until late afternoon, so I took my wife for a walk. One of her few pleasures was walking in the sunlight. We were just turning out of the forest when we saw coaches with the insignia of the Okhrana heading toward the house, and we hid in the woods all that night and the next day. We only came out when we heard Semyon calling us. They had beaten him for word of us, and he told them I'd gone to Novgorod on an emergency with my wife's health and didn't know the name of the doctor. They waited for us twenty-four hours. When Semyon was certain they were gone, he went to the root cellar where we'd hidden my money and jewels, packed it all with a few of my wife's treasures . . ." He pointed to the photographs, china and books. "And we never went back to that house. Semyon knew some peasants to the south who were true, and we walked all that day. How Semyon found the way, I'll never know. Anyway, the peasants were good to us. By then, my wife had fallen into her silence, you see. She never uttered a word after that. She never even looked at me. She just sat and stared at her hands."

"And Dmitri?" Misha asked, his heart racing.

"Well, I never heard from him again."

An almost uncontrollable rage was heating Misha's body. Unable to contain himself, he leapt to his feet. "I will kill Dmitri! As God is my witness, I will kill him one day!"

Ryabushinsky gazed at him quizzically, and then he said slowly, "Yes, I have often dreamed of doing the same myself. I never thought I was a vengeful man. It was only that I never knew hatred until the day I was betrayed. Not only me, Misha, but so many. My God . . ." His voice trembled. "I think of our beloved Alexei Yakovlevich and how he trusted Dmitri Andreievich. I think of the pain he would have suffered if he'd known the truth. Praise God, he was at least spared that."

"Tell me, have you told anyone of this?"

"Just Volk and Semyon. That's why I'm in hiding. If Dmitri is connected to the Okhrana, then absolute secrecy is the only way to survive. You see, I have but one goal left in my life—to keep arranging shipments of guns and ammunition for the revolution until my money runs out. That's why you are here. Volk tells me you're working with the Soviet."

"Yes. I'm helping to organize the *druzhinniki*. We're desperate for guns and ammunition. And I don't mean suitcases filled with Brownings, Alexander Ilyitch. We have to move beyond that if we're to survive. We have to build an arsenal."

"That's difficult. Not the buying of the guns. They can always be bought, but getting them into the country is another matter. Since Khrustalev's arrest, some of my best contacts at the borders have grown scared. As an example, we have a very large shipment of repeating rifles, Mausers, Brownings, and boxes of ammunition just sitting in a barn outside of Prague, but we haven't been able to move them across the border."

"How large?"

"Several carriages full. Enough to begin your arsenal."

"What would it take to get them here?"

"Either a very daring plan or some clear victories of the

revolution. As the Czar strikes back harder and harder, people grow afraid to take risks. There is little trust anymore.''

CHAPTER FIFTY-THREE

''In truth, Misha, I've yet to see you give serious thought to a strategy to find Dmitri, and now this insane plot about some arsenal in Prague.'' Marta frowned. ''There are many others expert at gun-running.''

''Not for a shipment like this,'' Schmidt interjected. ''Personally, I think we're about the only ones who can do it. Imagine, getting a haul like that to Petersburg . . .''

''*If.*'' Marta eyed Schmidt impatiently. ''That's a pretty big if.'' Her cheeks were reddening. ''Considering Misha won't even tell us whom he's working with other than this gun-runner Volk.''

''I explained, I can't. Anonymity is the only condition my contact laid down.''

''You're asking us to risk our lives on the basis of your estimation of a man who might very well be sending us into an ambush. Have you thought of that?''

''Quite honestly, the thought never crossed my mind. I trust this man absolutely.''

''Only a fool would trust anyone absolutely these days, Misha. You above all should know that. I shall talk to Trotsky about this.''

''I already have,'' Misha advised. ''We've his complete support. Of course, Marta, if you've no heart for the plan, you needn't come with us.''

''You'd like that, wouldn't you, Misha—to be in control all by yourself.''

''Funny, I thought he already was,'' Schmidt quipped.

Volk worked meticulously on the details of the plan with Misha. Volk's role was to have the shipment transported from Prague to as close to the border as possible, to provide an itinerary of the best route through Russia and to arrange partisan protection along the way. Misha, Schmidt, Marta, and

the others would cross the border in specially designed
coaches and wagons that Benya was arranging with Ryabushinsky's money. Schmidt argued that it would be safer and
more expedient to have the transports fitted out in Prague,
but Benya had precise ideas of how the work was to be done.
Patrols were becoming expert at sounding out false bottoms
and other means of hiding weapons.

Benya supervised the work personally in an abandoned
carriage house. The first transport was an elegant coach fitted with false walls and roof which, although hollow, would
be padded so as not to give the slightest echo of emptiness.
Schmidt and a man from Misha's *druzhina* named Vasia
would drive. Marta, dressed in aristocratic finery, would
ride inside, accompanied on the return trip by a young
woman and her four-year-old daughter. The woman, Marie
Balmesheva, was a Bolshevik and in charge of organizing
the movement of the guns from Prague to the border. Her
four-year-old daughter was her cover. Misha balked at the
idea. He didn't want the responsibility of a child, but com-
munications with Prague were difficult at best.

The second transport, a rougher, peasant wagon, would be
loaded with a coffin and a supply of turnips. The coffin would
in fact carry a dead body, and in false bottoms under the load
of turnips would be the rifles. Benya and Nadia, dressed as
peasants, were drivers of this wagon.

Misha and Nikita, dressed as priests, would ride in the
third carriage, also fitted with false sides and roof. Two men
from the *druzhinniki* were their drivers.

The date for the squad to leave Petersburg was set for December 2, but as November drew to a close, the tension of
completing their plans on such a tight schedule was exacer-
bated by the escalating moves of both the Czar and the Soviets. Nicholas was granting audiences to the most reactionary
representatives of the church, landowners, and merchants,
who demanded punishment not only for revolutionaries but
also for those liberals in "high places," such as Count Witte.
The Czar designated the delegation "true sons of Russia"
and promised a subsidy to a Black Hundred-based organization known as the Union of the Russian People. In retaliation,
the Petersburg Soviet issued a Financial Manifesto calling
upon workers to demand wages in gold and to withdraw their
savings from the bank. A run on the banks ensued, causing
some banks to lock their doors.

On the morning of December 2, the eight revolutionary
papers in Petersburg that printed the Soviet's Financial Manifesto were raided, their presses smashed. At the same time,

the Czar declared it illegal for railroad, postal and telegraph workers to strike, under threat of four years' imprisonment.

It was four-thirty on the afternoon of December 2, and Misha was getting ready to leave his flat for the rendezvous at the carriage house when there was a frantic banging on the door. "It's me, Benya! Open up!"

Benya was wild.

Nikita, behind him, was terrified.

"They've arrested all the Soviet!" Benya burst out. "Hundreds of troops swept down on the building where they were meeting. Two hundred and fifty people, all the leadership, the Presidium, the Executive Committee, they've all been arrested. The streets are swarming with troops. They're stopping everyone, smashing up workers' meeting places and any press they can find. Half the troops are stinking drunk."

"What happened to the Soviet? Wasn't there any resistance?"

"Resistance would have meant an all-out slaughter. The meeting hall was jam-packed, and mostly what people had with them were Brownings—no match against the rifles and cannon of the troops. Trotsky called for everyone to smash their guns, so at least the police couldn't get them. They had barely time for that. Come on, we'd better get out of here while we still have a chance."

As Misha put on his coat, he noticed Nikita standing almost frozen, his face white with fear. "Hey, hey, it's going to be okay," he whispered, wrapping an arm about him. "Just stay close, and whatever you do, don't allow anyone or anything to separate us. We're going to make it to the carriage house, you understand. Then we're going to make it to Prague."

Nikita nodded blankly.

"Concentrate on Prague and the guns, Nikita. New leadership will take the place of those they've arrested today, but without guns, the *druzhinniki* won't be able to regroup. Prague is our only answer, and you must believe we're going to succeed."

"I want to . . ." Nikita said fearfully.

"Listen, brother, we've been through worse than this in skirmishes. We'll be out of Petersburg by daybreak. I promise you."

The carriage house was on the outskirts of Petersburg, where the city begins to turn into country. The road was off the main thoroughfare and speckled with a few houses belonging to middle-class merchants, all of whom had fled Petersburg months before. Not only was the neighborhood presently uninhabited, but the carriage house itself was set back from the road, in woods behind the abandoned main house. There was no one to notice the work going on there over the past weeks, no one to wonder about horses being stabled. The carriage house was not only a perfect meeting place, but would be a safe hideaway should there be any trouble in getting away from the city.

Misha, Benya, and Nikita were the first to arrive. Vasia and Galin, from Misha's *druzhina*, were next, followed by Marta, Nadia, and then Afonka and Kolenka, Benya's men. By six-thirty, everyone but Schmidt had arrived. They waited. Minutes passed with agonizing slowness.

"I don't think we should stay here," Afonka suggested as he sat on the running board of the coach meant for Marta and Schmidt. He was holding his rifle firmly between his knees. It was dark in the cavernous carriage house except for a lantern placed on the floor. From the back stalls, a horse neighed and pawed the straw. "We're sitting ducks if someone's ratted on us."

"Schmidt, you mean," Marta suggested. "He's the only one not here."

Everyone looked at Misha, as if waiting for him to defend Schmidt.

Misha hesitated, then snapped the order: "Afonka, you and Galin take the first watch. Go down to the main house and watch from there. Benya, you and Nikita take the back door."

"I'll check the road," Marta said.

"Stay well out of sight," Misha cautioned.

Marta hesitated, then turned to Misha. "I hope you're right about Schmidt," she said.

"I'd bet my last kopeck on his loyalty."

"You would have bet that on Dmitri's at one time too."

To Misha's relief, Schmidt sauntered in just after ten that night. "Praise God, but it's good to see you." Misha embraced him.

"I was caught in a sweep, but there weren't enough police vans to cart us all off, so they held us in some basement. The guards were drinking like pigs in slop. Some bright fellow jimmied the lock and we jumped the guards. They hardly knew what hit them and we all got the hell out of there. But Vasilievsky Island is like a fortress. They've drawn up the bridges. Troops are patrolling on the ice now . . . Hell!" He grinned broadly. "I see everyone else made it."

"Hours ago," Marta said.

"And you waited for me. I'm touched."

Later, when Misha was standing guard with Schmidt, Schmidt said, "Listen, pal, I've some bad news for you. Word is the workers' hospital was seized and your grandmother and her staff arrested."

Misha nodded and didn't respond.

"You all right?" Schmidt asked after a while.

Staring into the starless night, Misha said angrily, "We're going to get the guns, and then were going to blast them all to hell."

Just before dawn, Misha called everyone into the carriage house to change into their disguises and hitch the horses. Marta wore the fine dress, coat, fur hat and muff befitting the daughter of a wealthy landlord. Schmidt and Afonka and the other two drivers changed into the suits of coachmen. Benya and Nadia wore rough peasant clothes; Misha dressed as a priest and Nikita as a novitiate.

"Schmidt, you go first," Misha said. "Benya and Nadia will follow a few minutes later."

"With our friend Igor," Schmidt said, referring to the nickname he'd given the corpse.

Nikita laughed stiffly. "Don't think he'll be much company, though."

"Nikita and I, and Galin and Kolenka will pull out last. And don't worry if other wagons get behind us. If we get separated, we'll all meet at the Horse and Rider Tavern outside of Lubosk. And remember, the signal for trouble is one shot if it's from Schmidt's carriage, two if it's from Benya's and Nadia's, and three if it's from ours. Everyone got that?"

Heads nodded.

"Well, that's it, then, comrades. May God be with us."

Kolenka and Galin crossed themselves.

Marta eyed Misha with a hint of softness and smiled. As she climbed into the coach, Nadia and Nikita opened the doors of the carriage house. A line of police were waiting outside with guns pointed.

"Don't even think of it," Marta commanded, pulling her pistol from her coat as she backed away from the coach, swinging in a circle in case anyone was near. Waving her gun, she walked toward the police and motioned them inside.

"That one and that one . . ." She pointed to Misha and Benya. "They've all the names of the partisans and meeting places in their heads. I don't give a damn about the others, but I want those two unharmed."

Schmidt's arm sliced the air and he shot, hitting Marta squarely in the forehead.

In the confusion, the others scrambled to the cover of carriages and the police fell back into the courtyard.

"Schmidt, Benya, come with me." Misha motioned toward the back entrance. As they opened the door, bullets rang out.

"Upstairs!" Benya pointed up at the hayloft.

"I'm coming with you!" Nikita cried, racing toward Misha, and as he did, a bullet hit him. His body arched, then crumpled, and he lay motionless.

"Oh, God!" Misha shrieked.

Schmidt held him back. "You'll be no good to him dead. Come on!"

A barrage of bullets allowed Misha no time to argue. Breathing so heavily he thought he would choke, he followed Schmidt and Benya up to the hayloft. Schmidt pulled him onto the thick layer of hay covering the floor. "Don't think about any of it, Misha!" Schmidt ordered, grabbing Misha's shoulders. "Don't think about Nikita. Concentrate on the bitch Marta. See her face in every one of those bastards you kill."

"They've got us surrounded—"

"Yes, but we've got the advantage, especially out front. There are few places for them to hide in that courtyard. You're the marksman, Misha. Go on, pick them off one by one. Don't let them get so much as an arm raised before you shoot. Kill them, Misha, do you understand? We have to kill them until they start to run."

Schmidt motioned Benya to the back window and then he hurried back downstairs. Bullets were ripping through the front window and Misha got on all fours, crawling past a huge pile of hay that filled a third of the loft, and smashed out what was left of the window with the butt of his gun. Pressing his back against the wall, he peered carefully outside. Police edged the courtyard, twenty or thirty of them. He saw a group setting up an automatic rifle just where the road curved from the main house. Schmidt was right. The cops were sitting ducks.

Misha picked his first target and shot. The victim fell. Almost immediately, a spray of bullets from the automatic showered the front of the carriage house. Misha fell back, and when he looked again, several policemen were racing toward the front doors, shooting as they went. He picked one to target and fired. The victim fell and the others darted out of his sight. The automatic rifle exploded again and there was a frenzied neighing of horses. Misha slapped back against the wall and then leaned forward to take aim. Like a machine, he kept shooting, stopping only to reload his gun; but the police kept coming. It didn't matter how many he felled, more kept coming. The second time he reloaded, he saw Benya sprawled on the floor at the other side of the loft, blood puddling about his head and shoulders.

Misha stared at Benya as if he were some bizarre oil painting, and he listened, trying to distinguish how many guns were still shooting from downstairs. It was impossible to tell, and he went back to his post against the window and took aim; almost every shot hit its target, and a rhythm began to build. Shoot, rest, look, take aim. Shoot, rest, look, take aim. His mind was empty except for this rhythm, and for counting his bullets so he knew when to reload. He was reloading when he heard the guns downstairs silenced and a single pair of boots bounding up the stairs.

"It's me, Schmidt," came a hoarse voice. "I'm almost out of ammo, and no one else is moving down there." He crawled over to Misha and leaned flush against the wall. "There's no way we're going to shoot our way out of here. They're swarming out of the woods behind."

"Then we'll die shooting," Misha said hurriedly, and not wanting to lose his rhythm, he leaned forward, only to see the police starting toward the front door. "Get back there!" He shoved Schmidt toward Benya's post and took aim out the window again, but his bullet ran wild. Schmidt was breaking his concentration. "Goddammit, Schmidt, take Benya's post!"

"I don't know about you, pal, but I'm not ready to die or spend the rest of my life in some filthy Czarist jail." He swerved around as if looking for something, and stopped as his eye caught sight of the huge hay pile. "There!" He pointed.

Footsteps pounded on the floor below.

Schmidt crawled for the hay and started digging himself in. "Don't be a fucking hero, Kalinin!" he warned before disappearing into the hay.

Misha heard a voice from below. "Ain't a one still breathing."

"Check upstairs, but go slowly!" snapped another.

Misha stood frozen as the boots pounding on the steps neared. He listened and the boots edged closer. The gunman was hesitant, most likely afraid. He was right to be afraid. Misha would shoot the first one who showed his head. Misha would die where he stood, as the others had died.

The boots drew nearer.

Misha pointed the gun, then at the last moment, without any forethought, dove under the hay pile after Schmidt. He shrank like a turtle into its shell, and the thudding of boots made the loft shake.

More and more boots followed; footsteps drew closer. "There's one up here. Dead. Nothing else."

Someone rushed up the stairs, pounding heavily. A voice, chilling Misha to his core, snarled, "That's not Kalinin! I want Kalinin! He's got to be here! Him and another. There were nine, and there are only seven bodies. Pyatnitsky, take your men and search every inch of this goddamned place. Chesnokov, you take the rest of the men and search the outside. And don't come back if you can't find them. They can't have gotten far."

"Yes, sir!"

"The rafters, the carriages, the water barrels, the roof, the goddamned hay pile, Pyatnitsky!" Dmitri ordered. "Find them!"

Dmitri's words cracked like gun shots against Misha's skull. Dmitri's men scurried about at his command. The reality of Ryabushinsky's story settled sickeningly about him. Dmitri was the police, the Okhrana, himself.

"That pile of hay," someone snapped. "If they're up here, it's the only damn place they could be."

Hands began pulling at the hay.

"Stab it with your bayonets," came the order.

Bayonets pounded and slashed. The hay shifted. Misha thought for sure it would simply collapse, split like the Red Sea, and expose them. He wanted to move, to dig down deeper, to curl into a small ball. He wanted to survive, to remain free. He had to be free to kill Dmitri. The bayonets stabbed again and again. A blade slashed the hay less than an inch from his eye. He winced as the bayonet stabbed about him. He ground his teeth to keep himself from making a sound. He listened for a groan from Schmidt. Nothing, only the huffing of the soldiers.

"Nothing here, sir," came a voice.

The men returned downstairs and slowly the pounding of the boots silenced and the loft was still except for the shivering inside Misha. He listened, unable to make out words or movements from downstairs. He listened for a long time, and slowly an awareness of total silence settled like a peaceful awakening about him. Dmitri was gone; the police were gone; they had been gone for a while, and he thought of Nikita lying downstairs. Perhaps he wasn't dead. If Misha went down now, he might save Nikita, but he couldn't move. *Hold on, little brother,* he silently pleaded. *Don't die, don't go away. Please, don't you go away too.*

"Misha, hey, Kalinin, are you alive in there?" Schmidt's voice knocked faintly at the edges of his consciousness.

He couldn't answer.

"Misha!" Schmidt's voice was growing frantic as he pulled at the hay. "Misha, my comrade!" he cried as he uncovered an arm. "Are you all right?" He pulled gently. "Dear God, let him be all right . . ."

The misery in Schmidt's voice made him raise his arm.

Schmidt began madly shoving the hay aside.

Misha pushed himself to his feet.

Schmidt embraced him, kissed him, and then, catching him in a bear hug, twirled him about until they both fell on the hay pile again. "Speak to me, Kalinin!"

Misha looked up, but no words came out of his mouth.

"They're gone! I swear! My God, I don't believe it, we're alive!" He pulled Misha to his feet. "We're alive! Come on, Misha, say something. Speak to me!"

Misha reached to pick up his gun, and walked over to where Benya had fallen. All that was left was Benya's hat lying in his blood. He walked downstairs. The bodies were gone; bullet holes and blood were everywhere. The two horses hitched to the first carriage were dead. The front doors of the carriage house were wide open. Outside was calm; the day was gray, threatening snow. Misha stood in the place where Nikita had fallen; then he walked back to the stalls. One of the horses there was dead; the other three stood quietly, as if the horror had never happened. A large bay nuzzled him as he passed.

Misha stared at Schmidt's coachman's uniform and then down at himself; he was still wearing his priest's robes. He absently rubbed the horse's forehead and said to Schmidt, "We can still get the guns. We can still rendezvous with Marie Balmesheva." Without waiting for a reply, he went to inspect the carriage in which he and Nikita were to have ridden. Crawling out from underneath it, he said, "As far as I can see, there are only two bullet holes, and they're both inconspicuous."

Schmidt nodded his understanding. He hitched up a team of horses while Misha stood guard. "All set." Schmidt yanked himself into the driver's seat.

"Take the back roads," Misha ordered, climbing up beside him.

They passed through deserted farmland covered under layers of snow. After several hours they had to cut into a main highway, crowded with people fleeing Petersburg. Misha went inside the coach. They had been traveling twenty minutes when Schmidt knocked twice on the roof, the signal for a roadblock, and Misha slipped his gun inside his robes. The roadblock created a huge traffic jam, and while people waited, they stood around exchanging information and stories. Misha stayed in the carriage and Schmidt talked to no one.

"Papers!" a harried guard barked, tearing open the door of the carriage. His expression softened when he saw Misha. "Sorry, Father. Didn't know it was a priest. Have to ask to see your papers anyway."

"Of course." Misha smiled beatifically and handed him newly forged papers identifying him as the priest, Father Filip, and marked with Akimov's chameleon. The guard snapped to attention and hurriedly motioned Schmidt to move on.

CHAPTER FIFTY-FOUR

Anna sat in the taxi going over every detail of the day. She and Victoria Ghent had been Christmas shopping, and had had the loveliest of times. Victoria had taken her to small, out-of-the-way shops with unique but inexpensive gifts. Anna bought a brightly colored jack-in-the-box for Irinushka, presents for Larisa Filipovna, Marc Antonovich and their six children, as well as a lace-edged handkerchief for Mrs. Ghent and some Italian glass earrings which she'd seen Victoria admiring. She felt quite clever purchasing the earrings without Victoria ever being the wiser, and then they stopped in a sweet shop for tea.

Suddenly Victoria grew inexplicably quiet and serious.

"What is it?" Anna questioned.

Victoria shook her head.

"The Baron," Anna guessed. She'd learned that when the shadow of sorrow passed over Victoria's eyes, she was thinking of her Baron. Anna pulled her chair closer and whispered, "Is he coming to Geneva? Did you tell him it was all right?"

Victoria fumbled for her handkerchief, and hiding her face in her hands, she wept, "I fear he's the only man I'll ever love."

Anna's motherly instincts came to the fore, and she thought to admonish Victoria to keep her virtue, but then she thought about Irina, who always had seemed to flourish in the expression of her passion. She recalled her own painfully thwarted months of hopelessly desiring Alexei, and of the delirious glory that followed. "Victoria," she began dryly, "how deep is your passion?"

Victoria took her hands from her tearstained face, and leaning close to Anna, whispered ardently, "Very, *very* deep."

"When is the Baron coming?"

"After Christmas and before New Year's Eve. He can only stay one day and night, but he says he can't greet the new year without seeing me. He's taken a suite at the Grand Hotel."

"Well." Anna sighed as if she'd come to a decision. "I had a friend once, a very dear, the dearest friend, who was also my cousin. I named Irinushka after her. Anyway, she lived for her passion."

"Oh . . ." Victoria clasped her hands tightly together. "And is she terribly happy?"

Anna hesitated and said softly, "She died in the revolution."

"Oh, Anna, you've lost so much—I feel so guilty sitting here talking about love with all the terrible things going on in Russia. You must worry about the lives of your loved ones and . . ."

Anna waved her hand to quiet Victoria. One of the reasons she enjoyed Victoria's company was that Victoria didn't have a thought about current events in her head. With Larisa Filipovna and Marc Antonovich the talk was only of the dying revolution and the brutality of the Czar's reprisals; even alone, Anna couldn't still her worries about Misha and Zhenya Kirilovna. She feared for her brother, Petya, too, and scoured the newspapers for word of people she knew in Russia.

"Irina was a great believer in passion, you see," Anna reiterated. She sat very straight and looked directly at Victoria. "So think, Victoria, just think if she *hadn't* followed her passion."

"Then you think I should meet with the Baron?"

"I can't tell you what to do."

"But you must, Anna. I've no one else to turn to. At least, if you can't tell me what I should do, tell me what you would do."

"I don't know, Victoria. I just don't know. But I suspect in your heart you know what's best for you."

Anna rolled down the window of the cab so she could hear the Christmas carols from street-corner musicians; the scene might easily have been from St. Petersburg and she might be hurrying home with an armload of Christmas gifts to share with Alexei. Her thoughts spun to last Christmas and the lovely porcelain piano and girl that Alexei had commissioned Fabergé to make for her. Anna wondered where the piano was now. Perhaps Helena had it, with the rest of Anna's most beloved possessions. Anna thought if she could get back anything, it would be the porcelain piano, and the ruby brooch Alexei had sent her when she was still at Smolny.

The memories choked like a fine gray dust, and she forced her thoughts to Irinushka, who must be starving. Anna was already forty-five minutes later than she'd planned. She had her fare carefully counted out when the cab pulled up in front of the house, and was no sooner in the front door than she heard Irinushka's hungry cries from behind Larisa Filipovna's door. Leaving her bundles with Larisa Filipovna, Anna hurried upstairs, and soon Irinushka was quietly feeding. Anna rocked slowly, floating with the peace and the touch of Irinushka against her skin. She smoothed her fingers on the downy black curls and bent her head to smell her daughter's sweet scent. How Alexei would have loved being a father, she mused wistfully. How he would have spoiled Irinushka! Anna would have had to be the authoritarian, of that she was certain, although she couldn't imagine Irinushka ever doing anything wrong. More, she couldn't imagine ever being lonely so long as she had Irinushka.

That's what Misha had said to her in his letter, and he was right. Anna reached for the book on the table by the rocker and slipped out Misha's letter, which, although written almost a month earlier, had reached Anna only the day before.

My dearest Anna,

Please forgive me for not writing sooner, but events are moving at such a rapid pace here, it is hard to find time to do anything for just sheer pleasure. Grandmother talks of you and Irinushka constantly and prays for the day when she will see you both.

How are Larisa Filipovna and all her brood? How are you? Did you ever put that ad in the newspaper to give lessons? I think it a fine idea and you a marvelous teacher. Also, music will generally make you feel better. I hope you

*are not too lonely, although I can't imagine you being lonely
with an angel like Irinushka.*

*I hold you in my heart, Anna, and pray that you will
remain my dearest friend. That is what is really the most
important, I think, that we should never stop being friends.*

God bless and keep you and Irinushka.

> *With fondest affections,*
> *Misha*

Friendship, yes, perhaps that's what she should have told
Victoria. If only she had a telephone she would call Victoria.
Keep the Baron your friend only, she would tell Victoria.
That way, when he leaves, as he inevitably will, the pain of
his going won't be nearly so bad as it will be if you're lovers.

"You in there—your papers!" The guard rapped smartly
on the carriage door. Misha and Schmidt were at a roadblock
just outside of Pskov, one of many they'd successfully passed
through since leaving Petersburg.

The guard pulled open the door.

Misha, his hand readied on the gun slipped inside the sleeve
of his cassock, handed him the papers.

"Would you please step out, Father."

"Of course." Cautiously Misha climbed from the carriage. A bitter late-afternoon wind was whipping across the
barren field bordering one side of the road; on the other side
the woods stood black and stark against the deep orange band
of the setting sun. A long line of travelers waited behind
Misha's and Schmidt's carriage. The roadblock and the city
of Pskov were before them.

Schmidt was still sitting in the driver's seat. Misha could
just make out his worried expression in the darkening afternoon shadows. Misha was worried too. The guard was taking
too long with his papers. The chameleon should have allowed
them to pass right through. "Is there a problem?"

"Please, Father . . . your driver." He motioned to Schmidt
to come down.

"Father is on a mission of mercy. Time is of the essence,"
Schmidt advised as he jumped from the driver's seat.

"This won't take long." The guard's eyes looked everywhere but at Misha and Schmidt. His lips were twitching
slightly. "Come with me." The words had the edge of an
order.

"I'm not sure I want to play this one out," Schmidt murmured, falling in step beside Misha.

Misha nodded his agreement as two guards who had been chatting beside a bonfire snapped to attention.

The travelers sensed an incident building too. An uneasy hush settled on the line.

Misha and Schmidt slowed their pace as two more guards came out of a hut. "The woods," Misha whispered.

"Now!" Schmidt tugged at his sleeve and the two of them bolted.

There were screams behind them and a loud voice commanded, "Shoot!"

Misha and Schmidt kept running. It seemed an eternity before the volley came. Schmidt jerked, almost tripped, and grabbed his arm.

"You all right?" Misha grabbed him, pulled him as they ran.

"Nothing. Just grazed me. Keep the hell going!"

More shots rang out, but this time they bounced off trees. The forest was deep and protecting. Any moment now, darkness would be complete.

Anna was sitting on the floor of Larisa Filipovna's parlor making Christmas decorations with the children and talking about ice slides. Irinushka lay on a blanket beside her, watching her fingers move, and Larisa Filipovna was in the kitchen baking bread. "What we need is some happy project to get everyone's mind off the terrible news from home," Anna said. They had just heard of the arrest of the Petersburg Soviet and the bitter reprisals that had followed. The Czar had retaken his capital with a vengeance. The revolution had been all but crushed in Petersburg.

"It's not *all* bad," Gerald insisted, bombarding his sister, Marinka, with a piece of popcorn. "They say the best revolutionaries have gone to Moscow. They say half of the garrison there supports the rebels. They say even if the Czar sends in the Semyonovsky Guards, the revolution will spread from Moscow like the charge to a stick of dynamite!"

"We're making Christmas decorations, Gerald," Anna scolded. "Do you think we can put off talk of dynamite and such for a little while at least?"

"I don't care about these stupid decorations!" Gerald flared. "People are dying at home and we're talking about decorations and ice slides! And . . . and it's easy for you to talk, Anna Petrovna! You've been there. You've been in the middle of everything. But me, I'll probably be stuck here in Geneva and never get to fight. Never!"

Anna was sobered by Gerald's outburst. He was usually

such an amenable boy. Before she could think of an appropriate response, there was a knocking at the door.

"Marinka, be a good girl and see who it is," Larisa Filipovna called from the kitchen. "I'm a fright."

Moments later Marinka returned. "It's for you, Anna Petrovna, some old lady, but she wouldn't tell me her name."

"For me?" Anna hurried to the front hall.

Zhenya Kirilovna was standing there, her babushka-covered head layered with snow. She seemed enormous in a black oversize coat. One small bag was by her feet.

"Mother!" Anna cried, running with open arms.

"Anna, Anna . . ." Zhenya hugged her fiercely and kissed her again and again. "Show me my granddaughter," she said assertively. "Show me my Irinushka. . . ."

Larisa Filipovna brought out her best china and sent Gerald to the bakery for sweet cakes. Zhenya Kirilovna, who refused to take off her coat or babushka, settled herself on an overstuffed chair with Irina. Tears kept watering her eyes as she stared down at the infant, cradling her. "I can't tell you how much she looks like Alexei when he was this age. Ah, how she takes me back. She's a beauty, she is. They used to mistake Alexei for a girl then, what with his black curls and big eyes. His eyes turned quickly dark, but I think she's got your blue ones, Anna. Is she a good baby?"

"The best, Mother." Anna leaned forward and took Zhenya Kirilovna's large hand in her own. She kissed the palm, wanting to ask about Misha. There were so many questions she wanted to ask, but all she said was, "Are you sure you won't take off your scarf and coat?"

"I'm fine, just fine," Zhenya insisted, even though little beads of sweat were forming about her face.

Before taking off her coat and babushka, Zhenya checked the lock on Anna's apartment door and explored each of the three tiny rooms twice, looking in closets and under the bed. She groaned and muttered as she knelt and bent under the weight of her bulky coat.

"What are you doing, Mother?" Anna asked, certain Zhenya had lost her mind.

"Can't be too careful, Anna, even here in Geneva. It's terrible what's happening, just terrible. Let's go into the bedroom. There's no window onto the street there." She led Anna into the bedroom and closed the door behind them. She took Irina, who had fallen asleep in Anna's arms, and laid her gently in the cradle. Only then did she begin to unknot her babushka. "Ah, that feels good," she sighed as the scarf came off. Her hair was braided unusually high on top of her head. "Haven't had that off for over a week."

"Why?" Anna blinked her eyes, wondering that Zhenya's hair had grown so full, as full as her body seemed to have grown wide.

"This either." Zhenya slipped off her coat and laid it carefully on the bed. "Watch this . . ." She eyed Anna expectantly and grinned mischievously as she slowly began pulling out the hairpins. Her braids fell heavily across her shoulders.

Anna peered, thinking she saw sparkling colors woven in the braids.

Zhenya plowed her fingers through her braids and shook her head. A diamond necklace fell out of one braid, an emerald necklace out of the other.

Anna gaped.

"Scissors?" Zhenya asked.

"Yes." Anna pulled out her sewing box from under the bed.

Zhenya began cutting stitches from the hem of her dress. Inside were more jewels, which she dumped on the bed. "Some of these are yours, my love, and some mine." Zhenya began looking through the glittering pile on the bed. "Ah, here it is! Almost thought I'd forgotten it." She handed Anna the ruby brooch from Alexei. "That's one piece we won't sell, unless we're desperate. But I don't think that will be."

Zhenya spread open her coat and began cutting the seam. The inside was padded with rubles. "I've got the name of a man here in Geneva who'll help us get the best rate of exchange on the rubles and the jewels. There are thousands and thousands here, Anna. What I hid over the years. Never did trust banks, you know, and it's a lucky thing. No one's been able to get any money from the banks for weeks."

Finally she unpacked her bag. Inside were a few clothes, but most of what she carried were photographs, pictures of the family, many of which Anna had never seen. There were several recent ones of Alexei, including Anna's and Alexei's wedding pictures, along with photographs of the Kalinin family over the years, even one from when Yakov was alive. "That was Alexei's eleventh name day," Zhenya explained, "just before he and Yakov were to leave on their trip to Petersburg. It was a fine trip, first-class all the way. I didn't go. Our Mousia, as you can see, was sickly."

Anna stared intently at the photograph. She had never seen the unmentionable Yakov before, but from the few comments she'd heard, she'd imagined him a big, rough man like Tolya. To her surprise, he was a rather short, sad, even gentle-looking man. Zhenya and Alexei dominated the family photograph. Zhenya stood in between a rigid Yakov and a churlish Tolya, but she stood alone, her thick braids wound loosely about her head, which was thrown slightly back; she appeared carefree; her buxom figure in its peasant blouse and wide skirt was inviting. Yakov was somber; he stood very straight. In one hand he held his hat. His other hand grasped Alexei's shoulder. Alexei was grinning happily, almost laughing as he hugged a small, sickly little girl standing in front of him. Even at eleven Alexei flaunted a dark romanticism. Despite his new suit and starched collar, he seemed a Gypsy, ready to bound from the photograph, grab Anna in his arms, and twirl her in a wild dance.

"Mother," Anna asked, pressing the pictures to her, "how's Misha? Have you seen him?"

Zhenya Kirilovna hesitated. "To tell you the truth, I don't know. The last I saw him was the morning of the day the Czar's troops arrested the Soviet. When the hospital was invaded, I was certain I was to be killed. Such shooting and bloodshed. Ach . . ." She crossed herself. "It is a miracle any of us are alive. Then this policeman took me aside and said he was sent to see I got out of Petersburg. I was certain it was some kind of ploy, but he told me if I gave him the least bit of trouble, I would never see you or my granddaughter again. I had no choice but to go with him. He took me to our palace in Petersburg and said we wouldn't be leaving until dark and I should pack what I needed. Then he took me to the Finnish border, where I was met by partisans who took me to Berlin, and the train brought me here."

"Dmitri Andreievich—was it he who helped you escape?"

"I don't know," she said gravely. "What have you heard from him? "

"Nothing other than my allowance, which arrives by messenger every month. Perhaps we can ask the messenger if he has word of Misha."

"No! You must not ask Dmitri's messenger anything of Misha. And if we hear from Misha, you must mention it to no one."

"But why?"

Zhenya was quiet, as if collecting her thoughts. "I must tell you, Anna. Our Misha is on a very dangerous mission. It would be best if you knew no more."

Anna nodded and stared down at the photographs spread across the bed. Her eyes settled on a picture of Alexei and herself on their wedding day. He was gazing at her with such love. His eyes, it seemed, might turn any moment and see her now. Pressing the photo to her, she asked in a small, hesitant voice, "Mother, tell me truthfully—do you think Alexei is really dead?"

"How do you mean?" Zhenya Kirilovna asked cautiously.

"I sometimes think . . . well . . ." She looked at Zhenya then with desperation. "There are so many truths and untruths. Could they have lied to us? Could they have just told us that Alexei was killed? They lie about so much."

"Oh, my sweet child." Zhenya reached for Anna's hand. "Alexei's gone. I buried my son. He's gone."

Anna nodded and her lips quivered. "It's what I thought, of course," she said stoically. "But without proof, there was always that glimmer of hope." She slipped her hand free of Zhenya's and stared at the photograph once more. "May I keep this one, Mother?"

"Of course, my love. They're for you, all for you and Irinushka."

The bullet which had barely grazed Schmidt's upper arm had lodged in the padding of his heavy coachman's coat. Schmidt insisted he wanted to keep it there as a memento. They were in a barn where they'd taken secret refuge; Schmidt had stolen some eggs from a hen and they'd eaten them raw.

"All we need is a little vodka and this place would be real homey." Schmidt smiled as he settled into the warm comfort of some hay. His expression grew serious. "What the hell happened back there?"

Misha breathed deeply, knowing he should have told Schmidt about Dmitri earlier. He hadn't been able to. Even now he wasn't certain Schmidt was going to believe him. "It must have been my papers," he began, relating all the details about Akimov and the mark of the chameleon. Then he told him about Dmitri, about Trotsky's suspicions, about Ryabushinsky's narrow escape, and about the voice in the carriage house.

Schmidt sat dumbfounded.

"You don't believe me."

"It's just hard to take in. Dmitri Andreievich a traitor. Can you be so certain it was his voice—after all we'd been through?"

"I'd know Dmitri's voice anywhere. Look, Schmidt, I've made a decision, and I don't expect you to agree with it, but since we can't get the guns anymore, I'm going back to Petersburg. Dmitri's there. I know he is. I've got to find him."

CHAPTER FIFTY-FIVE

Victoria threw her arms about Anna. "Oh, my friend, I've missed you so. I thought I should never see you again, that you wanted nothing more to do with me."

"Whatever for? I told you my mother-in-law had unexpectedly arrived."

"But three weeks, Anna. I feared you despised me because of the Baron." Victoria's cheeks turned rosy and she bit her lower lip apprehensively.

Anna bent close. "Then you went to him?"

"Oh, yes!" Excitement edged Victoria's uneasiness. In a hoarse whisper she added, "We are more united than ever—"

The intimacy of the moment was broken off by Mrs. Ghent hobbling into the front hall. Her face was seething with stern reprimand.

Victoria stiffened proudly and assumed a stance of exaggerated confidence.

"Well, Anna Petrovna, are you here to give my granddaughter a lesson?" Mrs. Ghent angrily questioned.

"Of course Anna's here to give me a lesson, Grandmother. But first we need some time alone. It's been so long. Come, Anna." She ushered a confused Anna into the parlor and not only closed but also locked the doors. "Prying old biddy," Victoria mumbled as she sat next to Anna on the couch.

"What is going on, Victoria?"

"Well." Victoria's face filled with determination. "Freddy is buying a house for me here in Geneva. I've invited my grandmother to come, but she refuses. Freddy's getting married in the spring, you see."

Anna looked for some sign of emotion in Victoria but there was only cold resolve.

"Do you think I'm despicable too?" Victoria demanded.

"Oh, no, no!" Anna took Victoria's hands warmly. "Not if you're happy. Not if it's what you want."

"Oh, it is, Anna!" Victoria's face softened. Her lips trembled. "I love Freddy so desperately. It matters little that I

599

shall never have his name so long as I have his love. I feel I am the luckiest woman in the world!''

"Then I couldn't be happier for you, truly.'' Anna smiled, feeling genuinely happy for Victoria.

"And you will come to our first party? Freddy says the house will be all ready by the end of the month and he wants to have a housewarming. He knows so many people in Geneva, all the finest people, and he says they will never scorn our love. Will you come too, Anna? I'm so desperate for you to meet Freddy. I've told him all about your talent. He's eager to hear you play.''

"Why, yes,'' Anna said without hesitation. "I should love to come to your party. And if you like, I'll play for your guests.''

"Oh, Anna, would you really?'' Victoria gasped. "Oh, Anna, I think I shall die with excitement! Oh, Anna!'' She grabbed Anna's hand and pressed it to her heart. "Feel it pound. I think I shall burst!''

Misha and Schmidt looked little better than peddlers themselves in their shaggy beards and nondescript clothes. They were nursing beers in a workingmen's tavern on Sadovaya Street when a man Schmidt recognized walked in. "Praise God, that's Reitzel,'' Schmidt whispered as the man settled at the bar. "We were in the same prison camp in Siberia. He's a Bolshevik. If anyone's true, he is. Wait here.'' Schmidt downed his beer and went to the bar for a refill.

Reitzel recognized him and with a quick movement of his eyes cautioned against making contact. Schmidt took his beer back to the table, and after a while Reitzel sauntered out. In a few minutes Schmidt followed. When it was clear no one noticed either man's leaving, Misha put on his hat, pulling the flaps down over his ears, and left too.

He stood in the dark, bitterly cold street outside the tavern, trying to decide which way to go, and a noise, like the banging of cans, caught his attention. He turned to the left.

"In here,'' Schmidt's voice whispered as he neared an alley.

"We're safe,'' Misha assured. "Let's go back to the hut where we can talk.''

They went back to the storage hut behind Tailors' Row where they'd taken residency, sleeping under fabric to keep warm.

Schmidt lit a lantern as they settled on bolts for chairs. Misha took out a flask and passed it around. "What brought

you two back to Petersburg?" Reitzel asked. "You must know
your lives aren't worth a kopeck if you're found."

"We've a story to tell you, Reitzel. One you will find hard
to believe." Schmidt nodded to Misha to begin.

Anna smiled at herself in the mirror, the formal smile of
greeting. She rearranged the diamond necklace and tucked a
wisp of hair in place under the diamond-spray hairpin. Then
she stepped back to make one last check, and nodded approvingly. She smoothed her hands along the full crimson
velvet of the skirt, and looked down at her breasts swelling
from the low neckline. It seemed so long since she'd dressed
for a formal affair; she felt naked. Still, she was confident
about her gown; she and Victoria had been to all the finest
shops in Geneva. Larisa Filipovna had carefully designed the
gown after the one Anna and Victoria had liked best.

A knock on the door startled her.

"It's me," Zhenya Kirilovna called.

"Come in, Mother." Anna turned to the door.

Zhenya Kirilovna gasped. "Oh, how magnificent! You shall
be the shining star of the evening. Anna, I have only the best
feelings about this evening. I think it's grand you want to step
out into society again. And you must always remember that
you're Alexei Yakovlevich's wife. It is a name to be proud of.
But also . . ." Zhenya's face twisted as if she were scolding
herself. "Also remember that Alexei is gone, my dear. Have a
good time. There's nothing wrong with that. Larisa Filipovna
tells me the fete is the talk of the society pages. You've even
been mentioned—Anna Marks, the young Swiss pianist, they
call you. Are you nervous?" Zhenya wrung her hands.

"Not about the concert. But I am terrified to meet people
again. Every time I think of it, my stomach flutters horribly.
What if it's not the right thing to do, Mother? You know, I
never did have much experience in society, and—"

The ringing of the doorbell cut her short. "There's Larisa
Filipovna and her family." Zhenya kissed her quickly. "Now,
no more nonsense about whether you should go. You are going. I'll answer the door. You wait until I knock. Then make
your entrance. Oh, Anna, Anna—Alexei would be so proud.
I can just see you dancing in his arms. Ach, what a mad
dream life is! One must not struggle too hard to make sense
of it, my dear." Zhenya gazed as if enraptured, then hurried
to answer the door.

"Look, I'm not saying you're a liar, Kalinin. But a man
would be a fool to condemn Dmitri Andreievich on the

strength of a rumor spawned in Petersburg these days. Perhaps if Trotsky could vouch for you, but God knows when he'll see the outside of a prison cell again.''

"We're not asking you to believe us, Reitzel. All we need is for you to get the word out that Misha wants to meet with Dmitri.''

"If he has turned, he's not going to want to talk with you, or if he does, it will be to kill you.''

"That's a chance I'm willing to take.''

Reitzel was quiet, as if considering. Finally he said, "I've heard Mayakovsky is recruiting for the Brigade again. Some say Gapon's been targeted.''

"Why would the Brigade target Gapon?'' Misha questioned in disbelief.

"It seems the priest has become something of a liability. He's everyone's pawn since he returned. The police, the revolution. No one trusts him.''

"Akimov,'' Misha exclaimed. His face hardened. "I'll stake my life it's Akimov who wants Gapon dead and the Brigade who'll do the dirty work. It's just like the Yermolov assassination. Akimov and Dmitri are like a hand in a glove.''

"If you repeat that, you're going to get a reputation as a lunatic,'' Reitzel warned. "But look, I'll see what I can do, for old times' sake.'' He nodded toward Schmidt. "Where can I say you can be reached?''

"Behind the Haymarket. We'll be there at three o'clock every day.''

"Give it a couple of days, a week at the most. If nothing comes up by the end of the week, you know the contact fell through.''

Although Anna had never asked Victoria her lover's age, she'd always expected the Baron to be an older man, but Freddy was only twenty-five, tall and handsomely aristocratic, very Prussian with fine cheekbones, white-blond hair and sky-blue eyes. He had a contagious smile, was quick to put everyone immediately at ease, and he clearly adored Victoria. Despite his impending marriage, or perhaps because of it, he managed to spend almost all of February in Geneva and Anna became a frequent guest. Freddy's friend Willy Bekendorf, heir to the Bekendorf publishing fortune, was also there whenever Anna came.

Anna liked Willy. He was dark, not so good-looking as Freddy, but he had an interesting face. His nose was jagged and his eyes brooding and deeply set. On the surface, he was far more serious than Freddy, but he could always make Anna laugh. Like Freddy, Willy was a devotee of music, and an afternoon or evening when the four of them were together never passed without Anna playing. She wouldn't see Willy alone, however, and refused to allow him to take her home or pick her up; she refused to attend parties and dinners with him. In fact, except for Victoria's and Freddy's fetes, Anna turned down all the many invitations she was receiving.

"Geneva society has fallen for you, Anna, and you turn your back on it," Victoria scolded. "Just as you turn your back on Willy Bekendorf. He's quite mad for you. Why won't you give him any encouragement?"

"Because it would be wrong. I like Willy, I do. I enjoy his company, but my feelings don't go beyond that, Victoria. And as for society, it's truly painful for me. It reminds me of all I've lost."

"I haven't told a soul your true identity, not even Freddy, although he shall be very cross with me if he discovers the truth." Victoria pouted and shook her head.

"Really, let's talk of something else. This is becoming dreadfully boring. And as for Willy, if you think I'm misleading him, then perhaps I should stop seeing him altogether."

"But, Anna, you can't. We have such fun together."

"Anyway, I've been spending too much time away from Irinushka lately, and from my mother-in-law. I really think I shouldn't come to tea so often. We'll have our lessons, of course. And you and I can have our chats. But as for the men, well, I'm afraid I shan't be able to participate anymore."

Two days later, Anna was home alone with Irinushka. Zhenya Kirilovna was off to one of her political meetings, to which she went several times a week. Anna was cooking when the doorbell rang. Thinking it was Zhenya Kirilovna forgetting her key, as she often did, Anna opened the door without hesitation. To her horror, Willy Bekendorf was standing there with several dozen roses.

"For you, madame!" He smiled happily and bowed, handing her the roses.

"Willy! What are you doing here?" she cried, not knowing whether to tear off her apron or cover her face. She was in her oldest dress and had barely combed her hair that day.

"May I come in?"

Anna paled. No one, not even Victoria, had ever seen where she lived. "How did you find me?" she asked.

"I followed you. In fact, I've followed you several times,

to make sure you got home all right. You really ought to put those in water, you know.'' His eyes were fixed on Anna.

''This is all very embarrassing—''

''Don't be silly. I know who you really are—Anna Petrovna Kalinina.'' Willy was giddy as if he were unveiling a surprise.

''Victoria told you!''

''No, she never mentioned it, but it seems everyone in your neighborhood knows you. You're some kind of heroine, I'm told.''

''You must never talk about that to anyone, Willy—promise me.''

''Why not? It's terribly romantic. The daughter of a Russian count marries one of the richest, most mysterious men in Russia, becomes a terrorist, kills the head of the secret police, and escapes amid bullets flying. One would never think all that to look at you, Anna.''

''It's not me. None of that was me!'' she flared, her temper catching her up as it hadn't since her first months in Geneva. ''Now I want you to leave—and take your flowers!'' She pressed them back in his arms.

As she did, Willy embraced her. ''God, Anna, you're ravishing. You're the most ravishing woman I've ever known.''

''Leave me alone, Willy!'' She tore from him as Irinushka's cries erupted from the other room. ''I expect you to be gone when I come out!'' she ordered as she hurried into the bedroom.

Willy was sitting on the couch smoking a cigarette when Anna returned carrying Irinushka. The roses were in a vase in the middle of the table. He put down his cigarette and walked toward Anna. He smiled at Irinushka. ''She's beautiful, Anna, absolutely beautiful.''

Irinushka smiled back.

''Why aren't you gone?'' Anna held the baby protectively.

''Please, just a few moments. I . . . I was horribly out of place before. I'm sorry. I just have such feelings for you.'' He pressed his hand to his forehead as if trying to collect his thoughts. ''It's maddening. I think of you day and night . . .''

''Willy, you're making this—''

''You're right, you're right. That's not what I came here to say to you. And I only came because Victoria said you wouldn't be seeing me again.''

''Willy, you must go. I have to feed the baby.''

Willy shoved his hands into his pockets. For a moment he seemed at a loss for words. ''Well, you see,'' he began, ''what I've come to tell you is that I've spoken to some friends of my father about you. They run the Chamber Music Society here in Geneva. They promised that if you're half as spectacular as I told them you are, they would set up a recital for you.''

Anna opened her mouth to respond.

''No, please, don't say anything yet. Just think about it. You're such a brilliant pianist, Anna. You deserve to be heard and applauded. Don't confuse your anger at me with what might be a beginning of a whole new life. I can help you, Anna. My family has connections in the art world throughout Europe. I want to help you, Anna, I so desperately do. And I promise, I shall never so much as try to hold your hand if you don't want me to.''

Misha and Schmidt watched the Haymarket Square from the second story of the bazaar every day, but no one suspicious showed up. On the fifth day, they were walking up Nevsky Prospect at dusk when Misha noticed a fancy black coach following them.

''We should split up,'' he suggested. ''You take Sadovaya. I'll stay on Nevsky. Then you cut back through the alley.''

''Right.'' Schmidt crossed the wide boulevard and turned at the next corner.

The coach followed Misha. He kept walking.

''You there!'' the coachman called as Misha passed a fashionable teahouse.

Misha looked up.

The coach slowed to a stop. The carriage door swung open. ''Greetings, Misha.'' Dmitri held out his hand.

Misha spun around. A very tall, brutish man reminding Misha of Kolesnikov was standing behind him. Schmidt was just coming out of the alley.

Dmitri saw him too. ''Tell your comrade to leave us alone, or I'll tell Naglovsky here to arrest him, and you too. It would be quite messy and it's totally avoidable.''

''I'm all right!'' Misha shouted to Schmidt. ''Really. Go on, get out of here.''

Schmidt hesitated.

''Show him you still have your gun, Misha.''

''Here, in the middle of Nevsky Prospect?''

''Yes, wave it quickly and then get inside. But remember, Naglovsky will be behind you, and if you try to shoot me, he'll shoot you first.''

Naglovsky reached out and grabbed Misha's gun as soon as he stepped inside the carriage. The movement was swift, leaving Misha no time to think before Naglovsky shoved him into the seat opposite Dmitri and pulled shut the door. The carriage took off at a fast clip.

It was luxurious inside; Misha had forgotten how clean and lush luxury could be. Dmitri, looking thinner and his face more lined, was wearing a black fur-collared greatcoat; a sable blanket lay across his lap. "I got your message, Misha." His voice was bland, his face devoid of any expression which might give away his thoughts.

Misha felt his mouth twitch. His hatred of the man was almost unbearable; it pulsated through his veins and muscles and strained against his head and skin like too much air inside a balloon.

Dmitri seemed not to notice. He was relaxed. He smiled and said, "But before you tell me what's on your mind, let me ask you a question. How did you and Schmidt escape the carriage-house fiasco?"

"We were in the hay pile."

"You must have had a good chuckle on us."

"Humor was the last thing on my mind."

"I'm terribly sorry about Nikita. I didn't mean there to be such bloodshed. I had to stop you from bringing in those guns, of course. Which we eventually did. Your mistake was in forging the chameleon on your documents. So few young men travel under Akimov's personal protection, you see. And, on the outside chance you continued to use the chameleon, I had every checkpoint guard in Russia on the lookout. In the end, though, it was all so much wasted energy. Even had you managed to get in the guns, the revolution would have been defeated."

"*Nothing* was wasted. The revolution will rise again."

"Youth is so filled with ideals and fight. Look at you, look how you've toughened up, broadened out. War does that to a man. With a shower and a shave, I'd say you'd look more like Alexei than ever. You know, your grandmother is safe. I saw to that. She's in Geneva with Anna and the baby."

"Is that supposed to fill me with some overwhelming feeling of gratitude?"

"I don't want to kill you. I won't, unless you force me to."

"Is that why you had Marta set us up?"

Dmitri seemed to be considering his reply. "You see," he began, "when I first invited you back to Petersburg from Geneva, I thought I could use you. But . . ." He shrugged. "I underestimated your abilities and your determination, Misha. You've became a rather unpleasant needle in my side. I want you to stop being that. I must insist that you stop being that. It's the only way I can allow you to live."

"Why are you so philanthropic about my life? Is it just because of Uncle Alexei?"

"Yes, precisely, but even that has its limits."

Misha snorted. "You hardly seem like the kind of man who holds his allegiances sacred."

"It was different between Alexei Yakovlevich and me. And I want you to know, he knew nothing of my other life."

"That thought never crossed my mind."

Dmitri opened his mouth to speak, then hesitated and took a deep breath. There was a hint of sadness about his eyes. His shoulders rounded and, for a moment, he might have been the old Dmitri.

Misha looked away quickly, biting his lip as if to cut out unwanted memories. Dmitri was the enemy. He had always been the enemy. Misha would kill him. He needed to leave it at that. He needed to keep the old Dmitri dead and buried, but he couldn't. The man across from him, the traitor and the enemy, had also been a teacher; he had changed the course of Misha's life and helped shape Misha into the man he was. He had also destroyed almost everyone Misha loved.

"How, Dmitri?" Misha found himself asking, his voice husky in confusion. "How could you have done this to us? How can you live with yourself, knowing that your cohort Akimov killed the finest man that any of us will ever know? Yes, you see, I know Akimov killed Uncle Alexei, so don't try denying it. Tell me how you can work with a man who killed a friend so true? Ah, but I forget!" Misha laughed bitterly. "Such morality is like water off a duck's back to you. Otherwise, how could you have set us up? Even Anna." Misha wanted to sound angry, but the mention of Anna pained him, and the question came out mournfully. "Did you bring her into our plan only to destroy her life too?"

Dmitri glared at Misha. "Listen to me." His voice was hard. "I owe you no explanation. Perhaps when you have lived as long as I have lived, and known what I have known, perhaps then I would talk to you."

"You're wrong. You do owe me an explanation." Misha's hands gripped and ungripped the edges of the carriage seat.

"I have none for you."

"And Uncle Alexei—would you have one for him? Will you explain to him as you plead with God to let you into heaven—will you explain to Uncle Alexei how you lived out your life befriending his murderer?" Misha was shouting.

Naglovsky made a threatening motion, and Dmitri held

him at bay. Sadness again clouded his eyes, and when he spoke, his voice quivered with unexpected emotion. "Hell itself will never absolve me of my hideous connection to Alexei Yakovlevich's death. He was an honorable man. He deserved better than me."

The admission of guilt maddened Misha and he lunged as he screamed, "Bastard!" His movement was so quick and unexpected, he managed to wring his fingers about Dmitri's neck before Naglovsky's fist pounded the small of Misha's back, causing him to recoil.

Throwing Misha back against the seat, Naglovsky slammed his massive fists into Misha's face, chest, and shoulders with such force, it seemed to Misha that his bones were shattering. He was helpless to defend himself against the powerful blows.

"Let him go," Dmitri finally rasped.

Naglovsky fell back and Dmitri stood, bent over Misha, and yanked him to a sitting position. The movement sent an excruciating pain throughout Misha's body. Blood seeped from above his eyes, blurring his vision.

"Listen to me, Misha." Dmitri held on to Misha's lapels. His voice was coarse and menacing. "You have no idea the power I wield. I am invulnerable to a worm such as you. You'll never touch me, never see me again unless I want to see *you*. And if you keep up your ranting that I'm a double agent, you'll soon be seen as far more the madman than the revolutionary hero." He knocked three times on the roof and sat down, gingerly fingering his throat where Misha's fingers had clamped down.

The carriage turned a corner and came slowly to a stop.

"Naglovsky, deposit our friend here, will you?" Dmitri said, pulling the sable rug about him.

Naglovsky opened the carriage door, grabbed Misha, and hurled him out. He landed facedown in the snow, groaning at the impact. He tried to turn as the carriage pulled away, but the smallest movement caused too much pain. He wanted to call something to Dmitri, a threat, a curse, but the cold snow felt sweetly numbing against his throbbing face, and he closed his eyes, feeling himself sink into blackness.

CHAPTER FIFTY-SIX

ANNA MARKS PERFORMS WITH THE STUTTGART CHAMBER MUSIC SOCIETY

April 1, 1907. Anna Marks, the young Swiss pianist who captured the hearts of music critics and audiences alike in Geneva, Zurich, and Bern last season, enthralled an audience of almost one hundred in Stuttgart tonight. Miss Marks, who was a pupil of the Russian master Rimsky-Korsakov, performed an exacting program combining Bach and Mozart with the works of some of today's most avant-garde composers. Her patron, Wilhelm Bekendorf III, son of publishing magnate Wilhelm Bekendorf II, says Miss Marks will be performing in Heidelberg and Frankfurt and will arrive in Berlin for a series of concerts presented by the Berlin Chamber Music Society in June.

Misha's eyes fixed on the photograph of Anna. She looked older than he remembered, and he quickly computed the time since he'd last seen her, October 1905, a year and a half before. He ran his finger across her face. It was Anna and not Anna. She appeared statically beautiful; the picture captured none of her life.

"What's the matter?" Schmidt asked from across the table of the dreary room they shared in a Berlin rooming house.

Misha handed him the paper. "The picture of the pianist Anna Marks." He pointed. "That's my uncle's wife, Anna Petrovna."

Schmidt whistled. "She's a looker."

Misha stood and glanced over Schmidt's shoulder at the paper. "She's really doing well for herself. I'm glad."

"She's the one you first escaped with. How come you never talk to me about her?"

"What's to talk about? Look, I'm going out. I've some things to do before work. By the way, I'm working a double

shift, so I won't be back till morning. That gives you and
Genevieve the place the whole night. Have fun.''

"And you.''

"Sure.'' Misha grimaced. "I love standing in front of fiery
pits pouring molten iron all night.''

"I think you do.''

Misha looked at Schmidt as if he were insane, and left,
stopping at the bathroom down the hall before heading out.
He stared at his reflection in the small square mirror and
rubbed his hand across his mouth; the hardened blisters on
his palm snagged on his lips. Three days' growth shadowed
his chin and cheeks. He needed a bath. He pressed the broad
bump on the bridge of his nose, which had never healed right
after Naglovsky broke it along with two ribs.

Misha might have frozen to death if Schmidt hadn't found
him in that alleyway, had his chest wrapped tightly, and
whisked him out of Russia while he was still too weak to
argue. Or perhaps he didn't care to argue. Dmitri was the
undisputed victor. Dmitri was alive while Irina, Uncle Alexei,
Nikita and countless others were dead. Dmitri was untouchable, while the revolution was ground into the dirt under the
heels of the Czar. How could it have ended like this? How
could so many have fought and died so heroically for nothing? How could Dmitri Andreievich be working with Arkady
Akimov? In the face of such colossal enigmas, how could
anything matter anymore?

Life was meaningless, absurd. That was the constant argument Misha had with Schmidt. The meaning of life. Poor,
deluded Schmidt still believed in the revolution. He believed
the bloodied remnants would rise again. That's why he'd
brought Misha to Berlin, where the survivors had run one
step ahead of the soldiers' bullets. There was work to be done
in Berlin, organizing.

While Misha drudged twelve, fourteen, and sometimes
eighteen numbing hours a day at an iron-works plant on the
outskirts of Berlin, Schmidt waited tables in a restaurant near
the university. He argued politics and wrote for a revolutionary newspaper that no one read. Lately Schmidt talked of
going to Paris, where socialists were gathering. Revolutionaries of the world unite in cafés and talk of yesterday's brave
deeds and tomorrow's bold dreams.

Misha despised Schmidt's friends. Sometimes he thought
he despised Schmidt for the naive stupidity of his belief in
the revolution resurrected. He thought if Schmidt didn't leave
soon, he would. Either he'd die of exhaustion at the factory
one day, or just take off, hop a train and begin walking to

anyplace. He had more money than he needed. It had been his plan to send most of it to Anna and his grandmother. But what need did they have for his miserable savings when Anna's patron was Wilhelm Bekendorf III?

"Why don't we go to Paris like we've been talking about?" Schmidt suggested as he eyed Misha over morning tea.

"Well, to tell you the truth, I've been thinking, Paris isn't really where I want to be. But you go if you want."

Schmidt took his time buttering his roll. "It's that woman, isn't it, that pianist, your uncle's wife."

"It has nothing to do with Anna."

"You haven't been the same since you read that article about her. I swear it's like you're pining away for her, lying on your cot staring up at the damned ceiling. And now her concerts. She'll be here in a few weeks, won't she?"

"My mood has nothing to do with Anna. Why should it?"

"That's what I'm asking."

"We escaped together, that's all. She was my uncle's wife, but I hardly knew her. I assure you, she can be in Berlin and it won't matter in the least to me."

Schmidt chuckled. "Jesus, you're a miserable liar. What do you think—I don't know you after all the time we've been together?"

"Don't kid yourself. No one knows me." He dumped two lumps of sugar in his tea.

"I know what makes you tick a whole lot better than you do. I think you feel so damn guilty about surviving—"

"Don't push me—"

"Look at you—glaring at me like I'm your enemy. That's what you need, isn't it? An enemy. I'm your enemy. The guy who still believes in the revolution—"

"The revolution's over, Schmidt, or haven't you noticed? We lost. L-o-s-t. Lost. Why the hell are you and your comrades sweating over words that nobody cares about anymore?"

"Someone like you doesn't just turn off caring."

"I told you, Schmidt, stop trying to get inside me!"

Schmidt laughed bitterly. "I guess maybe I was wrong about your friend Anna. You don't need a woman. You need another war to fight. It'd be much better than breaking your back shoveling iron. And since you can't touch Dmitri, why don't you open today's newspaper—you'll find a place where they'll give you a gun. And maybe this time you'll even manage to get yourself killed!"

Misha lunged for Schmidt and they rolled about the floor, knocking over the table and chairs, hitting each other until they were exhausted, each sitting in a corner of the room gasping for breath.

"Get out of my life, Schmidt. Take the afternoon train to Paris. Just get out of my life!"

"Fine. Okay. I'm on my way, pal!" He jumped to his feet and stormed about the room, stuffing his few belongings into his tattered bag, and when he was finished, he stared in confusion at Misha. "You know what, I wish I could say I'm never going to think about you again. But I'm going to miss you like hell, you son of a bitch. See, like it or not, we been living inside each other's heads for the last year and a half. I'm alive because of you, and you're alive because of me. That means something, Misha. Alive! You got that?"

Misha sat quietly. Schmidt's words bounced off him. He wouldn't listen. He didn't care. He watched Schmidt's feet. He watched Schmidt leave. Then he started to dress.

An envelope had been shoved under the door when Misha came home from work the next morning. Inside was a ticket to the Thursday afternoon concert of Miss Anna Marks at the Chamber Music Society on June 15, and a note.

> *Be good to yourself for a change. Go see her. First get a haircut and buy yourself some decent clothes. If you're ever in Paris, look me up. Somebody will always know me. Good luck, comrade. Long live the revolution!*
>
> *Schmidt*

He wasn't going to go; he told himself he wasn't going, but he went shopping for a new suit, shirt, tie, and shoes in one of the finest haberdasheries in Berlin and told his foreman he needed the day off to go to a funeral in Brandenburg. At the last minute, he panicked and couldn't enter the elegant home of the Berlin Chamber Music Society. He stood outside smoking until just before two, then dashed in, horrified to find the concert was being held in a room not much bigger than his mother's parlor. There were only some thirty chairs, and no way he could meld with the crowd, no way Anna would not see him; he raced from the room, practically knocking over a couple as he started down the wide marble staircase.

"My God, Misha!" Anna called. "Is that you?"

He swerved about.

Anna's hand was on her mouth; her eyes were wide in astonishment. Despite her shock, she appeared ethereal in a delicate gown of pale blue silk; she wore an exquisite sapphire necklace with matching earrings. Her hair was done up, with wisps of small curls about her forehead and cheeks. The color, which had faded from her cheeks, was rapidly rising.

"Is it really you, Misha?" She dropped hold of the arm of her escort and reached for Misha, hesitating only a moment before embracing him in an exuberant greeting. "Misha, Misha . . ." She repeated his name breathlessly, and seemed not so fragile in his arms. She was soft and full, and smelled of sweetness such as he had forgotten existed. He touched her cheek to feel her life. She laughed and nuzzled his hand between her shoulder and chin. The moment came and went so quickly, hardly noticed, yet absorbed. They stood in the heat of their coming together. Then she was holding him at arm's length, laughing and crying and fumbling in her sleeve for her handkerchief. "Misha, my God, we thought you were dead."

"Well, as you can see, I'm not!" He was giddy with the joyous spontaneity of her greeting, and he held her hands to kiss them, stunned by the glitter of the large diamond-and-emerald engagement ring on her finger.

She pulled her hands away and quickly turned the ring about so it was hidden under her finger; but the moment was gone, time raced backward, and there was nothing to say.

"Excuse me, Anna," her escort interrupted.

"Oh, Willy, I'm sorry. I'm just so shocked." Thankful for the intrusion, she reached for his hand. "Wilhelm Bekendorf . . . Mikhail Anatolyevich Kalinin—Misha. We call him Misha. You remember, Willy, I told you about Misha." Anna was flustered. Perspiration beaded on her forehead.

"Did you come to hear Anna perform?" Willy asked haughtily, slipping his arm proprietarily through Anna's.

Misha wanted to dismiss Willy, a rather unremarkable-looking man; surely he couldn't be Anna's fiancé.

"Why didn't you let me know you were coming?" Anna insisted, regaining her composure. "And where were you racing to just now? You practically knocked Willy and me down."

"To get some flowers, actually," Misha said, reaching for the first thing that came to his mind. "I wanted to have some flowers for you afterward."

William Bekendorf III straightened to take command of the situation. "Anna, I really think we should be going inside. You should have begun five minutes ago." His tone was patronizing, as if chiding a child.

"Of course—but you will be here when I'm done, Misha?"

"Where else would I be?"

"There's so much we need to talk about. Oh, Misha." Her smile relaxed and she kissed his cheek once more, lingering a moment. "You've never heard me play, have you?"

"Just a little, when we were in the Crimea."

"Goodness, I was so ill then. Come." She reached for his hand. "I shall dedicate this performance to you, is that all right? Can I do that? I shall say to a friend, a dear, dear friend."

Misha had to concentrate very hard on staying in his seat. He had to concentrate very hard on not fleeing into the Berlin streets and forgetting he'd ever seen Anna. This was a mistake. Anna was engaged, and the world of Wilhelm Bekendorf III, the world which once had been Misha's too, the world he despised as Irina had despised it, adored her. After the concert, the audience flocked about her, sycophants, some of them seeming only to want to touch Anna or breathe her air. It was twenty minutes before she could break away, with Willy by her side.

"You were wonderful, Anna."

"I wanted to be wonderful for you, Misha. Willy, would you mind terribly if I begged off from the party tonight? I would like to have dinner with Misha . . . that is, if you'd like to." She turned, beaming, to Misha.

"But really, I don't want to keep you from your plans . . ."

"Why not have Misha come to the party, my dear?" Willy was solicitous, but the undertone of authority was clear.

Anna ignored Willy. "Misha, you will take me out to dinner, won't you? Willy, give him one of your cards. I'd like to go back and change. I'm staying at Willy's parents' house."

With a curt nod of his head, Willy handed Misha his embossed calling card.

"Seven-thirty," Anna said. "I can hardly wait. We've so much to talk about."

"My grandmother—I heard she was with you."

"Oh, yes, and she's fine, wonderful, active as ever. She's involved in all sorts of things."

"And Irinushka."

"You wouldn't believe how she's grown. Here . . ." She fumbled in her purse. "I never go anyplace without a picture of her." She handed Misha a photograph. The child was immediately a Kalinin. Although she was small and delicate, her beauty had none of Anna's serenity. Irinushka was dark; her curls defied the ribbons. She stared directly at the camera with a carefree smile and laughing eyes.

"She's beautiful." Misha handed her back the photograph.

"You may keep it if you like. I have plenty."

"Well, thank you. Yes, I'd like to have it."

"I'll tell you about her tonight. But you have to promise to let me know if I go on too much. Sometimes I bore people with talk of Irinushka."

"I doubt I could ever be bored."

"Oh, Misha." She embraced him, trembling as she did. "This is surely a dream come true."

Anna's mind filled with thoughts of Misha, memories and fantasies of all that was to come. She thought he didn't look well, and his hands were terribly coarse. Who knew what stories he had to tell. Well, he was back, and that's all that mattered. He'd return to Geneva with her, of course. Zhenya Kirilovna would be mad with happiness. The new apartment was big enough for all of them. There was even an extra room nobody slept in. Neither Zhenya nor Anna had ever said what the room was for, but they both knew. In their hearts, they knew. *Thank you, Lord, thank you. . . .* She smiled, leaning her head against the back of the car. *Thank you for sending him back to us.*

"Anna!" The gruffness of Willy's tone startled her. "We're home."

She looked up to see the car pulling up the drive of the Bekendorf mansion, and turned to Willy, whose face was gray with tension. "You're angry," she said with surprise.

"How can I be angry when you played so magnificently today?" he replied coldly. "I only wish my presence could instill such passion."

There was no time to answer before the driver opened the door. Willy held Anna's arm tightly as they walked up the stairs, leading her like a wayward child. He waved away the servant at the door, and ushered Anna into the drawing room. Closing the door, he demanded, "Who is that man?"

"I told you. He's Alexei's nephew. We escaped from Russia together. He returned to fight in the revolution and we haven't heard from him in . . . well, in a year and a half. We thought he was dead."

"You're in love with him," Willy accused, his voice low, but his jaw tight, his eyes wild, as Anna had never seen him.

"What?" Her body burned.

"I saw more passion in those few minutes you were with him than I've seen in all the months we've been together. I saw more happiness in your face when you looked at him than I've ever seen when you look at me. And to say you're not coming to a party that my parents' closest friends are holding in your honor. My God, Anna! How far can I be pushed?"

"You must understand, Willy . . ." Anna was trying to compose her thoughts. "Misha and I went through a tremendous lot together. He's my family and we thought him dead. Of course I'm happy to see him."

"I know what family happiness is, Anna. Family happiness isn't passion. Tell me . . ." His eyes menaced and his tone rose audibly. "Were you lovers? Have you kept me from your bed in the hopes that he would return?"

"How dare you?" She slapped his face.

"Well, I suppose I've my answer!"

Before Anna could respond, there was a loud rapping on the door and Willy's mother, the Baroness, walked in. "What is going on here?" She directed the question to Willy.

He averted his eyes. "Nothing, Mother," he said like a boy caught in his naughtiness.

"Nothing? You sound like banshees. I will not have it in my house, you know that, Willy. Under no circumstances will I allow such rude behavior in my house."

"I'm sorry, Madame Bekendorf." Anna had to force herself to sound polite. She felt like screaming that they were all insane—not to be able to raise one's voice in one's own house!

As Misha stumbled from the bed, he saw he still had on the trousers and shirt he'd worn to Anna's concert. The jacket and tie lay on the floor and one of his new shoes was propped on the windowsill. He tried to bend to look under the bed for the other, but his head pounded pitiably. He had a roaring hangover. He wondered how long he'd been drinking and how long he'd been sleeping. It was light out, bright daylight, and he peered at his watch, which had stopped at eight-eleven.

Sheets of paper were strewn about the table and floor, paper and empty bottles of vodka, a half-eaten salami attracting flies, and a gnawed loaf of bread. Some of the papers were crumpled in balls, other were covered with writing, and since the bathroom seemed an exceedingly far distance to go in his present condition, he sat at the table and picked up a page. On it, in his handwriting, was a poem called *Fire*.

> *To talk of love and have no fire*
> *is eyes without sight.*
> *To burn and never scorch the petal*
> *is a gift.*
> *She rippled like a lake,*
> *and shamed the scented lilac in spring.*

He thought, at first, the poem was about Irina. He read it again and shuddered as the shadow of Anna swept over him. As a beggar racing after fallen money, he gathered up the papers in his arms, even the crumpled ones; he spread them open and made a pile. Some of the poems were clearly about Irina, about living with her, loving her, marching with her, laughing with her. Others, like the one called *Fire*, might have been about either Irina or Anna. How insane. How could he have confused the two? How, even drunk, could he think about loving Anna? She was engaged to a man who could give her luxury such as Misha would never know again. Damn Schmidt for ever having given him that ticket.

He folded the poems roughly and put them under a book where he kept the newspaper articles about Anna. Inside the book, on top of the article, was the picture of Irinushka. In a flash, he remembered his dinner date with Anna. He remembered he'd never gone.

He leaned out the window. The streets of the teeming émigré neighborhood were steaming from a June heat. Women in flowered babushkas were arguing in Russian with street vendors. Misha looked through the crowd until he spied someone he knew. "Hey, you, Lara Ivanovna!" he called to a young woman selling scarves. "Can you tell me what day it is?"

"Monday, of course."

"What date?"

"June 18."

"June 18 . . ." he muttered, aghast, and drew back inside. Anna's concert had been on June 15. He had no memory of the days in between.

CHAPTER FIFTY-SEVEN

Misha didn't need to read the numbers on the houses to find the one he was looking for. Strains of Mozart streamed from an open window of a second-floor apartment of a gray-and-white building midway down the wide, tree-lined street. Flowers spilled from window boxes.

"Please don't announce my arrival to Mademoiselle Marks," Misha whispered conspiratorially to the doorman. "This is a surprise visit." There was an elevator in the building, but Misha chose to walk. He climbed the stairs slowly and when he reached the carpeted landing, he sat, his head against the wall, listening to Anna play. He'd been so glad for the time and the music to calm his nerves. He'd been so certain of why he'd come back. He had it all worked out in his mind, and suddenly he couldn't remember—except he had to apologize for never taking Anna to dinner that night, and he needed to see Irinushka and his grandmother again.

The music stopped and Misha took a deep breath. Clutching his present for Irinushka, he stood, forcing his finger on the doorbell before he changed his mind. He knew from the footsteps, Anna would open the door.

"Oh, God," was all she said. The words came out low, like mourning.

"Anna, please, can I talk to you?"

"Of course." She looked pale and thin in a peach cotton dress. Her hair was haphazardly pinned on her head and long, straight golden strands hung down her neck. Her face was expressionless. She led him into a bright, sunny parlor where a grand piano stood. The parlor itself was three times the size of the old apartment they'd shared. The furniture was new and expensive. Plants curtained the window.

"My grandmother and Irinushka?"

"They're at the park. They go every day at this time so I can practice."

Misha held out the box he carried. "This is for Irinushka. It's a black bear dressed like a Russian coachman, and when you wind it up, it walks."

"She'll like that!" For a fleeting second Anna's smile seemed genuine; then she grew solemn and they fell into an awkward silence. "Can I get you something to drink? Some lemonade, perhaps. It's terribly warm."

"Yes, that would be nice. Can I help you?"

"Oh, no, you stay here. I'll only be a moment." She hurried out of the room.

Misha listened to the noises coming from the kitchen. He wiped the sweat from his face. The apartment was very warm. He wanted to take off his jacket or loosen his tie.

Suddenly there was a crash and the sound of glass splintering. Anna cried out and Misha ran to the kitchen. She was standing, bewildered, in a puddle of lemonade, the glass from the pitcher all about her.

"Let me help . . ." He started toward her.

"No, no, I'm fine!" she shouted, and held up her hand.
She bent to pick up a piece of glass and blood trickled from
her finger. "Leave me alone, I'm fine. It's just a cut, just a
cut!" She grabbed a towel and pressed it to the wound.

"Anna—" He wanted to help.

She cut him off, demanding, "Why didn't you come that
night?" Her voice was stern, like a schoolteacher's.

"You're engaged to him!"

She shook her head as if to say that made no difference.

"Don't you see—we're in such different worlds. I could
never be like that again."

"Who was asking you to?"

He threw up his arms in despair. This wasn't working out
the way he'd planned. "I should never have come, I can see
that now. I'd better go." He turned to the door.

"I think," she began authoritatively, "I think you should
stay. Your grandmother and Irinushka will be back in a while.
Your grandmother will be distraught if you leave." She looked
at the lemonade and glass about her and, shaking her head,
she reached for a dish towel and haphazardly mopped up the
mess. Wordlessly, she strode by him to the parlor and sat
down at the piano and began playing.

He stood by the window, listening to her playing and not
listening. The sun on his skin was almost unbearably hot.

"Have you come home for good? Or is this just a visit?"
An almost imperceptible tremor, like dry wind in heated
beach grass, fluttered through Anna's voice.

Misha was startled to find her standing beside him. He
hadn't realized she'd stopped playing. "I don't know."

"What happened to your nose?"

"It got broken."

She frowned. "Well, you look awful. Is Nikita with you?
Your grandmother said you were together."

"Nikita's dead." He was surprised how easy it was to say
the words, *Nikita's dead*. "I saw him die. We were fighting
and he was shot," he reported starkly.

"Poor Nikita." Her eyes grew watery. "He was such a
fine boy. We had such fun together in Peterhof. He took me
on the ice slide. Did I ever tell you . . ."

Anna's words drifted, and Misha asked, "Do you ever
wonder why you lived?"

"For Irinushka," she said without hesitation.

Yes, of course, she had her child, and soon a husband, a
real family again. The thought of her marriage filled him with
an overwhelming sadness and he turned to look out the window, wiping his eyes as if the sun had made them tear. What

right did he have to feel sad over her happiness? Thank God she was marrying Bekendorf. Thank God her life would be whole again.

He heard a small whimper and turned. Anna had been too absorbed in her own sadness to notice his. Her hands were covering her face. "I'm sorry." Her voice was childlike. "I just can't believe Nikita's gone too. So many gone." She breathed deeply and became still.

She was all right, he thought. She didn't need his comforting and he stared back out the window, trying to remember if he'd ever cried for Nikita. He wasn't sure. He could scarcely remember Nikita's death, or Nadia's or Benya's or the countless others he'd seen die. Only Irina's stayed clear. There was something empty in the rest, in the killing, the dying, the heroism, and the betrayal. Irina was different. Irina was outside the forsaken landscape, buried deeply within his soul. He wondered if Anna crawled inside him, if she would vanish too, or if her touch would add texture to his life once more. Was that what he'd returned for? Some madness that his life was here, with Anna? Some madness that he could win her from Bekendorf?

Time passed slowly and awkwardly. Anna sat on a chair and Misha on the couch. Anna held her hands tightly together. Misha loosened his tie. "I saw Larisa Filipovna," he said finally. "She told me your wedding is set for next month. That's wonderful. I'm sure you'll be very happy."

Her eyes flashed wildly as he spoke and her reply snapped like rifle shots. "Willy's terribly fond of Irinushka. I'm quite fortunate to have found someone like him, you see. Of course, Willy's not Alexei." She was on her feet, her arms wrapped tightly about herself. "I could never love him as I loved Alexei, but how can one expect to be so fortunate a second time? No, I'm very content with Willy. Perhaps we should all be friends someday and you'll come to dinner. I think you two should like each other. Of course, Willy can be terribly serious, but . . ." She paused as if her breath had been cut off and she pushed past Misha to the piano. Her fingers gripped the edges and she swerved, her arms pressed about her waist again. "I have to know, Misha. Are you just flying in and out of my life as you did in Berlin? Should I close my eyes and pretend you never came?"

He looked at her warily.

"You told me you loved me once!" she burst out. "Here, in Geneva, you held me in your arms and told me you could never leave me, but you did! Do you think I've forgotten that?"

The unexpected passion brought him to his feet. He shifted uneasily, not knowing where to look.

"Well, I haven't. It was all that got me through the loneliness and fear those many months. And even now . . ." Her lips quivered and her eyes filled with tears as she walked slowly toward him. "Every time Willy holds me, I think of you and wish I had one-tenth of the feelings for him I had for you that night."

He couldn't speak.

"Answer me!" she shouted, shaking him. "Say something!" She raised her arms and he thought she was going to pummel him. Instead, she embraced him, pressing against him with startling desperation. "Hold me, Misha. Please hold me. Hold me very tight . . ." Her heart was pounding, and as his arms enveloped her, she breathed in the clean starchy smell of his shirt mixing with the muskiness of his skin. "Misha . . ." she whispered just to hear his name, and in the quiet, Anna thought she felt the drying edges of time grow moist.

Misha shuddered. An unexpected terror left him cold, like a starving child crouched inside a locked tomb. When he spoke, his voice was miserably forlorn. "I've nothing to give you, Anna. You've everything with Bekendorf—Irinushka, and your music. You're so talented, and . . ."

She drew away as if repelled. "Oh, God, don't *you* say that! I don't think I could bear hearing that from you too."

He looked confused.

"It's why Alexei loved me. It's why Willy loves me. 'Oh, you're so talented, Anna. Oh, you can be adored by all Europe. People will love you. They'll throw roses at your feet. Bravo, Anna. Bravo!' " she said bitterly, pulling at her engagement ring, yanking it off, and hurling it at the piano. "They don't know me! Not even Alexei really knew me. But you, I thought you did, Misha. You never even heard me play until Berlin. I thought my music never mattered to you—only what we did and who we are!"

Misha gazed in dismay. Her passion seemed to know no bounds. "I don't know what you're talking about, Anna," he said softly, apologetically.

She drew in a deep breath. "I'm saying I can't marry Willy Bekendorf. I think I knew that even before you walked through that door. I could never have gone through with the marriage. It would be a prison as horrid as any I've known."

"But you don't want me. Surely you don't want me . . ." He was backing away from her. "I've changed since I was last in Geneva. Everything has changed . . ." He wanted desperately to tell her about Dmitri. He wanted to sit beside her on the couch as they used to do in their little apartment, and he would talk, even cry, and she would hold his hand and understand. Dmitri. He felt sick as images of the man flashed past him: Dmitri as his leader, Dmitri in the carriage house, Dmitri in his sable-collared coat, untouchable. "We've nothing to fight for anymore, Anna. The revolution is dead." The words he'd said in bitterness to Schmidt so many times, twisted from him like a lament.

Anna held his hand and her voice was gentle. "I won't let you talk like that, not you, Misha, of all people. Don't you remember how you used to talk to me and read to me and—"

"That was before, when there was still hope."

"And now?"

"Now the Czar is more powerful than even when we began. There is no hope. There's only betrayal."

"How dare you say that!" Her face paled in horror. "How dare you say that Alexei and Irina and Nikita and all the others died in vain? I shall never believe that and neither shall your grandmother nor Irinushka when she's old enough to understand. She will know that her namesake and father died for a great cause! Her father . . . ." Her voice quivered and tears filled her eyes. "The most brave and noble Alexei Yakovlevich, who could have quietly kept to the matters of his own life, chose to fight for the people whose blood flows through my baby and through you, Mikhail Anatolyevich. Praise God, have you forgotten who you are? Have you forgotten all your brave words about the peasants and your roots? Do you forsake them now, when they need fighters more than ever?" She trembled as she spoke, and wiped a few escaping tears from her cheeks.

Before Misha could respond, the sound of childish laughter floated up from the street.

"That's Irinushka," Anna warned, drying her eyes. "No more of such talk. Don't let your grandmother know you have forsaken her."

"Mama! Mama!" Irinushka's voice called excitedly.

Anna started to the window.

"No, wait!" He grabbed her arm. "Since when have you become the great champion of the revolution? As I recall, you used to cover your ears when I talked. You wanted to hear nothing of the revolution that you said killed Uncle Alexei and Irina. What changed your mind, Anna? I have the right to know, when only moments before you accused me more harshly than I ever would have accused you."

Misha's words subdued her. It seemed impossible that she could have turned on him so virulently. "I'm sorry, you're right." Her voice was hushed. Her eyes as they rested on his shifted in the colors of a crystal dawn. "I never want to be harsh with you. I think I didn't know myself how strongly I felt about the revolution. It's your grandmother, I suppose." She half-smiled and felt a bit giddy. "Her devotion is unwavering. She reminds me so of you when we lived together here in Geneva. She goes to meetings several times a week, and would you believe it, I'm teaching her how to read."

"Grandma's learning how to read?" he asked incredulously.

"And write. She's a devoted student. She wants to start her own newspaper someday. Geneva is flooded with political exiles. Your grandmother says it's like Petersburg all over again. People haven't given up, Misha. You must believe that."

His eyes burned with tears. Wiping them away, he murmured, "I don't know why I'm crying. This is so absurd."

"It's your grandmother! She has the most extraordinary effect on people. I must have been insane to think of leaving her for Willy Bekendorf. It seems suddenly so clear. Everything I love is bound up in Russia. Someday I want to return with Irinushka. It's our country. Her heritage is there. We will go back one day, won't we, Misha? We'll go back in freedom."

"Mama! Mama, come! Mama!" Irinushka was growing impatient.

"I must go to her." Anna glanced down at Misha's hand still holding her arm, but softly now. "I always have to wave to her from the window before she comes up."

"Can I come too?" His brows furrowed with the question. Suddenly he wanted to see Irinushka very much.

They squeezed together into the window. "Hello, my dove!" Anna waved and threw a kiss.

"Mama!" Irinushka jumped up and down, her little legs clumsy, her curls bouncing. She held Zhenya Kirilovna's hand tightly. "Mama! Mama! I home!" She radiated joy. Then her little face scrunched up. "Who dat?" She pointed to Misha.

"An old friend, my sweet. Besides me, he's the oldest friend you have."

"Misha!" Zhenya Kirilovna gasped. "Misha, is that you?" She squinted to see. "Irinushka, it's our Misha!"

"Misha! Misha!" Irinushka repeated happily as she toddled after her grandmother.

Misha stepped back from the window. "She's wonderful,

Anna!'' He felt breathless. It seemed hard to believe that little person was the same infant he'd left.

"Wait until you really get to know her. She's love, pure love, and she needs you, Misha. She needs a father.''

"I don't know, Anna. I don't know if I'd be any good anymore. What if—''

"Shush . . .'' She pressed her fingers on his lips. "All that matters is that we're together, a family. I don't think any of us can survive alone anymore.''

She was close to him then, embracing him. They kissed and she tasted like a lover, ripe and fragile as the moment; he was washed in a stream of connectedness.

"Mama! Mama!'' Irinushka's little fist pounded on the door.

"Oh, do hurry, Anna!'' Zhenya insisted. "I've forgotten my keys again!''

Reluctantly Misha and Anna separated. She laughed softly. Her hair spread about her shoulders in a fine golden spray. She took his hand and held it to her cheeks. "Am I too bold, Misha?''

"No.'' He smiled in wonder.

"It's just that I've waited for you so long.''

"What's going on in there? Anna! Misha! If I have to wait another moment, I shall never forgive you.''

Anna smoothed her dress and hair. "Tell me, Misha, tell me now. Are you staying? Are you home for good?''

Silently he reached for her and pulled her toward him once more. As her arms slipped about him, the purpose of his leaving so long ago seemed suddenly fulfilled. The purpose was in returning. "I love you, Anna, and I'll stay with you for as long as you want me.''

"That will be forever, I promise. I'll never let you leave again.''

They kissed, and kissed again.

Zhenya Kirilovna pounded on the door. "Now I must insist—Misha, if you're playing one of your games, I shall never speak to you again!''

Reluctantly Anna pushed him away. "Go on, you open it.''

"Coming, Grandma,'' Misha assured as he walked backward, his eyes not leaving Anna's.

AN AFTERWORD ON
HISTORICAL CHARACTERS

SERGEI WITTE was made a count for his efforts in negotiating the end of the Russo-Japanese War. Less than a year later, the Czar asked for his resignation. Witte never returned to the government and died in 1915. The Czar remarked, "Count Witte's death has been a great relief to me. I also regard it as a sign from God."

CZAR NICHOLAS II and his entire family were executed by the Bolsheviks on July 16, 1918.

FATHER GAPON returned to Russia in 1906 in hopes of reestablishing his Society of Workers. He tried to meet with Witte, who refused, fearing Gapon would assassinate him. Gapon was then naively involved in plots of double and triple betrayals and was executed in 1907 by terrorists on the orders of Yevno Azef, the man on whom Arkady Akimov is based.

YEVNO AZEF *(Arkady Akimov)* was, after years of rumor and suspicion, finally exposed by revolutionaries, who hunted him relentlessly. There are two accounts of his death: in one, he escaped to Germany, where he died during World War I; in the other, he was tried and executed by the revolutionaries.

LEON TROTSKY was a leader, along with Lenin, of the 1917 Bolshevik Revolution. He organized and led the Red Army during the civil war that followed. He was exiled by Stalin in 1929 and finally emigrated to Mexico where he was murdered in 1940. All evidence suggests that this was yet another of Stalin's political assassinations.

ABOUT THE AUTHOR

Emily Hanlon lives in Westchester County, New York, with her husband and two children. She is at work on another novel.